Ian Gosling was born in Buckinghamshire and brought up in Cambridgeshire. He moved to Rutland – England's smallest county – 20 years ago, with his wife Maggie and their three children. The Puppet Master is his first novel.

To Anita

The Puppet Master

Best Wishes

Ian Gosling

Ian Gosling

The Puppet Master

Vanguard Press

VANGUARD PAPERBACK

© Copyright 2008
Ian Gosling

The right of Ian Gosling to be identified as author of
this work has been asserted by him in accordance with the
Copyright, Designs and Patents Act 1988.

A CIP catalogue record for this title is
available from the British Library.

ISBN: 978 1 84386 386 1

Vanguard Press is an imprint of
Pegasus Elliot MacKenzie Publishers Ltd.
www.pegasuspublishers.com

First Published in 2008

Vanguard Press
Sheraton House Castle Park
Cambridge England

Printed & Bound in Great Britain

To Maggie for her encouragement and support

AUTHOR'S NOTES

The events in this book are the invention of the author, but the inspiration came from actual reported cases. One only has to turn on the news or read a newspaper to know that, unfortunately, real life can often be more terrible than fiction. The criminal organisations involved in the illegal trafficking of drugs and human beings are like cancers eating away at our society; making huge profits from their trade in human misery and devastating the lives of countless numbers of innocent people. Law enforcement agencies around the world are engaged in a seemingly never-ending war, in which the enemy is assisted by modern communications technologies, the growing *global economy*, corrupt administrations, greedy businessmen and weak politicians.

For several years the British Government's main police agencies against organised crime were the National Crime Squad, and its counterpart the Scottish Crime Squad. Established in April 1998, the NCS was responsible for many successful operations against international drug trafficking, money laundering and organised immigration crime. In 2006 the NCS was merged with a number of other agencies to form the Serious and Organised Crime Agency (SOCA).

All the characters in the book are fictitious, but many of the locations are real: the cities, towns and villages, streets, pubs and hotels, the Tate Modern and other landmark buildings. Other places exist only in the pages of this book, so don't waste any time looking for the Palace Club or the Puppet Master's villa. Although in Austin Friars, just a few yards from the hustle and bustle of the City, you might imagine yourself standing outside the offices of Blanchard's bank.

Prologue

Tuesday 6th May 2003

The flight gave Barton time to reflect on the events of the last few days.

Four men had died. But they'd had it coming and deserved to die painfully, victims only of their own greed. The world was a better, safer place without them. He gave them no more thought.

He allowed himself to shed a tear or two, as he thought about the girls – maybe he could have saved them – Innocent, vulnerable girls; taken from their homes and their families, by a man who had promised them a new life; a better life. But the man had lied, just like he lied to all the others. They'd been shipped across Europe, like cattle, crammed together for days, inside dark, stinking, filthy metal compartments, hidden in the walls of a container truck, with barely enough food and water to keep them alive. And then he had sold them to other men; again and again and again. The man who had done this to them was dead now, but Barton would never be able to tell them that. He closed his eyes and saw Naida again; her cold lifeless body, lying battered and bloody at his feet. And her sister: *Only fourteen years old, for God's sake!* They'd found her in the bath, the waters stained red as the blood flowed slowly from her open veins. There was no *'maybe'* – if he'd just been satisfied with what they already had, and made a move earlier – he could have saved them. But he'd wanted more.

He thought about the team of people he'd left behind; his team. He could still see the looks of disappointment when they realised that it might all be over, and the relief when they learned that they'd been given more time. They'd given everything, but they still wanted to give more: *And for what?* Months of work had been had been screwed up in a weekend: *And what had they got?* Not the great result that he'd promised: *Another month?* They were getting very close, and that just might have been long enough. But it had all gone wrong. It wasn't their fault, no one could have anticipated it; it had just happened. But then, he'd made the wrong call and it had turned into a disaster – Why hadn't he agreed to close it down when he had the chance? Why had he been so sure that he could get more? – They deserved better than the second prize, and now it was up to him to turn it round.

Then he thought of Grace; selfishly at first, because he needed her to help him get through the next few weeks, like she always did at this time of the year. And he needed her to guide him and help him to understand what he was up against. Understand how a man could be like that. But he hadn't been fair to her and he couldn't go on being selfish. He had to put things right. There was so much that they needed to talk about. So much that had to change. Things had already changed, but he had to give her a lot more. This wasn't a good time for them to be apart. What his wife needed most now was for him to be with her, to support her, to show how much he loved her. She needed him to give her his time; but he didn't have any of that to give. Not yet.

As the plane flew low over the mountains, beginning its descent towards the coast, he looked out of the window. Somewhere down there, lived a man who enjoyed a life a million miles removed from the hell, that Naida and the others had endured. The man he had to find if he was to put an end to this.

He wasn't sure what he would feel when he met him again, but he knew it would be hard to put his personal feelings aside. They'd met before; twenty years earlier, but he doubted that the man would remember. Barton would never forget, and it was going to be difficult. But he knew he had to keep focussed – somehow he had to shut the ghost out of his mind – and concentrate on the job.

Why was he so sure about this man? He had no evidence, just coincidences, speculation, and gut feeling. He was going out on a limb, but his instincts had served him well in the past and something told him that this time was no different. He was certain this was the man.

He'd come to find out what the man knew; to ask questions, and find clues that would help prove his suspicions. And, he had to give him a message. A message from a man lying in a hospital bed; tubes sticking out of his broken body, electrodes stuck to his skin, his face creased with pain, knowing that this his life was over. Just a few words, whispered by a dying man: '*Lenny… talk to Lenny… I let him down… tell him, I'm sorry… tell him… I love him'.*

PART ONE

Chapter 1

Monday 28th April 2003

Dagenham, East London – 04:00 BST

Detective Constable Phil Fellows eased off the accelerator, and watched as the black Mercedes turned off the main road and led the two vans into industrial estate. He carried on past the turning and parked his car at the side of the road. He knew where they were going and followed on foot, calling in his position as he walked towards the truck depot. By the time he got to the gates, the three vehicles were already in the yard, hidden from view by the rows of parked trailers. He kept low, creeping beneath the trailers until he found a good vantage point. There was no moon, and the scene in front of him was illuminated only by the yellow glow of the streetlamps, in the road behind the yard, and the reflections in the windscreens.

The rear doors of the vans were open, and a group of men were standing by the car. The driver of the car got out, and for a few seconds a bulky figure in the back seat was visible in the soft glow of the car's interior light. The driver had his back to Fellows the smooth skin of his shaven head reflecting the glow of the streetlamps. But, although he couldn't see the man's face, he knew who he was. Marcus Preston was a giant of a man and he towered above the others, as he spoke to them and pointed towards a large box trailer. Two of the men returned to the vans, and the others followed Preston as he walked to the trailer. He unlocked the back, and the men disappeared inside, as the vans reversed towards to the trailer.

Fellows watched as they transferred the cargo. He was in his shirtsleeves and shivered in the chill night air. As it began to rain – small puddles appearing on the ground, giving the streetlamps a hundred new mirrors to reflect their light – he regretted leaving his coat in the car. The men were unloaded first and herded into one of the vans, then a dozen girls, and several large packages were packed into the other. He'd witnessed similar exchanges before. He knew that, the men probably had another long, uncomfortable journey ahead of them; the girls and the drugs had only a few more miles to travel. One of the men threw a bundle from the back of the trailer. In the darkness, Fellows couldn't make out whether it was a man or a woman. Preston bent down and shook the lifeless figure; then he shook his head, picked up the body, and bundled it back into the trailer. He locked the trailer doors, and ran to the car, followed by the two van drivers. The man in the back seat lowered the rear window and spoke to them; his face hidden in the shadows.

Fellows had seen enough. And, as the rain became heavier, turning the small puddles into larger pools and running streams, he retreated to the shelter of his car, and called his control room.

National Crime Squad, Hertfordshire Branch – 06:25 BST

Detective Chief Inspector Mike Barton was a worried man. He'd been worrying since he got the call from the Assistant Chief Constable's office last week. Barton had been running Operation De Niro for nearly a year and this was only the second time that the ACC had asked for a full briefing and an early morning one too. Barton knew it spelt trouble.

He knew why the ACC was coming this morning, his boss had told him last week: *'Harris is getting a lot of pressure from the Home Office, they want to see results. Next to terrorism... drugs and illegal immigration are top of their agenda. They need to show the public that something is being done'.*

Barton understood their agenda, but he wondered if the men at the Home Office really understood what the war against organised crime involved. It wasn't like on the TV, where at the end of an hour the police have solved the case and arrested the villains. The TV cop shows made it look so simple; so easy.

The men behind the drug trade and the human trafficking weren't out on the streets amongst the dealers and the pimps. They operated from comfortable offices, hiding behind legitimate business fronts, organising their trade across international borders and moving millions of pounds around the global banking system.

To track them down and make a solid case took months of painstaking work; running surveillance on suspects for days, weeks, months on end. It took dozens of officers working behind the scenes – gathering intelligence, searching the files, sifting mountains of paperwork, and sitting in front of computer screen for hours, inputting every scrap of information – patiently putting together the pieces of the puzzle. But, those things wouldn't make good television – not enough action.

But those were the things that Barton and his team had been doing, and they had achieved a lot; they were very close. And now he was afraid that he was going to be ordered to make his move before he was ready. He needed the ACC to give him more time.

Yes, Barton was a very worried man that morning, as he sat alone in his office, running over the notes he had prepared for the meeting.

Barton was expecting the call and picked up the phone before it rang a second time, "Barton here," he said.

"I'll be with you in about fifteen minutes, Mike," said the voice at the other end of the line, "make sure your team is ready. Has the ACC arrived yet?"

"He got here a couple of minutes ago, Trevor. Sally's just gone down to meet him."

"You know he's got to be away by eight forty-five, so we need to start on time. Get everyone into the briefing room and I'll come straight up when I get there."

"We'll be ready, Trevor. See you soon," said Barton. As he put the phone down there was a knock on the door. He looked up and saw the attractive figure of Detective Inspector Sally Parkinson standing in the open doorway with their visitor. The sight of Sally smiling was always a welcome start to the day. Barton wished he could say the same about the about the man standing beside her. But the sight of Assistant Chief Constable Malcolm Harris was one that Barton avoided whenever he could.

"Come in, sir," said Barton, getting up from his chair and walking round the desk, to greet his visitor. "Thanks Sally. Can you tell everyone to be in the briefing room in five minutes, please?"

"Good morning, Mike. Good to see you again," said the Assistant Chief Constable as the two men shook hands.

"The Chief Super just phoned; he'll be here in a few minutes. Shall we go along to the briefing room and get some coffee?"

They walked out of the office and along the short corridor. Barton opened the door and stood to one side. "After you, sir," he said, and then followed the ACC into the room.

The room had been rearranged for the ACC's benefit. Several desks had been moved together to form a large table, and the chairs set around three sides. A laptop computer was connected to a projector, which was casting a blurred image onto a large screen at the far end of the room. There were several large whiteboards, arranged on one side of the screen, one covered by a large diagram – a tangled web of blue and red lines connecting to coloured circles – the others displaying photographs, and maps covered with clusters of coloured dots. All totally unnecessary as far as Barton was concerned, but Harris liked a show.

Some of the team were already there. Detective Sergeant Dave Connor was standing by the coffee maker, sharing a joke with Detective Constable Phil Fellows, who was sitting on the corner of a desk. Detective Sergeant Lorna McLean was sitting at the big table, in front of the laptop, adjusting the focus of the projector. As the two men walked into the room they all looked up. "Good morning, sir," they said in unison.

"Coffee?" said Connor, as he picked up one of the jugs and started to pour. Looking at the ACC, he asked, "How do you like yours, sir?"

"Thanks. Strong, black with no sugar thank you," said Harris, politely; wondering what sort of foul brew he was about to be served.

Connor handed him a cup; "Best way to drink it, sir," he said as he poured another cup, which he handed to Barton.

The ACC took a sip of the coffee and smiled. Years on the force had conditioned him to expect the worst. He had never understood why most police officers seemed unable to make a decent cup of coffee. But this was good, very good. "Excellent coffee," he remarked.

Thank you, sir," said Connor, who was not the sort to pass up a compliment. "It's a special blend. I grind the beans myself," he added, with a smile.

"Really," said Harris with surprise. "I'm impressed," he said, looking down at Connor's ID badge. "Ever thought of applying for a job at HQ, Sergeant Connor?" he asked. "You ought to look out, Mike, or we might transfer this man." Harris and Connor both laughed. Barton forced a smile; he had never really got on with Harris; he didn't like way that he patronised people. Harris stereotyped people as well; as soon as Connor had opened his mouth he had probably put him in a compartment, along with Guinness, potatoes and Molly Malone. He would have been surprised had he read Connor's last assessment, which said that he was an excellent detective, highly intelligent with all the necessary leadership qualities for a higher rank. And it would never have occurred to him that the young, rather scruffy looking, Irishman, might be a cordon bleu chef with a passion for architecture and the opera.

It wasn't that Harris was prejudiced; just conditioned, like many of his generation, who had made life so difficult for Barton's father. There were still too many officers openly resentful about working alongside anyone of a different colour. Barton had learned to accept that, but he resented people like Harris, people who felt that they were doing him a favour. People, who talked about diversity, quoted statistics and used him as an example to demonstrate their commitment to equal opportunities. Barton needed to believe that he had achieved his position on his own merits; he couldn't bear to think that someone, in order to meet some sort of quota, had selected his name because it was on a list headed 'Afro-Caribbean'.

The rest of the team arrived, headed straight for the coffee, and then proceeded to take their places around the table, leaving just two empty chairs at the end, facing the screen. Barton gestured to the vacant seats. "If you would sit there please, sir, we can begin as soon as the Chief Super arrives." Formal briefings like this weren't Barton's style. Sure, he could do them standing on his head; he'd done so many. But it just seemed an awful lot of fuss and effort, just to impress, and in this case, the man had probably made up his mind already: *Come on, Trevor, where are you. I want to get this over with.* As he was about to sit down the door opened and everyone, except Harris, started to rise to their feet.

"No need for that, sit down everyone," said Detective Chief Superintendent Trevor Miller, as he walked into the room. He sat next to Harris, and reached across for the nearest coffee jug. "Sorry I'm late. Carry on please, Chief Inspector."

"Thank you, sir, and good morning everyone," said Barton, as he stood up. "As you all know we've been asked to give Assistant Chief Constable Harris the run down on Operation De Niro." He glanced at his watch; six-fifty. "OK, the ACC has to leave for another meeting at quarter to nine, which gives us just under two hours, so let's keep to the important points. I'll give a brief overview and then the rest of you can fill in the details. Is that OK, sir?"

Harris nodded, "Carry on, Chief Inspector," he said.

Barton started to speak, wondering if the meeting was going to have any effect on the decision that the two men in front of him had to take. He knew that Harris had been a good policeman in his time with the Met and the old Regional Crime Squad; a good old fashioned thief-taker. But he'd been slow to progress to the top ranks and now, at the age of fifty-five, the best he could hope for was one final promotion to boost his pension. He'd been with the NCS since its creation five years earlier, initially doing what was now Miller's job, as Chief Superintendent in charge of the Eastern Operational Command Unit. For the past three years, he had been the ACC Operations, with overall responsibility for all three OCUs. Barton, and many of his colleagues, thought that Harris was losing touch with the men and women on the ground. He had become more of a politician than a policeman, and, it seemed to them that, he was more interested in pleasing the Home Office than supporting his officers.

"As you know, about ten months ago, we identified a connection between two international criminal organisations and a London businessman, Robert King. What we're talking about is the import and distribution of large quantities of class A drugs – cocaine and heroin – and human-trafficking on a major scale.

The cocaine originates in Colombia, passing through a number of countries in Central America, North Africa and several Eastern European states, before entering the UK via ports in Holland and Germany. The syndicate's headman over here is Enrique Herrera, a Colombian national.

The human-traffickers are bringing in large numbers of men and women, mainly from Eastern Europe, but also from North Africa. The younger ones are forced to work as prostitutes and rent boys. Gang-masters hire out the older men and women, as contract labour. The people behind this have links to the Russian Mafia, and they're also smuggling in heroin, which we think comes from Afghanistan. Their man here is Vladan Milosevic, a Serb.

We first made the connection between Milosevic and King after NCIS learned that a container lorry, carrying a number of illegal immigrants and a quantity of heroin, was en route to Harwich from Rotterdam. Interpol had tracked the container from Albania. We picked it up when it came off the ferry, and followed it to a depot in Dagenham, where it was met by Milosevic, who we'd already been watching for a couple of months. The depot is owned by London Orbital Storage Ltd, part of Essex Distribution Ltd, and ownership of that company was traced back to a holding company owned by Robert King."

Barton paused for a moment, giving the senior officers an opportunity to ask questions. Harris nodded, signalling for him to continue. "Operation De Niro was originally set up to investigate human trafficking and Milosevic. We increased the scope to investigate the involvement of King and his associates. A couple of months later, we uncovered the connection with the Colombians.

I've got two operational teams working on this. DI Paul Timms has been concentrating on King and his people and DI Sally Parkinson is in charge of the other team. They've been keeping tabs on Milosevic and Herrera. There's also a support team, responsible for liaison with NCIS, Northern and Western OCUs, and the Scottish Crime Squad. We've now got a lot of evidence of the links between King, Herrera, and Milosevic, and we've identified over two hundred individuals who are involved across the country."

Barton stopped speaking and looked at the two senior officers. "Now, unless you have any questions sir," he said, "I'll hand you over to DI Timms."

"No, everything's clear so far," said Harris, "carry on, please."

"Thank you, sir," said Timms, picking up a wad of cards. He'd learned it all by heart and he didn't really need the briefing notes that his team had prepared, but he wanted to look good for Harris, and would refer to the cards, and the thick file that lay on the table, throughout his presentation.

Timms took a couple of paces towards the boards, and pointed to the diagram. "Each of these coloured circles represents one of our targets," he explained. "The lines show all of the connections that have been established." He pointed to the first photograph. Simultaneously, Lorna clicked the mouse and the same picture, of a man in his sixties, appeared on the screen. "Robert 'Bobby' King, codename *Godfather*," said Timms, and he started to outline Robert King's background. As he gave a brief run down of King's criminal record, he was interrupted by the ACC.

"I was on that case," said Harris. "King and some of his heavies beat up two men in an alley. There was a witness. He ran off before they saw him and almost got himself run over in the next street by a patrol car. They called up the troops, but one man was dead by the time they got there. The other one spent three months in hospital. We charged King and two others with murder, but the witness later said in court that the dead man had a knife and started the fight. We all knew they'd got to him, but King's brief convinced the jury that it was self-defence."

Everyone around the table could see that Timms was annoyed. His train of thought had been interrupted. Barton smiled at him, and shrugged his shoulders: *Just what I need. If bloody Harris is going to start reminiscing about his days at the sharp end, we'll never get to the end of this.*

"Sorry, Inspector, I don't suppose that's got any relevance to this case," said Harris. "Carry on please."

Timms collected his thoughts and continued. "Apart from that there's never been enough evidence to make anything stick. Every time a case has been put together, key witnesses have either disappeared or lost their memories. Over the years, he's built up a sizeable business empire. Some of it's legitimate – car dealers, heavy plant hire, property development, security and courier firms. Some on the edge – nightclubs, lap-dancing bars, massage parlours, pornography and sex shops – and the Met have always suspected that he's got a hand in prostitution and drugs. Although there's been no direct contact, we've connected several people who work for him with both Herrera and Milosevic.

A couple of years ago he had a heart operation, and took, what I'd suppose you'd call, early retirement… leaving two of his associates – Underwood and Nichols – to manage the day-to-day business. He hardly ever goes near his old patch any more, and spends most of his time playing golf these days…"

Timms continued to talk for about twenty minutes, giving brief summaries of each of King's associates, and answering questions from Harris; who'd had previous dealings with some of them and, to Barton's annoyance, had interrupted Timms three times, with amusing, but completely irrelevant, anecdotes.

"Last slide please, Lorna." Lorna switched the projector back on, to display the face of an attractive woman, in her mid-thirties.

"This is Deborah King, codename *Jackie Brown*. She's Bobby King's daughter. Very dutiful, she visits him every Sunday. Quite an interesting lady, she was married to a car dealer, divorced eight years ago. It seems that she used to put herself about a bit… liked a bit of rough, by all accounts… probably why her husband left. She's got a nice house in Maida Vale that King bought for her after the divorce. She likes the high life – smart clubs, fancy restaurants, posh parties – got busted by the Drug Squad a few years ago… caught her at a city banker's party in Chelsea – with a rolled up, twenty-pound note stuck up her nose."

Harris whispered something to Dave Connor, who immediately burst out laughing; Timms's face reddened; the others, who hadn't heard the remark, looked bemused. Barton glared at the senior officer: *For God's sake! Harris, we don't need this. Just shut up and let him get on with it.*

Timms gathered his composure again and carried on, pretending not have noticed the interruption. "The main reason Debbie King comes into the frame is that for the last three months she has been having an affair with Herrera. We don't know if she actually knows anything about his business dealings, but I think we can be fairly sure that she samples the merchandise… maybe she's in charge of quality control. Eh!" He chuckled and looked pleased, when he saw that his remark had raised a few smiles around the table.

"We did some more digging and found that she owns an escort agency, under her married name, Deborah Jackson. Top end of the market – five hundred or more for a night, a lot of big-shot clients, mainly diplomats and foreign businessmen. A lot of the girls they employ are from Eastern Europe, and we're fairly sure that she gets some of them through Milosevic." Timms put away his notes and sat down. "That's it, sir, any questions?" he asked.

"Not at the moment," said Harris. "I'd like to wait until DI Parkinson has told us more about our two foreign gentlemen. Just one thing though, who's the Robert De Niro fan?"

"What…? Oh! That's the boss, sir," Timms replied with a noticeable air of resignation – he'd suggested calling the operation Grand Prix, and naming the targets for racing drivers, but he'd been outvoted.

"Thank you, Inspector. That was most informative," said Harris, smiling, making a mental note of a common interest; shared with Barton. "Now, let's hear what DI Parkinson has got for us."

Sally stood up and it was Barton's turn to smile, as he noticed that she had left her notes on the table; he knew she wasn't bothered about impressing the brass. Barton stopped smiling though, when he noticed the way that Harris was looking at her. He'd was obviously put her into one of his compartments: *Which one Harris, Bimbo or Crumpet?*

"You've already met DS Connor, sir… and this is DC Phil Fellows… they're both on my operational team. We've been keeping surveillance on Herrera and Milosevic, who we've called *Jacknife* and *Ronin*." Phil's just got back from watching Milosevic. Sally paused until Lorna turned the projector on again; a picture of a man appeared on the screen; he looked about thirty-five, swarthy and quite handsome, with long, thick, black hair.

"Let's start with Enrique Herrera. He lives in a rented, penthouse apartment in Docklands, and seems to spend half his day sleeping off last night's party, although not always in his own bed. The day shift don't get very much excitement, but he does get the odd visitor in the afternoons... including a few known drug dealers who visit quite regularly. For the last three months, he's been staying at Debbie King's several times a week. The rest of the time, she's at his place. Most nights he'll go to a bar or a club, then on to a party or bring a crowd back to his place. Herrera mixes with a lot of well heeled city types – bankers, brokers, corporate lawyers, high fliers – you know... the sort who'll put away a couple of bottles of champagne or a dozen shooters in the bar after work... before going on to something stronger. We've identified several regulars, but apart from their coke habit, they all seem clean. We're talking about guys who can earn seven figure bonuses, by screwing people legally. If Herrera's been out all night, he'll get home anytime between six a.m. and midday, and we don't usually see him again until the evening. If he's at home at night, he usually has guests. Before he got involved with Debbie, the parties went on all night and some of them didn't leave until lunchtime... now it's more usually about three or four in the morning."

Lorna switched off the projector and Sally looked at the ACC, waiting for a flippant comment, but it seemed that Barton's warning look earlier had done the trick and Harris remained silent.

"He stays in London most of the time, but he's taken the Eurostar to Paris a few times, and made a couple of trips to Italy."

As Sally continued, Lorna turned on the projector again, to display an image of two men sitting in a bar. "As Paul has already said, King's contact with Herrera is through David Nichols. They meet regularly, every two or three weeks, in city wine bars. Herrera is usually alone, but a couple of times he has taken Fernando Marquez along. Marquez is the son of one of the top men in the Colombian drugs cartel. Interpol believe he runs most of their operations in Europe and he travels around a lot – Spain, France, Italy, Germany, Holland..."

Sally went on to explain the main evidence gathered from the surveillance on Herrera. And, as before, Harris interrupted frequently with questions, mostly concerning small details; most of which Sally answered without needing to consult her notes, letting Connor answer the few that she couldn't. Barton was growing impatient and looked at his watch as Harris asked an irrelevant question about Marquez: *I wouldn't put it past Harris to tell us that he knows him as well.*

Harris asked more questions as Sally gave the run down on Milosevic and the human-trafficking operation, but after a while, he stopped interrupting and started looking at his watch. Barton signalled to Sally to move things along.

Sally got up and stood by one of the boards. She moved her finger across a large map of Britain, pointing to the clusters of coloured dots. "Milosevic has been seen in all of these cities... sometimes with Nichols... often in the company of known drug dealers, pimps, and gang-masters. He's always got two or three of Jarvis's men with him on these trips… including Marcus Preston, who seems to be his minder. Sources in most of these places, have also confirmed that new supplies of cocaine and heroin often hit the streets, shortly after Milosevic has been in town.

Although they have local men on the ground in all the cities, Milosevic sometimes visits the houses and flats and has been seen talking to a few of the girls. He's also been seen visiting houses in London, which are owned by one of the property companies that Nichols runs."

Sally pointed to the maps again, "The dots represent all sightings of Herrera, and Milosevic in the last three months and, as you can see… they both get about a bit."

Harris didn't have any more questions and Sally sat down, breathed a sigh of relief and poured herself another cup of coffee.

Harris stood up, walked to the front, and looked briefly at each of the boards. "So let me try and sum this up," he said. "Nichols is the common factor connecting King to both Herrera and Milosevic. You've seen him doing deals with both of them. We also have both of them running around in Underwood's cars, using Jarvis's men as minders. The people Milosevic brings in are moved around the country by King's people, they live in King's properties, and it looks like Jarvis supplies Milosevic with muscle to help keep them in order. You've tracked consignments from the ports and seen the drugs handed over. From what you've told me, you've got enough to pull them in… so why haven't you asked HQ for the go ahead?"

This was the question Barton had been expecting; the question he had been hoping wouldn't be asked. "Two reasons, sir. First, we've been doing the sums, and we reckon that their operations are turning over three to five million a week. We've seen some cash changing hands – King's people collecting from dealers and pimps – and we know that goes back to Jarvis. But that's it… we don't know how the bulk of the money gets back to Herrera's friends in Colombia, or… to the Russians. We think that King's turning over some of it through his legitimate business and that he's getting his cut through the property deals, but the accounts add up. There aren't any unusual transfers out. Apart from what they've been spending – and that's only small change – there's no trace. They have to be laundering the cash somehow but every lead we've followed comes up blank. To be honest, sir, in that respect… we're not much further forward than when we started."

Harris frowned; he was hoping that he'd have something more positive to report back, to the men at the Home Office. "And the other reason?"

"I don't think that King's organised all of this on his own. He's never operated outside his own patch before. It's just too big, too well organised for a bunch of old-school gangsters. This isn't in their league. I think there's somebody else pulling their strings." Barton nodded to Lorna and another picture appeared on the screen; a silhouette of a man's head, with a question mark where his nose should have been. "Someone who's connected to King, somehow, somebody with enough clout to control him. I couldn't find a fitting De Niro film, so I'm calling him *The Puppet Master*. We're still ploughing through a pretty tangled web of holding companies and offshore accounts. It'll take time, but if we can follow the money... I think we can find him."

Harris looked at Miller. "Well, Chief Superintendent, it looks as though someone's got a decision to make. Go with what you've got, and worry about recovering the money and finding this Puppet Master later... or let it run until we've got everything."

"Trouble is," said Miller, "...if we let it run too long we could lose the whole lot."

"I know," replied Harris, "it's a tough call to make." He looked at his watch; eight thirty-five. "Time I was leaving," he said. "Thank you, everyone, it's been very interesting."

Miller got up and followed Harris to the door. "I'll see you in your office later, Mike," he said, as they left the room.

Sally was the first to speak, as soon as the two senior officers were safely out of earshot. "Do you think they're going to pull the plug, sir?" She looked as disappointed as she sounded.

"Hard to say, Sally, I probably would if I were in the ACC's position, but let's wait and see what the Chief Super has to say," said Barton. But, he didn't sound too hopeful. Like everyone else in the room, as he'd listened to Harris's last remarks, he could tell what the decision was going to be.

Chapter 2

Tuesday 29th April 2003

National Crime Squad, Hertfordshire Branch – 09:30 BST

Barton sat at his desk, listening to his boss relaying the conversation he'd just had with the ACC. It hadn't gone well and Trevor Miller was in sombre mood: *'I'll give you the bottom line, Mike... we can't give you any more time. The budget's tight and twenty-four-seven ops cost a lot of money... cards on the table... how close are you?'*

"I'm not sure, we're following up new leads every day... but I don't know where they'll take us. King's been getting away with it for years... and whoever he's got doing the laundry, they're bloody good."

"Harris has told the Home Office that if we move now, we'll break up the biggest organised crime operation since the squad was set up, and throw some big spanners into the works of the two international rings," said Miller.

"Yes sir, but what about the money?"

"He's not going to take the risk. Harris wants to impress people. So does the Home Office. He's told them what he knows he can deliver... it's enough for them. The public likes to see a big drugs bust... they want to see the criminals caught and locked up. They're not bothered that most of the people we'll pick up are victims themselves, they just want to see something done about illegal immigration. Harris wants you to close it down now. He's looking for a big story for the media this week. The bastard's booked a space in his diary on Friday and he's already got the PR team preparing the press release. I don't like it any more than you, Mike. But that's the way it is... OK... so we don't get the money... well two out of three will just have to do. Anyway, if you add up all the loose change they've got lying around, it'll come to quite a few million."

"But, Trevor. If we don't get to the man who's really behind this, the big money laundering operation will stay intact. They'll be able to use it again. We might put this lot away... but it's only a matter of time before the Colombians and Milosevic's people find another Bobby King and start up again."

"I know, Mike... but my hands are tied. Miller said. He started to get up, indicating that the meeting was over, "I'll talk to Harris again... see if can get you some more time, but don't bank on it... meantime you'd better set the ball rolling."

28

"OK, Trevor, but please try and change his mind," said Barton. He leaned forward and looked at Miller. "Tell him I'll pull out all the stops." Barton's eyes were wide open; like windows, inviting Miller to look inside and see his thoughts. His eyes were pleading: *I know what you're thinking, Trevor. But you have to trust me.*

Miller hadn't put a much of an argument to Harris – mainly, because the ACC hadn't been listening, but partly because he was worried about Barton. Miller hated clichés, but the words *rock* and *hard place* seemed appropriate in this situation. Miller doubted that the operation would make any significant progress without Barton's leadership, but at the same time, he wasn't sure if Barton could cope with the extra pressure that a fixed deadline would bring. It wasn't that he had any real doubts about him, but he knew that, even without all this, the next few weeks would be difficult for him. He saw it every year at this time; Barton would become withdrawn, distant, impatient, and short tempered. He'd push himself beyond the limits, as if he had to prove something. Miller understood and wished that he could help; but he knew he had to let Barton come to terms with it in his own way and in his own time. It was his tragedy, his ghost, and they – the people who cared for him – knew they had to keep their distance and let him deal with it.

"I know you will. I'll give you a call later," said Miller, he didn't like the situation any more than Barton did: *Bloody politicians, if it was down to me, I'd let you do it... get a result... get the Puppet Master.*

Crouch End, North London – 11:30 BST

David Nichols closed his briefcase and told his secretary that he was going out for lunch. "I won't have my mobile on, so if anyone calls take a message. I'll be back about three."

He left the office building by the back door and walked down the road to Crouch End Hill. The man, watching him, started the engine of the builder's van and followed: *Regular as clockwork.*

"Alpha-Two to control, *Taxi Driver* is on his way." He pulled in to the kerb and waited as Nichols hailed a taxi. He watched as the taxi did a U-turn and then followed as it turned into a side road.

"Control to Alpha-Two, understood. Confirm direction. Alpha-Six is following *Deer Hunter*."

Detective Sergeant Matt Brady stopped at the junction and turned onto the main road. "Going south down Crouch Hill towards Seven Sisters."

Brady lost sight of them for a while, but he caught up when the taxi stopped near Finsbury Park. Nichols got out and walked round the corner, where he hailed another cab.

Not that it mattered, he knew where Nichols was going – Brady had written the notes for yesterday's briefing – it was the same every Tuesday. Nichols was on his way to a pub in Highbury, to meet George Underwood for lunch.

Briefing Note: DAVID NICHOLS – 'Taxi Driver'
Age: 43 – 11/06/59
Home Address: ... Barnet, EN4
Marital Status: married no children
Business Address: RJK Property Holdings, Crouch End, N8 & Leeds, LS2
CRO: none
Relationship to Robert King: Business associate (since 1984 King bought out the property development company he worked for, and kept Nichols on the payroll) – Managing Director of several property companies incl.: RJK Property Holdings / King Estates / Northern Home Renewals. Front-man for most of King's business deals – travels around the country buying run-down property for development (accommodation for Milosevic's illegal workers?) – see map
Relationship with other targets: business meeting with Underwood every week – regular meetings with Herrera and Milosevic – (see p2)

Briefing Note: GEORGE UNDERWOOD – 'Deer Hunter'
Age: 65 – 29/03/38
Home address: ... Epping, EN9
Marital Status: divorced
Business Address: East London Motors, Stratford, E15
CRO: 1959, assault, 6 months (suspended) – 1966, GBH, 2 yrs (acquitted on appeal) – 1969 armed robbery, 5 yrs (served 3yrs)
Relationship to Robert King: Underwood and King were at school together. Business partners since 1960's – started with a house clearance business – more than just clearing out the furniture – clients included Mr P Rackman)
Managing Director – RJK Transport Group (distribution and ware housing, van couriers and heavy plant hire) and RJK Motors (motor dealers, car hire, mini-cabs)
King's right-hand man – ran the whole show when King was inside (1987-96)

Relationship with other targets: *Nichol – business meeting with every week. Warren Jarvis – old school friends, drinking partners, football – they have had the same pair of seats at Arsenal for 20 years.*

Highbury, North London – 12:15 BST

Nichols sat at their usual table, in a corner at the back of the pub, out of sight of the bar. The barman put two glasses on the table. Nichols picked up the lager and sipped it slowly.

Brady ordered a half pint of Guinness leaned on the corner of the bar, and watched for a few minutes. He slipped the barman a ten-pound note and made his exit by the back door, when he saw Underwood's car pull up outside. Nichols wouldn't know he was being followed if you were riding on his back, but Underwood was old-school and could smell Old Bill a mile away. The barman would call Brady later and let him know if he overheard anything.

The two men ordered lunch and another pint of bitter for Underwood. The pub was Underwood's choice; one of several that they used – all within walking distance of Underwood's place of worship. The walls of the bar were decorated pictures of the supermen, past and present, that he had worshipped since he was a boy – Adams, Armstrong, Bergkamp, Drake, George, Mee, Mercer, Whittaker, Wenger, Wright and a hundred more – gods attired in the red and white strip of Arsenal Football Club. When most of the kids in East London were following local heroes – The Hammers, The Orient and The Lions of Millwall – Underwood was standing, next to his father, on the terraces at Highbury, cheering on The Gunners. Nichols looked at the walls of the shrine and cringed; he supported Spurs and this was enemy territory.

Nichols opened his briefcase and gave Underwood a sheaf of papers. While Nichols talked, Underwood studied the papers, nodding and asking the odd question. This was a routine, they went through every week; agreeing and amending the report before Nichols took it to King. Both men knew that King had long since stopped bothering about figures. But they weren't for him.

George Underwood had recognised Nichols' potential when they had first met. The younger man had a good business brain and the two men had quickly set about transforming a miscellany of small businesses into a coherent group of successful companies. King and Underwood were impressed enough to make Nichols a full partner, with a ten percent share of the profits, and by the time King was sent down, the legitimate side of their business was turning over more than enough to secure a comfortable retirement from their life of crime. But while

Bobby King was preparing for his six-year holiday in the Scrubs, Underwood found out that it wasn't King who called the shots. Mid-way through the trial someone else started calling Underwood and giving him instructions, and by the time King came out the business had trebled in size. Underwood and Nichols both knew that for over twenty years, someone else had been pulling all the strings, and he wanted every penny accounted for. Nichols had never dared to ask questions and didn't know who his real boss was. Only a few people knew his identity, and George Underwood was one of them.

"So, when's all this cloak and dagger stuff going to stop, George? All this going out the back door, changing taxis. I've still not seen anyone following me."

"That's because you don't know what to look for. There's a blue Astra parked outside right now. It followed me all the way from Stratford."

"Well, it's making me nervous. Can't we ease off for a while?"

"He'll tell us when it's time. Don't worry they're not ready to move in yet. And we'll get enough notice when the time comes. We'll be clear away when they come. He's got it all worked out." *The sooner, the better though. It's time I retired.*

Nichols nodded and shrugged his shoulders. "I suppose so, but it doesn't stop me worrying about it." But he was more worried about how his wife would react when he told her to drop everything and meet him at the airport.

"Shut up, Dave. Let's get on with the job in hand. What are you doing this week?"

Nichols got out his diary and read out his appointments. When he had finished he got up and left Underwood to finish his third pint.

"Blue Astra, Dave, but don't look at them. They don't know that we know," said Underwood as he picked up his glass.

National Crime Squad, Hertfordshire Branch – 13:45 BST

Barton was staring out of the window when they came in. He didn't hear them; but he sensed their presence and turned round, "Sorry, didn't hear you knock, I was miles away."

"The door was open, sir," said Timms, as he placed a grease-stained brown bag and a paper napkin on the desk. "Here's your bacon roll?"

"You look miles away," said Sally, "What were you thinking about, sir?"

Barton smiled; he thought it was funny, the way that she always seemed to call him '*sir*' when Paul was around. It didn't sound right somehow, when she addressed the rank, rather than the man – the man who had once talked of sharing his life with her; the man who had once shared her bed. That part of their relationship was over; it was over long before he met Grace, but the bond of friendship that had led to the affair had been too strong, too important to be discarded. They had parted amicably and after a short period of readjustment they had started again; much the same as before, but without the sex. Friends had warned them of the dangers; his wife had sometimes openly expressed her resentment of '*his other woman*'; and he had to admit that there were times, when he still felt a spark of the old electricity. But it worked, most of the time; it just didn't sound right when she called him '*sir*'.

"Just daydreaming… I had this picture in my head… Bobby King laughing at us… dancing on a big pile of cash… except it wasn't King. It was a doll with King's face… like a puppet on strings."

He picked up the bag and took out the bacon sandwich, looked at it and put it back in the bag. "Sorry," he said. "I've lost my appetite."

They were all hoping that he'd got them some more time and Sally thought that Barton looked a bit happier than when he'd spoken to them earlier, but his face wasn't giving much away. "So, what did the Chief Super say?" she asked apprehensively.

Barton consigned the greasy bag into the bin. "He's talked to Harris again," he said with an air of resignation. "We've got another month."

Chapter 3

Wednesday 30th April 2003

London, Docklands -12:30 BST

Herrera got out of bed and made his way to the bathroom. He stood in front of the mirror and ran his fingers through his hair. He moved his hand down and felt the rough, dark stubble on his face; contemplated for a moment, then decided not to bother shaving. Continuing his morning routine, he flexed his arms and felt his firm biceps, breathed in to expand his chest and patted his trim stomach, nodding in approval as he admired his naked body. Finally, and with great satisfaction, he held his penis in the palm of his hand, stroking it fondly, as he emptied his bladder: *No wonder the lady is satisfied.*

"Christ, Ricky! Do you always have to piss with the door open?" Debbie King called out, as she rolled over in the bed and reached for a cigarette: *Why do men have to fart when they piss?*

Herrera ignored her and flushed the toilet. He turned on the shower and sang as he washed away the traces of their lovemaking.

"And if you have to sing, you could at least be in tune," she shouted.

Herrera ignored her again and carried on singing as the powerful jets of water massaged his body: *Women! Three months and she's already nagging.* But, he'd never been with a woman like this before; never been with a woman for this long. He wondered how much longer it would be before one of them got bored. His friends back home had told him that English women weren't very exciting – too inhibited, lazy in bed – but, they hadn't met this one. He was thirty-six and had been with more women than he could even begin to count – American, European, Asian… black, brown, white… tall, short… skinny, voluptuous – and none had pleased him like this one. And she was insatiable. He wasn't looking anywhere else at the moment: *Not yet. Not while she still screws like a bitch on heat.*

He wrapped a towel around his waist and went back into the bedroom, and sat on the edge of the bed. Debbie lit a cigarette and passed it to him as he spoke to someone on the phone. He watched her as she got up and walked to the dressing table. There was still some white powder on the mirror, left from the night before. She picked up one of her credit cards, cut a few lines, and rolled up a ten-pound note. She inhaled deeply, and then sat for a moment, exhilarated by the rush that she felt in her brain. She picked up the mirror and took it back to the bed. "Want some?" she asked.

Herrera took the mirror and finished off the remaining lines. "I've got to go out and meet someone." He stood up and dropped his towel onto the floor.

"What time's the car coming?"

"Two o'clock."

"That's plenty of time, then," she said, with a wicked look on her face. He closed his eyes, and counted his blessings, as she pushed him onto the bed and sat astride him.

Briefing Note: ENRIQUE HERRERA – 'Jacknife'
Age: 36 (from immigration records – Colombian national – first entered UK from Malaga, Spain, March 2001)
Home address: ... Docklands, E15
Marital Status: single?
Business Address: n/a
Relationship to Robert King: Sleeping with King's daughter – Deborah
Relationship with other targets: Nichols and Milosevic – regular meetings. Fernando Marquez (Interpol target) – cousins. Warren Jarvis – provides drives/minders – Underwood – provides cars – Herrera travels everywhere by car – usually a Mercedes S Class supplied by Highgate Executive Car Hire – never drives himself – Jarvis's boys take it in turns to be his chauffeur

Today Herrera's driver was a well-dressed young man called Errol Preston, younger brother of Marcus; who according to his business card was Head of Operations for Jarvis Security. In reality, Marcus Preston was no more than a thug in a thousand-pound suit. But he was brighter than most and Warren Jarvis trusted him with the jobs that he would have done himself in the old days. And because Jarvis trusted Marcus, he also trusted Errol.

Usually Errol would have noticed that he was being followed, but Herrera had kept him waiting and was now sitting in the back of the Mercedes, urging him to make up time. And – as he drove along Westferry Road towards Limehouse, accelerating to forty whenever he could – he was too busy, concentrating on the traffic in front, to look into his mirrors. If he had been paying attention, he would have seen a green Volkswagen Golf; the one that had been parked round the corner when he'd arrived at Herrera's.

"Bravo-Two to control, I'm following *Jacknife* along Commercial Road, heading for the City, and he's in a hurry," said Phil Fellows, as put his foot down to keep up.

City of London -14:30 BST

Phil Fellows called in again, to say that he stuck in the traffic near Tower Hill. The message was relayed to Matt Brady as he watched the blue BMW 7 series, pull up alongside the kerb: *Sod it!* Nichols, as always, was on time and Brady knew that Phil Fellows was still about ten minutes away, so he would have to follow Nichols to the meeting place. Phil would have the easy job of following Herrera's car to the car park. It wasn't that the he minded the walking; the difficult bit was finding somewhere to park. He wasn't worried about getting a ticket, but the parking wardens were all private contractors and didn't care who they clamped. He found a space, stuck a note on the windscreen, and hoped for best. "Alpha-Two to control, I'm on foot following *Taxi Driver* along Devonshire Row towards Bishopsgate. Tell Bravo-Two to stick with the car after *Jacknife* gets out."

He watched, as Nichols turned right onto Bishopsgate, ran to catch up with him, and followed him to Liverpool Street. As usual, Nichols was taking a roundabout route; taking notice of what Underwood had told him. He walked past the station, then along Sun Street Passage and Broad Lane, before turning into Appold Street, where he went into a bar. He headed straight for the gents and then, having relieved himself, walked back out into the street and crossed the road, almost bumping into Brady, who was standing at the pedestrian crossing.

Brady followed Nichols a short distance, then stopped, and watched as he entered The Broadgate Exchange. The pub was crowded with office workers and, after ordering a drink at the bar, Nichols was having some difficulty finding a table. Brady watched from outside as Nichols looked around for somewhere to sit. After a few minutes three girls got up to leave and he elbowed his way in and claimed his prize, putting his briefcase on the table to mark his territory. Brady watched from the bar in amusement, as Nichols, looking increasingly nervous shook his head and waved his hand in response to anyone who asked if the seats were free. It was fifteen minutes before Herrera arrived to join him, and by then Nichols had valiantly defended the space against at least a twenty people. Taking advantage of the crowd Brady moved closer and sat at the next table, with his back to them.

He couldn't hear much over the noise, but by the time that the two men got up to leave forty minutes later, he'd heard enough.

Briefing Note: ENRIQUE HERRERA – Codename 'Jacknife'
... Nothing is ever actually exchanged between Nichols and Herrera. Both men make and receive calls on their mobiles during the meetings. They always arrive at the bar on foot, having got out of their cars a couple of streets away. The two drivers go to a car park -the underground in Finsbury Square is a favourite. Each driver gets a phone call (presumably from N&H to tell them that the deal has been done) and Herrera's driver will take several parcels from the boot and put them in the other car – each parcel estimated to contain about 10 kilos. After the transfer, the drivers make brief calls (to N&H?), and then the cars leave about five minutes apart and pick up their passengers – always in a different street to the one where they were dropped off.

Phil Fellows parked the car in the square and took the stairs down to the underground car park, where he saw Nichols's BMW parked in a bay on the far side. Errol Preston had parked the Mercedes at right angles to it, blocking three spaces, so that the rear ends of the two cars were close to each other. Fellows watched as Nichols' driver got out and opened the boot of the BMW. Errol put his phone back into his pocket, and opened the boot of the Mercedes. He started unloading, tossing the parcels to the other driver; Fellows counted fifteen parcels.

As soon as they'd made the exchange, Fellows returned to his car and waited. Forty-five minutes later he pulled in behind a cab outside Spitalfields market and watched as Nichols got into the back of the BMW, now being driven by Errol Preston. From there it was a straight run to Tottenham.

When Nichols arrived at the club, Brady was still following Herrera on foot. He'd walked further than usual, down Old Broad Street towards the heart of the City. Brady lost him by the Stock Exchange – he was only about thirty metres behind, but he got to the bend in the alley too late, and didn't see Herrera disappearing into the bank.

Tottenham, North London – 16:30 BST

Nichols waited impatiently in the bar while Errol unloaded the car. He never felt comfortable in these places; this was the seedy side of Bobby King's business, catering to the dirty raincoat brigade. The strip clubs and the massage parlours were a reminder of the past; relics that had little place in the world they moved in now. They made a nice contribution to the profits, but Nichols was worried that it kept them too close to the front line. If he'd had his way, they'd have been sold off long ago. He'd worked out the figures and shown them to Bobby; if they sold them all off they could take a profit of several million on the deal; and the new owners would still need a supply of girls and drugs. Nevertheless, Bobby and Warren had insisted, partly because it reminded them of the old days; mainly it kept their sons occupied and out of the way.

Nichols was anxious to get away, but Warren had come down from the office and taken Errol upstairs. He was amusing himself, fondling the breasts of the girl sitting on his lap, when a man slapped him on the back. Then he smelt the garlic and heard the voice of Vladan Milosevic.

Briefing Note: VLADAN MILOSEVIC – Codename 'Ronin'
Age: 45 *(from immigration records – Serbian national - entered UK June 2001)*
Home address: *lives in hotels – currently Hotel Russell in Russell Square, WC1. Uses a rented flat for business/entertaining? Roseberry Avenue, EC1*
Marital status: *not known*
Business address: *see above*
Relationship to Robert King: *no evidence of direct contact*
Relationship with other targets: *Nichols and Herrera – regular business contacts (see p2). Terry King and Barry Jarvis – social (see p3) – regular customer at the Palace Club. Warren Jarvis – regular meetings at JSL offices – interviewing staff? He uses a car supplied by Highgate Executive Cars (part of RJK Motors) and drivers/minders supplied by Jarvis Security – Marcus Preston and Kevin Grant*

...Meetings between Milosevic and Nichols usually take place in London (Wine bars in the City) – within a day of Nichols meeting Herrera. The arrangements for his meetings with Nichols are similar to Herrera's meetings, but, Milosevic prefers North London pubs (seems to have developed a taste for real ale?)

... Milosevic spends a few days each week travelling around the country (sometimes meeting up with Nichols). He personally supervises the local arrangements for the illegals and meets up with gang-masters and pimps, in various cities. He also regularly visits the houses where his girls live and (according to informants) beats them up himself if they get out of line. Sometimes after he has visited, an Eastern European girl turns up at the local casualty department – claiming to have been attacked by muggers or beaten up by a boyfriend? Only two – a Bosnian Serb and an Albanian – have ever made an official complaint (both girls are in protective custody)

... Often seen with TK and BJ – clubs, casinos and parties (heavy drinker and cocaine user) – executive boxes at football matches and the races. Loves gambling – very large bets – hates losing. August 2002; barred from a West End casino – lost £75k at Blackjack and assaulted a croupier – February 2003; banned from Doncaster race course – lost £20k on a big race and threatened the jockey and one of the stewards in the ring (TK and BJ were also there)

"Hello David," said Milosevic, his slow pronunciation and thick accent, distorting Nichols's name – *'Daa-veed'*. "They said you were here. Put the girl down, we have to talk." As Milosevic sat down and the girl made a hasty exit; she didn't need telling - the look on the Pig's face gave her the message.

"Vlad! What are you doing here?" said Nichols, alarmed by the man's presence. He hadn't been expecting Milosevic; they'd never met here before, and the alarm bells started ringing. Ever since Underwood had told him they were being followed, he'd been particularly careful about his meetings with the two foreigners. He turned his head away as Milosevic leaned across the table, and the stench of garlic attacked his nostrils. Acting as the go-between with Milosevic was one of the least pleasant aspects of Nichols' work. He'd heard that the girls called him the Pig, and thought it was very appropriate. – bad-mannered, ill-tempered and foul-mouthed, stinking of garlic and stale sweat; he had greasy hair, bad skin and dressed like a slob – Nichols found it hard to imagine a more disgusting example of the human race.

"We have to talk David. I need more places. I send some more people to Liverpool this morning, but now the houses are full. No room for any more."

"OK I know. I'm trying to sort it out. I'm going to Leeds tomorrow. We'll talk about it, but not here," Nichols said angrily. "Friday, OK?"

Nichols started to get up, but Milosevic grabbed his wrist. "Friday... don't fuck with me... you better have something," he tightened his grip, and snarled. "My friends are getting impatient. They will not be pleased... if you... you make them wait."

Cheshunt, Hertfordshire – 19:00 BST

Briefing note: ROBERT 'BOBBY' KING – 'Godfather'
Age: *65 – 27/12/37*
Home Address: *... Cheshunt, Herts, EN8*
Marital Status: *widowed*

Business Address: -

CRO: *1950's & 60's several convictions for assault etc. 1974 GBH 2 yrs - 1987 manslaughter 10 yrs (served 7yrs)*

Background: *Involved with organised crime since he was a kid (ran errands for the Krays) and got a reputation as a hard man ('evicted' tenants for Rackman in the 60's) Professional criminal – extortion, protection, prostitution, armed robbery, drugs, pornography – never charged with anything. AKA 'the Waste Disposal Man – he has been prime suspect in several murder investigations (contract killings?), but never enough evidence for charges.*

King leafed through the papers that Nichols had brought him. He wasn't really interested; he already had more money than he could ever spend, but as always he listened attentively as Nichols tried to explain the figures. He knew that Lenny would go over them with a fine toothcomb when he got them, and he always had questions.

"So what's this? That's a lot more than last week. Won't that push the price down?" he asked. He'd never been that good at maths, but he could multiply by two and he knew about supply and demand.

"Don't worry… it's not all going out at once. Were stockpiling, ready for when we have to pull out," replied Nichols, wondering how much King had been told: *Maybe it is time for him to retire.* He wasn't the only one who had noticed that King seemed to be losing touch.

"It's OK… George told me… I'd forgotten. Carry on," said King, trying not to sound confused: *What's he doing? Why hasn't anyone told me?*

"They're doubling the amount on each shipment, and Herrera's people are sending four loads next month. So that'll be four times as much next month. It's a lot of money."

"What about Milosevic?"

"He's got about sixty people waiting, but we can't take many more until we've got some more houses sorted. We've still got the last lot at the warehouse… we can put a few more in there for a while, but they won't be earning. I've got some of flats near King's Cross to sort out next week and I'm going up to Leeds tonight to move things along up there. I'm taking Michael with me to sort out the contracts."

"How long will you be away?"

"It'll take a couple of days I've got to meet Milosevic in Liverpool. One of the agents called me yesterday. He's got some empty property available that we should be able to move into quickly. We can rent them until the contracts go through. I thought I'd come back on Monday."

"Have you still got that woman up there? She'll have to go without... we're playing a foursome with George and Michael on Sunday morning. Tee off at eight-thirty... don't be late and make sure that Michael isn't either."

"OK, I'll be back on Saturday night. Five hundred quid says we'll thrash you."

"Make it a grand and bring your wallet."

Stoke Newington, North London - 21:30 BST

Jasmina was alone in the small one bedroom flat. She looked out of the window of the room, which she had shared with four other girls for nearly six months. She could see lots of people in the street – walking, talking to each other, crossing the street, looking in the shop windows, going about their business; whatever that meant, it was just phrase, she'd picked up from someone, for what people did, but it sounded interesting – and the traffic – cars, vans, motorcycles, bicycles and buses – so much traffic. They'd told her that there were many places to see in the big city, but she didn't even know where the red buses had come from or where they were going. The names on the route signs meant nothing to her – Tottenham, Wood Green, Hackney –not even if she had been able to read English. The view that she was looking at, was all she had seen of London. All she knew was this place and the place that they took her to every day, in the back of the van with no windows: *Oh! To be able to cross the street, ride on a bus ... to anywhere, away from this place.*

She went into the other, larger, room; where another six girls slept and the curtains were always closed. Apart from the mattresses on the floor, the wooden table by the window was the only piece of furniture in the flat. She climbed on top, opened the curtains, and looked out of the window. Earlier this morning she'd heard the Imam's call to prayer and she hoped, that from a different vantage point, that she might see a glimpse of the mosque, that she knew must be close by. She let out a cry of disappointment when she saw that the view was the same.

She rolled up the ragged prayer mat and put it under her mattress. She didn't mind being alone; three times today she'd been able perform the ritual salah; to cleanse and cover her body before her prayers. Three times, she'd praised Allah, in the way she had been taught as a small child. But she'd committed so many sins since she'd been here; she'd been with so many men, displayed her treasures to all and, although it was haram, she'd learned that alcohol and drugs could dull the pain. She knew that she'd never be able to correct the balance. Allah would judge her and she feared that her burden would be too great; but how could he punish her more than she was already being punished?

The other girls had been taken to work, as usual, but she'd been left on her own all day. She couldn't go out, the door was locked, and the windows were barred. One of the other girls had told her that she'd tried to get out through the window. She'd fallen three floors and broken many bones. She couldn't work for a long time and now, because she had to pay them back, they wouldn't send any money to her family. After that, they put up the bars.

It hadn't been the usual man this morning, she liked him; he was nice to them and he sometimes brought them nice things. The man they called the Pig had come for them today and he'd told her that she didn't have to work. One of the other girls told her not to be afraid.

The Pig had come back in the afternoon and she'd cowered in the corner, expecting a beating: *For what?* She'd done everything he'd asked, and he'd told her that all the men were pleased with her. But she knew that he hurt the girls for his pleasure; the more that they cried for him to stop, the more he enjoyed it. But today he'd spoken kindly to her; he'd told her she was special, that he wanted her to please some important men. And afterwards he would take her to her sister. He gave her a new dress and things to make her body smell sweet. He gave her food; the packets were sealed and from the labels, she knew it was halal. And he'd told her to be ready at ten o'clock.

As she sat and waited, for the Pig to return, Jasmina was happy for the first time in months. Soon, insha'Allah, she would be with Naida again.

Chapter 4

Thursday 1st May 2003

Tottenham, North London -10:30 BST

Terry King put down the control pad and held out his hand; his friend had just been beaten again and owed him another twenty pounds. He could never have beaten Barry in a real fight, but he always had the upper hand in the virtual world. Clenched into fists, Barry's podgy hands were lethal weapons, but his stubby fingers lacked the dexterity required to master the PlayStation. In real life, Barry had always fought Terry's street battles, but he always lost when they played Street Fighter on the screen, and he always paid up.

"Double or quits," said Barry, pressing the reset button: *So what? There's plenty of cash in the safe.* "I'll be Ibuki."

"OK, one more. Then we've got to sort those films out. What time is your old man coming round?"

Briefing note: TERRY KING – 'Goodfella
Age: 39 – 21/09/63
Home address: ... Tottenham, N15
Marital status: single
Business address: The Palace Club, Tottenham, N15
CRO: 1982 car theft & assault 9 months - 2 driving bans
Relationship to Robert King: Son. Managing Director – The RJK Group (that's what the records at Companies House show, but it's Underwood and Nichols who really run things. Terry just does as he's told – they don't let him get involved with much except the clubs)
Relationship with other targets: Barry Jarvis – cousins, went to school together, share an office at the Palace Club. Milosevic – social

Briefing Note: BARRY JARVIS – 'Mad Dog'
Age: 39 – 24/01/64
Home address: ... Tottenham, N15
Marital status: divorced

Business address: *The Palace Club, Tottenham, N15*
CRO: *too much to fit on the page – including three stretches for GBH. He's a real hard man - nasty temper – like his old man but worse*
Relationship to Robert King: *Nephew*
Relationship with other targets: *Warren Jarvis's son – works for his dad. Milosevic – social. Terry King – cousin, close friend – Barry and Terry share an office and do some of the drugs distribution, through the clubs – they also fancy themselves as film producers and make rather bad (amateurish) porn films.*

Barton's team had dubbed them *'The Terrible Twins'* and at the briefing Timms had summed them up in a few words: *'both fat and lazy... hardly a brain cell between them and too thick to be given anything really important to do'.*

One more game had become two, and then ten, and then the morning had gone; they didn't hear Warren Jarvis come into the office.

"Fucking hell, Barry! Don't you two ever do anything, but fuck about?" Without waiting for an answer, Warren Jarvis walked over to TV set and pulled the plug out of the socket. "Have you got those fucking DVDs sorted out yet? Marcus is coming over soon and they'd better be ready."

"We were just going to do it, Dad," said Barry, red faced – embarrassed at being taken to task in front of his friend. If anyone else had spoken to him, like that, they'd have been lying on the floor by now; but there was one person he didn't argue with.

"Well, fuck off and do it then. I've got some calls to make."

The *Terrible Twins* got up and walked out of the office. "And, shut the fucking door behind you," Jarvis ordered. "I'll give you a shout when Marcus gets here."

Briefing Note: WARREN JARVIS – 'Raging Bull'
Age: *64 – 03/04/39*
Home address: *... Highbury, N5*
Marital Status: *divorced*
Business Address: *Jarvis Security, Stoke Newington, N16*
CRO: *1950's & 1960's – several convictions for assault – fine, short (mostly suspended) sentences 1978 – GBH 3 yrs (served full term – assaulted another prisoner)*
Relationship to Robert King: *Brother-in-law (they were at school together and married twin-sisters). King's minder*

Managing Director – Jarvis Security Ltd. (King owns 60%) – provides doormen and security to club, pubs etc. across London. JSL employs all the heavies who look after the women and the other illegals. Jarvis also controls a lot of the distribution of drugs and hard-core porn. **Note:** *two of Jarvis's employees were convicted with King in 1987 manslaughter case*

Relationship with other targets: *George Underwood – old school friends, drinking partners, football – Arsenal season tickets in adjacent seats. Jarvis Security provides all the drivers (minders) for King, Underwood, Nichols, Herrera and Milosevic. Barry Jarvis – son*

Warren Jarvis had given up on his son long ago – Barry was a big disappointment to him, and he knew that, although he and Bobby didn't always see eye-to-eye, they were of one mind when it came to their opinions about their sons – Barry and Terry were a pair of clowns; good for running errands and not much else. Jarvis always referred to them as *Laurel and Hardy*, he couldn't make his mind up about who was who; and it would have been a fine call to find any redeeming feature that might favour one over the other. Their fathers had managed to keep them well away from things over the years, and between them, they knew less about the business than some of the morons employed by Jarvis. But they were family, their incompetence was tolerated, and they got a share of the profits – but not forever – Bobby King's will, left everything to his daughter. Warren Jarvis had also made a will and Barry wasn't going to get a penny; he was leaving his share of Jarvis Security to Marcus Preston, and his money to football charities.

The centre of operations of '*Jarvis and King Video Productions*' was in the basement under the lap dancing club. On two walls, floor to ceiling racking held dozens of DVD recorders; Barry often came down here and would sometimes stand in front of the racks for hours, watching the flashing lights on the machines as they copied the images that he'd captured with his camera. He wrote the scripts with Terry, but he was the cameraman and director.

Against another wall were shelves full of the finished goods. Three fast, colour laser printers were whirring away at one end of the room; one printing labels; the other two printing the box covers. Four girls were standing at a large table in the middle of the room; one was putting labels onto the silver discs, another was putting the discs into plastic boxes, the third was putting on the covers and the last one put each case into a cellophane wrapper. Sometimes, when business upstairs was slack, the production line was much busier and there'd be up to a dozen girls round the table. The operation was tiny compared to some – Barry had heard about a place in Germany with four-hundred recorders – but they'd only been going a couple of years, and it was all their own work.

Well almost. Neither man had a clue how the technology worked, how to code the discs so that they couldn't be copied, edit Barry's amateur camerawork into something that looked at least semi-professional, or overdub the sound so that the girls sounded like they were enjoying it. And they hadn't even thought of the idea themselves. *The Terrible Twins* had been struggling to compete; they were still making tapes when everyone wanted DVD. They'd probably still be making tapes that nobody wanted if Barry hadn't met some students in a pub. Two of them were now sitting at the desks in the corner, in front of the PCs from where they controlled the recorders and printers, edited the films, and designed the labels and covers. Every so often one got up and walked up and down the bank of recorders, changing the discs. Initially they'd been happy to work for free beer, a bit of gear and their pick of girls, but as sales had increased, they'd given up their degree courses and now they worked full time, in the dingy, airless basement, making more money than they could ever have imagined. They'd negotiated a thirty percent share of the profits. Terry had only wanted to give them twenty-percent; and Barry had to give them the other ten-percent from his share, but he didn't mind that; he still had thirty-percent; and they could all thrash Terry on the PlayStation.

Terry walked over to the desks, "Have you packed the Liverpool order?" he asked.

The man at the desk didn't answer and continued staring at the film that was running on the PC screen. Terry pulled the earpieces from the man's ears and shouted, "Hello is anyone home!"

The man turned round with a start, "Oh! Hi Terry, I didn't realise you were there. I've got that order ready. Over there in the corner, the demos are in the small box."

"Thanks, what are you watching?"

"The one Barry gave me to edit this morning?"

"Can I have a couple of copies?"

"I've only just started on it. It's not ready."

"Never mind, burn me a couple of copies. I'll take it as it is."

Stoke Newington, North London – 12:45 BST

Jasmina had showered three times that morning, but still she didn't feel clean; she would never feel clean. She had returned from the club at three o'clock in the morning: physically and mentally exhausted; and the Pig had told her she could rest today. Every part of her body hurt, but the physical pain was nothing compared to the agonies inside her tortured mind. She felt more ashamed and degraded than ever. Thoughts of what she had been forced to do last night sickened and disgusted her. As she felt the poison inside, in every cell of her body, consuming her, only two thoughts helped to ease the pain.

The Pig was pleased; the men had been satisfied and had paid him well. Now, at last, she would see her beloved sister Naida. And Naida would take care of her.

And she believed. Her faith told her that her suffering had a higher purpose. She knew that she was being tested and she had been taught how to bear her trials: *Seek Allah's help with patient perseverance and prayer.* She covered her head with a scarf. The clothes she wore were not appropriate, and so she wrapped a sheet around her body. And then, as she began to recite her prayers, *"Allahu Akbar…"* the pain inside subsided.

National Crime Squad, Hertfordshire Branch – 13:00 BST

Barton sat in his office with Sally and Timms, reviewing a stack of surveillance reports. He put a form to one side and picked up the phone, "Lorna is Matt Brady in yet…? OK, tell him to come over to my office. I want to go over his report for yesterday," said Barton. He put down the phone and looked at Brady's report again. "I don't like this, there's too much happening all at the same time."

"Yes, all this activity is putting pressure on us. Maybe they're expanding," said Timms. "If they are, then we could use some more bodies."

"I wasn't thinking about that, Paul. I'm more concerned with why," said Barton as he read the report for a third time. There was a knock on the door and he looked up. "Come in, Matt."

Brady was still embarrassed about losing Herrera and was hoping that they wouldn't make a big deal over it. "I managed to pick up some of what they said. I couldn't hear a lot, sir," he said. "It was very noisy in the pub, but I managed to get a lot closer than usual. Most times, we can't hear anything. Herrera definitely said something about extra shipments next month, and I think he said they'd be two hundred kilo loads. Yes… I'm pretty sure."

"What's this about Milosevic and Nichols going to Liverpool? Have you got that right? It's a bit sudden, they were only up there a couple of weeks ago."

"Maybe something urgent came up. It might explain why Milosevic was at the club when Nichols got there," Sally offered. "That's the first time the two of them have been there at the same time. And Warren Jarvis was there as well.

Dave and John Perry said that they both left about ten minutes after Nichols. What, exactly, did Nichols say, Matt?"

"All I heard was something about houses. Nichols was complaining about having to spend all day looking at houses. Something about needing to find more space, quickly." Brady thought for a moment, trying to think if he'd missed anything. "Oh yes...! yes... he said something about taking someone called Stevens with him... to sort out the contacts."

"Stevens... who's he?" asked Sally.

"Well the only Stevens that I can think of is Michael Stevens," said Timms, "...you know... King's lawyer. But I wouldn't have thought he'd be going all the way up to Liverpool to do paperwork."

"Give his office a call when we've finished and see if he's there," said Barton. "Now, Matt, tell me exactly how you lost Herrera. Do you think he could have seen you and given you the slip deliberately?"

"No, I'm sure about that, he didn't look back once. It was my fault, I let him get too far ahead, and then I almost walked past the alley. It's got a bend in it and there are several ways out. I was too slow that's all. I'm sorry, sir."

"That's OK, Matt, it happens. Anyway, I think what you got in the pub more than makes up for it. And he got back to his flat just a few minutes after you got there, so no real harm done. That's all, thanks,"

Timms put down the phone and added to the puzzle. "Stevens is out of the office until Tuesday ... they wouldn't say where he was."

Tottenham, North London – 15:00 BST

Warren Jarvis sat in the office above the Palace Club; he had been briefing his lieutenant for an hour. He got up from behind and walked over to the window. "So you've got all that Marcus?"

"Yes, we take Milosevic to Liverpool tonight... then tomorrow... take him to wherever he has to meet Mr Nichols."

Briefing Note: DAVID NICHOLS – 'Taxi Driver'
                  VLADAN MILOSEVIC – 'Ronin'

– seen together, in Newcastle, Manchester, Leeds, Liverpool, Birmingham, Bristol, Cardiff, Portsmouth, Glasgow and Edinburgh.
– 3 years ago, King bought a Leeds based property development company – Northern Home Renewals - they've been buying up run-down houses and flats in all of these cities. The properties are modernised and resold within a year – at a

big profit. It is usually several months before contractors start work - according to local council tax records, the houses are unoccupied during that time, it's quite usual and nobody bothers to check – at the moment the company owns over one hundred empty properties. Most of them are actually occupied either by a few women or by larger groups of men and women – mainly Eastern Europeans – as many as twenty in one house.
– going rate for Milosevic's girls £1500 a week pimps and brothels and £2000+ escort agencies in London and Birmingham
- pimps paying up to £6000 a week rent for a two-bed flat with 4 girls included

"Then I've got to meet up with Errol somewhere and give him twenty kilos to take to Leeds... run Milosevic around, wherever he wants... shift all the other gear... deliver Barry's DVDs and collect the money. With all that extra running around, I'll need to hire another car when we get there and split the boys up... is that OK, Warren?"

"Whatever it takes," said Jarvis. "Just don't let that mad bastard Leroy drive."

"Where's the stuff?"

"In the basement... Laurel and Hardy are down there now sorting it out. Have a good weekend. I'll see you on Monday."

Preston looked at the pile of boxes in the corner of the basement and shook his head. "Bloody hell! We'll never get that lot in the car. There's four of us and luggage."

"That's OK, you can leave the Merc and take my Land Cruiser," said Barry. "Come on let's get this lot loaded up."

The two men, who had come down to the basement with Preston, each picked up a box and followed Jarvis upstairs. Preston started to browse the shelves of DVDs. "Got anything new, Terry."

"Help yourself, Marcus. The latest ones are on the first rack and there's some demo disks over there on the desk."

Chapter 5

Friday 2nd May 2003

Liverpool – 09:00 BST

Milosevic and Marcus Preston were sitting in the hotel dining room eating breakfast. Preston listened while Milosevic took a phone call. "…alright… yes OK… it had better be a good deal… nine-thirty at the dock… OK." Milosevic was annoyed; he didn't like having his plans changed.

"Fuck!" Milosevic swore as Nichols ended the call. He carried on swearing as he made several short calls, barking down the phone and becoming increasingly agitated. As Milosevic rescheduled his plans, Preston picked up enough to work out what was going on, and he knew that Milosevic would be in a bad mood for the rest of the day. He'd have to tell the boys to tread carefully. Milosevic had a short fuse and it didn't take much get him going; one wrong word, one traffic hold up, was all it would take to set him off.

Preston poured another coffee and lit a cigarette; he passed the pack across the table to Milosevic. "So he wants you to go to Manchester, will it take long?"

"That depends on Mr Nichols, but I don't want to be long. I've got more business here this afternoon."

"I need to see Errol some time. I've got to load up some gear for him to take to Leeds."

"Well you'll have to do that while we're looking at houses this morning," snapped Milosevic. "…or when you come to pick me up in Manchester… I don't care, just make sure it doesn't hold me up."

"Probably better this morning, then. Where are these houses, you're looking at?"

"I don't know. I'll call you when we get there. Now I have to go, Mr Nichols is meeting me in ten minutes." Milosevic got up and stormed off, cursing, pushing past waiters, and ignoring the stares of the other diners. Preston shook his head as a warning, and watched as Leroy and Kevin stood aside to let Milosevic pass them on his way to the lobby. He called them over to the table and gave them the bad news. Something told him that it wasn't going to be a good weekend.

For the third day, Jasmina was alone in the flat again. She lay on the dirty mattress, her eyes wide open; staring but seeing nothing. The pain was beyond bearing; there could be no relief. She had no tears left.

She got up and wandered trancelike around the squalid flat that had been her home for the past six months, stepping over the mattresses and the discarded clothes on the floor; the clothes that the all girls shared, but rarely had time to wash. She stared at the bare walls, the torn curtains, and the bars at the windows of her prison. She looked at herself in the mirror – the girl that her mother and sister would recognise was gone – and she saw only what the Pig had made her; unclean, a filthy whore, an animal. She turned on the kitchen tap and watched the water run for a while: *Something in this hell that is pure and clean.*

All hope was gone. The Pig had come back and told her. He was going to sell her to one of the men she had pleased. He had offered a good price and the Pig had accepted. She would be his; available day and night, whenever he felt the need to satisfy his lust. The Pig had laughed and told her that she was lucky; the man was rich and she would live well. The Pig had lied to her and he told her how she stupid was to have believed that he would take her to Naida. He told her that Naida was dead. He told her that he lied to make her happy, so she would please the men. The Pig had lied about everything. He'd lied about the money, he'd sent her family nothing; the Pig had kept it all. And he'd sneered and laughed as he taunted her with the truth. And he laughed as he locked the door and left her alone again.

She couldn't bear to see the Pig again; she had to keep him out, but there were no bolts on the inside. So she dragged the mattresses across the floor and piled them against the door. She went into the bathroom, took the clothes from the bath, and pulled the plug. She watched the water drain away as she folded the wet clothes, and put them on the rail. Then, she sat on the edge of the bath; watching the water drip from the clothes, forming a pool on the floor. She turned on the taps to fill the bath, and picked up the bottle of bath oil – the present that the Pig had given her when he told his lies. The dirty, damp bathroom always stank of piss and shit; but now – as she emptied the bottle under the tap and the oil mixed into the water – the sweet smell of honeysuckle filled the air.

She went back to the kitchen and searched through the drawers; in vain. There were no knives in the flat. She remembered the small pair of scissors that one of the other girls kept hidden, and searched the two rooms until she found them under a mattress.

She bolted the bathroom door; undressed and stepped into the bath. She immersed herself in the hot water and put her head back; her long black hair floating on the oily surface. As the water warmed her body and eased her inner pain, she opened the scissors and twisted the point of a blade deep into her wrist. It was painful but she had already endured much worse. She dragged the blade through her flesh; making a deep ragged gash. It was more difficult to make the next cut, but she managed at the second attempt, to open the veins in her other wrist. She had failed the test and, as the water slowly turned red, she closed her eyes, knowing that they would never open again. Jasmina began to say a final prayer, "Forgive me Allah, I have failed you... I am truly sorry for my sins... Allah, forgive me..." And she prayed that she would soon be re-united with Nadia.

National Crime Squad, Hertfordshire Branch – 16:00

Barton called Timms and Sally into his office. He'd read their latest reports, and wanted to confirm that they knew where everyone was. "...and Milosevic and Nichols are both up North, so we don't have to bother with them, Northern OCU can take care of them. You're sure that Herrera's away for the whole weekend?"

"Yes, with Debbie. They checked into the Randolph Hotel in Oxford an hour ago. They've got the room till Monday," said Sally.

"Well in that case, let's stand down the surveillance for a couple of days. Get everyone who's on the roster over the weekend to come into the office. Get them going through files again. Be thorough... tell them to look for ..."

Timms interrupted and started to argue, feeling that Barton was in some way criticising him; suggesting that he hadn't been through enough. "That'll be a bundle of fun for them. What's the point?" he said dismissively. "Do you think they'll find anything? Are you suggesting we've missed something?"

"No, Paul, I'm not suggesting anything. But there might be something... if we look hard enough... we might find something, some little detail that might be significant... maybe, if we look at it from a different angle. Concentrate on King's connections, his businesses. Dig back through all the background stuff. Tell them to look outside the box. Let's have some lateral thinking."

"Mike's right, Paul, there's a lot of stuff there," said Sally. "If we swap the files round... give them to people who aren't familiar... fresh minds and all that."

"Yes that's what I mean, thanks Sally," said Barton, grateful, as always, for her support. "Right let's get on with it then. Straight shifts, minimum overtime... let's give them a bit of free time over the weekend. I'm going to clear up my desk and go home early today and I suggest you two do the same. Get back fresh in the morning. Then we can have a nice quiet weekend, just sitting in the office doing the paperwork without any distractions. I can't see that much is going happen."

Timms and Sally went to give everyone the news leaving Barton alone in his office. He opened a desk drawer and took out the silver photo frame that his mother had given him as a graduation present. She'd spent days hunting around the antique shops in Oxford looking for one that was just right and when she'd found it she'd had it engraved. He unfolded the frame and looked at the three photographs. The centre photograph was of himself, in his cap and gown; standing tall and proud, between his mother and his little sister. His mother had left the frame on the right empty; it now held a picture of his wife, Grace. In the third frame, his mother had placed a picture of another man, also standing tall and proud, in his dress uniform. A man who had missed what should have been their proudest day, and who was the reason that Barton had chosen to do what he did.

"Am I doing the right thing, Dad," he said. "What would you have done?" Barton closed his eyes and talked to his father, in the only way that he could now; the only way he had been able to talk to him for twenty years. And it was well after midnight when he got up to go home.

Chapter 6

Saturday 3rd May 2003

Liverpool – 01:30 BST

The young woman crept out of the bedroom; she winced with every step. She was exhausted, and needed to get away from the man who had hurt her; the man that all the girls knew only as the Pig. She knew that he'd want her again, but she had to get away from his stench if only for a few minutes. The man in the bedroom was an animal. The girls were right to call him the Pig. He'd made them into an animals; whores. She'd been in this city nearly six months; she'd stopped counting the men after a week.

As she bent down to pick her dress up from the floor, she noticed the spots of blood, marking her path from the bedroom. He had mounted her like an animal, forcing her buttocks apart, ignoring her cries of pain, tearing her inside as he violated her. She pushed her long black hair away from her face and hobbled around the room; looking for something to dull the pain, but she couldn't see the bottle.

She was also scared of the man who was sitting on the sofa, so she spoke softly, not wanting to anger him "Where is the vodka?" she asked.

Without taking his eyes off the TV screen, Marcus Preston gestured to the table by the window. "Over there, take it and get out," he barked.

She picked the bottle from the floor and walked back to the sofa; buttoning her dress to cover her nakedness, reaching down to pick up a packet of cigarettes from the side table. She walked over to the armchair, where a naked teenage girl was sleeping. She felt a stab of pain as she sat down on the arm of the chair. She looked at the TV and she lit a cigarette. She wasn't really watching, just putting off going back to the man in the bedroom. As she drank from the bottle, the alcohol eased the pain and she lit another cigarette. If the Pig wanted her again, he could come and get her.

Suddenly she gasped and stared at the screen in silence, as if in a trance. She sat there for what seemed an eternity. As the tears ran down her cheeks, she wiped them away with the palms of her hands, leaving black streaks on her face. When she could take no more, she got to her feet and started to walk away. She said something under her breath and then cried aloud, "Jasmina…! No!"

"Shut the fuck up and get out," hissed Preston, lashing out at her with the back of his hand. He was a big man and even though he was sitting down the force of the blow made her stagger. Before he could stop her she had picked up the table lamp and thrown it at the TV set. The heavy metal base shattered the screen into a thousand pieces. She turned and ran back into the bedroom.

"Bastard…! Bastard!" she shrieked, picking up an ashtray and hurling it at the man on the bed. The missile missed his head by inches, and smashed into the bedside table; knocking the packet of white powder to the floor.

Milosevic leapt from the bed, "Bitch! You fucking bitch! You'll pay for that. I'll get you," he cried as he flung himself across the room.

He caught her by the wrist but she pulled away and stumbled to the door. He lashed out and struck her across the face; the blow sent her reeling to the floor. She tried to crawl away, but he twisted his fingers in her hair and pulled her to her feet; pushed her back against the wall and punched her in the face.

"Bastard!" she screamed again, and she jerked her knee upwards, into his groin, with all the force she could muster.

As he sank to his knees, she collapsed to the floor and crawled out of the bedroom, blood streaming from her broken nose. Milosevic grabbed at a chair and started to pull himself up.

"Bitch…! Come here," he snarled, fumbling in the pocket of the leather jacket that was draped over the back of the chair.

She saw the knife in his hand and cowered behind the armchair. The other girl, now awake and hysterical, was on her hands and knees, gathering up her clothes from the floor and moving towards the door. Milosevic saw her and shouted, to Preston, "Get her out of here!"

Preston got off the sofa and tried to hurdle the armchair, but kicked it over and crashed to the floor. "Shit!" he cried as he reached out and tried to grab the girl by the ankle. He wasn't fast enough and she stood up and ran to the door, screaming.

"Get her, you idiot. Stop the bitch! Shut her up!" Milosevic shouted as he glared at Preston.

Preston got to his feet, "Shut the fuck up, you'll wake up the whole of fuckin' Liverpool," he shouted as he grabbed the frightened girl. She tried to scream again, but he put a hand over her mouth. "It's OK," he said, "nobody's gonna to hurt you." He opened the door and as he pushed her out into the corridor; she turned to look back and saw the Pig smashing her friend's face, with his huge fists.

Preston dragged the girl along the corridor, and hammered on the door of the next room. "Come on, Kev, open the fuckin' door," he cried.

"Alright, keep your bloody hair on. I'm coming. Who is it?" a voice shouted from inside the room.

"It's me, Marcus. Let me in."

"What the fuck do you want?"

"Just open the fuckin' door."

The door opened and Marcus pushed the girl into the room; followed her in and slammed the door shut behind him. Kev was standing naked by the open bathroom door and stepped aside to let them pass. A girl was sitting up in the bed drinking a glass of champagne. The hysterical girl ran, wailing and sobbing, across to the bed and put her arms around her friend; who caressed her head and comforted her with words that the men did not understand.

"He's gone fuckin' mental," said Marcus as he picked up a bottle of Scotch. He put the bottle to his lips, tipped back his head, and gulped down the whisky.

"Give me your mobile," he said and took another swig from the bottle.

The other man picked up a phone from the side of the bed and tossed it across the room. "What are you doing?" he asked.

"I'm calling the boss. You go next door. Get Leroy and the other girl."

"What shall I tell them?"

"Just get them in here. And put some bloody clothes on."

Marcus dialled a number and waited. The boss wasn't going to be pleased, but he'd know what to do. The phone rang and rang: *Come on Warren, answer the fucking phone.* Eventually Warren Jarvis answered.

"Warren, it's Marcus. We've got trouble... big trouble."

"Marcus what are you calling me for? Where are you?"

"We're at the hotel in Liverpool, with the Russian. He's gone fucking crazy. He's beating up one of the girls."

"What happened?"

"We were watching one of Barry's films... all of a sudden this girl starts screaming and shouting at him. Next thing he's shouting at her and belting her. I got out and called you."

"Where is he now?"

"Still in the suite... he's got a knife... I think he's going to kill her."

"Marcus, you've got to try and stop him. Get him out of there. Get him away."

"Where shall we take him?"

"Just get him out, now! Just get away as fast as you can. Get onto the motorway."

"Which one?"

"It doesn't matter, just drive. I'll sort it out and call you back. How many girls have you got there?"

"Four… the other three are OK."

"Get them out. Get one of the boys to take them back to their house… tell him to make sure they don't talk to anyone… give them something to keep them quiet."

As Marcus switched off the phone, Kev came back into the room. "They're just coming," he said.

A couple of minutes later another man and a teenage girl entered the room. "Jesus Christ! What's going on, Marcus?" he asked, "I was asleep, can't this wait till the morning?"

"We're leaving. Now!" Marcus, barked out his orders at the two men, in a way that left them in no doubt that he meant business. "Kev, tell them to get dressed. Leroy, call a taxi and get the bags."

"Where are we going?" asked Leroy.

"Take the girls back to the house… make sure they don't talk to anyone. They're probably shit scared already… but give them a bottle and some smack to keep them quiet. Tell them if they talk to the cops they're dead meat."

"What are you going to do?"

"We've got to get him out of here. We'll meet you at the racecourse."

"Then what?"

"I don't know yet. The boss is going to sort something out. Now call that fucking taxi. Kev, you come with me."

The two men stood outside the suite. Marcus put his ear to the door; everything seemed quiet. He still had the key card in his pocket and he took it out and put it in the slot. As the green light came on, he gingerly turned the doorknob. He opened the door slowly and looked into the room; he couldn't see anyone.

As Kev followed Marcus into the room, something crunched under his foot; he looked down at the broken glass on the floor. "Christ! What a mess," he said, as he looked around the wrecked room.

Marcus was already in the bedroom. "Kev, get some towels and come in here and help me get him dressed," he said.

As he walked into the bedroom, Kev saw the man was lying face down on the bed. Then he saw the red stains on the carpet in front of the bathroom doorway. He opened the door and looked inside. "Fucking hell!" he cried, before he threw up. Kev had knocked a few girls about in his time but he'd never seen anything like this. He'd seen this sort of the thing on TV, but this was real. He retched again and ran into the bedroom, wiping his mouth with a towel, "Fucking hell! Have you seen it, Marcus…? Have you seen what he's done to her?"

"Leave it Kev. There's nothing we can do about her. It's not our fucking problem, but he will be if we don't move. Let's get him out here. Now!"

Sally was awakened by a buzzing sound. She stretched out an arm and groped around the bedside table for the source of the noise. She found her mobile phone and pressed one of the buttons. "Sally Parkinson here," she yawned, as she turned on the light, "…who's that?"

"Dave Connor. Sorry to wake you up, Sally. But the shit's about to hit the fan and I think you'd better come in."

She listened as Connor repeated the message that he had just received from the unit in Liverpool. By the time he had finished she was out of bed and opening the bathroom door.

"Thanks for calling, Dave. I'll be there in half an hour."

She switched off the phone and tossed it onto the bed. She looked longingly at the man snoring under the crumpled duvet, knowing that their plans for a quiet weekend together would have to wait. She turned away and switched on the bathroom light. Ten minutes later; showered and dressed, she bent over and gently kissed the sleeping man on the cheek. She found a pen and hastily scribbled a note which she placed on the pillow beside him, turned off the light and quietly crept out of the room.

As she drove to the office, she wondered if she should call Mike, but decided to wait until she got to the office. Maybe it would turn out to be a false alarm. Maybe the local guy had overreacted and they'd already come back. Maybe it was a mistake and she could go home to bed. Maybe not, but she'd wait and not call him until she knew for sure.

Sally was unaware that, while she had been talking to Connor, the man they knew as the Puppet Master had also been learning of the events in Liverpool.

"What do you want me to do, Lenny?"

"You'd better sort it out, Warren. The police are already poking around in my business. Sort it out, before the bastard completely screws it up."

"They said he's bleeding all over the place. What do you them to do with him?"

"I don't care. Whatever it takes… just make sure the police don't find him. And tell them to keep him well away from London."

"What about the Russians?"

"Leave them to me. Just get him away from there. Call me back when you've got him safe and I'll tell you what to do."

Warren Jarvis put down the phone. A couple of minutes later he made another call; this time, he spoke to Marcus Preston.

Chapter 7

Saturday 3rd May 2003

Duxford, Cambridgeshire – 05:15 BST

Grace Barton was woken by the sound of running water. She turned over and put out her arm, hoping that she was dreaming and that her husband was still lying beside her. But Barton's side of the bed was empty, as it had been every morning for the past two weeks. She rolled over, opened her eyes, and saw the light under the bathroom door. Reaching out in the darkness, she fumbled for the switch on the bedside lamp. She screwed up her eyes a couple of times adjusting them to the light, then looked at the alarm clock on the bedside table; it was quarter past five.

She got out of bed and went downstairs to the kitchen. Switching on the lights, she was momentarily blinded by the glare of the bright halogen spot lamps in the ceiling. She walked over to the sink and filled the kettle; opened the fridge and took out a carton of orange juice, a container of milk and a tub of butter. She took two mugs from the hooks on the dresser and opened a tin; it was empty and she swore under her breath, "Bugger! No tea bags." She walked to the pantry; returning a few seconds later with a new box of Earl Grey. Ignoring the tear off strip, she ripped open the box, spilling most of the contents over the floor. She was really pissed off now, and didn't bother to bend down and pick them up; she just swore, "Bugger! Bugger! Bugger!"

Sometimes – and this was definitely one of those times – she wished that she'd married someone with a normal job: *Nobody gets up at this time on a Saturday morning... or if they do... they could at least come home at a decent time the night before.*

She put a teabag into each of the mugs and poured boiling water over them; picked up a glass from the draining board, rinsed it and filled it with orange juice. Then she took a loaf from a cupboard, took out two slices, and put them in the toaster. He hated sliced bread, but it was quick and she couldn't be bothered to mess about with a fresh loaf and crumbs all over the worktop at this time of the morning; he probably wouldn't eat it anyway.

She stirred the mugs, took out the teabags, dropped them into the sink, and poured milk into each mug. He always said he preferred tea, but she knew that this would be his only cup of the day; he'd spend the rest of the day drinking coffee. The slices of toast sprang up in their slots. She took them out, put them on a plate, and spread butter on them. There was a jar of Marmite on the worktop and she spread a thin layer on each slice. It wasn't as messy as marmalade or jam, and she knew that if he ate it at all it would be as he walked out to the car.

She left the tea orange juice and toast on the worktop; she knew that he wouldn't bother to sit down. She sat down at the table and sipped her tea. She looked at the large, scrubbed pine, farmhouse table surrounded by an assortment of wooden chairs. They'd bought them at auction – paying rather more than they had intended – intending the huge kitchen to be used for entertaining: *'we can have great parties, we'll get loads of people round that,'* she'd said, to justify the expense. Now, it all seemed a bit pointless; they rarely had guests and she tried hard to remember the last time that they'd actually sat down for a meal together: *It must have been three, no four weeks ago.*

Barton came into the kitchen. "Hi," he said, without looking at her, and picked up the glass of orange juice, "…did I wake you up? Sorry, you didn't need to get up."

"I was awake anyway," she said sarcastically, "and don't give me that, did I wake you up, shit. If you don't want to wake me up, why don't you use one of the other bathrooms?"

"I'm sorry…" he said meekly, but she cut him off before he could say any more.

"Sorry…! You're always bloody sorry… sorry really doesn't mean a lot. Does it! And while I think of it, you might as well use another fucking bedroom as well … you spend precious little time in ours."

"Hey, take it easy. What's brought all this on?"

"Oh…! Come on Mike, you're the bloody detective work it out. I've hardly seen you for two weeks… you're out of the house before five-thirty every morning… don't get back until gone midnight. God knows what time you came in last night?"

"About one, I think."

"So who was that creeping up the stairs and getting into my bed at half past two then? The fucking tooth fairy!"

Barton picked up a slice of toast and folded it in two; he hadn't touched his tea. "Look, I know you're upset, but I don't have time now. Can we talk about this later?" he said as he walked towards the door.

Grace sat and watched as he walked through the hall and out the front door. As the door shut, she got up and ran into the hall. She flung open the door and shouted after him, tears in her eyes. "And when is later going to be? After you fucking retire! When I'm too old to care?"

Barton didn't hear her; the stereo came on, and a CD started to play as soon as he turned the key in the ignition. It was the end of the track, the last words of the song: *'That's all I want, that's all I need, I'm satisfied'*. He thought it hardly appropriate under the circumstances and reached forward to switch it off. But as the track faded, he remembered what was coming next, something altogether more suitable, and as he turned out of the driveway, a soulful voice sang: *'I've been working. I've been working so hard…'*

'You've got it right, there, Van,' he said to himself. He started to hum along to the music and he smiled as he thought of how he'd been introduced to Van the Man. Just after they met, Grace had taken him to a concert in Cambridge. He'd told her it wasn't his kind of music, but she'd insisted that he'd enjoy it and she'd been right. He'd never heard a white man sing like that, and he'd bought a CD after the concert; the first of many. He smiled again: Stereotypes. I wonder what Harris would make of my Van Morrison collection.

He'd always remember that concert; that was the night that he'd fallen in love with her: *It must be nearly nine years ago. And now,* he sighed, as he came back to reality… *what the hell is happening to us?* Something was wrong; she'd never been like this before: *It can't just be the job*

She had always known, right from the start, how it would be. He'd seen too many colleagues with broken marriages and he didn't want it to happen to them. He'd told her what it would be like; given her the chance to back out. Told her about why he'd joined the police; about how the job consumed you, how good it made him feel when it went well and how it tore him up inside when things went wrong. Told her how he could never give it up, not even for her. Eight years ago, the eighteenth of June 1996, on her twenty-sixth birthday, she'd taken him 'for better, for worse'. Eight years without a word of complaint, nor any hint of resentment – the long hours, the forgotten birthdays and anniversaries, the cancelled restaurant bookings, the dinner guests embarrassed by the empty chair; so many times she could have complained with good reason – she had always forgiven him, always accepted it and told him that she understood: *So why now? Why is it falling apart now?*

He remembered the first time that they met. He was a DI with the Met's Serious Crime Squad at the time; seconded to Cambridgeshire CID to assist with a murder enquiry. Four women had been brutally assaulted and murdered; their mutilated bodies, dumped by the banks of the Cam. Grace was a young forensic psychologist, studying for her PhD at the university, and had offered to help the investigating team. Her profile of the killer was uncannily accurate and, had not only saved them months of work in tracking the man down, but, almost certainly saved other lives.

The following year, Barton applied for a transfer to Cambridge. His boss had tried to dissuade him, telling him that it would set back his career: *'It's a backwater Mike; they're still living in the dark ages out in the Fens. Stay in the big city, where the action is. Don't go; you'll regret it.'*

Well, he'd gone, and it probably had set his career back a bit. But he was only just thirty-four when he made DCI, and he'd never regretted it; not for one moment. He'd often wondered what it would be like if he had to live without the job; but he couldn't even begin to imagine living without Grace.

He'd always remember the joy in his mother's eyes when he told her they were married; a look that he'd not seen for many years. They were on honeymoon, he'd taken her home, and, as they walked on the beach in front of his mother's house, the smile on Grace's face had seemed to light up the dark moonless night. They shared the joy of his journey of rediscovery, as together they'd explored the island that, in his heart, had been his home for so many years. Home; though he'd never lived there and it had always seemed so far away for years his home had always been where his mother was. But not any more; for the last eight years and for the rest of his life, home was with Grace.

So why is it going wrong? What's happening to us? Whatever it was had started weeks ago, long before the meeting with Harris, so it couldn't just be down to the extra pressure he was under. He was glad in a way that he'd been given the deadline. Four weeks to go, then maybe they could spend some time together to talk about things.

"Fuck Bobby King! Fuck them all!" he cursed, loudly. "Why can't they all just fucking die?"'

National Crime Squad, Hertfordshire Branch – 06:30 BST

Barton pulled into the car park, unable to recall how he'd got there. It was like that sometimes; like driving on autopilot. The wipers were on full speed – somewhere along the way it must have started to rain – but he didn't notice until he got out of the car. He dashed across the car park to the office. Most of the NCS branches were based in semi-covert locations; anonymous offices, well away from the nearest public police site. No signs, no uniforms, no blue lights, no cars with Day-Glo stripes, just ordinary looking office buildings; just like this one.

"Good morning, sir. Is it still raining out there?" said the girl behind the desk as he walked in. "DI Parkinson's looking for you, she's been trying to phone but your mobile must be switched off."

"Thanks," he said, "do you know where she is?"

"Upstairs, sir, waiting in your office."

Barton walked up the stairs. "Sod it!" he swore. His mobile wasn't switched off; it was sitting on the kitchen table. This stuff with Grace was really getting to him.

Sally Parkinson was sitting at Barton's desk, talking to someone on the phone. She looked up as he walked into his office; "I'll call you back," she said and put the phone down.

"Good morning, Mike," she said, starting to get up.

"Hi, Sally. It's OK, you stay there, I'll sit here," he said, pulling a chair across to the desk. "You're in early."

"Been here since about four," she said. "Dave," she called out as Connor walked past the door, "can you get the boss a coffee, please?" She gave Barton a worried look, "Although, I think you might need something stronger in a minute," she said.

"What's up Sally?" he asked. "Vicky told me you've been trying to get me on the mobile. Sorry... I had a bit of a row with Grace this morning... think I left it in the kitchen. It must be important for them to have got you in so early. I thought you were taking the day off."

"You're not going to like this, Mike... we lost Milosevic this morning."

"Shit! Just when you think things can't get any worse."

"What's that, sir?" said Connor, as he brought in the coffee. He put a tray down on the desk; there were three mugs on it.

"Oh! Nothing," said Barton, "just thinking out loud."

Sally picked up a mug. "I've asked Dave to sit in," she said. "He's got some details from Northern OCU. They've been feeding stuff through as quickly as they can get it."

"OK, Dave, what's going on?" asked Barton.

"Milosevic was in Liverpool all day yesterday," said Connor as he opened a file and started to read from the report inside. "This is what we've got so far. Milosevic left the hotel about nine-thirty, and walked to Albert Dock where he met Nichols... they drove out to Toxteth where they met another man and looked at a couple of empty houses. The other man's been checked out... he's a local estate agent... guy called Foster. Then the estate agent took them to look at a couple of other places. Nichols's driver picked them up at about eleven-thirty, and drove them Manchester, where they visited two more houses and a block of flats."

"OK," said Barton, making a mental note to ask some more questions about Nichols later. "Carry on."

"A driver picked Milosevic up at two and took him back to Liverpool. Nichols went back to Leeds... straight to his hotel... went out to the casino at nine... back in the hotel before midnight and he's been there all night."

63

Connor looked at the report again. "Milosevic had a late lunch in the hotel bar and then visited some of his girls… then they went to a couple of pubs near the hotel in the early evening. You won't believe this… the hotel's just around the corner from Merseyside Police HQ… I wonder if he's been drinking in the same bars as the local brass. Anyway, they went onto a strip club at about eight… and met up with a couple of dealers…left at half ten and went back to the hotel."

Barton looked surprised, Milosevic was supposed to be a party animal, "What, having an early night!"

"Well, he might have been going to bed early, but I doubt he was planning to get much sleep." Connor closed the file and put it on the desk. "Yesterday was Friday… right… if Milosevic goes up north on a Friday he's probably planning to have a good time… he makes a lads' weekend of it," he picked up the file and turned over a couple of pages. "Yeah…the hotel has confirmed he was booked in for three nights."

"Get on with it, Dave," said Sally.

"Now as we know a good time for Milosevic involves lots of sex, booze and drugs… and a bit of sport… you know racing or football. There's a match at Anfield today and he's bound to have tickets. As far as the sex is concerned… he uses these weekends away to treat his favourite girls… the ones who don't give him any trouble. Gives them a couple of days of luxury… away from the dumps he's got them living in… lets them pamper themselves in the beauty salon or spa… spoils them with room service, while he's out during the day. Mind, you can bet they have to work for it… he's always got two or three of Jarvis's boys with him, if you know what I mean."

He started reading the file again. "Ten-forty… Preston dropped Milosevic and two other men at the front of the hotel."

"Preston? Which one?"

"Marcus… he's been travelling regularly with Milosevic for about six months now. The other one, Errol… he's driving Nichols."

"What about the other two?"

Sally answered. "We don't know who they are yet, but it'll be more of Jarvis' lads. If Liverpool can't confirm, we'll have to cross check descriptions on file with the log for yesterday morning."

Connor continued to read from the report. "They had a couple of drinks in the bar, and went upstairs. At eleven-fifteen, someone called room service from Milosevic's suite and ordered several bottles of champagne, vodka, and whisky. The girl who took it up says there were three men in the room… watching something on TV. One of them gave her a twenty quid tip. About ten minutes later, Preston came back to the hotel, with four girls in the car. One of the others came down to meet them and took them upstairs while Preston parked the car. Just after eleven-thirty, Preston came back and took the lift upstairs."

"So seven hours ago, Milosevic is about to have a party in his room... and a few hours later they've lost him." Barton banged his fist on the desk, "How? What's been going on?" he demanded.

"I'm just getting to that, sir," said Connor calmly, wishing that he could be somewhere else when the boss heard the rest of the story.

"At about two-thirty a taxi pulled up outside the hotel and a man came out with three or four women. They were all shouting at each other... the man bundled the women into the cab and got in with them... then it drove off."

Barton interrupted, "Hang on. What do you mean three or four women... can't they count in Liverpool?"

"The guy who was watching the hotel... he's sure they were the same women who went in with Preston... but he's not sure how many got in the cab... they're looking for the cab driver to check."

"OK, carry on, Dave; let's hear the rest of it."

"Well, about five minutes later... Milosevic and Preston came out with another man. Milosevic looked like he was either pissed or high... whatever... he was staggering all over the place and they were holding him to stop him falling over. They went to the car park and a couple of minutes later the car came through the barrier... and I mean, through the barrier... broke it right off. Preston drove the wrong way down the one-way street and through a red light. To cut a long story short by the time our man had turned his car round they'd gone."

"Thanks, Dave. I've got a feeling that today's going to get a lot worse before it gets better," Barton sighed. "Let's get another coffee. Then we can start to work out how we're going to handle this... So much for a quiet weekend!"

As they walked into the main office, Detective Constable Jane Barclay called to Sally. "Liverpool have just been on again, ma'am. It's about the taxi driver."

Sally ran to Jane's desk. "What's he told them? Did they say?"

"He's making a statement at the moment. So far, we know he that dropped the women off at an address in Bootle and then took the man to Aintree race course, where another car was waiting for him."

"Call Liverpool back and find out if the other car was the one that Milosevic was using, and make sure they've got someone watching that house. They might go back there. Oh! And, see if you can find me a map of Merseyside. Let's try and work out where they might have gone."

She walked back over to where Barton and Connor were standing. Connor was pouring more coffee. "They've found the taxi driver," she said. She picked up a mug and repeated what Jane had just told her.

Phil Fellows came over with a road atlas. "Jane said you wanted this," he said, opening the book to a double page map of the Liverpool area, "and I've checked that Bootle address, it's one of King's places." Sally took the book and laid it on the desk.

"Thanks Phil," said Barton, "can you ask Jane to let me know as soon as she's got anything on the car."

"Anyone got any ideas?" asked Sally as they looked at the map.

Connor was the first to make a contribution, "The taxi took the man to the racecourse. There," he said, pointing to the map. "Now, we know they've not been back to the hotel, so let's assume that they didn't go back to the city. Look… it's only about two miles from the motorway."

He ran his finger along a blue line on the map. "They could have taken the M57 south to pick up the M62. That would take them out to the M6 and then south. Shit! They could be back in London by now. On the other hand, they could have stayed on the M62 to Manchester, or Leeds. They might have gone to see Nichols."

"Or they might have gone to Birmingham," said Barton "or they might have taken the M58 and gone north. They could be in Glasgow by now. Let's face it, they could be anywhere."

"I know, but once we've got the car registration, we might be able to get a fix from the traffic cameras," replied Connor. "No, that'll take ages… but they might have stopped at a service station. If they did, it wouldn't have been very busy and someone might remember seeing them… and they've all got CCTV."

"OK, Dave get all the services checked out," said Barton, "and get someone to find out if Nichols has had any visitors this morning."

"Yes, sir, I'll get someone onto it right way."

"What do you make of this, Sally?" asked Barton, but she didn't answer. She was miles away; staring out of the window.

"Sally, are you still with us?"

"What! Oh! Sorry Mike, I was just thinking."

"Care to share it?"

"Well, I was wondering what made Milosevic take off like that in the middle of the night. I mean, wherever they were going, they were in a hurry." She smiled, "I'd have loved to have seen the look on that copper's face when they crashed through the car park barrier… just like on TV. Eh!"

As Sally was speaking, Jane Barclay came back. She was holding a sheet of paper, "We've got the taxi driver's statement, sir," she said, and started to read from fax.

"He picked up a man and three teenage girls at the hotel, and took them to the house in Bootle. They all went inside... he heard some shouting, and then, after a few minutes, the man came out alone. Then they drove to Aintree... a car was waiting... three men were in it... the man got out of the taxi gave the driver forty pounds and ran to the car... got into the back seat and they drove off north on the A59."

"Towards the motorway," said Sally, "did they get details on the car?"

"Yes, ma'am, a big four-by-four, Land Cruiser or something like that, dark coloured, maybe blue or black... the taxi driver thinks the index number began R-T-5-2... he couldn't be sure... but that matches Milosevic's car, so it's a good bet it was the same one."

"Let me see that. Barton took the fax from Jane and quickly read it through, "Three girls... only three. So what does that mean? The copper at the hotel couldn't be sure if there were three or four. But, you'd expect a cabbie to know... wouldn't you... how many passengers he's got in the back?"

"Which means," said Sally, "...that we're missing a girl as well. Maybe she's still at the hotel. What if she's waiting for them to come back?"

She called over to Jane Barclay, "Jane, has anyone been anywhere near the hotel rooms or spoken to any of the hotel staff yet?"

"No, they're waiting for clearance from you," replied Jane, confidently. Her usual job involved liaison with the other OCUs and collating surveillance reports, all fairly mundane stuff, and she was beginning to enjoy being in the thick of things. She didn't get much opportunity to talk to the boss and this was a good opportunity to impress. "No one's spoken to any of the staff yet, apart from the local patrol that turned up when the hotel security man called in about the broken barrier. Oh! The local man on surveillance had spoken to the girl who took the drinks up to the room... before I put the block on."

"Who's in charge up there?" asked Barton.

"Bill Thomas," said Sally, "that's right, isn't it, Jane?"

"Get him on the phone, Jane, and put it through to my office," said Barton. He turned and walked towards his office, gesturing to Sally to follow him.

"Sit down, Sal. Let's try and make some sense of this," he said after she'd closed the door. "Why do a runner in the middle of the night?"

"What if King needed them somewhere else? What if something came up and..." she stopped abruptly. She was answering one question with more questions again.

"Maybe, but as far as we know King doesn't order Milosevic around."

"OK, so maybe Jarvis needed his heavies to sort something, or someone out?"

"But, why take Milosevic? If he was pissed or drugged up, why not leave him in the hotel with the girl… let him sleep it off?"

"Mike?" Sally said pensively, "…what if we're looking at this the wrong way. What if it doesn't matter where they were going? What if they weren't in a hurry to get somewhere? What if they were in a hurry to get away? What if something happened at the hotel… Oh God! What if…"

Before she could finish, the phone rang. Barton picked up the receiver. It was Jane, "I've got DI Thomas for you, sir," she said.

"Thanks, put him through," said Barton. He put down the handset and switched on the speaker, "Barton, here."

A loud voice, with a Liverpool accent, boomed through the speaker "Morning sir, Bill Thomas here, I'm sorry about all this."

Barton turned down the volume, "That's OK, Bill. These things happen, he'll turn up. I need you to get a look at those hotel rooms. Be discreet, they might be back… but if Sally's right," Barton looked at Sally who nodded, "we don't think that's very likely."

Sally nodded again and he continued to speak. "Four young women were seen entering the hotel with Preston, only three came out. We need to find the other girl. Our guess is that she's still in the hotel, and that she's in no state to be going anywhere."

"OK, sir, "said Thomas, "I'll talk to the duty manager at the hotel and get a couple of my team over there to check the rooms. I'll get back to you as soon as they've got anything. I hope you're wrong though, sir."

"So do I, Bill," he said, "…so do I." But, as he switched off the phone, he feared the worst.

Chapter 8

Saturday 3rd May 2003

National Crime Squad, Hertfordshire Branch – 07:30 BST

The first report came in from Leeds; Jane Barclay took the message and went to look for her boss. Sally was downstairs, outside the front door. It was still pouring with rain and she was huddled in the doorway trying not to get wet. As Jane approached, she threw a cigarette end into a puddle at the side of the step and immediately took another cigarette from the packet.

"Can I have one of those?" asked Jane. "I shouldn't really, but it's going to be one of those days, isn't it?"

Sally gave the packet and a lighter to Jane, who lit a cigarette and drew on it, inhaling the smoke deep into her lungs. She immediately started to cough, "That's good," and then she laughed. "First one for over a week," she said.

"Any news?" asked Sally.

"Leeds have been on," said Jane, "That's what I came out here to tell you. There's not much though. Nichols has been in his room all night, no visitors and no calls to or from the room."

"I didn't really expect anything else," said Sally.

The two women chatted for a couple of minutes. "Come on, we'd better get back inside," said Sally, as she finished her cigarette. Jane took a final drag on hers and threw the butt into the puddle.

Phil Fellows was talking on the phone when they got back to the office. He looked up and saw Sally, gesturing for her to come over to his desk. "OK... got to go now mate. Thanks, I'll call you back later to get the rest of the details," he said putting down the phone.

"That was the Lancashire police, boss," he sounded excited. "One of their motorway patrols has just checked out Forton Services... that's on the M6 near Lancaster. There's been a definite sighting of Milosevic's car."

"Great, what have you got?" asked Sally.

"They filled up at the northbound petrol station just before four," said Fellows, reading from his hastily scribbled notes. "...the attendant remembered them because three men went to the toilets... one looked like he was drunk. He checks the toilets on the hour... went in just after they left, and it's in a right state... blood and puke in the basins and on the floor... one of the bogs was

69

stuffed with paper towels. He'd cleaned it up by the time the traffic guys got there They've got the security video... the car's definitely Milosevic's... and they've got clear shots of two of the men."

"Get back to them, Phil. See if you can get a copy of the tape... and make sure they get a full statement from the attendant. I wonder whose blood it was... maybe Milosevic has been injured."

"I've already asked them to get the SOCOs out there to see what they can find," said Fellows. "But we won't get anything for a few hours."

"Good work, Phil," said Sally. She looked around for Dave Connor. He was standing talking to a couple of DCs and she walked over to them, and gave him the news. "Dave, Milosevic is heading north on the M6. Get someone to call Scottish Crime Squad and let them know what's going on. Let's see if someone up there can find him."

Connor looked down at the desk; the road atlas was still open at the map of Merseyside. He turned to the front pages and looked at a map of the whole major road network. "They might not have gone that far, the might have turned off," he said pointing to Carlisle and running his finger along the red line of the A69. "We'll check Newcastle as well."

Barton was lost in thought, wondering what he was going to say to Grace. Should he phone her before she left for work, or wait until tonight. Then he remembered it was Saturday, she wouldn't be going to work. He looked at his watch, eight-thirty; three hours since he'd left the house: *Long enough for her to have cooled off?* He started to pick up the phone: *But, maybe not.* He didn't want another row, not at moment: *...Better leave it a bit longer.*

The sound of the phone ringing, interrupted his thoughts, and he spun around in his chair, kicking over the waste bin as he grabbed at the phone. "Fuck it...! er... sorry, Barton here."

"You OK, sir," said Jane Barclay, "...I've got DI Thomas on the line, sir. I think you'd better talk to him."

"Thanks, Jane," he said. There was a click on the line and he heard Bill Thomas's voice. "We've got a body, sir... girl about nineteen or twenty... in Milosevic's suite. The..."

"Oh shit!" Barton exclaimed before Thomas got any further. "Sorry Bill, can you hang on a minute while I find Sally Parkinson, she needs to hear this."

When Sally came into the office Barton switched on the speakerphone and they both listened as the Liverpool policeman told them what they had found at the hotel. At eight o'clock four officers had gone to the top floor of the hotel, dressed as hotel housekeeping staff. Milosevic had been booked into a suite; the other men had three separate rooms on the same corridor. Each of the rooms had a Do-Not-Disturb sign hanging from the doorknob. According to the hotel manager, the staff had followed their regular instructions; not to service the rooms, or disturb Mr Sabic, as Milosevic was known or any of his colleagues at any time during their stay unless they called for room service. The staff expected the rooms to be in bit of a state afterwards, although not as bad as after footballers or rock groups, but they always left a large tip in each room for the housekeepers. Not this morning though. In two of the rooms, the beds had been used and some stuff had been left in the bathrooms; otherwise, they were relatively tidy, apart from a few empty bottles lying on the floor. The third room looked as though no one had been there, except for a holdall on the bed.

In Milosevic's suite, on the other hand, it looked like there'd been a riot. The furniture was upended, the TV screen smashed, broken bottles and glasses littered the floor and clothes were scattered all over the place. In the bedroom, there was a heap of bloodstained towels on the bed, and a trail of red footprints led across the floor from the bathroom and into the lounge. Behind the bathroom door, they'd found the body of a young woman, lying on the floor. The pool of blood had spread under the door and soaked into the bedroom carpet. Her dress was torn exposing her breasts, which appeared to have been slashed by a sharp blade; her hands and forearms were covered in cuts, as if she had tried to defend herself from the knife attack. Around her neck was a man's tie, twisted and pulled tight. Beside her, on the floor, they'd found a knife and a pair of scissors, both bloodstained.

"I've seen worse," said Thomas "but it's not what you expect in a two hundred quid a night hotel suite, a few hundred yards from the police headquarters."

"We're coming up," said Barton "I don't want anyone to know about this until I get there. How long can you keep the lid on this?"

"Sir, with respect, this is going to be taken out of our hands," Thomas said, surprised at Barton's question. "There's been a murder, sir, that's local CID territory… it's up to them."

"Not, if it compromises my operation," Barton said angrily. "We've got to keep things low key; I don't want any uniforms there and unmarked cars only. And nobody talks to the press. Who else knows about this?"

"Apart from you and me… about six of my team… we haven't told the local division yet. But, we can't keep this to ourselves for long, sir… we've got to seal off the crime scene… and the SOCOs are going to need to check out all the rooms… the corridor, the lift, the car park… you know the routine. The hotel's full, sir… people are going to realise something's going on. I've got to let the local CID know."

"You haven't got to do anything, Inspector," Barton shouted at the phone. "You just sit on this until I say otherwise. Give me a name in CID and I'll talk to them and…" Then he saw the disapproving look on Sally's face; telling him to back off. He read her lips as she mouthed, almost silently "Give him a break, Mike. We're not the FBI."

"Sorry, Bill, I know you're in a tight spot, but we can't afford to let this get out yet," he said, his voice lower and sounding calmer. Sally winked at him.

"Hello, Bill," she said. "Milosevic and his friends won't be expecting anyone to check the room until Monday. Chances are the minders have already told Jarvis… so we'd better assume King knows. They mustn't know we've found anything or they might start wondering how we found out."

"I know," said Thomas, "look… I know the local DCI really well… we go back a long way. He's sound… let me talk to him. It'll be OK. I'll get him to ring you."

"OK, Bill," said Barton, "get him to call me on Sally's mobile; we'll be in the car. See you later." Barton switched off the phone and put on his jacket. "Come on Sally, can we take your car."

"Do we have a choice?" she said sarcastically, "Unless you've got a new car, I'm not going in yours. You don't think I'd trust that heap to get us to Liverpool. Do you?"

On the way out, Barton stopped to tell Dave Connor what had happened. "…call DI Thomas if you want to know any more. Get hold of DI Timms and let him know what's going on… no tell him to come in… and tell everyone that I want hourly status checks on all main targets, starting now… we don't want to lose anybody else. And call us if you get anything new on Milosevic."

"Yes sir," said Connor, "…yes sir, three bags full sir," he muttered as Barton walked towards the door.

Barton looked back over his shoulder, "Sorry, Sergeant? I didn't quite catch that."

"Nothing, sir," Connor grinned, "…I was just wondering if there was anything else I could do for you."

But, Barton was already out of the door. "Just get on with it, Dave," said Sally, glaring at her subordinate.

As they got to Sally's car, she unlocked the doors with the remote and threw him the keys. "You can drive, Mike, I've been up since three, and I need a rest."

Before Barton could say anything, she had opened the door. She was reclining in the passenger seat by the time he opened the driver's door. He took off his jacket, threw it onto the back seat, and got into the car. He started to grope around under the front of the seat. "It's electric, remember … there's a switch on the door… press number three," she yawned. "It's set for Richard, so it should be about right for you."

He pressed the button and the seat moved backwards, and reclined slightly. "I suppose that'll do," he grunted, as he turned the key in the ignition. He reversed out of the parking space and started to drive out of the car park.

"Handbrake!" she snapped, "I know yours doesn't work, but…" She stopped speaking as she felt his arm brush against hers, and the car forwards moved again.

"Seat belt," her voice grated, in an irritating, patronising sort of way, as they turned onto the road. He reached over his shoulder, grabbed the belt, pulled it across his body, and fumbled to find the buckle.

"I'll do it," she said. "You concentrate on the road. Wipers!"

He flicked the switch and the blades swept across the windscreen. "Leave it out Sal. I used to have an old Austin Maestro with an electronic voice that told me what to do… it sounded just like you… I pulled the bloody fuse out, so just watch it, OK." He smiled and drove off.

Barton smiled again; he liked driving Sally's car. Not that he'd ever admit it to her, of course; but it was the sort of car that made you smile. It always did exactly what you wanted. Simple things like starting when you turned the key and not stopping unless you wanted it to. And he loved the way the engine responded when he floored the accelerator pedal, and the way he could take a tight bend fast and not have to worry about where the back end was going. Yes, he could get used to a car like this.

Sally was right; his car was a heap of shit. It sort of got you from A to B; just about. But it rattled and shook and the engine sometimes sounded like a bag of nails. He was always telling people that it was a classic, but the fact was it was just old and knackered and he couldn't afford a new one. But you had to make choices in this life, and when Grace had shown him the old farmhouse for the first time, he had made the right choice. The house that was far too big for two people and had suffered years of neglect, but they fell in love with it and both had willingly agreed to make the necessary sacrifices. Sacrifices like not having a decent car or new furniture; never spending more than three quid on a bottle of wine; no expensive holidays and not starting a family. It was the only way they'd been able to afford the mortgage payments, heating bills, and the army of tradesmen – builders, electricians, plumbers, decorators, all with their respective mates and labourers – needed to get the house in order. Next year maybe they'd have some cash to spare. But it seemed that it was always going to be next year.

He looked at the dashboard, "Shit! Typical bloody woman," he said under his breath. He turned to say something to Sally, but she was already asleep. Ten minutes later, he turned off and stopped. Sally opened her eyes, "Where are we?" she asked. "Why have we stopped?

Barton had opened the door and was already out of the car. "That bloody light's been on since we left, we need some petrol."

Sally leaned across to say something but it was too late; Barton already had the pump nozzle in the filler pipe. She got out and started to walk across the forecourt. "I'll pay," she called out, "do you want anything from the shop?" Barton said something, but she decided to ignore it.

After he'd filled the tank, Barton pulled up in front of the shop. Sally got in and put a bag on the floor. "Do you know how much that was?" she snapped, as they drove off. "Why did you stop here? There's a supermarket just up road, it's much cheaper there."

He laughed out loud. "Sal, I just don't understand you," he sighed. "You can afford to pay thirty grand for a car… but you're annoyed with me because I didn't buy the cheapest petrol. Come on how much extra did it cost? "

"About a pound," she sulked and silently conceded the point: *Love – fifteen.* "But that's not the point," she protested. "Why pay more than you need to?"

"I seem to remember saying something similar when you bought the car, Sal. It probably depreciated more in the first month than I paid for mine."

Sally sighed, "At this point in the conversation, I could make some wise remark like… don't tell me you actually paid for that thing… and then you could try and tell me it's a classic car or something like that. Let's not go there again Mike… just face up to it… this is a real car, and you drive a heap of junk." She smiled: *Fifteen all.*

"OK, I give up. What's in the bag?"

"Breakfast, what do you want Mars bar or Snickers?"

"But, I asked for a blueberry muffin." he said, sounding disappointed.

"I know, and I'm not having crumbs all over the car," she said.

"I'll have a Mars bar then. Did you get my coffee?"

"You can't drink hot coffee while you're driving… Coke or Red Bull?"

"Christ, Sal. I'm beginning to wish I'd left you behind and brought Dave Connor."

Sally didn't reply. It was too early in the morning to let this turn into another one of their duels. They both thrived on these silly games of tit-for-tat. Childish really, but she loved it. She knew he'd never choose Dave Connor or anyone else for that matter; not if she was available: *You're not getting away with this. It's still fifteen-all. I'm just calling time out for a bit.*

For a bank holiday weekend, the motorways were fairly quiet and the journey passed quickly. They speculated as to where Milosevic might be. Sally imagined him holed up in a scruffy Glasgow tenement. Barton had an idea that he'd made for the coast or an airport and was maybe looking to get out of the country. They tried to picture what had happened in the hotel. Why Milosevic had killed the girl. Why the minders hadn't stopped him. Of course it might not have been Milosevic. One of the minders might have killed her, or maybe more than one of them. What about the blood at the petrol station? Had Milosevic been injured? Theories, speculation, all a bit pointless really, this wasn't their case; Liverpool CID would handle the murder investigation. It was their job to find out what happened in the hotel.

"So, why exactly are we going to Liverpool?" asked Sally, already knowing the answer but wanting Barton to confirm why he needed her.

"One, to make sure that the local CID knows the score... and don't go making waves until Monday, that's my job. Two... you know more about Milosevic than anyone, so you can give them something in return for their co-operation."

"We could have done that on the phone," she said wistfully. "Come on, get on with it... just tell me."

"OK... I need you to talk to the other girls... they're probably scared shitless at the moment... but we have to find out what went on. You're good at dealing with that sort of thing." He glanced over; saw her smile and knew what she was thinking.

They were on the M6 just past Coventry, about halfway to Liverpool, when Barton pulled into the services. "I need the gents," he said, "I won't be a minute."

"I'll wait here," she said getting out of the car, lighting a cigarette as soon as the door was open.

Sally was on the phone when Barton returned about five minutes later carrying a McDonald's bag.

"...Hang on. He's here now, sir," she said and handed the phone to Barton. "It's DCI Briggs, from Liverpool CID."

Barton took the phone and gave her the bag in return. He spent the next five minutes going over the conversation that he'd had with Bill Thomas a couple of hours earlier; explaining why he and Sally were on their way to Liverpool. When he switched the phone off he spoke to Sally. "Bill was right, he's OK," said Barton, sounding relieved. "He'll keep a lid on it for us. But he wants to know about Milosevic and the others."

Sally was already drinking a cup of coffee as she handed him the McDonald's bag. Barton opened the bag and took out the other cup and a burger, placing them both on the bonnet of the car. He gave the bag back to Sally, "I got you a chicken one," he said.

Barton lit a cigarette and took a sip of coffee. "He sounds like a good bloke... he's going to arrange for the girls to be brought in and they're going to get the uniforms to turn over a few other houses in the area as well... not just King's places... they'll make it look like one of their regular clampdowns.."

He finished his cigarette and took a bite of the burger. "I don't suppose I'm allowed to eat this in the car either?" he said and without waiting for the answer he walked over to a bin: *Thirty-fifteen.*

When he got back to the car, Sally was in the driving seat. Barton got in to the passenger seat and fiddled with the seat adjusters. "Are we sitting comfortably?" asked Sally patronisingly. She turned the key and the engine roared into life as she pushed the pedal to the floor.

"Christ, Sal this isn't Le Mans!"

She smiled as she lifted her foot off the pedal and put the car into gear. "I know, but it's a nice noise isn't it?"

"I could have carried on driving," said Barton as they drove down the slip road, "I thought you were tired."

"I know, but I want to get there today," she replied as the car accelerated onto the motorway.

Barton glanced over at the dashboard; the speedometer needle was hovering over the hundred mark. "I think you'll find that they can take your licence away if you're clocked at this speed... being a Detective Inspector doesn't impress the uniforms these days you know."

"Spoilsport," she said, easing off the accelerator. They cruised along at a steady ninety until the road works began.

"So how much time did we save then?" Barton asked, as they drove through the contra-flow, behind a van doing forty. Before she had time to speak he'd answered his own question, "...must be a whole minute," he said. "What's the score?"

She saw the self-satisfied grin on his face, and grudgingly gave him the point. "OK, Thirty-all."

They eventually caught up with the holiday traffic and it was slow going on the M6 around Birmingham. And it didn't get much better the further north they went. "Bloody bank holidays," cursed Sally. "They ought to ban bloody caravans."

North of Stoke the traffic got lighter and Sally put her foot down again. "Don't say a word, don't even think about it," she said. "It's my licence."

Barton turned on the stereo, pressing buttons, listening briefly to each station before switching to the next and giving a running commentary as he did so. "Bloody rubbish... can't stand him... boring... bloody adverts... crap... not in the mood for that..." After trying a dozen stations, he switched over to the CD player. "Let's see if you taste in music has improved," he said. "Bloody hell! What's this?"

"Ibiza Beach Party. I bought it a couple of weeks ago."

"You paid for that!" Barton pressed a button and there was a short silence as the auto-changer selected another disc. "Oh God! This one's the same."

"No it's not, that's Ibiza Chill Out."

"How can you chill out to that noise?"

Sally didn't answer; there wasn't any point. Barton was already pushing the buttons again. "Not another one. Haven't you got any proper music?" Again there was no reply. The next CD started to play and he started to listen. "Hey. This is better," he said approvingly "Who's this?"

"Robbie Williams."

"Don't like him... mmm... not bad though, it'll do." To Sally's amazement Barton listened to the whole album without further comment. They were on the M62 about fifteen miles from Liverpool, when the last track finished.

"Mmm... That was quite good," he said. The next CD started to play; this time Barton didn't need to ask who it was. "Shit! No! Why didn't you tell me you had this? I've just had forty five minutes of bloody Robbie Williams... and I could have been listening to this."

"You didn't ask me what I'd got, did you? Anyway, you just said that Robbie was quite good."

"Well in way I suppose... but I didn't know then that I could have been listening to Marvin Gaye. Don't you know this is a classic... one of the greatest soul albums ever made?"

"Yes... you told me when you gave it to me. It's quite good I suppose... if you like the same sort of music as your parents." She smiled at him, with the sort of smile that told him exactly what she was thinking: *Don't even think about it, mate. I'm winding you up, and you know it. Forty-thirty.*

As they approached the city, she asked him to switch on the satellite navigation system and programme in the hotel address. Barton fiddled around for a few minutes and then gave up. "I can't get the hang of this... I'm trying to set it for where we're going to... and it keeps showing me where we are now. Bloody gadgets, what's the point? You've got a perfectly good road atlas on the back seat." He reached behind his seat and found the atlas, which he opened to a detailed map of Merseyside. "OK... it's easy. Just carry straight on at the end of the motorway... follow the road all the way into the city centre... the hotel is somewhere near the Albert Dock... it'll be signposted when we get nearer."

Twenty-five minutes later, having driven round the city's one-way system several times, they arrived at the hotel. "Good, no signs of any policemen," said Sally, as she drove past the entrance and turned into the multi-storey car park next door.

As they drove round the car park looking for a space, Barton picked up the mobile and selected the first number from the received calls list. "Hi, is that Ken

Briggs?" he said, "Mike Barton here. We're in the car park. Where shall we meet you?"

As they got out of the car, she looked at him and smiled. "Mmm... Yes, that was really easy, Mike. Oh! And thanks for the sightseeing tour."

Barton said nothing, as they walked to the lift. It was just a game; one they'd played many times before, and he always let her win. "Doesn't matter," he mumbled, "I'm still the boss."

"Men," she said, feigning admiration, "...what would we poor girls do without you?" *Game, set and match.*

They walked into the hotel lobby and headed straight for the lifts; Sally pressed the call button. An Out-of-Order sign was taped to the doors of two of lifts; the doors of the third opened immediately. They got in and the doors closed behind them. "Top floor," said Barton to the lift attendant.

"Sorry, sir, the top floor is closed, there's a fault in the air conditioning system."

"It's OK," said Barton, showing the man his warrant card, "DCI Briggs is expecting us. DCI Barton and DI Parkinson, and you are?"

"PC Mills, sir," said the policeman pressing a button on the panel, "what's all the fuss about?"

"You'll find out soon enough, Constable, but, in the meantime the fewer people that know the better. How do you like being a lift attendant?"

"It makes a change from walking the streets, sir. It's not a bad number really; I've already made about twenty quid in tips."

"I'll pretend that I didn't hear that. Now where's DCI Briggs?"

The lift jolted to a halt, and the doors opened. Mills stepped out of the lift with them and pointed to the end of the corridor. "It's the last door on the left, sir."

Half of the corridor was cordoned off with crime scene tape. As they walked along the remaining narrow walkway, they noticed a number of marks on the opposite wall. "Blood on the walls," said Sally, stopping for a moment to take a closer look at the smudged handprints "Hers or his?"

They were about halfway along the corridor when a man dressed in a white coverall came out of the room. As he walked towards them, he put up his hand, signalling them to stop. "Sorry, you can't go any further without one of these," he said tugging at his white suit. "The SOCOs are still in there. I'm DS Poole, sir. I take it you're DCI Barton, and you must be DI Parkinson. Come in here and get suited up."

He opened a door and showed them into a room. There were a couple of piles of coveralls on the bed, each in a cellophane wrapper, and another pile of smaller packets. Poole walked over to the bed and sorted through the piles. He picked up four packets and turned towards the two detectives. He gave Sally one of the larger packets. "Medium, I think that should be right Inspector, and if you could slip these on over your shoes please," he said giving her one of the small bags.

"Large one for you, sir... you can hang your coats in the wardrobe here." He opened a door and took out two coat hangers.

Barton and Sally took off their jackets and put them on the hangers. "I hate these things," said Sally, as she tore open the cellophane wrapper. She wriggled into the suit, zipped it up, and twirled around. "Bet my bum looks big in this?" They both laughed.

Sally walked out of the room, rolling up her sleeves, and spoke to Poole. "I think small would have been better, Sergeant."

"Sorry we haven't got any. Now if you're ready we'll go and find the DCI."

Poole led the way out of the room and along the corridor. "The body is still in there," he said. "We haven't worked out how to get her out of the hotel yet. I'll warn you now she's in a real mess."

They walked into the room, and were met by a scene much as Bill Thomas had described. The only piece of furniture that looked in place was a large leather sofa. A dining table was lying on its side, a leather armchair on its back; the shattered remains of a glass tabletop lay on the floor beneath its metal frame. There was a black hole where the TV screen had been; the metal table lamp that had smashed it was on the floor. Broken glass, clothing, and papers littered the floor. Two men in white suits were on their hands and knees on the far side of the room, carefully picking through the debris.

Sally gasped, "I haven't seen anything like this since I was in uniform. We were once called out to a hotel in the West End... someone had complained about a rock band having a party... some party."

A man in his early fifties came into the room, and held out his hand towards Barton. "Ken Briggs," he said, "welcome to Liverpool, Barton. You'd better come this way and see the rest of it." Briggs led them through into the bedroom. Apart from an upset bedside lamp, the stained towels on the bed and a broken mirror, this room was comparatively tidy.

Sally looked around and saw a covering of white powder on the bedside table. There was more powder on the floor beneath the table, and a half full plastic bag. A man was picking up a large glass ashtray. She pointed across the room. "That powder... coke do you think?"

Barton looked at the table "Yeah… the ashtray probably missed whoever it was aimed at and split the bag open. Judging by the size of it, whoever threw it must have been pretty mad about something."

Briggs was standing by the bathroom door. "She's in here," he said. "You can take a look if you want to…" He looked at Sally, "…or if you'd rather Inspector, you can see the SOCOs Polaroid's instead."

"It's all right, I've got a strong stomach," said Sally: *I've seen worse than anything you've got to show me, you patronising bastard.*

The door was open wide, and they looked in. The tiled floor of the bathroom was covered in blood, and a white plastic sheet covered the body. Sally could smell vomit and looked on apprehensively as Briggs lifted the sheet. She gasped and put a hand to her mouth. She'd seen worse, but it never got any easier. "I thought she was strangled… where did all the blood come from?" asked Sally.

"Seen enough?" said Briggs, as he covered the corpse. "When they found her it looked as though the knife wounds were fairly superficial… just the slashes to the breasts and arms. But the pathologist was here earlier and he found a deep wound in her back. She was lying on her back, so they didn't see it at first. But, that's where most of the blood came from. It could be she bled to death. Either way she was beaten up pretty badly before he killed her; broken jaw, busted nose, at least four broken ribs. Whoever did this was an evil bastard."

"Do we have any idea of what happened?" asked Sally as they walked back through the bedroom and into the lounge.

Briggs shook his head, "It's going to take a while to work it, and I don't expect to get a report from the SOCOs until tomorrow. So we're only speculating at the moment. It looks as though she was beaten up in here, see there's blood on the wall there… and over there on the windowsill… but we don't know if it's all hers. There are scratches around the bedroom doorframe… could be that she tried to hold onto it as she was dragged into the bedroom. She's got a couple of broken fingernails."

"I understand that you've brought the other three girls in," said Sally. "Can I talk to them? They might be able tell us what happened, do you think they'll talk to me?"

"They're in shock and very scared. I wouldn't hold out too much hope of anything today," replied Briggs. "We're still trying to sort out a translator. I'll get Poole to see if they've found anyone yet."

"What's that?" asked Barton, pointing to a slim, silver coloured box lying on the floor under the shattered TV set.

Poole asked one of the SOCOs to pick it up. The man brought it over to them. "It's a portable DVD player," he said "there's a disk still inside."

"Bag them separately," said Briggs, "and give me the disc."

Poole was looking at the TV. "Look," he said, "there's a video cable still plugged into the back. I bet they were watching porn movies."

The SOCO brought over a clear plastic evidence bag. Inside was the disc that he had removed from DVD player. Briggs took the bag, looked at the disc, and handed it to Barton. "What do you make of it?"

Barton looked at the disc; a recordable DVD; written on one side in black ink - *Demo 10/4/03 JKVP*. "Could be an amateur job… but demo probably means it's a pre-release copy of a commercial DVD."

"Maybe JKVP is some kind of reference code," said Briggs.

Barton nodded; he'd seen the code somewhere before, "Have you got any more of these?" he asked the SOCO.

"About a dozen, sir… some are recordable ones like that in plain cases. The rest are commercial copies in retail boxes."

"Can I have a look, please?" The man went over to the sofa and came back with a two large plastic bags. Barton took them from him and handed one to Briggs.

"These are all the same," Barton said looking at the four discs in the bag. They were all in plain clear plastic cases. "They've all have got Demo, a date and JKVP written on them. What about yours?"

"Finished versions for sale, I'd say," said Briggs. "Definitely the extreme end of hard core judging by the photos on the covers. Bet the censors have never seen these. The small print says they're made and distributed by *JK Video Productions, www.sweetyoungthings.com*."

Barton gave his bag of DVDs to Briggs. "I'll hang onto this one… if that's OK with you," he said, putting the other disc into his pocket, "…we can have a look at it later… if you don't mind."

Briggs did mind , and he was about to say what he was thinking – it was his case and his evidence and he wasn't happy about having some hot shot from the NCS sticking his nose in – as far as he was concerned it was just another murder investigation. But then, seeing an opportunity to get Barton out of his way, he changed his mind, "There's not really much else for you to see here. Why don't you try to talk to those women? Sergeant Poole will take you over to the station… you can use my office," he said. "I'll stay here until we can move the body."

Barton and Sally walked towards the door. As Poole followed them, Briggs tapped him on the shoulder. "Keep an eye on them, Gerry… and make sure that you get that disc back."

Chapter 9

Saturday 3rd May 2003

Leeds – 13:30 BST

The barman walked over to two men eating lunch at a table by the window. "There's a telephone call for you Mr Nichols. You can take it on the house phone in the booth over there."

David Nichols got up and walked over to the booth. He picked up the phone and the barman switched the call through. "Nichols here, who's that?" he said brusquely.

"It's Adrian Foster, Mr Nichols... Foster and Cole in Liverpool... we met yesterday."

"Yes, I remember. What can I do for you?"

"Well, I was wondering if you'd seen your colleague, Mr Sabic, today. I was supposed to meet him at twelve, but he didn't show up. I phoned his hotel but they couldn't get a reply from his room."

"Did they say where he'd gone?" asked Nichols. "Have you tried his mobile?"

"No, I've lost the number. The hotel didn't know where he was. That's why I'm ringing. I thought he might be with you."

"Sorry, I haven't seen him. Maybe he's been called away on business."

"This really is most inconvenient. He was going to look at a couple of houses. Look... if you see him... can you tell him that I've got another party interested... and I'll have to let them go if I get an offer. I've got to go now, I'm meeting someone."

"Hang on, there must be a mistake. We saw the houses yesterday and we've agreed the price. We're not interested in any more at the moment."

"Quite sure... there's a nice pair of semis in Walton. Mr Sabic said he was buying for a relative."

"Oh! Of course... I'd forgotten. Thanks for calling. I'm sorry, but I don't know where Mr Sabic is."

Foster hung up and dialled another number: *Damn the man, I've got better things to do than chase around after him.* "Hello, is that Mrs Williams. Good news it looks as though you've got yourself a house. Which one did you want?"

Nichols put down the phone and walked back to other man. He sat down at the table and picked up his drink. He thought of asking Errol, if he knew anything, his brother was supposed to be looking after Milosevic. Then he thought again: *He'd have said something, wouldn't he?* He needed Errol here, he didn't want him running off, looking for his brother.

"Problem, Mr Nichols?"

"No nothing... just my wife checking up on me. She wants to know if I'm coming home tonight... doesn't trust me since that thing with Debbie King."

"Huh! That was years ago... think she'd have forgotten by now. So are we going back?"

"Not yet... but I'll go to Harvey Nichols later and buy her something...useless but expensive. Get me another drink, Errol. I'm just going to call Mr Stevens... there's something I forgot to tell him before he caught the train."

Liverpool – 14:00 BST

Poole showed them into a small office. "Wait here, sir," he said. "I'll go and check on the interpreter. Do you need anything?"

"Be nice if you could find some coffee," said Barton. He looked at the laptop computer on the desk. "Do you mind if I borrow this?"

"I'm not sure. It's the DCI's," replied Poole. "What do you want it for, sir?"

"It's got a DVD drive. I thought I'd take a look at this while we're waiting," said Barton, taking the plastic bag containing the DVD from his pocket.

"OK, I suppose it'll be alright."

After Poole had gone, Barton took the DVD out of its case and looked at it as he opened the drive tray on the side of the computer. *JKVP,* Barton remembered where he'd see the code before; he'd seen a couple of their efforts before. "It's one of theirs, the Terrible Twins. You don't have to watch...if you don't want to," he said as he put the disc into the tray.

"Don't patronise me, Mike. What is it with you men?" Sally said indignantly "I've been in this job sixteen years. I've seen it all. Another one won't make any difference." She angled the screen so that they could both see it. "Now, let's see what they were watching. It can't be any worse than what we've just seen in the hotel." She was soon going to discover that it was a lot worse.

Barton closed the tray and they waited in anticipation, listening to the faint whirring noise as the disc started to spin in the drive. The movie started, the camera panning across a small stage where a couple of naked girls were pole dancing. Groups of men were sitting at tables in front of the stage, cheering and whistling. Others were standing at the bar; scantily dressed waitresses ran the gauntlet of groping hands. The camera followed a man and a girl into a private booth; it moved in close and focussed on the girl as she writhed around, teasing him for a couple of minutes, before he slipped a banknote into her G-string and she walked away. They watched another man and girl in a similar scene. After a couple of minutes, Sally said, "Raunchy, but not exactly hard-core. You get more explicit stuff on Channel Five these days."

"Looks like an ad for one of their clubs," said Barton as he fast-forwarded the film. He started it at normal speed when the scene changed. The stage was now empty and unlit; the crowd had disappeared and only three men remained in the bar; seated at a table, a few feet from the stage, with their backs to the camera. Another man approached the table. He sat down and said, "Ready for the special event, gents."

As the camera panned across the stage, the spotlights came on and music started. In a corner of the stage a man appeared from behind the curtains, holding what appeared to be a rope in his hands. He yanked on the rope and pulled a girl onto the stage. She was on all fours; naked except for a suspender belt, stockings, high-heeled shoes and a collar to which the rope was attached. She wore a blindfold and it was difficult to see her face, but they could tell that she was very young. "Oh God! She's just a child," gasped Sally, "...fourteen, fifteen maybe?"

They watched as she groped her way along the floor towards the man; he pulled on the rope again, sending her sprawling, her face on the floor. He dragged her towards a pole and grabbed the collar; forcing her to stand up. He put her arms around the pole and pulled her forward; squashing one of her breasts tight against it. One of the men stood up and threw something onto the stage; a pair of handcuffs landed at the girl's feet. The man picked them up and manacled one of the girl's wrists to the pole. The camera zoomed in as the man grabbed her hair and forced her to her knees; he removed her blindfold and untied the rope, coiled it up and stood back. They could now see that the 'rope' was a long whip. "Now, dance!" he shouted.

Music started playing. "Dance!" he shouted again and cracked the whip twice. The camera zoomed in again, focussing on the blood that was oozing from stripes on the girl's buttocks. The girl stood up and started to sway to the hypnotic rhythm of the music. The music got louder; the rhythm faster; she danced as if possessed. The whip cracked repeatedly, its tip only inches from her body, as the watching men cheered and banged their fists on the table. The girl danced on, her face stained with black streaks as the tears washed her eye makeup down her cheeks. To Sally's relief, Barton pressed fast forward again. The film restarted as the girl fell to the floor. There were more lash marks now across her back and shoulders. The man cracked the whip again, the tip tearing through the skin on her back. He shouted again. "Get up bitch! Dance!" But she didn't move.

The man grabbed her hair, pulling her to her feet; and then the camera caught his face, as he turned his head. It was only a glimpse, but enough for the watching detectives to know who it was. "Milosevic!" cried Sally. "God, we knew he was a vicious bastard, but this is really sick."

As she spoke, another man's voice shouted, "Party time, enjoy yourselves." Three men leapt onto the stage and Milosevic stepped down and joined the other man at the table. One of the men on the stage took off his trousers as the other two pulled the girl onto her hands and knees.

Sally watched as each man took his turn, cheered on by the voyeurs at the table. And, each time the acts became more violent, more extreme, as if they were competing.

Sally suddenly turned away. "Mike, I can't watch any more of this," she said and she walked towards the door. She felt sick, put her hand over her mouth, and ran into the corridor.

Barton called after her, "That's OK, Sal, go and get some air." They'd both had to watch this sort of thing, many times, before; it was part of the job. You learned not to let it get to you; shut off your senses; but it only worked up to a point. His own stomach was churning and he could only imagine how she felt.

She returned a few minutes later to find her boss staring at the screen. Barton had frozen the frame, and she looked over his shoulder and saw a close up of the girl's face, as she lay on the floor. Her eyes stared into the camera. "Recognise her?" he asked. She shook her head. "Look at the eyes," he said.

Sally had seen those eyes before; beautiful dark eyes, almost black; eyes that would forever look in terror; staring at her as Briggs had pulled the sheet back in the hotel bathroom.

"But it can't be... she's too young. The girl in the hotel was older... nineteen, twenty... It can't be the same girl."

"No, I don't think so," said Barton, "but a family resemblance... sisters maybe?"

"Could be... you think she saw this?" asked Sally, and for a moment, she thought of her own sister: *Oh God! If I saw this happening to her...*

"Maybe," she said, wiping away a tear, "...maybe she was watching... saw Milosevic on the film and lost it... maybe she attacked him... But he didn't have to kill her."

"Why not?" said Barton gravely, he fast forwarded the disc, and pressed the play button again, "Don't think it bother him... looks like they might have killed this one."

They watched the closing shots. The three men were laughing, adjusting their clothing, and standing over the now motionless girl as she lay curled up on the floor weeping. She screamed as one of them kicked her in the face and then she was quiet. She made no more sound as he kicked her again and the other men followed his example. As the men disappeared from view, one of the voyeurs left the table and jumped onto the stage. Although his face was half hidden by shadows, Sally thought she'd seen him before.

"Can you freeze it there, Mike?" she said and stared at the screen. "I'm sure I've seen him before. Who is he?" She couldn't remember and Barton started the film again.

Another man came into view and joined Milosevic as he stepped onto the stage. Milosevic unlocked the handcuffs and watched as the other two men dragged her away; towards the camera. Barton froze the frame again. Sally looked hard at the screen. The lighting was poor, but she could make out their faces and she knew who they were – Terry King and Barry Jarvis.

Wiping away her tears, she looked at Barton; the lump in her throat made it difficult to speak and she struggled to get her words out. "We've got to get them Mike... for this if nothing else."

By the time Poole returned, Sally was starting to feel better; or at least that's what she kept telling herself. Poole entered the office, accompanied by an attractive, professional looking, middle-aged woman. "Sir, this is Dr Sylvia Land, from the School of Eastern European Studies at the university. She's going to interpret for us."

Barton got up and shook the woman's hand. "Pleased to meet you, Dr Land, I'm Detective Chief Inspector Mike Barton and this is my colleague Detective Inspector Sally Parkinson."

"Please call me Sylvia, Chief Inspector. Now, Sergeant Poole has already explained things to me, and I hope I can be of some help."

Poole intervened, "The girls are waiting in the interview rooms downstairs. They're scared... really scared. I don't know if we'll get much from them."

"OK," said Barton, "but, it might be better if DI Parkinson and the doctor do this. They might feel safer talking to women."

Barton looked at Sally. "Is that alright with you?" he asked. She nodded and got up to join Poole and Dr Land. "Come on," she said, "let's get this started."

As they walked towards the stairs, Barton spoke to Sally. "Are you alright?" he asked. "You don't have to do this."

"It's OK, Mike," she said, "Don't worry I'll be fine. I'm OK." She was trying to put on a brave face, but her voice didn't match, and her eyes told Barton that she was far from OK.

He squeezed her hand and said, "Take it easy… just find out what you can. I'll see you later."

Poole opened the door of the first interview room, and Sally and Sylvia Land walked in. A young woman was sitting at a table, smoking a cigarette. The WPC sitting opposite her got up and spoke to them. "She speaks a little English, enough to tell me her name… she's called Asija."

"Thanks," said Sally. "Is this being recorded?"

The WPC nodded towards the video camera on the wall, and moved across the room and sat on a chair by the door. Sally whispered something to Sylvia and the two women sat down opposite Asija.

Sylvia Land said something to the girl. Her voice was soft, friendly and reassuring. The girl shook her head. Sylvia held her hand and spoke again. This time the girl nodded and half smiled. Sylvia started to speak again, patiently trying to gain the girl's trust. Finally, the girl replied and they talked for a while, the girl becoming agitated and gesturing with her hands.

The girl stopped and lit a cigarette as Sylvia turned and spoke to Sally. "She says her name is Asija Jasarevic, she's seventeen years old. She's from a small village in Bosnia; near the Serbian border… she's been in England for about six months. A man came last night and took her and three other women to a hotel… she'd never been there before. Another man took her to a room and they had sex… she says that he was nice to her and gave her champagne to drink… she'd never had champagne before and she got drunk. She was fast asleep when one of the other men came into the room. He took them to another room… where two of her friends were… there was a lot of shouting and then they left in a taxi."

"Does she know what happened to the other girl?"

Sylvia repeated the question to Asija, and the girl spoke to her again

"No, she didn't go into that room, but she says that her friend Naida was there… with another girl called Fahrija and two men. The one they call the Pig and a black man."

"What happened after they left the hotel?"

"She says they went back to the house with the man she had been with. He gave them some money and left."

"Does she know where the man went? Did she hear any names?"

Sylvia spoke to Asija again. The girl looked frightened. She spoke quickly and then drew her hand across her throat.

"She says she doesn't know. She's afraid… and she wants to know where her friend Naida is… the man said he would kill them if they said anything."

"Tell her it's alright… we won't let anything happen to her. She's safe here."

"I'll try, but she's very frightened," said Sylvia, turning to speak to the girl again.

She spoke in a quiet, reassuring voice. When she had finished the girl said a few words and then drew her hand across her throat again.

"I'm sorry Inspector, she won't say any more. She doesn't believe us... she thinks the man will come back to kill her."

"OK, tell her that's enough... ask her if she wants anything."

Sylvia spoke with the girl and then turned to Sally. "She'd like another cup of tea and some chocolate... and some more cigarettes."

Sally took a packet of cigarettes from her pocket and put it on the table, she smiled at the girl and said "Thank you."

"Tell her I'll get somebody to bring her some tea and chocolate."

Leeds – 15:30 BST

The two men finished their lunch and Nichols signed the bill. "I'm going up to my room, I've got a couple of calls to make... then I think I'll watch the football for a bit."

"Don't forget, Harvey Nicks."

"What? Oh! Yes," Nichols said absentmindedly "...thanks Errol. I'll see you back here later... say about eight. Thought we could go to the casino... see if we can pick up a couple of women... what do you think?"

"See you later."

He sat on the edge of the bed and dialled the number of the hotel in Liverpool. "Could I speak to Mr Sabic please?" he asked when the operator answered. He waited impatiently as she tried to connect him to the room.

"There's no reply sir."

"What about the people he was with?"

"I'll just check, sir. Do you know their names?"

"Er... um, I not sure, try Marcus Preston." Nichols drummed his fingers on the table, muttering to himself as he waited: *Come on, come on Marcus, where are you?*

"No sir, he seems to be out as well."

"Did they leave any messages?"

"I don't know sir, would you like to speak to the duty manager?"

"No thanks. I'll call Mr Sabic on his mobile."

Mr Sabic didn't answer the call; he couldn't; his mobile phone was in a plastic evidence bag, waiting to be taken to the Merseyside Police forensics lab. "Don't answer that," said Briggs as a young detective constable picked up the bag. "Give it to me."

He took the bag and looked at the phone display, *Nichols Calling.* The ringing stopped and the display changed *Missed Call,* and about thirty seconds later it changed again, *New Voice Message.*

Briggs said something to the DC and then took out his own mobile phone and called his office. "Isn't technology wonderful," he said when Barton answered the phone.

"What do you mean?"

"Someone called Nichols has just phoned and left a message on that mobile we found."

"What did he say?"

"Listen."

Briggs punched the keys through the plastic and connected to the voicemail service. He held the mobile close to his own handset, so that Barton could listen to message. "Vlad, it's Dave Nichols. Where the hell are you? What's going on? Give me a call when you get this."

Briggs spoke to Barton again. "Do you know this Nichols character?"

"Yes," replied Barton. "He was with Milosevic yesterday. And he obviously doesn't know what's going on."

"I've got someone checking with the hotel switchboard to see if any one has called. Hang on a minute."

The DC had come back into the room. He spoke to Briggs. "Two calls sir…Adrian Foster, from a firm called Foster and Cole… called about forty minutes ago… and another man called a few minutes before the mobile rang… didn't leave a name."

"Thanks," said Briggs. "Did you hear that Barton?"

"Yes. Can you get someone to find this Foster bloke? I'll see you later."

In the second interview room, Mina Hadjic was waiting for them. She was a couple of years older than Asija and, although she too was scared, she told them quite a bit more. She had come to England with her cousin Fahrija; about a year earlier. They had come to London at first, and then lived in Leeds for a few months before coming to Liverpool. She knew Milosevic – all the women knew him and, without exception, they hated and feared him in equal measure – they called him the Pig. She had seen the black man called Marcus a few times; he had been to the house with Milosevic. She hadn't been in Milosevic's room, but Fahrija had been there with Marcus, and later, she had told her what had happened. She was worried about Fahrija, who was only sixteen and very frightened, and she asked if she could see her.

Sally asked the WPC to bring the girl from the other interview room. When they came back Fahrija ran into the room and hugged her cousin. She sat down next to the older girl and held her hand, gripping it tight between both her hands.

Sylvia spoke to the two girls, stopping occasionally to tell Sally what was being said. Slowly Fahrija told her story, never letting go of her cousin's hand, looking at her for reassurance as she spoke.

When they had finished, Sylvia asked Sally if she could stay with them. "They need help," she said. "Let me talk to them a bit longer."

"OK, try and get them to tell you some more about how themselves and how they got here. We need them to tell us all they know. I'll get someone to bring Asija in."

London – 16:00 BST

Underwood finally picked up his phone; he looked at the display and saw Nichols's number. "What the fuck do you want?" he said angrily, before Nichols had chance to speak.

"Where have you been, George? I've been trying to reach you for over an hour."

"I've been playing golf. You know I always leave it switched off. Now what's so fucking important that you have to ring me here?"

"I was hoping that you could tell me. Milosevic has disappeared. He was supposed to be staying in Liverpool until Monday, but I can't reach him. Have you got any idea where he is?"

"No. Why should I know?"

"Something's going on. He got his mobile switched on, but he's not answering. This guy rang me... said he was supposed to meet Milosevic, but he didn't show up."

"What guy?"

"An estate agent... we did a deal with him on a couple of houses yesterday. He said Milosevic was looking for some more houses for himself... I think maybe he's trying to cut a deal without us."

"He'd better not be. They'll cut his balls off. Where are you?"

"Leeds."

"Stay there. I'll call Warren... he ought to know where his boys are."

Liverpool – 16:00 BST

Sally found Barton in the canteen talking to Gerry Poole and Bill Thomas. "How did it go, Sal?" asked Barton. The jaded look on her face told him it had been tough.

"Can we go somewhere else? I need a cigarette." She handed a sheet of notepaper to Bill Thomas. "Could you check these names for me Bill?"

They walked outside to the car park. Barton took out a packet of cigarettes and offered one to Sally. "Come on," he said, "let's go and find a pub, you look like you could use a drink."

"Thanks, Mike… And, I could use a hug too," she said as she blinked back another tear and put her arms around him.

They walked through the streets; slowly, in silence, each wrapped in their own thoughts. Neither of them knew where they were going, but they soon found themselves in Matthew Street. Barton dropped his cigarette butt on the ground and crushed it under his foot, "Did you know this street is famous… look, that's the Cavern Club over there, where the Beatles started?" Barton said, trying to think of something to talk about; something to distract her for a while, "Just imagine, John Lennon, Paul McCartney…"

Sally interrupted, "Doesn't mean a lot to me. I was only two years old when they split up." She crossed the narrow street and idly looked into a shop window. "My mum was a big fan though, she always liked Ringo the best," she said, looking at the display of sixties memorabilia. "Hang on a minute." Sally disappeared inside the shop. Barton lit another cigarette and waited. A few minutes later, she came out holding a small carrier bag. She took out a framed photograph. "I don't suppose he really signed this," she said. "But she'll like it anyway. Now let's have that drink."

They walked round the corner and stood outside a pub. "This looks nice," said Barton, opening the door. Stepping inside the White Star, for the first time, gave Barton a warm feeling. It was an old Victorian pub with wood panelling, a huge mahogany bar, and a quarry-tiled floor. Pictures covered almost every square inch of wall space, photographs of ships and the old docks, advertising posters and photos of sixties pop groups. Barton loved places like this; Sally would rather they had stopped at one of the several wine bars; they had passed on the way from the hotel. There were too many people in the bar for them to talk privately so they walked through to the back room. Furnished with leather banquettes, several low stools, and round tables, a rather threadbare, patterned carpet on the floor and dark, heavy drapes at the window, the room had witnessed more rowdy parties and old-fashioned knees-ups than intimate conversations. Around the walls were more pictures and on the back wall a huge mirror, advertising, *Bass – On Draught & In Bottle.*

"This is very nice," said Sally, sarcastically, "My granddad would like it here… and Gran's got a carpet like this in her front room."

Barton didn't reply: *What is it with women? Why can't they appreciate a good old-fashioned pub?* He walked through to the bar and ordered their drinks. When he returned, he found Sally looking at the pictures on the wall; he put the drinks on a table and stood beside her.

"Actually these are quite interesting. Look at this one," she said pointing to an old photo of cargo ships at the docks. "Didn't you tell me once, that your dad came to England on one of these?"

"Yes," he said, remembering the stories he'd listened to as a boy. "That was over fifty years ago. He came here with my grandparents. They didn't come to Liverpool though."

They sat at the table, and Sally told Barton about the interviews with the girls. They were all from Bosnia; Muslim refugees. It was ironic; they'd survived the horrors inflicted on their people by a man called Milosevic, only to end up in the hands of his namesake. "It's so awful, Mike, they'd already suffered so much. Mina told us that she'd seen the soldiers rape her mother and her aunt. And then they killed her whole family. She and her cousin Fahrija were the only ones who survived. They'd been in the barn when the soldiers came and hidden under the floor. They stayed there for three days before they dared to come out. Mina was seven years old, Fahrija was only four."

Fahrija had told them that she had fallen asleep, while the man called Marcus was watching the film. Naida's crying had woken her, and then Naida had smashed the TV set and screamed at Milosevic. How Marcus had taken her out of the room after the fight started, and how one of the other men had taken them home in a taxi, given them some heroin, and threatened to hurt them if they told anybody what had happened.

"You were right about the girl on the film. Fahrija recognised her… Her name is Jasmina Ajanovic, she's Naida's sister… and she's only just fourteen. She came to England with the others, but Milosevic kept her in London. He'd told Naida that Jasmina was ill and that she couldn't join them in Liverpool until she got better."

"Anything else?" asked Barton. He was grateful that he'd not had to hear this first hand, but he felt bad about having put Sally through it. "Did they have any idea where Milosevic has gone?"

"No, but the older girl… Mina, heard Preston… he was talking on the phone to someone… like he was asking what they should do… then he was telling the others something about the boss sorting things out. Oh! She gave me some names… the other two men were called Leroy and Kev… I've asked Bill to check them out."

"Come on, Sal, drink up. It's time we were getting back. Better see Briggs before we go." They left their glasses on the table; Sally hadn't touched hers.

"Can we get something to eat?" she asked. "I'm starving and I don't fancy stopping on the motorway."

"Canteen, OK?"

"It'll do," she said. She didn't really care.

"By the way Nichols has been trying to contact Milosevic… called the hotel first and then left a message on his mobile… he sounded a bit rattled, obviously doesn't know what's going on," said Barton. He told her that he'd contacted the estate agent Adrian Foster, who'd told him that he'd called Nichols. "Funny thing though… Foster said Nichols seemed surprised, as if he didn't know that Milosevic was looking at more houses."

"Maybe, he's planning to branch out of his own. They won't like that."

Back at the police station, they went to look for Briggs. He was standing at the top of the stairs talking to Sylvia Land. They shook hands and she walked down, stopping on the landing to talk to Barton and Sally. Sylvia looked tired, worn out; as if all her energy had been drained away.

"How are they?" asked Sally, "and are you alright, you look tired."

"It's been a difficult afternoon. They've settled a bit, but they're still frightened and confused. They keep asking about Naida… they want to know where she is and why they can't see her."

"Did they say much, after I left?"

"Mina, did… she told me a lot. She says there are lots of other girls like them… that awful man Milosevic treats them like slaves."

Now there was anger in her voice, "I've seen women like these in the refugee camps. They've lost everything… they've been beaten and abused at home… then they come here… hoping to escape… start a new life and it starts all over again. It's so cruel… someone has to do something. Someone has to stop this evil. Why don't the police do something? Why don't you do anything?"

Sally didn't have any answers, nor did Sylvia expect them. "I'm sorry, Sylvia," she said, forlornly; knowing that *sorry* wasn't going to help anyone.

"I'm sorry, Sally. I know there's nothing much that you can do." Sylvia's voice softened and became plaintive as she looked into Sally's eyes. "But, governments, politicians… the system treats women like these as criminals… but they're not. Why don't they do something about the real criminals, the people responsible for all this suffering?"

"I don't know," Sally replied; she couldn't think of anything else to say, "...I really don't know."

Sylvia took a card from her pocket and gave it to Sally. "My phone numbers... home and office... if there's anything I can do to help please call me... anything at all."

"I will. Thanks, Sylvia."

Sylvia Land turned and walked down the stairs. At the bottom, she looked back at the two detectives and called out, "Look after them."

"We will," said Sally, "I'll call you."

They walked to the top of the stairs, where Briggs was waiting and followed him to his office. "We've moved the body," said Briggs, "I'm going over to the morgue now; the pathologist is ready to start the post mortem."

"Have the SOCOs finished yet?" asked Sally.

"Still bagging and tagging; but they've already sent a lot of stuff over to the lab."

"Better make sure that they get that one," said Barton pointing to the disc in the bag on Briggs' desk.

"Have you looked at it?"

"Yes... not exactly family viewing. We need a copy though... and copies of the other discs and the women's interview tapes."

"I'll arrange it. Anything else you want?"

"Not at the moment thanks, we're going back soon. Give me a call later."

Barton was enjoying his mixed grill. "This is good, Sal, you should have had some. Good job Grace isn't here though... heart attack on a plate, she'd call this," he said as he bit into a sausage: *Grace. Oh no!* He'd not phoned her yet.

Sally smiled and picked at her tuna salad. Her stomach told her that she was still hungry, but her mind was somewhere else. "Sorry," she said, pushing the plate away. "I've lost my appetite."

"This is really getting to you, isn't it?"

"I can't help it Mike. I can't get over meeting those women. I wonder if they ever smile. Do you know what I saw when I looked into their eyes...? Nothing... nothing at all... it was as though they weren't really there. Don't you think that's awful?"

"Come on, Sal. Get over it, there's nothing you can do."

"That's the point," she said bitterly. "Sylvia's right. What do we do? Nothing... not a bloody thing! We just stand on the sidelines and watch... we've been watching this for a fucking year! I know we have to get the bastards who are doing this... but what about the people they're doing it to... who's going to help them? What's going to happen to those women, Mike?"

"That's up to the local police and the immigration people... I suppose they'll be sent home."

I know that," she said tearfully. "But in the mean time they'll be locked up somewhere. But they're not criminals, Mike... they're the victims. And there's nobody to help them. All that they've got is people like Sylvia. At least she cares... but there's not much she can do."

"You know what it's about, Sal. It's always about money... Drugs, illegal immigrants, prostitution; it'll never stop... not as long as someone out there can make money from it. There'll always be more girls... more addicts... more people getting hurt," he said, with a shrug of resignation. "But Sylvia's wrong... the government is doing something about the people responsible. That's why we're doing this Sal. And if we can get the big guys... the little people might have a better chance." *God! That sounds so clichéd. But it's what I have to believe.*

"I know, Mike. I know... I keep telling myself. But I'm just not sure, that I believe it any more... Come on, let's get out of here. I want to go home."

Edinburgh – 17:15 BST

Marcus Preston opened another can of lager and looked at his watch. They'd been in the flat all day and he was still waiting for the phone to ring. He went to the window, and stared through the glass, looking down onto the street below. The football supporters were pouring out of the side streets leading onto Easter Road. It must have been a good game; he'd heard the cheers from the ground. He'd counted four goals and judging by the volume he reckoned that Hibs had won, 3 – 1. It had started raining again, and the fans were taking cover in every available doorway: *God I hate this place, it's always raining.* The pub on the corner was full to bursting and offered no shelter to those who had waited for the referee to blow the final whistle. Marcus allowed himself a moment or two of philosophical reflection, as he contemplated the dilemma that hundreds of thousands struggled, with every Saturday afternoon, sitting on the edge of their seats, with one eye on the clock – *'If I go now, I'll get to the bar before the rush... but, they might get a late goal'*.

Further down the road he could see Leroy, he was easy to pick out: a lone black face, struggling against the tide of green and white that was flowing towards Leith Links. Leroy had a carrier bag in each hand and, every so often he lifted them above his head, to ease his passage through the crowd. Marcus watched with amusement, as Leroy stopped outside a shop and tried to fight his way through the doorway: *Idiot, I told him to get the beer first.*

Kev came into the room and picked up a beer can. He sat down on an armchair and looked at his shirt. "Fuck! I've got his blood all down my shirt." He glanced round the room. "Where's Leroy?" he asked.

"I sent him out to get some more beer and a takeaway. How's the Russian?"

"Sleeping, but he's in a bad way. Shouldn't we get him to a doctor?" asked Kev. "How long have we got to stay in this rat-hole, anyway?"

"I told you already," said Marcus. "We wait here until Jarvis tells us what to do. But let's hope it's soon. I want to get back."

"So do I, mate. Arsenal are at home tomorrow. I need my fix of football and we've already missed seeing Liverpool today because of that bastard."

The door buzzer sounded and Preston looked out of the window.

"It's Leroy. Go and let him in."

Leroy came in and put four carrier bags down on the kitchen worktop.

"It's pissin' down out there. I'm bleedin' soaked," he said as he walked into the bathroom. He came out rubbing his head with a towel and sat down in an armchair. He put his feet up on the coffee table and opened a beer can. "...and have you seen the fuckin' road out there... it's crawling with fuckin' jocks. I had a bastard of a time getting by them, they won't move out of the fuckin' way... and then I had to queue for fuckin' ages at the fuckin' off licence."

Kev had already emptied the carrier bags and put the beer in the fridge. "Let's see what we've got," he said as he started to take the lids off the foil containers, calling out the contents to his friends. "Chicken Balti... Tikka Masala... lamb Madras... something with prawns... rice, bhajis, samosas, naan bread... that's it. Huh! Nice one Leroy you forgot the poppadums again."

"No I didn't... I don't like fuckin' poppadums. If you want them, you can fuck off and get them."

"Typical," said Kev. "You just can't get the staff these days... Eh! Marcus?"

"Shut up you two and bring it over here."

Kev picked up some of the containers and carried them over as Marcus swept the empty cans onto the floor to make room on the table. "Move your feet Leroy, get up and help Kev."

"Hey Kev," said Leroy. "Here's a good one... the guy in the takeaway... he had a scotch accent."

"We're in fuckin' Scotland, what do expect arsehole?"

"I know that. What do you think... I'm fuckin' stupid?" said Leroy angrily. "No I mean... like he's a Paki... he's wearing a fuckin' turban, but he's talking like a jock. I tell you man, it was fuckin' weird... I mean it ain't right is it? It's not like he's a proper Paki."

"Christ you don't half talk some shit, Leroy," said Marcus. "What do mean not a proper Paki? It's the colour that makes them Pakis, not the way they talk. You talk like Kev… so what's that make you, then?"

"What do reckon, Kev?" Marcus looked at Kev and they both laughed. "Is Leroy proper black… or just some white boy pretending?"

"Fuck off!"

As they started to eat, the phone rang. Preston picked it up. "Christ, Warren you took your time… we've been in this crummy flat for hours."

"Sorry, Marcus I've been busy. The boss is very pissed off."

"What? Like it's our fault? I told you man… the guy was fuckin' nuts."

"OK, Marcus, take it easy. He's not blaming you. But I need to know everything in detail… starting with when you got there on Friday."

Marcus gave him the whole story, all the places, and names he could remember. "…and then this girl went crazy… she smashed the fuckin' TV set, man. Then she had a go at him, and he fuckin' killed her."

"Are you sure she was dead?"

"Well I didn't stop to take her pulse or nothing… but she looked pretty brown bread to me. Kev will tell you, he saw her too… he spilled his guts all over her."

"What about the hotel, Marcus. Did anyone else come up to the room?"

"Only the girl from room service. That was before I brought the girls back."

"What about when you left?"

"There was a crowd of people in the bar, but I don't think anyone saw us. The desk clerk was watching TV in the office."

"Did you leave anything behind, apart from a dead girl that is?"

"We didn't have time to clean up, man. But we got all the important stuff… we've got his wallet and briefcase… and the dead girl's bag so there's nothing to ID anyone. And I've got the money and most of the coke… apart from the bag he'd opened… and that got spilt all over the floor. All that got left behind was Leroy's DVD player and some discs."

"What about his phone? People have been trying to ring him."

"Didn't see it, he's probably got it in his pocket."

"You better check, and the DVDs, what were they?"

"Just a few from stock and some demos that Terry gave me."

"What?"

"Terry gave me a couple of demo discs… I was watching one when that girl went apeshit… a new one with the Russian and his Indiana Jones whip."

"Fuck, and you left it behind, didn't you see the end?"

"No… I told you the girl smashed the telly. What's the big deal?"

"It's not a fuckin' demo it's a private one… it was only for the punters who were there. Laurel and Hardy have got their fucking faces in it."

"Sorry, Warren, I didn't know."

"Marcus… I know… it's not your fault. But you'd better just pray that Mr King sees it that way."

"What do you want us to do?"

"Stay put. I'll call you back."

Marcus put down the phone, and picked up his plate. "Get me another beer, Leroy. This could be a long night."

Liverpool – 19:30 BST

They left the city centre and headed home, stopping at one of the petrol stations on Edge Lane, before they joined the motorway. "Get me some chocolate." Sally called to Barton, as he went to pay at the kiosk. She hadn't eaten more than a couple of mouthfuls in the canteen and, although she still didn't feel much like eating, she needed something to give her an energy boost.

They didn't speak as the car raced along the motorway. Barton drove; much faster than usual, keeping to the fast lane. He just wanted to get home as quickly as possible; he needed to see Grace. Sally reclined in the passenger seat and dozed. In her dream she saw their faces - Naida, Asija, Fahrija, Fahrija, Jasmina, and the all the others Hundreds, maybe thousands, of women all with the same look on their faces – frightened, helpless, hopeless. She woke several times, and every time she closed her eyes, again the faces were there.

She switched on the radio and listened for a while; then changed over to the CD: *The greatest soul album ever made?* She pressed a button to start it from the first track, turned up the volume and listened; listened to every word. Words written for a different time, in another country, and sadly still relevant today: *'What's going on…? What's happening brother…? Save the children…? Mercy, Mercy, Me…'* Sally closed her eyes again and wondered if it was always going to be like this.

Barton was thinking about Grace. What with all that stuff with Sally in the canteen; he'd forgotten to phone her before they left. He couldn't phone from the car. He didn't want another row; not in front of Sally. As the music faded, he spoke to his passenger. "Sally, are you awake?"

"Mmm… sort of… where are we?"

"Near Coventry… coming up to the services. Do you want to stop for a coffee or something?"

"No, I'm OK. Let's just get back."

"Do you mind if we take a detour? You can drop me off at home and I'll get a car in the morning."

Edinburgh – 22:00 BST

Warren Jarvis had made some more calls and had eventually, been given his instructions. They were all at risk, thanks to the foreigners, and he had to do something about it. Sitting in his office with a large whisky, he thought for a while about the possible consequences – something that he rarely did.

He picked up the phone again. This time he called Marcus Preston, who had been waiting all evening, staring at the phone in his hand, willing it to ring.

"Marcus, you've got to leave now."

"What about Mr King?"

"He's not very pleased Marcus... not at all. But don't worry I've squared things with him. Now he wants you back here... we've got a waste disposal job for you."

"OK, but what about the Russian? He needs a doctor."

"Too late for that, Marcus... he's been a bad boy."

"What do you mean?"

"I mean... you come back... he doesn't."

"OK, so how? Where?"

"That's up to you, just finish it. I want you back here in the morning."

Duxford, Cambridgeshire – 23:30 BST

Barton pulled the car off the road, and parked in the driveway. Sally opened her eyes and yawned. "Where are we?" she asked sleepily.

"My house," he said, opening the car door.

"All the lights are off, Mike."

"Grace must be in bed. Goodnight, see you in the morning." He gave her a peck on the cheek and got out of the car, leaving the engine running. Sally watched as he opened the front door and turned on the light in the hallway.

He didn't really want to wake Grace, but they had to talk. She wasn't in bed. He looked in the other bedrooms; he ran down the stairs and into the lounge, then the study; she wasn't there. He remembered his mobile phone and ran into the kitchen. It wasn't on the table where he thought he'd left it that morning. He looked on the worktops, he was sure he'd left it in here. Then he saw it in on the floor in the corner of the room and picked it up; the case was cracked. He scrolled though the call list; six missed calls. He looked at the numbers, four from Sally, one that he didn't recognise, and one from his own house phone.

Barton called the answer phone, and listened to the first message. "Hi Mike, it's Sally, call me when you get this." He pressed a button, *delete*; "Mike, it's Sally again, where are you?" *delete*; "Hello, Mr Barton, we've got your new starter motor." *delete; delete; delete.*

"Mike, it's me... your wife, remember. Where are you? Mike, we've got to talk... but you have to make time for me... I'm not waiting around here... I'm going to see Mum. Call me later.... Mike, I love you."

He switched off the phone and sat down at the table. As he sat with his head in his hands, he heard Sally's voice. "Are you OK, Mike?" she said. He looked up and saw her standing in the doorway. "You left the front door wide open."

"What are you doing here? I thought you'd gone home. She's not here, Sal."

"I know, didn't you notice her car's not here."

"Shit, I'm really messing this up."

Sally walked to the dresser, opened a door, and rummaged through the bottles, until she found the one she was looking for. "I don't know about you, but I need a drink," she said as she poured two large measures of Bushmills malt.

"Thanks," said Barton, taking one of the glasses from her.

"Mike, I know you're the boss, but that's never stopped us being mates. We look out for each other... I'll always be there for you, Mike. Never forget that. Do you want to talk about it?"

"Yeah, I'd like that... Oh God! I feel tired," he yawned and leaned back in the chair, "...but I might fall asleep on you."

"Well you can't go to sleep here, not in that chair, you'll fall off. Let's go and sit in the study."

"OK, bring the bottle."

Chapter 10

Sunday 4th May 2003

Duxford, Cambridgeshire – 06:30 BST

Barton rolled over in the bed and looked at his watch; half-past six, he couldn't remember the last time that he'd woken up this late. Nor could he remember going to bed. He stumbled out of bed and opened the curtains; bright sunlight flooded into the room. His head was aching and he searched in the bathroom cabinet for some aspirin. As he showered and dressed, the throbbing behind his eyes started to ease. He opened the bedroom door and smelt the aroma of fresh coffee wafting up the stairs. At first, he thought that Grace was back. Then he remembered; Sally. He looked at the crumpled bed; he couldn't remember: *Oh no…! No…! No!*

"Morning," said Sally as Barton walked into the kitchen, "did you sleep well?"

"Not really. How long have you been up?"

"Not long," she said, "I've only just made the coffee."

"Did I drink all that?" He asked pointing to the empty bottle on the table.

"I helped you a bit. You look rough, and you've forgotten to shave. Did you know you've got some grey in your beard?" She laughed at the frown on his face, "Don't worry, everyone gets old, even you. Sit down and have some coffee, I'm just going out to the car for a minute."

Barton picked up the empty bottle and put it in the bin. He turned on the tap. Sally had already washed the glasses, but for some reason he rinsed them again, carefully wiped them dry and put them back into the cupboard. He opened the fridge and took out a bottle of orange juice, unscrewed the top and drank from the bottle. He put the bottle down on the worktop and poured himself a mug of coffee: *Why doesn't she say something?*

When Sally came back, he was sitting at the table; still worrying. She was carrying a small holdall. She put it down on the table and poured herself some coffee.

"What's in the bag?" he asked.

"Change of clothes, make up, girls stuff. I'm a single girl Mike, we have to be prepared you know," she laughed again; she felt happy this morning; *Must be being with him… Yesterday I thought I'd never laugh again.* She finished her coffee and picked up the holdall. "Mind if I take a shower and freshen up?"

He only half heard the question, his mind was somewhere else. "What? Er… no, go ahead," he said: *Shit!*

"Are you sure that you're OK, Mike?" she asked, concerned: *Stupid question Sally. Of course he's not, that's why you ended up here.*

"What am I going to do Sal… about Grace… I mean… I…"

She bent down and kissed his forehead. "Stop worrying Mike. Give her a ring when we get to the office. It'll be alright. Trust me."

He followed her upstairs. After he'd shaved, he picked up the phone by the bed; the tone told him there was a message. He dialled 1-5-7-1 and listened as the recorded voice told him that he had two new messages. Probably for Grace, he thought; people usually called him in his mobile. He pressed a button and listened to Grace's voice.

"Mike, are you OK? I'm at Mum's… I needed to get away… I'm staying here tonight. Call me… please… I need to see you… I've got something to tell you. I love you."

He listened to the message again, just to hear her voice. He smiled, and thought about driving over to Grantchester to see her, then wondered what she'd told her parents and had second thoughts. He didn't have time for a big family argument; not this morning. But, Sally was probably right. Whatever the problem was they'd get over it. He'd call her later. He listened to the second short message

"Mike, it's me again. Sorry, forgot to tell you, your mobile is on the kitchen floor somewhere. Sorry, if I've broken it. Love you. Bye."

He walked out of the bedroom and heard the bathroom door opening. Sally came out, and walked towards the stairs, "That's better," she said, "…can't have the boss, turning up looking like a tramp in the morning." Then she laughed, "That's Dave Connor's job."

"Do you want some toast?" he asked.

She looked at her watch. "Shouldn't we be getting to work?"

"No hurry, it's Sunday, it will only take forty minutes. Less if you drive. Can you see if the paper's come?" He looked at her, hoping to see something in her face; anything that might tell him: *Say something… please say something. Tell me what we did last night.*

Barton put some bread into the toaster and switched on the radio to listen to the news – a train derailment near Swindon, the Prime Minister spending the weekend at Chequers with some European leaders, Bank Holiday traffic, and football – no mention of a dead body in a Liverpool hotel. Not that there should have been, if Briggs had managed to keep it quiet. Sally came back in with the

Sunday Times; took the main paper and put the rest in the middle of the table. Barton picked up the sports section and turned to the football results.

"Anything interesting in the paper, Sal?"

"Nothing much, usual Sunday rubbish," she replied. "No dead bodies if that's what you mean." She handed him the paper, "...here have a look." Then she poured the last of the coffee into her mug.

National Crime Squad, Hertfordshire Branch – 08:15 BST

They got to the office just after eight; the latest that either of them had arrived at work for weeks and the car park was already full of cars. Neither of them had said much in the car. Barton had been worrying; fearing the worst: *When is she going to say something? What's she so happy about*

And, Sally had felt happy – singing along to the radio, ignoring the speed limits; as usual – as if, for a while, she hadn't a care in the world.

But all she said was, "I'll go up first, you follow... we don't want to set tongues wagging."

Sally walked into the main office; it was a hive of activity. "You wouldn't think it was bank holiday Sunday," she said as she walked past Matt Brady.

Paul Timms was already at his desk, reading reports. "Morning, Paul is there anything interesting in that lot?" asked Sally, sitting down on the corner of her colleague's desk.

"Not a lot, Sally. Usual stuff so far, nothing out of the ordinary. Most of these are from yesterday's two-to-ten shifts. The night reports aren't in yet. Standing down surveillance. Huh...! That was a joke."

"Have you got anything there on Nichols? He was trying to get hold of Milosevic yesterday afternoon."

"No, we know he's in Leeds, but they've not sent anything in yet."

While they were talking one of the OCU liaison team officers, Detective Constable Sandra Pierce, approached them, carrying some manila files.

"Morning, Sandra, what have you got there?" asked Sally.

"We've had these reports faxed down from Liverpool. I thought the DCI might like to have a look. Is he in yet?"

"I'm not sure," she said: *Well, a little white lie won't do any harm.* "His car's outside, but I've not seen him. What's in those reports, anything interesting?"

Sandra held up the files. "This one's the post mortem report on the dead girl. This one's full of forensics reports. They've been coming in all night."

While they'd been talking, Barton had come into the room and was walking towards them. "Good morning, sir," said Sandra, "I was just on my way to bring you these."

"Thanks, Sandra put them on my desk. I'll have a look at them in a minute." As she walked away, Barton called her back. "Sandra."

"Yes, sir."

"When you've done that, can you get onto Leeds? See if they've got anything on Nichols."

"OK, sir."

Barton stood behind Timms, "Who's on surveillance at the moment, Paul?" he asked.

"I'll have to check the duties, sir. The shift's just changed over," said Timms. He opened a file and looked at the duty roster, "Let's have a look." He started to read out the entries. "Bobby King … Jeff Starkey went on at seven… Underwood…" Timms carried reading through the list. "…Warren Jarvis… he's Brenda Cooper's today. That's the lot," he said closing the file. "Oh! And Nichols is in Leeds of course."

"Thanks Paul, I want all the logs for last night in by nine," said Barton, "…and get someone round to Milosevic's flat, in case he comes back. We'd better cover Marcus Preston's place as well, it's a long shot, but they might turn up there."

"OK sir, I've got a couple of DCs due on at ten. I'll ring them and get them to go there now."

"Can you get everyone in the briefing room at nine-fifteen? If anyone wants me I'll be in my office reading those reports from Liverpool." Barton walked over to the coffee maker and poured himself a cup; it tasted awful: *Dave Connor's not in yet.*

Barton was walking back to his office, when Dave Connor and Lorna McLean came through the door, together. Barton looked at his watch. "Good afternoon," he said sarcastically. "Good of you to join us."

"Sorry, boss. The car…"

"No excuses, Dave, I've heard them all before."

Lorna glared at Connor. "Sorry, sir, he overslept."

Barton looked at them, standing in the doorway looking embarrassed, like a pair of school kids caught behind the bike sheds. They'd been seeing each other for about six months, and although neither would admit it, everyone on the team knew that Connor was practically living at Lorna's house. Barton wondered if she'd told her father.

They seemed an unlikely couple. Lorna, always neat and businesslike, her conservative, practical wardrobe, perfectly complimenting her no-nonsense, down-to-earth nature and her quiet, reserved demeanour – qualities that are, of course, expected of their daughters, by Scottish Presbyterian ministers; and much approved of by the ladies of their congregations; particularly in Crieff, the small Perthshire town, where she had grown up – looked strangely out of place, next to the fun-loving, dishevelled Irishman.

Connor's colleagues often joked about his appearance. – mismatched jackets and trousers, crumpled shirts, unruly hair and now that ridiculous red beard – some even suspected that it was all part of a carefully cultivated image; but not those who really knew him.

And, the few people who really knew Lorna would tell you that, behind the dour exterior, she had another side – which she rarely showed in public, and would never have dared to reveal in Crieff – and, to his good fortune, Connor had scratched the surface and found a witty, vivacious, and very sexy lady.

The pathologist had been thorough. Every injury described in detail; broken ribs, smashed nose, broken jaw, broken wrist, every cut and bruise; pages of them. Barton skimmed over the report; he'd seen the body, and didn't need to read the details. Some of it was interesting though; some of the blood on the girl's hands wasn't hers; also traces of skin and blood under her fingernails. Over the page there was evidence of a third person in the bathroom; vomit on the floor and in the girl's hair. He'd not noticed that when he'd looked at the body: *God that's disgusting.*

The cause of death wasn't strangulation. The tie hadn't been pulled tight enough and the bruising around her neck was fairly light. Marks on her fingers suggested that she had tried to pull the ligature away from her throat. The knife wound in her back had killed her; she'd bled to death. The time of death was approximately five o'clock: *The bastards left her there to die on her own. Shit, if they'd gone straight in after Milosevic left, she might still be alive. If the report had definitely said three girls in the taxi... Sally might have... No, she wouldn't have done anything, differently.*

Observe and record; don't break cover; that was the order. He wouldn't tell her though; if he'd thought that, so would she. He thought it better for her not to know; she'd been through enough already.

He turned to the forensic reports, looking at the times on the faxes. Sandra was right they'd been coming in all night. Piece by piece the evidence was building up to give a picture of what had happened in the hotel suite.

There was a knock at the door, and he looked up to see Sally standing in the doorway. "Everyone's ready to start, Mike. Are you coming?"

"Be with you in a minute," he said gathering up the papers and putting them back into the folder, hoping that she wouldn't want to read them.

Barton walked into the briefing room where about twenty officers were waiting and made his way to the front of the room. "Right, let's get started. First, for those that don't know yet, we've lost one of our targets. Milosevic disappeared last night."

A couple of faces showed surprise, but most nodded to indicate that they already knew. "He's left behind a dead girl and a wrecked hotel room… Liverpool CID are now running a murder investigation. Milosevic left the hotel at about two-forty-five… last seen heading north on the M6. He's travelling with three other men. One is Marcus Preston… we're still waiting for positive IDs on the other two. We think he may have been headed to Glasgow or Edinburgh… we've alerted the SCS. But, we're also checking known locations in Newcastle and we've got somebody watching his flat in London. That's all we know for the moment… And, unless you're on surveillance, finding him has got to be your top priority today."

Sandra Pierce raised her hand, "Sir, you haven't mentioned that he might be injured."

"Yes, sorry. That seems very likely now. Forensics identified some blood samples that don't match the dead girl. And it looks as though she may have stabbed him with a pair of scissors."

"That would explain the blood at the motorway services," said DS Matt Brady. "He might have gone to a hospital if it was bad. What about checking with A&E departments?"

"Might be worth a try, you can make a few calls, Matt. But if I were him I wouldn't risk a hospital," said Barton, "…too many questions to answer. Now, what else have we got Sandra?"

"We put an alert out on the car yesterday, but nothing's turned up yet. Liverpool CID are sending over some stills from the CCTV at the hotel and the motorway services," said Sandra, opening a file, "…might help identify the other two men. We've got a couple of names from the girls as well," she looked at the file, "Kev and Leroy… if that rings any bells."

"Thanks, Sandra," said Sally. "Oh! And another thing… they had the rooms booked through to Monday and the press haven't got hold of this yet… so there's a good chance they think the girl's not been found yet."

Several of the team contributed ideas about where Milosevic might be or what he was doing. Others asked questions about the murder. "Let's all understand the priority here," said Barton, "we're not investigating a murder… that's Liverpool's job. We've lost a primary target… we need to find him… and we need to make sure that this doesn't compromise the rest of the operation." He looked around the room and, when he was sure that everyone had had their say, he continued.

"Next. Nichols tried to contact Milosevic yesterday. We've got a voice message on Milosevic's mobile. Nichols doesn't know what's happened, but he's worried. He also had a call from a Liverpool estate agent yesterday and it's possible that he thinks Milosevic is doing deals behind King's back. Nichols is in Leeds at the moment, but I'll bet he's told King."

Lorna McLean spoke before Barton could continue, "Sir, if Nichols has been in contact with King. Do you think King would have told him why Milosevic is missing?" she asked.

"Good point, Lorna. If he knows what's happened he's probably getting worried. He'll know that it won't take long for us to find out that he was with Milosevic. Question is… is he going to wait for the knock on the door and try to bluff it out… or will he run?"

"Well he's not running yet," said Timms "Sandra spoke to a DS in Leeds half an hour ago. He said that Nichols was still at the hotel."

"Good, tell them not to let him out of their sight. Do we know who's been driving for him at the moment?"

"Errol Preston," said Timms.

"That's Marcus Preston's kid brother," said Lorna, "Maybe they've talked to each other, sir… and I can't see either of them doing anything without clearing it with Jarvis first."

After a couple of minutes of general speculation about who might have said what and to whom, Barton moved on to his final item. "Liverpool CID are sending down copies of some DVDs found in Milosevic's room. I looked at one yesterday with DI Parkinson. It's an unedited version and there are a couple of shots of Milosevic and Terry King together. And if Terry King and Milosevic are taking part, then there might be some others we know. I want someone to make a still copy of every face on the disc. Some of you have seen targets at close quarters and might recognise people."

Timms ended the meeting with a brief summary of the previous day's surveillance reports. There hadn't been much activity, and he was soon finished. "That's all folks. Apart from Milosevic and Nichols, nothing out of the ordinary, everyone else is accounted for."

"Let's keep it that way," said Barton picking up his papers. "Thanks everyone. Let's get back to work."

Barton sat in his office with Sally and Timms, trying to fit the pieces together. He doodled on a notepad as they talked; a pattern of circles and lines like a web.

He looked up, "So let's think about this'" he said. "Let's put Milosevic to one side for the moment and concentrate on the others. What do we actually know? And what are we assuming?"

Timms started the ball rolling. "We know that Nichols tried to contact Milosevic yesterday afternoon. We're assuming that he's contacted King. He's still in Leeds… so let's assume someone's told him to keep his head down. The estate agent can link him to Milosevic… which means that sooner or later the murder investigation will make the connection… so they'll want him out of the way for a while."

"But Foster called him at the hotel," said Sally. "So why is he still there? Why hasn't he run?"

"Good question," said Barton. He looked at Timms. "Paul, are you sure that he's still at the hotel?"

Timms looked at the report he'd received earlier. "Nichols and Preston came back to the hotel just after midnight, with two women… Nichols went straight up to the fourth floor… Preston stayed in the bar, with one of the women, for about an hour… then they went up. They haven't come down yet."

"So he's not actually been seen since midnight," said Barton, "What level of cover have you got on him?"

"DC or a DS, on a twenty-four-seven shift," said Timms, "…four-hourly check-ins. I've asked them to check in on the hour today, and as soon as they see him."

"So we've got one man covering, what… the hotel lobby area?"

"Yes, that's what we normally do," replied Timms, sensing that his boss was not happy with what he'd just told him.

Barton exploded, "Christ Paul! This isn't normal! If he wants to lose himself, he's not likely to use the bloody main entrance!"

"Sorry, sir, I'll ask Sandra to ring through to Leeds and get some extra cover put on."

"Not your fault Paul… I'm sorry… I should have thought of it yesterday afternoon," said Barton; although he didn't really know why he was letting Timms off the hook.

Timms picked up the phone, "Sandra, ring Leeds and tell them that we think Nichols might do a runner through the back door. Get some extra bodies to cover the hotel and get them to check that he's still in his room."

"Now what about the others?" asked Barton. "Who else would know where Milosevic is?"

"My money's on Warren Jarvis," said Sally. "I don't think Preston would have taken off like that without calling him first. What do you think, Paul?"

"Yes I agree. When all's said and done Preston's just hired help. Yes, he'd probably call Jarvis."

"OK," said Barton, "...let's assume that Preston called Jarvis for instructions... before they got Milosevic out of the hotel. That means that Jarvis probably knows where they are."

"And if Jarvis knew what was going on yesterday morning... he'd have told King..." Sally sounded uncertain, as if she was questioning what she was saying "I mean... Milosevic is a big player... if he got pulled for murder it would screw things up for them... Wouldn't it?"

"What are you thinking, Sally?" asked Barton.

"Well... if King knew... why didn't they tell Nichols? I mean... we're assuming that he knows now... but he didn't yesterday afternoon. Why would they leave him in the dark for so long?"

Timms answered, "Maybe Jarvis didn't tell King. Maybe he couldn't get hold of him... perhaps he thought he could get it sorted out and tell him later. After all if Jarvis is supposed to look after guys like Milosevic and Herrera... you know keep them out of trouble... then he's fucked up big time... King won't like that."

"Still doesn't explain why he didn't tell Nichols though," said Sally.

Barton thought for a minute, remembering the surveillance reports that Timms had told them about earlier. "Put yourself in Nichols's shoes... you get a call from Foster... which gets you thinking that Milosevic is doing his own deals... so you call Milosevic... but you can't reach him. What are you going to do next?"

"Phone King," said Sally, as she started to see what this was leading to.

"And if you can't get him? He was at the races, yesterday."

Timms looked confused, "What are you getting at, sir?"

"Well I can't see him calling Jarvis... Nichols tends to keep his distance from that side of the business... Terry's not going to be any use... that leaves Underwood."

"And he'd tell King," said Timms, "of course!"

"That may be one assumption too many," said Barton. "So lets make some more." He was on a roll, and fired off questions, neither waiting for, nor needing anyone to answer. "What if King doesn't know what's going on? What if he's not in the loop? What if someone else is telling them what to do?"

"Oh! Come on, sir. That's taking it a bit far. I..." Sally stopped, wishing she'd thought before speaking. "No, forget it; I can see what you're getting at now. This Puppet Master, whoever he is… you think he could be bypassing King altogether."

Barton carried on, ignoring the interruption. "We've been so focussed on King and his crew that we've forgotten the big picture. Milosevic may be a bit of a head-case, but he's an important man with some powerful friends. You were right, both of you. This kind of trouble could really fuck things up for them. But not just for King. Milosevic works for the Russians, not King. What if our Puppet Master is taking a much closer interest than we thought and is pulling everyone's strings?"

Stoke Newington, North London – 11:00 BST

The small café was crowded, as it always was on Sunday morning. People had time on a Sunday; time to relax, eat a proper breakfast, read the papers and catch up with world. Couples were sitting talking; some having their only real conversation of the week. A tall, athletic looking man walked in and looked around for an empty table. He saw a young couple by the window were getting up to leave. The girl was wearing high heels and a black evening dress; Marcus Preston wasn't the only one who'd been up all night.

He sat down at the table and picked up one of the papers they had left behind, turning to the back pages. After a couple of minutes the waitress came over carrying a tray and cleared away the remains of the last order.

"I'll just get rid of this lot and I'll be with you in a minute," she said as she picked up a pile of discarded papers, supplements and magazines, balancing them on top of the empty cups and plates.

"Get me a black coffee, while you're at it," said Preston.

When she returned, she wiped the table, before putting the cup in front of him; and then took out her notepad.

"Bacon, sausage, two eggs, beans and hash browns, more coffee and orange juice," he said; looking at the blackboard, behind the counter; he was starving. "…and I'll have some toast as well, please."

'Come straight here. I'll meet you in the café on the corner.' Warren had told him. He hadn't given Preston any hint of what it was all about or why it couldn't wait.

The waitress came back to the table carrying a jug of coffee, and started to refill his cup. "Leave the jug, please, two cups won't be enough this morning," he said. He'd been on the road since four o'clock and needed a shower and his bed. He'd had about four hours sleep since Friday and he was totally knackered.

Preston had finished eating, and was on his fourth cup of coffee when Warren Jarvis sat down opposite him. "You got back all right then?"

"Yeah, job done. Do you want to know where he is?" asked Preston.

"No not really."

"So what's the big deal that's keeping me from getting to my bed then?"

"Well like I said, I've got a job for you."

Preston looked up at the attractive young woman who had just walked by the table. "Whoa! Look at that. I wouldn't mind giving her one," he said, loud enough for her to hear.

There was an empty chair at the table behind Jarvis; she sat down, pushed the empty cups aside, and opened a paper. She woman smiled and laughed "Only one? Is that all a big boy like you can manage?"

"Bitch," muttered Preston.

"Leave it out, Marcus. Don't take any notice of him love."

She ignored them and spoke to the waitress. "Large cappuccino and a toasted bagel, with strawberry jam please." For the next ten minutes, she eavesdropped, as Jarvis explained the job to Preston.

"So who is it?" asked Preston, when Jarvis had finished speaking.

"You don't need to know. Take Errol… he should be on his way from Leeds by now. Give him a call when we're done here. But if he can't get back in time you'll have to get a couple of the boys." Jarvis got up to leave. "Now, go and get your head down, I need you awake tonight," he said sternly. "…I don't want any more mistakes."

"I'm sorry about the Russian," said Preston. "…there was nothing I could do. Have you sorted it with Mr King?"

"Just get this job right, Marcus. You don't have to worry about Mr King," said Jarvis as he walked to the door.

Preston got up and put his hand into his jacket pocket. He took out a handful of cash and put a five-pound note and some change on the table.

Detective Constable Brenda Cooper put down her paper and watched the two men, as they walked out of the café and crossed the street. Preston got into his car and drove off. Brenda finished her coffee and her eyes followed Jarvis as he walked to the corner and disappeared into the newsagents.

National Crime Squad, Hertfordshire Branch – 11:00 BST

Sandra Pierce swore as she put down the phone. She looked around the office: *Where's the DI? The boss isn't going to like this. Why does it always have to be me? Can't someone else tell him?*

Barton wasn't in his office either. She found them both outside in the car park, standing in a cloud of smoke. Barton was just lighting another cigarette when he saw her.

"Hi, Sandra, did you talk to Leeds?" he asked.

"Yes sir. It's too late though," she said apprehensively.

She jumped back as he barked, "What?"

"They just called back," she replied. They got housekeeping to check the room. A woman was asleep in the bed, but Nichols had gone, taken his bag and briefcase with him."

"Do they know when he left?"

"The woman said he was up at eight. She went to the bathroom and he was gone when she came out. That was at about eight-thirty."

"What about his driver, Preston?" Sally asked.

"No, he's still in bed. He had room service take up breakfast for two at about half nine. But the car's gone."

"Shit! I don't believe this happening," he said, "…it gets worse. Two hours! He could be a hundred miles away. Have you put out an alert on the car?"

"Yes sir, report sighting, follow, but don't approach or stop."

"Thanks, Sandra. Let me know as soon as you hear anything." Barton threw his cigarette onto the ground and followed her back into the building. "Come on Sal, lets get back to it," he said; although he wasn't sure what *it* was.

Cheshunt, Hertfordshire – 12:00 BST

Bobby King was fuming; Nichols hadn't turned up and nobody seemed to know where he was. His game had been all over the place; he'd packed up after the ninth hole and left Underwood and Stevens to finish without him. He was in the locker room when the phone rang. He opened the locker room door and walked outside

"Hello, Lenny. What's going on?"

"Just listen, Bobby. Don't say anything, just listen." King did as he was told and listened as he was given the news about Milosevic. "…It's OK. Milosevic has been taken care of. Don't worry, his bosses sanctioned it. But now you've got some clearing up to do… our friend Herrera."

"What?"

"Shut up and listen. He's in trouble… fucking your daughter was bad enough… it complicates things… got him too close to you. Fucking foreigners, they're more trouble than they're worth. But now he's been ripping us off and we can't allow that. I want him taken out tonight. Get him well out town. I don't want him to be found. You've still got plant on that motorway site, haven't you? There must be some nice big holes there. Bury him!"

"Why tonight, what's the hurry?"

"No questions, Bobby. Just do it. I want you to handle this one personally, just like in the old days. Make a proper job of it, just like you used to. I can't trust anyone else, so it's got to be you. I know you won't let me down."

"Of course I won't, Lenny. Leave it to me, they'll never find him."

King hung up, and then phoned his son. "Terry, where are you? Is Barry with you? Good, I've got a job for you…"

Then he made another call, but Nichols didn't answer. He switched off the phone, put into his pocket and went back into the locker room. He looked around to make sure he was alone, opened a locker, and took out a small notebook.

Later as they were driving back to the house, King told Underwood about the phone call. "Lenny wants us to get rid of Herrera… it's going to be tonight, and he wants me to do it. Do you want to come along for the ride?"

"Don't be daft," Underwood replied. "Don't you think we're getting a bit old for that sort of thing? Why don't you just get Warren to sort it? He'll be none the wiser."

"You're going soft George. I haven't done one myself for a long time… anyway, it's not your daughter the little greaseball's had his dirty hands all over… of course I'm going to do it and I'm going to enjoy it."

London, Docklands – 12:30 BST

Detective Constable Shona Moore wished that the she'd bought the Mail; it was hard to turn the pages of the Sunday Telegraph, sitting behind the wheel of the car, even with the seat pushed right back. She kept one eye on the apartment block. She knew what was going to happen; any minute now the front door would open, Debbie King would kiss her lover and walk across to the Mercedes. Then she would drive to Cheshunt, stopping on the way to pick up her brother. It was the same every Sunday, except that sometimes she started out from Maida Vale: *God this is boring.*

She smiled and turned on the radio; she'd have nothing to do for the rest of the shift, she was off at four and Herrera wouldn't be out until much later. She hadn't noticed the black BMW arrive, so she didn't know how long it had been there. She only saw it now, in the door mirror, as she leaned across to get a CD out of the glove compartment. She picked up her mobile phone and called Connor. "Hi, it's Shona. I'm outside Herrera's place, and… this is really weird…

I've got a black BMW parked about fifty feet behind me. There's three men in it... and I'd swear one of them is Terry King."

"It is," said Connor, "John Perry just followed him there. Have you seen him?"

"What's he driving?"

"The blue Rover, I think."

"Yeah, he drove past me a few minutes ago. He must be up the road a bit... Hang on a minute... I think Debbie's coming out." Shona put the phone down and watched the woman get into the Mercedes SL. The roof retracted into the boot and she drove off. "OK, she's gone. The BMW's just started to move... driving past me now... they're parking in front of the flats."

"Keep an eye on them. I'm going to phone John."

A couple of minutes later Shona's phone rang. "Hi Shona, it's John Perry. Can you see anything?"

"King's just gone into the flats... he's got Barry Jarvis with him. The other bloke's still sitting in the car."

"OK, let's wait."

They didn't have to wait very long. A few minutes later King and Jarvis came out of the door with Herrera and got into the waiting car. "They're on the move, John. Herrera's sitting in the back with King. They're coming towards you."

"OK, Shona, let's see where they're going. I'll call it in."

Connor was talking to Sally when the call came. He went back to his desk and took the call. "OK, John, I've got that. Keep with them." He put the phone down and went back to Sally's office. "That was John Perry. He's been following Terry King and Barry Jarvis. They've just picked up Herrera."

"Thanks Dave, we'd better tell the boss."

"And Brenda called in earlier... she's seen Marcus Preston, with Warren Jarvis."

"Come on, he'll want to know about that too."

National Crime Squad, Hertfordshire Branch – 12:45 BST

"They found his body this morning," said Sally. "Sandra's on the phone to SCS now getting details."

"Where was he?" asked Barton; not that it mattered any more.

"Edinburgh, he was lying at the bottom of a flight of stairs in a derelict warehouse near Leith docks. Some kids found him."

"Are they sure it's our man?"

"We think so. He didn't have any ID on him, but they found a registration card from the hotel in his pocket, name of Sabic. The local station called SCS. They've sent someone round to the mortuary to identify him from photographs."

"Bottom of the stairs, Eh! An accident... or maybe made to look like one?"

"They don't know. The pathologist hasn't seen him yet."

Barton stared out of the window. "So Milosevic is dead, and the first thing that Preston does when he gets back is meet Jarvis. Accident?" he shook his head, "...I don't think so."

Tottenham, North London – 14:30 BST

Herrera woke up and tried to remember where he was. His ribs hurt and his jaw was aching; he could taste the blood in his mouth, and he could feel with his tongue that two of his teeth were missing. He couldn't move; his ankles tied to the legs of the chair, wrists bound behind his back. They'd taken his clothes, leaving him in just a T-shirt and shorts. He heard a voice say, "He's awake, Baz, get the man a drink." He opened his eyes and raised his head to see Terry King standing over him.

King looked at him, "You'd like a drink, wouldn't you, Ricky? Straight Scotch alright?"

King took the glass from Jarvis and flung it in Herrera's face. The liquid stung his eyes and ran down his cheeks. "You've been a bad boy, Ricky... we don't like it when people rip us off. Now, where's our fucking money?"

Herrera leaned back; looked up at King and spat in his face. "*Vete al carajo! Chinga tu madre!*" he shouted.

"That doesn't sound very nice," said King wiping the blood and saliva from his cheek. "What did he say, Baz?"

"I think he told you to go to hell, and fuck your mother," said Jarvis, trying to suppress a laugh. "I'll have to remember that, it's a good one."

"But it's not very nice way to talk to friends, Ricky. You could get into all kinds of trouble talking to people like that," King snarled. He put his heel onto the seat, between the Colombian's legs and kicked the chair backwards, sending it and the man crashing to the floor.

"Pick him up, Baz. We haven't even started yet. Go and get your video camera. I want Dad to see this."

He walked over to the desk and lit a cigar. "Don't look so worried Ricky... I'm not going to kill you... my old man wants you alive. You've got to tell him where his money is."

Jarvis came back with a video camera, switched it on and pointed it towards Herrera, blinding him for a moment. The bright light reflected in his terrified eyes, as King bent down and grabbed his crotch. "Now let's have a look at what you've been giving my little sister."

He tore the silk shorts away. "Oh! Isn't he a big boy, Baz? Lucky Debbie, I bet she enjoys that. What a shame she won't be getting any more."

He drew hard on the cigar, and the tip glowed bright red. "They say that smoking is bad for your sex life, Ricky. Did you know that?"

King moved closer and Herrera winced as he felt the heat from the red-hot tip; screamed as it burnt into his flesh. King drew on the cigar again, and applied the glowing tip again; and again. Herrera's screams continued to echo round the basement as King finished the cigar. Then, as he stubbed it out, slowly grinding the hot ashes into Herrera's scrotum, the Colombian lost consciousness again.

National Crime Squad, Hertfordshire Branch – 16:30 BST

It was time to put a few more pieces of the puzzle in place and Barton had assembled the team in the briefing room. "OK, a lot's been happening today. Let's see what we've got."

"Where do you want to start sir?" asked Timms.

"Let's kick off with the easy ones first. Who's still where they should be?"

"Right, let's see'" said Timms. "Bobby King's at home having lunch with Deborah, as usual. Terry's not there, but we know where he is. Underwood's gone to the match. Where's Warren Jarvis, Brenda? "

"He's down at Highbury with Underwood, watching the Arsenal," she replied, "… do you want me to tell you about the meeting in the café?"

"Not yet, Brenda. Let's get the roll call out of the way first." Timms continued, "Terry King, Barry Jarvis and Herrera are at the club. Shona says they went straight there from Herrera's place… they've been there since about two… I wish we knew what Herrera's doing there."

"Thanks, Paul. Now what about the Nichols?"

"No sign yet, sir. But Errol Preston's still in Leeds. He's at the station waiting for a train to King's Cross."

"So, we've got five of them where we'd expect them to be," said Barton. "Terry King's not with his dad, which is unusual, and Herrera's definitely in the wrong place. Nichols is missing and Milosevic is dead. Got any more news about him yet Sandra?"

"Yes sir. The pathologist hasn't finished yet, but we've got a preliminary report from Leith CID." She read from the top page, "Time of death between two and three this morning, cause of death, broken neck."

"An accident then, he fell down the stairs," said Timms.

Brenda flipped through the pages; quickly scanning the report. "They don't think so, sir... if he'd fallen down the stairs there'd have been bruises... maybe some abrasions on his hands from where he tried to stop the fall... maybe a head wound. There weren't any... but he had some bruising around the neck. At the moment the pathologist thinks someone stood behind him and snapped his neck... commando style. He had a deep wound in his side... and he'd been bleeding a lot. According to the forensics report, there was blood round the doorway and on the floor... but none on the stairs... in fact there were no signs that anyone had been upstairs recently. It looks like he was dumped there." She looked at Barton. "They're fairly sure he was murdered, sir."

"Thanks, Sandra," said Barton. "OK, Brenda, tell us about Preston and Jarvis."

Brenda Cooper gave an account of the breakfast meeting. "They met just after eleven... in a café just round the corner from Jarvis's flat... Preston was already there waiting, when Jarvis got there. I didn't hear much... but they were planning something."

"What did you hear?" asked Timms.

"Like I said, sir, not much... Jarvis did most of the talking and he had his back to me. But he definitely said it was tonight and something about the motorway... the M4... something about road works... and something about motorbikes... he said it would be easier to get away on bikes. And he said something about Herrera and Errol, but I couldn't hear what."

Barton went back to his office; he had some urgent calls to make.

"Merseyside CID, Detective Sergeant Poole speaking."

"Hi Gerry, it's DCI Barton. We've found Milosevic... tell your boss he's dead. If you ring Lothian and Borders CID at Leith they'll fill you in with the details."

"Thanks' sir. Can we tell the press anything yet? We've had some reporters sniffing round, seems someone got a tip off from the mortuary."

"No, wait a bit longer. It's a holiday tomorrow, tell Briggs that he can organise a press briefing for Tuesday. You can tell the girls though. They might be willing to talk a bit more if they know he's out of the way."

"OK, sir. By the way we've had those DVDs copied, you should get them tomorrow. And we've got a list of the numbers in his phone memory. I'll get it faxed through."

Barton's next call was to Detective Chief Superintendent Miller. "…so that's it Trevor. I'm not too worried about Nichols at the moment. He'll turn up sooner or later. But I'd like to know why they killed Milosevic. I've got an idea but…"

"Come on then, Mike… tell me. Your hunches are usually pretty good."

"They couldn't take the risk that we'd get to him… he knew too much. They could have kept him hidden until they were able get him out of the country… but Jarvis needs a job doing tonight and he wants Preston to do it… so they couldn't baby-sit Milosevic. Now he may have been expendable but… I don't think they'd have killed him, without telling his bosses… He's a big player… the Russians must have agreed and that means someone convinced them that it was the only option."

"I'm not sure where this is going Mike, but carry on."

"Well it's this thing with Herrera that's bugging me. It's one thing for him to be at the clubs having a good time, but… why would he be there with Terry King and Barry Jarvis on a Sunday afternoon… when the place is closed? I'm guessing that… maybe they see Milosevic and Herrera as the weak links… they put themselves about too much. They've got rid of Milosevic… now Herrera's under wraps… because something big is going down tonight… drug shipment maybe and they need Preston… someone they can trust to handle it…"

Miller interrupted; he didn't need to hear any more of Barton's theories, it was time to act. "Mike, I know that I gave you until the end of the month, but you're going to have to make a move now."

"I know. We can't afford to lose Herrera. But, I want to see what happens tonight and then move in on them in the morning."

"It's your call Mike. You know that this means you probably won't get the Puppet Master, now."

"Yes, but if we don't move in, we could lose it all."

"So that's it. We pull them in tomorrow morning," said Barton, after he'd told them the plan. "I don't think we've got any choice. I want double manning on all the primary targets starting now… and everybody ready to move in at six. "

"What about the club," asked Sally, "…there's three of them there."

"Yes, and they might move separately, so keep it well covered. Herrera's your man Sally, so you organise it," said Barton. "…and Paul you'd better get someone on Preston."

"Might be difficult to follow if he's using a bike," said Sally. .

"I know, but Jarvis said something about the M4, so even if we lose him in London, we should be able to pick him up on the motorway."

"Trouble is we don't know how far he's going," said Sally, "...we should arrange some backup cover on the motorway..." she stopped speaking and looked at Timms. "Paul, you're very quiet what are you thinking?"

"Well, if it's a big shipment of drugs they could be coming up from Southampton. And, they'd use the A34 to get to the M4. There's a motorway services at the junction, a good place for a meet. And it fits with what Brenda said about road works... there's a big construction site near there at the moment... so if we put someone out there..."

"Good idea, Paul. If Preston shows up there we'll be one step ahead," said Sally. "And if they're meeting a shipment we'll be able move in on them as soon as he makes contact."

"We're going to need help," said Barton. "We can't cover everything, but maybe we can fix the odds in our favour... Paul, get on to Thames Valley traffic control. We need them watching all the motorway cameras on their patch. You know the form." He stopped and thought for a moment; he wasn't sure how big this was going to be, but he wasn't going to take any chances. "...and get some uniforms on standby... a couple of ARVs, and...."

They finalised the plan, and the two DIs left to brief their teams. Sally stopped outside the door, "I'll catch up in a minute, Paul. I've left my notebook on his desk."

Barton was standing by window when she came back into his office. "Mike, I know you've got a lot on your mind," she sounded concerned, "...but have you phoned Grace yet?"

"Haven't had time," he said, shrugging his shoulders.

"Why don't you go and see her? We've got everything under control here and anyway I can't see anything going down until after dark. That gives you a few hours at least. We'll call you if anything happens," she said. "...don't worry I'll cover for you."

"But..."

"No buts, Mike," she said firmly, "...just go."

Chapter 11

Sunday 4th May 2003

Grantchester, Cambridgeshire – 16:30pm BST

Grace's parents lived in Grantchester, just south of Cambridge. The traffic was light and he got there in less than an hour. He'd phoned on the way and spoken to Grace's mother. "Hello Kate, it's Mike, can I speak to Grace?"

"And about time too! She's very upset. I don't know how you can do this to her." Kate Faulkner sounded very angry "She's in the garden, Michael. She can't come to the phone at the moment…"

This wasn't going to be easy; he hadn't bargained on Kate. "Please just tell her I'm coming to see her…"

Grace heard the car and ran from the garden to meet him. She slowed her pace, before she reached the gate: *I'm not going to make this easy for him.* She ambled slowly towards the gate, stopped, and watched him get out of the car: *Why should I run to him?*

He thought how beautiful she looked standing there under the yew tree. He walked towards her and stretched out his arms to hug her, but she drew away. Her clenched fists pounded against his chest as she cried "I hate you! I hate you…!" over and over again; tears pouring down her face.

Barton just stood there, not knowing what to say. Gradually the force of the blows subsided and when they stopped, he put a hand to her face to wipe away the tears. "Why?" she sobbed, "…why didn't you phone…? I've been so worried… where have you been? I…"

"I'm sorry…" he said, feebly: *Why do I always say that? Why can't I just for once…*

She stopped sobbing, and let fly. "Not again, Mike!" I'm not interested! I don't care!" she cried. "…How many times! When will you learn! Saying sorry isn't enough. It just doesn't mean anything!"

"I'm sorry. I meant to phone but I've had a lot on. I…"

"And I'm not important! I mean so little to you, that you can't even be bothered to pick up the phone."

"I didn't mean that."

"No! So what exactly do you mean then?"

Barton had never seen her like this; he struggled to find his words. "I mean... I didn't mean to upset you. I mean... I love you... Oh! I mean... you know... I'd never do anything to hurt you. I love you..." He tried to take her hand but she pulled away.

"How do I know Mike? It's just words. It's what you do that counts," her anger had turned to exasperation. "Don't you understand? ...I needed you and you weren't there." She started to walk away. "It's too late now Mike. Just go away."

He watched her walk into the garden, part of him wanting to run after her; part wanting to get away. He didn't know what he should do. He didn't know what she wanted him to do. He didn't need this, not now, not today: *Bloody women! Why do they always talk in riddles? Bloody Sally!* She'd got him into this: *'Go and see her Mike'*. Why hadn't he just phoned? He decided to take the easy way out, and started back to his car.

"Move a step closer to that car, and I'll belt you so hard, you'll still be on the floor tomorrow." He turned around and saw his father-in-law standing behind him. Dr Julian Faulkner was a big man, physically fit and younger looking than his sixty-five years. He was quite capable of carrying out the threat, and the look on his face told Barton that he was deadly serious.

"You're a bloody fool Michael. I know you don't mean it, but if you hurt my girl, you'll have to answer to me for it. I think you'd better come into the house."

As Barton followed Julian to the kitchen, Kate Faulkner passed them in the hallway. She didn't say anything, just glared at him; her eyes said it all.

Julian opened the fridge, "Sit down. Do you want a beer?" he asked. Barton nodded obediently and sat at the table. Julian took two bottles of lager from the fridge; opened them and handed one to Barton. "Now tell me what the hell's going on. Grace turned up here in tears yesterday morning. She's spent hours talking to Kate, but neither of them will tell me anything. All I know is that you've had some kind of row."

Barton tried his best to explain. He told him about the row they'd had, and about how things hadn't seemed right for weeks. "I don't know Julian, something's just not right but she won't tell me."

"Maybe you haven't been there to listen."

"I know I'm not always there, it's the job. But she knows that," said Barton, bewildered, "...but she's never been like this before. I don't..."

"Well whatever it is Michael, you'd better do something," said Julian, looking at the anguish in Barton's eyes, "...or you'll come home one day and find that she's packed more than just an overnight bag."

"She wouldn't. Would she?" said Barton in disbelief. "She knows how much I love her."

"Maybe that's not enough, son."

"What do you mean?"

"You've got to work at it," said Julian. There was no hint of reproach in the remark. He knew how much this man loved his daughter, and he wanted to help them. "Kate and I have been married for nearly forty years... but don't think that we've not had bad times. But we've always worked things out... talked things through... made time for each other. You know, I look at Grace and I can see her mother in her... independent, stubborn... bloody obtuse at times. But, she doesn't really ask a lot of you... and when she does you have to be able to give... I know it's not as easy for you, in your job... but you've got to be there."

"Thanks Julian, thanks for understanding," said Barton, but I'm still not sure that I do, he thought. Why does everyone else make it sound so easy?

He was still asking himself questions as Julian spoke again. "Michael, you know that Kate and I love you like you were our own. All we want is for the two of you to be happy. But Grace is all we've got. She's the most precious thing in the world to us. Don't make us take sides, son." He stood up and put his hand on Barton's shoulder. "Now, I think you'd better go and find her."

He couldn't see her, at first. She was sitting on the old swing that hung beneath from the branches of the weeping ash. The ends of the branches trailed on the ground, forming a green curtain, hiding the trunk of the tree. It was Grace's secret place, hidden under the arching branches, a place for her private thoughts, where she had always hidden as a little girl – when mummy and daddy were cross with her; she pretending that she couldn't hear her parents calling and them pretending that they couldn't find her – although of course, she wasn't really hiding. They'd always known where she was and Mike would too.

"Hello. Can I come in?"

"Go away. I'm not here."

"Funny. It looks like you." Barton stood behind the swing, held the ropes, and gently pushed her away.

"You're still here then. Daddy hasn't shot you."

"No, but I saw your mum and if looks could kill..."

"What did you expect, the red carpet?"

"Can we talk?"

She put her feet on the ground, bringing the swing to a halt. "Not if you're going to stand there. Or are you afraid to look me in the face."

He stepped in front of the swing, to face her. "That's better," she said

"I'm sorry," he said, "and before you say anything. I really do mean it. I just don't know what else to say. I just can't bear to see you like this." His eyes were telling her far more than words ever could, and Grace could see that he was hurting as much as she was, "...but you have to tell me what's wrong."

"Nothing's wrong with me Mike. That's the whole point... there's nothing wrong... I just needed you to be there."

"Hang on I don't get this. You say nothing's wrong, but..." He was confused: *Now, she's talking in riddles again.* "But you've not been yourself for weeks."

"It's OK. It's nothing, "she said reassuringly, "...it's quite normal."

"What do you mean normal?"

"I mean it's normal for someone in my condition."

There she goes again, what's she talking about? "Your condition?" he said, probing. "Now you're really not making sense. I thought you just said nothing was wrong with you."

"You really haven't got the faintest idea, have you," she sighed "Are all men this thick, or is it just you? There's nothing wrong with me... I'm pregnant."

There was an awkward silence as it slowly sank in. It started to make sense now, he should have realised. She'd been like this before, but he'd buried the memory. "What? Are you sure?" Confusion gave way to excitement and the words tumbled out of his mouth. "But I thought, I mean after last time. That's fantastic. God! That's amazing. Why didn't you tell me? How long?"

"About three months," she said smiling, sharing his delight. "I wanted to tell you as soon as I knew. But after last time I wanted to be sure, that it was going to be alright. I waited until they'd done all the tests." Suddenly she felt sad again and her smile disappeared. "But when I was ready to tell you... you weren't there... you've hardly been at home."

He reached out and took her hands, gently pulling her to her feet. "But, you know I love you."

She put her arms around his neck and kissed him. "And I love you, you bastard, but why do you make it so difficult?"

"I love you... I'm so sorry," he was choking on the words, "...I didn't realise... I'm so sorry." He kissed her again, and took her hand. "Do your mum and dad know?" he asked.

"Mummy knows... well, I think she's guessed. Daddy doesn't know yet," she said. "I wanted you to be the first to know, Mike."

"We'd better go and tell him. He's worried, the way he was talking earlier, like he thinks we're on the verge of a divorce."

"You came this close, mate," she said, holding her forefinger and thumb, half an inch apart, in front of his face. "Come on. We've got some more talking to do first. Let's go for a walk by the river."

They walked out from under the tree. The canopy of branches was so dense that they hadn't realised it had started to rain. "It's only a shower," she said smiling, "…come on. I like the garden like this. It's like in that song."

He kissed her again and he knew it was going to be OK. He took her hand and they walked together – towards the gate and beyond that, the path that led to the meadows – through the garden that she loved so much. As the words of the song ran through his head, he knew that wherever he was he only had to close his eyes and they would be there: *'…After a summer shower, when I saw you standing in the garden… in the garden wet with rain…'*

Cheshunt, Hertfordshire – 23:00 BST

The two men sat in the dark; the interior of the car lit only by the orange glow of the dashboard lights. They had been parked for about two hours and could barely see out of the misted windows. The driver pressed down on the stalk to wipe the windscreen, again; the other man took off his baseball cap and used it to wipe the inside. He peered through the smeared glass and looked at the houses on the other side of the road.

"Well we're not going to see him again tonight. Lucky sod! We're sitting here freezing our balls off and he's tucked up in his bed."

"That's where I should be," said Phil Fellows, "…tucked up in bed with Dawn."

"Who?"

"Dawn, you know the new girl in records, the one who started last month."

"Thought you didn't fancy her," said Connor, seizing on the chance of a bit of gossip to relieve the boredom, "…you said she was too thin."

"That was before she came on to me in the canteen last week. She's alright," said Fellows, as he started to tell his companion the details. "…we had a good night out on Friday… We went to that new pub in the High Street for a couple of drinks… nice meal at the Lotus Garden… then on to Maxim's. She's not a bad little mover on the dance floor… good body too… I know it's a bit skinny, but all the right bits are in the right places. She can keep going too…"

"Then what?"

"She does quite a nice breakfast… got all these fancy fruit juices and yoghurt things in her fridge… good coffee, not quite up to yours. No bacon though."

"So you shagged her then?"

"I said… we had breakfast… anything else is for me to know and you to guess. I'm a gentleman you know… can't betray a lady's confidence."

Connor laughed. "You wouldn't know a lady if one sat on your face."

"Well at least they'd sit on mine. They wouldn't go near yours," said Fellows laughing, "…when are you going to shave that stupid beard off?"

"Lorna says it makes me look interesting."

"That's probably because she loves you, and doesn't want to hurt your feelings," Fellows said wistfully. "But I don't, so believe me… it makes you look like a garden gnome."

The two men sat and watched, exchanging stories to pass the time. Connor was in full flow, when the crackle of the radio interrupted him. "Delta-Four to control… *Goodfella* is on the move, he's just left the club. He's in a Black BMW seven series… index, Tango-Kilo-Zero-Two-Bravo-Mike-Whisky… turning north onto the A10… Bravo-One, it looks like he's coming your way… Control, he's in a hurry, pass the word… we don't want any uniforms pulling him over for speeding."

Connor looked across the street to the house. Someone had switched on an upstairs light and as he watched, he saw another light behind the front door. The curtains in a downstairs room moved and he saw a face at the window. He picked up the handset, "Bravo-One to control… *Godfather* is up and about… lights on in the house… target is looking out of the window."

The curtains closed and Fellows started the car, "Better move, just in case he's seen us… get down." he said, switching on the headlights and pulling away from the kerb.

Connor slid down in his seat. Fellows deliberately revved the engine as he drove the car past the house. Connor looked up and in the rear view mirror, he saw someone at the window again. "He's seen us now," he said.

"That's right," said the Fellows, "…he's just seen me leaving." Surveillance ops in this sort of residential area were always tricky, it was too quiet; not enough passing traffic for a strange car to go unnoticed for very long. Phil Fellows was an old hand and he drove past the first couple of side roads and then turned off to the left. He took the next left; drove past the next turning and then turned left again. He switched off the headlamps and guided the car towards the junction ahead. He pulled the car in to the kerb and switched off the engine. The rain had stopped. "Perfect," he said. Looking out of the side window, he could see the house about fifty yards away, on the opposite side of the street.

"I wonder why Terry is coming to see his old man in the middle of night. What's the time Phil?" asked Connor.

Fellows looked at his watch. "Quarter to one," he said.

"How long do you reckon before they get here?"

"Straight run from Tottenham at this time of night. About twenty minutes, thirty at the outside. I could do it in fifteen on the bike."

Connor spluttered, almost choking on his coffee; Phil's bike was a standing joke. "In your dreams mate," he laughed. "Assuming that it'll start in the first place… when was the last time you did more than five miles without something falling off?"

Although Fellows was used to being the butt of their jokes, he always became very protective when his treasured the 1962 Triumph Bonneville was derided in this way. "I'll have you know, that bike is a masterpiece of British engineering…a work of art. She's a classic and I know she might not be perfect, but…"

"They don't build them like that any more." Connor interjected. "Is that what you told the Chief Super when all that crap sprayed out the exhaust and over his new Jag last month?" Connor was laughing almost uncontrollably. "Christ! I hope you didn't take Dawn out on the pillion on Friday."

"Of course not, what do you think I am. Women can't be expected to appreciate a classic like that. Anyway she's off the road at moment."

"Again," laughed Connor."

"Fuck off." Fellows looked at his watch again. "They should be here soon. Better check with the others."

Connor picked up the radio mike, "Bravo-One to Delta-Four… how long?"

The speaker crackled, and a voice replied. "About five minutes."

"How many in the car?"

"Three… The driver and two in the back… *Goodfella*… and the other one could be *Jacknife.*"

"OK, we're parked in a side street opposite the house. We'll let you know as soon as we see them."

They saw a light in the window of the house, Fellows wound down his window so that he could get a better view. "He's at the window again, Dave, looks like he's expecting them."

"As the two men waited, the rain started falling again. It was coming in through the open window and Fellows pulled up the collar of his jacket, and muttered something under his breath. Connor only caught a couple of words, "…bloody rain."

Connor got on the radio as the BMW pulled up at the kerb. "Bravo-One to Delta-Four… we've got him… drive on and turn up one of the side roads."

"Now what's he doing?" said Fellows, as he watched the car reverse into the drive.

The drive was suddenly lit up in the blaze of the security lights. "Well at least we can see what's going on," said Connor, "...who's that getting out?"

"It's Barry Jarvis," said Fellows, peering through the rain-streaked windscreen. "What's he doing here? Hang on a minute. That's King coming out of the house." They watched as Jarvis walked around the car and opened the passenger door. King hurried from the house and got into the car. Jarvis got back behind the wheel and the car pulled out of the drive, heading back in the direction it had come from.

"Now where are they going? Come on Phil let's follow them. Drop me off by my car. I'd better call the DI."

As Fellows pulled out of the side street into the road, he could see the rear lights of the BMW a few hundred yards ahead. "They don't seem to be in too much of a hurry," he said, "...where's your car?"

"Just down here, in that street on the left. Drop me on the corner."

Fellows stopped the car and Connor got out. "OK, Phil, keep with them. I'll call you in a minute." He ran to his car, got in and picked up the radio. "Bravo-One to control... message for DI Timms."

"Timms here, Dave, what's happening?"

"*Godfather's* on the move. *Goodfella* and *Mad Dog* have just picked him up. There's another man in the back of the car. It could be *Jacknife*, but we didn't get a good look. Phil's tailing them."

"OK, Dave. Thanks you'd better keep on them as well. Let me know as soon as you've got some idea where they're going."

"Will do, sir, what about Delta-Four they're here as well?" asked Connor.

"Better take them along for the ride, until you know what's going on," said Timms. Time to call the boss, he thought.

Fellows had followed the car through the town and he was now driving down the A10 towards London. He called in his position. "Delta-Six to control... the targets are moving south on the A10... approaching the motorway junction."

"Bravo-One to Delta-Six... Delta-Four is following you, Phil. And I'm about a mile behind. I'll try and catch up, and get in front of you on the other side of the junction."

"They're turning onto the M25 heading west."

"Ok, Phil... when they're on the motorway you drop back... and I'll pick them up." Connor put his foot down, and after a couple of miles he caught up with Fellows and overtook him.

Grantchester, Cambridgeshire – 01:15 BST

The ringing woke Grace first. She turned over and shook Barton's shoulder. "Phone, Mike," she said as she switched on the light.

He sat up in the bed and picked up his mobile. "Barton here."

"It's, Paul. Something's going on, I thought you should know."

"OK, Paul, let's have it. What's the time?"

"Quarter-past one. I thought you'd better know that King's on the move... "

Timms quickly told Barton what had been happening "...that's all we've got so far, sir. I just wish I knew what they were doing?"

"So do I Paul. I'm coming in. I'll see you in about an hour."

"Do you have to go?" asked Grace rubbing her eyes.

"Yes. I'm sorry but something's not right," he said, as he leaned over and kissed her. "I'll call you later... promise."

"Make sure you do... you're still on probation... Remember."

"I promise. Now go back to sleep... you need your rest."

Grace smiled and closed her eyes as Barton kissed her. It was always going to be like this. She knew he'd never leave the job; she didn't really want him to, but now, she hoped, the rules had changed. "I love you, be careful," she said, as she turned over and switched off the light.

M25, South Mimms, Hertfordshire – 00:30 BST

"Bravo-One to Delta-Six... they're turning off, Phil. Try to keep close... we don't want to lose them on the junction." Connor followed the BMW down the slip road as it left the motorway and negotiated the junction. The car went through the green light and passed the first turning. "They're on the roundabout... they've gone past the first turn off. There's a red light ahead... they're in the centre lane. Get in front of me, Phil." He eased off the accelerator and let Fellows pass him. The BMW pulled away from the lights and carried on past the next exit.

"Delta-Six to Bravo-One... they're going right round... No... they've turned off to the service area." Fellows followed the car into the almost deserted car park and watched, as it parked in front of the main building. He stopped and turned off his engine and lights; in his rear view mirror, he saw Connor's car stop about twenty yards away.

"Bravo-One to Delta-Four... targets are out to the vehicle... we've got them covered... go round and park near the exit." Connor got out of his car and watched as four men ran across to the entrance of the service building. As soon as they were inside, he walked over to Fellows' car, opened the passenger door, and got in.

"So what do you reckon?" asked Fellows.

"I don't know Phil. Go inside and take a look… I'm going to call in."

When Timms answered, Connor told him where they were. "Phil's gone inside. I'll call you again when he comes back."

He didn't have to wait long. Fellows ran back across the car park and got into the car. "Bloody hell it's chucking it down out there, I'm soaked."

"I don't want to know about the weather. What are they doing in there?"

"Sitting at a table," replied Fellows "…eating burgers."

"What, that's all about! They've come all the way out here just to go to Burger King."

"Looks like it."

"Doesn't make sense, Phil, unless… they're on to us, and they're taking the piss."

"So what now?" asked Fellows, "sit and wait?"

"Yeah, I'll call the DI. Did you get a look at the other guy?"

"No he had his back to me. Could have been Herrera, same sort of build, but I'm not sure."

Connor called Timms again. "Keep watching, Dave," said Timms. "At least we know where they are. The boss is on his way in. We'll decide what to do when he gets here."

Fellows reached behind the seat and found a flask. He opened it and poured the last of the coffee. "Bloody great, they're inside feeding their faces, and all we've got is half a cup of coffee."

Connor put his hand into his pocket and took out a hip flask. "Give it here… we might as well fill it up. At least this will hide the taste of your coffee." He poured some of the honey coloured liquid into the cup and took couple of mouthfuls, before handing it to Fellows. "That's better. Here you are, finish it off before it gets cold. Now come on… tell me more about the lovely Dawn."

Connor was talking on the phone to Barton, when Barry Jarvis came out of the building. Jarvis pulled his jacket over his head and made dash for the BMW. "Hang on, sir, something's happening. Barry Jarvis just got into the car."

He watched as Jarvis drove onto the pavement in front of the entrance, as the doors opened and three men came out. Ten seconds later, they were all in the car.

"They're on the move."

"OK, get after them, Dave. Let me know as soon as you know where they're going."

Connor opened the car door. "Follow them Phil and tell Delta-Four to follow you. I'll catch up in a minute."

Connor got into the Vectra and started the engine. He put his foot down, but as he drove towards the exit, the engine spluttered and died. He turned the key in the ignition. The engine started and died again. He turned the key again; nothing. As he tried again, he looked at the dashboard. He'd been meaning to have the fuel gauge fixed for weeks; it had shown half full that morning, but now it was reading empty. "Bravo-One to Delta-Six... I've got car trouble... I've run out of petrol. Let me know where you're going. I'll follow as soon as I've filled up."

He got out, and opened the boot. The spare petrol can was missing; he'd left it in the shed with the lawnmower. "Trouble, mate?" said a voice from some distance away. He looked round to see two teenagers, sitting in a customised Peugeot.

"No petrol. Can give me a push to the pumps?" He pointed to the filling station about a hundred yards away.

Connor saw the Jaguar as he was walking back from the shop. He watched in disbelief, as it drove past the petrol station towards the exit: *No, it can't be. Oh Fuck!*

He ran back to his car and grabbed the radio, "Bravo-One to control... Get Timms or Barton on now!" he shouted. He put the car into gear and put his foot down, turning the wheel sharply to avoid a large van that was filling up at the next pump. Not sharp enough, the side of the car scraped the van's rear bumper. The van driver sounded his horn; Connor ignored it and carried on, following the Jaguar towards the motorway.

Timms' voice came over the radio, "Dave, it's Paul. What's up?"

"They've done a bloody switch. I've just seen *Godfather* and *Goodfella* driving off in a Jag, with two other guys. I'm just coming out of the services ... but they could be going anywhere... I can't see them... I think I've lost them."

"Dave, this is Barton... I think I know where they're going. Get on the M25 westbound... If you see them, just drive past."

Sitting in the back of the Jaguar, Bobby King turned to his son and laughed. "Bloody amateurs... who do they think they're dealing with? I've been one step ahead of Old Bill my whole life. They're not getting me now." He leaned back into the seat and lit a cigar. "OK, boys, let's get this job done. Keep your speed down Errol... we don't want to get picked up by the traffic cops."

Terry King smiled and took a small video camera out of his pocket. "Want to see a movie Dad? Baz filmed it this afternoon. I think you'll like it."

Barton sat in his office, trying to work out what was going on. He had a pretty good idea where King was going. But he couldn't think why. He had a bad feeling about this. Something didn't add up: *What's King playing at?*

He went into the squad room, poured himself another coffee, and sat down on Sally's desk. "Where's Paul?" he asked.

"On the radio to Dave, I think." replied Sally.

"Has he caught up with them yet?"

"I don't think so," she said. "Of course they might not be going that way."

"I know. But there's a good chance he is. We've got the Preston brothers waiting for someone, somewhere on the M4... and now, King's out for a drive in the middle of the night."

"He could just be playing games with us," said Sally, "...I mean if they think we're onto them."

"Maybe," said Barton "...but I can't see King being out at this hour just for fun."

"What about the car switch?"

"Maybe the other guys brought something with them? Cash? Drugs? Something to do with the meet on the M4?"

"Whatever it is it must be big," said Sally, "...if King's getting his hands dirty."

"That's what's worrying me," said Barton.

Paul Timms came out of the control room. "Dave's seen them, sir. He got past them at junction nineteen, turned off and then got back on at twenty. He's caught up again, and he's about a half a mile behind them now."

"Have we got everyone else covered?"

"Yes," replied Sally, "we're ready to pull them in as soon as you give the word."

"Good. Now, it's my guess that this thing with Milosevic has got someone rattled, and they're worried enough for King to be taking charge tonight. We've got to make sure that we pull everybody in at the same time," said Barton, "...we can't afford any more slip ups."

"Everyone's covered," she said, "...we've got over two-hundred officers waiting to move in. The cells are going to be full this morning."

"Check everything again, Sally. Just to make sure. Paul, I want you to get down to Chieveley now and take charge down there. I'll get onto Thames Valley and make sure their guys are ready."

Connor called Barton when the Jaguar turned off the motorway. "Looks like you were right, boss. Is the backup here?"

"Two ARVs... parked in the police compound behind the services, and a couple of transits full of uniforms, waiting about a mile up the A34. Timms is on his way, but you might have to call it Dave. Just wait till they park and let me know as soon as..."

Connor cut him off before he could finish "Shit! They're not slowing down... They've gone past the services." Ahead of him, he could see the Jaguar slowing down, before making a sharp turn to the left. "Now, they're pulling off... they're going into the construction site."

Barton slammed his fist onto the desk, "Bloody hell! What are they doing?"

Connor switched off his lights as he pulled the Vectra off the road and, keeping his revs low, he followed the tail-lights of the Jaguar into the site. He parked next to a site hut and watched the Jaguar as it stopped about two hundred yards further on. He could see the in headlights that it had stopped in front of a large embankment, near a group of parked vehicles. He inched the car forward another hundred yards, until he reached some large concrete blocks, "I can see them, they've stopped, I'll get out and take a look."

"No, Dave, wait. Tell me exactly where you are," said Barton. "Don't move until you've got some backup."

As Connor described his position he saw the Jaguar's interior lights come on as one of the doors opened, "Something's happening. I can't see. I'm going to get out and get a bit closer," he said. "It's OK. I've got plenty of cover. I'll call back on the mobile." He got out of the car and moved carefully between the concrete blocks, and then dashed across the site taking cover from the construction plant until he was standing behind a bulldozer, about sixty feet from the Jaguar.

As he dialled Barton's number, Connor heard the sound of a diesel engine starting. For a moment, the scene in front of him was illuminated and he could see the Jaguar had stopped next to a large pit, about ten feet wide and thirty feet long. He heard a man shout and the lights went out again as a JCB started to move towards the pit. It stopped behind the Jaguar, partially blocking Connor's view of the car. Next moment he heard the sound of a much more powerful diesel engine roaring into life. "What the fuck was that!" he cried, as the ground shook. He dropped to his knees. In his surprise, he had dropped his radio and now he groped around in the darkness, looking for it. As he picked it out of the puddle, he wondered if it was waterproof. He stood up and used his shirt-tail to wipe the mud off the set.

"Are you still there?

"What's going on Dave?"

"I don't know, they seem to be..." he froze as the area ahead of him was suddenly flooded with light and he saw the giant truck, headlamps blazing, moving at speed towards the parked Jaguar. He heard gunfire and looked up, in the direction it was coming from. He could see the muzzle flashes of the top of the embankment, and two shadows with automatic weapons raining bullets down onto the car. The driver of the JCB jumped down from the cab and ran towards Connor, and disappeared behind a site hut. "Christ! Where's that backup?" he shouted. A car horn sounded, and two men leapt out of the Jaguar. There were more gunshots, one of the truck's headlamps went out, and then a man screamed in pain.

A bullet hit the cab of the bulldozer, shattering the glass, and as Connor ducked for cover, another ricocheted off the tracks: *That was bloody close!* – There was a slight burning sensation in his cheek – *Very close.*

Then – crouched low behind the blade of the bulldozer, no longer able to view the scene – he heard more gun shots, and more screams; of terror rather than pain, followed by the gut wrenching sound of the mangled metal and breaking bodies, as one of the truck's huge front tyres crushed the car.

Suddenly, it was all over – the shooting stopped, the engine of the truck died, there were no more screams – and for a moment, there was silence. Then the sound of another engine as powerful trail bike appeared from behind the site hut and sped towards the truck.

Connor raced back to his car and heard Barton's voice on the radio. "What was that? What's happening Dave?"

The shrieking of sirens drowned out Connor's answer. Two cars drove past him lights ablaze and blue lights flashing. Eight officers in body armour leapt out of the cars and took up position; guns aimed in the direction of the truck.

A voice barked through a loud speaker, "Armed Police! Don't move. Drop your weapons."

The shadowy figures on the embankment answered with two long bursts of fire, as Preston jumped onto the pillion of the trail bike. The bike accelerated away, into the darkness, racing up the embankment to join the others. Preston held on to the pillion grip with one hand and emptied the Uzi's magazine; firing wildly in the direction of the blue lights, taking out the radiator and windscreen of one of the cars, before discarding his weapon.

"Christ! It's like a battlefield," Connor shouted, as he watched the two bikes disappear into the distance. Then, regaining his composure, he said calmly, "I think that you'd better get over here, boss," and walked slowly towards the police cars."

Chapter 12

Monday 5th May 2003

Chieveley, Berkshire – 04:30 BST

The dawn was breaking when Barton arrived at the site, the weak rays of the early morning sun, backlighting the dark rain-clouds that were gathering ominously in the distance. A uniformed PC flagged down Barton's car as he turned into the site entrance. Barton wound down the window and handed the officer his warrant card. "OK, sir, go straight on about for a hundred yards… turn left after that big mound. Everyone's parked just behind it."

Barton drove through the site until he saw a white mini bus, a police van, and several cars. He got out of the car and surveyed at the scene. Two ambulances were parked just ahead with their rear doors open and beyond them; he could see two fire trucks. Powerful halogen lamps set on poles, were flooding the area in front of him with light. As he walked towards the lights, another ambulance passed him, blue lights flashing.

A group of uniformed policemen were standing next to the van, smoking and drinking from paper cups. He approached them and spoke to a Sergeant. "DCI Barton, NCS. Do you know where I can find DI Timms?"

"He's over there somewhere with our Inspector sir. Hang on a minute… I'll get one of the lads to find them." He said something to a young constable who immediately headed off in the direction of the fire trucks.

"Do you want some tea or coffee sir?"

Barton looked in the back of the van and saw several vacuum flasks and a stack of paper cups. "Coffee please, Sergeant."

A few minutes later, the constable returned followed by Timms and another uniformed officer. "Hi Paul," said Barton. "What the hell's been going on?"

"It's a bloody mess, sir. This is Inspector Jeff Hunter, Thames Valley … he got here just after the shooting stopped."

Hunter stepped forward and shook Barton's hand. "Come on we'll show you," he said. "…watch your step though, the ground's very uneven."

As they walked towards the fire trucks, they passed Dave Connor's car. "Where's Dave?" asked Barton.

"He's in the ambulance that just left."

"What…? Is he hurt?"

"Nothing too serious… he got clipped by a bullet… only a scratch, though. They're taking him to casualty at Reading."

"One of our blokes is with him," said Hunter, "…caught a bullet in the arm. Luckily it's only a flesh wound… could have been a lot worse. The blokes who got away were using Uzis." He pointed to the police car that they were walking past; the windscreen was shattered, and there were bullet holes in the bonnet and doors. "We'll send you the repair bill, for that," he said,

Barton could here the sound of cutting equipment, but at first all he could see, behind the cordon tape that encircled a large area of the site, was a huge yellow tractor, blocking their view. Then as they walked round to the front of the JCB, the full horror of the scene confronted him.

Timms tried to explain what had happened. "From what Dave has told us, they used the JCB to block them in… then… see that big truck over there," he pointed to a giant yellow dump truck, with a shattered windscreen; it looked the size of a small house. "That was on top of the Jag when I got here. It just drove straight at them."

Hunter pointed towards a large pit just beyond the car. "Looks like they were going to push the Jag into that big hole over there… With the embankment in front and the JCB behind… they had nowhere to go."

"From the look of that truck's windscreen someone got a few rounds off before it hit them." said Barton.

"Yes," said Paul, "Terry King had a gun in his hand when we found him, and there was another one on the ground near the Jag. We think that the guy driving the truck was wounded… there's some blood on the seat… so we'll be able to get a DNA sample. That'll help."

Barton looked at what was left of the Jaguar. The fire crew had already cut away part of the roof, and were working on the doors. One of the paramedics had managed to get into the back of the car, and was trying to treat one of the occupants.

"The guys in the front didn't have a chance, sir," said Timms. "The truck rode right up over the front half of the roof and the bonnet. If he'd taken a straighter line, King would probably be dead as well."

"Where is he now, Paul?"

"He's still trapped in the back of the car, sir. It looks like he was trying to get out when the truck hit them. The truck shoved the car over… smashed the door shut on him. Trapped one of his legs and his arm's caught up under the front seat. The paramedics are trying to keep him alive until they can get him out."

"And Terry?"

"On his way to hospital, he must have got out of the car before the truck hit it… but he's in a bad way."

"One of my chaps found him over there," said Hunter pointing to some marker flags a few feet from the car, "...he was unconscious. He'd been hit a few times... including one to the head."

"What about the other two?"

"Dead before the paramedics got here. They were really smashed up... didn't stand a chance," said Timms.

"And there was nobody else here?"

"Not apart from the four who got away. They had two big trail bikes and rode off through the site. We haven't found them yet."

"No other vehicles... a van or a truck maybe?"

"No," said Hunter, "...we sealed off the service area and we've checked every vehicle that's parked in there. We're still taking statements... but so far nothing."

"Thanks, Inspector. I don't think there's much use us hanging round here in the rain. Let's go and sit in the car."

Hunter opened the back doors of a mini bus. "There's more room in here," he said. Barton and Timms got in, while Hunter went to talk to the officers who were standing by the van. He returned carrying three paper cups.

"We can't do much until it gets lighter," said Hunter. "The SOCOs are on their way... they won't want the area disturbing any more than necessary."

"OK," said Barton. "We'll leave you to it, for the moment. Where will they take King when they get him out?"

"Reading. The other man should be there already."

"Thanks, we'll see you later. Come on, Paul, let's go, and see how Dave is. We'll take your car." Barton called Sally from the car. "How did it go?"

"We're still rounding up all the illegals... there's still a lot of houses and flats we haven't got round to yet. We got most of the targets... but Herrera's disappeared... and Warren Jarvis has slipped through as well.

"We've got a couple of mangled bodies here... one of them's still in what's left of the front passenger seat, it might be Herrera. King's still here, Terry's on his way to hospital. The Prestons got away... that's assuming it was them."

"So what do you want us to do now?" asked Sally.

"Keep watching Preston's flat... and Jarvis' place in case they go there... I want teams searching houses and offices, as soon as possible... you've got the list... nobody comes or goes until we've finished. Now, what about Nichols?"

"Still missing... but, they're bringing his wife in now."

"Good. And where's Deborah King?"

"I'll have to check which station she's been taken to, wait a minute."

136

"No, don't bother now. They're going to take Bobby King to the Royal Berkshire in Reading... Terry's already there. They're both in a bad way, so get someone to take her over there. We can interview her later."

Reading, Royal Berkshire Hospital – 05:30 BST

The nurse pulled back the curtain and Barton saw that Connor was sitting on the edge of the bed, wearing a hospital gown "Are you OK, Dave," he asked. "Paul's parking the car... he should be along in a minute, then we'll see about getting you home.

"I'm fine boss," he said, "...it's only a scratch," said Connor pointing to the dressing on his left cheek. "The doc says I can go, but I can't get dressed yet... they've got my kit."

An orderly came in carrying a bundle of clothes. "I've dried these out for you Mr Connor," he said.

"Thanks mate. I'll be with you in a minute, boss."

"You look like a tramp, Dave," said Timms, as Connor emerged from the cubicle; his suit was covered in dried mud, and the trousers were torn at the knee. "Trust you to go falling over."

"Thanks for your concern Paul. I'll be sure to bring you flowers next time you get shot at," laughed Connor. "And for your information I didn't fall over. Those firearms guys don't mess around. One minute I'm just walking over to the cars. Next, I've got three shooters pointing at me and someone shouting at me to lie down. So, just make sure you sign the expenses claim when I put in for a new suit."

"How's the other fellow?" asked Barton.

"He's in the cubicle over there. One of his mates is with him... I think they're keeping him in for a bit."

Barton walked over to the cubicle and pulled the curtain aside. "Hi, I'm DCI Barton," he said. "How are you, PC...?"

"Evans, sir, I'll be fine. The bullet got me in the shoulder and cracked the bone. They say I'll be off for a while, but I'll be OK... lucky really... a few inches higher and it could have been my head."

"Well, I'm glad you're OK. I just wanted to say thanks for your help tonight and good luck."

"Thanks, sir. And can you tell your DS that the lads said to tell him they're sorry for rolling him in the mud?"

As they drove back to Chieveley, they discussed their next steps. Timms would stay at the scene with Hunter and talk to the SOCOs; Barton and Connor were going back to the hospital at Reading.

"You sure you're up to it Dave?" asked Barton. "You can get off home if you want to."

"No sir, I'll be fine sir. I need a lift anyway. My car's going to need a garage."

An ambulance passed them and sped away towards the site entrance. Jeff Hunter had seen them drive in and was waiting to greet them. He pointed in the direction of the ambulance. "They're taking King to hospital now. One of the paramedics told me that they don't think he'll last long... he's lost a lot of blood, they had to take his leg off."

"I'm going back to the hospital now, with Sergeant Connor," said Barton. "...I want to be there if he comes round. Paul's going to stay here and see what the SOCOs can make of this. Thanks for your help... sorry if we've messed up your weekend."

"That's alright sir," said Hunter, smiling. "I'm rather enjoying it... I don't normally see this much action. Come on, Paul... I'll take you to meet the head SOCO."

Timms looked towards Barton's car and whispered to Connor. "Rather you than me, Dave... I wouldn't want to ride in that heap. You sure you don't want me to organise you a lift home in a nice comfy patrol car."

"See you later Paul. I've survived a gun battle tonight," said Connor, "...the boss's car can't be any worse."

"What was that?" said Barton as he got into the car and leaned across to open the passenger door.

"Nothing sir," said Connor, winking at Timms.

Barton looked at Connor and smiled. "Have you looked in a mirror since they patched you up Dave?

"No... Why?"

Chapter 13

Monday 5th May

Reading, Royal Berkshire Hospital – 07:15 BST

Barton introduced himself and Connor to the girl at the A&E department reception desk and asked her about the casualties. She gave their warrant cards a cursory glance and checked the admission details on her computer, then asked them to wait while she called a nurse.

While Barton talked to the receptionist, Connor looked around the room. It was pretty dreary, with a tiled floor, stark white walls with just a few posters for relief, harsh lighting and rows of uncomfortable looking grey plastic chairs, not really the sort of place that you'd want stay for long. Like in most hospitals, the room was too warm, and he wondered how much money the NHS could save by turning down the thermostats a couple of degrees. There were about a twenty people waiting, mostly in pairs, which meant that there probably a dozen waiting for treatment. They all seemed to be sitting as far away from anybody else as possible; each marking out their territory by placing coats and bags on the adjacent seats.

A man, with a bloodstained bandage on his hand, pointed to the sign above the reception desk – a message in red lights rolled across the screen, telling patients that the waiting time was approximately ninety minutes – and interrupted the receptionist, who was talking to a nurse. "Is that right?" he asked.

"I'm afraid so, sir, a doctor will see you as soon as possible," said the girl politely.

"I saw the nurse an hour ago, that's what he told me. What about him?" the man shouted angrily. He pointed to a man in a wheelchair; being wheeled through the swing doors to the treatment area. "He got here after me. Why is he getting seen?"

"I'm sorry sir... you'll be seen as soon as possible. Now, please wait over there," she said; not quite as politely this time.

"Bloody NHS!" he said loudly to Barton, "I wouldn't bother mate... you'll probably be dead by the time they get off their arses."

"Busy night?" asked Connor, smiling at the girl

"Not really, we're just short staffed as usual," she said, "...trouble is, the people waiting in here... they don't realise that we've got casualties coming in by ambulance at the back. They think they're the only ones here. One minute that sign's telling them they've got to wait twenty minutes... then we get some serious casualties come in... like your two, and everybody's rushed off their feet."

"I suppose you've been on all night. When do you get off?" asked Connor, smiling again.

"In about an hour, and then I'm home to my bed," she said wearily.

"Don't even think about it, Dave," whispered Barton.

A young nurse arrived and asked them to follow her to the office. As they walked through the swing doors, the man with the bandaged hand got up and shouted at the receptionist, "Hey, that's not fair they've only been here two minutes."

The nurse showed them into a small office and told them that Terry King was on his way to the operating theatre. "What about Robert King?"

"He's in the emergency room now... the doctors are trying to stabilise him. I'll get one of them to come and see you as soon as they can."

"Can I use a phone please?"

"Use the one in here, you need to dial zero for a line."

Barton picked up the phone. "Hi, Sally. It's Mike... we're at the hospital... is Debbie King on her way?"

"Yes, and according to Brenda Cooper she's being a real bitch. They left about forty minutes ago. She should be there soon."

"Call them up... tell them to bring her to the A&E department. We'll meet her here."

He put the phone down and turned to Connor. "Dave, you go and wait in reception. See if they've got a room you can put her in when she gets here. I'll wait here for the doctor... and Dave ..."

"Yes, boss."

"Try to keep your hands off that receptionist."

Edward Simms was tired and irritable. He'd been on shift for over twelve hours and he wanted to get home and get some sleep. The last thing he needed was policemen trampling all over his department, and there were two of them standing outside his emergency room; getting in everyone's way: *Why do they have to wait there?*

After all the man they'd come in with wasn't going anywhere. It had been the same with the other two who he guessed were now probably camped outside the theatre suite. And now there were two detectives waiting in his office. He put some coins in the vending machine, stooped and picked up a can from the tray at the bottom: *I really don't need all this*

He opened the door to his office and walked in. At least there was only one of them here now, which meant that there was an empty chair. He sat down; said nothing as he opened the can of Coke and then looked at Barton. "I take it you're the policeman who wants to talk to me?" he said brusquely.

"Yes sir. Detective Chief Inspector Mike Barton."

"I'm Edward Simms… A&E Consultant. I'm in charge of this mad house… what can I do for you?"

"You've had two men brought in this morning. A Mr Robert King and his son Terrence King… I was hoping that you could tell me how they are."

"Well, I've just left Robert King. We've done all that we can for him… he's stable at the moment… we're just waiting to send him up to theatre. He's in a very critical condition. He's lost his right leg… his right arm was crushed and there may be internal injuries. To be honest… I'm amazed the paramedics got him here alive. It took them a long time to get him out of the car… he lost a lot of blood."

"What about the other one?"

"He's in theatre at the moment. Most of the bullet wounds were superficial… we patched them up down here. But he's got a bullet in his chest and another in his head… nasty… could be some brain damage."

Brain… what brain? Barton chuckled, but the look on Simms's face told him that he wasn't in any mood for frivolity this morning. "Sorry, sir… when will I be able to talk to them?"

"Your guess is as good as mine, Inspector. We'll know more once they're out of theatre and in intensive care… if I were you I'd prepare myself for a long wait."

"Thank you sir, we're used to that."

"Well if there's nothing else, I'll say goodbye," said Simms opening the door.

"There is one more thing sir. Robert King's daughter is on her way. Could you tell her about them?"

"OK, I'll see her when she arrives. What's her name?"

"Deborah… she's under arrest so there will have to be an officer present when you talk to her."

"Is that really necessary? This is going to be very distressing for her… her father and her brother… you know… it's not good… for either of them."

"I'm sorry sir, but we can't take any chances."

"OK, if you must. Ask the receptionist to take her to the relatives' room when she gets here. I'll talk to her in there. Now, if you'll excuse me, I must get back. I've got other patients."

"Thank you for your time, sir... I'll try and make sure that we're not too intrusive."

"Too late for that Inspector," said Simms with an air of resignation.

Barton was standing outside in the car park, smoking a cigarette and talking on his mobile, when the car drew up. He recognised the driver and went over to the car. As Brenda Cooper got out of the driver's seat, he saw that a WPC was sitting in the back with another woman. "Hello, sir," said Brenda. "I've got Debbie King in the car. Where do you want her?"

"Morning Brenda, follow me. The doctor's got to talk to her. Dave Connor's waiting inside." Brenda opened the rear door of the car and the WPC got out, followed closely by the other woman, who was handcuffed to her. Barton had only seen Debbie King in photographs, and close up she looked just as he had expected. She was a very attractive woman in her mid thirties; tall and slim, dressed in smart designer clothes and, even at this time of the morning, well groomed without a hair out of place. In spite of her situation, she looked calm and self-assured, almost arrogant. Everything about her said spoilt rich bitch.

"Hello, you must be Deborah King, I'm DCI Barton," he spoke quietly, with genuine consideration. After all, it didn't matter who she was, her father and brother were both seriously ill, and she deserved some compassion, "...please come this way. I'll take you see the doctor who's been treating your father. I'm sorry..."

She didn't give him chance to finish. In an instant, her demeanour changed. Suddenly the gangster's daughter revealed herself as she spat out a reply. "I'll give you sorry you bastard... you fucking bastard...! As if you bloody care... why don't you fucking leave us alone? My Dad's not done anything." She raised her hands and lunged at him, almost pulling the policewoman off her feet. "I'd fucking do you if I wasn't chained to this cow... I'll fucking have you... you piece of shit..."

Her eyes were wet with tears and Barton stepped back and said nothing; letting the torrent of abuse continue until she started to gasp for breath. "I can't breathe... asthma... where's my inhaler..." The WPC took an inhaler from her pocket and gave it to Debbie. She put it to her mouth and took several deep breaths.

As she slowly regained her composure, Barton spoke to her again, "I'm sorry, Miss King... I appreciate that this must be very upsetting for you. But you're not going to do your father any good... not if you carry on behaving like this. Now if you can behave with a little more decorum, I'll take you to see the doctor. Otherwise, I think it would be better if you waited in the car."

She nodded and they walked towards the building, Barton leading the way, Debbie King a few paces behind, with the policewomen on either side, although, she was much taller than her escorts and had difficulty keeping in step. When they came to a kerb, she tripped and Brenda put out a hand to steady her. "Don't touch me you bitch!" she spat, pushing Brenda away. "I don't need your fucking help bitch… keep your fucking hands off me."

When they got to the building, Connor was waiting by the door and held it open for them.

"Thanks Dave. Can you take Miss King and the WPC to the relatives' room? I'll tell the receptionist that she's here."

"Cow! So much for an expensive private education… I bet she didn't learn to swear like that at Roedean…" said Brenda Cooper, when they were out of earshot, "…you saw sir… she pushed me. I could do her for assault."

"Watch it Brenda," he said, "…how would you feel right now… if you were her?"

"You should have heard her in the car sir," said Brenda, "…like butter wouldn't melt in her mouth… playing the concerned daughter… pretending not to have the slightest idea what was going on. Christ…! The way she was talking about King… you'd think he was a saint."

"That's enough Brenda. Now get back to her… and tell Sergeant Connor to come back here. You stay with her… and take those handcuffs off her."

"Sir? You saw what she's like… she tried to attack you. Don't you think we should leave the cuffs on?"

"I don't think that she'll be in any mood for fighting… once she hears what the doctor's got to say. Don't worry… I'll be right here with Sergeant Connor."

"OK, sir, if you say so."

"And I want you to make a note of everything she says."

Brenda disappeared into the room, and a minute later Connor joined Barton at the reception desk. "Would you let Mr Simms know that Miss King is here please? He's expecting her," said Barton.

The girl picked up a phone and asked someone to give Mr Simms a message. When she had finished, Barton spoke to her again. "Mr Simms said that they'd both be taken to intensive care. Can you tell me how to get there, please?" he asked.

The girl gave him a small plan of the hospital and pointed to some doors. "Through those doors, take the lift to the fourth floor and follow the signs."

"Thanks. Could you tell them that we'll be coming up?"

Terry King was lying motionless on a bed in the corner of the ward; a sheet covered his body from the waist down; apart from the bandages, his torso and arms were bare; there was no colour at all in his face. A tube in his mouth led to a machine; wires taped to his head and chest were connected to monitors, the coloured tracers moving slowly, hypnotically, across the screens. A bag hung from the side of his bed, half filled with the fluid that was draining into it from a narrow tube in his side. More tubes ran from the bags hanging above the bed to the IV needles in his arms. A uniformed constable was sitting beside the bed, reading a paper. He looked up as Barton approached. "Good morning Constable, I'm DCI Barton. Can you wait outside please?"

The policeman got up and walked towards the doors. Barton raised a hand and waved to Connor who was looking through the glass panel in the door. He opened the door and Debbie King, handcuffed to the WPC again, came into the ward. When she saw her brother, Debbie raised her free hand to her mouth to stifle a scream. She stumbled towards a chair and held the back for support. Barton could tell that this was no act. The composure, the arrogance, the bravado were all gone; this was a frightened woman. At that moment she seemed almost as helpless as the man lying on the bed. Barton whispered something to the WPC and made his exit.

Outside in the corridor Barton spoke to the constable. "What's your name, son?" he asked.

"PC Nick Kirwan, sir."

"Are you here on your own, Kirwan?"

"No sir, my mate's gone to the canteen," replied the young PC, "…he should be back in a minute."

"Do you know who came in with the other man?"

"No… there are two of them… but I don't know them. I think they're from Newbury, I'm based here at Reading."

"Do you know where they are now?"

"They were outside the operating theatre when we came down here."

"Thanks," said Barton, "Now I don't think that it needs four of you, so a couple of you can get off… How did you get here?"

"In the ambulance, sir," replied Kirwan, "…but it's OK, my mate will give me a lift back to the station at the end of the shift."

Another PC walked down the corridor carrying a plastic cup. "This is my mate coming now, sir," said Kirwan pointing towards his colleague.

"Danny, this is DCI Barton… Mr Barton, this is Danny Carr."

"OK, Kirwan you stay here," said Barton, "…keep an eye on them from the door. Don't go in unless the WPC needs you."

He looked at the other constable. "PC Carr, could you show DS Connor where the operating theatres are?" he asked.

"Yes sir. I think I can find the way back."

Connor, who was leaning against the wall, stepped forward "Morning, Danny, I'm Dave Connor… come on show me the way."

"Dave, when you get up there you can send the other two fellows home," said Barton, "…PC Carr can wait up there with you…come back when they bring King down."

As the two men walked down the corridor, Barton called to Connor. "We'll meet you in the canteen, when you're done."

He turned to Kirwan, "What time are you due off?" he asked.

"Eight, sir."

"It's past that now… I'll call the station and make sure that they send someone to relieve you. Get someone to call us if they bring King down before we get back."

He looked at Brenda Cooper, "Come on, Brenda, let's get something to eat," he said.

As they walked to the hospital canteen Barton took out his mobile and started to dial the number, he'd been given for Reading Divisional HQ. "You're not supposed to use that in here, sir," said Brenda reproachfully.

"I won't tell, if you don't," he said with a smile.

"Penny for them, sir," said Brenda, noticing that Barton wasn't eating.

He was staring at the mess on his plate, Full English Breakfast, it said on the menu over the counter – a rubbery egg, two thin, greasy slices of bacon, a tiny sausage, a pile of beans and a cold slice of toast. – thinking that if ever there were a contest to find the worst institutional catering, this place would win by a mile. "Oh! Nothing Brenda… just wondering if this tastes as bad as it looks."

Barton got up and went to the counter for another cup of tea. When he got back to the table Connor was sitting there. "That looks good," he said.

"Have it if you want Dave. I don't feel like eating."

"Thanks," said Connor, sliding the tray across the table.

"Have you finished Brenda… don't you want those beans… Oh! And get me a coffee."

"Please would be, nice," said Brenda as got up.

Connor didn't notice her scowling at him, as he scraped the beans from her plate; adding them to the pile on his.

"So what's the news on King?" asked Barton.

"He's still in there sir. I talked to one of the theatre nurses… she reckoned it could be a while yet."

Barton's mobile rang. Before he could answer it he heard a voice behind him, "You can't use that in here. Switch it off." He turned around and saw two nurses standing behind him. They stood and watched him while he switched the phone off and put it back into his pocket.

"What's the matter with these people," said one, as they walked towards the counter, raising her voice as she spoke, "…can't they read the bloody signs?"

Barton finished his tea and stood up. "Dave, when you've finished go back to the ICU with Brenda," he said, "I've got a couple of calls to make. I'll see you there soon."

Chieveley, Berkshire – 08:00 BST

Paul Timms had been talking to Jeff Hunter, when the woman in a white coverall ran towards them. "Inspector Hunter… I think you'd better come and see this," she said.

She led them, through the crime scene, to the wreckage of the car. The boot was open and a man was taking photographs. He looked up and called them over. "We've just opened the boot," he said. "…I thought we'd better have a look inside before we put the car on the lorry."

"What have you got?" asked Timms, "Drugs?"

"A body sir… a man… about thirty five I'd say."

Timms leaned forwards, over the boot, to get a better look. "Anyone you know?" asked Hunter.

"I'm not sure, it's hard to tell," replied Timms, "…his face… looks like he's gone ten rounds with the Terminator."

The woman looked at Timms, "I've called an ambulance sir," she said.

"I think he's beyond that," said Hunter. "You'd better call your boss."

Reading, Royal Berkshire Hospital – 08:45 BST

Barton walked across the car park and lit a cigarette. The screen on his phone showed the number of the call that he'd just missed.

He called Timms, "Hi, Paul. Sorry I missed your call… hospital rules… they won't let you use mobiles inside. Anything from the SOCOs yet."

Paul told him about the body in the boot. "The SOCOs have taken his prints to get an ID... look, sir, I can't be certain... his face is a bloody mess... but I think we've found Herrera."

"When will you know for sure?" asked Barton.

"They're sending his prints down to Newbury, shouldn't take them too long to check."

"OK, call me as soon as you've got an ID... Anything else?"

"Not a lot yet," said Timms, "...the SOCOs are taking the car to the police garage now... they've got loads of prints to check. We don't know where the bikes went yet... there are some good tyre tracks through the site... leading to a B road about two miles from here. But they could have gone anywhere from there."

"Thanks, Paul, you'd better stay there till the SOCOs have finished. I'm going to call Sally and fill her in."

When Barton got back to the Intensive Care Unit, he found Dave Connor standing in the corridor talking to Kirwan.

"Hello, Kirwan, still here?" said Barton.

"Yeah, I've got to wait till ten for my relief. Never mind," the young PC said cheerfully, "...I'm on overtime now."

"Do you know where the mortuary is?"

"Sorry, sir, I've only been stationed here a week... first time I've been to this place. Danny ought to know."

"Is he still upstairs?"

"He should be down here soon," said Connor, "...one of the nurses just told us that King's on his way from the operating theatre."

"Good. Where's Brenda?"

"In that office over there with one of the nurses," said Connor, pointing to a door, "...she's gone to look through Terry's stuff."

"Wait here."

Barton walked into the office; Brenda was arguing with a nurse and they didn't notice him. "...and you're obstructing a police investigation. Now will you show me or do I have to fetch my boss?" Brenda said angrily.

"He's already here," said Barton, "...now what's going on?"

"She won't let me look at the stuff that Terry King had on him when he came in." said Brenda, pointing to a large plastic bag full of clothes.

The nurse looked at Barton "I'm sorry, sir, "she said officiously, "...but these are Mr King's personal belongings... and I've already explained that I can only release them to him... or to his next of kin. That's the hospital policy."

147

"OK Brenda," said Barton, "...I'll deal with this. Go and wait with DS Connor."

"Thank you," said the nurse, "...now if that's all."

"No I'm afraid it's not," he said, "...now look here nurse," he paused and looked at her badge. "...Sorry... Charge Nurse Chambers... Can I call you Jane? Three men were murdered this morning, and one of the only people who might be able to tell us why, is lying next door fighting for his life. So, Jane, I'm sure that you understand... we need anything that might help us... including the clothes that Mr King was wearing when he came in, and everything that was in his pockets."

"I understand Chief Inspector," she said, "...but I don't have the authority. I need Mr King's consent... or, you'll need a search warrant."

"I don't have time for that. For God's sake whose side are you on?"

"It's not about taking sides. My only concern is for my patients. We have rules... I can't just ignore them. I'm sorry."

Barton shrugged his shoulders. This was getting him nowhere. He started towards the door and then stopped. "Is there a private room that I could use for a while?" he asked.

"You can use this office." She picked up the bag of clothes and put it into a locker. "I'll just lock this away first," she said self-righteously. As Barton left and went back to his colleagues, Jane Chambers smiled, congratulating herself on her little victory, and put the locker key into her pocket.

"How did you get on, boss?" asked Connor.

"Miss Goody-Two-Shoes in there isn't going to give in," replied Barton. "Never mind, there's another way. Go and get Debbie King... and bring her to the office." As he spoke the lift doors opened. A nurse got out first, and then two porters pushed a bed into the corridor, followed by PC Carr. They watched as the unconscious Bobby King was wheeled past them and into the ward. Barton put his hand on Brenda's arm as she started to follow. "No... better wait a minute," he said, "...let her see the old man first."

They watched through the window, as the porters moved the bed into the space next to Terry King. Debbie stood up and took her father's hand. "Oh! Isn't that nice... a family reunion," said Brenda sarcastically.

Two nurses walked towards them. "Ah! Charge Nurse Chambers," said Barton, "...just who I wanted see. Could you do me a favour?"

"Not now Inspector. Can't you see we're busy?"

"I just want you to ask Miss King to leave the room for a while," he said, "...tell her she's in the way or something."

"Look who's talking... pity I can't ask you lot to leave," said the nurse.

Barton took Connor to one side. "Dave, there's another body on the way," he said, "...it might be Herrera... He was in the boot of the Jag."

"Christ...! So that's why King was out there."

"We don't know it's him yet... Paul's only seen him in photographs," said Barton, "...but you've seen him at close quarters a few times... that's why I want you to get down to the mortuary. Get PC Carr to take you."

"Then what?"

"If you can identify him let me know straight away. It'll give us another card to play with Miss King."

Barton was waiting in the office when the three women came in. He spoke to the WPC first. "You can take those cuffs off her now. Go and get yourself a cup of tea... we'll look after her."

"Thanks, sir. I'm parched. The air conditioning in these places doesn't half make you thirsty."

"Sit down please, Miss King. We need to talk."

"I've got nothing to say to you, copper," she said defiantly; but without the vitriol of their previous encounter.

"That's alright, I don't want to ask you any questions... I just want you to listen?" he said not trying to sound too threatening.

"Have you got a fag?"

"You can't smoke in here," snapped Brenda.

"It's alright, Brenda... I'm sure Charge Nurse Chambers won't mind... in the circumstances," he winked at Debbie and took a pack of cigarettes from his pocket. He offered the packet to her and she took a cigarette. He would have liked one himself, but thought that might be pushing his luck too far. They would probably be there for hours and he didn't want to antagonise Jane Chambers any more than necessary.

"OK, so what have you got to tell me?" she asked, leaning her head back and blowing a cloud of grey smoke into the air.

"I don't know how much you've been told," he said, "...but this wasn't an accident. Someone tried to kill your father and brother. Three other men are dead... and I need to find out who's responsible... and why they wanted to kill your father. I'm sure that you want to know as well. But I need your help. There's no point us arguing about this... I'm sure that we both want the same thing."

"So what do you expect me to tell you? I don't know anything," she said, shrugging her shoulders, "Why would anyone want to kill my dad?"

"I was hoping that you might be able to tell me," he said. "We think he was set up."

149

"Well I don't know. For all I know it was you lot."

"So you've no idea what he was doing at a motorway construction site in the middle of the night?"

"No. Now can I go back and see my dad now?"

"The nurse will come and tell you when they've got him settled. But first I want you to do something."

"What do you want? Why should I help you?"

"I need you to give your permission for the hospital to hand over their clothes and other belongings for examination."

"What if I say no?"

"Then I'll get a search warrant. It'll take a bit longer but we'll still get what we want. In the meantime, though… whoever did this is getting away. All you've got to do is tell the charge nurse to give the stuff to us."

There was a knock at the door; Brenda opened it and a nurse came in. "You can come back to the ward and see your father now Miss King," she said.

"Don't forget," said Barton as she left the room.

Barton and Brenda were looking through the contents of the plastic bags when Connor came into the office. "Well is it Herrera?" asked Barton.

"Don't know… I haven't seen him yet."

"Then what are you doing here?"

"He's not dead," said Connor.

"What do mean, he's not dead!"

"Well, we waited at the mortuary, but they didn't bring him in. So I phoned the ambulance control to see what the delay was. They said that they were taking him to A&E. Carr's down there now. I thought I'd better come and tell you."

"Right, come with me. Let's go see what's going on."

He looked at the two piles of clothes on the desk. "Better get that stuff back in the bags, Brenda," said Barton, "…and see if you can get someone from forensics to come and pick it up."

Outside in the corridor, Kirwan was talking to three other PCs. Barton spoke to him. "Is this your relief, Kirwan?"

"Yes, sir, is it OK if I get off now?"

Barton looked through the glass panel in the door. Debbie King appeared to be talking to her father, but as far as Barton could make out, he wasn't responding. "Have either of them come round yet?" he asked

"No, sir, they're both still out," said Kirwan.

"OK, one of you can stay here. The rest of you come with us."

Carr was in the A&E reception talking to a couple of paramedics. He broke off when he saw Barton and walked towards him. "They're the ones who brought your man in sir. I thought you might want to talk to them," he said.

"Thanks Carr, you and Kirwan can get off now."

Barton approached the two paramedics. "DCI Barton," he said, "I understand that you brought in the man in the boot."

"That's right, sir," said one of the men, "we thought he was dead at first... but my mate found a weak pulse after we got him into the ambulance."

"I managed to resuscitate him," said the other man. "He's in a bad way, but he was still alive when we got him here."

"Well done. Did he say anything to you?

"No, he's been unconscious the whole time."

"Where is he now?"

"Through there with the doctor," he said, pointing to the emergency room.

Barton heard a bleeping sound and one of the men looked at his pager. "Got to go, sir, we've got another shout." The paramedics left and Barton went to talk to the receptionist.

Edward Simms came into the office and Connor started to get up from his chair. "No, that's alright. I'm dead on my feet, if I sit down I might not get up again," said the consultant.

"Thought you'd have gone by now," said Barton.

"I was just leaving, when they brought your man in," said Simms, "...I do hope there aren't going go be any more, Inspector."

"Me too, now what can you tell me about this one?"

"Well, he's very lucky. The ambulance crew saved his life. They got him here just in time, but he should recover... eventually. From some of his injuries, I'd say he'd been tortured."

"What makes you say that?"

Simms described the extent of the man's injuries. "...but this wasn't just a violent attack, you understand. The burns are particularly nasty and were inflicted slowly and methodically, probably over a period of hours..."

"Any idea who he is?" asked Connor.

"No, he didn't have anything on him. He was naked, except for a T-shirt."

"Can we see him?"

"I'll take you through," said the consultant. "You won't be able to talk to him for a while. He's heavily sedated, and I need to get the orthopaedic surgeon to take a look him."

Simms led the way to a cubicle and pulled the curtain aside. The man was sleeping; breathing oxygen through a tube in his nostril. At first Connor wasn't sure; the nurses had cleaned him up a bit, wiped away most of the blood, but the man's face was badly bruised and swollen. Then, Connor nodded to Barton and closed the curtain. "Thank you, doctor, that'll be all for now," said Barton, "I'll send a PC in to sit with him."

They went back into reception where Barton spoke briefly to the Constable; then made their way back to the ICU. "Definitely Herrera," said Connor, as they got into the lift.

"Keep it quiet, Dave," said Barton. "I think it might be a good idea to let people think he's dead. The fewer people who know he's still alive, the better."

"Glad you're back, sir. I was coming to find you. Bobby King's just woken up," said Brenda as she walked towards them. Barton opened the door and looked into the room. He could see some nurses and a doctor standing by King's bed; there was no sign of Debbie or the WPC.

"Where's Debbie?" he asked.

"They sent her out a minute ago. She's in the office."

"Stay here you two," he said, as he walked into the ward.

Charge Nurse Chambers stopped him before he got any further. "You can't come in Inspector. Mr King's only just come round and the doctor's doing some tests. You can wait in the office with Miss King."

Barton went into the office, where he found Debbie King talking to a doctor. The WPC was standing a few feet from them. "What's going on?" he whispered.

"I'm not sure, sir. King woke up, but I think something's wrong," she said quietly. "The nurse called the doctor and they sent us out."

"Has King said anything?"

"No, sir he was trying to talk, but nothing came out."

Debbie put her head in her hands as the doctor finished speaking. Barton just caught his last few words. "...I'm really sorry, Miss King. We'll keep him as comfortable as we can. But I don't think there's anything else we can do. It's too late."

She looked up at him and nodded. "Thanks, can I see him now?"

"I'll send a nurse to get you when we're ready."

Barton whispered to the WPC, "Keep an eye on her." Then he followed the doctor out of the office.

"How's King?" he asked.

"He's dying Chief Inspector and there's nothing we can do about it."

"How long has he got?"

"It's hard to say... not long... a day, or... maybe just a few hours. There's always a risk in this sort of case. If blood clots get into the brain... or the lungs, the body just can't get enough oxygen. It's just a matter of time now."

"Can I talk to him?"

"Well he's very weak, he won't be able to say much. But I suppose if you must. I'll get one of the nurses to let you know if he wakes up."

Connor waited outside with the uniformed officers, as a nurse escorted Barton and Brenda back to the ward. Debbie was sitting at King's bedside holding his hand. King opened his eyes and smiled weakly as his daughter squeezed his hand. "How do you feel, Dad?" she asked.

"I've had better days love," he croaked, gasping for breath. "...Who's this?"

"I'm Detective Chief Inspector Barton, Mr King. I've got a few questions to ask you."

"I know all about you Barton... got what you want now?" King said slowly, fighting for his breath and slurring his words. Barton found it hard to believe that this pathetic creature was the same man; Bobby King the hard man was gone; this man wasn't going to hurt anyone ever again. "I like to know... who's poking around in my business... so I know all about you... know what you want... led you on a good chase... so, why should I tell you anything, copper?"

Barton felt a sort of begrudging respect for the old gangster. King was a professional; he'd never given anything, willingly, to the police before; so why should he start now: *He doesn't know how to give up. Fighting to the end* "Clear your conscience maybe? Come on King it's over."

"I ain't got a conscience... never did... can't afford one in my line of business," said King, his mouth forming into a weak smile. He tried to laugh, but it turned into a cough.

"Do you know who did this to you?" asked Barton.

"No."

"What were you doing this morning?"

"Taking a drive in the country," said King, his voice was becoming weaker, but the defiance still there in his eyes.

"But Herrera wasn't going to come back, was he," said Barton, his tone changing, becoming more menacing. "...come on King... give me a name... Who was it...? Who told you to get rid of him?"

Kings face tightened, his eyes giving away his surprise. He started gasping for breath, as his daughter interrupted.

"What do you mean? Ricky wasn't with them. Was he Dad?"

"So he didn't tell you, they were planning to kill your boyfriend?"

"It's not true!" she screamed, "You're lying. Dad, tell him... tell him it's not true. Dad..." But as she looked into her father's eyes, for a sign that would tell her that Barton was lying; all she could see the truth.

"You bastard! How could you do that to me!" she cried, "I loved him… Why! What's he ever…"

"Please, Miss King. If you can't control yourself you'll have to leave," said the nurse.

She was still shouting as Barton leaned closer to King. "He's still alive Bobby. But, it wasn't him they wanted was it?" he said.

The old man didn't respond; the tracers on the monitor slowed, as his breathing became more laboured, and his eyes closed.

"That's enough, Inspector. You'll have to leave now. You too, Miss King," said Jane Chambers, who had been standing by the door witnessing the scene. Barton apologised and ushered Debbie towards the door, as the nurse walked over to her patient.

"What's up, sir?" asked Connor as they came out.

"She's had a bit of a shock," replied Barton, "Brenda, can you go and find her a cup of tea? We'll be in the office."

"You bastard!" said Debbie King as she sat down, "…You lot don't give a shit, do you? What was that all about?"

"It's true Debbie. We found Herrera in the boot of your car. We thought he was dead at first."

"What! He's alive?"

"Yes. He's downstairs in casualty. I'll let you see him later, maybe… if…"

"If what… if I cooperate with you, grass up my dad?"

"Something like that. Come on Debbie… you're a big girl… you know that's the way it works. You help me and I'll help you."

Before she could say anything, the door opened and Brenda came in with a plastic cup. Barton told her to put it down on the desk and asked her to wait outside.

Debbie King picked up the cup and took a sip of tea. She thought for a minute before speaking again. "Do I have a choice?"

"This way at least you'll get to visit Herrera when he's on the inside. If you're lucky, the Home Office might not deport him. But, you won't get to see him at all if you're in Holloway."

"I'm not doing any deals without my lawyer."

"I can understand that, "he said, "but I need something now. Have you got any idea why your dad would want to kill Herrera?"

"No. I know he didn't like him and he wasn't too pleased when he found out about us. But he never let personal stuff get in the way of business before… someone must have set it up."

"And you've no idea who that might be?" he asked, "This is serious Debbie...right now there are only four people who know Herrera's still alive... I'll keep it that way as long as I can... but if someone set this up... they'll try again. "

"I don't know, maybe... no... that's all you're getting until I see my lawyer. I don't trust you... I need to be sure that I'll be safe."

"We'll get you a lawyer, but I don't want you talking to anyone connected with your father."

"That's OK," she said, picking up a pen from the desk and writing a number on a slip of paper, "...give this guy a call. He's straight. Now give me another cigarette."

Jane Chambers could smell the cigarette smoke from the corridor. She burst into her office, "You're really trying my patience Inspector! You're not allowed to smoke in here," she said angrily.

"I know. Hospital rules and all that... What would you do without them? Anyway I'm not smoking. Surely you don't mind if Miss King does though?"

"But I do mind," said the nurse, "I'm sorry, Miss King, I know this is a difficult time, but you still can't smoke in the hospital."

Barton looked at the woman sitting opposite him. This wasn't the same woman; she was broken; in the last few hours, her whole life had crashed around her. At that moment, it didn't matter who she was or what she'd done. That could wait. Her hand trembled as she put the cigarette to her lips for the last time before dropping it into the half-empty cup. He wondered what the charge nurse was thinking, behind that smug look on her face; maybe she enjoyed scoring points by enforcing bureaucratic rules. "So much for the caring profession," he said, under his breath.

"Did you say something Inspector?"

"No, nothing, I was just thinking."

"Anyway, I came to tell you that you can go back in now. He's asking for you Miss King, you too, Inspector. Just make sure that there's no more trouble."

Debbie King sat next to the bed, holding her father's hand. The detectives sat together on the opposite side; within earshot, but far enough away to afford father and daughter some degree of privacy. Debbie talked to her father; questions mainly, not appearing to notice when didn't answer. And when the dying man did reply, Barton had to strain to listen. They'd been at the bedside for two hours and, with every question, Barton became more convinced that she really didn't know much, about the business that her father had been involved in.

Maybe it was a coincidence, and she had met Herrera at a party; not knowing until later about his business with her father.

But she was still a vital link, and he knew that he would have to get her to talk; to dig into her memory for clues, however insignificant and however painful. He knew that King wasn't going to say anything. Deathbed confessions were the stuff of fiction. Whatever he knew, he'd take with him.

"Why did you do it Dad?" she'd repeated the question a dozen times or more.

"I had to… I didn't want to hurt you… but I had to."

"I don't understand," she said.

"Can't explain… just had to do it… always had to do it for him," He gasped for breath again, struggling to speak, "Is that copper still here?"

"He's over there."

King turned his head slowly towards Barton. "See she's looked after Barton… she's got nobody else now… she's got no part in this."

He was struggling to speak, his breathing becoming more difficult. "It's not her fault… she can't help… who she is… who I am. You can't blame her… for what I've done."

"The sins of the father," said Barton quietly.

The tracers on the monitor were moving more slowly. "You must let him rest now," said the nurse, "he's too weak to talk."

"No… let me finish," gasped King.

"It's alright Dad, don't say anymore." Debbie's eyes were full of tears as she spoke.

King closed his eyes and spoke in a whisper; every word an effort. "Lenny… talk to Lenny… I let him down… tell him… I'm sorry."

Talk to Lenny. Barton's skipped a beat. The machine in his hand was recording King's words, but he wasn't really listening any more: *Talk to Lenny* King might have just given him the Puppet Master?

"…tell him… I love him… tell him… Barton, I'm sorry… I did it for him." King's voice was fading, "…Barton… I'm sorry… I didn't want to… I'm sorry, Barton… I had to do it."

King rambled incoherently as the tracers on the screen slowed, the peaks getting smaller until they finally disappeared and the lines on the screen stopped moving. Barton got up, and switched off his tape recorder; there was no reason for him to stay, nothing more for him here. He looked at Debbie King and put his hand on her shoulder; "I'm sorry, I'll leave you alone with him now." She nodded as he walked towards the door.

"Stay with her Brenda," he whispered. "I'll be outside."

Chapter 14

Monday 5th May

Reading – 16:40 BST

It was a couple of hours before they were ready to leave the hospital. Brenda had stayed with Debbie King for over an hour after her father died, and then briefed the WPC who had been sent to relieve her escort. Barton had visited Herrera and then called Sally to arrange a briefing for that evening. Connor had arranged reliefs for himself and Brenda, checked that the uniforms were OK, and called Paul Timms to get a scene of crime and forensics update.

"You can go home, Dave. Take Brenda's car. I'll see you tomorrow," said Barton, as they walked across the car park.

As she handed over the keys, Connor smiled and pointed to Barton's car. "Looks like you've drawn the short straw, Brenda," he said with a laugh.

"There's nothing wrong with my car," said Barton, "...come on Brenda let's go."

"Don't mind him sir. I know people joke about it, but I like it. It's a Lotus Elite, isn't it?"

"Yes, how did you know?"

"I like old sports cars. My dad's got a couple," she said.

"This one used to belong to my father-in-law."

"So it's a bit of a family heirloom then," she laughed.

"You could say that I suppose, he bought it new in nineteen-seventy-six."

"Same age as me," she said. "Can I drive, sir?"

"OK. Be careful though... it hasn't got power steering and the brakes aren't that good," said Barton, surprised to have found anyone who actually wanted to drive his car.

"Don't worry, sir, I'm used to that. I drive my dad's cars, so I know what I'm doing."

Barton couldn't remember the last time he'd sat in the passenger seat, nor the last time that the old Lotus had run so well; it must have been the woman's touch. She was right, she did know what she was doing, and she was a good driver.

Barton just sat back and relaxed. They didn't say much to each other. Brenda was busy concentrating on the traffic. "I don't like talking when I'm driving," she said, "it's too distracting. I hope you don't mind, sir."

He didn't mind at all, he was tired, and he had a lot to think about. This was going to be a very long day. He reclined his seat, closed his eyes and the questions started running through his mind: *Who? What if? Why? Always bloody questions. I need some answers.*

But all he got was another question, as Brenda stopped behind a queue of traffic. "Who's Lenny?" she asked.

Barton had dozed off, and awoke with a start, "What?" He rubbed his eyes and yawned. "Sorry what did you say?"

"Who's Lenny? You know, King said something about telling Lenny. I was just wondering what he meant."

"I think he meant his brother," said Barton. As soon as King had said it, Barton had thought he recognised the name, and the look on Debbie King's face had confirmed it.

"I didn't know King had a brother," she said in surprise.

"No... Not many people do, but... Look the traffic's moving. I'll tell you about it later."

National Crime Squad, Hertfordshire Branch – 17:30 BST

"I enjoyed that," said Brenda as they got out of the car, "...you ought to get the carburettors adjusted though, to get rid of that flat spot. The clutch is slipping and the starter motor's knackered, but otherwise it's not bad for its age."

"Glad someone appreciates it."

"Let me know if you ever want to sell it."

"Now, you're joking."

"No, seriously, I like it. With a bit of work it could be a very nice car."

As they walked across the car park, Barton stopped and looked at Brenda. "Remember," he said, "not a word... not to anyone."

"OK, sir. Just one thing though."

"What's that?"

"Why has Sergeant Connor only got half a beard?"

Lorna McLean came to meet him as he walked into the main office. Barton looked round the room; it was almost empty. "Hello, Lorna. Have they left you in charge?"

"Yes sir, Paul went straight home on his way back from Oxford, and Sally went off a couple of hours ago. They'll both be back around six. Almost everyone else is still out interviewing King's mob."

"How long have you been here?"

"I didn't come on until two. I missed all the action."

"Never mind, this isn't finished yet. We've still got a lot of work to do. Get in touch with everyone and tell them to wrap up the interviews for today. I want everyone who is still on duty back here for seven... and get all the DSs in even if they're off duty. I want to brief everyone this evening. I'm not going to be around for a few days."

"Where are you going to be, sir?" asked Lorna.

"I'll tell you later. Now I need some of the files on Bobby King. Not the recent ones... I want all the old background stuff. Leave them in my office. I've got to phone the Chief Super and then I'm going out for a couple of hours."

Lorna caught Barton just as he was leaving. "This has just come in from Matt Brady, sir. I thought you ought to know about it. When they broke into one of the London flats this morning, they found the body of a girl in the bath. Suicide... she'd been dead a couple of days. It was one of the flats where they kept the girls who worked for Terry King. They found her passport in King's safe at the club... she's Jasmina Ajanovic."

Amersham, Buckinghamshire – 18:25 BST

It had taken Barton less than forty minutes to drive to Amersham and Irene Miller greeted him at the door, "Good to see you again, Mike," she said, as she wiped her hands on her apron. "Come inside." She looked at her reflection in the hall mirror. "Goodness, I do look a mess, whatever must you think."

The kitchen door was open and Barton could see that she was obviously in the middle of preparing dinner. Through another door he saw the dining table, set for a large dinner party. "I'm awfully sorry, Irene," he said, "I didn't realise that you were expecting company."

"Just a few friends for dinner. Don't worry they won't be here for a couple of hours yet. Talking of dinner isn't it about time that you and Grace came over. You cancelled last time, remember."

"I'm sorry about that," he said, "something came up at the last moment. Grace was really disappointed."

"You policemen, you're all the same," she sighed. "Trevor's in the garden. Why don't you go through to the study? I'll go and get him. Would you like some tea?"

159

"Thanks that would be nice."

Trevor Miller's study was a very private place, not visited by many; although Barton had been invited here several times before. And, as always, while he waited he walked around the room, looking at the walls, that were covered with mementoes of Trevor Miller's career in the service – photographs, framed newspaper articles, commendation certificates, the medals in the small case – a record of the achievements of, perhaps, the finest police officer that Barton had ever known. Chief Superintendent Trevor Miller was a senior policeman who had never forgotten where he had come from; who had never lost touch with the men and women on the front line. He had risen through the ranks, driven not by ambition, but by a passion for the service and a desire to serve the public and his colleagues. He commanded the Eastern OCU, leading by example, and from the front, not from behind a desk. Trevor Miller was a role model for every officer that served with him and Barton felt honoured to know him as a friend.

"You've been busy," said Miller, after Barton had given him a run down of the day's events. "Shame about King... but you've still done enough to mess their operations up for a long time."

"We've still got a lot to do, sir. Not counting all the illegals that Immigration are dealing with, we've got over seventy people in custody. The main problem is that we had to move so fast, without getting all other agencies lined up first, I reckon that we'll be able to start processing them through the magistrates' courts tomorrow, but there's a mass of paperwork. We need to make sure that nobody gets bailed, so we need to talk to the CPS."

"Do you need any help?"

"Not really. I'm going to have plenty of people available, now that we've finished the surveillance ops. But I could do with your support on a few things."

"Like what?"

"Well, I might have a lead on the Puppet Master... thing is I need to take myself out of the frame for a few days, to follow it up... I have to handle this personally, but I need your backing. He's got friends in very high places and he could make a lot of waves."

"Who is he, Mike?"

"I was hoping that you wouldn't ask me that. I'd rather not tell you at moment. Not until I'm sure."

"Bloody hell! You can't expect me to," Miller looked at Barton and saw that he was serious, "...you do. Don't you...? OK, how long do you need?"

"Can you just give me a few days? I'll tell you everything as soon as I can. Trust me."

"Well, I just hope you know what you're doing. If it goes wrong I might not be able to help you," said Miller, although he didn't have the slightest doubt in his mind. Barton wasn't the sort of man to let down people who put their trust in him. He took risks, but he was never reckless.

Barton also had other qualities that marked him out as a great criminal investigator. Most detectives learned their skills in the way that Miller had, but Barton had great intuition; a sixth sense almost. You had to be born with that, and if Mike Barton asked you trust him, you'd be a fool to say no.

"Thanks sir. Now there are a couple of other things that I need."

"Come on then, tell me about it."

"Well for starters, I want you to talk to the CPS about Debbie King… I've sort of offered her a deal… I reckon she's nearly ready to cooperate. She may not have known much about all this. But I'm sure she's got a lot of secrets tucked away in her memory."

Barton paused for a moment looking for a reaction, wondering how far he could push this. Miller nodded.

"We haven't had a chance to talk to Herrera yet, but he'll probably do a deal too… after what King did to him… and his bosses in Colombia must have agreed to it… so he'll be pretty pissed off with them as well. If we play him right, he could help blow the whole syndicate wide open. Obviously we'd need to get him and Debbie King under witness protection… but I think it'll be worth it… especially if they help us get the Puppet Master."

"OK, I'll see what I can do," said Miller, "…no promises though. Herrera could be a tough one. He's a foreign national and the Home Office will want to deport him at the first opportunity."

"He's a dead man if they do," said Barton gravely.

"I'll make sure they're aware of that."

"Can we keep all this on a need to know basis?" asked Barton, "…I don't want to publicise the fact that Herrera's still alive. Something King said… he knew we were onto him. We've got a leak somewhere."

"It'll be hard to keep quiet. Who else knows about Herrera?"

"We didn't tell the hospital who he was, so apart from Debbie King… it's only DS Connor and DC Cooper and they've been told not to say anything."

"I'll see what I can do to keep it quiet. But no promises."

"I understand," said Barton. "Now just one more, then I'll get out of your hair. I want Sally to concentrate on Debbie King and Herrera, while I'm away. I thought Paul could take over the team for bit, but he's going to need another DI to support him."

"You sure Paul will be OK?" asked Miller.

"Well he's not the greatest of detectives, but he's a good manager and great at the details when it comes to the paperwork. That's what's needed if we've gong to get all those case files prepared for the CPS."

"Alright, there shouldn't be a problem. I'll find you a DI by Wednesday."

"Thanks, sir. I've got to get back now and brief the troops. I won't be around for a few days."

National Crime Squad, Hertfordshire Branch – 20:10 BST

"I'm going to be away for a while," said Barton. "I've asked the Chief Super to put Paul in charge. I haven't told him yet, I wanted to talk to you first."

"I don't know what to say, Mike," said Sally, "Why Paul? I thought..."

"Don't look at me like that, Sal. No one's putting Paul ahead of you. It's just that I need you for something else. Now listen carefully, it's important that you understand what I'm planning to do..."

"So what about the branch?" she asked, when he had finished telling her about Herrera and Debbie King.

"The Chief is bringing in another DI to replace you, but Paul will still have to run his own team. I'll brief everyone about this when I've seen Paul. Now go and work out who else we need. We've got to have Dave and Brenda, because they already know what went on at the hospital. Pick a couple more DCs who you can rely on... but nobody else can know... not even Paul."

After the briefing, Sally went back to Barton's office with Connor. Barton picked up a pile of files that Lorna had given him earlier, and put them on the table. "This is where it starts," he said. "Have you decided on the team Sally?"

"Yes, I think we can cover it with five of us; me and Dave... Brenda of course, and then I thought Jane Barclay and Phil Fellows. They're both really good officers. Do you agree Dave?"

"Yes, they'll work well together and they can keep things to themselves," said Connor.

"Can you bring them in, Sally? Give me a few minutes... I want a word with Dave."

"What's up, Mike," asked Connor after Sally had left.

"You and Lorna, you know if your relationship continues, I'm going to have look at transferring one of you," said Barton seriously.

"But, I thought we were..."

"What? Thought you were being discreet. Come on, Dave the whole bloody branch knows about it... I'm sorry, but sooner or later it'll start to affect your work and that's not acceptable."

Yeah, I know," said Connor. "It's alright, we've talked about it. My secondment has only got another six months to run so we thought it would sort itself out."

"OK, we'll talk about that later. In the meantime, I need to be a hundred and ten percent certain about the security around this investigation. That means that you can't discuss anything that you see or hear with Lorna, until this is over. Got it?"

"Yes Mike, you can trust me," said Connor, wondering what he was going to tell Lorna.

"I know what you're thinking Dave. Don't worry. We're all going to have to tell the same story. I'll explain it all when Sally comes back."

The small team was gathered around the table in Barton's office, waiting in anticipation; some of them still wondering what was going on.

"Right, now let's get one thing straight from the start," said Barton. "Apart from the Chief Super... nobody outside of this room knows what I'm going to tell you... and it's got to stay that way. Firstly, what you just heard about Herrera at the briefing was for the benefit of DI Timms and the rest of the branch. Herrera isn't missing... he's in hospital in Reading And at the moment only nine people know, the six of us... the Chief Super, Debbie King... and Herrera of course. I'm hoping that Herrera's own people think that he's dead... Because, it looks like that's what King was planning. I think Herrera is going to be pretty pissed off with his bosses... and so we might be able to do a deal with him. Debbie King's already prepared to talk... after what they did to her boyfriend. The Chief Super has still got to square it with the powers that be... but in the meantime we keep Herrera under wraps and nobody goes near him until we can move him from Reading. Now as far as the rest of the team are concerned you're doing two things... interviewing Debbie King and looking for Herrera. But what you're also doing is helping me get the Puppet Master."

"But why all the secrecy?" asked Fellows.

"Because there's a leak... now I'm not suggesting that it's anyone in this branch... I'm not even suggesting that it's deliberate. But somehow, information has been getting back to King. I've suspected it for a while, and something he said today has made me sure about it."

"So what's this about the Puppet Master, then?" asked Connor. "Are you saying that you know who he is?"

"No, it's just a hunch and, even if I'm right, proving it's going to be difficult. It's going to take a lot of digging... starting with these," said Barton, pointing to the stack of files.

"Is this something to do with what King said? You know... about someone called Lenny?" asked Brenda, "You said you were going to tell me who he was talking about."

"Yes, that's exactly what it's about, Brenda. If I'm right Lenny is Bobby King's brother... a man called Leonard Anthony King... although he's not been called that for a long time."

"I didn't know King had a brother," said Connor, "why isn't he in the files?"

"Oh! But he is... it's just that you've got to go back a long way... that's the first job for you tomorrow. I want you to start with King's trial in 1987 and work back, thirty years if you have to. I want every name, every company, every business deal, checking out... because somewhere there's got to be a connection with Sir Anthony Naismith... that's what Leonard King calls himself now."

"Do you know where he is?" asked Connor.

"He lives in Spain, the Costa del Sol, and I'm going to see him tomorrow... and by the way Dave, I want you to bring me copies of everything tomorrow evening."

"Bloody hell sir, that's a bit short notice. What shall I tell...?"

Barton cut him off. "Same as I've told DI Timms. As far as anyone else is concerned we've had a tip off that that's where Herrera's gone."

Duxford, Cambridgeshire – 23:55 BST

They'd sat in the kitchen, eating their first proper meal together for weeks and he'd talked for over an hour, telling Grace about the events of the weekend and his plans for the week ahead. He was sure that he was on the right trail, but he felt uneasy. He was going out on a limb, and if it all went wrong, he'd be on his own. The Chief Super was bending the rules, but he could only help him up to a point. Sir Anthony Naismith had powerful friends; people who could put pressure on and make things very difficult for Barton's superiors. He knew that he was going to make waves, and he wondered how big they would be.

"What sort of man am I going to be dealing with?" asked Barton as he refilled their wine glasses.

"A very dangerous one," she replied, "if you're right, he's prepared to go to any lengths to protect himself."

"But killing his brother?"

"Why not? The first murderer killed his brother… remember the Bible story… Cain and Abel?"

"But Cain killed Abel because he was jealous of him. I can't see Naismith being jealous of Bobby King."

"That's not it… Cain killed Abel because he was insecure… afraid that he was losing his position… your man's insecure too, although he wouldn't see it that way. He's probably a classic control freak… he needs to be in control… on top… Let's go through to the lounge and I'll try to explain," Grace said, picking up her glass.

Barton listened intently as Grace gave him a psychology lesson. "You make him sound like a psychopath," he said.

"In a way, I suppose. But for a psychopath the act of violence, murder, rape, whatever, is the means of control… and it's usually a very personal, intimate. Men like your puppet master keeps their hands clean and get others to do their dirty work."

"But apart from that, this guy has to exercise control over others, and doesn't care who he hurts in the process.

"Yes… and one of the ways that he ensures that is by removing anything, or anyone, that threatens him. Maybe he saw King as a threat… because he might lead you to him."

"But why kill him? Why not just warn him?"

"Probably because King had failed in some way, it's on the tape: '…*I let him down'*. The sort of man I'm talking about can't tolerate failure… he controls people… manipulates them, and if they fail him it means that he's not in control… he's failed… and he can't admit that. He's got to maintain his position. King will be an example to others."

"But why would a man like that… you know, a successful, rich businessman, be involved in this… he doesn't need the money… he doesn't need to prove anything… so why's he doing it… controlling all these people… pulling their strings?"

"It's not about money. It's all about power." Grace picked up her empty glass and rolled the stem between her fingers as she spoke. "Because he can, Mike… because he can get away with it… because that's how he gets his kicks."

Barton drained his glass and, noticing Grace's empty glass in her hand, he read a message that wasn't there, and got up to fetch another bottle.

"What if I'm wrong?" he asked, when he returned. "After all, King didn't say much. Maybe I'm reading too much into it."

"Then you're going to annoy a lot of people," said Grace wearily, "and maybe put a blot on your copybook. But that's not going to happen is it?"

"I wish I could be sure, but..." he said, looking into space, not paying attention to the corkscrew that he was pulling from the neck of the bottle, "Shit! The bloody cork's broken."

"I didn't want any more anyway, I'm pregnant remember," she said.

She was worried that something else was bothering him; something that he didn't want to talk about. "Look Mike, for as long as I've known you, you've gone with your instincts. Remember that first case that I helped you with?"

"Yes, of course. I couldn't have cracked that case without you."

"But all I did was to give you a profile... described the sort of man that you were looking for. It could have been anyone, but you already knew it was Keith Lake, didn't you?" All that I did was give you a way of getting to him... I'm only a psychologist Mike... I can help you get inside people's heads, tell you what makes them tick. But that's no good unless you've got someone to match the profile to. You're the detective... you had to find the clues and fit the pieces of the puzzle together. You notice things, Mike... things that other people miss and you've got the courage to make that leap and follow your instincts. "

"I know. You're right as usual, but..."

"What is it Mike... come on Trevor wouldn't let you do this unless he thought you were on the right track."

"It's not that. I'm just not sure I want to dig up old skeletons. There are things that Trevor and Sally don't know about. Things that I'd rather not think about... I'm worried that I might not be able to keep this at arms length..."

"You've lost me, Mike," she said. And then she remembered something he'd told her, years ago. "You blame him don't you?" It was something they never talked about, "...for your dad... it was an accident Mike."

Grace reached across the table and took his hand. He was trembling and, when she looked into his eyes, she didn't see the man she knew. She looked for the strong, confident, mature man, she knew and loved; the father of her unborn child. But from behind the tears, a frightened, confused young man was looking back at her; a young man, grieving for his father.

She got up and felt his grip tighten, holding her back. "Come on, "she said softly, "...that's enough talking... lets go to bed. You've got a plane to catch in the morning."

He looked at her and nodded. He was glad that she was here, "Thanks," he said, letting go of her hand as he stood up. "Thanks for being here."

"I'm always here, Mike... It's just that sometimes... you forget. Now stop thinking about him... he can wait until tomorrow."

"I can't help it. I've not had to think about it for years, but the feelings are still there. Dad was only there because of him."

Grace put her arms around her husband and held him. "Be careful Mike," she said, "You mustn't let this man get inside your head... If you do you'll get hurt."

PART TWO

Chapter 15

Tuesday 6th May 2003

Marbella, Costa del Sol – 14:00 CET

Barton hired a car at the airport and made a couple of calls before heading west along the new motorway. He'd decided to go straight there; Connor wasn't arriving until the evening, so he had time to sort out a hotel later. The girl he had spoken to on the phone had given him directions, and forty-five minutes after leaving the airport, he'd turned off the motorway and driven up into the hills. Along the road, were advertising hoardings; new golf resorts, hotels, and residential developments. After a few kilometres he came to the turning; a large hoarding advertised the '*Jardines de las Montanas Golf and Vacation Resort*', and a large red arrow pointed to the left indicating that his destination was two kilometres further along the newly surfaced road. Five minutes later, he parked the car and walked in to the hotel.

It was just a few minutes after two and he stopped briefly at the reception desk, before making his way to the bar. Four men were standing at the bar ordering drinks, but otherwise the huge room was empty. Barton looked around the room; like the reception lobby that he had just walked through, the bar was decorated in neutral colours with expensive modern furnishings. There were about a dozen circular, glass topped tables, each with four chairs, which appeared to have been designed more for style than comfort. Several low leather armchairs and sofas grouped were around low tables. Everything looked brand new and very expensive. Large, framed, black and white photographs of famous golfers, playing famous courses, adorned the walls. The place had been decorated for immediate impact, but felt cold and unwelcoming. Only the vast expanses of marble flooring differentiated this place from the many similar resort hotels he had been to back home. It was the sort of place that his bosses had hired for conferences and 'bonding weekends'. Given the choice, he would have headed for the nearest local bar. Barton preferred the character and shabby comfort of old pubs and small hotels; this wasn't really his sort of place. But this was a working trip and he knew that Naismith would be here.

Light flooded into the room through the large glass sliding doors; all of which were open, effectively extending the room out onto the large paved terrace, where large parasols gave shade to the marble topped tables and cane chairs.

Barton stepped outside, immediately feeling the heat of the sun, as he left the chill of the air-conditioned room, and walked over to the balustrade on the far side of the terrace, then looked around for a few moments, taking in the view.

The golf course spread out in front of him; lush, green fairways lying between artificial lakes, shaded in places by the tall palms, each leading to a patch of immaculately manicured emerald green turf, with a small red flag flapping in the breeze. A fountain in the middle of one of the lakes sent a stream of water some fifty feet into the air, and a small waterfall fed a stream that separated the 18th green from the fairway. The surrounding hills looked dry and barren with only bare brown earth beneath the olive trees, reminding him that this oasis was man made. The foundations of the new roads scarred the hillsides, linking vast terraces where more buildings were in various stages of completion, and would soon be yielding new crops – euros, pounds, dollars – as tourists and ex-pats flooded in. And towering above the construction sites, the huge cranes dominated the view; those at the very tops of the hills, silhouetted against the sky, like giant sentries keeping guard.

For years, the Costa del Sol had been a huge construction site, and the boundaries of the old towns. – Torremolinos, Fuengirola, Marbella, Estepona – were no longer distinguishable as they merged with the new resorts and urbanisations, strung along the coast. The developments had brought huge increases in traffic and the coast road had gained notoriety as one of the most dangerous in Europe. Now, a new motorway that took the traffic away from the coast and further back into the hills, was also giving the developers easier access to the old white villages and the fincas with their olive groves. Barton and Grace had taken some package holidays here and every time he returned a little bit more of 'the real Spain' had disappeared, as the cranes and the earthmovers moved back into the hills and towards the mountains. He'd never really stopped to think about where all the money came from, until now. Now he wondered how much of this was financed by men like the one he was here to meet.

The scale of investment was huge. The roads came first, then the golf courses, followed by hotels, villas, townhouses and apartments; whole communities growing from nothing in a couple of years. Except that these were not real communities; most of the permanent residents were retired, wealthy middle class couples with good pensions and private incomes who had left behind the cold winters and wet summers of Northern Europe, for the all year sunshine of Andalucía. Thousands of new neighbours came and went every week, their rental cars filling the driveways of the rented villas and holiday apartments. Barton wondered at the lifestyle of the residents. What did they do with their time? Surely they didn't play golf every day?

Barton walked back towards the bar; to his right behind another glass wall he could see what looked like hotel restaurant. He sat at one of the tables, closest to the bar, and gestured to the waiter.

"*Quisiera una cerveza, por favor*," he said, using one of the few Spanish phrases that he knew without consulting the phrase book. Not that it really mattered; almost everyone, in every bar on the Costa del Sol could speak English better than he spoke Spanish. But Barton liked to practice and after all, it was only a simple courtesy; to make the effort; to try to address someone in their own language; he had no right to expect them to speak his. In any case it was always a good ice-breaker, especially when he got it hopelessly wrong. His pathetic attempts at pronunciation, often preceded by a flick through the pages of phrase book, usually raised a smile before the exchange inevitably switched into English. At least he tried, unlike many of his fellow countrymen, who still seemed to think that the answer to any language difficulty, anywhere in the world, was to shout louder.

From where he was sitting, he could see, without turning his head, the bar, and the 18th green. Out of the corner of his eye, he could see the buggy park and a corner of the car park. Turning his head slightly the fairway came into view and in the distance the 18th tee. A small eye movement the other way brought the entrance to the restaurant into view. As he congratulated himself on his choice of vantage point, the waiter appeared in front of him bearing a tray on which sat a glass of pale beer and a small dish of olives.

"*Gracias,*" said Barton

"*De nada,*" replied the waiter.

"*Cómo se llama?*" enquired Barton.

The man smiled, "*Manolo, señor.*"

"*Hola Manolo, me llamo Barton. Habla inglés?*"

"*Si señor.*"

"Do you know *Señor* Naismith?"

"*Si señor*, he owns this place."

"Is he here, today?"

"*Si señor*, he is playing golf now, but he will come here after he is finished. Would you like me to tell him you are here?"

"*Non gracias*; but please let me know when he comes in."

Barton took a sip of the ice-cold beer, and settled down to wait and watch. He was good at people watching; looking at their faces and body language, looking for the involuntary movements that said so much. Listening, not so much to what was said, but for things that people left unsaid. He could tell a lot from the silences and the pauses; filling the gaps and listening for the changes in tone that often betrayed a person's real thoughts. Seeing and hearing things that most people didn't notice or didn't even look for. Reading lips; listening without hearing. Reading faces; looking into someone's eyes and seeing the lie before it was spoken. Noticing the unconscious movements and gestures, that can give someone away. Years of surveillance, investigations, interviewing witnesses and interrogating suspects couldn't help but make you notice everything. Barton was a professional, one of the best; he enjoyed watching.

Watching – the four men, who had been at the bar, now sitting at a table on the other side of the terrace. When he had first seen them, he'd immediately assumed that they were Scotsmen. They'd ordered Irn Bru to mix with their spirits. But then he'd remembered that his wife liked to dink vodka mixed with the sickly, sugary beverage and gave himself a silent reprimand for jumping to conclusions.

Watching – the two women who had just entered the bar, engrossed in conversation. He watched them walk across to a table in a corner. By the time they taken their seats, Manolo had placed a wine cooler at the side of the table, set two glasses and a dish of olives on the table and was already opening a bottle of white Rioja. The blonde tasted the wine, nodded her head and carried on talking to her companion without so much as a glance at Manolo, as he poured the wine and placed the bottle into the ice bucket. Neither woman had uttered even a single word to the attentive young man. As he returned to the bar, the look on his face, said what he was thinking. Barton nodded in agreement.

Ladies who lunch, he thought. Rich, obviously; Barton didn't know much about fashion, but he could see the logos – Gucci, Dior, Chanel, Louis Vuitton, and Prada – and knew enough to know they didn't shop at M&S. The clothes they were wearing would have cost more than Barton's entire wardrobe, their jewellery could probably have paid for his pension, and he imagined that they'd spent more than he earned in a week on make up and hairdos. He reckoned that they were both in their early fifties; still trying, without success, to look forty. Strange, he thought, how money and good taste were so often at odds. He thought of Grace, who looked fabulous in nothing more than Gap jeans and T-shirt, and still looked as young and beautiful as when they had first met nearly ten years ago.

Watching, the four golfers again, replaying every hole of the game they had just finished – he smiled as they raised their voices and their accents, confirmed his original assumption regarding ethnicity – all joking and laughing. Then each silenced, in turn as the others made a big thing of the missed putt, the lost ball, or a disaster in the sand trap. Then all laughing and joking again as the obviously exaggerated account of the morning's play continued.

174

One of the men called out to the waiter. A moment later Manolo walked over to their table carrying a tray of drinks, which he placed in front of them. The man looked up, took a banknote from his wallet, and said something to the waiter. Barton couldn't hear what was said, but there was a big smile on Manolo's face as he walked away, pocketing the tip, a smile that said that these customers would be looked after.

Watching – the two golfers, as they rode in their buggy towards the final hole, stopping on the edge of the fairway, and only walking the last few yards to where their balls were lying: *So much for exercise.*

Watching – with a big smile on his face – as the first man played towards the green and then held his head in his hands as the ball landed in bunker. Then the other man played his shot and waved his club in the air as the ball landed about six feet from the flag.

Watching – the two women as they each smoked a cigarette and sipped their wine; their actions almost perfectly synchronised. The blonde seemed to be doing most of the talking; her companion was starting to look bored. He saw that their glasses and the bottle were almost empty: *God they can put it away, they've only been there about twenty minutes.*

Watching – the two golfers on the 18th again, one sitting in the shade of the buggy, also watching, as his companion wielded a sand iron; striking the ball too hard, so it bounced past the flag to the rough grass at the back of the green.

Barton finished his beer and catching Manolo's eye, waved the empty glass. The barman brought another beer. "Will there be anything else, *señor?*"

Barton looked across the room. "Those two ladies, do you know them?" he asked.

"*Si señor*, the lady in blue is *Señora* Naismith. The other lady, I think is her sister. I'm not sure."

"*Gracias,*" said Barton, and then as the waiter turned to leave he asked, "Do you have any cigarettes at the bar?"

"There is a machine near the reception desk, *señor.*"

"Can you give me some change?" Barton asked, taking a fifty-euro note from his wallet, he got up to follow the waiter to the bar. "Enough for two packs please."

Manolo took some notes and coins from the till and pointed in the direction of the reception area. "The machine is on the left, *señor.*"

"*Gracias,*" said Barton, handing back one of the notes.

Barton walked through to reception and found the cigarette machine in an alcove next to the desk. He put three coins in the slot, pressed the selection button, and took the pack and his change from the tray. He repeated the process, put one pack into his jacket pocket, and, tore the cellophane wrapper from the other as he walked back into the bar. Flipping the lid open, he pulled out the silver paper, took out a cigarette, and put it into his mouth. Then he fumbled in his pockets. He had a lighter in the pocket of his chinos, but asking for a light was always a good way to engineer an introduction. As he passed the two women, he stopped and fumbled in his pockets again.

"Excuse me, but could I trouble you for a light?" he asked.

The blonde turned and looked at him. She smiled, picked up her lighter, and raised her hand. Barton bent towards her and she lit his cigarette.

"Thanks," he said. "Is it always as quiet as this in here?"

"It generally picks up towards three," she replied. "I take it that you haven't been here before."

"No, I just got in this morning. I came here straight from the airport."

"Are you staying here at the resort?" she enquired, seizing on the opportunity to start a new conversation.

"I don't know, I had to fly out at short notice and I haven't made any arrangements yet."

"Well," she said, "I can highly recommend this hotel, the rooms are beautiful and the food is out of this world; reasonably priced as well."

Barton had enquired about the price of a room when he'd arrived: *Reasonable! You obviously live on a different planet to the one I inhabit.*

"Take no notice of her," said her companion. "She would say that. Her husband owns the place."

"But it's true darling, everyone says this is the best hotel for miles."

"That's because it's the only hotel for miles. If I were you, I'd stay in town. It's so boring here; all they talk about is bloody golf. You should stay at the El Fuerte, it's very good."

Barton and Grace had once had a couple of drinks in one of the Hotel el Fuerte's elegant bars and he'd almost choked on an olive when he was given the bill. "I know it," he said, "but, I'm not sure that my budget would stretch to that."

"Oh! Don't worry about that. Just tell the manager that you know us. I'm sure he'll give you a very good rate."

The blonde looked at Barton and enquired, "Are you on your own, Mr...?"

"Barton... Mike Barton. And yes, I'm alone at the moment but I'm meeting a colleague later this evening."

"Well, why don't you join us then? My horoscope said that I was going to meet a dark, handsome man today," she said laughing. She waved to the waiter. "Manolo, bring the gentleman's drink over here."

Barton pulled up a chair and sat between the two women, facing the bar, with his back to the terrace.

"So your husband owns all of this," he said, with interest, wondering how much he could learn from the woman, without appearing too prying. He needn't have worried; she didn't need any further prompting.

"Well, not exactly... his company owns the hotel and the two golf courses, but most of the villas and apartments are privately owned," she informed him, with a self-satisfied smile on her face as she spoke. "Oh! And of course he owns the development company that is building the whole resort," she paused, looking at Barton's face for a sign that he was suitably impressed; none was evident, but she carried on anyway, "...bought the whole site for peanuts over ten years ago; now it's worth millions He's..."

The other woman interrupted her, "Oh! Helen, do stop. I'm sure that Mr Barton isn't the least bit interested in Tony's boring business."

Turning to Barton she said, "I'm terribly sorry, Mr Barton you must think us awfully rude, we haven't even introduced ourselves. I'm Jean Browning and this is my sister-in-law Helen Naismith."

"Please call me Mike," he said. "And can I get you ladies another bottle of wine." Without waiting for an answer he called to the waiter, "Manolo, another bottle of wine please, and another glass." He leaned back slightly in his chair; feeling rather pleased with himself. This was going better than expected. "I'll join you in a glass of wine, if you don't mind, this beer's not really to my liking."

Helen Naismith obviously liked to show off and didn't waste much time in letting him know that she was 'Lady Naismith'. "You've probably heard of my husband... Sir Anthony Naismith... but don't worry... we don't go in for all that pretentious title stuff out here."

Jean launched a stream of questions, "Are you here on business Mike? Did you say that you were meeting someone later? What is it that you do? Are you going to be here long?" she asked, not pausing for long enough to allow Barton to answer.

Now, it was Helen's turn to interrupt. "Jean, now who's being rude?" she said sharply.

"I'm sorry Mike, but she's always like this, giving complete strangers the third degree treatment. She's like a one woman Spanish Inquisition."

They all laughed; although Jean, embarrassed by her friend's comment, looked rather uncomfortable.

"It's all right Jean, I don't mind," said Barton, seeing that Helen was obviously the dominant half of this pair.

Jean smiled demurely; she'd taken quite a fancy to the polite, handsome man, who was brightening up a rather boring day. "Thank you Mike, you're very kind," she said.

He turned his attention back to Helen. "Actually, Helen, I've come to Spain to meet your husband, and I'm not sure how long I'll be staying."

"You've come all the way to Spain to see my husband, and this is the first place you come to. There's a lucky coincidence," said Helen. "He's on the course at the moment, but they should be finished any minute now."

"Not exactly luck," replied Barton. "I phoned his office from the airport and they said he'd be here."

"Well, he won't have a lot of time, he's supposed to be taking us to lunch and be warned. If he's just lost he'll be in no mood to talk business," she said in a warning tone.

"That's OK. I just want to let him know that I'm here. His secretary has made an appointment for me at his office tomorrow. Now ladies tell me something about yourselves and what you do in Marbella."

The two women needed no further prompting and spent the next ten minutes telling him where they lived; how long the had lived there, how many rooms their houses had. He soon knew how much Helen's house worth, what cars were in the driveway, who had the biggest pool, Helen conceding that Jean's was the larger, "...although, of course, we do have an indoor one as well." As if that mattered to him.

Then for another ten minutes, Barton was given the complete guide to Marbella. The places to be seen and the places to avoid; the best bars and restaurants, graded not by to the quality of the food or the service but according to whom you might see there.

"Oh! No, Helen. Surely not...? Nobody goes there any more," exclaimed Jean with surprise.

"Well last week I'm sure that I saw... Oh...! What's her name, you know the model... the one who's just married that dishy French actor? Well, she was there with Patricia's daughter." Helen seemed almost oblivious to Barton's presence as she rolled off lists of where to shop, where to stay, the nightlife, the best beaches, the health clubs.

Jean was constantly looking at him; saying much less than Helen, but flirting quite openly. "You really must go shopping, while you're here. I saw some beautiful shirts this morning... of course my husband couldn't wear them, he's a bit too old, and overweight. But I bet they'd look great on you," she said, smiling seductively.

Barton smiled back, and pretended to be fascinated by their chatter. He'd given up looking around the bar; he knew that, if he sat here, the man he wanted would come to him. Besides, it would have been bad manners to give his companions any sign that he wasn't interested in their gossip. But he was starting to weary and wondered how much more of this he could take; he hoped the man would arrive soon.

The bar had suddenly become quite busy and at first, he didn't see the two men approaching the table. They were the two golfers he'd seen earlier playing the 18th; fresh from the locker room, showered and smelling of expensive eau de cologne. One of the men was in his late sixties; the other looked several years younger. Both wore dark polo shirts, pale chinos, and loafers. The older man was quite slim and athletic looking, six feet tall; maybe a bit more, the slight stoop made it difficult to be sure. His well cut clothes were expensive but discreet, not drawing attention to his wealth; unlike the large white gold Rolex on his wrist. He was sporting the kind of tan that resulted from years of living in the sun, and his face had the sort of self-important, arrogant look that, cast disdainfully on others, said: *'I'm a better man than you.'*

The other man, a couple of inches shorter and more than just a few pounds overweight, bent down and gave Jean a peck on the cheek.

"Who won darling?" said Jean.

"Tony," he said. "Can't you tell from the bloody smile on his face?"

"Gave you every chance you old bugger, even put my ball into the sand to help you out." said the other man. "Would you believe it, six feet from the flag and he takes three putts to put the bloody thing away."

"Well if you got your people to cut the bloody grass properly, the ball might go where it's supposed to."

"Now then boys, it's only a game," said Helen. She looked at Barton, "Although I sometimes think that for Tony it's a matter of life and death." Both women and the younger man laughed at the remark. The other man, who Barton assumed to be Naismith, grunted and looked away.

"Come and meet our new friend," said Jean.

"Mike, this is Peter, my husband," she said, standing up to introduce them properly.

Peter Browning reached out and took Barton's hand; his grip was firm and he shook Barton's hand vigorously. "Pleased to meet you, Mike, thanks for keeping the ladies entertained," he said warmly. "Sorry girls that last hole took a bit longer than usual."

Helen turned towards the other man, who was still keeping his distance. His face had taken on a rather sullen look. "Tony, don't be so rude, say hello," she said. "Mike," she said, "I'd like you to meet my husband, Tony."

Barton moved towards the man and held out his hand, "Pleased to meet you, Sir Anthony," he said.

Naismith hesitated before grudgingly taking Barton's hand; his grip felt cold and limp. "No need to be so formal, my friends call me Tony," he said. But the tone of his voice and the look in his eyes told Barton that he wasn't to consider himself a friend. "Sorry, didn't catch your last name."

"Barton... Mike Barton."

Peter Browning sat down next to his wife, but Naismith remained standing. He looked anxious, and Barton sensed that he knew who he was. "Well Mr Barton," he said impatiently. "It's been nice to meet you, but we have to go now."

Helen touched her husband's arm. "There's no hurry Tony," she said, annoyed at her husband's rudeness. "Lunch can wait. Sit down and have a drink. Mike's come all this way to see you."

Naismith looked at Barton and the muscles in the face tightened slightly, forming an insincere smile; his shoulders straightened as he spoke. "And what exactly do you want, Mr Barton? People who want to do business with me usually call at my office." His tone was unfriendly, almost confrontational, leaving Barton in no doubt that his presence was not welcome.

"I'm a police officer, sir. Detective Chief Inspector, with the National Crime Squad and I have to talk to you about your brother."

There was a brief, but uncomfortable silence before Naismith spoke. His voice softened, "Give me a moment please, Inspector." Turning to Browning he said, "Peter, could you and Jean drive Helen back to town, I'll join you at the restaurant as soon as I can."

As the others got up to leave, Barton looked at Naismith. "Is there somewhere that we could talk more privately?" he asked.

"You'd better come this way," said Naismith and he gestured towards the door that led to the reception area. He led the way, walked behind the reception desk, and opened a door. "We'll use the manager's office; it's upstairs," He gestured to Barton, who followed him through the door. As Naismith closed the door, he was studying Barton's face. "I can't think of any reason that I would know you, but your face looks familiar. Have we met before?" he asked.

"A long time ago, sir, in 1983, but I don't expect you'd remember me."

The office was at the end of a short corridor. Naismith opened the door and Barton went inside. Naismith followed and closed the door. An oak desk dominated the office; behind it was a large leather chair. The sun poured in through the large windows, casting dark shadows behind the desk. In front of the windows were a round table and a couple of comfortable looking armchairs. Naismith took the chair behind the desk and sat down. Barton crossed over to the window – looking out he could see the view that he had seen earlier from the terrace – and turned one of the armchairs to face the desk. Moving it a little closer, he sat down and waited for Naismith to speak.

Naismith scowled at Barton. "Well, Inspector, this had better be good," he said. He sounded calm and composed, but Barton could see the small beads of sweat, gathering in the furrows of his forehead, and glistening in the bright sunlight.

"I'm afraid that I have some bad news, sir," said Barton, hesitating for a moment before he dropped his bombshell. "…I'm very sorry to have to tell you, that your brother died yesterday."

Even behind the tan, Barton could tell that the colour had drained from Naismith's face. As the man slumped back into the chair, he suddenly looked much older; the arrogance gone. "There must be a mistake," he spluttered, "you can't have…"

He stopped in mid sentence, got to his feet and walked over to a large oak cabinet. Hands shaking, he opened the door and reached for a bottle of Lagavulin. He pulled out the cork, dropping it on the floor and poured the whisky into a tumbler; more spilling on the floor than ended up in the glass. He downed the drink in one and slammed the glass down hard onto the desk. He winced as the glass shattered; picked a shard of glass from his palm and licked the blood that trickled from the cut.

Barton took a couple of clean tissues from his pocket and offered them across the desk. As Naismith wrapped the tissues around his hand, Barton went over to the cabinet and poured another whisky. He put it in on the desk in front of Naismith and sat down again. Naismith picked up the glass and walked to the window. He stared into the distance and spoke slowly, quietly, his voice trembling slightly. "Excuse me… but I can't believe this… When did it happen… are you sure it was my brother?"

"I'm afraid, there's no mistake sir. He died in hospital just after three o'clock yesterday afternoon. I was with him when he died."

"Could I have one of your cigarettes?" Naismith asked. He moved towards Barton and sat in the other armchair. "I usually smoke cigars, but it doesn't seem appropriate… given the circumstances."

Barton got up, took a cigarette packet, and lighter from his pocket and placed them on the table. Naismith took a cigarette and lit it, drawing deeply. Barton, turned his chair to face the table, but didn't move it closer. He sat about six feet away from Naismith, and watched him as he raised the glass and drained the contents. The arrogant look had returned and he stared at Barton, waiting for the policeman to speak again.

"Your brother was involved in an incident at the weekend. He was in a car with three other men. One was his son, Terry. We haven't been able to identify the others yet. Your nephew is still in a coma, and the other two were dead before the paramedics arrived." Barton paused, looking for some response, but the old man just stared at him; his eyes, cold and piercing.

"I think that you should know that your brother and a number of his business associates were the subjects of a police investigation," said Barton, speaking slowly; using the sombre, measured tone that all good policemen reserve for such occasions. "At the time of the incident he was under surveillance. The incident was witnessed by several police officers," Barton saw a tiny flicker of movement in the man's eyes and paused for a moment, "…and I have to tell you that we are treating the deaths as murder."

Naismith still said nothing. He took another cigarette from the pack, lighting it from the glowing tip of the first, which he stubbed out slowly and deliberately, grinding the butt into the large glass ashtray.

Barton continued, "Obviously we will be pursuing a number of lines of enquiry… But it would seem that your brother was not a popular man, and we already have several suspects. In the meantime I was hoping that you may be able to help me… Can you think of anyone who might have wanted your brother dead?"

Naismith rose to his feet. "I'm afraid that I'm not going to be much help, Inspector… my brother and I were never close… we don't… didn't… keep in touch. In fact, I haven't seen him for over forty years."

"I appreciate that this has come as a shock, sir, and I won't keep you any longer," said Barton. "But if you can think of anything… however insignificant it might seem, it may help us to find out who was responsible for his death. I phoned your office earlier and you secretary has made me an appointment… perhaps you could think about it overnight, and then we can talk again in the morning."

"Thank you Inspector, but I think that you'll be wasting your time. Now, I really must be going. I have to meet my wife and our friends."

Naismith stood up, walked to the door; and opened it, without waiting for a response. Barton followed, and the two men walked down the stairs and through the reception lobby in silence.

They stepped out of the cool air-conditioned building and into the afternoon heat. Barton started to sweat as he followed Naismith towards a row of expensive cars parked opposite the hotel. When Barton had arrived there had been several empty spaces there; but a uniformed security man waving and shouting 'reservado!' had made it obvious that they were not to be used, and he had parked the hire car in the main car park at the side of the hotel. Now, directly in front of him was a dark green Aston Martin and he noticed the letters '*AN*' painted on the paving.

Naismith took out a remote control and pointed it at the Aston; the indicator lights flashed twice and he moved towards the car door. "Nice car," said Barton, admiring the sleek lines of the powerful coupé.

Naismith smiled; but it wasn't the forced, tight-lipped, grudging apology for a smile that he had shown Barton earlier; now he was beaming, and grinning like the Cheshire cat.

"Aston Martin Vanquish, six litre V12, a real beast, a hundred and ninety miles an hour, nought to sixty in five seconds, much better than any of that Italian rubbish." He looked at Barton as he opened the car door. "Best car money can buy... But I don't suppose that's relevant to you. A hundred and fifty grand would be a bit much on a policeman's salary," he said patronisingly. He slapped Barton across the shoulder and laughed. "See you tomorrow, Inspector."

Barton started to walk away, then suddenly stopped and turned back. He had another card to play; he was about to up the stakes. He called out, "Oh! Lenny! I nearly forgot to tell you..."

Before he could finish, Naismith exploded. "What was that? Nobody calls me Lenny! And certainly not a jumped up piece of shit like you! Your kind are all the same... they can put you in a uniform... give you a bloody badge... it doesn't make you like us... it doesn't give you the right to..." he shouted angrily, waving his fist. "You call me Sir Anthony or just plain bloody sir. Do you understand! Just you remember that... show some respect or I'll see you back in a bloody panda car."

Barton tried to suppress the smile. This wasn't the response he had expected; it was better than he could possibly have hoped for.

"Are you fucking laughing at me boy? I'm warning you, I know a lot of important people... people who'll see to it... put you in your place, before you've even got on the plane to go home."

"I'm sorry sir. I didn't mean to cause offence, I'm just doing my job," said Barton as he turned his back and started to walk away again.

Naismith shouted after him, "Don't you walk away from me boy. What were you going to tell me?"

Barton carried on walking, without turning his head, "Never mind sir, it can wait until tomorrow," he said with a satisfied look on his face.

The big V12 roared into life and Naismith reversed the car from the parking space. He accelerated hard as he drove off, the rear wheels spinning, creating a cloud of dust and tyre smoke. He was fuming, his heart thumping, his eyes filled with rage. Nobody had used that name for a long time. The mere thought of it made his stomach turn, reminding him of a man he had hated all his life, a man he wanted to forget, a man he would never forgive. He had tolerated Bobby and some of the others, but that was different, they'd always called him by that name. But a stranger... one of them... they were all the same... no respect. He'd made other men pay for insulting him. This one would too. And then he remembered, as the ghost fleetingly appeared; he remembered where he'd seen the policeman before.

The charade he'd been playing for the past hour had taken it out of him, and Barton was feeling quite tired by the time he got back to his car. Or maybe it was just the heat? He got in and started the engine. For a few moments, he closed his eyes and relaxed as the chilled air streamed through the vents. Then, feeling refreshed, he took out his mobile and called the office.

"National Crime Squad, Detective Constable Fellows speaking."

"Hi, Phil, it's DCI Barton. Has Dave Connor left for the airport yet?"

"No, sir, he's waiting for a car. His flight leaves at four. Do you want to speak to him?"

Barton looked at his watch, quarter to four; quarter to three in England, "Yes, put him on please."

"Hello, Mike," said the unmistakable voice of Dave Connor, "I've got those files you wanted, and Jane's putting some more stuff together. She can send it out tomorrow, if you need it. How's it going at your end?"

"Fine, Dave... the old man got a bit wound up though. I'll let him cool off for a bit before tomorrow. Oh! I've just met his brother-in-law, Peter Browning, is there anything in the files about him?"

"I think I've seen a briefing note somewhere. I don't think there's much. Do you want me to ask Jane to dig out some more on him?"

"Yes please. Right, I'll see you later. What time does your plane get in?"

"About seven-thirty."

"Fine, I'll be waiting," said Barton. He turned off the phone. He had plenty of time to find a hotel in Marbella, have a shower and a shave before driving to the airport. As he drove towards the coast he thought about the message he had come to give to the Naismith; the message from his dead brother.

Chapter 16

Tuesday 6th May 2003

London Colney, Hertfordshire – 15:00 BST

Deborah King wiped her eyes again and looked across the room at the police officer, who was at this moment, in this place, the only friend she could turn to. She shook her head.

"I still can't believe it," she said, "it's like a dream. I keep thinking that I'm going to wake up and none of this has happened. Poor Ricky, I can't believe they did that to him... not my Dad. I know he's never been... you know... but I didn't think he'd ever do anything to hurt me... not like this." She shook her head again. "Sorry, you don't want to hear all this."

"That's alright," said Brenda Cooper as she poured the tea. "Let's go and sit in the lounge. You can talk about it all you want, no notes, no tape recorder, we'll do that later."

Brenda was still trying to work out if it was all an act. Yesterday the woman had been arrogant and abusive; now she was talking to her as if she were a friend. The tears seemed genuine enough, and the way she'd spoken of her father and brother, with hatred in her voice and in her eyes; that had to be real. The doctor had told them that she was in shock and would probably be confused for a while. The DI had said that they'd give her a few days to come to terms with the situation, and then the questions would start.

Maybe she really did love the Colombian, but was that enough for her give them everything? Only time would tell.

Marbella, Costa Del Sol – 16:30 CET

It took Barton about half an hour to drive to the centre of Marbella. The Hotel el Fuerte overlooked the beach, very close to the old town. It wasn't really his sort of hotel – too flashy, too comfortable, too smart; too impersonal; all perfectly good reasons for preferring small hotels, without admitting you couldn't afford to stay in a place like this – but it had its own car park and Helen had told him that it was also quite close to Naismith's office. He parked the car and made his way to reception, stopping to take a quick look as his phrase book before he got to the desk.

"*Hola*," he said as one of the receptionists looked towards him. "*Buenos tardes señorita, quisiera dos habitaćion individual, por favor.*"

The receptionist glanced at the passport in Barton's hand, "*Si señor,*" she replied. "You are English, yes? But you speak *español* very well. Yes we have two rooms."

"Thank you," said Barton. He'd made the effort again and now he could revert to his own language. "My name is Barton... Mike Barton. The other room is for Mr David Connor... he'll be arriving later."

"*Señor* Barton, but of course, your room is already reserved. *Señora* Naismith, she telephoned... but she said nothing of *Señor* Connor. I can give him a nice room... but I'm sorry... it will not be on the same floor."

"That will be OK," said Barton, "I'll check in now, Mr Connor will be arriving at about nine."

Barton opened the door of his room to find that Helen Naismith had booked him into large penthouse suite. Very nice, but even if he could get Miller to sign the expenses claim, how was he going to he get it past the finance officer? For a moment he considered calling reception and asking for a cheaper room. Then he thought again; it would make up for all the expenses that he'd forgotten to claim.

After unpacking, he took a shower and helped himself to a beer from the mini bar. He sat on the balcony, studying the street plan of Marbella that the receptionist had given him. Naismith's office was only about a ten-minute walk from the hotel, so he wouldn't have to bother with the car in the morning. He made a couple of phone calls, first to Sally and then to Grace.

"How was the flight?" asked Grace.

"Not bad," he replied. "In fact I didn't really notice. Guess I had a lot on my mind. I can't even remember taking off."

"That makes a change; you're usually a bag of nerves. Do you remember when we went to Spain, last spring? You kept on looking at all the golf clubs that people were checking in, and worrying that the plane would be too heavy to get off the ground. And last time we went to see your mum..."

"OK, that's enough. I can't help it if I don't like flying. Anyway how was your day?" he asked, "Are you alright?"

"So-so, I didn't go into work today... I was feeling a bit sick this morning. I didn't have any clients to see so I stayed at home and wrote up some notes. How about you, did you meet him?"

"Yes, briefly. I'm seeing him again at his office tomorrow."

"How did it go? What was he like?"

"I'd say it was pretty uncomfortable for both of us." he replied, and proceeded to tell her about the meeting; finishing with the episode in the car park.

"Sounds like you really touched a nerve there Mike." She sounded concerned, "I'm worried about you... take it easy tomorrow. Be careful not to push him too far."

"Don't worry I know what I'm doing. I'll take it slowly."

He hung up the phone and looked at his watch. He didn't need to leave for the airport until just before seven and there was plenty of time to go for a walk; time to think about his next move. He was certain that Naismith would be thinking about his.

The drive to the airport took him just under an hour and by seven-forty he was standing in the arrivals hall, looking at the flight information screens;\the flight from Stansted was about five minutes early. There was a small café in the corner, so he bought a coffee and sat a table, which had a good view of the doors leading from the baggage handling area. Just after eight, he spotted Dave Connor walking through the doors and got up to meet him.

"Hi Mike. Have you had a good day?" asked Connor, as he walked up to Barton.

Barton nodded and took one of his bags. "God this is heavy, what have you got in here?" he asked. "We're only here for a couple of days."

"That's full of your files... this is my stuff," replied Connor, holding up a small holdall. "I brought a laptop as well... downloaded some stuff that might be useful."

"Come on then, the car's this way. We've got to call in at the car hire office first to get you on the insurance. Then we'll get back to the hotel and have something to eat. Are you hungry?"

"Starving and I could murder a beer. I'll tell you what's been going on today on the way."

As they drove to Marbella, Connor updated Barton on the day's activities. Sally had already given him the headlines, but he asked Connor to fill in the details.

"We've got Debbie King in a safe house, Brenda's still with her. Sally hasn't started questioning her yet... they'll start tomorrow when her lawyer's available. He's been away for the weekend... didn't get back until this afternoon. Jane checked him out today. He's clean, no connections to King or anyone else... partner in a firm in Kensington... knows Debbie socially."

"Has she seen Herrera yet?"

"Brenda took her over to Reading this morning. She spent a couple of hours with him... they didn't say much to each other... he's still heavily sedated, and the doc told Brenda he won't be up to talking for a few of days yet."

"Any idea how long they're going to keep him in?"

"Doctor says he should be well enough to be discharged by the weekend. Sally's trying to find somewhere to put him. She said to tell you that she'll need a couple more DCs to mind him."

"I know... she's already asked me... I told her to talk to the Chief Super," said Barton. "Did Debbie visit Terry when she was at the hospital?"

"No... wasn't interested... didn't even ask about him," replied Connor. "Brenda had a word with the charge nurse in ICU, though... he's still in a coma. Debbie said she didn't care if he never woke up. She's really pissed off with them all. Brenda reckons she'll tell us anything we want to know, just to get back at them."

"Good, that's what I was hoping. Now what's Timms been up to?"

"He's not getting very far," said Connor. "He was looking a bit ragged when I left. Lorna says they're going round in circles, nobody's talking."

"Don't think I would in their position. Not yet anyway. What about Nichols?"

"There's no sign of him yet and his wife is pleading ignorance... says that she doesn't know anything about her husband's business... or where he is. We know from the phone records that he's contacted her... two calls from a mobile on Sunday and another one yesterday. Wherever he is, he can't go far, we've got his passport."

"What have the searches turned up, anything interesting?"

"Nothing much... they've taken away loads of files and papers but it's going to take ages to go through it all. They found a kilo of coke at Terry's place and a load more at Jarvis'...and they're still bringing stuff in from all the offices and clubs."

"Alright, that'll do for now, we're here," said Barton as he turned into the hotel car park. "Let's get you checked in."

"Whoa! This place is the business," said Connor as they walked into the hotel.

"I'm glad that you approve," said Barton. "Now get yourself sorted out. I'll meet you in the bar... shall we say, about ten? I'll have a beer waiting, OK."

Barton sat at a table and ordered a beer. Someone had left a copy of the Telegraph on the table, with the crossword half completed. He picked it up and stared at the clues. He started looking at the words that were already filled in, and their clues; most were anagrams, which he usually found easy. The cryptic ones, where you sometimes needed to get inside the compiler's head, were the ones he liked best.

'*Most important and correspondingly rubricated (3-6)*'. Rubricated? What the bloody hell was that? He hated it whenever his vocabulary was challenged. He already had some letters, but they didn't seem to be much help: *E -D / ----- R.*

After staring at the page for about five of minutes, he put down the paper and lit a cigarette; his 'thinking stick' as Grace would say. As he picked up the paper again, he heard a woman's voice.

"Excuse me... you have a lighter please?"

He turned round and saw a woman of about thirty, taking a pack of cigarettes from her bag. "Sure," he said and offered her his lighter. He thought back to his meeting with the ladies that afternoon and wondered how non-smokers got by.

"Oh! *Una crucigrama*... you must be very clever. I am very bad with words... and I... er... *no comprendo* the questions."

"I'm trying to do the crossword," he said diplomatically, "but I'm not very good."

"Please... can I sit with you?" she asked. "I am waiting for my friend, but I do not like to be alone here. Some of the men... they may think I am a bad girl."

"Not at all," said Barton. "Be my guest. But I may not be here for long. I am also waiting for someone."

"Then we are the same, we both wait. Are you waiting for a *senorita*? Is she very pretty?"

"No, unfortunately... he's a big, ugly Irish policeman. What about you, are you waiting for your boyfriend?" He couldn't think what else to say; he'd already worked out why she was there. He wasn't in the market for that, but she would be a pleasant diversion while he waited and he could think of worse ways to spend the time.

"I am meeting a girlfriend... we are going to a late show at the theatre."

Theatre; Barton picked up the crossword again. Eight across, *T-H-E-A-T-E-R*, it was spelt wrong; maybe an American had been filling in the grid earlier. That made the first letter of his clue an *R*, not *E*, and the first word was, *Red... of course! Red Letter.*

"Thank you," he said with a smile. "Oh! I'm sorry that was very rude of me."

"I have helped you?" she asked, smiling seductively.

"Just something you said. Now would you like a drink?"

"I shouldn't drink with strange men," she laughed. "What is your name?"

"My name is Mike," he replied, "and you?"

"I am Juanita. And now that we are not strangers, you may buy me a Cuba libré."

Barton signalled to the waiter. As he was about to order their drinks he noticed that Connor had just walked into the bar. *"Dos cervezas grande, y una Cuba libré, por favor."*

"Is that for your friend? Will he be here soon?" she asked.

"He's here now." A soft Irish brogue announced Dave Connor's presence. "Who's your gorgeous friend, Mike?" he asked.

"Hi Dave, this is Juanita. I've been keeping her company while she waits for her friend."

"I'm very pleased to meet you Juanita… I hope your friend is as lovely as you. Are you doing anything this evening?" asked Connor, turning on his Irish charm. "How would you like to come to dinner with us?"

"Behave yourself, Dave," said Barton sharply.

"Yes she is very beautiful, you will like her," said Juanita as she took out her mobile. "Please excuse me… I must ring her… she is late." She dialled a number and after a short pause, she spoke into the phone. *"Maria, dondé estas? Es muy tarde."*

"Is she coming?" asked Connor.

"Yes, she will be here in a minute."

A couple of minutes Maria arrived. Juanita got up and kissed her on both cheeks. "Maria," she said, "these are my new friends Mike and Dave."

"Pleased to meet you Maria," said Barton getting to his feet and offering the girl his hand.

Connor was drooling; thinking he'd much rather spend the evening with the girls than his boss: *Señoritas… or Mike talking shop? No contest.* "Very pleased to meet you Maria, we were just wondering if you lovely ladies would like to join us for dinner," he said, feeling sharp kick on his left ankle.

"Give it a rest, Dave. Juanita and Maria have tickets for the theatre," growled Barton.

He finished his drink and spoke to Juanita. "We have to go now… enjoy your show… I'm sorry about my friend."

"Hasta luego," said Maria

"Very soon I hope," added Juanita as she kissed Barton on both cheeks.

"I don't think that's very likely… *Adiós, señoritas*," said Barton firmly, ushering Connor towards the door.

"Bloody hell Mike… what's the matter with you?" asked Connor when they were outside. "We were in there. Come on it's not as if Grace and Lorna would ever to find out."

"Don't be a prat, Dave, they're hookers," said Barton. "God you can be dense sometimes."

"They seemed OK... nice girls... bit of class... they were gorgeous. What makes you think that they're tarts?"

"They're working the hotel... that Maria wasn't late... she was standing by the lifts when we came in. Come on let's go and eat. And think yourself lucky ... you couldn't afford them anyway."

"Where are we eating?" asked Connor, as the thought of food took over from his interest in the girls.

"Well any where but here. Let's walk up into the old town and find somewhere. I think there are some pretty good places around Orange Square."

"Ah...! *La Plaza de los Naranjos*," said Connor, showing off. "I fancy a really good steak... I'm bloody famished. It's not too far is it?"

"No, about five minutes," said Barton. "Let's go."

They soon found the large square, surrounded on all sides by bars and restaurants. Even though it was late, most of the tables were occupied, with waiters hurrying between them carrying plates and glasses. Barton stopped at each doorway they passed to look at the menus.

Connor was looking at what other people were eating. "This'll do," he said. "Would you look at the size of that fillet steak the big fella's eating? I'll have one of those. Look that table under the tree's empty."

Without waiting for a response from his boss, he weaved his way between the other diners, making his way towards the empty table. Barton stopped for a moment to speak to a waiter, who was carrying some empty glasses towards the bar, then made his way over to the table.

"I've just ordered a couple of pints of San Miguel," said Barton. "Is that OK?"

"That'll do for me, Mike. What are you having?"

"Cut it out Dave, you're not on holiday," groaned Barton.

Nevertheless, having Dave along would help lighten things up a bit. Barton knew that the afternoon's encounter with Naismith had only been a taste of what was to come and Connor would provide some welcome relief; and support if the going got tough.

Carefree – but not careless, loud and rude – but never offensive, obsessed by detail – but easily distracted by trivia; Dave Connor delighted and annoyed his colleagues in equal measure. The two men had known each other a few years and had become good friends. The difference in their ranks, respected by Connor when it mattered, didn't interfere with their relationship.

They were another oddly matched pair. Connor, several years younger, was Barton's equal in many things; his superior in some. But, whilst Barton had consciously strived to keep out of the box, that people like Harris would have put him in; Connor played up to his stereotype. He was a rough diamond – the hard-drinking, working class boy from East Belfast; always the first with a witty remark and a song for every occasion – one of the lads

Early on, they had found a common bond. Both had lost their fathers, in violent circumstances. Both had been policemen; Sergeant Liam Connor, blown up, along with another RUC officer, in an IRA ambush in the bandit country of South Armagh; Inspector James Barton, the accidental victim of a shooting in leafy Buckinghamshire.

But, the way they dealt with their tragedies was different and Barton often envied Connor, who wore his like a badge of honour, a life to be celebrated and a death that was part of who he was; part of his heritage. Barton rarely spoke of his father, and at times, his ghost was an unbearable burden.

The waiter came to the table with their beer and two menus. Connor ordered for both of them, impressing Barton with his fluent Spanish. "So what's on the agenda for tomorrow, Mike?" he asked, as they waited for their meal to arrive.

"Well, I've got an appointment with Naismith at eleven. I thought you could put your Spanish to good use," said Barton. He continued, pausing frequently to give Connor time to take notes. "I want you to start poking about into Naismith's business… you could start at the town hall… see what you can find… planning applications… property that he owns… that sort of thing… I had a walk up to his office earlier… looks like he's got several companies operating from the building. I made a list." Connor took the list and put it into his notebook. He jotted down notes as Barton continued giving him instructions, "…just poke around… that should keep you busy… Oh! What about…"

"I'd have to go to Malaga for some of this," said Connor. "That's the provincial capital where all the government offices are."

"That's alright, you can take the car… I won't need it tomorrow. I'm going to spend some time going through those files after I've seen Naismith."

"I still don't get it though," said Connor. "There's nothing in the files to suggest that this Naismith has got anything to do with King. They may be brothers, but they grew up in totally different worlds. Your man went to live in the country, with his aunt during the war and never went home again. His brother was only three, when he left, and turned into a right tearaway. He was running errands for gangsters before he was out of short pants. Naismith went to grammar school and became a respectable businessman… local councillor, chairman of a Police Authority… Tory MP…"

Connor stopped and looked at his boss: *We're wasting our time.* From what he'd read in the files there wasn't any connection and he didn't like the idea that he'd come all this way to be Barton's bagman on a wild goose chase. "Come on Mike, you know he spent nearly twenty years standing against everything that Bobby King represented."

Barton was impressed; Connor had obviously been doing his homework. "So what are you getting at Dave?" he asked.

"Well, nobody even knew they were brothers until King was up on that murder charge," said Connor. "Look at all the stuff he's been involved in over the years. All the times he's been pulled in, there's nothing to suggest any involvement with his brother. No, they might have had the same mother and father, but that's all."

"Maybe, that's exactly what they wanted us to think," said Barton.

Chapter 17

Wednesday 7th May 2003

Marbella, Costa del Sol – 11:00 CET

The girl at the desk told Barton that Sir Anthony was busy and asked him to wait. He walked across the marble-floored reception area and sat in a black leather armchair. The table in front of him was covered in glossy magazines and marketing brochures. A glossy brochure for the Jardines de las Montanas Golf and Vacation Resort caught his eye; as he picked it up the receptionist brought him a cup of coffee. "What did you think of it?" she asked.

"Sorry," he said, turning around with a start, "I didn't catch that."

"The new resort, didn't you say you were going there yesterday?"

"Oh! Yes… very impressive."

"Sir Anthony says it will be the finest resort in the area when it's finished. But not for long, we've already started building the next one," she said proudly.

"Where's that?"

"Down the coast towards Estepona, there's a lot of new development there, it's like Marbella was ten years ago. The mayors of Marbella and Estepona are cousins. Everyone says that they're competing with each other. Of course, Sir Anthony knows them both. I think he plays them off one against the other sometimes." The girl laughed. "When we opened a five-star hotel in Estepona a year ago the mayor of Marbella wouldn't speak to him for a month."

Barton made a mental note to send Connor to ask some questions in Estepona, and leafed through the brochure. He'd always thought that property in Spain was quite cheap. These prices made his eyes water; over three hundred grand for a two bed apartment, that was London money. He scanned the pages; small town houses at half a million, villas starting at a million. He started to realise just how much money must be changing hands in this part of the world. There were new developments everywhere; hundreds, no thousands of new properties, the market must be worth billions: *How much of it is dirty money? I bet you could launder a lot of cash out here if you know the right people.*

"Mr Barton, Sir Anthony will see you now. Take the lift to the top floor, he'll meet you there," said the receptionist, pointing in the direction of the lift.

The lift doors opened directly into Naismith's office, which took up the whole of the top floor of the building. The room was about sixty feet long; at one end a huge conference table with chairs for twenty people and at the other a seating area with leather sofas and armchairs, not unlike those in the reception lobby at the resort. Between these two areas was Naismith's desk, an impressive piece of antique Spanish furniture, a massive slab of oak almost the size of a snooker table. Naismith got up from his chair and walked round to the front of the desk as Barton got out of the lift.

"Barton, come in, good to see you," he said reaching out his hand. The handshake was as little firmer, not as cold as before, but still half-hearted and very brief. Barton sensed that, although he was hiding it well, the man was feeling uncomfortable.

"Good morning, Sir Anthony, good of you to see me."

Naismith moved towards the sofas. "We'll sit over here. It's more comfortable," he said. His demeanour had changed since their previous encounter. He'd had time to prepare this time; he wasn't likely to let his guard slip again. Today he was confident and relaxed, looking every bit the archetypal English businessman, in an expensive hand tailored, lightweight, suit. He'd thought of sitting at his desk; a barrier, a useful device to make people feel uncomfortable, inferior, but he'd made a mistake yesterday and he wanted to show the policeman that he didn't need to hide. He was smarter than any policeman; he'd find out what this one wanted, find how much he knew; maybe find out if he had a price. This man had already cost him a lot of money, but there was no need to antagonise him; he'd cooperate; answer all of his questions politely, but tell him nothing. The sooner that he could get rid of him the better.

They sat opposite each other, saying nothing as they sized each other up. Barton had spent hours working out how to play this. He'd rattled the old man yesterday, which would give him the upper hand for a while. But now he'd had time to think and would be prepared; wouldn't be giving anything away. He guessed that the man would have already been making his own enquiries; calling in favours, finding out who he was dealing with and would have his strategy worked out. Any advantage that Barton had would be short lived. It was going to be like playing chess, except that his opponent now controlled all the pieces. Naismith knew what Barton could only suspect.

"I'm sorry about that outburst yesterday," said Naismith, "I don't know what came over me."

"That's alright sir. Think nothing of it. I know the news about your brother must have come as a shock," said Barton, sensing that the man wasn't listening.

He was right. Naismith continued with his own train of thought, seemingly oblivious to Barton's presence, almost as if he was talking to himself. "It's just that I haven't been called that by anyone for so long," he said. "I've always hated that damned name and... well I'm sorry I lost my temper. You weren't to know. But I'd like to know why you said it."

"I'm sorry about that sir," Barton replied, believing that there was something more to this; something he would explore later. "I didn't know what it meant; it was just something that your brother said to me."

"Oh! Yes, you said that you had something to tell me," said Naismith giving his attention to Barton again.

"Well sir I'm not sure that it will make any sense. You have to understand that your brother was dying and had difficulty talking." Barton took a small tape recorder from his pocket. "It's probably better if you listen to this," he said, switching on the machine. He'd already cued the tape to start at the right place.

They both listened as the tape played Bobby King's dying words: *'Lenny... talk to Lenny... I let him down... tell him... I'm sorry... .tell him... I love him'.*

Barton switched off the tape, before it ended; he didn't want Naismith to hear the rest. Not yet: *'I did it for him',* he'd play that card later. "That's it, sir. That's all he said. I don't know what it means. I was hoping that you might be able to shed some light on it. Can you think what he might have meant?"

"I'm afraid I have no idea. I can't think what he meant about being sorry. Unless..."

"Yes, sir," Barton said, encouraging the man to continue.

"Well I'm sure that you must already know about this... but he ruined my political career. He was charged with murder in1987. I was a Home Office minister at the time, had a bloody good chance of getting into the Cabinet... and then this sleazy little reporter from one of the Sunday scandal sheets found out that we were brothers. Well, that was it... at least his editor had the decency to call me before they went to press... but I couldn't stay on. Not with an election in the offing... much too embarrassing for the party... and I felt I'd let Margaret down. Of course the men in grey suits had words with me... they were very supportive... but I'd already decided to resign... I thought it best to get right away, so I sold up and came here."

"So you think he wanted to say sorry for that, for ending your career in politics?" said Barton, wondering if a man like Bobby King would really give a damn: *No there's something else. King wouldn't have been asked for me just to tell me that.*

"Well, I can't think of anything else. It bloody well took him long enough though... I mean it's been sixteen years. I didn't get anything from him at the time not even a bloody note... but then you don't expect anything from people like that."

"Like what, sir?"

"Criminals, gangsters, whatever it is you people call them these days... Oh! I knew about him alright," said Naismith starting to become rather animated. "He was bloody lucky that he didn't come anywhere near me when he was alive. They say that blood is thicker than water Chief Inspector, but not in this case. He might have been my brother. But he was still scum, just like the rest of his kind. They should have locked him up and thrown away the key. But instead, he did what...? Six years... then they let him out. It was a bloody disgrace. The courts are too bloody soft on them. If I'd had my way..."

He looked at Barton, and realised that he was maybe playing the righteous indignation card a bit too strongly. "I'm sorry Barton; I'm starting to sound like a politician. You didn't come here to hear me sounding off."

"I gather you had something of a reputation for that when you were an MP," said Barton: *Come on, play on his vanity, and keep him on a roll. You never know what he'll let slip.* Barton opened another door, to see where it would lead. "There were a lot of coppers who'd have liked to have seen you as Home Secretary. I think you would have made a big difference."

"That's what I'd hoped for too, but that's all in the past now. In a way he did me a favour... I don't think I'd have lasted long in the party after '87. It wasn't the same as when we first got in. In the old days being a Tory meant something... there was a sense of duty... wanting to serve your country, and give something back. You're probably too young to remember Margaret when she first got in... but she made this speech on the steps of Number 10... quoted Saint Francis of Assisi. OK, I know a lot of people thought it was a bit over the top, a bit too much humility... but that's what it was all about. That first appearance as Prime Minister... that was a defining moment... She was a very caring person, who loved the country and the British people. You probably remember her in later years...as the Iron Lady. And she was... she was prepared to defend her country against any threat, whoever the enemy, and whatever the cost.

'But I digress. We weren't in it for ourselves... the country was on its knees... and we had to repair all the damage that those bloody socialists and their bleeding heart liberal friends had done. People used to talk about being one of us... you might have heard the phrase... it was usually twisted by our opponents to sound like something sinister... they tried to make us out to be like a bunch of Freemasons. But let me tell you... it meant something much more than that... people of a like mind sharing common ideals... there I go again. Sorry, Barton... I'm not boring you, am I?"

"Not at all sir, "said Barton: W*hat a load of bullshit.* He'd heard it all before, and it always sounded the same; politicians using a lot of words to say nothing important. But he encouraged Naismith to say more. "It's fascinating, sir."

197

"Well... as I was saying, we had ideals and a sense of purpose. I suppose that you might think me old fashioned... I suppose I am. But, I was brought up in the old school, where we didn't go into politics for what we could get out of it... it was what you put back that mattered. Later, of course, all that started to change... old values started to disappear, and men like Carrington, Whitelaw, Joseph... they were getting old. We thought we were going to be in government for ever... and like many others, I suppose that I was too concerned with waiting to step into the shoes of the old guard... men I admired, like Gerald Browning, you know, my wife's father. We didn't see that there was a new breed, climbing on the bandwagon. By the third election, the party was full of the wrong types... people who'd made a quick buck and wanted more... they were only in it for themselves and they didn't give a toss about duty to the country. Then of course it all started to go wrong... it wasn't Margaret's fault... she was already becoming isolated... surrounded by people she couldn't trust anymore, weak little men with no sense of loyalty... she eventually became a caricature of the leader who delivered us from socialism. And then... look at what those spineless scumbags did to her... they stabbed her in the back and let that bloody man Major and his sleazy cronies take over. Yes, I was glad I got out when I did."

"And of course... you've done pretty well out here," Barton remarked flippantly; intentionally, to get a reaction.

"You've got a bloody cheek Inspector," said Naismith, brushing the remark aside with a shrug of his shoulders. He was angered by Barton's impertinence, but chose not to rise to the bait. "But you're right of course. I couldn't have made this much money if I'd ridden out the storm and stayed on... And I've certainly made more out here than I would have done in England."

A secretary appeared with coffee, the interruption was welcome, giving both men an opportunity collect their thoughts "Have you ever thought of going back? Barton asked, idly. "Things are different now."

"Oh! You think so. Just look at what Blair's doing to the country... Third Way, no bloody idea which way, if you ask me... with their nanny state and political bloody correctness... pandering to all those bloody foreigners... human rights..."

Barton immediately started to regret his question, as Naismith, now refreshed, launched into another diatribe.

"...And then the way they let the bloody EU walk all over them... licking the arses of bureaucrats in Brussels... I suppose you know that everyone else just pays lip service to their directives. But not the British, we play by the rules and naively believe that everyone else will too. So our businesses get shackled by all those bloody awful employment laws... health and safety... working hours directives... equal opportunities... For God's sake...! In my day you made your own opportunities. Mind you I don't really blame the socialists... they're just carrying on where Major left off."

Naismith paused for a moment and glanced at the wall clock: *I could go on like this all day, just keep on running down the clock old boy.* He started to brag, "Yes... I got out at the right time. Land was dirt-cheap back then. Bloody Spaniards didn't have a clue about what it was really worth. I just bought the right sites and sat on them... watched the value increase. It's hard to believe that this whole coast was once just a string of small fishing villages. It still would be if it wasn't for people like me. And look at it now... property developer's heaven. Go back... Never."

He laughed, "I'm sorry Barton... now you've got me on my other favourite subject. I've always loved the thrill I get from making money... and when you're as good at it as I am... well it just seems to multiply by itself. It's an easy life over here. Look at all this... this isn't hard work. It just needs a nose for a good deal. Come over here and have a look."

He got up and led the way to the conference table. Barton saw that the bank of glass display cases, lining the wall behind the table, contained architect's models – hotels, golf courses, shopping malls, office buildings – each labelled with a date and location. "This is only a few. If I had them all out they'd fill the room," Naismith said proudly. "Look at this one, the first five-star hotel on the Costa del Sol."

"Yes, your receptionist told me that the mayor of Marbella was none too pleased about that," said Barton.

"Oh! Juan Delgado, he's just like all these bloody Spaniards... you know, they're like children. If one of them gets a new toy the others sulk until you give them a better one."

"Isn't this where we were yesterday?" asked Barton pointing to the end case.

"Yes, impressive isn't it? But wait till you see this one." Naismith pressed a button on the side of the table. A section of the top opened and a glass case rose silently from below. If it was meant to impress, it certainly didn't fail.

"Wow!" was all that Barton could say.

"Three golf courses, Ballesteros designed one of them. Five-star hotel, conference centre with two more hotels, villas, apartments, shopping mall..." Naismith was bursting with pride as he listed resort's facilities. "Estepona's getting this... you should have seen Delgado's face when he found out."

Naismith looked at his watch: *So far so good.* It was time to play another card and throw the policeman off a bit more. "I'm sorry Barton, but I'll have to call a halt, now. I've got some guests coming for lunch on the yacht."

"That's OK, sir, I need to get back to the hotel and make some phone calls," said Barton, silently congratulating his opponent, neither man had given anything away: *Honours even, maybe I'm still just ahead.* He was wondering where and when they'd play the next round; unaware that, as Naismith played his next card, he already had that planned.

"Oh! If you're going back to the hotel could you do me small favour. One of our charities is having a big fund raising do, the manager's a good friend of mine and he always manages to sell a couple of hundred tickets for us." Naismith walked back to his desk and opened a drawer. He took out a large envelope. "I was going to drop these off this morning, but I was late. You wouldn't mind would you?" he said.

"Of course not, sir," said Barton taking the envelope.

"I'm sure that I know you from somewhere Barton," said Naismith as he pressed the button to call the lift. "You said something yesterday. That we'd met before?"

"Yes, sir, you were at my father's funeral."

"Barton… Barton… Yes of course, I thought the name was familiar. It was your father… the policeman who was killed. God that was twenty years ago… Terrible, tragic business… it should have been me, you know, but I was lucky. Still at least the bastard who did it is still rotting in jail… they'll never let him out. Even Blair's lot wouldn't dare."

Barton shivered as the ghost awakened. He couldn't tell if the last remark was contrived or merely a slip of the tongue. Either way, it betrayed Naismith's insincerity, and told him to be careful. "I try not to think about it too much, sir… It's better that way," he said, letting his head drop slightly, avoiding contact with Naismith's eyes. He didn't want this man to see how much the memories could still hurt.

"Of course, it must have been difficult for you. He was a good man. I'm sorry for bringing back bad memories," said Naismith gravely. He sounded sincere; but, an ex-politician with years of practice? "Look, if you're not doing anything this afternoon, why don't you come and join us for lunch."

"Thank you, sir. I've never had lunch on a yacht."

"I'll see you in about an hour then. You'll find us in the marina at Puerto Banus. Just ask for the Lady Margaret."

Barton shook Naismith's hand and got into the lift, wondering whether the lunch invitation was as spontaneous as it seemed or contrived.

Barton walked back to the hotel, deep in thought. He cursed himself for bringing up the past; he'd been the one who prompted it the day before. Why couldn't he have just told Naismith that he was mistaken; that they'd never met?

He hadn't realised how much it would hurt. He needed to keep his mind focussed on the reason that he was here. He couldn't afford to let his father's ghost distract him. But now the memories came flooding back again.

His grandparents had left their home in the Caribbean in the fifties, with their son James. They'd come to England, like so many others; seeking opportunities for a better life and to help rebuild their mother nation. What they found were poorly paid jobs, bad housing, and prejudice. Against all the odds Barton's father had gained a good education and, after serving in the army, became one of the first black officers in the Metropolitan Police. When Barton had been about ten years old, his father had transferred to the Buckinghamshire force and worked his way up the ranks to Inspector. Although he had never been able to tell him, Barton would always be proud to be his father's son.

Twenty years ago, during the General Election campaign, he had been on duty when an attempt was made on the life of the Conservative candidate. The gunman's first shot had almost missed its target, leaving Anthony Naismith MP with just a minor flesh wound; the second shot would probably have killed him if James Barton hadn't got in the way.

Politicians of all parties called a truce until the day of the funeral. The Home Secretary represented the Government, but it was Anthony Naismith who gave an address on behalf of all the parties; a eulogy to the man who had saved his life. As a young man, Barton had experienced mixed emotions that day; a great sadness, tempered by the memories that, even in his grief, brought moments of joy and happiness. There'd been humility and admiration as he saw the dignity with which his mother carried herself; and pride as he listened to the tributes of his father's colleagues and honour at meeting men that his father had admired. But he'd felt anger and revulsion as Naismith's tribute turned into an election speech; feelings that grew stronger in the days that followed as the political circus played to full houses and his father's death became a cause célèbre in the race to win votes. He couldn't hold Naismith responsible for his father's death, but he still blamed him. And he'd made Barton's pain worse by playing his political games.

The anaesthesia of time had dulled the pain, but he had never stopped grieving, and the memories always returned at this time of the year, inflaming the wounds that had never really healed. He'd known, even before he'd spoken to Trevor; there was something inside telling him that seeing Naismith would heal the wounds and lay the ghost to rest. He hadn't dared to admit it; Trevor would have stopped him. Grace had understood and she'd warned him to be careful; she knew that he wouldn't be able to ignore his feelings. He thought that he could deal with it but, as he walked into the hotel, the hate, that he'd once felt for Naismith, stirred inside him again.

He was still holding the envelope and he went to the desk and asked for the manager. As he handed him the envelope, it dawned on him what a fool he'd been. He didn't believe in coincidences; this was all a part of the game they were playing. It was all about truth and lies; he was here to find the truth and he had a feeling that he'd just fallen for one of the Puppet Master's lies.

Chapter 18

Wednesday 7th May 2003

Marbella, Costa del Sol – 14:30 CET

Barton ordered a taxi at the hotel reception for the short journey to Puerto Banus, a few kilometres to the west of Marbella. In less than thirty years the town had grown from nothing into a bustling playground for the rich and famous. Barton had been here a few years earlier on one of their rare holidays. They hadn't stayed here; it was way out of their price range. Like most visitors they'd come on one of the package company's day trips. Throughout the year the place was full of tourists; sitting outside the bars, watching the expensive cars that drove slowly by day and night, or walking around the vast marina looking longingly at the yachts. Others spent their time window shopping at the designer stores on the waterfront or wandering around El Corte Ingles shopping mall. Barton had neither the time nor the inclination for any of these pursuits today; he had to find the yacht.

He knew that Naismith's yacht would be large and expensive, but that didn't make it easy to find; there were hundreds of them. Row upon row of gleaming white hulls, equipped with state of the art navigation systems and powerful engines; mostly superfluous; there were yachts here that could probably cross the Atlantic, certainly cruise the length and breadth of the Mediterranean with ease, but the most never ventured out of the harbour. The beautiful, luxurious craft were statements of wealth; kept here because it was the place to be seen, a place to entertain and impress. Somewhere amongst this huge fleet was the Lady Margaret, and Barton made his way to the harbourmaster's office to ask where she was berthed.

He was directed to a pier on the far side of the marina, and walked slowly past the boats, glancing to the left and right in turn, looking at the name and port of registration painted on the stern of each yacht that he passed. About halfway along the pier, a group of holidaymakers asked him if he could take their picture. They gave him a digital camera and posed in front of a large motor cruiser making faces and pointing to the name on the transom, 'Bronwen – Cardiff'. "See that, she's come all the way from Wales," said one of the men, as he took back the camera. "Isn't she a beauty," he said proudly, as though the photograph conferred on him some sort of ownership, "Bronwen, that's my mam's name you know. She's from Cardiff too." Barton smiled, but he doubted the vessel had ever been anywhere near Wales.

Before he reached the next yacht, he heard a voice behind him. "Mike… Mike Barton, what on earth are you doing here?"

He turned around and found himself looking at a familiar face. "Colin," he said, after the moment of surprise had left him, "fancy seeing you. How are you?"

Colin Marshall looked a picture of health, his face, and arms displaying the deep, all year tan that immediately distinguishes the residents from the tourists. For a man who'd retired eight years earlier due to poor health, he looked remarkably fit.

"I'm very well thanks," said Marshall, "it's hard not to be out here. Get out of the job and head south for the sun as soon as you can, that's my advice. Are you on holiday? You should have called… you could have stayed with us."

"No I'm afraid I'm working… just here for a couple of days."

"Well you still should have called. We've got a lot of catching up to do. What is it… seven, eight years? Anyway what are you doing hanging around the marina?"

"Sorry, Colin, I forgot you'd moved out here. Look, I'll call you later. I can't stop now. I'm meeting someone for lunch, if I can find his yacht."

"Well things must be looking up," said Marshall. "Who do you know who owns a yacht?"

"Well I don't really know him, I told you, Colin it's work. I'm meeting Sir Anthony Naismith."

"No, you're kidding. That's where I'm going. Come on, it's just along here on the right. But tell me, what does the NCS want with Tony Naismith?"

"Nothing much, I'm just making some enquiries about his brother."

Barton expected the ex-policeman to show some sort of interest. He knew that Marshall had gone up against King several times during his career and thought that he'd be well aware of the connection. But Marshall made no comment and simply pointed to a yacht. "There it is," he said, "not bad. Eh!"

"Wow! This must have set him back a bit," said Barton, reckoning that The Lady Margaret was about thirty metres; not as big as some of the neighbouring yachts, but still very impressive.

"About six million," said Marshall, "…if you think the outside looks good, wait till he shows you round inside. It's like a floating villa."

"Come on board," shouted Naismith, looking down from the upper deck. "We're all up here. You know the way, Colin."

Marshall led the way through the main saloon and up the staircase to the bridge. Naismith was standing at the top of the stairs, talking to Peter Browning and two other men. Marshall said something to them as he walked past and made his way towards a group of women. He greeted each of the women with a kiss on the cheek and poured himself a glass of wine.

Barton hesitated at the top of the stairs. The game was on again and he wondered how Naismith would explain a policeman's presence to this gathering; or were they playing the game too? Naismith left the two men he was talking to and moved towards Barton. "Glad you could make it Barton," he said, "…come and get a drink, and then I'll introduce you to everyone…wine or beer?"

Barton looked around and saw that, apart from Colin Marshall, all the men were drinking beer. "I'll have a beer thanks," he said.

Naismith opened the fridge and displayed a selection of lagers to Barton. "Thank you, sir," said Barton as he took the first bottle that came to hand.

"I think that, for the sake of appearances, we had better use first names, so call me Tony," said Naismith. "Now, what about some introductions?"

Barton shook hands with Peter Browning, and the other two men, who were introduced as Brian Jackson and Martin Davenport. Then Naismith steered him towards the table where the women were sitting. "I take it you already know Colin," he said as they approached the table.

"Yes, sir, he used to be my boss."

"Small world, what!" exclaimed Naismith. "And you can drop the sir, remember, it's Tony and Mike, OK?"

"Helen, why don't you introduce Mike to your friends? If you'll excuse me for a few minutes, Mike, I've got some business to discuss before lunch." He signalled to Marshall and the two men walked towards the stairs, following the other three men, who were already making their way down to the lower deck.

Helen looked up and smiled, "Hi Mike, nice to see you again," she said. The other two women were younger than Helen and Jean. One was forty-ish, with a similar dress sense to the older women; although her clothes were only first division, rather than the premier league designer originals sported by her three companions. Barton thought that he'd seen her somewhere before, but couldn't think where. The other woman was casually dressed, wearing a pair of tight jeans and a cotton halter top; she was about thirty and looked very out of place in this company. But, Barton knew exactly where he'd seen her before.

"Ladies, let me introduce you to my handsome friend," said Helen, then she laughed, "…but keep off, I saw him first."

"Mike, this is Angela Marshall," she said.

"Angela? Oh! Of course," he said, he recognised her now. "…you're Colin's wife. Good to see you again," said Barton. The last time they'd met, she'd been in uniform.

"Nice to see you again, I didn't expect you to remember me," she said.

Barton remembered her as WPC Angela Evans. There'd been quite a scandal when the Commander's affair with a junior officer became public knowledge. Marshall's wife had left him and Angela had been around to provide comfort. Rumours had spread, but they'd been very discreet, and it wasn't until after Marshall announced his intention to retire, that their relationship became more open. Colin Marshall was married to the job, which was why his wife had left him; the sort that keeps on going forever. His early retirement on grounds of ill health surprised even his closest colleagues, and when Angela resigned, only a few days later, the tongues started wagging. The following week Colin Marshall, a stickler for formalities of rank and the rule book, was seen in his office, locked in a passionate embrace with the WPC, fifteen years his junior. They'd already put in their papers so the top brass couldn't do much about it. They both left quietly, a period of 'gardening leave' filling the remainder of their service. And now here they were having lunch with a multi-millionaire.

"Sounds as if you two have some catching up to do, "said Helen, "But first you must meet Juanita."

"We've already met," he said. "It's nice to see you again, señorita. This is a coincidence. How was the show last night?"

"And I'm very pleased to meet you again Mike. We missed the show, because Maria was late. What a pity. We could have come to dinner with you and your friend. Now sit next to me so that I can get to know you better." said Juanita, as she patted the seat next to hers.

Barton accepted her invitation; he was intrigued: *Marshall and now this girl? This can't be coincidence.* Whatever the game was, Naismith had upped the stakes. Suddenly, Barton felt vulnerable; he was used to being in control, but in this situation, he was the one being controlled. Here he was in a foreign country, following up a hunch, driven by a ghost that had haunted him for twenty years. He'd not had a scrap of evidence; just gone with his instincts, and now this: *What's Naismith playing at, bringing me here?*

"Do you live here in Marbella?" asked Barton, making small talk and wishing he was somewhere else.

"For part of the year, yes," she said, "...my family have many friends in Andalucía and I visit them often... I come to Marbella to buy clothes... I love all the designer shops here... their clothes are so sexy."

Barton glanced down at her legs. She obviously didn't buy those jeans in Gap, he thought. "You like my legs?" she said, "...maybe we can go to the beach later and you can see them properly."

Barton tried to hide his embarrassment; he wasn't used to beautiful women flirting with him. "I'm sorry," he said, "...I don't think I'll have time for the beach. I've got to meet someone later."

"Maybe you would rather come to my apartment," she said seductively, turning her head and pointing to one of the apartment blocks overlooking the marina. "It's very close, just over there. It wouldn't take us a moment to get there. My bedroom has views of the harbour and the sea."

Helen interrupted, "Juanita, you're embarrassing Mike," she said crossly, "...do you have to flirt like that with every man you meet."

Juanita pouted and looked at Helen. "I'm sorry'" she said, "...I didn't mean anything. I was just being friendly."

She looked at Barton "Would you pour me another glass of wine, please?" she asked.

Barton reached across the table and took a wine bottle from the cooler; it was empty. He stood up and reached across for another bottle; also empty.

Jean smiled at him, "There's some more bottles in the fridge over there, Mike," she said. Barton walked over to the fridge, bent down and took out a bottle of wine. As he stood up he felt a hand on his waist. Before he could turn around, Juanita spoke. "Bitch, she's just jealous. She hasn't had a man for ages. You know they sleep in separate rooms."

Her hand moved from Barton's waist and slid into his pocket. He turned quickly and moved away from her. "But I'm sure you could make a girl very happy, Mike," she whispered, "...I bet you could keep it up all night. I've never had a man like you. Is it true what they say, about you black men?"

Barton didn't know what to say; nor did he have time to say anything. Juanita threw her arms around his neck, and kissed him hard on the lips, her tongue forcing its way into his mouth. She pressed her body against his, gyrating her hips; Barton cast a glance across to the table. The other three women were talking and laughing; none of them seemed aware of the scene being acted out just ten feet away.

The cavalry arrived just in time. Barton heard footsteps on the wooden stairs. A steward carrying a large tray appeared and Juanita pulled away. She patted his crotch and winked at him. "Another time big boy," she said playfully. She took the bottle of wine from his hand, turned and walked back to the table, followed by the steward.

Over lunch, Barton learned a little more about his fellow guests. Colin Marshall and Angela had married shortly after they left the Met. "Sorry we didn't invite you to the wedding, we decided to keep it to family. Given the circumstances, it didn't seem right to invite any of our former colleagues. I know that you were OK about it, Mike. But some of our so called friends said some pretty nasty things about us at the time."

They'd moved to Marbella where Marshall had set up a small security business, advising wealthy clients on how to protect their properties. "Didn't really know bugger all about all the technology. You know, alarm systems, CCTV and all that. I left all that stuff to the specialists. But you'd be surprised how much some people will pay just to have an ex-commander from the Met spend a few hours poking about their house and telling them how easy it would be for someone to get in."

Within a year, he had bought out a couple of local alarm companies and a couple of years later he branched out into security guarding. "That's where the real money is in this game. Everywhere you go on the Costa... the hotels, shopping malls, apartment blocks, holiday complexes... you'll see guys in uniforms... and if you're with a twenty kilometre radius of Marbella there's a good chance that they work for me. That's how I met Tony. He needed security for one of his developments and we got the job."

Brian Jackson was an arrogant bastard, who talked about nothing but cars and money, neither of which would have been Barton's chosen subject on Mastermind. The Londoner was much younger than the other men, about forty five; and like Juanita he seemed a bit out of place in this company, but it turned out that he too had business contacts with Naismith and the others. He ran a luxury car dealership with branches in Marbella and Malaga. A few years earlier Naismith had bought a share in the company when Jackson needed capital to fund the development of new showrooms. He and Marshall had recently set up a new company installing high-tech car security systems.

"Rollers, Ferrari, Porsche..." he said rolling off a huge list of expensive marques, "...you name any car you like and a good thief can crack the manufacturers' systems. Now the stuff we do... biometrics, it's all state of the art stuff. You could park the bloody thing, with the doors open, the keys and the engine running, and it'll still be there when you get back. Unless it's programmed for the person in the diving seat, everything shuts down. Of course, if the pros, stealing to order, really want it, they'll still take it. But they'll usually look for something that's easier."

"I'd have thought that if someone's car gets stolen, it'd be good for your new car business," said Barton, trying to contribute to the conversation, "...I mean, if a car's pinched, they've got to buy a new one, right."

"Not a lot of money in selling new cars Mike. Even at the top end the margins aren't what they were, the real money is in servicing and trade-ins. I might only make what... twenty grand on a new Ferrari... less if it's an insurance job, but I'll make that much again servicing it over two years. Then I'll give the guy seventy-five grand... for a car that he paid a hundred and twenty five for...

and sell it on for ninety-five. I can tell you there are plenty of people out here who don't know, or don't care that their 'prancing horse' is going to cost them thirty grand a year. And for what? … Maybe three thousand kilometres a year… that's about ten quid a mile."

Barton didn't think much to Jackson's maths, but he wasn't really been listening. He was deep in thought; trying to remember where he had come across this man before.

Naismith engaged him in a conversation that he was having with Browning. "I was just saying to Peter, that it's about time he sold up and came out here permanently. What do you think, Mike?"

He couldn't think why Naismith should ask his opinion, but readily joined in; anything to get away from the obnoxious Jackson. "Sorry, I thought you lived here already, Peter," he said. "Jean said you had a villa."

"We do. Jean spends most of the year over here, but I still have a business at home. Then there's my father…"

"Oh! Come on Peter. The old man doesn't need you, that's just an excuse." said Naismith, The truth is, Peter's still labouring under the belief that the Tories will get back in and put everything back as it was, and he wants to keep his options open."

"I thought that you'd want to see that, too." said Barton.

"Of course I do, but I'm a realist. It won't happen in my life time, not with the people running the party now," said Naismith. "No, as I said this morning the country's gone to the dogs."

"So is there anything that would make you go back?" asked Barton.

"Well, unlike most of people running the party, I'd start by giving give the Scots their independence. We've nothing to lose, and we've had all their oil anyway… And you'd get rid of Blair and half the Labour cabinet into the bargain… Let the Welsh and Irish go as well and maybe the government will start thinking of the English for once…"

"Oh! Tony, I've never heard such rubbish," said Martin Douglas.

"No, I mean it… and it's about time people started to take it seriously… or there won't be anyone English left… just look at it, they keep letting all those bloody foreigners in, there'll soon be more mosques than churches. Do you know, I read something in the Times last week… white people are soon going to be a minority in Leicester…"

"Tony, that's enough!" said Helen angrily. "I'm sorry, Mike."

"Sorry, Mike," said Naismith, "I've nothing against you, personally… but surely even someone like you can see what mess it all is. I didn't mean to cause any offence."

"None taken," said Barton; he'd heard it all before.

After lunch, Barton found himself sitting alone with Martin Davenport. It occurred to Barton that these men, Naismith, Marshall, and Jackson, all had something in common. They all loved making money, and telling people about it, and he found it quite refreshing to talk to Davenport, who didn't seem to share anything in common with the others; neither money nor politics.

Martin Davenport QC was nearly seventy; he'd retired twelve years earlier due to his wife's poor health. They had moved to Spain for the climate and a quieter pace of life.

"We had a villa about thirty miles off the coast," he said, "...up in the mountains. The air's very good up there. We bought the house about fifteen years ago... when Felicity first became ill... we found this wonderful spa in a place called Tolox. People come from all over Spain to take the waters. We made many good friends and moved there permanently when I retired. For a while, it was idyllic and I had plenty of time for walking, reading, and..."

But, his wife had died only a couple of years later and he had moved to the coast where he now lived alone. "I know that it sounds callous old boy... but I sometimes think that I should have waited... I was a bloody good silk... I might have been a judge by now. But it was too late to go back and there was nobody there for me anyway."

Barton enjoyed Davenport's company; he was cultured and intelligent and spoke with a passion about the history and culture of the region, urging Barton to come back and visit the places that the tourists didn't go to. Barton wondered what he had in common with these arrogant money-grabbers, but it turned out that his relationship with the others was also a business one.

"After my wife died," he explained, "...I just needed to do something to occupy my mind and keep me busy. The only thing that I know is the law... but I couldn't practice law in Spain. If I'd been ten years younger I might have taken the Spanish bar exam... but I was too old for all that. When I moved to the Costa I found that were are a lot of English businessmen... who didn't trust Spanish lawyers." He smiled and chuckled, "...not that they really trust English ones either, but at least we speak the same language. Anyway, I make quite a nice living... acting as a sort of go between...giving people like Tony some reassurance that they aren't being cheated in their legal affairs. Not really necessary of course... the average Spanish lawyer is no more likely to cheat you than a solicitor back home." He smiled again, "...it's just that they seem to take even longer to do it."

A little later as Barton was leaving the game took another turn. After taking his leave of the other guests, he walked down the stairs and through the saloon with Naismith. It occurred to him that after his outburst at the golf club, the old man had been remarkably civil today, even friendly towards him, although he was sure that the 'someone like you' remark was intended to keep him at a distance. He was even starting to wonder if maybe he'd got it wrong. Maybe Naismith wasn't playing games; maybe Colin Marshall and Juanita were exactly what they seemed and there presence here was pure coincidence.

"I'm sorry that we didn't get much of a chance to speak privately today," said Naismith. "When are you going back to England?"

"Friday morning… unless I can get a flight tomorrow."

"Well I'm going to have a day off tomorrow. Why don't you come up to the house? Nobody else will be there… Helen's going to see friends… so we'll be on our own. I think that there are a few loose ends that we should clear up." He handed Barton a business card.

"I've already got one of these," said Barton.

"That one has got my address and private phone number on the back. See you tomorrow."

Barton was halfway along the pier when he heard Juanita. "Mike! Wait for me," she called out. He pretended not to hear and carried on walking, but she caught him up and took his arm.

She pouted and said, "Mike, I am very cross with you. You didn't speak to me at lunch… and you didn't say goodbye. But I saw you looking at me… do you like me? Wouldn't you like to spend a nice time with me?" She smiled seductively, "Maybe we could have a little fun."

He tried to stop, but she still had her arm through his and carried on walking. "Look," he said firmly, "…I don't know what's going on, but I'm not interested. I've got a wife at home, who I love very much… and I'm not about to cheat on her. And certainly not with a spoilt little tart like you." He immediately wished that he hadn't said that. She wasn't really interested in him; just playing the old man's game, whatever that was.

"I'm sorry, Mike… Helen is right, I am *una coqueta*… I am always, what do you say…? Flirting. But it doesn't mean anything… I just like men. Those people they are all very boring, but you are different… interesting. Let me walk with you… Please."

The way that she said *'plee-ease'* Barton could tell that she was used to getting her own way with men. He felt flattered and although he knew, it was a game he saw no harm in going along with it for a few minutes. She also seemed a little bit drunk, and the heels that she was wearing were not the most suitable footwear on the planks of the pier. She was holding onto his arm for support, and as they walked side by side past the shops that fronted the harbour, he hardly noticed that she had taken his hand. "So, why were you at lunch with a bunch of people who you obviously dislike so much?" he asked, knowing that whatever she said would probably be a lie. But he had a feeling that he'd learn the real answer before this was all over.

"Oh! My uncle has some business with Tony. I don't know about those things... it's so boring... but every time I come to Marbella, they invite me to spend time with them. You know... lunch on the boat, dinner at the villa, shopping with Helen and her boring friends. But I have to do it because I love my uncle... and they are his friends... and I think my uncle arranges it... he worries that I may be a bad girl." She sighed and said, "I shall be so pleased when Fernando is back... and we can go home, or to Italy perhaps. I love Milano."

"Who's Fernando...? Your husband? Boyfriend?" he asked.

"What kind of girl do you think I am?" she exclaimed. "I am a good Catholic... do you think that I would be here with you if I was married?" She laughed out loud, "Fernando is my brother."

She stopped outside a bar and pulled him towards a table under the awning. "Buy me a drink," she said, turning on the spoilt little girl again.

"Don't you think that you've had enough," said Barton, thinking that the game had gone on too long and that it was now time to get away.

"Please... just one. This is such a nice bar and those sofas look so comfortable... I could curl up and go to sleep. Please... just a little one."

'Plee-ease'. He gave in. "OK, but just coffee and then I must go," he said firmly. They sat on a sofa and Barton called to the waiter. "*Dos café solo, por favor.*" By the time that their coffee arrived, she was asleep, with her head resting on Barton's shoulder. And, after the huge lunch and a couple of beers too many, Barton was starting to feel drowsy himself.

The coffee was very strong and hit the spot. He ordered again and the second cup seemed to revitalise Juanita. "Oh! Those boring people," she looked at her watch and sighed, "...I've wasted so much of the day. Look it's past four, and I haven't been shopping yet."

As he told Connor later that evening, Barton really couldn't remember much about the next two hours. After a while, all the shops had looked the same. He remembered some of the price tags though, and the astronomical sums that had rung up on the cash tills. It had been a lesson in Power Shopping.

He remembered the last boutique; that was where he had finally put his foot down. "No, Juanita. You can't buy any more shoes. How the hell are we going to carry them?"

"We'll get a taxi," she said, and, without giving Barton a chance for further protest, she sat down and started pointing to shoes, "*Esos, rojo y esos... y esos... dos, blanco y rosa...*" snapping her orders as the shop assistant, obediently ran back and forth, carrying boxes. Juanita tried on each pair for no more than a few seconds, accepting or rejecting them with barely a glance at her feet. Within fifteen minutes, the floor was littered with boxes and another three carriers were added to Barton's burden.

He didn't tell Connor everything. There were some things that he could remember, but wished he could forget; better still if they hadn't happened at all. Things that he knew people would read the wrong way; things that he might live to regret.

Her apartment was on the top floor and he had found himself standing at her door laden with carriers. "Put them in there," she said opening a door, "...just leave them on the bed."

Oh! God. What am I doing? Now he was in her bedroom; and all he wanted to do was get out, fast. But she took his hand and pulled him over to the window.

"Please... you must see my beautiful view now that you are here," she said.

'*Plee-ease', s*he was doing it again. "No stop!" he protested.

She took no notice threw open the doors and gently pushed him out onto the balcony. She stood behind him and nuzzled the back of his neck. He felt her hands slide down below from waist and into his trouser pockets. He moved away.

"I'm sorry," she said coyly, "...I am a bad girl."

She pointed towards the sea. "Look over there... you can see the mountains in Africa," she said excitely "...and over there is Gibraltar. I told you I had a beautiful view?"

"It's lovely and you have a beautiful apartment, but now I must go." He said, trying to put on his serious policeman's face: G*et out, now! Walk away!* But his feet didn't seem to be taking any notice.

"I know... but let me thank you for my nice time."

He knew what was about to happen, and later he told himself that he just hadn't been quick enough on his feet. The episode on the boat was about to be repeated. Her arms wrapped tightly around his neck, and her tongue snaked into his mouth. She put one of her arms behind her neck for a moment and drew away from him. Her top fell to her waist, exposing her breasts. Although she had released her hold on his neck, he didn't move away. Later he would curse himself for not seizing the opportunity to turn and run.

She pulled herself close to him again, greedily kissing his mouth. This time he responded and his tongue started to explore her hungry mouth. She dropped a hand to his waist. Her hand moved down towards his groin and she gasped, "It is true… it's so big." She kissed him again and then, took hold of his belt and led him back into the room.

She smiled and said, "And now it is time," she paused and laughed "…for you to go." Barton watched as she covered her breasts and ran her fingers through her thick black hair. At that moment, he didn't know whether he was relieved or disappointed. "I'm sorry Mike… It's a game… do you know that they can see us from the boat? I hope that bitch Helen got a good look."

She led him to the door and walked to the lift with him, they rode to the ground floor in silence. As he stepped out into the street, she leaned towards him and kissed him on the cheek. "Thank you'" she sighed, "…I had a lovely day. You are a beautiful man."

"Goodbye, Juanita," he said, and turned to walk away. "It was nice meeting you, but…"

She took his hand, pulled him back, and put her arms round his waist. "I would love to fuck with you… even though I'm a good Catholic girl," she said and kissed him again; this time on the lips.

"But, I'm sorry I told you a little lie… I have a husband. And he is very jealous. I shouldn't have brought you here… someone might see and tell him. Then he would kill me."

Barton took a taxi back to the hotel, wondering whose game he'd just been playing, Naismith's or Juanita's; or maybe it was some kind of weird, one sided mixed doubles. He got out of the cab and reached into his pocket for his wallet; as he took it out a small white card fell to the ground. He bent down and picked it up without looking at it, thinking that it was the one Naismith had given to him. He paid the cab driver and walked into the hotel lobby.

It had been a strange day, and maybe he was making too much of it. Maybe he was letting his ghosts get the better of his judgement. Maybe Naismith wasn't playing games. Maybe it was just coincidence, Colin Marshall being there; and maybe Juanita was just a spoilt little rich girl with too much time on her hands.

He walked through to the bar where Connor was standing talking to the barman. "Hi Dave, get me a pint of San Miguel please," he said. "…I'll find a table outside."

Connor came out of the bar and sat at the table. "The beers are coming," he said. "…now what shall we talk about first… your day or mine?"

Barton didn't answer he was looking at the card that was still in his hand. It was her calling card – *Juanita Herrera-Marquez* – she must have slipped it into his pocket, when they were on the boat, or maybe at the apartment. Under the name were two addresses and phone numbers; the Puerto Banus apartment and an address in Bogotá, Colombia.

"What's that?" asked Connor.

Barton turned the card over and saw that she'd written something on the back – *I want you – call me* – he slipped the card into his wallet. "Oh! Nothing, Dave... it's just a souvenir."

"God! That woman could shop... you've never seen anything like it. If it was an Olympic Sport..."

"Did you buy anything?"

"You must be joking... at those prices?" Barton replied. "But what am I going to do with this tie, Dave?"

"Wear it. Why not?"

"But it cost over a hundred quid. Look at the label. What do I tell Grace? That I saw it in the shop and I just had to buy it... Christ! She'd go mad."

"Well she'd probably kill you if you told her the truth. You can give it to me. I won't tell if you don't," said Connor. "Now when are we going to eat? In case you've forgotten... one of us has actually been working today."

"You're really sure about this, aren't you?" said Connor, as they sat on the hotel terrace after dinner. "But we still haven't really got anything on him."

"You're right this might be a wild goose chase. But look at it another way... we've got a picture... OK, I know it's not much... But the sort of man we're looking for... he's got to be hiding behind a legitimate business front... something big given the huge amounts of money he's got to move. He's well connected... these international syndicates don't just get into bed with anyone... he has to be able give them something in return, like contacts in high places? He's probably someone who has no record... totally clean... above suspicion. There could be hundreds, thousands of people who fit the bill... But, only one of them is Bobby King's brother."

"We're going to need more than that Mike," said Connor.

"I know that's why we're here. I'm sure we're onto something. We've just got to dig until we find it. But there was something he said yesterday... something about him... it's been niggling away at me all day."

"What was that?"

"Well... not so much what he said... but the way he reacted, a couple of things that didn't seem right. He seemed to know who I was... as soon we met, before I told him I was a policeman... like he knew. And then when I told him about King... he seemed really shocked."

"Well so would you be... if someone told you your brother had just died."

215

"No I don't mean that Dave… I mean it was as if he already knew… but he seemed surprised that I did. Maybe…" Barton hesitated and shook his head. *It still doesn't prove anything. Maybe I just thought I saw something because I wanted to.* "Oh! I don't know."

"Neither do I, Mike," said Connor. "I'm just along for ride."

Barton gazed out over the sea, turning his thoughts to Juanita Herrera-Marquez: *OK, so she's Colombian, and she's got the same name as Herrera … and she's got a brother or husband called Fernando, it doesn't mean he's the same Fernando Marquez; there must be thousands of people called Herrera and Marquez in Colombia. It could all be coincidence.* And as he looked into the distance, he wondered if Connor could also see the flock of pigs, flying over the sea towards the mountains of Africa.

Chapter 19

Thursday 8th May

Potters Bar, Hertfordshire – 05:30 BST

"Can you get that?" she yawned, "Tell them I'm not awake yet."

The man reached for the phone. "Who the hell's calling you at this time of the morning?" he asked.

"I don't know. Tell them I'll call back later.

"She'll call you later," he mumbled, and put the receiver down.

"Who was it?"

"Him again... who else would it be?"

Sally jumped out of bed and searched in her bag. She found her mobile phone and called Barton's number. The man sat up and listened to one half of the conversation.

"What time do you call this...? I should think so too. What do want...? Hang on let me get a pen... OK. I've got all that. Is there any more...? Believe me you will be..."

"Is there still something going on between you two?" he asked.

"I told you it was over a long time ago," said Sally angrily.

"Come on. All the time you spend together... all these phone calls."

"Well if you showed a bit more commitment to this relationship... maybe I'd spend a bit more time with you," she said, walking towards the bathroom.

"Where are you going? Aren't you coming back to bed?"

"I'm awake now. I won't get back to sleep now. I might as well get dressed and go to work."

"I wasn't thinking about sleep," he said as she stepped into the shower.

Men! She turned on the shower and relaxed as the warm water caressed her body: *I wish you could wash them away.* Her affair with Richard had been an on and off thing for months. The current on phase was in its second week. But she had to honest with herself; the lack of commitment wasn't all on his part. Like all the others, he was only a temporary substitute for the one she'd lost.

Marbella, Costa del Sol – 10:30 CET

Barton hadn't slept well, lying awake for hours in the huge bed with a jumble of thoughts swirling around in his head. Wondering how he was he going to prove his suspicions about Naismith. Replaying yesterday's conversations; trying to separate the truth from the lies. Trying to think out his next moves in the bizarre game, they were playing. Worrying about going home to Grace, she'd know at once that something wasn't right. What could he tell her? He wasn't good at hiding things from her. He wanted to feel ashamed, guilty, but he felt strangely exited – *I want you – call me* – it was only a game and yet part of him wanted to call the number on the card. Maybe she meant it. Maybe it wasn't the same game to her. Maybe she meant she couldn't be unfaithful, to her husband because they were in their apartment. That didn't mean she wouldn't. Maybe she was just a high-class hooker after all; hired by the hour to be a pawn in Naismith's game. Then he felt guilty, because he'd been tempted. And he felt ashamed, because part of him had wanted to.

He'd thought of the people who had died, and wondered how many more there had been. Images of faces flashed through his mind, some were fleeting, but others wouldn't go away. The dead – his father lying in a pool of blood; a girl staring at him from the floor of the hotel bathroom; and a vicious evil man reduced to a pathetic shell gasping for the last breaths of life. The living – Grace the love of his life, her face streaked with tears; the politician delivering his victory speech from a stage still stained with blood; a policeman counting his blood money; and an angry young man standing at his father's grave, trying to comfort his grieving mother and sister.

When sleep had come, the thoughts carried on in his dreams. She came to him, naked, calling him – *'plee-ease, plee-ease take me'* – her body writhing, jerking uncontrollably, as the puppet master manipulated the strings. As he turned and ran to the door, the puppet master pulled more strings, and Bobby King rose from his death bed to stand and block his way, laughing: *'I know all about you Barton'.* Turning round he saw a man in uniform, holding out a bundle of bloodstained banknotes, goading him: *'It's easy Mike, after you've taken the money the first time… it's so easy'.*

More puppets appeared in the macabre – young girls with fear in their eyes, unable to resist as the men used their bodies; Deborah King swearing and spitting blood, her arms wrapped around her bruised and battered lover; Martin Davenport in his wig and gown, pleading the innocence of the guilty. – And, as these puppets performed their dance, choreographed by the unseen hands of the puppet master, his other puppets watched; faceless men – businessmen, politicians, lawyers, bankers, accountants – counting their money and not asking where it came from.

And then Barton felt something tug at his arms and realised that he too was a puppet. He looked up, and his eyes traced the strings upwards, higher and higher until, at last, he saw the face of the Puppet Master; and looking into Naismith's eyes, he saw his own end.

As he prepared to meet Naismith again, the dream continued to haunt him. The ghosts of the past were dancing with the ghosts of the present, and calling on him to set them free, to help them rest. Driving him to seek the truth, to give them justice; and revenge.

He felt uneasy; vulnerable. At their first meeting, he had the advantage, the element of surprise. He had caught the man off guard and had seen a glimpse of what lay behind the façade. But now, Naismith was calling the shots. Barton was convinced that yesterday's lunch invitation was not a spontaneous gesture. He thought Marshall could still have been a coincidence; he wanted to believe that, but he was starting to come to terms with the truth. He didn't know what if any significance there was in the presence of the others, but he had a feeling that he would find out before very long.

Right now, Juanita was his main worry. Yesterday he had let his guard drop and his animal instincts had taken over from rational thinking. No wonder he was still struggling to sort out the truth from the lies. He would normally have been analysing every word of the conversations that he'd had on the boat; filling in the gaps, studying their expressions and body language. But his brain had been in his trousers. Naismith had planned the whole thing; he was sure about that. But there was more to it. It might have all been an act. There were hundreds of beautiful women in Marbella who could have played out that little charade; flaunted themselves and played with a man's ego, ensuring that his mind was not on the job in hand. But if this woman really was related to Fernando Marquez she could prove the link between Naismith and the Colombian drugs cartel: *'My uncle has some business with Tony'*. The more he thought about it, the surer he was that she was the real thing and the more worried he became. Naismith was handing him evidence on a plate and he wanted to know why. He could only think of one reason; and he was desperately searching for an alternative.

Naismith's villa was in the hills to the east of Marbella and Barton asked the hotel receptionist for directions. "Go past the hospital and then after five kilometres turn off at the Don Carlos Hotel, *señor*... the sign is for Elviria," said the girl. "...you will see signs for the International School. Follow the road... it is very easy and not possible to get lost."

"Anything is possible," he mused.

"*Perdóneme señor*, I do not understand."

"*De nada*," he said, "*gracias por su ayuda.*"

He drove out the town and joined the main coast road, heading in the direction of Fuengirola and Malaga. A few minutes later, he passed the Hospital Costa Del Sol. It was a free public hospital, with excellent modern facilities, serving the whole of the Costa del Sol. Barton didn't think that it looked very big considering the size of the population spread along the coast. He thought of Colin Marshall's remark about it being hard not to be well out here. Maybe they didn't need many hospital beds.

He remembered his conversation with Martin Davenport. This was where his wife had died; where the lawyer had spent hours sitting at her bedside; reading aloud her favourite poetry when she was awake, and gazing out of the window whilst she slept, looking at the mountains that rose up in the distance.

Davenport had given up smoking during those long days and nights, but had discovered that unlike their NHS counterparts the public cafeterias in Spanish hospitals sold alcohol. Night after night, the pain of watching his wife's life slipping away had been deadened by copious quantities of cheap wine and beer; his fall into alcoholism had followed with a predictable inevitability.

A few minutes later, he turned off the main road. '*Go past the houses, and drive up the hill'.*

The road ahead now climbed steeply, with wide sweeping bends, hugging the contours of the hillside. He dropped a gear, and made rapid progress over the smooth surface of the new road. There were no houses at all on this stretch and he hadn't seen another vehicle since he had been on this road; although when he had turned off the main road he had seen the cranes and new buildings rising high up in the hills and no doubt the new developments would soon change things.

He pulled over to the side the road, got out of the car and looked at the view. The golf course was below him, in a valley that stretched right down to the coast. On the far side of the valley, amongst the trees, he could see a large house. There were no other houses anywhere near; it had to be Naismith's villa. He got back into the car and drove half a kilometre further up the hill, until he came to a wide gateway. A pair of metal gates, eight feet high, blocked his way; on each gatepost was a CCTV camera and a large halogen security light; and on one the panel for an intercom system. He got out and pressed the button, there was no reply, but a couple of electric motors whirred and the gates opened.

He drove though the gates, along the driveway that wound through the trees, and parked in front of the house. Naismith was waiting at the door. "Good, you found it alright," he said. Barton noticed that there was no handshake today.

"The hotel gave me some directions," said Barton. "It's quite a place you've got here."

"It serves a purpose," said Naismith dismissively. "Come inside, I'll give you the grand tour and then we'll talk." For a moment, as Barton looked at Naismith, an image from his dream flashed through his mind. His host led him into the house and as he followed, a couple of steps behind he felt the Puppet Master pulling at the strings.

The house was huge and quite beautiful. Barton lost count of the number of large, expensively furnished rooms. Everything in the house looked new and unused; more like a show house than a real home. Upstairs there were two large suites; not only did the Naismiths have separate rooms but they were at opposite ends of the house. There were also a further six bedrooms and Barton had to remind himself that all of this was for just two people. Downstairs in the massive basement, Naismith had installed a leisure complex with a private cinema, billiard room, indoor pool, sauna, steam room, and a gym; the equipment looked as though it was never used.

"This is where I keep my toys," said Naismith proudly as the entered the enormous garage. "Take a closer look if you want."

Besides the Aston there were another seven cars, parked two deep, including a brand new Range Rover, and a short wheelbase open Land Rover in full off-road trim. The other five were shrouded in dust covers; one looked like it might be a Rolls Royce, but knowing Naismith it was more likely that it was a Bentley. The others were low sports cars and as Barton peered under a couple of the covers, Naismith looked on with a smile and gave a running commentary.

'McLaren F1, the best car in the world in its time, and it's British... Mercedes SL, but not the standard job like Helen drives. This one's a bit special... there are only three in the world like it... all built to special order for some Arab... he paid a fifty percent deposit, but changed his mind and never took delivery. Brian got this one for a less than a hundred grand."

"I don't believe this," said Barton, as he approached another car. Even under the dust cover, the shape was unmistakeable. "I've got one of these."

"I've had it since it was new... it was the second one off the production line... couldn't get the first one." said Naismith. "I haven't driven it for years... the bloody thing would probably break down before I got to the gates. I only keep it for sentimental reasons. Barton pulled back the cover; the Lotus was immaculate: *Mine must have looked like this once. I keep it because I can't afford anything else.*

Barton took a last look around before they walked out into the sunlight. He smiled as he tried to picture Sir Anthony and Lady Helen on the pair of quad bikes, which were parked in the corner. He did a quick sum in his head and reckoned that Naismith had over a million pounds worth of 'toys' in his garage. And, though he wouldn't have chosen the same toys, Barton couldn't help feeling a touch of envy.

Barton had thought the house impressive, but he could only describe the grounds as stunning; and without his guide to show the way, he could easily have lost himself. The main gardens were set out on the hillside, in a series of formal landscaped terraces. The views were spectacular; looking over Marbella, to the coast and across the sea, where on the horizon the Atlas Mountains rose up in North Africa. On the slopes to the north side of the property, the formal gardens gave way to acres of woodland. As they walked under the shade of the oaks, eucalyptus and cork trees, Naismith told Barton some more about the property.

"The hillside was all like this when we bought the land, all the way down into the valley. There was nothing out here then... just a couple of run down farms... the owners slaving away to make a basic living. I bought as much land as I could, it was very cheap back then... but I still drove a hard bargain. If only they'd had the sense to realise that there was a property boom coming... but I suppose that to the farmers it was like winning the lottery. That's how you make money in this game Barton... you've got to see the opportunity before anyone else does."

"Don't you ever think that the most of Spanish have lost out as we've taken over their Costa?" asked Barton. "I mean most of the people with money around here seem to be British, German, Dutch, Arab, all incomers. The Spanish don't seem to have gained a lot."

Naismith had been asked the question many times before. "Not my problem Barton. Look they're a lot better off than they were before we came. Do you think they could have done all of this without us. They were fishermen, and farmers not businessmen. We've built the economy down here... brought new jobs... new opportunities. It's up to them to put the work in to get their share. Some have, but the rest won't get anything without the right attitude. They're too lazy, and there's no place in business for the three hour *siesta* and the *mañana* mentality."

Barton thought of the farmers, who had once had all this, many now they were living in the dreary apartment blocks, in the parts of Marbella that were not visited by tourists; their families still working long hours, serving the incomers, in the hotels, bars and shops. He wasn't convinced that they'd see it the way that Naismith did.

They carried on walking and came to one of the lawns that overlooked the valley, where they stopped to admire the view. "I built the golf course first," said Naismith pointing down to the expanse of green in front of them, "…it was my first one and I have to admit that I made quite a few mistakes. A couple of the holes have never really been right… still, it's not a bad round… and I learnt some valuable lessons for the future. It was Helen's idea to build the house… I was going to develop apartments and villas… but she loved the site and it meant that we could ensure complete privacy."

He turned around and pointed up the hill. "Nobody is going to build up there," said Naismith, "I own it all. I rent the olive groves to a farmer… I reckon that over the years, I've got back everything that I paid for the land. And I'm still making money; did you notice all the cranes right at the top, that's a new development, very exclusive, individual villas. But, I own all the land, and I'm selling nothing within two kilometres of here."

There were two other buildings in the grounds. The five-bedroom guesthouse was set quite close to the main house, but well hidden amongst the trees. Further away, and accessed from the road by a separate driveway, was a large garage-cum-workshop, full of the machinery needed to maintain the vast estate; and above this an apartment where the head gardener lived.

Working for Naismith was a family affair; the head gardener's wife was employed as a cook, and their two sons worked in the grounds with their father. Maria the housekeeper, who Barton had met on the tour of the house, lived in an apartment, over the garage, which adjoined the main house. Her husband worked as a general handyman, and their daughter helped in the house. '*Nobody else will be there*', Naismith had said. Obviously seven staff didn't count.

All this just for two people! Barton felt angry rather than envious as they walked back to the house. Naismith led the way to the terrace, where the huge circular swimming pool glistened in the sunlight. Maria had set the table for lunch and was walking out of the house carrying a tray. Barton looked at his watch. He couldn't believe it; he'd been here over two hours, and all Naismith had really talked about so far was money. In every reference to the house, the grounds, the staff, and his '*toys*', he hadn't failed to mention how much it had all cost. It was a blatant unashamed display of wealth, clearly meant to impress. And, as if to demonstrate how good he was at business deals, he boasted of how nearly everything had been built or acquired at less than the going rate.

Maria set the tray down on the table and poured two glasses of wine. By the time they reached the table she was on her way back to the house. "Sit down Barton," said Naismith as he handed one of the glasses to his guest.

A few minutes later Maria returned with a large two-tier trolley laden with food – Serrano ham, chorizo, cheeses, Spanish omelette, salads, breads and a huge bowl of fresh fruit – Naismith gave it a cursory inspection and nodded his head. Then the housekeeper turned away from them and walked back to the house. Barton couldn't fail to notice that not a word had been exchanged between master and servant.

"Help yourself," said Naismith gesturing towards the trolley. "I thought we'd keep it simple after yesterday's spread. I have to watch my weight."

"You call this simple," said Barton. "I could live for a week on this lot."

"Maybe… but, I bet you could get used to living like this… believe me it wouldn't take you very long. This is the way to live, Barton… But of course, you couldn't even think about it on a policeman's pay. Forgive me for rubbing it in… but I'll never understand how anyone as smart as you can be satisfied working for peanuts… when you could have so much more…"

Barton was tempted to rise to the bait, but he could see where this was leading; Naismith was probing to see if he had a price. Instead, he took another mouthful of omelette and shrugged his shoulders.

"Sorry, Barton… Am I making you feel uncomfortable. Some people just don't have the drive. I can't understand it, but I suppose you're content with what you have. But this isn't why you are here is it?"

Before Barton could answer, Naismith continued. "Look I understand that you've got a job to do. And I know that you had to come out here to find out if I knew anything that might shed some light on my brother's death. But to be frank, it's a bloody nuisance and I'll be glad to see the back of you. I've…"

"I appreciate that this is an inconvenience, sir, but…"

Naismith interrupted, "Let me finish. The reason that I asked you here today, is that I want settle this now… because I don't want a procession of flatfoots, coming backwards and forwards to Marbella, asking questions. I may still have friends in high places… but I've also made enemies over the years… some of whom would take great pleasure in leaning on your bosses to make sure that this never finishes. I've got better things to do… and I'm sure that your undermanned police force has got better ways to spend its time. Who will it benefit? The airlines, a few local hotels and bars… and a lot of bastards who'd like to get back at me. And another thing… I've got my reputation, and position in the community, over here to think about. You know as well as I do that there some real crooks living over here. They might think that they've got some sort of respectability now, but they're still the same scum that they always were. Some of them still get the occasional visit from your colleagues, and the last thing that I want is for my friends to think that in some way I might be associated them. Your presence here is an embarrassment to me. I've put up with it so far… played along with you… I'm sure that you've realised that I've also played a couple of little games at your expense. Caught you on the hop yesterday, Eh? Meeting your old boss... I bet that was a bit of a shock. Well it's been an amusing diversion, but..."

"I'm not sure where this is leading," said Barton, letting the tone of his voice give away that he was a getting pissed off. He didn't need a lecture.

Ignoring the interruption, Naismith carried on. "So let's get to the point... You're not going to let this go until I give you something. People like you... you never do," Barton felt a chill; there was something in the way Naismith said *'people like you'*, something in his voice; the way that the words were enunciated; precise and deliberate, piercing into Barton's brain like needles.

"You've got to prove something. And before you say anything... I'm not going to try and buy you... Don't think I haven't thought of it... but I know that you're not that kind. No, you need something that you can take back to your bosses... enough to satisfy them that there is nothing more to be gained from this line of enquiry... enough to satisfy you... that I had no association with my brother."

Naismith reached for a bottle, and filled his glass. "So, while we enjoy some more of this excellent Rioja, I'm going to have to tell you some things that nobody else knows... not even Helen."

Barton followed suit and poured himself another glass, as Naismith continued. "That's why I asked you to come here today... this is very personal and very private... I'm not going to put you on the spot by asking you to keep everything off the record... because I know that's not possible. But you have to give me your word... that you'll only tell those who absolutely need to know... and that I can rely on your discretion only to tell them what is necessary."

"OK, I suppose so," said Barton, half-heartedly, realising too late that this reply wasn't appropriate.

Naismith's face reddened. "OK! You suppose so! If that's the best you can do Barton, you can fuck off now." As he shouted, Barton saw the man in the golf club car park again. "This is about my fucking life! You bastard!"

The tirade over, Naismith lowered his voice, the tone still angry, but now challenging; testing the policeman. "I didn't have you down as stupid. Come on man... we both know that whoever they send next time will settle for a lot less than I'm prepared to give you... I told you this was going to be very personal and private. There are some bloody painful memories... things I prefer not to remember... and when I ask you to give me you word, all you can say is OK. Well forget it. OK doesn't even come close to being enough."

Barton felt acutely embarrassed, and angry with himself. He wasn't concentrating on the game today. He was tired, but lack of sleep last night wasn't an excuse. The man had just set down some new rules and he'd ignored him. He felt the strings tugging again and he could do nothing about it.

"I'm sorry sir, I didn't mean to offend you," he said, the words sticking in his throat. Apologising to a Naismith; it felt like he was selling his soul to the devil and he wondered how he was ever going to cut the strings.

"Apology accepted," said Naismith. The anger had subsided; never really there behind the façade. But the arrogance remained; that wasn't an act. "Now let me repeat my request... Will you give me your word that you will keep what I am going to tell you confidential?"

"Yes sir, you have my word... I won't betray your confidence," said Barton contritely, the only way that he knew would be accepted. He hated himself as he heard his own words. It didn't matter that he was only acting, nor that Naismith knew it was a charade. It still felt bad. But the game was still on, and, even though he was losing, he was still in with a chance.

"That's better, Barton," said Naismith, with a wry smile. "Now this is going to take some time, so let's open another bottle. Don't worry about driving back, I'll send one of the boys into town to fetch your Sergeant."

Barton felt the strings again. He hadn't once mentioned to Naismith that Connor was in Marbella with him: *The hotel? He knows the manager. Juanita maybe? She met Dave at the hotel... I even told her that he was a policeman.*

Barton emptied the glass and poured another. "Thank you, sir, but you don't have to go to any trouble, I can ring for a taxi," he said. He was regaining his composure, and trying to get back in the game.

"It's no trouble... anyway it's the boy who's going, not me. And as I said, I want to see the back of you. We don't want you to have to come back to collect your car in the morning. Do we?" Naismith said, with another wry smile. "You might miss your flight...and be stuck here all weekend."

"That's very considerate of you," said Barton as he saw the game slipping further from his grasp: *Oh! What the hell.*

"Look, sir," he said, suddenly feeling very tired, "I'm not sure I can take in much more... so if this is as important as you say, would you mind if I take some notes... I've got a notebook in the car."

Naismith smiled; he'd won this hand, and would now be magnanimous in victory. "I have no objection... provided that they are for your personal use," he said. "But, why do you need a notebook? Where's that little recorder that you had yesterday...? You know the one that you played to me... the one that you recorded my guests with," asked Naismith, giving the strings yet another tug.

"In the car," replied Barton, "I'll go and get it."

He walked to his car, wondering if the strings were long enough to allow him to reach it, half-expecting Naismith to pull him back at any moment. As he got into the car, he was tempted to give up there and then, start the engine, and drive away. He wasn't sure how much longer he could last, or what purpose it was going to serve. He thought about some of the other policemen he knew; the ones who would have taken what they had a few days ago; wrapped things up and been satisfied with a result; any result. The only one he could think of who would have followed it this far, was sitting there in the car; punishing himself, wondering, why he had to be different, and what was so wrong with taking the easy way? He was a bloody good detective but nobody expected him to be some kind of superman. He was putting himself through all this shit. He knew why and it had nothing to do with the case. It was a memory of something that had happened a long time ago; a ghost that had to be laid to rest.

Barton retraced his steps back to the terrace, where he found Naismith standing, looking out at the view. Barton stood beside him for a few minutes; neither man spoke. This was a tough game and had taken it's taken its toll on both players; they needed a time out.

Naismith broke the silence. "Magnificent view, isn't it? Did I tell you that was my first golf course down there? I could never leave this place you know." He spoke with real feeling, no act, and no strings.

"I can see that," said Barton, suddenly feeling very tired. "Could we get this over with now please?"

As they sat down Naismith said "There's something special about life out here… something that people like you, could never appreciate." Barton felt another tug at the strings, and another needle pierced his brain: *'People like you'.*

Barton filled four tapes during the next two hours, as Naismith told the story of his early life and of the events that had separated him from his brother. The old man spoke slowly, hesitantly at times. He paused frequently; sometimes to refresh his glass, sometimes to wipe a tear from his eye, but mostly to look at the policeman as if to check that he was paying attention.

Apart from asking one question, and asking Naismith to wait while he changed the tape, Barton didn't say anything. He listened intently, taking in every word; watching and listening for the smallest signs that would help him distinguish the truth from the lies. As Naismith related the episodes from his early life, Barton wondered how long he'd spent rehearsing, for he was sure that he had. But there were times, when the old man's voice had changed, and it seemed as though a small boy was talking; and he thought that surely even he couldn't have rehearsed that.

When he had finished, Naismith stood up and said, "That's all. You now know things about my past that no one else does. Don't forget, you've given me you word."

"Thank you, sir. I won't forget."

A young man appeared on the lawn and walked towards the terrace, followed by Dave Connor. Naismith didn't bother to get up as he greeted him. "Detective Sergeant Connor I presume. Now you must look after your boss. I'm afraid that we've had rather a lot to drink," he said, pointing to the four empty wine bottles. Barton hadn't realised that they'd drunk so much, although he remembered that his glass had never seemed empty. And now, strangely, he felt as sober as a judge.

I won't walk to the car with you," said Naismith, "you know the way." With that final remark, the two men shook hands and Barton turned his back and walked away.

As they disappeared from view, Naismith breathed a sigh of relief. He'd played out the charade, as he'd planned; he'd gambled that Barton would go back and play the tape to his bosses. Who could possibly imagine he had anything to do with his brother after that performance? But something told him that whilst the game was over for now, there would be a rematch before very long. This policeman was one of the clever ones. He'd even started to respect him in a grudging way, but as far as he was concerned he was just like all the others, and he hated him: *Thank God that's over. I'll never see that bastard again.*

He wished that it were true, although he knew it wasn't over. But for now he could savour his victory and think about revenge He could end it all now if he wanted; a couple of calls, a fatal accident maybe or perhaps just a quick clinical shooting. But killing was too kind for this one. He couldn't make him suffer if he was dead, and the media would end up making the bastard into some kind of hero. Anyway, he didn't have Bobby to do his dirty work any more. No, he wanted to see this man crushed, humiliated; totally destroyed. That way he wouldn't get any sympathy; he'd be hounded and vilified. Another example of what happens when the ignorant lefties and liberals turned their backs on decent people and encouraged the vermin to flourish. No, he would continue with the game. He didn't even stop to consider the possibility that he might lose. Losing to one of them just wasn't an option.

He barked at Maria who was clearing the table. "Throw it all away… everything." Naismith walked back into the house and into the reception hall. He opened the door of the cloakroom, and swore. The bastard had pissed in there; he'd have to get Maria to scrub it clean. He lifted the toilet lid and looked down. He pictured Barton's face staring up from the pan and laughed out loud as he watched his nemesis drown in a stream of piss. Then he heard a voice in his head; a voice from long ago: *'I told you not to touch them. They're dirty, how d'ya think they got that colour. Wash your hands, boy… give them a good scrubbing'.*

Naismith turned on the basin taps, picked up a nailbrush and scrubbed; scrubbed until the skin was red.

"Thanks for coming to pick me up Dave," said Barton as they drove down the hill. "I'm all in. I feel like I could sleep for a week."

"So I can take it that you don't fancy a night on the town. I suppose that I'll have to amuse myself," said Connor. "I wonder if I can find that Maria."

"Don't even think about it. The game's over."

"Game; what do you mean?"

"I'm too tired to explain now. I'll tell you about it some other time."

"Well for what it's worth… while you've been playing games I've been doing some real police work. In case you've forgotten what that is… I'll remind you. It's about knocking on doors… asking questions and filling the pages of a little black notebook," said Connor bitterly. "You're not the only one who's tired. And I'm getting bloody tired of all this."

"Don't you take that bloody tone with me Sergeant… we may be friends, but I'm still your senior officer and I won't have it," said Barton angrily. "I'll have you show a little more respect."

"With respect… sir," said Connor grudgingly. "You've dragged me all the way out here… carrying your bags. And I bet that you haven't even bothered to look at any of that stuff I brought out for you… I've spent two days running around for you, while you've been living it up… lunches on fucking yachts, while I have to make do with a sandwich in a bar… shopping for Christ's sake! And you still haven't really told me what it's all about. And now you tell me it's all a bloody game. Well I'm sorry Mike, but respect goes both ways."

Barton knew that Dave was right. This wasn't how he treated people. He had always encouraged his team to speak their minds, and respect the person not their position. He hated people who demanded respect without ever making the effort to earn it. And now here he was behaving just like one of them; like the man, he had just left. "I'm sorry Dave," he said. "I'm letting this get to me. Look, I'm grateful for your help. Let me get a couple of hours' sleep and then maybe we'll talk about it. We'll have a few beers and you can let me know what you've found out."

"Well that won't take very long," said Connor. "I might have filled a lot of pages in the notebook, but I can't see that any of it's going to be of use."

"We'll see," said Barton. "You never know."

Connor stopped the car outside the main entrance to the hotel. "I'll drop you off here," he said. He was still annoyed and needed some time to think. "If you don't need me for anything else, I thought I'd go for drive. Go up into the hills maybe. I might have a walk… If that's OK with you?"

"Yeah… you go and enjoy yourself, Dave."

"I'll see you in a couple of hours then."

"Let's make it three. I've got some thinking to do," Barton replied, "and you were wrong about the files, by the way. They made interesting bedtime reading."

As Barton got out of the car, he felt something fall out of his pocket. Connor picked the recorder off the seat, looked at it pensively, and handed it to his boss. "What have you been recording?" he asked.

"Truth and lies, Dave," Barton replied. "Truth and lies… the trouble is I don't know which is which." Barton shut the car door and watched Connor drive off: *I just have to sort out the truth from the lies. If only it was that simple.*

Barton went up to his room and drew the curtains; he took a bottle of cold water from the mini bar and lay on the bed. He switched on the recorder and lay there with his eyes closed; listening once more to the story, he'd been told that afternoon.

At one point, Naismith paused and Barton heard his own voice, asking his only question. Not so much a question as a comment, he thought, as he listened again to Naismith's response.

'Yes, I'm sorry about that. It was unforgivable… the way I reacted the other day. But hope that now you can see why. I know it's irrational, but even after all these years I still can't bear to hear that name. It makes me think of him and it triggers something inside me. All the anger comes back. Do you understand? I wasn't angry at you… it's him, the bastard still makes me feel that way… even after all this time'.

He turned off the recorder and looked at his watch. Two hours and so little said; so few words. It had been a masterly performance; full of pauses and long silences, for dramatic effect as Naismith had waited for signs of acknowledgment from his audience. Barton realised how much he was missing. He'd got all the words, but he wished that he could have made a record of what had been in the man's eyes as he'd spoken them. As he'd listened to the recording, he'd tried to picture the man's face as he'd poured out his cocktail of truth and lies. In his mind, he pictured the times when the arrogant man had appeared to shrink in stature, becoming a confused small boy again. He'd never forget that; Naismith hadn't put that on. But he was struggling to remember the other signs; the images he needed to go with the words; clues to help him see the truth that was hiding somewhere amongst the lies.

There was time to have a shower and make his calls to Grace and Sally, before meeting Connor. He just hoped that the Irishman was behaving himself. He half expected to find him in the bar, turning on the charm for the *señoritas*. But he knew that for all the bravado, Dave Connor wasn't one to let it go further than a bit of harmless flirting. Connor was a good man, faithful, and when Barton saw him looking at Lorna, he could tell, because Barton looked at Grace in the same way. Then he felt guilty again as he remembered Juanita.

In common with most men, Barton wasn't very good at long telephone conversations with his wife and his call to Grace was brief. Just long enough to let her know that he loved her and missed her, and tell her when he'd be back. It was alright if she had something to tell him; he could listen for ages. But he never felt able to say much when he couldn't see her; he needed to see her face, look into her eyes, and touch her; it helped him open up. He didn't like having personal conversations on the phone; it always felt anonymous, too distant. It would be good to get home; he had a lot he needed to talk about with Grace. He still had to work out how to tell her some of it, but he would think about that tomorrow.

The call to Sally took longer, but work always did. It would have taken even longer if she had asked him to explain his requests, but, as usual, she didn't ask and, as he had been so many times before, he was grateful for her trust.

Then he turned his thoughts back to Naismith: Truth and lies. Separating them wasn't really all that difficult. The half-truths were the hardest to work out.

231

Chapter 20

Friday 9th May

Flight number EZY3116 – Malaga to London Stansted – 16:00 CET

Connor hated budget short haul flights; they didn't have any in flight entertainment and he always found it difficult read on a plane. He sat in the window seat and idly looked down at the ground, watching as the people became like ants, the cars like toys, and the details of the landscape became harder to distinguish as the plane gained altitude. Then they were cruising above the clouds and there was nothing more to see, and nothing to do; he was bored.

In the next seat Barton was already stating to nod off. Connor nudged him, "Can I listen to those tapes you made yesterday?" he asked: *I want to know about this fella, too.*

"In my bag," said Barton without opening his eyes. He was tired; they hadn't got back to the hotel until after two and then, he hadn't slept well; as the dream had returned, more vivid than before. He reclined his seat back, and the ghosts tormented him, mercilessly, as he spent the rest of the flight in the dark swirling mists that blur the boundaries between waking and sleep.

Barton liked a lot of legroom and as EasyJet didn't allocate seats they had been first in the queue at the gate to ensure seats in the front row. And Connor was able to get up and open the overhead locker without disturbing his boss. He found the tape recorder and the tapes, and returned to his seat: *Four tapes, that'll last till we get there.* He plugged the earpiece lead into the tape recorder, switched on the first tape and listened to the voice of a man he'd never met.

'As you are probably aware I've always tried to keep my personal life very private. It's important not to let people get too close. That also goes for business and politics you have to keep them separate to avoid a conflict of interest.

'Bobby was a piece of baggage that I had to carry… the skeleton in the closet. I couldn't do much about it because he was my brother… and I couldn't change that. But I had to build walls to keep him out. I couldn't afford it to be made public. I did a good job too. Nobody knew… not until that sleazy little journalist started digging in eighty-seven. Most of what he wrote was true, but a lot of it was innuendo and there were quite a few downright lies. My wife was devastated. I'd never told her you see. It was particularly difficult for her, all of

her so-called friends started to shut her out. That's one of the reasons that I decided to get away. That's what they do... these journalists, they don't care who they hurt.

'Did you know that the slimy little bastard went round all the old folks' homes in East London, trying to track down my mother's old friends? He even managed to trace the man that she married after the war. I had to take an out an injunction to stop him pestering my aunt.

'Anyway, I said that I'd tell you some very personal and private things. You might have read about some of them before, but at least this way you'll know the truth. Then, hopefully, you'll understand at least something, about my relationship with my brother, and see why it ended so long ago. I suppose that the best place to start would be the beginning.

'I was born on the 15th of August 1934, in my grandparents' house in the East End... in the bed that my mother and aunt were both born in' ... my brother too, later on. It's so long since I last went back. The house isn't there now. We were bombed out during the Blitz, and had to move in with my grandparents. I don't really remember much about my early childhood. Most of what I know about the first few years is what I was told later by my aunt.

'At first, we lived in our own house. I think that it must have been quite near to my grandmother's, as my mother would leave me there all day while she went to work. She had to work because my father was unemployed... he spent all of his time and her money in the pub. I was scared of him. He never hit me mind... never laid a finger on me. I don't think that he ever touched me at all. I can't remember ever being picked up and held by him.

'But he was always shouting at my mother and that frightened me. I remember him coming home drunk and shouting at her every night. I can't really remember if he hit her, but I knew that she was afraid of him. And Aunt Mary told me later that he'd often hurt her... once very badly. When she heard him come in at night she would come into my room and get into my bed. She used to hold me close and I could feel the tears running down her cheeks. Once she told me not to be afraid. She said, 'He won't hurt you, you're his little soldier'. Sometimes he wouldn't come up. I could hear him as he crashed about downstairs. Those were the times when she would still be in my bed in the morning. We'd go down together and he'd be asleep in a chair, or on the floor... snoring like a pig. There were other times when he would burst into the room and grab her arms or by the hair and pull her out of the bed. Then he would shove her out of the room and slam the door. I used to lie in bed afraid that he'd come for me... listening to her crying all night.

233

'I remember that my aunt lived with my grandparents. Aunt Mary was much younger than my mother, and she used to come to our house on her way home from school. My first real memory is of a day when I was about three years old and she took me to play in the park near our house. It was a beautiful day, bright sunshine... there was a small fair with a roundabout and rides... and she bought me a toffee apple. On the way home, I fell over and hurt my knee. She took out her hanky and wiped the blood away, and when I looked up at her the sun was making her hair sparkle and I thought she was an angel... I thought she'd come to take me to heaven.

'My brother was born in December 1937. Things were worse by then, I remember how angry my father was when my mother found out that she was pregnant, and how he left the house and didn't come back for days. After Bobby was born he was even worse and I was terrified that he would hurt us. It was like that right up until the war.

'My father left us just after the war started. My mother told me that he'd gone to fight the Germans. It was only some years later that I learned the truth.

My poor mother tried hard to cope, but after a few months, she gave up. She had a toddler, and a five year old and she was still working. My aunt told me later that she was beside herself with worry, not having heard from my father for months. Despite all the abuse, she still loved him and it broke her heart when he left.

'I didn't tell you, did I? He didn't leave us to go to war; he ran away to avoid the call up. My aunt told me the truth a few years later. I was so ashamed. I realised that I'd spent the war lying to my friends, telling them that he was a hero... away fighting. When all the time he was nothing more than a miserable coward who'd run away, leaving his wife and his sons. While decent, hard working men were laying down their lives for their country, my father abandoned his family, his King and his country... so that he could save his own pathetic skin. It still sickens me to think that I share the same blood... that and his wretched name. I only ever saw him once again. I don't know how he died in the end, but I hope it was slow and painful and that he's rotting in hell.

'Once, when I was about twenty, I tried to find out what had happened to him. I tried to find out where he was buried... I wanted to piss on his grave.

'In the summer of 1940 we were bombed out. Our whole street was turned to rubble and we went to live with my grandparents. My aunt had left home the previous year. She'd been swept off her feet by a young RAF officer and was now married. The three of us moved into her old bedroom, the same room that she had once shared with my mother.

'Eight months later my grandfather was killed during an air raid, the day before his 49th birthday. He'd already served his country once... joined up in 1914 and served right through the Great War. Twenty-eight men from his street left to fight that... he was the only one who came back. My grandmother once told me that he'd felt guilty about that for the rest of his life. She once said it made our family special. She believed that we were blessed in some way and that because my grandfather had been spared it meant that his children and grandchildren were special. Soon after the start of the war, he gave up his job at the market and joined the fire brigade, so he could do his bit again. I can remember watching him once after an air raid, disappearing into a cellar... risking his own life to save others buried under the rubble.

'It's ironic, don't you think? I thought that my father was a hero, away fighting... he was always shouting and hitting people, and I thought that's what soldiers did. I didn't realise that the kind, quietly spoken man who had taken us in was the real hero... twice over.

'My grandmother went to pieces after that and my mother was struggling to cope. After six months, she was just worn out. Lots of kids were being evacuated at that time and they asked my aunt if she would take me in for a while.

'My aunt and uncle came for Christmas dinner and I remember how smart he looked in his blue uniform. I was a bit scared of him at first because of the scars on his face, but he was very kind to us. They brought sweets and presents for us. My uncle had made a model Spitfire for me, from balsa wood and tissue. It was the best present that I'd ever had. My brother had a set of coloured wooden building blocks and an extra present that had to remain wrapped until his birthday two days later.

'I will always remember that day. My grandmother cooked the goose that Aunt Mary had brought and everyone got a coin in their pudding. We had sweets and ginger beer and we sang carols and played games. It was the first time for months that my grandmother hadn't cried, and my mother seemed so happy too. In the afternoon, my uncle took us to the park and even though it was only a few streets away, we went in his car. It was the first time we'd been in a car and we pressed our faces against the window and poked out our tongues whenever we passed someone we knew.

'That night they slept in our room. My mother made up a bed for me on the sofa, and she slept in my grandmother's bed with my little brother between them.

'Next morning we had to get up early as my uncle was on duty later in the day. As they were about to leave, my grandmother picked me up and hugged me... so hard I thought that I would suffocate.

'You have to go now with your Aunt Mary', she said, 'I'm sorry, Lenny but we can't look after you any more'.

'I put on my coat and my grandmother gave me another hug... she was crying; so were my mother and aunt. My little brother started to cry as well even though he didn't know why. I didn't cry, I don't think that I really understood what was happening, I thought I was just going for a visit. My uncle took my case and gas mask and put them in the car. I hugged my mother and then my brother, but he pulled away from me, clenching his fists, beating them on my chest, and then pulled at my sleeve, sobbing. My grandmother had to pull him away and I told him not to be a crybaby.

'I got into the back of the car with Aunt Mary, and my mother leaned in and kissed me goodbye. 'Don't be sad,' she said, 'it's not for long, you can come home to mummy soon.'

'I kneeled on the seat and looked out of the back window. As the car started down the street, I saw my brother run from the house carrying something in his hand. It was my model Spitfire. Aunt Mary told my uncle to stop the car, but as she got out of the car to go back for it, the little bastard threw it to the ground and smashed it. I ran from the car and picked up the pieces. I hated him and I wanted to hit him but my aunt stopped me.

'My uncle was stationed at High Wycombe. He had already done his bit. He'd flown a Spitfire in the Battle of Britain, but one day his plane was shot up quite badly. He'd managed to get back to his base, but he'd been blinded in one eye by a shard of Perspex from his shattered cockpit cover. He couldn't fly anymore after that and when he came out of hospital, he had been transferred to back room duties at Wycombe.

'I was six years old and this was the furthest from my home that I had ever been. The car journey seemed to take forever, and we had to stop several times for me to be sick. I was asleep by the time we reached their house and my aunt put me to bed with my clothes still on.

'Next morning when I woke up I opened the curtains and looked out of the window. I could see for miles. I had never seen anything like it before, the largest open space I had ever seen was the local park. The white frost covered fields and trees were glistening in the morning sun. I thought that my aunt must really be an angel and that this was heaven.

'My aunt made me some breakfast and took me for a walk. It was freezing cold, but I didn't notice. I was totally entranced by this wonderland that she had brought me to. We walked about a mile to a farm where we bought some milk and eggs. It was the first time that I'd ever seen a cow... it had huge horns and I thought it was some kind of monster.

236

'I spent the whole day exploring every nook and cranny of the house and its small garden. I was so excited that it wasn't until evening that I started to miss my mother. When I did, I cried uncontrollably. My aunt found me sitting alone in the corner of my room and sat on the floor next to me. She put her arm around me and I laid my head on her breast. It felt nice... I loved Aunt Mary. But I wanted to know when I could go home. I wanted my mother and I wanted to thump my brother for breaking my aeroplane.

'The house was a small cottage just outside a village called Downley, about two miles from High Wycombe. At the time it seemed huge compared to the two up-two down that I had left the day before, and the next nearest house was about a quarter of a mile away, not the other side of the wall. It seemed a world away from the East End. As the days and weeks passed and I gradually settled, I didn't cry as much. I went to the village school and made new friends; after a time, I found that whole days went by without me hardly thinking of my mother and at times, I almost forgot my brother completely.

'It was strange at first; everybody spoke differently. I had trouble understanding the teacher at school and although I was quite clever, she would call me stupid. Some of the boys bullied me because I didn't talk like them. Nothing too bad, just name calling and a bit of shoving in the playground. I would sit in my room for hours, talking to myself; trying to imitate the way that they spoke.

'One day I got into a fight with an older boy. He was always picking on me. I usually ignored it but this time he'd said something about my mother not wanting me and I punched him. He was bigger than me, of course and gave me a black eye. When I got home, I had to tell Aunt Mary what had happened. The next day my uncle took me to school in his car. He walked into the classroom and spoke to the teacher. I don't know what he said to her, but she never called me stupid again. Of course, most of the other children already knew my uncle; he was the local hero. After they knew who I was, nobody bullied me again.

'My uncle was my hero too. He was everything my own father wasn't. He was devoted to my aunt and treated me just like his own son. Every day he'd read the paper to me, telling me what was happening in the war. He made model aeroplanes for me. He had a book of scale plans of all sorts of aircraft and would spend hours sitting at the kitchen table carefully shaping tiny pieces of balsa wood, assembling the miniature airframes and then covering them with tissue paper. When they were finished, he would hang them by threads from the ceiling of my bedroom. I remember bringing my friends home and charging them a ha'penny to see my private air force ... a penny if they wanted to touch one.

'I still saw my mother and brother occasionally; birthdays, Christmas, the odd weekend. We usually visited them as my grandmother was always ill, and my *mother didn't like leave her for long. Once they were supposed to come and visit us for the weekend, I think it was my aunt's birthday. But my brother wandered off and got lost on Marylebone station, and they missed the train. I waited for hours with my aunt at the station, but they didn't come. After that, I don't think that my brother visited us again until the end of the war.*

'Anyway, it wasn't the same as before. I was growing up in a different world. As time went by, although I thought of my mother every day, I didn't really feel part of that family any more.

'Towards the end of the war, we saw a bit more of them. Well my mother anyway. She met an American Air Force Sergeant, called Henry Patterson. He didn't fly though... he said he was in charge of the ground crew. I remember at the time, I didn't think that was fair, I'd wanted my mother to have a hero too, someone like my uncle.

'Henry had a motorcycle and they would ride over to see us on it. I remember the first time they came. We weren't expecting them. I was in my bedroom reading and I heard the sound of the engine. I looked out and saw the motorbike coming up the lane; she was sitting on the pillion, her skirts billowing, and her long hair streaming behind her.

'Of course, they couldn't bring my brother with them, but I didn't care. I knew that every time I heard the sound of the motor bike it meant treats... Hershey bars, chewing gum, and comics for me ... nylon stockings for my aunt and cigarettes for my uncle.

'I really liked Henry, he was good fun, and he told me all sorts of stories about the farm in Mississippi where his family lived and about his brothers and sisters. He told me about a world that I had never known. He said that they had lots of people working on the farm... people who were different to the ones I knew. I'd only ever seen a few people like that, but he said where he came from there were lots of them to do the work. Henry told me that he had servants in the house and I thought that he must be very rich. He told me that he'd joined the army because he wanted to fight the Japanese. But they'd sent him to England instead. I don't think that he got on with my uncle, I used to hear them arguing with each other. I think that Henry was jealous because my uncle had been a pilot and was an officer.

'I always wanted to go on the motor bike, but Aunt Mary and my mother said it wasn't safe. One day, when they were in the kitchen talking, I sneaked out with Henry and he took me for a ride round the lanes. They were so angry with him when we came back.

'And then one day...my father came back. The war had just ended and he came crawling out of his hole, expecting to pick up where he had left off. Of course our house wasn't there any more, so he went to my Grandmother's. He banged on the door and shouted at her, but she wouldn't let him. He went round to the house several times, but my mother wasn't there that day. I think that one of the neighbours must have told him where she was.

'Henry had borrowed a car so that they could bring my brother with them. They'd arrived without any notice, just like they always did and announced that they'd come to stay for a few days... I remember that I took my brother to play in the woods and showed him my secret den. I had to make him promise not to tell any one. And I took him to the farm to see the monsters... the cows. One of them came really close and licked his face, it was so funny. He was really scared and he cried and ran away.

'A couple of days later, we were all sitting in the kitchen having tea, when the door burst open. I didn't recognise him at first, but my aunt and mother were terrified. And then he said something like, 'What's the matter Lenny, aren't you going to say hello to your old dad?' My brother clung to his mother and started to cry... of course he'd been too young... he didn't know who it was.

'I shouted at him; something like. 'Go away, you're not my father. You ran away. You're a coward'

He caught me across the cheek with back of his hand. 'Don't talk to me like that you little bastard!' he shouted and hit me again, so hard that I fell off the chair. He pulled my brother away from his mother and grabbed her by the arm, tearing her dress: 'You're coming with me!' he shouted, even louder.

'It all happened so fast... but I think Henry and my uncle grabbed hold of him. Next thing I knew, they'd taken him outside. My brother and I watched them through the window... They kicked the shit out of the bastard. I thought they were going to kill him. I wish they had. Then my brother stopped crying, ran outside, and started to cheer.

'We watched them pick him up and bundle him out of the gate where they left him lying in the lane. He lay there for a while motionless and I thought he really was dead. Then he pulled himself to his feet and limped away. That was the last we ever saw of him.

'A couple of months later my mother called my aunt and asked her to bring me up to London. I remember that we caught the train and when we got to my grandmother's house Henry's motorbike was parked outside.

'Henry took us boys to the park, while the women talked. An hour later when we returned they were sitting in the front parlour. I knew something important was happening; my grandmother hardly ever used that room. My mother and grandmother both looked happy, but Aunt Mary was crying.

'She explained that she had just learned that my father was dead. She said that Henry's unit was leaving after Christmas and he'd asked her to marry him. We were all going to live in America. Henry had to go back first and we would be able go a few months later. She didn't know how long it would take, there were a lot of immigration papers to fill in, but she told us that we were going across the sea on a big ship.

'She married Henry Patterson at Millwall registry office on the 25th of January 1946. We had a big party in the room above the pub, a typical East End knees up. Afterwards, Henry took her to a hotel in the West End and, we went back to my grandmother's house, where the party carried on after we were sent to bed. Lots of Henry's friends came to the wedding and that night we sat in bed counting our haul of Hershey bars and gum. Four weeks later Henry went back to the States.

'She left us in June 1946. She was pregnant with Henry's baby, when she sailed for America on the Queen Mary, There'd been a mix up with the paperwork or something and my brother, and I couldn't go with her. We all went to Southampton in my uncle's car to see her go. She kissed me goodbye first, I remember that I was very angry that she was leaving us. But I don't remember being sad, I suppose that by then I didn't really know her any more. Then Bobby's mother picked him up and held him tight for what seemed like ages. Of course, she didn't know that it was for the last time. 'Be a good boy for your Gran, Bobby', she said. 'I'll send for you soon'. I remember that they were both crying as she let go of his hand. We stood on the dockside and watched as she waved from the rail. We stood and waved until the ship was out of sight and then my uncle drove us home.

'She died on the 20th of December 1946. I was at school when my aunt got the news. Henry sent her a telegram. She was crossing the street. They said the truck that hit her was speeding and that the boy driving was drunk. My baby sister, who I had never seen, was thrown into the air, and died the instant that her head hit the road. It took three days for my mother to die. The night that she died Henry and his two brothers went to the jail. The deputy didn't even try to stop them... just gave them the keys. They dragged the boy from his cell and beat him up, right there in the jail. Next morning they found him hanging in the woods. That was the way it worked back then in the South.

'Henry later told me that he'd have been found guilty anyway, so it saved wasting money on a trial. I don't know if what they said about the boy was true ... it didn't matter... he'd killed them... he deserved what he got. Henry was proud *of what he'd done... he hated the man of course... you couldn't blame him. Strange though... I didn't really hate him... I don't think I even thought about him. As far as I was concerned, it was my father's fault. If he hadn't deserted us she wouldn't have been in that street on the other side of the world. She would have still been at home with us.*

'*They buried her in the family cemetery on Henry's farm. Of course, we couldn't go to her funeral; it was too far. But a few months later Henry wrote to my Aunt and sent boat tickets so that we could visit. I went to America that summer with Aunt Mary and my brother. We stayed with Henry and his family for about four weeks. I shared an attic room with my brother and I remember that he didn't like it because it was at the back of the house and we could see the cemetery from the window, I think he was afraid that there were ghosts. Henry must have really loved his wife and the baby, he made sure that the boys kept their graves tidy and there were fresh flowers every day. I liked staying with Henry he took me and my brother for rides in his truck and on a tractor. We went fishing and played games with his nephews. There were other children as well, but we didn't play with them. I wanted to stay longer because Henry was good fun. He took me to lots of places and showed me things I'd never seen. But Aunt Mary said we had to go home. I don't think she ever liked Henry, because he didn't like my uncle.*

'*My aunt and uncle had decided to adopt me and on the 16th of September 1947, Leonard Anthony King ceased to exist. I was now Anthony Naismith. The change of name didn't matter to anyone else. My aunt had always called me Anthony, as did all my school friends. It was my grandfather's name. It was the name my mother wanted me to have, but when my father registered the birth, he had given me his name instead. And ignoring my mother's protests, he had always insisted that she called me Lenny. I remember that he got very angry with her one day, just before he left. I was about four years old...we were at my grandmother's house and he hit her when he heard her calling me Anthony.*

'*I can't tell you how good it felt... I was so glad to be able to cast off that name and with it all connection to the bullying coward who had destroyed our family*

'*...anyway, enough of that, let me continue...*

'*That same year, I started at the Royal Grammar School in High Wycombe and I saw even less of my brother. We had to go to school on Saturday morning and there were sports in the afternoon. So there wasn't much time to visit London. But it didn't matter to me... I didn't really want to see my little brother.*

It's strange isn't it how big an age gap of three years seems when you're thirteen. I felt that I was grown up and he was just a little boy. I did well at school excelling in English and history. I loved history, all those stories of the great men who built our country and made us masters of the world.

'When we did visit my grandmother, more often than not my brother wouldn't be there anyway. My grandmother had never really recovered from her husband's death and although she was only in her fifties, she looked like an old woman. She found it increasingly difficult to control my brother, who spent most of his time running wild with a gang of boys, most of whose fathers had not returned from the war.

'The East End was a bleak place after the war. There were so many derelict sites where houses and workplaces had once stood. But the bombing had destroyed more than bricks and mortar. Families had been devastated... close knit communities broken up for ever as people returned not to their old streets, but to the rows of hastily erected little prefabs, often miles away from their friends and relatives.

'I don't think that I was surprised that my brother turned out the way he did. Not that it's any excuse, there were plenty of others similarly affected who ended up as decent, hard working young men. But they didn't share my father's blood. Their fathers had been good, honest men. I've often looked back and thanked God that I inherited my grandfather's genes, and pitied my brother for being so much like our father.

'Our grandmother died in 1949, just a few months before my brother started at secondary school. It hadn't come as a surprise to anyone when he failed his grammar school exams... by that time nobody really expected much of him. He was already a waster. I remember that her funeral was a dismal affair and I will never forget the sadness in my aunt's eyes as they lay her mother to rest. I stood at her side and gripped her arm tightly; I didn't want to let go, she was all that I had left.

'My uncle said that my brother could come and live with us, but he ran away and they had to go to London to fetch him back. After he ran away for the third or fourth time, they gave up and he was taken into a council home in Stratford. At Stratford Secondary School, he went from bad to worse. He was constantly in trouble, always fighting or playing truant and generally making a nuisance of himself. We still kept in touch... well I would write to him and sometimes I'd get a couple of lines on postcard in return... but I hardly saw him. He never visited... even when my aunt sent the train fare.

'I remember visiting him once I think was after I started at the grammar school, because my aunt insisted that I wore my new blazer. He took me to play *football with some of his friends. I was surprised that they were mostly about my age. They told me to take off my blazer to use as a goalpost, and I folded it neatly and set it on the ground. Two boys picked sides…and as usual, I was the last one to be picked. During the game, I was tackled violently at every opportunity… at one point even by my brother… who was supposed to be on the same side. He barged me off the ball so hard that days later I still had the bruises. All the boys were laughing at me, they said that I was stuck up and called me lots of cruel names. After the game, one of the boys picked up my new blazer and waved it in the air like a flag. Then they started throwing it to each over and trampling on it when it fell to the ground. Finally, one boy threw it over a fence and I had to climb over and get it out of a bramble patch. I got stuck at the top but nobody would help me. They all just looked on laughing and calling me names. Then a boy grabbed my ankles and threw me over into the brambles. I had cuts and scratches all over my arms and legs and I tore my blazer as I climbed back. Do you know? All the time my brother was laughing. When we got home, we told my aunt that I'd fallen over playing football and she scolded me for tearing my blazer.*

'There was another time, I remember, we were on the way home when we saw a boy in the street. He was about ten or eleven, a little younger than my brother was. He ran away, but my brother caught him and tried to make him give us some money. The poor lad looked terrified. One of the other boys held his arms behind his back, while my brother went through his pockets. He didn't have any money on him, so my brother punched him hard in the stomach and told him he'd better pay up the next day or else.

'A few years later, he boasted to me that he knew some gangsters. He said they paid him to run errands for then. He was fourteen and he proudly showed me a flick knife and told me that he was going to use it to cut a teacher who'd caned him. He told me that he had a gun in the box at the back of his locker and that he was going to kill somebody one day. He said that one of his friends had already killed a man. I didn't believe him, but I was frightened. Can you believe that? I was seventeen years old and scared of my kid brother.

'Don't get me wrong, I was no angel. I got into my fair share of scrapes at school, just like any boy. But nothing serious… just harmless pranks. I learned very early on that words were a better weapon than fists. It was always better to negotiate than fight. I used to do some of the boys' homework for them in return for their sweet rations or pocket money. Then I'd pay other boys to do favours for me, little things like doing the errands that my aunt sent me on, or cleaning my football boots. I even had a couple of boys who would look out for me, if anyone

tried to bully me. I suppose that's when I found out that I was good at doing business deals.

'I suppose that I was lucky. I was never exposed to the kind of violence that my brother was used to. I think the worst that I ever saw was when I was in my second year at grammar school. A new boy started halfway through the first term. His parents were immigrants. There were hardly any of them around at that time and because he was different from the rest of us, some of the other boys used to pick on him. One day I found him lying on the ground outside a door surrounded by broken glass. Two boys were looking through the door laughing. They said he'd run into the door and made some stupid remark about there being no doors in the jungle. But he said that they'd pushed him. I remembered what it was like being different and told him not to worry. I don't think that they really meant any harm, but I thought of a way to pay them back. A couple of days later the two boys were called out in assembly, and given the cane for cheating with their homework. The head said that they must have copied each other as every answer, right or wrong, was exactly the same... of course I'd given them both the same answers.

'I told the boy later that I'd paid them back and after that, nobody touched him anymore. Do you know? He'd do anything for me after that, he used to follow me round everywhere like a little lap dog, fetching and carrying for me.

'When I was at grammar school, I visited the States and stayed with Henry for a few weeks each summer. We could never have afforded it, but he'd come into a lot of money and always paid for the tickets. He told my aunt that he thought of me and Bobby as family, the sons he'd never had. But Bobby never visited and I could never really understand why. I know that Henry invited him but he always seemed to have better things to do. But he always kept the money that Henry sent him to pay for the ticket... just like whenever my aunt sent him money for train fares. But he was like that... even when he was a boy... dishonest... always taking advantage of people. He missed a lot though... those visits to Mississippi became a highlight of my year and I looked forward to them.

'After I left school, my brother and I lost touch completely. I was planning to go to Oxford. I'd passed the entrance exams and been awarded a small bursary, but my uncle became very ill that year .It was something to do with his war injuries and he needed a lot of nursing. My aunt had to visit him every day at the hospital. She still corresponded with Henry and asked if I could visit him for the whole summer... I think she was worried that I would be bored at home.

'Henry wrote back to say he would be delighted and enclosed the money for tickets for Bobby and myself. But as usual, Bobby didn't want to come. I saw him before I left... to try to persuade him and we had a big argument. He said he wasn't interested. He said he'd been offered a job. God knows what it was, but it wasn't honest work. When I got back he'd been arrested and had his first conviction. I didn't even bother writing to him after that.

'Before that long summer visit, I had never really seen much apart from the farm and the area that surrounded the small town where Henry lived, but that year he took me on a river trip from Memphis to New Orleans. Have you ever seen the Mississippi river? It's an amazing waterway… makes the Thames look like a stream. It was good to see Henry and spend so much time with him. A lot had changed since my previous visit. He'd sold the family farm and had invested the money in an agricultural equipment and farm supplies business. He'd also gone into politics and was going to stand for the state senate. He was busy working a lot of the time and lent me a car so that I could drive myself around and explore… I covered hundreds of miles that summer. I also went back to Henry's old farm to visit my mother's grave again… Next to it was a tiny grave My sister Mary, I must have seen it before, but I cried when I saw it. So much was happening in my life that I'd forgotten I had a sister.

'After we returned, I decided not to go to Oxford. My aunt and uncle couldn't really afford it, and anyway I'd been awestruck by the prosperity in America. I don't mean the blacks and the poor people… everyone knows that they had a hard time. No different to the working classes at home really. But the middle class people like Henry's family had so much. Everywhere you went, even in quite small towns, there were so many businesses. And the shops in the big towns were full of all kinds of luxuries that hardly anyone had at home… things like TV sets and washing machines. And the cars were all new at a time when not many at home people even had cars.

'I decided that studying history for the next three years wasn't going to make me rich and that I would start my own business. I didn't have the faintest idea what I was going to do but I set myself a goal of buying a brand new car within a year… you have to set targets to aim for. You know… something to drive you on. My aunt was very disappointed and begged me to go to Oxford, but I was determined. I still had the money that my grandmother had left to me. It wasn't a lot, but I had invested it wisely, unlike my brother who had blown his. I bought some of old army trucks and did a deal with a local garage. They tidied them up a bit, repainted them and I sold them on. We split the profits sixty-forty. After a few months, we were buying and selling a dozen vehicles a month and making a tidy sum. You should have seen Aunt Mary's face the day I turned up in my new MG. I had so many vehicles at one time that I bought a small plot of land behind the garage to park them. I sold it later to a builder … for a big profit of course. That was my first property deal.

'But, my brother carried on the path that was ultimately going to lead him to where he is now, getting into all sorts of trouble with the police. He spent some time in borstal and then when he was about twenty he attacked someone in a pub and was sent to prison. The next time I saw him was when he invited me to his wedding in 1962... or was it 1963? What would that be...eight or nine years since I'd last seen him? He just phoned me out of the blue and said he had met Sandra and that he was going to marry her and make a fresh start. He said that he wanted to patch things up and asked me to be his best man.

'Like a fool I accepted. What a disaster. Sandra walked down the aisle with Terry already showing. Her parents didn't speak to Bobby all day. It was pretty obvious that her dad had arranged the whole thing with his shotgun. My brother got very drunk and accused me of fancying Sandra or something like that. He said he'd seen me eying her during my speech. We ended up having a blazing row and I stormed out. He called me a few days later to apologise, but I knew that he hadn't changed. I didn't even bother replying to the invitation to the christening.

'I met him only once more after that. It was 1966 I think... he'd just got out of prison and he came to my office asking for money. I think I gave him a couple of hundred pounds, and told him never to come near me again. That was the last time we ever spoke.

'I think I told you the other day that I hadn't seem my brother for nearly forty years... In all that time I haven't had the slightest interest in him or his sordid business.

'I know that you are only doing your job. But why anyone should think that I might know anything about the circumstances of his death... well it's beyond me.

'Most of the rest of my life is on the public record, somewhere, I'm sure that you can look it up if you want. My business dealings have always been above board. I've got where I am by hard work and a nose for a good deal. I've made a lot of money but there's nothing wrong with that. I spent nearly twenty years in the public eye in the service to the party and my country. My political career is well documented, and, as with my business dealing, I always played by the rules, showed respect to my opponents and spoke my mind... And if you'll bear with me a moment longer I'll speak my mind again.

'I don't know how my brother died, or why. And to tell you the truth I don't care. If you really want to know the truth, I'm glad. As far as I'm concerned, he died a long time ago when he chose to take the path that he followed.

The last tape ended as the plane began its descent to Stansted. When they landed, Connor took their bags from the overhead locker and put the tape recorder and the tapes back into Barton's bag. "And I thought I had the gift of the Blarney," he said, as he handed Barton his bag.

"So what did you think?" asked Barton.

"Good story… load of bollocks… but a good story."

"No I mean about him and King."

"Like I said… it's a load of bollocks. Are you sure, he didn't have it written down. I mean… well could you tell a story like that… all those details, off the top of your head?"

Chapter 21

Saturday 10th May

Duxford, Cambridge – 08:30 BST

They'd done a deal when he'd phoned from the airport; Grace had laid down her terms and he'd agreed. "It's not a lot to ask, Mike," she'd said. "It's either that or you come home to an empty house again." So they spent Friday night together at home; no phone calls, no talk of work; just a quiet romantic dinner and an early night. They'd talked into the small hours, just like they used to. Barton couldn't remember the last time that he'd felt so relaxed.

Grace was already up when he woke; the bedroom door was open and he could hear her singing along to the radio in the kitchen. He was in the shower when she came back, and didn't hear her; when he came out of the bathroom, he found her sitting by the window reading the paper. A breakfast tray was on the table and she put down the paper and poured him some tea. "What have I done to deserve this?" he asked, "I should be bringing you breakfast in bed."

"You haven't done anything," she replied with a smile. "You don't need to do anything, I'm just happy to have you back. Like I said, I just need you to be here. It wasn't that difficult, was it?"

"No, I could get used to this," he replied as he sat next to her on the sofa. "I'd forgotten what it's like to have breakfast with you."

They sat for about an hour, neither one saying much, just quietly enjoying each other's company and the feeling of being together. "So what are we going to do today?" he asked as she got up.

"I wish you'd put your bloody clothes away," she said, as she bent down to pick up his jacket. "What's this on the back, Mike?"

"Blood, Naismith cut his hand. Leave it out I'll take it to the cleaners on Monday."

"Now, I thought you wanted to tell me about Naismith," she said. "You've kept your part of the bargain and now I'm ready to listen."

"It's a long story."

"Don't worry, we've got all day. I really want to help you with this Mike."

Barton spent the rest of the morning telling Grace about his trip to Spain and his encounters with Naismith, although he left out the afternoon with Juanita. He still hadn't worked out how to tell her that, and he hoped that he wouldn't need to. She listened carefully, trying to build her own picture of the man. She didn't say much, but scribbled notes as he spoke; questions to ask him later.

"Can I listen to the recording?" she asked, when he had finished.

"It's quite long."

"That's OK. Why don't you make your calls? I'd like to listen to it alone."

"What calls?"

"The ones you've wanted to make ever since you got home yesterday," she replied. "Go on. Go and phone Sally and Trevor. And anyone else you need to, I don't mind."

Barton took the recorder from his briefcase and put it on the kitchen table. "Do you know how this works? This button…"

She interrupted him, "I'll work it out. Now go and let me listen to it in peace. I'll call you if I need you." Grace switched on the machine and waved him away.

Of course, she was right; he had calls to make. He couldn't believe that he'd waited so long. But last night she'd made everything else seem unimportant, and he was grateful for that. And this morning, talking to her had helped and he was thinking more clearly now. He opened the fridge, took out a bottle of Stella, and walked out into the garden.

"Hi Sally, it's Mike. How are you?" he said when the familiar voice answered.

"Hello stranger. I was beginning to think something had happened to you. I thought you'd have called me yesterday," said Sally casually. She hoped that her voice didn't give anything away. She couldn't tell him that she'd been worried sick; that she'd sat up half the night waiting for him to call and that she was angry with him for not calling.

"Sorry, Sal, I had a quiet evening in with Grace," he said. "What you girls call, quality time, I think. Anyway, I needed some time to think things through.

"That's OK, Mike. How are you feeling? You sounded awful when you called on Thursday," she sounded concerned. She knew from his calls that he'd had a tough time and she'd quizzed Connor when he came back to the office. He'd told her about the row he'd had with Barton and how he'd never seen him so unsettled before.

"I'm OK, Sal. It's good to be back. Now tell me what's been going on here."

"…That's about all, Mike," she said after she'd updated him on Debbie King and Herrera. "We've not really started with either of them yet, but I think they're ready to start talking."

"What about the files?" he asked. "Did you turn up much?"

"Jane's got a whole list of things that might fit," she replied. "I don't have any details with me though, everything's at the office. Are you going in tomorrow?"

"No, I thought I'd spend the day here. But why don't you come over for lunch. You could call in at the office on the way." He wanted to see what they'd found, but he wanted this weekend to last; he knew that this was just a brief respite and he wanted some more time with Grace. "I know. Why don't you bring the others? We'll have barbeque."

"It's a bit short notice, Mike. I'm not sure…" she said; the invitation had taken her by surprise: *What's he playing at? Why does he sound so happy?*

"Come on, Sal, I wouldn't be asking if this wasn't important. I really think that we all need to get together before we take this any further… And I'd rather not do it at the office."

"…Dave might not be able to make it… er… I think he's…" she stopped, there was no point arguing: *Why is it that all he has to do is ask?*

He knew, she'd always do anything he asked, and she knew that he wouldn't be asking if it wasn't important. OK, so Lorna would be annoyed, but that wasn't Sally's problem. "No I'll call him, and I'll try and get hold of Jane and Phil as well. Brenda's at the house with Debbie King and it will be a bit difficult to arrange for someone else to cover."

"That's OK," he said. It was Jane and Phil that he needed to talk to; they'd be the ones who knew what was in the files. He could do with finding out a bit more about Debbie King though. "The whole team Sal, including Brenda. I'm sure you can find someone who'd like a bit of overtime tomorrow."

"OK, I'll see what I can do," she said with an air of resignation.

"Fine, I'll see you all at about half twelve then. Oh! By the way, did you track down that journalist?"

"Yes, he's a TV news producer or something now. I've got his number."

Barton scribbled the phone number on a scrap of paper. "Thanks. I'll see you tomorrow. Enjoy your afternoon."

Sally hung up the phone: *Bloody man!* There wouldn't be much of the afternoon left to enjoy, by the time she'd finished making all the calls; retail therapy would have to wait another week. She picked up the phone and dialled the first number. "Richard… about lunch tomorrow…"

Barton looked up and saw Grace standing in the doorway. "How long have you been there?" he asked.

"Only a couple of minutes," she replied. "How's Sally?"

"She's OK. How did you know it was her?" he asked.

"Well I don't know anyone else that you talk to like that. Poor Sally I don't know why she lets you get away with it." She stopped speaking and closed her eyes for a moment: *Maybe I do know.* She hated herself for thinking it, and prayed she was wrong. "And what was that about a barbeque?"

"Well I just thought…"

"It's alright Mike, you don't have to explain. Anything that keeps you away from the office… but you can cook."

"What did you want anyway? You can't have finished listening to that recording already."

"No, I'm just having a break. God! It's heavy stuff, Mike, I can't imagine what it was like for you," she sighed. "I came to see if you wanted something to eat."

"No I'm not hungry, I've got a couple more call to make and then…" he hesitated; he didn't really want to ask this; not today, "I think I should go and see Trevor." There he'd done it; blown their quiet weekend together. Why couldn't he just wait?

"That's OK Mike. I'll need a couple of hours to go through that recording, anyway, I have to keep stopping and replaying bits." It's hard work; so much to take in; so many questions to ask. "And I'll need to go out and buy some food for tomorrow. How many are coming?"

"Five I think," he replied, feeling relieved to have been let off. "…But, only if you're sure it's OK. I'll just make a couple of quick calls and get off. I should be back by about five."

When she'd gone, he picked up the phone and called the TV studios.

Amersham, Buckinghamshire – 15:30 BST

Trevor Miller sat stony faced as he listened to Barton's story. "Bloody hell! Do you know what you're saying?" This was not what he'd been expecting; he could see the headlines now; feel the heat coming down from on high. "If you've got this wrong…"

"I know Trevor. If I'm wrong a lot of important people are going to be very pissed off with me," said Barton: *That's putting it mildly. If I'm wrong they'll hang me out to dry.*

"But Naismith… do you know who you're taking on? You know he's still got a lot of clout, and even if…"

251

"Yeah, I know. Even if I'm right, it doesn't mean that we'll be able to prove anything. His politician friends will close ranks and getting any hard evidence is going to be very difficult," said Barton. "You know it's ironic really. In a way, if it hadn't been for Naismith, I wouldn't be here now."

"What do you mean?"

"Do you remember a few years ago I told you why I'd joined the police?"

Trevor Miller thought for a moment. He remembered that Barton had joined the police shortly after his father was killed. James Barton had been shot while he was on security duty at an election meeting. The gunman was member of an extreme black activist group and his target had been Anthony Naismith MP. James Barton had saved Naismith's life and taken a bullet in the chest. His son had joined the force as some sort of tribute to his father. "Oh God! I'd forgotten about that," he said. "But what do you mean it's ironic?"

"Well I mean I'd have been a lawyer instead. You know I joined the force because of what happened to Dad, and if that man hadn't tried to kill Naismith... well you know," replied Barton. There was sadness in his voice as he remembered his mother's tears when she thought no one could see her; and how strong she had been in public at the funeral and the trial. It was at the trial that he had made his mind up. Sitting in the courtroom day after day, listening to the evidence being twisted first one way and then the other; his faith in the legal process was challenged and had been found wanting. *Innocent until proven guilty,* he realised then that he could never be a barrister. Guilty men had a right to be defended, but not by him.

"If things had been different, my Dad might still be here and I'd probably have made a lot of money defending people like Bobby King. See what I mean about irony?"

Miller didn't reply. He could see the anguish in Barton's face and could only imagine the painful memories that his encounters with Naismith must have raised. He was worried that Barton might be in danger of letting personal feelings get in the way, but he didn't say anything. Instead, he just nodded and changed the subject.

"And you're certain about Colin Marshall?" Miller asked. "I know the man, so do you... he was your boss... he always played it straight. I really find it hard to believe that he'd be involved in something like this." This was the part that Miller was finding it hardest to come to terms with; the thought of corrupt police officers always made him feel physically sick. The more senior they were, the worse it was; they were like a cancer, corrupting others with their lies and hypocrisy. But he also felt a touch of relief. If Barton was right about Marshall, it removed suspicion from his own officers. King hadn't been getting his information from anyone in the NCS. Marshall had his own source; someone else they knew, with access to the confidential records. "So what have you got in mind?" he asked.

"I've arranged to meet Andy for lunch tomorrow. I've not said anything to him," said Barton. "I just told him that I was going to be in town and needed a favour."

"Some favour!" exclaimed Miller. "You're going to ask one of your best friends to grass up his father. How do you know you can trust him?"

"I don't," replied Barton. "I'm not sure who I can trust anymore. But we've got to take the chance that he's straight and Marshall has been using him, without him knowing. You know, what it's like… coppers and ex-coppers. We talk about the job, and well… Andy would have known that his dad had a special interest in King. He might have just let something slip out without realising the significance. It's a risk we've got to take."

"What's with all this we, all of a sudden?" asked Miller. "Am I to assume that you want me to get involved in this?"

"Well, I just thought that an offer he can't refuse might sound better coming from a more senior officer." Barton winked at his boss. "After all, like you said, he's one of my best friends and if I've got to put his balls in the vice I could do with a bit of moral support."

"OK, so tell me where and when," said Miller with a sigh of resignation, "and you'd better tell me exactly how you want me to play this. I'm getting a bit old for the good cop, bad cop routine."

"Well, I'm meeting him in the Anchor at two…" said Barton as he explained the plan, what he was going to say, and the signal he would use to prompt Miller's intervention. He had it all worked out and he was sure that they wouldn't have to lean on his old pal too heavily. What he still hadn't worked out was how to tell his boss the next part; the part that he'd been putting off. But it couldn't wait any longer, not if he was going to get in with his side of things, before the Puppet Master played another card.

Miller could see that Barton looked worried and guessed that there was something else. *What next? How far out on the limb are we going here?* He didn't say anything. If it was important Barton would tell him in his own time.

"There's something else you need to know, Trevor," said Barton breaking the silence. There was a tremble in his voice. There was no easy way to say it; any way would sound bad. How do you tell your boss that you've been a complete prat; worse than that; that you may have dug yourself a hole that even he can't get you out of.

"While I was in Spain, I let myself get suckered into a couple of traps," he said, hesitantly: *Christ! Two, this is going to sound bad. Maybe the first one is just my imagination.* But he knew it wasn't, Naismith had set the trap, and he'd walked right in.

"I don't know what, if anything, Naismith is planning to do. But he could make a lot of waves and at best I could have seriously compromised the operation… at worst…"

"Just tell me Mike," said Miller seriously. "I'll be the one to judge how bad it might be." But he could already tell from the look on Barton's face, that he'd left the worst until last. He sat and listened carefully as Barton gave him the details. "Might be nothing," said Miller, supportively, while fuming inside at Barton's carelessness. "Just because a man gives you a fat brown envelope, doesn't mean that it's stuffed with cash. And anyway, it would only be his word against yours."

"Yes, but if there were pictures… you know from his CCTV… then it could be made to look like something else," said Barton, thinking of all the surveillance photos he'd seen of similar envelopes changing hands – all the payoffs, backhanders, sweeteners, bribes, bungs, hush-money – in exchange for anything and everything that could be bought, and no questions asked.

"We'll cross that bridge when and if we come to it," said Miller, still waiting for the big one. Barton looked even more worried now; there was more to come. "What's next?"

"This could be far worse, Trevor. I know that anyone can slip up, make a mistake, be caught on the wrong foot, like with the envelope, but…"

"Oh! Come on, Mike," Miller let his irritation show, he was used to this sort of prevarication from other officers, but not this one. Now he really was starting to get worried; wondering, how bad it could be, "…this is starting to sound like a confession. Now get on with it. Spit it out!"

"Well it's about Juanita Herrera-Marquez, assuming that's her real name. The crazy thing is that I knew it was a set up and I still let it happen…" said Barton nervously as he proceeded to give Miller an edited account of his indiscretion.

"For Christ's sake!" bawled Miller. "How could you be so fucking stupid? I can see the headlines now. If this comes out they'll crucify you."

"I know that's why I had to tell you before it does," said Barton, desperately looking at Miller for some sign of support. "I was hoping that we could work out how to deal with it."

"How to deal with it!" said Miller angrily. "I'll tell you how I ought to deal with it. I should suspend you right here and now. Because if it comes out and they find out that I knew about it and didn't do anything then we're both in the shit." He started to calm down, started to think how it would look. "Let's look at how bad this is. The police do a deal with a major drug dealer and a few days later the senior officer in charge of the case is seen in a compromising situation with the man's sister. It couldn't really be any worse. What the hell do you think the CPS is going to say about this? Your credibility as a witness will be wrecked."

"Maybe, but what if we could turn it around?" Barton was struggling to salvage something and an idea had just crossed his mind. He was clutching at straws, but it might be worth a try.

"What do you mean, turn it round?" asked Miller incredulously. "If this comes out, Mike, nobody will be able to get you out of it."

"Look, Trevor. We don't know for certain, that she is Herrera's sister. Naismith might have just got her to play the part. But let's for the moment, assume that she is," said Barton hesitantly, not sure that what he was about to suggest was feasible. "...and she doesn't know they tried to kill her brother. OK, if she's married to Marquez she might have divided loyalties, but let's hope that blood's thicker than water in this case. It would be worth having a word with Herrera. We'll have to get him to confirm she's his sister... he probably has a photo somewhere. And maybe we could get to her through him."

Miller had a puzzled look on his face as if he was trying to work out the implications of such an audacious suggestion. "So what you're saying is that we try to get her to turn against her husband. Why would she go for that?"

"What if she could be convinced that she was just as expendable as her brother... that this isn't a game," said Barton. He was beginning to feel a bit more confident now. "Sooner of later, they're going to find out that Herrera isn't dead. These people don't give a damn about anyone but themselves. They wouldn't think twice about using her to threaten Herrera. If we could get to her first though..."

"And just how do you propose to that?" asked Miller. "For all we know, she could be back in Colombia by now."

"Maybe not, she told me that she was waiting for Marquez to come back. She'll be in Spain at least until the end of the week. Now if we can find out where Marquez is, we could get him pulled at the airport... an immigration irregularity or something to get him out of the picture for a while." Barton's mind was racing now; seeing new possibilities, "If we could get to her, we might be able to get something without tipping them off about Herrera. She doesn't have to know he's alive... not at first... maybe we can get her to come to England to identify the body. If we can move quickly and get her here, we might even be able to get enough to hold onto Marquez..."

"That's a lot of ifs, Mike," said Miller. "Even if you could pull it off, it might not help you. If they've got pictures and the press get hold of them, things are still going to look bad for you. "

"I know, but this isn't just about getting me out of a hole. Pulling Marquez would be a real bonus," said Barton. And it'll buy me some time, he thought. "If anything comes out, and I'm pretty sure it will. You're going to have to react exactly as Naismith would expect. That mean's that you're going to have to suspend me. But at least this way I'll be able to maintain some sort of unofficial contact with the investigation without compromising any of the team."

"Don't ask me to make any promises Mike. I'm not sure that Harris and the others will go for it, and if they don't…"

"But you'll see what you can do, OK," said Barton. "You'll give it a try. Won't you?"

"Don't put me on the spot Mike. I said no promises." Miller, sighed, he wasn't at all sure that he could pull it off and he could already think of a few of people who would be quite pleased to see his star DCI take a fall.

Duxford, Cambridgeshire – 19:00 BST

The meeting with Trevor Miller had taken longer than expected and it was nearly seven when Barton arrived home. He found Grace sitting in the garden, eyes closed, a look of intense concentration on her face; she was still listening to the recording. She looked up with a start and switched off the machine. "Sorry, I didn't hear you coming," she said. "How did it go with Trevor?"

"Not too bad," said Barton, "I'll tell you about it later." He was still trying to work out what to say about Juanita; he didn't have much choice now, but it still wasn't going to be easy. "Are you still listening to that?"

"Yes, I'm just replaying some bits and making a few more notes. I've nearly finished, give me fifteen minutes," she said. "I thought we could just have some salad this evening, I bought loads of stuff this afternoon. You could sort it out while I'm finishing this and we can eat out here. Oh…! And can you get me something to drink? I've put some bottles of cranberry juice the in the fridge. Put some in a tall glass and top it up with fizzy water, please?"

As Barton prepared the salad, he thought back to the spreads that Naismith had laid on, just a couple of days ago. He looked at the thin slices of ham and salami, from the supermarket delicatessen. How the other half lived, he thought, as he remembered the whole Serrano ham brought to the table by the taciturn servant. Naismith was right, they did live in different worlds, and much as he hated to admit it, he felt more than a little envious. *'This is the way to live'*, the old man had said, *'…you couldn't even think about it on a policeman's pay…'* But of course he hadn't meant it that way. He'd been fishing, trying to find out if Barton had a price, like all the others. And of course, Barton had thought about it;

he was thinking about it now; thinking how easy it would have been. He'd only spent a few hours with Naismith, but it had been long enough to realise how the man operated; how he baited his trap and how readily his prey became enmeshed in the web. He could see them now: Marshall, Browning, Jackson, all playing their parts in Naismith's little charade on the yacht; each dangling the bait, letting Barton know much they had, and how easy it would be for him to have the same. And suddenly it didn't seem easy at all; to take Naismith's money and spend the rest of your life paying for it. With Naismith pulling your strings, always wondering when he'd call in the next payment, and knowing the price that would be exacted for stepping out of line. No, that wouldn't be easy to live with. Naismith was right; Barton couldn't be bought. But right now, he was frightened; scared at the thought of what he might be going to lose.

"Mike! What are you doing in there?"

Barton looked up and saw Grace standing in the doorway. "Sorry," he said, "I was miles away."

"I didn't ask where you were. I want to know what you're doing. How long does it take to open a bottle of juice?"

"Sorry. I forgot. I'll get it in a minute."

"Too late, Barton," she said, the tone of her voice conveyed a warning note. Barton grinned; then realised that was the wrong response and looked down at the table, trying to think of something to say. He was just about to say sorry again, but before he could open his mouth, she laughed and opened the fridge. She took out the bottles of juice and water, and put them on the table. "I suppose you want one as well," she said, as she opened the fridge again.

Barton nodded and muttered something unintelligible, as she opened a bottle of lager and put it in front of him. She found large jug, emptied a tray of ice cubes into it and then poured in the juice and water.

"And I'd better help you with that salad, or it'll be past it's sell by date." She picked up a knife and waved it menacingly at him. "Pass me those tomatoes."

"Sorry," he said.

"You will be," she laughed. "You know, every time we have one of these conversations I end up asking myself what men are for... I mean, what purpose do you really serve?"

"We have our uses," he said wistfully. "Or at least you seemed to think so last night."

"OK. But apart from that," she replied. She winked at him and deftly sliced a tomato in two, "...what use would you be without any balls?"

Barton winced as she brought the blade down hard across another fruit. "OK, you've made your point. But I wish you wouldn't look as though you're enjoying that."

She laughed and scooped the pieces of tomato into a bowl, tore up some basil leaves, which she sprinkled on top and poured some olive oil over the bowl.

She picked up the jug and a glass and walked towards the door. "You can bring the rest," she said. "Two minutes, OK!"

Barton watched her go. "Bloody women!" he muttered under his breath.

"Did you say something?"

"No, never mind." But at that moment, he was thinking that if women served any purpose, it was obviously to make men feel inadequate.

They talked while they ate, about nothing in particular, just anything to put off the serious conversations that they needed to have. After compiling a list of uses for men without balls, Grace had conceded that she preferred Barton with his manhood intact, and he'd promised not to hide the kitchen knives. They laughed and joked the way they had done the previous night, but this evening it was awkward somehow, not so relaxed, it seemed, almost, that they had to make an effort. Something had changed, but Barton couldn't work out what.

Grace wanted to talk about the baby and what he or she would be like; how their lives were going to change. She wanted to know if Barton would still want her to give up work. They'd talked about that the last time, but now she didn't want to. She'd been offered a new job, but she hadn't told him about that yet and now wasn't the right time. Grace knew that he wouldn't be able to think about them, their future, until he'd got Naismith out of his mind. She kept telling herself that she understood, that she didn't mind; but she was finding it hard. She drained her glass: *Better to get it over with.*

But, it was Barton, sensing that she was ready to talk, who spoke first. "Well, tell me what you made of it?" he asked,

"A very complex character, your Naismith," she mused. "There's a lot on that tape, and I don't think he meant to tell you as much as he did."

"How, do mean?" asked Barton. "I thought he'd pretty well rehearsed it all. You know, just enough to convince us that there wasn't anything between him and his brother."

"Oh Yes! Of course… what he gave you were a series of carefully selected anecdotes… and I'm sure that he'd rehearsed exactly what he was going to say. No, it's more about how he said it and the things that he didn't say."

"I've been thinking along those lines as well. I suppose that I needed you to confirm it," said Barton. "You know I wish I had more than the voice to go on. I've been trying really hard to play things back in my mind, trying to remember the look on his face as he spoke, the body language. But, he made pretty sure that I wasn't paying full attention, we got through four bottles of wine you know."

"There's still a lot in the voice, though," she said. "The bits that are really interesting are when he talks about his early life. Something's not right there. There are times when you can hear the voice of the small boy, vulnerable and afraid. You can really feel the fear and hatred when he mentions his father, and yet most of the time he talks about his mother with no sign of emotion."

"Yes, I thought that was a bit strange. I remember there was a point at which he stopped referring to 'my mother' and started using 'she', as if he was shutting her out. I think it's after he went to live with his aunt. And I'm sure he referred to her, as 'Bobby's mother' at one point, that's strange isn't it. Maybe, he felt that she'd deserted him as well."

"Very good... we'll make a psychologist of you yet. Yes, I picked that up too. It's as if he has no real feeling for her after that. And he was almost certainly jealous of his brother, who she kept with her."

"So he was screwed up by both his parents?"

"His father, definitely, although I think there's something else there as well. Something he didn't tell you. The hatred seems so intense, there has to something else, maybe he was abused. I don't know. And I still can't work out what it is about his mother. There's something missing, something else he didn't tell. But, I can't put my finger on it."

"And the rest of it?" he asked.

"Well the later stuff is much more matter of fact, in the way he tells it. You have to remember, that by the time he was in his teens he'd have settled down, gained confidence. And he's able to recount that as an adult. But even then, he couldn't hide his emotions, what he really felt about things. That comes over in the voice, at times it even sounded as if he was boasting."

"So how much of it do you think is true?"

Grace thought for a moment. "That depends on what you mean by true. I think most of it is true, embellished, distorted maybe, but still true. Or at least what he's come to believe is the truth, or wants to believe is true."

"That's a bit cryptic," said Barton.

"Let me try to explain. We agree that he had obviously rehearsed what he told you, selected anecdotes... snapshots of his life. He didn't have much time to prepare, so he had to tell you about things that actually happened. I don't think that he could have invented those things. But I'm not sure that everything happened the way he said, or that it even happened to him."

"So we're no further forward then."

"Oh! No, I wouldn't say that. No, he's told us quite a lot. Take this thing with his father for instance. The way he distances himself from the possibility that he could be anything like him. And everything, that was bad about his father, gets passed on to his brother. But, as children, we learn from the example of our parents. Bobby King never knew his father… he wasn't even two years old when he left. But, Naismith was old enough to understand some of what was going on… the bullying and the violence. He was exposed to it for longer, and I wouldn't mind betting it was worse than he says. He said that his father never hit him… I don't believe that. Many victims of abuse feel ashamed and denial is easier, than acceptance. No, if either of the brothers was going to turn out like the father, my money's on Naismith. And he can't bear the thought that he might be like the man he hates so much, so he transfers that onto his brother."

"But that doesn't fit the facts. We know all about Bobby King, he was a violent man… cruel, vicious. There's nothing to suggest that Naismith was anything like that."

"I'm not saying that he is, although we don't know for certain. But a person can be cruel and vindictive… hurt others, without using physical violence. He's a control freak… doesn't need to get his own hands dirty. He gets other people to do that for him."

"So where does that leave us."

"I'm not sure. But you have to be careful not to push him too far. You've already seen how he can turn. Remember what you told me about the first time that you met. How he reacted when you called him by his real name… his father's name."

"Yes, but I deliberately engineered that, caught him off guard."

"And for a moment you were in control, and he didn't like that."

Barton needed a break; this was getting very heavy. He needed to let it soak in, before they continued. "If there's more of this, I could do with another drink, before we go on," he said. "I'll just get another beer. Do you want anything, how about a glass of wine?"

"I shouldn't drink alcohol. It's not good for the baby."

"Of course you know that he's a racist. Don't you?" Grace said, in a very matter of fact way, as Barton came back from the kitchen.

The remark took Barton by surprise. "What do you mean?" he asked. Barton had encountered racism before; at school, at university and in the job. And, although it had been fairly obvious to him that Naismith was prejudiced, he hadn't put him down as a real racist; not like some people he'd come across.

"Well, I don't mean like your typical National Front or BNP type," she said. "But, from some of the things that you told me last night and some of the stuff on the tape… I'd say he was worse. Particularly, when I add it to what Charlie told me."

"Charlie?"

"Charles Henderson, he's a don at Trinity... modern history. He's an expert on right wing politics. I met him last week. I wanted to get some background on Naismith. He knows the sort of stuff that you haven't got in your files and that's kept out of the papers."

"And what did he tell you?" asked Barton eagerly.

"Quite a lot, you'd be surprised at some of the things that are hidden from the public. Like how Number Ten insisted on vetting all of his election addresses. He was kept under a pretty close watch by some of the high ups in the party. They needed him, he was popular with the rank and file, but they didn't trust him. Apparently, Mrs T loathed him. She let him get so far in government, but he was never going to get into her cabinet. She was worried that she might have another Enoch Powell on her hands. Besides, the Tories had a lot of financial support from the Asian business community, and they couldn't risk Naismith scaring them away. As long as he thought he was in favour and heading for the top, they were able to keep him in check."

"He seems to know a lot... this Charlie."

"Like I said, he's an expert. He's spent years researching this sort of stuff. He's written books about it."

"So how come he's not published anything about Naismith?"

"He's very careful not to name names. He couldn't afford to be sued for libel by someone as rich a Naismith. And besides, he's not really interested in exposing individuals. He's an academic, not a journalist."

"Are you sure he's not just another left wing university type, with an axe to grind."

"You couldn't be further off the mark if you tried. Charles Henderson is about sixty years old and joined the Tory party over forty years ago. He's a personal friend of Mrs T and he's been an advisor to central office. He knows almost everyone who's held a senior position in the party over the past twenty-five years, including Naismith. I think that you could say he's a reliable source," she said smugly.

"OK, so he knows what he's talking about. What else did he tell you?"

"Well, most of it's hearsay of course, none of them... Charlie's friends in the party, I mean... would ever talk to an outsider. They might not have liked Naismith, but he was still one of them and they always close ranks to protect their own. It's not in the interests of the party to let things like that get out. And besides, they've all got skeletons in their cupboards. But he did tell me something that was very interesting, and very disturbing."

"Come on! Get on with it," he said impatiently. "What is it? Does he eat babies, worship the devil, or something?"

"No, don't be stupid. During the seventies and eighties, he made regular trips to America. They were mostly official visits of some sort, but he nearly always extended his stay by a few days." Grace was looking exited; she was enjoying this; the slow build up to the bombshell. "Now, and this is on the record if, like Charlie, you know where to look. Naismith almost always visited the southern states, where he met with prominent local politicians and businessmen. Many of these visits were reported in local papers, Charlie has cuttings. The earliest is from the time that he was the chairman of the Police Authority… You know before he was an MP. I've been through all of the newspaper reports that Charlie has on his file and guess what? One name comes up more than any other does. Henry Patterson."

"That's not the same…"

"I don't know, but I suppose you could find out. Although, for all we know, he's dead by now."

"But if it was the same man, Naismith would have had a perfectly innocent reason to visit. His mother was buried out there, remember. So what's the big deal?"

"Well, this Henry Patterson was a Grand Wizard of the White Knights of the Cross… an extreme racist group… part of the Ku Klux Klan." With her bombshell dropped on target, Grace leaned forward in her chair and poured a glass of wine: *Just one will be OK.*

"Oh Shit!" That was all Barton could think of to say. And then he felt cold, as the ghost made its presence felt: *Oh God!*

Grace saw the tears welling up in his eyes as he spoke. "My dad… I was so proud of my dad. And I thought he died saving someone who really mattered. Do you know? In all these years… even though part of me has always blamed Naismith… hated him for a while. I never once wished it had been him instead. But… it was his fault, Grace, Naismith's fault. That's why they wanted to kill him. And Dad died because of him… he died to save a fucking racist."

"He was doing his job Mike," said Grace, reaching out and touching his hand. "Just like you would have done, and even if he'd known the man was a racist it wouldn't have changed anything. The same laws protect everyone; you can't choose who to apply them to."

Chapter 22

Sunday 11th May

Duxford, Cambridgeshire – 12:30 BST

Barton stood at the window and watched the blue BMW pull into the drive. The driver's door opened and Brenda Cooper stepped out of the car; grinning, like the cat that had got the cream. Barton guessed that a few speed limits had just been shattered. The other door opened; Sally got out first and tilted the seat forward to let Jane Barclay out of the back.

Barton went downstairs and opened the door. "I see you've got a new chauffeur then, Sal," he said as the three women walked into the hall.

"And she can drive too, unlike some people that I know," replied Sally.

"Nice car," said Brenda. "Very fast, but it's not really my style. I'd rather have one like yours, sir." Barton looked at Sally, licked his finger, and waved it at her: *Fifteen- love.*

Sally glared at him and mouthed, almost, silently, "Bastard."

"Are you alright, Jane?" he asked. "You look a bit pale."

"I'll be alright, sir. But I think I left my stomach somewhere near Harlow," she replied. "I've never been that fast, not even with the blue lights flashing." She laughed. "Next time these two offer me a lift, I think I'll catch the bus."

"Dave and Phil should be here soon, we passed then on the motorway about twenty minutes ago," said Sally.

He led them through the house and into the garden, where Grace was sitting under a tree, reading the paper. She got up as they approached, "Hi Grace, how are you?" said Sally, stretching out her arms and lightly placing her hands on Grace's shoulders. The two women briefly exchanged kisses, barely making contact. The greeting looked a little awkward, but they were acquaintances rather than friends and Grace preferred it that way.

Grace always felt uncomfortable when Sally was around. Maybe she was a bit jealous of her; she was a psychologist, she ought to have known, but she was never quite sure. Grace had lived her whole life in the country, and she liked the quiet life, or at least that's what she told herself. Barton was the only man she'd ever really had a relationship with; of course, there'd been a few boyfriends at school and university, but nothing serious, until she met him. Sally was a party girl with a liking for late nights, fast cars, and fast living. Grace was sure that there must be a word, some sort of '*–ist*', for women who collected men, but she couldn't think of it: *Tart, Whore, Slut, that'll do*. A bit unfair perhaps, but that's how she felt today.

Barton introduced Sandra and Jane. Grace hadn't met them before and she wasn't quite sure what she was supposed to do. She wasn't used to this. She'd been to a few social gatherings when Barton was in Cambridge, but this was different. She didn't really know how the boss's wife was supposed to act: '*Just be yourself, be natural*', he'd told her. But she'd heard one of the call him '*sir*' as they came out of the house. That always threw her; she didn't think she'd ever get used to people calling her husband '*sir*'. Strangers, shop assistants, waiters, that was OK, that was just politeness; but not people you work with every day, no that wasn't normal; at least not in the environment that she worked in. How could you have a proper conversation with someone who addressed their boss in a way that suggested they'd missed the twentieth century?

Barton had anticipated this and had told the two young DCs as they were walking through the kitchen. "Drop the '*sir*', OK, girls? It's a bit formal for my back garden. Just call me Mike, OK. And please don't call Grace '*Mrs Barton*' she hates it." He knew that they'd find it a bit awkward, and he tried to guess which one would lapse first.

He didn't have to wait long; less than thirty seconds. As they walked out of the kitchen door Jane said "What a fantastic garden, sir."

Barton left them talking and went to check on the barbecue. The flames and smoke had died away and the coals were ready, glowing red, beneath a dull grey coating of ash. He was putting some chicken pieces on the grill, when he heard Dave Connor's voice. "Hi, Mike, there was no answer at the door, so we came round by the side gate." Barton turned around and saw Connor and Phil standing on the lawn, Connor was half-hidden behind a huge pink soft toy.

"What's that?" asked Barton.

"A cuddly pig, it's a present for the baby. We had a whip round and Sally told us to get something appropriate," said Phil. "Look, we even got it a helmet."

"Very amusing," said Barton. "And what makes you think it's a boy?"

"Has to be, no doubt about it," said Connor. "John Perry's running a book. I've got ten quid on a boy, eight pounds two ounces."

"Hang on a minute, how many people know about this?"

"Oh! Not many… well maybe the whole of the NCS, and probably half the Met by now," laughed Phil. "If you wanted to keep it secret, why did you tell Dave? You might as well have put an advert in the papers."

"What are you suggesting mate? You know me… I'm the soul of discretion."

"That's enough you two. I think some of this is ready," said Barton, pointing to the barbeque. "Come on, we'll get you some beer and you can help me bring out the rest of the food."

The women had seen Connor and Phil arrive and were walking across the lawn to join them. "Oh my God!" exclaimed Sally, "Can't I trust you two to do anything? I'm sorry Grace, when I told them to buy something for the baby I thought they'd get something sensible."

Grace smiled, "Well I like it and I'm sure the baby will, once she gets over the shock."

"She? But I thought it was going to be a boy," said Connor. "Mike, you said it was a boy."

"No. You said it was a boy, Dave, we don't know yet."

"But haven't you had one of those test things that tells you?"

"Too early... but we don't want to know anyway. We want it to be a surprise," said Grace.

"But when you see John Perry you can put a tenner on for me. Girl, six pounds eleven ounces," said Barton with smile.

"Anything we can do to help Grace?" asked Brenda.

"No thanks," said Grace. "I think we can leave the men to cook. They seem to have things in hand." She frowned at Barton, "I see you've got yourselves a drink, what about us?"

"Sorry," said Barton. "What can I get you?"

"I'll drive back, if you two want to drink," said Sally.

"In that case I'll have a vodka and tonic please," said Brenda.

"Me too," said Jane.

Lunch was a relaxed affair, with everyone chatting and joking. Barton was pleased; they needed a break after the pressures of the past few weeks. Dave Connor had taken over the barbeque after Barton had incinerated the first batch of chicken pieces, and he'd spent most of the time on his feet carefully turning the food and cooking everything to perfection. Barton confined himself to bar duties, keeping the chef well lubricated and mixing jugs of brightly coloured fruit cocktails, for the women; although, as Sally was driving, Jane and Brenda added generous quantities of vodka to theirs.

After lunch, Grace got up and started towards her favourite seat under the birch tree. "I'll leave you to talk about work for a bit. He's going to make you pay for lunch now."

The others listened intently as Barton explained his suspicions and his plan. He answered their questions as best he could, without giving too much away. There were some things they didn't need to know, yet.

Sally gave a brief account of the situation on the home front, and their progress in following up all the enquiries that Barton and Connor had sent them from Spain. Finally, she confirmed that the arrangements were in place for moving Herrera to the safe house.

"I'm going over to Reading with a couple of the witness protection guys tonight," said Connor. "Debbie King's already at the house, but she doesn't know he's coming yet."

Barton asked a question. "Do you think that we can trust her?" A lot was riding on Debbie King, and he had to be sure.

"It's been slow going, but I think she's coming round," said Sally. "What do you think Brenda?"

"I wouldn't want to stake my life on it, but she's opened up quite a bit towards the end of the week." Brenda thought for a moment and nodded her head. "Yes... I think she'll be OK. She's mad as hell about what they did to Herrera. And I think she'll open up a bit more when she knows we're keeping our side of the deal."

"OK, we've got to go for it," said Barton. "But, be warned, the shit's going to hit the fan next week, and you might get some of the fall out."

"That's alright, Mike. We can handle it," said Connor. But there was a hint of doubt in his voice. Last week, he'd seen just how much this was getting to his boss and he was worried.

"Good, but if any of you have any second thoughts," Barton said seriously. "...If anybody wants out, just call the Chief Super."

Jane shook her head and looked at the others. "No worries, sir, we're all in this now." The young WPC looked at the man who was giving her the chance to do the biggest thing so far in her short career; there was no way that she was going to back out now. The others didn't need to speak; their faces said that she spoke for them all.

"Thanks," said Barton. "Now how about a walk to work off that lunch; the pub in the village should be open."

"I'll stay here," said Sally. "We can't all just go off and desert Grace." There was something they had to talk about; Sally wasn't sure what it was, but something was bugging Grace, and she knew that it couldn't be put off for much longer.

"They've gone to the pub. I Thought you might like a chat," said Sally as she sat on the bench. "What's up Grace?"

Grace leapt up from the bench. "What's up!" she shouted. "What's up is that you've been sleeping with my husband, you fucking tart. She was shaking, as she spat out the words. "You come here… to my house! As if nothing's happened… and you ask me what's up! How could you! How could you!"

Sally hadn't expected this and for a moment, she just sat speechless.

"Well, say something!" Grace demanded. "It's true… isn't it!"

"You've got it all wrong Grace. There's nothing," Sally stammered as she got to her feet. "…There's been nothing… not since…"

"Not since when? How long has this been going on? When?" Grace stopped and put her hand over her mouth "Oh God! It never stopped did it?"

"Grace, you've got it wrong. There's nothing. Nothing since before he met you." But, Sally's words went unheard as Grace ran towards the house. Sally sat on the bench, held her head in her hands, and cried. She wasn't sure how long she sat there, on her own. It seemed like hours, but she knew it was only a few minutes. She got up and walked across the lawn. She needed to settle this before Barton came back.

She found Grace sitting in the study. A CD was playing quietly, the volume turned so low that Sally didn't notice it at first. And Grace wasn't listening to it anyway. She was sobbing, talking to herself, asking a question to which she had no answer; one word repeated, over and over, "Why? Why? Why…?"

Sally said nothing as she sat down, and waited for Grace of become aware of her presence.

When Grace looked up, her anger had gone, replaced by sadness, and a look of hopelessness. "Why, Sally? He's all I ever wanted. You can have anyone. Why are you taking Mike away from me?"

"Grace, I don't know why you're thinking this," said Sally. "There's nothing going on between me and Mike. You have to believe me."

"You were here…" Grace spoke slowly, deliberately, choking back her tears "…last week… when I was away." She paused again and looked at Sally; she wanted to see the truth. "You slept with him, here in my house. Don't deny it. I found these. Your name's on the label." She threw a small packet at Sally. "You left them in the bathroom."

Sally bent down and picked up the packet of contraceptive pills. "I can explain…" she said.

Grace interrupted her, angrily. "Explain what… that you got careless… that I wasn't meant to find out. It's a good job you're on the fucking pill, or this might be an even bigger mess."

Now it was Sally's turn to get angry. "You're a bloody fool Grace. Where did you find them?"

"I told you. They were in the bathroom."

Sally stood up and crossed the room, "Which bathroom?"

"Does it matter?"

"Of course it bloody does," said Sally, grabbing Grace by the wrist and pulling her to her feet. "Come with me."

She pulled Grace through the doorway and pushed her towards the stairs. "Up!" she shouted.

She followed Grace upstairs, "Now show me. Show me which bathroom?"

Grace trembled as she pointed to an open doorway. "There, the one in the guest room."

"And this is where I slept," Sally said quietly, as she walked into the room. "Or at least, where I spent half of the night crying, because the man I love was asleep in the room next door... and I know that I can never have him... Because he's not interested... because he loves you."

Sally sat on the bed and looked at Grace. "If only you knew how lucky you are," she sighed; now it was her turn to cry.

"When we got back that night and you weren't here... I've never seen Mike so upset. He thought that you'd left him. We sat in the study and drank most of a bottle of whisky between us, and all he could think about was you. Yes, I stayed the night, but only because I was too drunk to drive home." Sally looked straight into Grace's eyes. Grace said nothing, but she could see that Sally was telling the truth, and she could see that she was hurting inside. "You have to believe me Grace. Nothing happened. I lost Mike years ago. I'd already lost him before he met you. Now come back downstairs, there's something else you need to know."

Grace, still silent, sat in an armchair as Sally walked over to the hi-fi. "Mike was sitting in that chair when I went to bed," said Sally. "I couldn't sleep and I came down at about half-past three. He was still awake, sitting there just staring into space. I made him go to bed." She stretched her hand out to the volume control on the hi-fi. "He was listening to this, over and over... he'd set it on repeat play... he said he was playing it for you."

Sally turned up the volume so that Grace could hear, and walked towards the door.

Grace cried as she heard the voice of Etta James coming from the speakers, then closed her eyes and listened to the song: '*I'd rather go blind than to see you walk away from me...*'

"You need to talk to him, Grace," said Sally, as she walked out of the door, not even trying to hide the sadness in her voice. "You're so lucky. I had to watch him walk away a long time ago."

PART THREE

Chapter 23

Monday 12th May

Clerkenwell, London – 10:15 BST

Barton took the train from Cambridge and arrived at King's Cross station just before ten. It was only a short distance from King's Cross to the offices at 200 Gray's Inn Road and Barton decided to walk. He crossed Euston Road and made his way along the busy road that runs between Bloomsbury to the west and Clerkenwell to the east. Fifteen minutes later, he was standing at the reception desk of the ITN offices. He wasn't sure how much he was going to learn, but he reckoned that the man he'd come to see knew more about Naismith than he'd ever been allowed to publish. He'd been waiting a few minutes when a young man in jeans and a T-shirt emerged from the lift and approached him.

"Mr Barton?" he said, holding out his hand. "Gary Mills, I'm Chris's PA. Would you like to follow me? I'll take you up to his office."

They took the lift to the fifth floor, and walked along the corridor. "Here," said the young man, stopping outside a door. "Go in and take a seat, Chris will be along in a minute. Help yourself to coffee."

Barton looked at the nameplate on the door, as he stepped into the office. 'Chris Fisher, Executive Producer, Home Affairs'.

As he drank his coffee, he stared out of the window. The back of the building overlooked the main Post Office at Mount Pleasant. He'd once been involved in an investigation there; years ago, when he was a DS. He recalled that it had something to do with credit cards being stolen from the mail. He smiled as he remembered the attractive young WPC who had brightened up the long, boring nights in the sorting office observation gallery; it was the first time that he had worked with Sally Parkinson. Happy days, life had seemed so simple back then.

He was lost in his thoughts and didn't hear the door open. As it closed he turned round with a start, slopping coffee into the saucer, and saw a tall, good looking, man in his early forties, immaculately groomed wearing a hand made suit, expensive shoes and a Rolex watch. Naismith's *'sleazy little reporter'* seemed to be doing quite well for himself. He extended his hand towards Barton. "Chris Fisher... and you must be Chief Inspector Barton."

Barton shook Fisher's hand. "Good of you to see me at such short notice, Mr Fisher."

"Chris, please. Now if I've got this right, you want to talk to me about Sir Anthony Naismith. Well, it's about time your lot caught up with that bastard. How can I help you Inspector."

Fisher's comment took Barton by surprise. He hadn't really expected much from this meeting, just background. He was used to dealing with journalists, and getting anything useful from them was sometimes like pulling teeth. But he sensed that Fisher was going to be different.

"I'm not really sure what I want from you, or how useful it will be, and for the moment this conversation is off the record," said Barton.

"But you are after Naismith?" said Fisher, "look, anything that I can do to help you nail that lying hypocrite, you just have to ask. If you only knew how long I've been waiting for this, Inspector."

"Like I said this is off the record. To say that we are, as you put it, 'after Naismith', might be stretching the point. You've no doubt heard that his brother, Bobby King, died last week. He was the subject of a major National Crime Squad investigation, and his death has left a lot of questions unanswered."

"And you think that Naismith is involved?"

"What I might think and what I can prove, are a very long way apart at the moment," said Barton. "Let's call this a fishing trip. I've read everything that you wrote when King was up for murder, but I'm getting the impression that there's more."

"Oh! Yes, there's a lot more," said Fisher with a nod and a knowing smile. "In my case there was a world of difference between what I knew and what I could publish."

"And will you tell me what you know?" asked Barton eagerly, "...on the record."

"On the record," said Fisher. "Although I'll need some guarantees, and you have to understand that in journalism the rules of evidence aren't as clear cut as they are in your job. I don't have to able to prove beyond a reasonable doubt that two plus two equals five, just as long as I can avoid a libel suit."

"Understood," said Barton with a smile. "And I suppose that with a man of Naismith's means, a libel suit is to be avoided at all costs. Is that why you didn't publish any more?"

"Partly, but there was a lot more to it than that," said Fisher solemnly. "There's always more than meets the eye where Naismith is involved. By the way, I've been doing some checking up on you. I like to know who I'm dealing with and I reckon that we've something in common."

"What do you mean?" asked Barton. He shouldn't have been surprised, but he was. He was the detective and the idea of someone checking up on him was a bit unnerving. But he wasn't surprised; some journalists were better investigators than many of the detectives he knew.

"Well, one way or another Naismith has blighted both of our lives."

"What do you mean?"

"I think you know, Inspector," he said bitterly. "We've both lost part of ourselves because of him. You lost your father, and I lost my self respect."

"My father? I don't blame him for that!" Barton protested, as he sensed that the conversation was going in a direction that he'd rather avoid.

"You should. The only way you're going to get Naismith is to make this personal," said Fisher wistfully. "If you keep it all in the line of duty, you'll end up making compromises. We all do, and that's how he wins."

"But we don't work like that. I can't go off on a personal vendetta. They'd hang me out to dry." Barton was becoming annoyed. So far Fisher had said nothing and he was beginning to think that this was a waste of time. "Look I'm sorry to press you Mr Fisher. But could you get to the point."

"Don't you see? The point is that he's already winning. If you fear the consequences, you'll make the compromise. You want this man. I can see it in your eyes. You may not know what he's done, but you're sure that he's done it."

"You're talking in riddles again. Now I need to know if you have anything that will help me prove a connection between Naismith and his brother. Because right now that's the only way I'm going to get to Naismith."

"I'm sorry Inspector, but I need to know how committed you are. I can tell you things that will ease my conscience, maybe help me regain some self respect. But if you don't nail him, I could end up dead. There are things that I know that will make it personal for you, whether you like it or not. I made the compromises and I've regretted it ever since. But I became quite good at pretending that it didn't matter a long time ago, and I'd like to live a bit longer yet."

"What do you mean?"

"Oh! Come on Inspector! You're not a fool. I mean that Naismith kills people. Oh! Of course, he doesn't actually get his hands dirty, but people who get in his way can end up dead. OK, so maybe it won't be quite so easy for him now his brother's gone, but he'll find others."

"Hold on. You're saying that Naismith and King…"

Fisher interrupted, "Yes, of course that's what I mean. That's why you're here isn't it."

"Yes. I suppose it is. I just didn't expect you to be quite so…"

"What? Honest, frank, co-operative? I have been waiting over fifteen years for a knock on the door. I waited, but the police never came, or at least they went through the motions but they never really wanted to know. I told you, I compromised and because of that, I'm still alive. But I believe that you really want to know. So tell me, will you make it personal if you have to? No compromises."

Both men already knew the answer. The conversation had been a fishing trip for both of them and now they knew that they could trust each other.

It was midday when Barton left the ITN offices. Fisher needed to prepare for an interview with a government minister, for the early evening news, and had to cut their meeting short. He'd said a lot, but there was more, and they'd agreed to meet again that evening, but for the time being there was enough to convince Barton that he was on the right track. Fisher had told him that he'd made copies of his notebooks, tape transcripts and other papers relating to Naismith: *'I left them with a solicitor for safe keeping... a sort of insurance'.* Just as well, because the originals had disappeared shortly after King's heavies paid their first visit.

*

Southwark, London – 12:30 BST

Barton's next appointment was going to be to be a lot more difficult, and he needed time to think. He'd arranged to meet Andy Marshall for lunch at two, so he had some time to kill. He cut through Mount Pleasant to Farringdon Road and took a short bus ride to Blackfriars Bridge, where he walked down the flight of steps in front of the Express building to the riverside path. Things had changed since he and Andy were last here; two young probationers, fresh out of Hendon patrolling the streets of Southwark. In those days much of the riverside, between Waterloo and Tower Bridge, was still a run down shambles of old warehouses, wharves and dingy streets – looking enviously across the river at the rich architecture of the Embankment and the City – and definitely not a place to linger. Most of the old warehouses were now gone, replaced by new buildings or converted to offices. Tourists now thronged the riverside walk, visiting attractions like the Globe Theatre and Borough Market, and the new bars and cafes were always busy.

The old Backside power station dominates the stretch of river between the bridges of Blackfriars and Southwark. Built in 1947, the bold modern design, of the massive brick fortress, had reflected the mood of the country, as post-war Britain embarked on the long and difficult task of re-construction. Facing it, on the opposite side of the river, partially obscured by the ugly erections of concrete and glass between the top of Ludgate Hill and the north bank, the ornate structure St. Paul's stood, as a reminder of an old order that was gone forever.

Now, a spectacular pedestrian bridge, constructed to mark the new millennium, linked the two sites. Its inspired design bringing them closer together, like two competing giants preparing to joust, and yet keeping them at a safe distance, so that neither can win the contest. The delicate span drawing the eye towards each in turn, inviting the viewer to choose his or her champion.

It was only a five minute walk from the here to the pub, but he wanted to get there early and set the alarm on his mobile for one-forty before entering the building

The old power station now housed one of the world's finest museums of modern art and had become one of the city's most visited sites. The Tate Modern was Barton's favourite London building and he visited whenever he could. This was a place where you could lose yourself, if only for a while; a place to let your imagination run free. It had taken him a long time to appreciate modern art, and as with so many things it was Grace who had opened his eyes: *'Use your imagination,'* she had told him: *'First, try to see what the artist saw, then look beyond and travel to wherever your mind takes you'*.

He never ceased to marvel at the vastness of the old turbine room, which extended for the full length and height of the building. In this incredible, daunting space – echoing with a hundred voices and ten-thousand footsteps – even the most massive of artworks are dwarfed; swallowed into the belly of a giant beast, to be slowly digested by swarms of micro-organisms – the thousands who visit daily – at least that was how Barton always imagined it; whenever he walked down the huge ramp. And today he felt as insignificant as a micro-organism as he stood on the central mezzanine, towered over by a massive bronze and steel sculpture, over thirty feet high. Then, he looked up at the giant spider and shuddered as he imagined Naismith; spinning his web of corruption and deceit.

Barton wasn't completely sold on the serious side of art; the idea that everything had to have a meaning. Amongst the exhibits, there are many examples of the bizarre, the ridiculous, and the comic; and he always found moments of light relief, when he wandered the Tate's maze of galleries. But he found none today. Instead, many familiar pieces provoked a sense of foreboding and shocking, disturbing imaginings. He stood transfixed in front of a piece titled *Exquisite Corpses* and remembered playing a game as a child; where each drew a head at the top of a sheet of paper, then folded it over and passed it round the circle. The next child drew a body and the next the legs, and when the papers were unfolded, the children had all laughed at the comical figures. These drawings took the game to extremes, with grotesque, disturbing images of distorted and tortured figures; hanging on the wall, like the marionettes, backstage in a puppet theatre; reminding him of the figures from his dream; Naismith's puppets?

In Chris Ofili's portrait of a proud and beautiful black woman, with tears running down her face, he saw his mother. Then, he looked again, and she became his sister. *No Woman, No Cry.* Sometimes – particularly at this time; the time when it always hurt the most – it seemed that they would always cry, and he wondered if they would ever stop grieving.

Barton stood at the entrance to a room that he loved and feared in equal measure. Loved for the way it freed his thoughts like no other place he knew; feared for the dark places it uncovered in the deepest recesses of his mind. And no matter how little time he had, there were always minutes that he could steal, to sit there for a while. Today he arrived in this place, with an acute awareness of his own vulnerability, and no recollection of how he came to be there.

In the cavernous, dimly lit room, massive wooden benches provided somewhere to sit and contemplate the nine huge canvases by Mark Rothko. These were, stark, featureless images, composed of bold, massive brush strokes, muted shades of dark red, and maroon, contrasting with the darkest black. Powerful images, dark and brooding, like Barton's thoughts on that day. Mysterious images that really could set your mind free to wander and explore the depths of imagination, Some were hard, and unforgiving, the shapes appearing as solid barriers like walls or locked doors. Others had a softer, ethereal quality, the shadowy rectangular frames appearing to float, in a sea of mist, inviting the viewer to enter the picture, and explore what lay beyond these doorways to the unknown; or maybe they were windows? Barton preferred to imagine windows – it was safer, just to look through a window.

But, today, Barton found himself in front of a doorway, staring into the mist, and powerless to resist the unseen force drawing him across the threshold, through the portal, to a place inside the image, a place beyond safety. It was a dark, cold, melancholy place, and through the layers of the swirling mists he saw the shadowy figures of men and women – running, pushing, stumbling, trying to escape, trying to find the door, but unable to break free and all calling out, forlornly, for help – and he couldn't help them; they were beyond help. Then in the half-light he could see their faces; faces from his dreams. He turned and tried to run, back towards the door, but the invisible strings tightened, entangling him, and holding him back; in sight of freedom, but beyond help. And then, he called out, to a man standing in the gallery, a man he recognised, begging him to reach in and pull him to safety. But the man just stared, into the mist, as he stepped through the doorway, and then he too was beyond help. And then, both called out in one voice, to a man standing in the gallery, a man they both recognised. But, Barton just stared, into the mist, and...

The vibration of the mobile phone in his pocket brought him back to reality. He rubbed his eyes and shook his head. At first, as he turned and walked away, he was trembling, and then as he left the gallery he started shaking and sweating. He took the shortest route that he could remember and hurried to the exit. Once outside, he ran to the riverside and took in large gulps of air, leaning on the railings for support. The last time he'd experienced a panic attack was twenty years ago, during the Trinity term, when the two policemen had come to his rooms at Pembroke College and given him the terrible news. The same feelings were inside his head now; he was angry and scared.

He drew more deep breaths and slowly composed himself. He remembered what the journalist had said: *'It has to be personal, no compromises'*. As he walked towards Southwark Bridge to meet his friend, he steeled himself, for what he had to do. And, by the time he passed the Globe, he was ready: *I'm sorry, Andy. But this is personal.*

The Anchor was one of Southwark's oldest pubs and had once been a regular haunt for the two young PCs. It stood in the shadow of the bridge, facing the river. Outside, on the opposite side of the street, there were tables and benches, all occupied by office workers and tourists enjoying lunch in the spring sunshine. Inside there were plenty of quiet corners for a discreet meeting. Barton had arranged to meet his friend in one of the small bars, but he entered by the main bar. He had chosen the time, after the lunchtime rush, to guarantee somewhere to sit and talk privately, but it was still busy enough for Trevor Miller to sit unnoticed until it was time to intervene; he nodded to Barton as he came in.

Barton made his way through to the other bar. It was still a few minutes before two; Andy Marshall was always punctual, he'd always walk through the door on the dot; not a minute early, not a minute late. Still feeling the aftershock of the panic attack, Barton ordered a large brandy and downed it in one. Then he ordered two pints of bitter, sat at a table and lit a cigarette. He sat with his back to the wall, so that Andy would have to sit with his back to the door to the main bar. He drew deeply on the cigarette, and felt a rush as the nicotine hit his system. He realised that it was his first of the day. 'Maybe I should give up,' he thought, 'if I can go half a day without one.'

At precisely two o'clock Andy Marshall walked into the bar. "Hi, Mike, this is just like old times," he said with a smile. "Well, not quite. I see you've bought the first round," he laughed.

"Good to see you, Andy," said Barton. "I can see that office work suits you." He prodded his friend gently in the stomach.

"It's only a few pounds," said Marshall, breathing in. "Anyway, we can't all be NCS super cops. Someone has to keep on top of all the paperwork that you lot create."

They hadn't seen each other for months and the verbal sparring continued for a several minutes. Two old friends enjoying a pint; at least that was what Andy Marshall was meant to think when he got the message that Barton left on his answering machine: *'Hi Andy, haven't seen you for ages. Look, there's a couple of things that I need to pick your brains over. I've got to come into town on Monday, and I'm going to have a couple of hours to spare in the afternoon. I could come over to NCIS. But what about meeting up at the Anchor for a pint? We can talk business and catch up on the gossip. How about two o'clock?'*

Poor Andy, he didn't even get a chance to say no. Not that he would have done. Although he was the older by a couple of years, he'd always looked up to Barton. The super cop, always where the action was; the sort of policeman that he'd wanted to be all those years ago at Hendon. But somewhere along the way he'd lost the drive and he'd become content with the quieter side of police work. Barton had often challenged him, but his answer was always the same: *'Why risk your neck out on the streets, when you could get paid the same for sitting behind a desk?'* And, he was good at paperwork; even enjoyed it. It hadn't taken much in those days to get fixed up with a nice little number in the collator's office and from there it had only been a short step to the NCIS. Still, he sometimes envied his friend and the others who got all the attention. NCIS was pretty anonymous, you weren't exactly going to get covered in glory sitting at a computer all day; but if he couldn't be a hero the next best thing was to have one for a best mate. And besides, he liked the regular hours.

Marshall finished his pint and stood up. "Same again?" he asked.

"Just a half," said Barton, gesturing to his half-empty glass.

"So what's it all about?" asked Marshall as he put the glasses on the table. "We've been getting so many priority requests coming in from your team this past week, we're starting to get a backlog, and other squads are complaining." He paused for a moment, looking slightly puzzled. "You said that you had to pick my brains. So is this about something else? I heard that you'd left Paul Timms in charge of the King investigation and that you were on a break. It was a bit of a surprise when you phoned. I thought you were on holiday in Spain."

"Now I wonder where you got that idea from?" said Barton, his tone had become serious.

"I spoke to Dad a couple of days ago and he said he'd seen you in Marbella. I just assumed that you were taking a bit of leave."

"Come on Andy, since when did you ever know me to go on leave in the middle of an investigation."

"But I thought you'd got the King case all wrapped up now. Dead and buried all bar the paper work, and we'll end up doing a lot of that," Marshall laughed, "Definitely dead and buried, as far as King's concerned."

"I'm glad that you think it's funny," said Barton. "But it's still a long way from over."

"So what have you been doing then?" asked Marshall. He sounded annoyed. "I'm supposed to know. NCIS, National Criminal Intelligence Service, mate. Criminal intelligence, that means that we need to know what's going on out there. You lot are meant to keep us informed. How are we supposed to do our job if you're playing at secret squirrel?"

"OK, Andy... you want to talk about secrets, well how about this one. We've been keeping information from NCIS for over a week. Do you want to know why?"

"What do you mean?" Marshall asked indignantly. "We've been getting stuff from Paul every day... loads of it."

"You don't get it do you? Of course, Paul's sending stuff over. King's dead, Milosevic is dead, they've arrested Underwood, Nichols, Jarvis and a small army of pimps and dealers, not to mention all the illegals. That generates a mountain of paperwork. But like I said it's not finished, in fact my team have only just started," Barton stressed 'my team' to make his point. "Who do you think has been generating all those requests for information?"

"What do you mean your team? Look mate if you're working on something new and haven't told us..."

"What? I'll be in trouble. You'll tell your boss and he'll tell my boss. Then what? I'll get a slap on the wrist!" Barton sneered; it was time to get personal. "You've been at a desk too long, mate. In the real world out there, people don't always play by the rules. But then you wouldn't know about real police work, you're just a fucking bureaucrat."

"Hold on. There's no call for that. I do a bloody important job and you know it. I was just saying..."

"And I was just about to tell you why we've not been giving you information. So shut up and listen. This isn't about playing games, this is serious." He looked Marshall in the eye and held the stare until he was sure that he had his full attention.

"OK, OK. I get the message. Now tell me."

"I... we are certain that information about the investigation has been leaked. It could explain why we hit so many dead ends."

"But you got King, surely if he'd known that you were on to him..."

"I thought that I told you to shut up and listen," said Barton sternly. "We didn't get King. Someone else got to him first. Their whole operation went pear shaped after Milosevic killed that woman, and somebody decided it was time to shut it down. Bit of luck for us really, because in the panic they've left a lot of loose ends that might otherwise have been tied up by the time that we went in.

Not to mention a few loose cannons, who'll soon be telling us a lot more, to try to save their own necks. If Milosevic hadn't screwed up, and we'd carried on co-ordinating intelligence through NCIS we might have lost the lot."

"Hang on. You're saying the leak is in NCIS. What about your lot? It could have been anyone…"

Barton ignored the interruption. "I know it's a leak from inside NCIS, and what's more I know who it is. I also know how the information got to King. And I'm fairly certain that the man calling the shots behind King's operation … the man, who had him killed, was his brother."

"What?" Marshall seemed to be genuinely surprised, and Barton didn't know if that was going to make things easier or more difficult.

"Yes, I saw your dad in Marbella last week, came as a bit of a shock… not meeting him, but where I met him, but I'm sure he told you that… we had lunch on Sir Anthony Naismith's yacht. Now I'm the suspicious type and not a great believer in coincidence, so when I see a retired commander, living a lifestyle that a police pension couldn't possibly support… rubbing shoulders with a multi-millionaire… who just happens to be the brother of my prime target. Well you don't have to be a genius to work that one out."

Marshall's expression altered; the surprised look had gone and he sat ashen faced as Barton continued. "And, as important as your dad may have been when he was in the job, he wouldn't be of much interest to a guy like Naismith now. Not unless… but I think even you can work that out."

"I didn't know Mike. You've got to believe me."

"Thought you'd say that," said Barton, "…and I'd like to believe you, I really would… for old times' sake. But, it's not me you have to convince, Andy." Barton glanced towards the bar, "Have you met my boss?"

The man leaning at the bar turned around and walked over to the table. "Andrew Marshall, I'm Chief Superintendent Trevor Miller, National Crime Squad. I'm arresting you on suspicion of perverting the course of justice. You do not have to say anything, but it may harm your defence if you do not mention when questioned something, which you later rely on in court. Anything you do say may be given in evidence."

Marshall sat for a moment in disbelief and then started to get up.

"Where are you going, Andy?" asked Barton.

"I don't know. I've never been arrested; I was looking round for the others."

"You watch too many cop shows on TV, Andy." said Barton, sarcastically. "This is real life… there aren't any others, just the three of us."

Miller pulled over a chair and sat down. "If you like, I can call for a couple of uniforms. I'm sure they'd be happy to give you a ride to the Yard or somewhere. Might even turn the blue lights on for you. Or maybe you'd rather just sit here and talk for a while. You look as though you could do with another drink. Could you do the honours please, Mike?"

Miller picked up Barton's packet of cigarettes. He took one out and offered the packet to Marshall. Neither of the men spoke as they lit the cigarettes. Barton came back from the bar with three glasses and set them on the table. He took out a cigarette and lit it as he sat down.

Miller broke the uneasy silence. "I'll be straight with you Marshall. I don't give a shit whether you passed the information knowingly or not, so there's no point protesting your innocence. I don't want you. I don't even want your old man. I want Naismith. We can charge you, and get the Spanish police to pick up your old man. We'll probably offer him a deal to get to Naismith. Worst-case scenario you both go down for a few years. Best case your old man does the decent thing and takes the full blame; you only lose your job and your pension. But there is an alternative that would save everyone a lot of trouble."

"What? You turn your back for a couple of minutes so that I can go jump in the river?"

"Grow up Andy. Real life, remember." said Barton.

"A deal," said Miller, "just a good old fashioned deal. First, you tell us everything, every detail of every conversation that you've had with your father since the King investigation started. And then you keep on talking to him about the investigation. You tell him everything that we tell you to say. I can't guarantee that your dad won't go down, that depends on how deeply he's involved. But you walk away from here today and you keep your job, until we get you out on early retirement. You've got until you finish that pint to make up your mind."

Marshall picked up his glass and gulped down the beer. "There's not really a lot to think about. Is there?" said Marshall. "I guess it's a deal."

"Wise decision, Andy," said Barton. "Now tell us what you've been talking to your dad about."

"I can't remember everything, but I suppose it started last year when you first set up the investigation. I just mentioned it in passing really. You know how dad had tried to nail King a couple of times, but never got a result. I thought he'd be interested that you lot were having a go. Anyway, he was really fired up by it. Reckoned that if you put him away, the only way he'd be coming out was in a box. After that, I suppose we talked about it every time we spoke, just snippets in the conversation really. Look it's not like I was giving away state secrets, passing him copies of confidential files or that sort of thing. He's my dad... he's interested in what I do... he's an ex-copper, and they all like to keep in the know... don't they?"

"Details, Andy, details. Dates, names, you know the score. Remember the details," said Barton, taking out his tape recorder. "If it helps, start with last week and work back. The big things will do for starters. We can go over it again later and fill in the gaps."

An hour later, Barton had filled the two tapes and Marshall was looking very tired; it was time to give him a break.

"OK, Phil, you can take over from here," said Barton.

"I thought that you said there was just the three of us," protested Marshall as Phil Fellows appeared from behind a corner. "Who's this?"

"Come on, Andy. You didn't think that we were just going to let you walk out of here on your own. This is DC Phil Fellows and he's going to be stuck to you like glue until this is over. First thing in the morning, you call in sick. Then you just sit tight at home and wait. And while you're waiting you can go over everything again, so that Phil can write it down."

Barton handed Fellows the small tape cassette. "Listen to this and get him to fill in the gaps." He looked at Marshall, "Details, Andy, details. We'll decide what's important. Oh! And while I think about it, give Phil your mobile. I don't want you making any calls that he doesn't know about."

"What do you think?" asked Miller, as they watched Marshall and Fellows leave.

"Lying through his teeth," replied Barton. "But it's a chance we have to take."

"So do you think he'll tell us anything useful?"

"Yes, if he thinks it will save him from prison. Don't get me wrong, Andy was a good friend, but he'll do anything for an easy life and he knows that he wouldn't last long inside."

"He could still end up there, you know. I haven't cleared this deal with anyone, and if Harris find out it won't be our call."

"That's tough," Barton said bitterly. Marshall had betrayed his trust; their twenty years of friendship had just ended, and he didn't really care what happened to him.

Miller opened his briefcase, "This arrived this morning Mike," he said, taking out a thick, padded envelope.

Barton took the envelope; it was addressed to Assistant Chief Constable Harris. He took out the contents – a photo of Naismith handing him an envelope, a copy of a bank deposit slip for €50,000 with his signature, a bank statement in his name showing three deposits each of €50,000, and a sealed polythene envelope, containing two €100 bank notes – examined each in turn. Then he looked at a hand written witness statement, and scanned the typed English translation; the gist of which was that Mr Michael Barton, a tall black man with an English accent, had made a large cash deposit into his account. There as also a copy of the police report, and a covering letter addressed to Harris.

"You've got to hand it to Naismith, he must have some clout to have set up a frame like this up in a couple of days," said Barton. "It's pretty convincing."

"Harris thinks so," said Miller.

"The signature on the deposit slip is a bloody good forgery."

"It had better not be the real thing," said Miller with a smile.

"I suppose those two notes have got my prints on them," said Barton: *And I bet they've also got some that belong to Juanita, fucking bitch, Marquez.* He remembered the shopping trip and the €500 cash point withdrawal he'd made for her: *'I don't like machines darling',* she'd said as she wrote down her PIN and gave him her card.

"So what happens now?" he asked. "Did you tell Harris what we discussed?"

"Yes, and he doesn't like it at all. He wants your balls."

"Well that's bloody typical."

"Hold on, Mike. I know you don't think a lot of him, but he's going along with it for now. He's got a lot to lose too… if it goes wrong. He'll make it official tomorrow, and give it to CIB. But as of now, you're AWOL. That way you get to hang on to your warrant card. Your little team will be in on it, but as far as anyone else will know, it's the real thing. So you've got to keep your head down. If you go anywhere near another copper, you'll be out of the game."

"Thanks, Trevor," said Barton.

Miller stood up to leave, "Let's just pray that the press don't get hold of this. But if he uses the girl as well, then all bets are off."

"Before you go you might be interested in the meeting I had this morning," said Barton.

Miller sat down again, "What? The journalist, did he tell you anything."

"Oh Yes! He told me a lot. He's had evidence linking King and Naismith for over fifteen years. Not enough to stand up in court, but plenty that could have pointed us in the right direction."

"So why didn't he published anything at the time?"

"The official version is that his editor pulled the follow up story on the advice of the paper's lawyers to avoid an expensive libel action. But that's bullshit. No, it was pressure from men in high places, protecting Naismith. And it was seriously heavy political pressure. He tried taking it to several other papers and nobody would touch it. In the end he had a choice, let it drop or never work again. He was an ambitious young journalist and he chose his career."

"So why's he talked now?"

"Let's just say that over the years he's had the odd visit from King's heavies. Nothing too physical, but enough to scare him… and he's kept his head down. No point being Journalist of the Year if it's awarded posthumously. Now that King's out of the way he's not so scared, but I still had to make some promises before he'd agree to go on the record."

"Promises? I don't like the sound of that. What promises?"

"That I'd make it personal and go after Naismith, no compromise."

"And I suppose you really struggled over that," said Miller with a wry smile.

Bloomsbury, London – 17:00 BST

After he left the pub, Barton walked back to the Tate, and crossed the Millennium Bridge; then made his way past St. Paul's to Ludgate Hill, and from there to Holborn Viaduct, where he caught a bus. The route held a certain attraction for Barton as it took him past the Central Criminal Court; better known as the Old Bailey; although that is the name of the street on which the court building stands. Many of Barton's cases had ended up there and it was where Barton had expected the final scenes of Operation De Niro to be played out. They still would be, but the cast list had changed and now, he had a new leading man.

Fisher had arranged to Barton meet in a quiet corner of Bloomsbury. He got off the bus at Kingsway and made his way to Queen Square, a quiet lane leading off Southampton Row. The pub was convenient for Fisher, only a few minutes walk from his office. Barton arrived just before five and phoned Sally; the place would also be easy for her to get to from King's Cross. "The Queen's Larder… round the corner from Russell Square tube station. I think we've been here before."

"Yes I remember, is it that one on the corner of the little square near the Children's Hospital."

"That's the one. I'll see you at about six."

He bought a drink and sat at one of the pavement tables, and waited for Fisher. He looked at the pint in front of him: *How many is that today?* He'd had a couple or three pints in The Anchor; and a brandy, but it didn't seem to be having much effect: *Must be the adrenalin, maybe it dilutes the alcohol?*

The journalist strolled towards him from Great Ormond Street at about ten past five. "Sorry I'm late. Have you been waiting long? Can I get you another?" he said, picking up Barton's empty glass.

"Pint please," replied Barton

"So how was your afternoon?" asked Fisher, making polite conversation. For some reason he felt more awkward about this second meeting, than he had this morning. He'd been having second thoughts on the way over and now he started to wonder what they were doing there: *Maybe this isn't such a good idea.*

"Not bad," said Barton in a way that indicated that he didn't want to talk about it. He'd just spent the best part of two hours putting one of his best friends through the wringer, and he didn't like the aftertaste.

"Mine was pretty awful. Two hours with that bloody little man. We had to do the interview a dozen times before he got it right. He changed his tie three times, because he didn't like the way it looked on the monitor. Just so he can get thirty seconds on the six o'clock, with some lame excuse for another government cock up. You know I really miss the papers. TV journalism isn't the same. In the old days I'd have spent ten minutes listening to his crap and two hours writing a real story."

"Can we get on with it?" said Barton irritably. He could sense something was wrong. This morning Fisher had made all the running: *Why is he holding back now?*

"Yes, sorry. Have you thought about what I told you this morning? Can you use it?"

"Well like you said your rules of evidence aren't quite the same as mine, but I'll get my team to start work on these in the morning," he said, holding out two small tape cassettes. "Let's see how much they can corroborate. But they'll need more than just your recollections of events. Did you talk to your solicitor?"

"Yes, I've told him that someone will be coming to collect them. Here's a letter of authorisation, the address is on the back." Fisher smiled. "As you'll see it's been right under their noses for all those years. Don't mention my name though... I call myself James Harrison."

Barton took the envelope, and put it into his pocket. "Thanks," he said. "Now you had something else to tell me."

"I'm not sure now," Fisher hesitated, clearly reluctant to continue. "Look, maybe it's nothing... maybe just coincidence. I'm not sure it's relevant."

"Let me be the judge of that."

"It's about how personal this is to you," said Fisher. "And how you deal with this is up to you. This morning you said that you don't blame Naismith for your father, but I think you do."

"It was an accident. He got in the way. OK, if Naismith had been someone else, a different politician, then maybe the guy wouldn't have taken a pop at him. But he did and he shot the wrong man. It took me a long time to come to terms with it but my dad was in the wrong place at the wrong time. End of story."

"So you've never thought about why?"

Barton was getting agitated. "Look Naismith was the target... my dad was just doing his job and got in the way. That's why. It's a risk that every copper takes, every day. Campbell put his hands up to it, there were over three hundred eye witnesses... open and shut case."

"This is about the eye witnesses," said Fisher, "...three-hundred and sixty-eight of them, if you want to be to be precise. The police sealed off the building, took down every name, and got every available officer to take statements. Some of the poor sods had to hang around for hours, waiting their turn."

"So? Standard procedure, each witness has to be questioned and make a formal statement, which is written out in longhand by the interviewing officer. The witness has to read it, correct it if necessary, and then sign it. It takes time... there'd have been lots of confused, distressed people. In that kind of situation, a good PC might get through four, maybe five statements in an hour."

"Closer to four in this case... twenty-nine officers took the statements, in just over three hours. The strange thing is that only three-hundred and fifty-six statements were put on the files."

"Twelve missing... it happens. What are you suggesting? For God's sake! Some nutter with a gun had just killed a police officer. I bet every copper there had half a mind on getting back to the station to give the bastard a good kicking. So, a few witnesses got missed out. I don't suppose anybody gave it a second thought. It was hardly going to change anything. Was it!" Barton ranted. "If this is all you've got to tell me, then you're wasting my time."

Fisher remained perfectly calm. "Sorry, I'll leave now, if that's the way you feel. I told you, that I wasn't sure I should be telling you this."

Barton took a deep breath. "No. I'm sorry. You obviously believe this is important. But I wish that you'd get to the bloody point though," he said. "And how come you know all these details."

"I had a good friend, a local TV reporter who was in the hall when it happened. He was up in the balcony with his cameraman... they were up there on their own... I don't think the police realised, because they missed them off the witness list. The cameraman left the tape running the whole time... it was never broadcast of course. Next day they went to the police station to give a copy of the tape to the detectives. My friend got the details a couple of weeks later when he was talking to the local collator. He told him that all the missing statements had been taken by the same officer, who swore blind that he'd filed them, and said that the collator had lost them. But you're right nobody else seemed bothered."

"So that's it?" asked Barton.

"Not quite. Most people would have let it go at that, but my friend hated loose ends. He told me that something didn't ring true. He knew the man very well and was sure that he wasn't the sort to lose paper work. He also knew the detective whose witness statements were missing and he wasn't the careless type either. So he decided to contact the witnesses himself. He told me it might make a good filler story, you know the sort of thing. Police inefficiency or something like that."

"And did he?"

"I don't think so. He probably never got round to it. You know how it is; something more important comes along. He died in a car accident a few months later. I helped his wife sort out his papers and she gave me all his work files and diaries. Took months to go through it all, I kept a few files and his diaries, but most of it was local interest stuff that I gave to a local archivist. I didn't find much to do with that story, just a folder with a copy of the list of witnesses, a receipt for the video tape and a few notes... the things that he'd already told me about. If he'd talked to any of the witnesses there would have been notes."

"So it looks like he let it go as well. So why did you think this was so important, and why were you in two minds about telling me?"

"Sorry Barton, I can't help it, I love a good story, and especially, when it's a mystery, with a twist in the tail. Just another minute, I promise, and then I have to get back to the office."

Barton had had enough and was about to tell Fisher what he thought of his story, when a hand tapped him on the shoulder. He turned his head to see Sally standing behind him.

"Don't let me interrupt, I love a good mystery," she said as she sat down. "Hello, you must be Chris, I'm Sally Parkinson, I work with Mike."

"Sorry, Chris," said Barton. "I forgot to mention that Inspector Parkinson would be joining us. She'll be going over your notes, so I thought you should meet."

"Nice to meet you, Inspector, or can I call you Sally?" Fisher took her hand and held it for rather longer than was needed for a polite handshake. "Pity you couldn't have joined us earlier, I've got to dash."

He took a business card from his wallet and wrote something on the back. "Here's my card, call me if you need anything."

"Aren't you going to tell us the end of the story?" she said.

"Sorry. Yes. A few months later, I took the receipt for the tape to the police station. But, they had no record of it. Apparently, they have numbered official receipts, but this was just on a sheet of headed paper, and the detective who issued it had left the area. Transferred to the Met, I think. What do you make of that?"

"Sounds a bit odd," said Sally.

"It's more than bloody odd. Mislaying a bit of paperwork is one thing, but losing a video recording of a murder." Barton got to his feet, knocking over his glass, as he shouted, "No! That just doesn't happen."

287

He lunged forward and grabbed Fisher by the lapel of his suit jacket. "Why the hell didn't you tell me this sooner? Why didn't you tell anyone at the time?"

Several heads had turned to see the commotion. "Calm down, Mike," said Sally pulling at his sleeve. "What's so special about this tape?"

"Sorry," said Barton, sitting down again. "Sorry, Chris, it's been a long day. But I think you know what this could mean. Is there anything else?" Suddenly he had all the time in the world to listen.

"No that's all. The file with the receipt and the witness list are with the papers at my solicitors, if that's any help. At the time, it didn't really seem very important. It was only when I did the King and Naismith story a few years later, that I realised what it could mean. But I was too much of a coward to say anything."

"You said the tape was a copy, do you know what happened to the original?"

"Probably recorded over, several times... this was twenty years ago and video tape was bloody expensive then."

"Can you find out?"

"It'll take a bit of digging, but I'll try. Now I really have to go. I'll give you a call if I get anywhere."

"Thanks," said Barton, "and if I'm not around call Sally."

The two men shook hands, and then Fisher put his arm round Barton's shoulder. "Good luck. I'll be in touch." Although they had only just met, he believed he could trust this policeman. A weight had been lifted and he would sleep easily tonight, for the first time in years.

"He fancies himself," said Sally, when Fisher had gone. "Look, he's written his home number on the back of the card. Do you want another drink?"

"No thanks, I've had enough today. But I'm starving, I haven't eaten all day," Barton gestured towards the little Italian restaurant, next to the pub, "How about some pasta?"

"Remember the last time we were here?" she asked, as they studied the menu.

Barton shook his head.

"You know. The night we went to that bloody awful musical. We left at the interval, and came here for a meal on the way back... you had the seafood." She frowned; this was how it was now. Whilst she remembered and cherished every detail of their past relationship, Mike had either forgotten; or he chose not to remember.

Barton wondered why it was, whenever he arranged to meet her, they always seemed to end up in a place they had been to before; before Grace. He shook his head again, "God that was years ago, how can you remember that."

Over the meal, Sally listened quietly as he described the meetings with Fisher and Marshall, trying to take it all in. They were drinking coffee when he got to the part about his imminent suspension. Before hearing the full story, she leapt to his defence. "It's not fair! Surely they can see it's a frame up?"

"It's OK, Sal. It's sorted," said Barton, and he told her the details. "You can tell the others tomorrow. If they need any confirmation, they can talk to Miller. And make sure that one of you gives Andy Marshall the official version, so he can tell his old man."

"So we're not going to see much of you for a while," she sounded worried. It was all very well for him, but she wasn't comfortable with the situation that he was putting her in.

"I know it puts a lot on you Sal, but…"

"It's not just me Mike, it's the others. There's only the four of them, and it's heavy going. Look I know they were all up for this yesterday. They don't want to let you down, but it's a big workload and they're all feeling the strain."

"I've thought about that, and I've asked the chief to let you have Lorna. I know it's only one extra pair of hands, but it should help. Besides, with her on the outside there's always a risk that Dave might let something slip. It'll take some of the pressure off him."

"It still won't be easy," she said. "I'm worried that I might not be able hold it together. They're doing this for you… not me."

They finished their coffee and Barton paid the bill. "Anyone waiting for you at home?" he asked.

"No," she lied; Richard was back, but it didn't matter.

"We've got a bit more to talk about," he said. "Let's take a walk… we can talk on the way."

They walked through to Theobald's Road and headed towards Clerkenwell. "We can get the tube from Farringdon," he said.

Barton stopped outside a door in one of the side streets. He took out the envelope that Fisher had given him and looked at the address on the back.

"What is it, Mike?" she asked.

"Fisher's solicitor… this is his office. Can you ask Jane to pick up Fisher's papers from here in the morning?" He gave her the envelope. "If you drop this in at her place on your way home, it'll save her going to the office first. Tell her to take the files home. I'll meet her there. And, send Lorna down to join us as soon as Miller has spoken to her. I think she deserves to get it from me first hand."

"What's in these files?"

"I don't know, but Fisher's been looking over his shoulder for the past fifteen years, so there has to be something. We're getting close, Sal."

As they walked, she put her arm through his. He pretended not to notice.

289

"How about a drink in the Eagle?" she said as they reached Farringdon Road. "If it's still there." She took his hand and led him round the corner, "Just up here if I remember."

"The tube's the other way," he protested. But it didn't do any good.

"This has changed... look at that menu," she said looking at the large boards behind the bar. "Bit different from when we on the Post Office job... nice wine too, let's get a bottle."

The bar was busy, but not crowded, and they managed to find an empty table. "First time you ever bought me a drink was in here," Sally said, wistfully, as Barton poured the wine. She didn't expect a response; she knew that it was no longer important to him.

"So what's this tape that you got so worked up about?" she asked, changing the subject back to the only thing he wanted to talk about. "I thought you were going to thump him."

"Sorry about that, Sal. You're not going to want to hear this, and I'm not sure I should involve you, but this is where it starts to get messy."

"What do you mean?"

"It's getting personal... very personal. You know what I said about Fisher... making me promise... *personal, no compromises*... that was his way of making sure. Otherwise, we wouldn't be getting those files tomorrow... he wouldn't have talked to us at all..."

"You're not making sense Mike."

"I mean he talked to me. He wouldn't talk to the police. He checked up on me before we met. He wouldn't have told anyone else." Barton paused while the full significance of Fisher's story sank in. "Just me. Because he knows that I'll never let it drop."

"But you can't make promises like that, Mike. They won't let you. I know we tread a pretty thin line at times, but the line's there and they'll have you out if you go too far over."

"Let me tell you what it's about. I'm not asking you to help. Just cover for me if you can."

Barton repeated the story that Fisher had told him, almost word for word. Sally wanted to ask questions; challenge things he said, but she knew Barton too well and this was not the time to interrupt.

"So you see why I have to do this," he said. "The missing statements, the missing tape, the journalist killed in a car accident... it's too much to be coincidence. My father was deliberately killed and somebody went to great lengths to cover it up."

"You don't know that Mike, and you certainly can't put it on Naismith. Why would he?"

"Because he could... power... control... that's what it's all about. Christ! Sal, the man had his own brother killed."

"We don't know that either. We've no proof, just your bloody gut feeling."

"Oh! I'll prove it. I'll prove it."

Highbury, North London – 11:45 BST

Warren Jarvis picked up the phone and called the number again. This time he got an answer, "Who's that?"

"It's Warren. Where've you been? I've been trying to reach you all night."

"I told you not to call unless it was important."

"This is bloody important. That journalist, Fisher had a visitor today... he's giving them his files... I thought you said you were taking care of Barton..."

"Don't worry, it's all in hand. He'll be off the investigation."

"As if that's going to stop him... I mean... if he's making this personal... it wouldn't stop me if..."

"Pull yourself together man. There's nothing in those papers... you got the originals... I've seen them... there's nothing in there about that."

"It's all right for you... you're well away. I'm still stuck here. You don't have to look over your shoulder every time you go outside... Christ! When are you going to get me out?"

"In good time... these things take time. But if you're that worried you'd better do something about it... time to tie up loose ends. I want you to..."

Jarvis listened as he was given his instructions. He always listened to Lenny.

"...and while you're about it you'd better get someone to see to young Mr Mills... he's served his purpose... and bloody well find Nichols too."

"OK... but then you have to get me out... if the Old Bill pick me up... you owe me Lenny..."

"I told you never call me that. Now just do it!"

Naismith slammed down the phone. "Insolent bastard!" he shouted: "How dare he threaten me?" *Another loose cannon. How many more?*

There were too many people who knew. The game was changing and, slowly but surely, Barton was cutting their strings: *I'll show them though. I'll show all those nobodies. Who do they think they are?*

Naismith picked up the phone again; there was no reply at the other end and he roared at the answering machine. "Colin, get hold of that boy of yours. Find out what the fuck is going on! What's Barton up to? I want some answers."

291

Chapter 24

Tuesday 13th May

Gartree Prison, Leicestershire – 08:00 BST

"Move it!" barked the uniformed man. "I haven't got all day."

Patrick Campbell lifted his head and looked around the dining hall. As usual he was the last at the table; the last in the room. He casually picked up the last slice of bread, folded it in half, and wiped the remains of his breakfast from his plate.

"I and I got all day Babylon," Campbell spoke deliberately and very quietly, almost in a whisper, "I and I got all di time in di world," He looked down again and slowly the put bread into his mouth.

"Come on get up."

Campbell licked the egg and ketchup from his fingers; one at a time; deliberately, defiantly; challenging the other man's authority. "When I and I is ready," he said. Then he leisurely raised a plastic mug to his mouth and drank the last dregs of his coffee.

It was a game; just a stupid game with no point; no winners and no losers. Just one of many games he played to relieve the monotony. Campbell was a lifer, and he knew that for him there was no prospect of an early release on licence. For what he had done, life could mean only one thing, and he knew that would never walk out of this place. But the little games showed that, at least in his mind, he was a free man. It didn't do any harm; just wound them up a bit. And, as long as he kept his nose clean and didn't make any trouble, they tolerated his small gestures of defiance.

He stood up, pushed back his greying dreadlocks, and shook his head. He towered above the other man and looked him in the eye. He ran his fingers through his grey streaked beard, and spoke again; softly, clearly; the rhythm of his words carrying no challenge; just an acceptance of his situation. "Ya nuh see? It never be finish for I, Babylon… Jah know, I and I is here for the rest of I life."

He shuffled towards the door, paused for a moment, and looked up at the clock. He never hurried anything; there wasn't any point, it wouldn't make the days any shorter. In twenty minutes, he'd go to the workshop. He'd be back here at twelve-thirty, and again six hours later. At nine the door would close, an hour later the lights would go out, and another day would be over. Just like every other day for the past twenty years. Just like every day would be for the rest of his life.

As he walked towards the workshops, he had no way of knowing that today would be different.

London Colney, Hertfordshire – 08:30 BST

Enrique Herrera got out of bed and winced as he limped towards the window. It was only a few feet, but the painkillers they'd given him the night before had worn off, and every step was agony. He pulled back the curtain and blinked as the bright sunlight flooded into the small bedroom. He didn't know where he was; it was dark when they got here last night, but they'd told him it was safe and at least it wasn't a prison. He could see that he was at the back of the house, overlooking a large garden surrounded by tall trees that obscured the view. He could have been anywhere.

Very slowly, he dragged his aching limbs across the room. He'd expected the door to be locked, but it opened when he turned the handle. As he stepped out of the room, he saw a man walking up the stairs; one of the policemen who had brought him from the hospital last night.

"Good morning," said Connor. "If you need the bathroom it's that door there. He pointed to a door at the top of the stairs. "You'll have to share with us… your girlfriend's got the en-suite."

"Deborah… she is here too?" said Herrera with surprise. "Can I see her?"

"She's downstairs. Come down when you've got dressed. There are some clean clothes in the cupboard in your room."

Herrera looked in the mirror; the bruises had almost gone, but the scars would be there for a long time. He splashed water on his face and dried himself with one of the clean towels. There was a new razor on the windowsill, but he left it there. Behind the stubble, the cuts on his face still smarted. One of the nurses had shaved him yesterday and another day wouldn't matter; he wasn't going anywhere.

He returned to the room and dressed. The clothes were cheap, but at least they were the right size. This was the first time that he had dressed himself for over a week. His face distorted as he pulled on a T-shirt, covering his battered torso, and then with great difficulty and more pain he put on a pair of jeans. Deciding against the socks, he slipped his bare feet into a pair of loafers, and made his way downstairs. He'd only been up for forty-five minutes and, already he felt exhausted. The simple routine of preparing for the day ahead had been a painful ordeal, an almost unbearable torture that had seemed to go on forever. By the time he walked into the kitchen it was twenty past nine.

Debbie King rushed towards door and threw her arms around him. "I'm so glad you're here." He cried out in pain and she pulled away, "Oh! I'm sorry Ricky... does it still hurt?"

"It's not so bad," he said.

"The hospital gave us these for you," said Connor, holding up a bottle of pills. "Just let us know when you need them."

"I'll have some now," said Herrera, taking the bottle. He sat at the table next to Debbie. "Is there anything to eat?"

While Herrera was eating, Connor explained where he was and what was going on. "This is a safe house... you don't need to know where. Nobody knows that you are here... in fact most people think you're missing or dead. It's better that way. You'll be here for as long as is necessary to ensure your safety, provided that you cooperate with us."

"Why should I tell you anything?" snarled Herrera.

Connor's tone became more serious, more formal. "Like I said, if you cooperate you'll stay here... tucked up nice and safe with your girlfriend. But if you'd rather... we'll charge you and get you down to the court. This case is getting a lot of publicity, and I'm sure that you'll be quite a celebrity on the remand wing."

"OK, I get it. What's the deal?"

"My boss will tell you later. In the meantime we've got a few rules here," said Connor. "First off, this is a safe house not a jail... during the day you've got a free run of the back of the house and the garden... but there will be three officers here at all times and the only time that you'll be left alone is when you go to bed or the bathroom. Under no circumstances do you go anywhere near the front of the house. When we're not interviewing you, you can spend as much time as you like with your girlfriend... but not alone... and don't get any ideas in the middle of the night. There's a camera in every room and all the outside doors and windows are alarmed. Understand... *comprendo*?"

"*Si, comprendo*," said Herrera.

"Behave yourself and we'll look after you," said Connor. "...I'll even ignore the fact that you're a scumbag who deserves to be dead."

Debbie put her hand on Herrera's arm preventing him from responding. "It's all right Ricky. Ignore it... it doesn't matter... we're safe."

Potters Bar, Hertfordshire – 11:00 BST

Barton had taken a taxi to the station, where he'd left his car the night before, and decided to get the train. The Cambridge trains stopped at Potters Bar, and Jane Barclay lived not too far from the station. She'd phoned him just before he got off the train to say that she'd just collected the files from Fisher's solicitor. 'I'm getting a cab back, sir. I didn't realise there'd be so much stuff. I'll be with you in about forty-five minutes.'

Barton used the time to carry out a couple of personal errands and he was sitting in a café waiting for the waitress to bring him another coffee when he called Sally. "Hi. Did you get home OK, last night... How's it going with Herrera?" he asked the second question without waiting for a reply to the first.

She told him that she had just returned from the safe house. "Dave's still there with Brenda... I'm going back later on... we're going to talk to him again this afternoon."

"Sounds good. What's the situation with Lorna?"

"She's just seen the Chief Super. I'll have a quick word with her and she'll be on her way. Paul's pretty pissed off though. He's just given me a real earful."

"I don't suppose that you'd be too happy in his situation... he'll get over it."

"Is there anything you need?"

"Not right now. I'll call you later if I think of anything, but you could ask Lorna to stop off and get some sandwiches."

He was waiting outside the front door when the Jane's taxi pulled up; and between them, they carried the boxes up to the first floor. "There's an awful lot here, sir," said Jane. "When the DI said to collect some files, I thought I'd be able to get them in my bag."

"Sorry, Jane, I didn't think there'd be this many. You don't mind doing this here do you? I'd rather not go into the office today."

"That's OK, sir. At least I won't be late getting home tonight."

Barton went downstairs to get the last box and paid the driver. When he got back to the flat, he found Jane sitting on the sofa looking at the pile of deed boxes.

"Where do we start, sir?" she asked. "What are we looking for?"

"According to the man I met yesterday, this lot contains details that will prove that King and Naismith have rather more in common than blood." said Barton. "Lorna should be along soon and I'll explain then. Meanwhile, I suggest we just open these one at a time and make a list of what's inside."

Jane cut the seal on the first box. Inside there was a single printed sheet of paper on top of a stack of manila folders. "Looks like we won't need to make a list," she said, as she handed him the sheet of paper. "He's already done it for us."

Barton looked at the sheet of paper.

1. *Naismith & King - Business Connections*
2. *Carrington International – Guernsey*
3. *Point One Properties - Spain*
4. *MVN Trust*
5. *Ridgeway Holdings*
6. *Marchmont Estates*
7. *Ashdown Developments…*

The list contained the names of another seventeen companies, and as Barton read out them Jane confirmed that there was a corresponding file for each one.

"Let's have a look at one, Jane," said Barton.

The file for Marchmont Estates contained a list of addresses, and copies of the Land Registry entries relating to each one. Under each address on the list was the name of a company. Barton nodded; he recognised a couple of the names. He handed the file to Jane.

"Right put those back in the box and we'll look at the next one."

"I've just noticed that boxes are numbered, sir," Jane said as she read a label on the side of the open box. She turned the box so that Barton could see the label.

Client Property to be held until further notice
JAMES HARRISON
PO BOX 1276, Mount Pleasant EC1A
Ref. D645/MPS/02/06/87
Box 4 of 6
Shaw, Stevens, Jefferies and Co.
15, Harpur St. London WC1

"This is number four. I'll find number one."

Jane opened each of the boxes in turn. Like the first each held a number of manila folders and an index sheet. With each box Jane checked the contents against the index sheet, while Barton quickly scanned through one of the files. Box 1 contained several files of press cuttings; 2 and 3 were full of Fisher's notes, all methodically filed and indexed. The fifth box contained a miscellany of documents, including extracts from company accounts, copies of letters and faxes, and a thick file with a one-word title, *CONNECTIONS.*

Barton silently thanked Fisher for being so methodical. He knew what would be in the last box. Jane didn't need to know but as she was about to open it, the bell rang; saving him from the need to make up an excuse.

"That must be Lorna," he said. I'll open the last one while you let her in."

The last box was smaller than the others and contained only a single folder and two sealed envelopes. The folder was full of press cuttings, and he put it back in the box; he'd probably read them all before. He felt the thicker of the two envelopes. There seemed to be some sort of notebook inside, he opened it and took out a small hardcover book, *NUJ Diary 1983.* Barton put the diary back into the envelope. Fisher had told him that he'd been given his friend's diaries, but he hadn't mentioned that one was with the files. He put the both envelopes into the box, and closed the lid.

"Hello, sir, I've got your sandwiches," said Lorna, putting two deli bags on the kitchen worktop, "…got some juice as well."

"Thanks Lorna. Bring them over here," said Barton, "…I'll explain what's going on while we eat."

"What's in the last box, sir?" asked Jane.

"Nothing to do with this," he lied. "Looks like some of his personal papers. I'll take them back to him, later."

Jane got some plates and glasses and they all sat at the small dining table as Barton explained what they were doing with Fisher's files.

"I had a meeting yesterday with a journalist, Chris Fisher. The name probably won't mean much to you, but he's the one who exposed Naismith as King's brother. He had a lot of other information that could have linked them, but he was stopped from publishing it," Barton explained.

"What he told me was that there were a lot of business deals that indirectly involved both men. That's what's in the files. It's mainly to do with King's business premises and other properties. According to Fisher he either bought them or leased them from Naismith… none of it in their own names of course… all through their companies."

"And none of this came out at the time?" said Jane.

"No, it was all hushed up. Even though Naismith had resigned, there could have been a lot of political fallout," replied Barton, "…and the police investigation wasn't looking for a connection. The case was pretty open and shut… the guy that King killed was just a punter at one of his clubs."

"So why has Fisher kept all these files?" asked Lorna.

"He obviously dug up stuff that was more than just embarrassing for Naismith. If it had been just that, he'd have published something when the political pressure was off, but he's had regular threats from King to keep him quiet. Fisher thought at the time that the business deals were some kind of tax evasion scheme, but I think it could be more than that."

"What do you mean?" asked Lorna.

"Fisher said the property deals were all at way over the market rate…that's why he thought it was a tax thing. But given what we now know about King's operations… I reckon they were money laundering… and you have to remember… back then we didn't have anything like the controls and intelligence that we do now."

"And it's all in there?" said Jane gesturing towards the boxes on the floor.

"That's what you two have to find out," said Barton. "I want you to go through everything and check it all. Looks like Fisher has given you a good start, but you'll need to cross-reference everything with our own files. Look for things like directors' names, registered addresses, and overseas companies, check out the dates… and let DI Parkinson know immediately if you turn up anything that looks out of place."

"How long have we got?"

"Till I get back," he said, "…about four days. But do it quicker if you can."

"That's not much time, sir."

"I know. Get help if you need it… we've plugged the leak…"

"Leak?" Lorna exclaimed. He'd forgotten that Lorna didn't know about that.

"The DI will tell you about that later Lorna. Anyway if you need anything from NCIS, Serious Fraud or anyone else, just shout, and the Chief Super will get it priority."

Barton got to his feet and bent down to pick up the last box. "I'll leave you to it then… see you in a few days."

When Barton had gone, Lorna took her laptop out of her case and placed it on the table. "Right," she said, "…we'd better get started."

Barton's mobile rang. "Where are you?" asked Sally, before he could say anything.

"Walking back to the station," said Barton. Fisher's *personal papers* were in his briefcase, and the empty box was at the bottom of Jane's refuse chute.

"Officially, I'm not supposed to be talking to you," said Sally. "They announced your suspension half an hour ago."

"Have you told anyone yet?"

"Only Dave and Brenda so far… I was waiting for you to call before I rang the others."

"Call them as soon as you can. And tell Phil that Andy Marshall has to make a phone call this evening… there are one or two things he needs share…"

Sally listened and made notes as Barton told her what he wanted Marshall to relay to the men in Spain. "OK, I've got all that. What about the files... any good?"

"There's loads of stuff, five boxes! I told the girls to give you a shout if they need help... or find anything particularly interesting."

"OK, I'll have a word with them in a minute."

"How did it go with Herrera?"

"Slow. We only spent a couple of hours there... he's still in a pretty bad state. We mainly talked about what kind of deal he might get... and what sort of charges he was facing if he didn't play the game. He knows that he's in big trouble... and I got the feeling that he's scared of going back to Colombia. We'll give him the night to sleep on it and start on the questions tomorrow."

"Good. Concentrate on what he knows about where the money goes," said Barton. He reeled off a list of questions, "...and I want you to find out all you can about his sister, and see if he's got a photo of her."

"Where are you going now?"

"Somewhere safe, I want to get Grace out of the way," said Barton with a sigh, "...a long way away."

"Be careful," said Sally, grateful that he couldn't see the tears welling in her eyes.

Barton bought a single ticket to Kings Cross, from where he planned to take the underground to the airport. He stood on the station platform and smoked a cigarette while he waited for the train. He knew that the phone signal wasn't very good on the line going south; too many tunnels. So he made a last call, before getting the train arrived.

"I'm all set," said Grace, "...I've packed you a bag, and I've got your passport. What time's the flight?"

"Not till the morning... I've booked us into the Holiday Inn for the night. You can park there... I'll meet you in the lobby in a couple of hours."

Heathrow Airport – 17:30 BST

Barton sat in the lobby of the Holiday Inn, wondering how he was going to pay for all this. He'd got the only available flight and he'd had to buy business class tickets. The card company had extended his credit limit, but he would still have to pay it back. He half wished that the €150,000 in the Spanish bank was his. It might have been enough for some, but no amount of Naismith's blood money would ever be enough to buy him.

He took an envelope out of his briefcase and looked at the contents again. On the third page of the witness list twelve names were underlined – Twelve missing witnesses including two names that he knew – alongside was the name of the policeman who should have filed the statements; the same policeman who had signed the receipt for a video tape. A policeman his father had regarded as a friend, and who Barton had once respected. He stared at the sheet of headed paper, still not really able to take it in. He didn't want to believe it. For the last hour he'd gone through all the possible reasons; all the things that might make it just a coincidence; none of them worked. There was only one explanation; and the ghost stirred again.

He still had the papers in his hand when Grace arrived with their luggage. She sat next to him on the sofa, and caught a glimpse of the top sheet as he hurriedly put the papers back into the envelope. "What's that… 1983?"

"Nothing… just something, someone thought I might be interested in," he replied. He knew that he'd have to tell her soon, but he wasn't ready to share it with her yet.

Gartree Prison, Leicestershire – 19:30 BST

"Break it up!" cried the prison officer as he drew his baton. The tall black man with the long black dreadlocks was unmistakeable, but the brawl had already drawn a large crowd of onlookers and he couldn't see who the man was fighting. "Break it up! Get back!" he shouted again, as he approached the men. He could see the three other officers running to his assistance and he pushed his way through the mob.

"Stay where you are Butler… you too Prentice… don't you bloody move," he shouted, as he reached the front of the crowd "…And the rest of you… stay put." He tripped on something and lost his balance; before he could steady himself, he felt a hand shove him in the back, and laughter erupted as he fell awkwardly to the ground. The crowd was already dispersing, as he got to his feet. He looked down and saw what had caused him to trip. The man with the dreadlocks was lying motionless on the floor. "You can get up too!" he shouted, prodding the prone figure with the toe of his boot. "Come on, get on you feet…"

The man didn't respond. "Get up!" bawled the officer. He bent down and shook the man by the shoulder. Then he noticed the small pool of blood that was gradually spreading across the concrete floor. He shouted for help; but it was too late. Patrick Campbell's sentence was over.

Chapter 25

Wednesday 14th May

National Crime Squad, Hertfordshire Branch – 08:30 BST

Sally heard a raised voice outside her office, and then a loud cheer. A moment later, the door opened and DI Paul Timms walked in, looking like the cat that had got the cream. "Guess what?" he said as he sat on the corner of his desk.

"You've won the lottery," she said sarcastically; she wasn't in the mood for playing at guessing games.

"We've got Nichols. He was picked up last night," said Timms excitedly, "…you'll never guess where."

Sally didn't reply. This would make things even worse. For the past week Timms had been unbearable. To hear him talk anyone would have thought that whole King investigation was his idea; like he'd broken the whole thing single-handed.

"About ten miles from here… bloody fool. Local boys picked him up at King's house."

Sally sat up, "What?"

"Yes, the neighbour phoned and reported an intruder. Nichols was in the garage, creeping round like a burglar… God knows what he thought he was going to find… you'd think he'd have realised that we'd have already taken away everything that was of any use."

"Maybe you missed something."

"Not a chance. We went over that place with a toothcomb. Papers, files, photos… we've got the lot. We…"

"If you say so," she said, indifferently; she could do without the details. "Now do you mind? I've got a lot to do."

"What's up? Sour grapes? Look it's not my fault they put me in charge of this. Or is this because I've got Nichols, and Herrera is still missing. Looks like you needed Lorna more than I did," he said sarcastically. "OK, don't let me keep you… get back to your babysitting."

"Bastard," she said under her breath, as he walked out of the door.

"Sticks and stones," he said, and Sally could see the smug grin on his face even though he had his back to her.

Sally was about to phone Barton with the news when Lorna walked into the room. "Paul looks pleased with himself," she said.

"Don't even ask," said Sally. "Hang on a minute while I phone Mike...you can listen in."

"No wonder he's pleased," said Lorna after Sally hung up the phone. "Another one in the bag, that only leaves Jarvis and Preston... wonder where they are?"

"Hiding under a stone at the bottom of a sewer somewhere," said Sally. "I hope Paul gets covered in shit looking for them."

"So what's the form for today then?" asked Lorna.

"Have you bought those files in?"

"They're in the car. Is Jane here yet?"

"I haven't seen her. But you two can carry on with Fisher's files, when she gets in. How's it going?"

"It's a bit heavy going, but I think he was onto something. I recognised a few of the addresses... I've seen some of the places and if they were really worth that kind of money, my little house must be worth a million. We still have masses of stuff to get through... there's loads of company records... accounts, directors lists, shareholders. Can we get some help from Serious Fraud? "

"I'll talk to Miller, It shouldn't be a problem," said Sally. "I'm going over to the house with Brenda. I assume Dave's on his way there already."

Lorna nodded. "Good," said Sally. She was quite pleased to have Lorna on board; she knew it would keep Dave on his toes. "There's something else. Mike wants to know what Nichols was looking for at King's house. I suppose Paul will find out eventually so keep your ear to the ground... and see if you can find out who turned King's place over... they might have missed something... funny place to be?"

"What?"

"The garage... that's where they found Nichols... ferreting around in the garage."

Heathrow Airport – 09:30 BST

Grace settled into the window seat, while Barton stowed the hand baggage in the locker. "This is nice," she said stretching out in the large seat. "I've never flown business class before. Do we get better food as well?"

"I don't know," said Barton as he took his seat beside her. We'd better... at this price, he thought. He hadn't told her how much the tickets had cost; he didn't want her worrying about anything else. All he wanted was to get her as far away as possible until this was over. Naismith wouldn't get to him through her.

They'd spent a pleasant, relaxed night at the hotel, enjoying each other's company. Barton had tried not to talk about Naismith and thankfully, Grace hadn't pressed him on the subject. Instead, they'd talked about the baby and made plans for the future: preparing the nursery, names, the christening, schools, and their unborn child's future siblings: *'Let's have this one first'*, he'd said when she got onto that. But all the time, nagging at the back of his mind, was the need to sort out the present and bury the past. Until he did that, the future would have to wait.

The four powerful engines roared into life and the plane started to move slowly towards the taxiway. Barton sat back in his seat and relaxed; he was sure that the place they were going to was out of Naismith's reach; he was going home.

National Crime Squad, Hertfordshire Branch – 10:30 BST

DC Jane Barclay was searching the Companies House register for details of the companies in Fisher's file. "That's odd," she said, looking up from her computer. "This company... Ashdown... the address... it's the same as Fisher's solicitor... look."

Lorna McLean looked at screen. "You sure it's the same?"

"I was there yesterday... 15 Harpur Street... look it's on the box labels."

Lorna read out the label on one of the boxes, "Shaw, Stevens, Jefferies and Co. 15, Harpur St. London WC1... yes. Lots of companies use a solicitor as their registered office... you'll probably find one of the partners is the company secretary."

"Was... they ceased trading ten years ago," said Jane as she clicked the mouse button. "Now let's see... yes, company secretary...Michael Peter Stevens, same address. Bit of a coincidence... Fisher choosing the same firm."

London Colney, Hertfordshire – 11:00 BST

The women were in the kitchen at the back of the old farmhouse, Herrera was still in bed, and Dave Connor was getting impatient. "Deal me out," he said. He was already twenty pounds down and the odds were stacked against him. He got up and went into the kitchen: *These witness protection guys must spend hours sitting around playing cards. They're too bloody good for me. I can't afford much more of this.*

"I've been sitting round for two hours," he said. "When can I get him up?"

"Give us another fifteen minutes, Dave," replied Sally, "...we're nearly ready." The other two women nodded. Sally looked at Debbie King, "...and you're sure he's ready?"

"I've never known him scared like this before," replied Debbie. "...you know... really frightened... he's sure that they'll kill him if he's sent back... or to prison. He knows this is his only chance."

National Crime Squad, Hertfordshire Branch – 16:30 BST

Jane sighed with relief. "Finished," she said, as she put the file back into the box and closed the lid. "Not a bad day's work. I hope the DI thinks so."

Lorna McLean nodded. "Well done. Print it off, we'll check it over before they get back," she said. She'd been impressed by Jane today; she'd a good eye for detail. "Hold on a minute, I'll print mine as well." She saved her own file and pressed the print button. She hadn't finished yet, but the picture that had emerged so far was fairly clear.

Jane came back with the copies from the printer. "Did you notice if DI Timms was out there?" asked Lorna.

"I didn't see him, but they're back, I've just seen Matt Brady. Do you want me to go and look for the DI?"

"No, leave it for now. I'm not his favourite person right now. But, go and have a word with Matt... see what you can find out."

Lorna picked up the printed pages, scanned though them, underlining some of the text with a red pen. Jane was right; this was a good day's work. Fisher's notes had got them off to a good start, but they'd put in a lot of effort themselves. Sally would be pleased.

"They didn't make much progress," said Jane, as she sat down. "Matt says they spent all morning waiting for his brief to turn up... and all afternoon about the only thing Nichols said was 'no comment'... his brief did most of the talking. He's in court in the morning."

"Did he say why he was at King's house?"

"Said it was none of their business... he had a key, and had every right to be there."

"I told you... I didn't find anything... the old girl across the street must have seen me and called the police. I didn't get much time, but it wasn't there," said Nichols. "Look, I'm not even sure that I was looking in the right place. Are you sure that was where he kept it."

"In the bag... that's all he told me. He said, *'Nobody would ever think of looking there'.*"

"But even if we do find it... where's the box?"

"I'm not sure, but I've got a good idea." *'You'll know where to find it.'*

"So what's in this box that's so bloody important?" Nichols demanded, trying to keep his temper. He'd been on his way, almost out of reach, when the phone call came. Asking him... no, ordering that he return to carry out the errand.

"I don't know, he said it was his insurance policy. He used to keep it at my office. He left it with me years ago... said if anything happened to him I'd know what to do with it. He was always coming and going... taking the box out... always sent me out of the room... couple of minutes later, he'd call me back, and I'd lock it away again. I saw him open it once... one of the panes in the door had been broken a few days earlier and we hadn't had it fixed... he didn't take anything out... just put something in. I couldn't really see much, but he took something out of his pocket and put it in the box."

"And you've never seen what was in this box?" asked Nichols. "You were never tempted to have a look."

"What do you think? He'd have bloody killed me. He used to lock it and put one of those plastic security seals on. There's no way I could have opened it without him knowing."

"So why do you think he took it away?"

"Your guess is as good as mine... look, I just take the money, like you do... no questions. All he said was that he wanted it closer to hand."

"So why all the bother? Whatever it is, he doesn't need it now."

"But someone else does. Let's just hope the police haven't got it... but if it wasn't at the house... then where did he put it?" Nichols's lawyer got up and closed his briefcase. "Think man... think where," he said as he walked to the door. "I'll see you in the morning."

The door was locked and he tapped it with his knuckles. "OK, we're finished now," he said in a loud voice.

Nichols looked over his shoulder as the policeman led him back to his cell. "You'll get me out of here... won't you, Michael?" he said.

But Michael Stevens wasn't listening; he had more important things on his mind.

"Well, that was an interesting day," said Sally as she walked into the office with Brenda and Connor.

"Expensive," said Connor, with a worried look on his face. By the time that Herrera had finally got up it was past noon, and Connor had lost another twenty-five pounds. "Don't tell Lorna I've been playing cards."

"She doesn't need to," said a voice from behind the bank of filing cabinets. "How much did you lose then?" asked Lorna, as she stood up, glaring at her partner.

"Debrief in five minutes," said Sally, rescuing Connor before he had time to reply. "My office, tell Jane and Phil."

"OK," said Lorna. She scowled at Connor: *I'll sort you out later.*

The six of them sat in Sally's small office sharing the outcomes of their day's work. "I know that name," said Connor. "Stevens... Paul said something about him the other day after they'd interviewed Underwood. I'm sure he said Stevens was his brief. Right clever bastard, nearly managed to get him bailed."

"Lorna," said Sally inquisitively, "...did Stevens represent any of King's companies, when they did the property deals?"

"I don't know. We cross referenced the company names to our records but we didn't check on the solicitors' details."

"Go and have a quick look Jane," said Sally as she picked up the phone and dialled Timms' extension. "Paul have you got a minute? Just want to check something with you."

A little white lie won't hurt, she thought as Timms came into the office. "Paul, what's the name of Underwood's solicitor?" she asked.

"Stevens. Why?"

"Michael Stevens... isn't he King's solicitor?"

"Yes, why are you interested?"

"Just that Debbie King's asked for a brief and she gave us his name."

"Well she'll have to join the queue. He's been with Nichols all day, and he's in court in the morning. He's a busy man at the moment. What with Nichols and Underwood... and I wouldn't be surprised if he turns out to be Jarvis' brief as well," said Timms.

"Have you picked Jarvis up yet?" asked Sally.

"No, but we've got Barry and he's bound to give something away… he's not smart enough… it won't take us long to find his old man." said Timms, confidently. "Scum always rises to the surface. Have you found Herrera yet?"

Sally shook her head.

"I bet he's long gone," said Timms, barely disguising his delight at his colleague's lack of progress. "Look, if I were you, I'd try and keep Stevens away from Debbie King for as long as possible. He's as bent as they come."

"Thanks, Paul," said Sally, satisfied in the knowledge that Debbie King had no intention of engaging the services of Michael Stevens.

Jane retuned with a couple of files in her hand. "Stevens," she said as she opened the Marchmont Estates file and showed a page to Lorna.

When Timms was gone, Sally stood up and started to write on the white board. She wrote the initials 'MPS' in the centre of the board and circled them. "So let's see," she said as she drew an arrow from the circle and wrote 'Naismith' at the head. "Fifteen years ago Stevens was Naismith's solicitor… or at least was involved with some of his companies." She drew another arrow and wrote 'Underwood' and another to 'Nichols'. "Now he turns up with these two… and… Lorna, who was King's brief at the murder trial?"

Lorna typed something into the computer and waited for a moment. "Michael Peter Stevens," she said. Sally drew another arrow and wrote 'King'.

"And Fisher kept his files with Stevens," said Sally as she drew another arrow. "Give him a call tomorrow, Jane. Ask him why… although I can probably guess."

"So what's this leading to?" asked Jane.

"More digging for you," replied Sally. "Fisher's files are all over fifteen years old and you said that most of the companies have ceased trading. Now you have to go through the details for Naismith's current businesses… and check all King's companies, including the ones in Fisher's files. Let's see what else our Mr Stevens is connected with."

Chapter 26

Thursday 15th May

London Colney, Hertfordshire – 09:00 BST

"So what did your father keep in the garage?" asked Sally

"That's a bloody strange question," Debbie King replied. "How should I know? Anyway he had lots of garages."

"No… not those… I mean at his house."

"I don't know. The usual stuff… lawn mower, barbeque, golf clubs… just stuff… you know?"

"Nothing else… no documents, papers… anything like that?"

"Why would anyone keep stuff like that in their garage?" asked Debbie. "Anyway what's this all about?"

"Oh! Sorry I forgot to tell you… we picked up another one of your father's associates the night before last. David Nichols… he was looking for something in your father's garage."

"Well I'll let you know if I think of anything," said Debbie brusquely. "Now if it's alright with you, I'm going to do my hair before we go."

National Crime Squad, Hertfordshire Branch – 09:30 BST

Jane broke off from her search of the company records and started to write on her notepad.

What's in the garage?
Something valuable?
Why take the risk?

She'd been going through it in her head most of the morning, and it still didn't make any sense: *Questions…Questions. Where are the answers? Come on Jane, think.*

She started to write again.

What's in the garage? *Something we missed. Something small?*

Something valuable? *What? Maybe only if you know what it is*

Why take the risk? *Something more important than getting caught?*

Threatened? – Ordered? - STAYING ALIVE?

What's not in the garage? CAR!!! What's in the car?

She crossed out what she had just written: *He's not that stupid. He'd have known that we'd have the car. But...*

She picked up the pen and wrote again. *WHAT WAS IN THE CAR?*

"Yes. That's it!" she exclaimed, as she picked up the phone.

"What are you doing?" asked Lorna.

"Hang on a minute and I'll tell you," replied Jane, and she started to talk into the phone.

"Thanks, that'll be great," she said as an officer at the Thames Valley forensics lab promised to fax the details over within the hour. She put down the phone and turned to Lorna. "I've had an idea about what Nichols might have been looking for," she said.

Lorna nodded as she listened to Jane's theory. "You might be onto something," she said. "Let's wait until we've got the list and then we'll talk to Sally."

Bournemouth, Dorset – 13.30 BST

"It's just up here on the left," said Debbie, "see those big gates just there?"

Sally turned the BMW off the road and stopped in front of the gates. She lowered the window and reached out to press the button on the intercom. "Deborah King to visit Mrs. Naismith," she said in reply to the disembodied voice that crackled from the speaker.

Inside the windowless basement control room the security guard looked up at the CCTV monitor and then at the clipboard on his desk. "You're not on my list," he said. "You'll have to wait while I check with the manager. Who else is with you?"

"A friend, Sally Parkinson," replied Sally. She turned to her companion, "You didn't tell me about this."

"Sorry," replied Debbie. "They like you to tell them in advance that you're coming. They're very hot on security here."

Sally looked at the massive iron gates and saw that there was a CCTV camera and a large security light on each gatepost. "I see what you mean. It's more like a prison than a retirement home."

"Except that this is to keep people out," said Debbie. "Old people like to feel safe."

After a couple of minutes, the speaker crackled again. "That's OK, Miss King. Please, park in one of the visitors' spaces and go to reception."

The gates opened silently and Sally drove into the grounds of Norbury Manor. The wide driveway had 5 MPH markers and six-inch high speed bumps at regular intervals. Sally negotiated them slowly – the 17 inch alloy wheels and low profile tyres fitted to the BMW were designed for speed; not speed bumps – the car jolting over every one; following the drive as it curved round through the trees and crossed a large, beautifully manicured lawn. A small sign pointed them in the direction of the visitors' car park, and she pulled the car up to a halt in the nearest space. As they got out, she noticed several more CCTV cameras attached to the exterior of the building: *Big Brother is watching.*

A pair of large plate glass doors parted as they approached, and Sally drew a sharp breath as they entered the reception area. "Wow, it's like a five-star hotel," she gasped.

"Nothing but the best," said Debbie, "…you don't think that my Dad would put his aunt anywhere cheap."

"Your father paid for all this?" asked Sally.

"Well not exactly. He arranged it all, but my uncle pays the bills," replied Debbie. "Just as well now that you've frozen Dad's bank accounts… or they'd be throwing her out."

"So how much does it cost for a place like this?" asked Sally as she thought of her grandmother, who'd had to sell her house to raise the three hundred pounds a week that she paid for a small room, in a run down nursing home in Worthing.

"About two grand a week, give or take," replied Debbie, "and believe me, these people know how to take. You should see the bills for extras."

A young girl in a black suit looked up as they stood in front of the desk. "Nice to see you again Miss King," she said politely. "I'm sorry you had to wait, but you know that we like you to call ahead."

"That's alright… I didn't know we were coming until this morning. Spur of the moment… you know," said Debbie. "I've brought my very dear friend Miss Parkinson to see Aunt Mary. I do hope that's alright." For a moment Sally was taken by surprise as Debbie put on her charming, sophisticated voice: *Is this the same woman I've been talking to for the past week?*

"Of course, Miss King," the girl turned the visitors' book to face Debbie and held out a pen, "…your aunt is in her room. If you'll both sign in, I'll get someone to take you through."

A young man in a crisp white uniform led them along a long corridor towards the back of the building. "All the best rooms are at the back," boasted Debbie, "…they overlook the gardens."

Sally looked at the signs above each of the doors as they passed: *Solarium, Spa, Gymnasium, Library, Games Room.* At the end of the corridor there were two pairs of glass doors. The man took out a card and swiped it through a reader next to doors on the left, which opened silently, then held out his arm, gesturing to them to pass through, to the *Residents' Suites*.

Halfway along the corridor the man stopped and pressed a button on an intercom panel next to a panelled oak door. "Hello, Mary," he said, "...it's William. I've brought your visitors."

A green light flashed on the panel and Sally heard the click of an electronic door lock. William pushed the door and held it open to let the two women through.

Mary Naismith was sitting in an armchair in front of a large window that overlooked the gardens; the remote control with which she had unlocked the door was still in her hand. She looked tired and pale, but her face lit up when she saw Debbie. Sally felt sorry for her; for all the luxury, this place wasn't really any different from the home where her grandmother was spending her last days. Three-hundred pounds or two-thousand, it didn't make any difference, the excuses were the same: *'she can't cope with the stairs any more... we'd look after him, but... it's for the best... she'll be happier with people of her own age'*.

Sally looked through the window at the people in the garden; they didn't look very happy. Put here by their relatives – out of sight and out of mind, looking at the same view every day, waiting for the end to come, waiting for the relatives to visit, and wondering which would come first – relatives whose consciences were eased by writing the cheques.

"Thank you William," she said, "...would you bring some tea. Earl Grey, I think... with some lemon." As the two women approached, she put the remote control down, stood up, and walked unsteadily across the room to greet them.

Debbie King kissed the old lady on both cheeks. "You're looking well today Aunt Mary," she said. "This is my friend Sally."

Mary Naismith gestured towards the window, "It's such a lovely day," she said, "why don't we sit outside."

As Sally looked out onto the terrace and then at the old lady, she wondered if she could go through with the story that she'd worked out with Barton. Debbie King had agreed to play along, but Sally could see there was genuine affection between these two women and she was starting to feel guilty about the deception that they had planned: *I can't do this. No more lies.*

"I think it would be better to stay in here," said Sally seriously, "...it's more private."

Debbie King looked at Sally and nodded. "Thank you," she whispered.

William returned with the tea and as the three women sat down at the table by the window. Debbie started to speak. "I'm sorry, Aunt Mary," she said. "I'm afraid that I wasn't completely honest with you when I rang." She sounded agitated and, although she took a deep breath before continuing, the words just tumbled out. "I'm in a lot of trouble. Dad's dead, Terry too for all I know, everything's a mess, Sally's a policewoman, I'm under arrest and..."

Mary Naismith reached across the table; her frail fingers clasped Debbie's hand tightly as she spoke slowly and calmly, "It's all right Debbie dear." She took a small handkerchief from her sleeve and gave it to Debbie. "Now wipe your eyes and drink your tea. Then you can start at the beginning. It's alright... I've been expecting this for a long time."

She turned to Sally. "Don't look so surprised, young lady. I may be old and ill but I'm not senile or stupid. I'll be eighty-three next month and according to the doctors I probably won't get to eighty-four, so maybe it's time to stop pretending. Perhaps you'd better start... I don't think Debbie will make a very good job of it."

St Lucia – 10:30 Eastern Standard Time

Their flight from Miami had been delayed, and then cancelled; they'd spent the night at an airport hotel and taken an early morning flight. As the house came into view, Barton could see the matronly figures of his mother and aunt standing on the porch; by the time that the taxi pulled up they were both standing at the roadside.

Julia Barton flung open the car door and barely gave her son a chance to get out before she enveloped him in her arms. "Welcome home Michael... it's been a long time," she said as she planted a large kiss on his cheek.

"Give the boy a break, Julia," laughed his aunt. But Barton didn't want a break. For the first time in ages, he felt completely at ease.

"It's OK, Aunty Lou, I'll survive," he said, with a big smile: *Everything is OK now.*

"Come up to the house," said Lou, taking Grace by the hand. "You must be starving you poor things. I'll make breakfast."

"I've got a surprise for you," said Julia. "Your sister's coming this evening and we're going to have a big party."

Barton shrugged. This wasn't exactly what he'd had in mind. He needed to spend some time alone with his mother; there were questions he had to ask. But the light in her eyes gave him a warm feeling. Maybe a party was what he needed right now. There'd be time to talk later.

Grace could here the sound of the waves breaking on the beach and she gazed out of the window as she unpacked. The slopes of the distant mountains, covered by the rain forest, were a vivid green colour that you didn't see in England. She loved this place; so peaceful, so beautiful. The wooden house next to the beach was dilapidated and the furnishings threadbare, but it was comfortable and always felt like home. The house had a small bathroom, but the shower was outside, and she watched her husband as he stood under the cascade in the yard. She smiled at him and he smiled back; she hadn't seen him so happy for a long time.

Julia and Aunty Lou had lived alone in the small house for nearly twenty years, except they were never alone, as for most of the time it was open house with relatives and friends calling at all hours; so long it was after ten in the morning. Grace remembered that Julia and Aunty Lou didn't do lunch, but breakfast was always late, big and leisurely.

The sisters had a way of doing things in the morning: up at six, cutting flowers from the garden by half-past, singing hymns as they walked the two miles to the small wooden church, arranging the flowers before the small congregation arrived, and after the service a leisurely walk home followed by breakfast. They had followed this routine, every day – although there were many days when they were the only members of the congregation for the eight o'clock service – for as long as anyone could remember.

Breakfast with Julia and Lou was an experience. On her first visit with Mike, Sunday breakfast had started at ten, after the sisters had returned from morning service, and they'd finished some time around three, by which time Grace had lost count of the number of people who'd just dropped by. Many bringing contributions to help restock the sisters' depleted larder, all welcomed like long lost friends.

Barton got dressed and they held hands as they went out to the front porch; the table was laden with food and several of the rickety chairs were already occupied. The next few minutes involved many enthusiastic handshakes, hugs and kisses, as friends and neighbours greeted them. As the morning progressed and more people arrived, Grace knew that breakfast would somehow last for the rest of the day, and that the evening party would never really start; it would just be a continuation.

Julia picked up two empty jugs from the table and Grace saw her opportunity. She stood up and took Barton's hand. "Come on," she said, "we'll tell her now."

Bournemouth, Dorset – 15:00 BST

Mary Naismith had listened in silence as Sally had explained the reason for their visit, the events of the past few days and the enquiries that they were

313

following. "I suppose that you've got quite a lot of questions," she said quietly when Sally had finished.

"Anything that you can think of that might help us," said Sally. The old lady was tired and frail, but throughout she had listened attentively, nodding and shaking her head; not in disbelief, but resignation.

"I'm sorry about your dad, Debbie," Mary said uneasily. "But we both knew that this was how he would probably end up. He was a bad lot, always was... just like his father. But now maybe you can get on with your life... go away... start again." She looked relieved: *Maybe it's time... Time it was all over.*

"'I'm afraid that Anthony hasn't been entirely honest with your boss," she said to Sally. "Yes it's true that he and Bobby never really got on, but they were a lot closer than that. Yes, he tried to make out that he was better... that his brother was the black sheep... but really they were like peas in a pod. Sons of the same father, you see. Anthony was always the clever one, but he had a nasty malicious streak in him. I don't know what's worse... doing bad things... or getting others to do it for you. Bobby adored him and he took advantage of it."

Debbie and Sally looked shocked, but before either of them could say anything, the old lady continued.

"You mustn't think I don't love him," she said. "I love him more than I could ever tell you. But that doesn't mean that I have to like my son." She pointed to the bedside table, "Debbie will you get me something from that drawer."

Debbie got up and opened the drawer, inside was a large bundle of paper, tied with a blue ribbon. She looked at the title on the top page – 'The *Business of Politics ~ An Autobiography ~ Sir Anthony Naismith ~ July 1994* – as she handed the manuscript to her aunt.

"He never published this. I told him that it was very badly written. Anthony was very clever, but literature wasn't his strongest subject. Bobby was always the writer in the family." Mary passed the manuscript to Sally. "Like most men, Anthony sometimes had difficulty distinguishing between the truth and what he wanted to be true. I'm afraid that his version of events is a little coloured. I didn't know much about his business after he grew up, but the first few chapters... well of course I was there and it wasn't quite like that."

Sally leafed though the top sheets and saw that almost every page had annotations in a neat delicate script.

"You have to understand that Anthony hated his brother... your father Debbie... so everything shows Bobby in a bad light... as the weak one... the bad one. But most of the time he was writing about himself."

"I don't understand," said Debbie. "Why did he hate Dad?"

"Because Bobby was my sister's favourite... because he stayed at home, when Anthony was sent away... because my sister loved Bobby and hated Anthony. Of course, she never said as much, but we all knew and she couldn't hide it from the boy. Things got worse after my sister went to America and Bobby lived on his own with his grandmother. My mother was very strict and did her best to keep him away from trouble. But, I'm afraid that I spoiled Anthony... always let have his own way. It's stupid I know... but I always felt that I had to make it up to him... it wasn't his fault. That's probably why I stood by and did nothing as that vile American poisoned his mind."

"What do you mean? What did you have to make up to him," asked Sally.

Mary Naismith held back the tears; she wasn't going to lose her dignity now. "I had to make up for giving him away... for denying who he was... for lying to my own son." Her voice faltered, but she carried on. "It has to come out," she said. "I've kept it in too long and maybe it will help people understand... and not judge him too harshly."

Debbie's head was reeling at the revelations and she looked into her aunt's eyes. "You don't have to do this Aunt Mary, it doesn't matter," she said.

"But I do... you see it's what made him the way he is... it wasn't his fault." She was very tired now, but there might never be another chance. She might not feel this brave again. "It started when I was twelve. My father worked at night and every Thursday evening when my mother and sister went to the pictures... they left me with my sister's husband... to keep an eye on me..." her voice trembled. "My brother-in-law...your grandfather, Debbie... came to the house every week and raped me. I was thirteen when I fell pregnant and they kept me indoors for months. Abortion was out of the question... it was 1934. Do you know that they locked girls like me up in mental homes? My mother made my sister pretend that she was pregnant... padding her out with more layers every few weeks. When Anthony was born they didn't even let me hold him... they just took him away. They even took away his name and called him after that awful man."

She stopped and took a sip of water. Sally and Debbie looked at each other but said nothing. There was nothing to say.

"Then all those years of pretending... watching him grow up... and the fear of losing him again when my sister took up with that American. She had a poor choice in men... your grandmother. I had to stand by while Henry Patterson filled the boys' heads with hate. Once he even told them, that he wished Hitler had been American, so that he could have dealt with their Jews and Negroes. But at least I stopped him taking them... my husband knew someone... he made sure that their papers were wrong. I know it's an awful thing to admit to, but I was so happy when my sister died, because it meant that I could keep him forever."

315

Sally spoke at last. "Does your son know who he is?" she asked, regretting the impertinence of the question.

"I couldn't tell him for a long time. Even after my husband died, I couldn't stand the shame. It was Christmas1962... and we were a little drunk. I don't know how it came out... he shouldn't have found out like that. Anthony was so angry... he shouted and stormed out. He was gone for days. When he came back, he packed his things. I tried to explain, but he didn't want to listen. It was two years before we spoke again."

The old lady looked exhausted. But something in her eyes told them that somehow she felt at peace with herself now; she looked relieved to have cast off the burden she had carried for so many years. "Now, I'm glad I've told someone. They say confession is good for the soul," she said, serenely. "Thank you for listening. I feel better now." She picked up a remote control and pressed a button. "Now, you'll have some more tea before you go."

"You said something about Dad," said Debbie, as she sipped the Earl Grey. "You said he was the writer. I don't understand he never struck me as that."

"He was when he was young, Debbie... especially before my mother died. He always kept a little diary... he showed me sometimes. He wrote about lots of things... all his little adventures... made a lot of it up I suppose... all little boys do. And every time he saw Anthony, he'd write about it... for days before... all the things that they were going to do. And afterwards, accounts of everything they'd done. He used to write long letters to Anthony too. He had a lovely way with words when he was a boy. He was a lovely boy. Mind you after my mother died, he went off the rails. I wish that we'd taken him in, but we had our hands full with Anthony. He still used to write to his brother but the letters changed... full of boasting about how bad he was... as if he was trying to impress."

"Sally looked at her watch, "Time we were leaving," she said. "We've got a long drive back."

At the door Mary took Sally's hand; her eyes were pleading. "Don't be too hard on him," she said. "It's not all his fault. They were both good boys who made the wrong choices."

Debbie hugged her aunt and kissed her on both cheeks. "Thanks Aunt Mary," she said. "Thanks for helping me understand."

"You'll probably find your dad's diaries somewhere when you're clearing the house," said Mary. "He told me he'd kept them. And the letters that he wrote to Anthony... I gave them back to him a few years ago. You should read them."

Aunty Lou had sensed that Barton needed some privacy and she'd somehow contrived to disperse the guests. They'd be back, but not for a while. Grace helped her to clear the table and they went into the kitchen to do the dishes, leaving Barton and Julia alone on the porch.

Julia took his hand and led him towards the steps. "Come on, Michael, let's walk a while. You can tell me all about it."

"I need to ask some questions, Mum… about Dad," he said cautiously.

"That's alright," she said. "Now take off those shoes, you don't want to get sand in them. And I want to know why you make me wait so long to find out I'm going to be a grandmother? You too busy to pick up the telephone. I know you, so don't try and fool me now," she laughed, as Barton shrugged his shoulders and hung his head. "And take that look off your face, you still not too big for me to give you a good whooping with the broom."

They walked along the shoreline; Julia had hitched up her skirts and Barton had rolled his trousers up to the knee. On any other day, walking hand-in-hand in the surf with his mother would have transported him back to his childhood. But today was different, he felt uneasy; uncertain about how to ask his questions; questions he desperately needed to ask: *Is it fair to rake over the past?*

Time heals, erasing, or at least obscuring, unpleasant memories; and he wondered if, after twenty years, he had he the right, to ask her to talk about such things.

"What's troubling you Michael?" she asked

And so he told her about the rows with Grace, the botched up operation and the meetings with Naismith; about being betrayed by people he trusted and the nightmares.

It was late as they walked back to the house, and he still hadn't asked her his questions. As the house came into view, he saw his sister in the distance, walking to meet them. He quickened his pace and started to run, but she grasped his hand and held him back. "Wait, there's still so much to talk about."

Julia knew why her son had come here, and she was ready. And she hoped that she would be able to give him some answers. She had waited twenty years and now it was time. But, Barton could never have anticipated what she was about to tell him.

"She came to see me, you know. That man Campbell's wife… she came to say she was sorry."

Barton stopped dead. "When? Why didn't you tell me?" His head started to reel. He clenched his fists, wanting to lash out at something; but there was only

Julia. He started pounding the sides of his head. He didn't know why; nothing made sense any more.

Julia reached out and stopped him, taking hold of his forearm, pulling him towards her. Then, she hugged him, her tears mingling with his.

"It's alright, Michael, it's all going to be OK," she said at last. She took a handkerchief from her apron pocket and wiped away their tears. "We'll talk again tomorrow, son. But, tonight let's be happy."

"But…" Barton forced a smile. "OK, Mum, I'll try." The man was still angry and confused, but the boy inside listened to his mother. And she was always right. "Now go see your sister, she's come all the way from Boston to see you. She's got good news too."

Chapter 27

Friday 16th May

Tottenham, North London – 09:15 BST

The policeman had seen the face before; recently, on a poster at the station. He couldn't remember what he was wanted for, but he knew there had been a warning not to approach the man. He took out his notebook and flicked back a couple of pages: *It's him... Marcus Preston.* He switched on his radio, and moments later, he was put through to the NCS control room.

"Yes I'm sure it's him, he's just gone into the pub."

"Stay there," said Paul Timms. "We'll get some armed back up. How many exits are there?"

"Two doors onto the street, and there's a delivery gate and fire escape in the alley at the back. The pub's not open yet, but someone let him in the back gate."

"OK, you stay watching from where you are; I'll get the station to send someone to watch the front. Do not... I repeat, do not go anywhere near him. We believe that he's armed and extremely dangerous."

National Crime Squad, Hertfordshire Branch – 10:15 BST

Jane signed for the packet and walked back to her desk. She opened the envelope and tipped the contents onto the desk; a black key fob with the initials *RJK,* scratched on one side and *Cheshunt Golf Club 31* in white lettering on the other. Attached to the ring were three small keys.

"Got it," she cried triumphantly, waving the keys at Lorna.

"What have you got?" asked Sally who had just walked in to the office.

"Hi, Sally," said Lorna. "We tried to reach you yesterday but your mobile was off. Jane's been doing some detective work."

"Well, that's what we're paid for," said Sally sarcastically. After yesterday, she wasn't in a mood for games. "Now what have you got there?"

"The keys to King's locker at the golf club... at least I think that's what they are. They were in his car," said Jane.

"We think they're what Nichols was looking for at King's house," added Lorna.

Sally smiled: *Something else that Paul has missed,* "Well, what are you doing still here? Go and get a warrant. Then get over there and see what they unlock."

Jane didn't need telling twice, "Are you coming Lorna?" she asked as she got up.

"I think you can manage on your own, Jane," said Sally. "I need Lorna to give me a full briefing on what you found in those files. We'll go over what I found out yesterday, when you get back."

"Another one in the bag," said Timms as he strutted through the office. "We've just picked up Preston. I'm off to interview him now. Have you found your man yet?"

Sally gritted her teeth. She wished she could tell the smug bastard that they weren't even looking; acting DCI Timms needed taking down a peg or two. She glared at her colleague. "No... looks like they gave you all the easy ones," she said.

"No need to be like that," said Timms. "He didn't come that easy; he's just put two uniforms in hospital."

"Better watch out then. If I were you, I'd stand well back... when you tell him about his brother?"

Cheshunt – 11:35 BST

Jane walked into the clubhouse and waited while the man at the desk finished talking to a couple of golfers. When he was free, she spoke to him.

"Hello, I'm Detective Constable Jane Barclay. Could you confirm that these belong to one of your members," she said, showing the man the keys.

"Yes that's one of our key fobs," said the man, holding out his hand. "I'll make sure that the member gets them back."

"You'll have a job mate. He's dead. But I'd like to see what's inside his locker."

"I'm sorry, but I can't let you into the members' locker room," the man protested. "I'll have to call the club secretary."

"Call who you like, but I've got a search warrant here that says I can open the locker and remove the contents. So if you'll just show me the way. I'm sure that we can do this without any fuss."

The man shrugged and led the way. "There are two locker keys, but I don't know what the other one is," he said.

"And why would someone want two lockers?" asked Jane.

"A lot of members do. They use one for clothes and stuff, and keep their clubs in the other. It saves carting them back and forth in the car, I suppose."

"So how secure are these lockers? What if I wanted to keep something valuable in one?"

"Well of course the club doesn't accept any responsibility, but the security is very good," said the man as they approached the door. "This is an electronic lock. The key fob activates it, like this," he said holding an identical fob up to a sensor by the door. "Every key fob has a different code, and if a member leaves or loses their fob the code is taken off the system so it can't be used until it's reactivated. Keeps out the riff raff, you see. We used to have a problem with kids getting in and nicking stuff, but not anymore, now we know exactly who's coming and going, and when. Bloody good these computers."

"Thanks, I'll find it myself from here," said Jane.

"I shouldn't leave you. Not in the gentlemen's locker room. I shouldn't really let a woman in here at all."

"Well I'm a big girl and I don't suppose I'll see anything I've not seen before. So why don't you go back to your desk and call your secretary or whoever," said Jane dismissively.

The man turned and left as Jane went through the doorway. A couple of minutes later she would be sorry that she hadn't let him stay.

Tottenham, North London – 11:45 BST

"He wants his brief," said the custody sergeant "won't talk to anyone until he gets here."

"Let me guess… Michael Stevens," said Timms. "I'm surprised he's not here already."

"Can't get hold of him. His office said he's playing golf with clients, and his mobile's switched off."

"Well he might not want to talk to us. But he can still listen. Where's the interview room?"

Marcus Preston was leaning back in his chair with both feet on the table. He looked away as Timms and Brady entered the room.

"You're wastin' your time. I ain't saying nothin' till my brief gets 'ere," he said, arrogantly, without looking at Timms.

Timms spoke to the two uniforms. "OK, we'll take it from here, but I want one of you outside the door."

He sat down, unwrapped two tapes and put them in the recorder. He switched on the machine. "Interview with Marcus Preston, Friday 16th of May commencing at," he glanced at his watch, "…11:48 a.m., officers present, Acting DCI Paul Timms and DS Matt Brady. Mr Preston has asked for his solicitor, but he is not present at this time. Mr Preston, I must remind you that you are still under caution."

"Dunno why you're botherin' with that. I ain't saying nothin'," said Preston defiantly. "And you ain't got nothin' so we'll just sit 'ere and wait for my brief. I got plenty of time."

Timms ignored the remark and continued. He'd met lots like Preston. Hard men, all front, and no brains. But he'd talk sooner or later. Prison didn't bother him, it went with the job; but he'd say something to keep the stretch as short as possible.

"Oh! I think we might have a bit more than nothing. How about murder… or, at least, conspiracy to murder? Did you know that the conspiracy bit can get you life even if you didn't actually do the murder?"

"No comment."

"Let's start with something easy. Will you confirm that you are Marcus Preston of 33a Church Street, Stoke Newington?"

"No comment."

"OK, well we don't really need you to answer that. So where were you between 10 a.m. on Friday, 2nd of May 2003 and 11 a.m. on Sunday, 3rd of May 2003?"

"No comment."

"No problem, we'll come back to that later. How about… between 11 a.m. and 11:45 a.m., on Sunday 4th of May? No need to answer that we know already. Did you enjoy your breakfast with Warren Jarvis? Bet you needed it after that long drive back from Edinburgh?"

"How did you? No comment."

"Careful Marcus…. You nearly gave me an answer there."

"Bastard!" Preston spat the word Timms; deliberately expelling a mouthful of saliva for good measure. "You think you're so fucking clever. Well you ain't getting' nothing'…you bastard."

Timms wiped his face and leaned across the table. "Don't be stupid Marcus, we've already got enough to put you away and throw away the key. Of course you could co-operate and make life a bit easier for all concerned."

"No comment."

"The record seems to be stuck, again, but don't worry. I'll talk and you can listen. You might even learn something," said Timms. "Like what a pathetic, stupid prick you are."

"Talk all you like, copper… I ain't listenin'. I'll be out of 'ere when my brief gets 'ere."

"Oh! It says something else. Let's try Monday 5th of May about three in the morning. Remember that?"

"No comment."

"This is getting boring. Matt, have you got those pictures?"

Brady opened his briefcase and took out a folder; inside was a bundle of A4 sized colour photographs. He took the top one and placed it on the table facing Preston.

"Recognise anyone Marcus?" asked Brady. The photograph showed a group of men in a hotel lobby. He pointed to the figure at the centre of the group. "Oh! That looks like you."

Preston stared straight ahead. "No comment."

"How about this man?" said Brady pointing to another figure, "Vladan Milosevic, do you recognise him?"

"No comment," said Preston, without even looking at the picture.

Brady laid down another picture. "What about this, do you recognise any of these women?" The photo showed a group of young women getting out of a car. Brady pointed to one of the faces, "Do you know her?"

Preston glanced at the picture. Brady's finger was pointing at the smiling face of Naida Ajanovic. "No comment."

Brady placed another picture carefully on the table, and looked away. Pictures like this one always made his stomach turn. Naida Ajanovic again; lying on a mortuary table.

"She's dead," said Timms coldly. "Look!"

Preston stared at the picture for a moment, and pushed it away.

"We know you didn't kill her, but can you say the same for these people?" Timms took the bundle from Brady and started to lay the photos on the table. As he placed each one in front of Preston, he slowly and deliberately said a name.

"Jasmina Ajanovic."

"No comment."

Milosevic, again, maybe you recognise him better like this?"

"No… fuckin'… comment."

"Robert King and Terence King… he's not dead, but looking at the state he's in this picture… he might as well be. Did you know they were in the car last week?" Did you know it was them you were going kill?

"No comment. You got fuck all."

"You think so! I'll tell you what I've fucking got!" Timms paused for a moment, before laying down the last picture. "Did they tell you who was driving for King that night? No, I bet they didn't. Well, take a good look… take a really good look," Timms slowly put the photograph on the table, "at what you did to Errol Preston."

Preston leapt to his feet. "Bastards! Fuckin' Bastards!" he shouted, as he lunged forward with his fists flailing.

Timms had expected a reaction, and moved aside. But he wasn't quite fast enough and crashed to floor as Preston's fist caught him on the cheek. Brady pressed the call button and a uniformed officer ran into the room. Between them, they managed to get Preston onto the floor and cuff him, before he could hit Timms again. Brady got to his feet and stepped over his boss to reach the recorder.

"For the benefit of the tape, Mr Preston has just assaulted DCI Timms. Interview suspended at 12:17 p.m."

He reached down and helped Timms to his feet. "Do you need a doctor, sir?" he asked.

"Bloody dentist, more like," said Timms as he spat out a tooth. "Come on let's get out of here, I need drink."

National Crime Squad, Hertfordshire Branch – 12:15 BST

"OK, thanks. We'll be right there." Lorna put down the phone and ran over to Sally's office.

"I've just had a call from Hertfordshire Police," said Lorna. "It's Jane, she's been attacked."

"What?"

"Jane, she was attacked at the golf club. She's on her way to casualty now."

"What happened?"

"They don't know… someone found her out cold on the floor of the locker room."

"OK, you get over to the hospital," said Sally. "I'll go to the golf club. Who called you?"

Lorna tore the top page off her notepad, and gave it to Sally. "PC Bryant, he's there now, that's his mobile number."

Sally dialled the number as she ran down the stairs.

"Hello, is that PC Bryant? This is DI Parkinson NCS; I'm on my way over now. Have you called in the SOCOs…? Good, and get someone from your CID down there… yes that's alright. Now don't let anyone leave or touch anything until I get there. I'm leaving now; I'll be about twenty minutes."

Sally stopped at the gates and flashed her warrant card at the uniform. "DI Parkinson, NCS. Who's in charge up there?"

"DS Hadley, ma'am, he's expecting you, I'll tell him you're here."

Sally parked in front of the clubhouse and a young man approached her as she was getting out of the car. "DS Hadley, ma'am," he said as he extended his hand. "You didn't waste any time, you didn't need to rush... we've got everything under control."

"One of my officers has just been attacked, Hadley. I'll decide when things are under control," she snapped. "Now show me where it happened."

"Bloody NCS," muttered Hadley as he led the way to the clubhouse. "...that's all I need."

"I heard that, Sergeant. Let's get on with it."

"This is where she was," said Hadley pointing to the area between two banks of lockers. Strips of blue and white tape obstructed the gaps at each end.

Sally moved as close as she could, and saw the small pool of blood on the floor between the lockers. Jane's bag was about ten feet away, its contents strewn across the floor. "She had a nasty cut on the back of her head. Golf club, I'll bet. Looks like someone was getting in a bit of driving practice, if you ask me," Hadley said with a snigger.

"Nobody's asking you, Sergeant. We'll let the experts tell us. Is this exactly as it was... all the lockers were shut?"

"Yes, nothing's been touched. Oh! PC Bryant found her warrant card over there... that's how he knew who she was... but he didn't touch anything else. Her purse looks to be missing and there's no sign of a mobile. If you ask me she was mugged."

"And I've already told you... I'm not asking for your opinion. Now where are your SOCOs?"

"Not here yet, they've been delayed. They won't get here for about an hour."

"Not good enough. Get onto your control... I want someone here... Now!"

"Now hang on a minute, ma'am. I can't..."

"Yes you can. My officer was here looking for evidence in connection with serious crime investigation. I need to see what's in those lockers and I can't touch a bloody thing until the SOCOs have done their stuff. So don't piss about. Get on the phone now! And while you're at it get your DI here." Sally stormed out of the locker room, without waiting for the young officer to reply.

"Fuck it," snarled Derek Hadley. He'd been a DS for just three days and was anxious to prove his worth. Now he had to call his boss out to a mugging because some bloody woman didn't think he was up to it.

Sally approached the reception desk where a man was arguing with a uniformed officer. "What's going on?" she asked.

"Who are you?" demanded the man angrily.

"Detective Inspector Parkinson... and you are?"

"Miles Kingston, I'm the club secretary and I'm trying to explain to this officer that we have members complaining that they can't leave and the gentlemen can't get into the locker room. God knows that's bad enough, but they're not letting anybody in the gates either. We've got an important, ladies four-ball competition today and half the players aren't here."

"Well, I'm sorry that your members are being inconvenienced, but one of my officers is in hospital and nobody comes or goes until I know what happened," said Sally as politely as she could: *Pompous prat*

Kingston opened his mouth to protest, but Sally didn't give him a chance to say anything. "We need to take statements from everyone who was here this morning and the locker room stays out of bounds until it's been cleared by our forensic team," said Sally. "Now I'd like you to send someone out on to the course and tell everyone to stop playing and return to the clubhouse immediately."

"Is this really necessary?" Kingston protested. "The members will be very annoyed,"

"Well make it up to them... give them all a free drink or something." Sally said dismissively as turned away to talk to the policeman.

PC Rob Bryant gave her an admiring look. "That told him, ma'am, he's a real pain in the arse. By the way, I'm PC Bryant, we spoke earlier."

"Were the first on the scene, Bryant?" asked Sally.

"Yes, we were only about a mile away when the call came in. We got here in a couple of minutes," Bryant said proudly.

"We, who was with you?"

"My partner, you would have seen him at the gate when you arrived. As soon as we realised what had happened he went down to the gate to stop anyone coming or going."

"Well, done Bryant. At least someone here knows what they're doing."

"I got them to get everyone together in the bar. They're all in there with one of our DCs at the moment. They're not very happy."

"How many are in there?"

"About twenty members and half a dozen staff, there are still a quite a few members out on the course... one of the green keepers is out there rounding them up now."

"Thanks, Bryant, you better get in there and start taking statements until reinforcements arrive," said Sally. "You've been very helpful."

"Just doing my job ma'am," replied Bryant. "By the way the security here is pretty good… they've got CCTV covering all the doors and the main gate. I was in the Crime Prevention Team last summer and checked it all out for them after it was installed."

"Thanks again," said Sally, thinking how much they relied on ordinary coppers like Bryant; just doing the job.

"Can I help you," asked the young man behind the desk.

"Yes, I'm DI Parkinson, have you been on the desk all morning?"

"Since about half-six, when we opened," the man replied.

"And you haven't left the area unattended at all?"

"Well I had to go to the loo a couple of times… and I had to show her where the locker room was."

"You mean DC Barclay?"

"Yes. Stroppy cow comes marching in here with her search warrant. Ordered me about like she owned the place," he said.

Sally let the remark pass without comment, but made a mental note to ask Bryant and Hadley to be particularly thorough with the man's interview. "Who found her?" she asked.

"Mr Bingham, one of the members. He came running in here in a right panic."

"And, you called the police?"

"No, Mr Bingham's partner called on his mobile. He was still in the locker room when I got there. Is that all?"

"Yes, for the time being," replied Sally. "But I assume that you can give me a list of everyone who has been here today."

"I can try," he said, "but members can come and go as they please. Only guests have to be signed in." He looked nervous, and his voice faltered a little. "I can remember most of the members I suppose. Give me a bit of time to think."

"And we'll need the CCTV tapes as well," said Sally.

Joe Turner had been expecting this request. He put his hand into his pocket and felt the wad of twenty-pound notes. "No problem, but a couple of them may be a bit dodgy. Some of the recorders are playing up, keep stopping for some reason." He crossed his fingers and hoped he had sounded convincing; he wasn't very good at lying.

Sally stayed around until the local DI arrived. She explained the situation, and told him what Jane had been doing at the club. Unlike Hadley, he seemed to know what he was doing and she felt confident to leave him in charge.

"Give me a call when the SOCOs have finished," she said. "And don't open King's lockers until I get back. I'll be at the hospital."

Tottenham, North London – 14:30 BST

"Come on Matt, finish that beer, we're on again," said Timms, putting his mobile back in his pocket. "Stevens has just turned up."

Ten minutes later Timms and Brady walked into the interview room. Preston and Stevens immediately stopped talking. Timms replaced the two tapes in the recorder and switched the machine on. "Interview with Marcus Preston, Friday 16th May resuming at 14:42... officers present, DCI Timms and DS Brady... also present is Mr Preston's solicitor, Mr Michael Stevens."

"Has my client been charged with anything?" asked Stevens.

"Not yet," said Timms. "At this stage he is assisting our investigation."

Preston leaned forward and glared at Timms. "I ain't assistin' you with nothin', 'cos you ain't got nothin'," he said confidently. "That's right Mr Stevens, ain't it?"

Stevens leaned over and whispered in Preston's ear. Preston nodded his head and leaned back in his chair.

The lawyer looked at Timms, "What my client means is that he knows of no reason why you should want to question him and that unfortunately, he cannot help you with your enquiries. So unless you intend to charge him I request that he is released without further delay," he said smugly, repeating the words of the mantra he'd chanted a thousand times before.

"Very well, if that's what you want," said Timms and he leaned over to the recorder. "Interview suspended at 14:46."

Preston looked at Timms in disbelief. "So I can go then?" he said rising from his chair. "Thanks Mr Stevens, that's sorted the bastards."

Stevens wasn't listening; he hadn't expected it to be as easy as this: *That's a relief. I've got better things to do than look after this moron. Not often you get lucky twice in a day.*

"Not so fast," said Timms. He pressed the call button and a uniform opened the door. "Matt, will you and the constable take Mr Preston to the custody sergeant. Charge him. Assault and resisting arrest, that'll do for now. Then put him back in the cells." He turned to Preston and smiled. "I'm afraid it's going to be a long time before you go anywhere Marcus."

Preston lunged forward, but Stevens put a hand on his arm. "Easy Marcus, it's all bluff. You'll be out soon."

Timms breathed a sigh of relief and rubbed his cheek. "I'll see you tomorrow," he said as he rubbed his aching face again, "...after I've been to the dentist."

Stevens closed his briefcase and got up to leave; there was no use in protesting.

"Stay there!" barked Timms, who was now standing with his back to the door. "I think that you and I need a little chat."

"Now hang on. You can't keep me here," said the lawyer. "I'll report you for harassment."

"I'll only keep you a minute, I'm not sure I can breathe the same air for much longer," said Timms. "Now sit down, you arrogant little shit!"

The lawyer stood his ground, "You can't talk to me like that," he said.

Timms licked at blood that trickled from the corner of his mouth as he spoke, menacingly, "No tapes... no witnesses... my word against yours..." he pulled back his sleeve and clenched his fist, "and who's going to believe you?"

Stevens looked terrified and fumbled for the chair, "Don't... please... don't hit me," he stammered. He scrambled onto the chair, "...you wouldn't... would you?"

Timms would have liked nothing more at that moment, but he said nothing as he sat down opposite the trembling man and calmly folded his arms across his broad chest.

"You won't get away with this," said Stevens defiantly.

Timms maintained his silence and looked the lawyer straight in the eyes. Eventually he started to speak. "Now listen carefully because I'm not going to repeat myself. King's dead, his whole organisation is fucked. We've got more coppers than you can imagine going over every dirty deal and scam that he's ever been involved in. Sooner or later your name's going to come up. And when it does, we'll be sitting here like this, again... only you'll be helping us with our enquiries... no doubt with some other smartarse brief sitting next to you. By the time we finish, I personally guarantee that you'll be going away for a long time. I'm going to make you regret the day that you met Bobby King. On the other hand... Well, just give me a call when you've thought about it."

Stevens sat in silence; his name was on hundreds of contracts and he knew that he was being offered a way out. "I'll need some time," he said submissively.

"You've got the weekend. Now piss off." said Timms, as he got up and opened the door.

Stevens looked a broken man as he shambled out of the room, thinking about the choices; the thought of prison really scared him, but so did Naismith. He didn't know if he dared to take the risk; and wondered if there would be anywhere for him to hide if he did. But, maybe, if he acted quickly, there was another option and that scared him too.

Timms called after him as he walked down the corridor, "Might be a good idea if you throw a sicky tomorrow... get one of your lackeys to represent that piece of shit in the cells."

North Middlesex Hospital – 15:00 BST

Jane opened her eyes and looked around the room. Everything was a bit blurred, but she just about could make out the two faces. She blinked and rubbed her eyes; Sally and Lorna came into focus.

"How's your head," asked Sally.

"Hurts like hell," replied Jane, forcing a smile. "Give me a bad hangover any day."

"We've been worried about you," said Lorna. "You've been out for ages."

"What happened?"

"Looks like someone used the back of your head to practise their golf swing," said Lorna.

"They're going to keep you in a few days... you've got a fractured skull and a bad concussion," said Sally. "Do you feel alright to talk, or do you want us to come back later?"

"I want you to get the bastard who did this," said Jane. "So let's get on with it." She put her hand to her head, "Christ! It hurts."

Lorna moved closer and held Jane's hand, "Can you remember anything?"

"I'd gone to the locker room, the bloke on the desk wanted to come in with me but I told him to go... big mistake." Jane laughed. "I told him I was a big girl and could look after myself. Hah! Anyway, I was opening King's locker, and... Wham! That's it. Next thing I know, I'm being carried out to an ambulance. Got some dishy PC holding my hand... at least his voice sounded gorgeous, I couldn't really make out his face. I'm sorry, I should have..."

Not your fault Jane," said Sally. "Now try and remember... did you see anyone in the room?"

"There were a couple of blokes, but they were just going out to the course as I got there... they had their backs to me. And there was another man... getting changed... funny... I'm sure I'd seen him somewhere... can't place him," Jane shook her head and closed her eyes, "...sorry, boss... can we leave this for a bit... I'm tired."

"That's alright," said Sally. She bent over and kissed Jane on the cheek. "It can wait, you get better."

"You won't leave me," said Jane; she sounded frightened. "What if he comes here?"

"Don't worry, Lorna will stay with you," said Sally. "But they got your purse and watch, looks like it was a chance mugging, probably some druggie."

Jane opened her eyes. "No it couldn't be, you can't get into the locker room without a special key... the bloke said... some kind of computer system... records it all..." Her words tailed off, as she closed her eyes again.

Sally turned to Lorna, "Stay here, I'm going back to Cheshunt, something's not right."

"I'll give you a call when she wakes up," said Lorna. "Is there anything else you want me to do?"

"Yes, get Phil and Brenda over here. Let them know what's happened and go over everything that we've got so far," Sally's mind was racing, and she fired off questions; hoping that one might hit the target. "What are we missing? Who's still out there? Who could have got to Jane? What..."

Cheshunt, Hertfordshire – 15:45 BST

Rob Bryant was still at the golf club when Sally arrived. "Sorry, ma'am, but the SOCOs are still at it. You can't go in yet," he said.

"That's, OK. It can wait. Where's your DI? Sorry, I've forgotten his name."

"It's DI Lennox, and he's in the office looking at the CCTV tapes," replied Bryant. "Do you want me to get him?"

"No, take me to him... I need to speak to both of you."

Bryant led the way into the office. Lennox had his back to them. He was staring intently at a TV screen. "DI Parkinson to see you, sir," said Bryant.

"Come in sit down," said Lennox. "I need a break."

"Anything on the CCTV," asked Sally.

"Not a lot, comings and goings. Kingston's been putting names to faces for us, most of them match the list I got from the chap on the desk, and we've already got statements from a lot of them. Pity about the bloody faulty recorders though, there's a few gaps."

"Yes he told me about that... said they kept stopping for no reason."

"Well they stopped just at the wrong time," said Lennox. "Look." He rewound the tape and started to play it again. "They're activated by motion sensors, so they only come on when they need to... it saves having to change the tape so often. Now look here, this is the gate. Now there's nothing between here... ten-thirty and just after twelve, when you can see Bryant arriving. But we know that at the very least there were eight cars in that time, your DC and seven of the members that we've interviewed. Then it goes off on and again until we took the tape out just before two. You can see the ambulance arriving, but not leaving... you arrived at about twelve-forty, but it doesn't show it, then there's me arriving and you leaving. It's the same for the other one."

"And the other one covers what?" asked Sally.

Bryant answered, "That'll be the front door. The system uses dual tape decks, and the main door and gate are on the same recorder."

"Thanks, Rob," said Sally. "What do you know about the locker room security?"

"It's a keyless entry system. All the members and the staff have a unique key fob. It works the car park barrier as well. I don't know the details but it's linked to their membership system. Mr Kingston would know," said Bryant.

"Go and find him," said Sally

After Bryant had gone, she spoke to Lennox. "I've got a bad feeling about this... it's just too much of a coincidence... those tapes."

"Turner said they'd had a problem for a while... very intermittent... works fine for days sometimes, then it stops. Look I'll put this one in... fourth of May," he fast-forwarded the tape. "See, ten-thirty the tape stops, it starts again at eleven... stops again just after four and starts again at five. Now that was a Sunday and the place would have been buzzing."

The door opened and Miles Kingston came into the office. He looked at Sally "Oh! You again," he said, barely disguising his annoyance. "You wanted to see me?"

"Yes, you can tell me about your key fob system," said Sally; it was more of an order than a request.

"Of course, we're very proud of that. State of the art you know," said Kingston, eagerly trying to impress. "At first we just used it to control access, but then company showed me how I could link it up to our member records. It can tell us exactly what time each member arrives and leaves... both the car park and the locker room. We don't bother much with the car park, but the locker room record is great. We know exactly when each member has played. That meant that I could introduce a corporate membership."

"What's that?" asked Sally.

"Well it means that we can give a business several key fobs, which any of their employees can use." Kingston was boasting now. "The system tells us how many rounds the business has played each month and we send them a bill for green fees... big discount of course."

"So you don't have a unique record for every member," said Sally, "...and that means, you can't be certain who was in the locker room this morning."

"Well we can see if it was a private member, but... What are you getting at?"

"It means that it would be quite easy for anyone to get hold of a fob and use it," said Lennox. "Not as secure as you thought."

"I suppose so," said a rather deflated Kingston. "But that's not the point, we trust our…"

Sally interrupted "That's enough. Can you show me the records?"

"Well, I don't know how it works." Kingston pointed to a computer. "I wouldn't even know how to switch it on. You'd have to ask the membership secretary, but she's on holiday."

"That's alright sir," said Sally. "I'll take it with me, we've got people…"

"You can't do that it's confidential information," protested Kingston. "I won't allow it."

"DC Barclay, who you may recall was viciously attacked in this club, came here with a warrant to search these premises and remove any items that could be used in evidence in connection with our investigations," said Sally seriously; she could sense that she was on to something and was in no mood fore niceties. "DI Lennox… would you like to arrest Mr Kingston for obstructing a police officer in the performance of their duty or shall I?" Sally got up and stood right in front of Kingston; any closer would have been an assault. "Do I make myself clear, sir!" she snapped.

"OK take the bloody thing," said Kingston angrily. "I've had about all I can take today."

As Kingston stormed out Sally smiled at Lennox. "Could you get one of your blokes to put that in my car please?" she said.

St Lucia – 10:45 Eastern Standard Time

The party had gone on until the early hours, and Aunty Lou had told everyone that they were going to break with tradition. Today, breakfast was going to be a strictly family affair.

Julia and Lou were up at six, as usual, and when Barton and Grace awoke the aroma of ham, eggs and coffee was already wafting through the house. They stumbled bleary eyed onto the porch, where they found Lizzie sitting at the table, drinking orange juice.

"Ughhh! Hi Lizzie," yawned Barton. "What time is it?"

"Good morning Bro, good morning Grace," chirped Lizzie. "It's a beautiful day… but it's nearly eleven and you've missed most of it."

Barton sat down and reached for the coffee pot. "Want some?" he grunted, looking at Grace.

"Strong and black, and keep it coming," she yawned. "What a night. Your mum knows how to party. Did you see her? Strutting her stuff with that big guy," she laughed. "Do you think she's got herself a toy boy?"

"The big guy belongs to me, so you tell your momma to keep her hands off, Michael."

They looked up to see Aunty Lou standing in the doorway. Barton and Lizzie burst out laughing, "Not another one Lou!" exclaimed Lizzie.

"Girl's gotta keep young somehow," laughed Lou. "An' you know I like 'em young."

Lou had been married and divorced three times, and seemed to have a different man every time Barton saw her. She had often told him: *'I get bored too easy, but I still love 'em all'*. And Barton had never had any reason to argue with that; ex-husbands and old lovers were always coming round for breakfast.

"Shame on you sister," Julia scolded, "an' you just been to church an' all. The Lord only knows what that new preacher must make of you girl." The assembled company erupted into uncontrollable laughter, reminding Barton, again, that he was at home.

"So what do you think?" Lizzie asked Barton.

"What, the new job or the new man?" he joked.

"Both you idiot, and Simon's not a new man. You met him last year."

Barton was in the mood for joking this morning and teased his sister. "What? Not a new man! You mean you'll have to cook and do the dishes?"

"If you can't be serious I won't invite you to the wedding." Lizzie pretended to sulk, but her face had cracked before she could finish.

"And look after all the baby violins, while he's down the pub," he giggled.

"Stop, stop it," pleaded Lizzie. "That's not funny. Tell him Grace."

But Grace was too busy laughing. Mr and Mrs Violin; she'd christened them last year, when Lizzie brought Simon to stay for a weekend. Simon Coleman, first violin with the London Philharmonic Orchestra, had known Lizzie for several years; and now that Lizzie had a new job, also playing violin with the LPO, she was returning to England, and they were going to get married. Grace didn't think she'd ever be able to think of them Mr and Mrs Coleman. No, they were going to be stuck with Mr and Mrs Violin for a long time.

Barton had just started eating his ham and eggs, when his mobile rang. He could hear it, but he didn't have a clue where it was, and by the time he found it the ringing had stopped. Then it beeped and he opened the text message – *big trouble – call sally asap – v urg – lorna.* – He walked back onto the porch, swearing, "Bugger! Bugger!"

"What's up?" asked Grace.

"Don't know. Got to call Sally," he showed Grace the text; then he dialled Sally's number.

Grace caught Barton's end of the conversation. "What…! No…! Is she OK…? Have you told the Chief Super?" Barton stood up and started pacing up and down the porch. "Call him now… better get him to call me… of course you did the right thing… Who…? Oh! Yes of course… What…? No?" Grace could see what was coming. "I'm coming back… no arguments … I don't know… tomorrow some time, I'll check the flights and let you know… thanks Sal, see you, bye." He put the phone down on the table, "Bugger!" he swore, and smashed his fist against the wall.

Everyone round the table had stopped eating; they were all sitting in silence, looking at Barton; nobody knew what to say. Finally, Grace said something, "So we're going home," she said bitterly; the new husband that she'd had only for a few days was gone: *Fuck the bloody job. Why can't you let go?*

Barton calmed down and sat at the table again. He took Grace's hands and clasped them tightly. "No, you have to stay here," he said, looking into her eyes. "It's too risky… I don't want anything happening to you?"

"Shouldn't you let me decide?" asked Grace "We agreed…"

"I know, but things have changed." Barton told her everything that Sally had said. When he'd finished he put his arms round her and held her close. "Please understand, I have to go back… Jane could have been killed today… I don't know what they might try next… you're already too involved and I'm not going to risk you anywhere near it. You're too precious. But, I opened this box and now I've got to close it."

Barton spent the next hour arranging flights and calling Sally to confirm when he'd be home. He also took a call from his Trevor Miller, who agreed he should come back, although they both knew that it wouldn't have made any difference if he'd said no.

When he'd finished, Barton went down to the beach to find Grace. She was sitting on the shoreline with the waves lapping over her legs. Sensing that he was there, she turned and smiled. "Sorry," she said. "I know you need to go."

Barton saw the tear tracks on her cheeks and bent down to kiss her. "No, I'm the one who ought to be sorry for putting you through this." He kissed her again. "Now let's try and enjoy the rest of the day."

She smiled and then laughed. "Who are you kidding? You're going to be worrying about this until you get home… and you haven't talked to Julia yet."

In all the drama, Barton had forgotten that he still had questions for his mother. "OK, but that can wait a while. Let's go for a walk." He took her hand and helped her to her feet, and they walked hand in hand along the shore. "Just one thing, before I forget," he said.

"Wow! That was a whole thirty seconds, what happened to the rest of the day?" she said, shrugging her shoulders. "Come on then, out with it and then not another word for at least an hour."

"I still need your help," he said. "Sally met the old lady, yesterday. You know Naismith's aunt. Except she's not... She's his mother. Anyway I need you to listen to Sally's tape and read through something that the old lady gave her... compare it with that story Naismith told me. Will you do that for me? Please?"

"Well I suppose it will give me something to do while I'm on my own," she said, trying not to sound too eager. "But you're going to owe me, big time, Barton. Oh boy...! Will you owe me."

"Great. Sally's sending copies by courier. You should get them tomorrow."

"You, bastard... you scheming, cheating bastard." Grace put her arms round his neck and kissed him. "God knows why. But, I love you, Mike Barton."

"And I love you... I just wish I could show you how much," he said wistfully as the resumed their walk. "I've got an idea," he said, excitedly. "Why don't I go and ask George if we can borrow the boat for a few hours."

"Yeah... why not?" mused Grace. She knew that George was sure to agree; he always did. "I'll go back to the house and get a picnic. I'll meet you at the jetty in half an hour."

True to his word, Barton hadn't said anything about the case all afternoon. As they lay side by side on the foredeck watching the sunset, he even started to have second thoughts about flying back in the morning.

Grace rolled over and stroked Barton's forehead. "Thanks Mike. It's been a wonderful afternoon and it's really good just to see you so relaxed," she said. "You know, I've been thinking... I might write a book, when this is all over. You and your Puppet Master will certainly give me enough material."

"It's not over yet though," he said, "and you might not like the ending. Your hero might not win."

"I wasn't thinking about that sort of book. I mean a serious academic study. Anyway it was only a thought."

"It's late," he said. "We should get back."

Grace frowned; she didn't want the day to end.

"OK maybe another five minutes." Barton rolled over and clamped her to the deck with his arm, "...well maybe ten," he said with a glint in his eye.

It was dark when they started back. Grace raised the anchor as Barton fiddled about under the hatch. After several attempts, the ancient diesel engine rattled and spluttered into life. Barton steered a course back to the jetty, navigating by the lights on the shore. As he sat at the wheel, Grace stood behind and put her arms around him. She cuddled up close and whispered softly, "Please give me a happy ending Mike,"

When they got back to the house, they found Julia, Lizzie, and Aunty Lou sitting on the porch. Each held a tall glass and there was a large pitcher on the table. "Mmm… is that what I think it is?" asked Grace, moving towards the pitcher. She frowned when she saw it was empty.

"Don't you worry girl, there's a whole new bowl waitin' for you in the kitchen. You just sit you down and take it easy while I fill this up," said Lou as she picked up the jug and disappeared into the house.

"Mmm… delicious," said Grace as she took a long swig of Aunty Lou's secret recipe punch. "I thought we might have had this last night."

"Too good to waste on all 'em good for nothin's," said Lou. "This is for us special people."

"Well then, here's a toast to us special people," said Grace, raising her glass. Then she winked at Lou. "And here's to Mike. It's not fair to leave him out."

The pitcher was nearly empty when Grace turned to Lizzie and whispered, "Mike needs to talk with Julia. Let's go inside and have a girl talk." Lizzie nodded and whispered to her aunt, and a few moments later Barton and Julia were alone on the porch. Lizzie reappeared briefly with another pitcher and disappeared again, without a word.

They talked for over an hour; or rather, Julia talked, prompted by a few questions. Barton mainly listened intently; trying to memorise her every word. This was stuff she'd never told him before; things that wouldn't have made much sense, until now. When she'd finished, Julia breathed a sigh of relief. She'd kept these things bottled up inside for twenty years, and she was glad to tell her son at last. Even now, she didn't really understand it all; she just knew that something wasn't right. And now she'd told her big grown up boy; and looking at his face she could see that he understood; and she prayed that he'd never need to tell her what it meant.

"Just one more thing," said Barton. He could see that his mother was tired, but he needed to know. "Yesterday… you said something about Nina Campbell… saying she was sorry."

Relief gave way to guilt, as Julia answered. "She was just a girl… sixteen maybe seventeen. She came to the house a few weeks after the funeral. First thing I thought was… well I won't say… but after what her man had done, I had every right. But that poor girl… she was soaked to the skin… been waitin' outside all day, waitin' in the rain for me to come home. Had her baby with her…little child can't have been more than a few months."

Julia paused and lifted her glass to her lips. She took a long draught of the punch, before continuing, "...said she knew how she must be the last person that I wanted to see... Good Lord! She got that right... Said she wanted to explain. She wanted me to know how sorry she was. She said that he'd done it for them... her an' the little baby... he had to..." Julia's voice trembled and faded to a whisper.

"Mum, are you alright," asked Barton. He could see how difficult this was for her, but he needed her to finish.

"Just tired boy," Julia sighed. "Oh! So tired... She said it was her fault... they'd made him do it cos of her. Didn't make any sense... she never said who they was. Then she asked me... asked me if I could find it in my heart to forgive him."

Julia's voice suddenly became louder; as anger mixed with anguish. "Well I tell her... I got angry with the girl... an' you know me son... I believe the word of the Lord. But I swear, I can never... not even if I burn in hellfire... I can never forgive that man for what he done to us. An' I tell her so... tell her to go."

Tears were rolling down Julia's cheeks as she struggled with the words. "Lord forgive me... I sent that girl an' her baby out into that night... never saw them again... Oh Lord! What did I do...? You know Michael... she was just a child herself... an' real scared... an' real brave too... just stood there while I was screamin' an' shoutin'... an' she never said one word back."

Barton put his arm round Julia's shoulder and caressed her hair. "Bitch," he spat. "What the hell was she playing at?"

Julia pulled away from her son. "You take that back boy!" she snapped. "Shame on you... You don't use bad language in this house. An' she don't deserve it neither."

Barton was taken aback and stammered "But..."

"But nothin' boy, I ain't done yet. An' you betta listen good... 'cos you gotta understan'... 'Cos I swear to God, I never did." There was strength in Julia's voice now and Barton knew he'd better listen. Julia took another sip from the glass, and when she spoke again she was calm and her words were clear and precise.

"You know what she said? Before she went out the door? With not a word of complaint nor pleadin', she just said... 'We both lost our men that day. They took 'em away from us an' we'll never get 'em back'." Julia stopped speaking and reached into the pocket of her dress. She took out a small package wrapped in a black ribbon and placed it on the table. "I want you to keep these. The last one came today an' that ain't right. You read 'em now, while I go see the ladies."

For a while, Barton just stared at the package, afraid to look inside. Then he undid the ribbon and carefully unfolded the paper. Inside were a number of black edged postcards and a folded envelope. He looked at the back of the first card. It was addressed to his mother in a delicate italic script, each letter perfectly formed; as if the obvious care that had taken been by the writer was meant as part of the message. It was postmarked: *'Oxford May 20th 1984'*. He turned it over and looked at the message, written by the same hand.

James Barton born 30~11~1942 died 25~05~1983

To my sister Julia who has to live without her beloved James
From Nina who has to live without her beloved Patrick

We both lost our men that day
They took them away from us and we'll never get them back

Patrick Campbell born 19~02~1963 taken away 25~05~1983
Every day I pray that you might forgive him

Barton set it on one side and looked at the other eighteen almost identical cards, one for each year, each posted a few days before the anniversary of his father's murder. Finally, he then unfolded the envelope. It had been posted by air courier and inside was another card. He took it out and looked at it. At first glance, it seemed identical to the others; until he looked more closely.

James Barton born 30~11~1942 died 25~05~1983

To my sister Julia who has to live without her beloved James
From Nina who has to live without her beloved Patrick

We both lost our men that day - Today I lost my man again
They took them away from us and we'll never get them back

Patrick Campbell born 19~02~1963 died 13~05~2003
I beg you to forgive him now

Barton read the card again, shaking his head in disbelief. He thought back to his meetings with the journalist. "No! No!" he shouted and buried his head in his hands. He felt a hand on his shoulder and looked up to see Julia standing behind him.

"What did she mean Michael? What did she mean?" she pleaded.

"I don't know mum... I don't know." Barton shook his head: *But I'm going to find out.*

Chapter 28

Saturday 17th May

Cheshunt, Hertfordshire – 10:00 BST

Sally had called at the hospital on her way to the golf club. She was a man down now; Jane was recovering well, but she'd been told to spend at least a week taking it easy. Sally had spoken to Lorna and the others the previous evening and it was clear that the task was getting more daunting by the hour. Debbie King was proving to be a rich source; she'd taken a liking to Brenda, who was gradually teasing more pieces of information from her. The problem was that everything needed to be followed up, and that required manpower. They were working round the clock and nobody had had more than a few hours' sleep for days. Something had to give. She'd told the Chief Super and Barton that they needed to pool resources with Timms, but neither had agreed. There was still too much of a risk with Jarvis still on the loose and Stevens roaming amongst all the big players. She'd decided have a go at Barton again when he was back.

The SOCOs had finished late in the evening and Sally read through the initial report that Lennox had faxed to her first thing in the morning. There wasn't much to go on. The only prints so far matched to the database belonged to King and Underwood and the last time they been there was two weeks ago. Which didn't say much for the cleaners; and then the thought had struck her.

Lennox was waiting for her in the car park. "Bit of a development last night, I called your office but you were already on the way," he said. "We nicked a young couple last night in a pub. She was trying to use a stolen credit card and he was hawking round an expensive watch."

"Jane's?" said Sally.

"You got it. They said that someone threw them out of a car, about ten minutes before we got the call from here." Lennox took some keys out of his pocket. "Their story checks out because we found these at the side of the road."

"I don't suppose you've traced the car,'" said Sally: *Come on I need a break*

"Well sort of, they said it was a big black Merc, and gave us a partial index. We've narrowed it down to four possibles. They're all registered to the same leasing company."

Have you contacted them yet?"

"Won't be necessary, I just got off the phone with one of your people. The leasing company is owned by the late Mr King, and apparently all their records are in your office. Someone's checking now."

"Let's hope it turns up something," said Sally. She glanced round the car park, "Trouble is everyone leases cars these days. I bet King's firm supplied quite a few of these. Now can we have a look at those lockers?"

A young man was waiting for them in the locker room. Lennox handed him the keys. "This is Sam, one of our SOCOs," he said.

"I don't suppose we'll find anything," said Sally. "But you might get some prints inside. What about the outside, Sam?"

"They're all a match to King. You can see that the areas round the locks have been wiped, but there's a good chance that whoever it was forgot to wipe the inside. Most people will open the door like this," Sam put the key in the lock and turned it. "See, you tend to pull the door open with the key, like this, and then push the door back, like this." He put his fingers behind the door and pushed it back flat against the adjacent locker. It's automatic, you probably don't realise you're doing it. When you close the door you push it from the outside, like this." He closed the door. "You know you've just touched the door so you wipe it, forgetting about the inside. By the way it's empty, apart from some shoes."

Sally looked inside, "Try the other one," she said.

Sam opened the top locker and looked inside. "Not much in here, only what you'd expect." He moved to one side so that Sally could get a closer look. There were a couple of photographs stuck to the back of the door, and inside she could see another pair of shoes, a few items clothing and some toiletries.

"Nothing here," said Lennox. "Bag it all, Sam, and dust both lockers for prints. We'll see you in the office."

"What did you do with the CCTV tapes?" asked Sally, as they sat in the office.

"We've got them back at the station, cross checking them against the witness statements."

"Just yesterday's?"

"Yeah, didn't seem any point in taking the others."

"Good. So the old one you showed me is still here?"

"It should be, why?"

"Just a hunch, let's have a look at it… and the other one from the same recorder."

Lennox opened a cupboard. "Can you remember what the date was?"

"Fourth of May," replied Sally; it was a date that she wouldn't forget in a hurry. "Run them though and make a note of the exact times of the breaks."

While Lennox found the tapes and put the first one into the video player, Sally picked up the phone. "Hi Paul, it's Sally. Can you do me a favour?"

Lennox had checked the first tape, and was part way through the second. "That's odd," he said. "The times don't match."

"What's that?"

"Give me a couple of minutes, to make sure," said Lennox, "and I'll show you."

Sally looked at the notepad. "Are you sure you copied the times down right?"

"Have a look yourself," said Lennox. But Sally didn't need to; it was what she had expected.

"Where's Turner today?" asked Sally.

"Haven't seen him," replied Lennox.

"Go and find Kingston then, see if he knows."

The fax had arrived by the time Lennox returned, and Sally was comparing the times that Lennox had taken from the tapes with the extracts from the NCS surveillance log for the same day. "Gotcha!" she exclaimed.

"Got who?" asked Lennox.

"Joe Turner. Did you find out where he is?"

"He's not here. Kingston said that he switched shifts before he left yesterday."

"Get a car round to his place and pick him up. Then come and see this."

Sally showed Lennox the copies of the surveillance logs on King and Underwood. "See, according to this they were both playing golf here on the fourth. King arrived at ten thirty-seven and Underwood at ten forty-nine. They both left at quarter to five. That's the gate times of course."

"So, neither their arrival nor departure was recorded... and," Lennox could already see what was going on, "...the slight discrepancy between times on the gate and door tapes suggest that the recorder didn't go wrong, but it was stopped by someone."

"I think we can safely assume that, if we have it checked out, they won't find anything wrong with it. Look at this." She showed him the last page of the fax; it was a hand written note from Timms.

Herts and Essex Alarms – record of faults reported by Cheshunt Golf Club
  Alarm system – 27 / 02/ 03 – faulty PIR
  Entry system – none
  CCTV – none
  Last routine maintenance visit 08 / 05/ 03

"Now wouldn't you expect a faulty recorder to have been reported, particularly as the system is less than a year old? And even if there was a fault on the fourth it would have been fixed on the eighth, when they came to do the maintenance." said Sally. "Somehow I don't think Mr Turner will be at home. How far back do these tapes go?"

"Two weeks and then they record over them. That one was due to go back on tomorrow."

"Never mind, the ones that we've got should do for evidence of tampering. Get the lab to check them thoroughly, and the machine. What about the other cameras, anything from them?"

"No they only switch them on when the place is closed."

"All finished, sir," said Sam, as he came into the office. "I've got some nice prints. Definitely more than one set inside each door. I'll let you have a report within the hour."

"I think that's me finished, too," Sally said to Lennox. "Can you run some checks on Turner... and talk to Kingston again, see how much he knows about him."

London Colney, Hertfordshire– 13:00 BST

"Well that was useful," said Sally. Connor had called earlier to say that Debbie King and Herrera wanted to talk to her, and she was sitting with Connor and Brenda Cooper in the kitchen at the safe house. "So let's go over that again," she said, "just to make sure we all got it. Brenda you start."

Brenda looked at her notepad, and started to underline some of the notes. "Herrera was dealing on the side, and King found out, that's why Terry pulled him that morning. He'd been selling to Jonathan Edwards. Debbie introduced them at a party. Edwards was an old boyfriend."

"The guy she got busted with a few years ago," interjected Connor, remembering where he'd seen Edwards' name before.

"They didn't mention that," said Brenda.

"It's on her record," said Connor. "I've got a good memory."

Brenda continued, "Debbie was introduced to Edwards by his boss, Phillip Jones or Johnson. I'm sure we can find out. Anyway, he's an investment banker, or something, and Debbie first met him about ten years ago. She thinks it was at her uncle's house in Spain. He was a friend of Peter Browning... Naismith's brother-in-law."

Connor looked at his notes, "Yeah, that's what I've got too. Except you missed something... Herrera said Edwards knows Nichols as well."

Brenda looked at her notepad again, "Sorry, I've got that down, just didn't underline it."

Sally looked out of the window at the couple walking hand-in-hand in the garden. She was finding it hard to believe that in the space of an hour they'd got so much out of them. "So that's another connection, rather tenuous I admit, between King's organisation and Naismith. But, I think we should pay a visit to the bank on Monday. This could be a lead to the money. Well done, both of you."

Brixton Prison, London – 13:30 BST

The prison officer stood in the cell doorway, "Your brief's here Underwood," he said. "Get a move on."

George Underwood folded his paper, got off the bed and put on his shoes, and muttered, "About bloody time," as he followed the officer. He had a bail hearing on Monday and had been waiting for Stevens all morning.

The lawyer was waiting in an interview room "You're late," said Underwood as he sat at the table.

"Sorry George, I had to see Warren this morning," said Stevens.

"Have they got him then?" asked Underwood.

"They haven't found him yet," said Stevens. "I've still got him somewhere safe."

"Well in that case you can concentrate on getting me out of this rat hole," snapped Underwood. "What's the plan for Monday?"

"Look George, we're just going through the motions… don't bank on getting out. I think you'd better make the best of it," sighed Stevens.

"What about my heart?"

"Doesn't make any difference, the doctor's report says that there's no increased risk."

"Bloody doctors! What do they know? I'm ill."

"Don't push it George, all they'll do is put you in the prison hospital, and I don't suppose that's any better than your cell."

"Don't know why you bothered coming if that's all you've got. Bloody hell, Mike! What do we pay you for?" Underwood got up and started pacing round the small room. It was a long time since he'd been inside and he knew that if he went down this time, he'd be an old man when he got out: *Some bloody retirement.* "Where've they got Dave? He's not in here."

"Chelmsford, they've got him on breaking and entering at the moment. They're charging him with everything else on Monday. They'll move him then. But not here, they'll keep you apart until the trial."

345

"What about Warren? Still out there? God! He's a slippery bastard."

"He's OK, that's really why I'm here. He told me about Bobby's diaries. That's how Dave got caught... he was looking for them at Bobby's house. But it doesn't matter, because I've got them now."

Underwood looked relieved: *Bobby's insurance policy, there's enough to put us all away for ever, and Lenny too.* He smiled at Stevens; maybe there was a deal to be done. "So what are you going to do with them?"

"I haven't read them yet, but from what Warren's told me they could be useful. Just don't say anything until I tell you."

"Make sure they're kept safe Mike... could be my way out of this. And don't worry about Dave... just remember who's been paying your wages for the last thirty years. This is just about me and Warren now. Dave's not one of us, not the old school," said Underwood. "Are we finished now? I want to watch the racing on TV."

The prison officer took Underwood back to the remand wing and Stevens was escorted back to the reception area. He smiled to himself as he walked out of the gate. He already knew what he was going to do with the diaries, and Jarvis and Underwood didn't have any part in it. Now he just had to deal with Jarvis. He stopped the car next to the first phone box he saw.

West Mersea, Essex – 16:00 BST

"Come on my beauty... come on... Oh! Yes!" Warren Jarvis was watching the racing from Newbury. The favourite, Hawk Wing, had just left the rest of the field standing in the three o'clock and he was now five-hundred pounds up. He looked at the race card on the teletext; he fancied an eight to one shot in the four-forty, it would be a nice little touch if it came in. And, Stevens had found the diaries; it was turning out to be a good day. In spite of what he'd told Naismith, he'd decided that Mersea Island wasn't such a bad place to hide out after all. The caravan was comfortable enough and there was a decent pub nearby. He thought he'd go out later; pick up his winnings, get some fish and chips and eat them out of the paper on the seafront; just like in the old days when he used to come here for weekends, with Janice and Barry. It was out of the way, safe enough, and he was happy to sit it out there for a while. He called the bookie again, "...that's right, put the lot on Night Kiss. I'll come in and pick up the winnings after the race."

Unfortunately for Jarvis, his luck had changed. Night Kiss came in third. Not that it mattered, because he wouldn't have been able to collect his winnings. He didn't even get to see the race; and it was going to be a long time before he ate fish and chips on the seafront again.

If he'd been looking out of the window, he might have seen them, as they bobbed and weaved between the rows of caravans. He might even have been able to make a run for it; although he wouldn't have got very far. But it was too late. Thirty seconds after he'd put the phone down; the caravan shook as a size ten boot kicked the door in and, before he realised what was happening, he was looking down the wrong end of a standard police issue Heckler and Koch MP5.

Chapter 29

Sunday 18th May

Amersham, Buckinghamshire – 08:30 BST

Barton opened his eyes as the car stopped. "Are we here already?" he yawned, as Trevor Miller switched off the engine. Barton got out and took his bag from the back seat.

Irene Miller opened the front door. "I've made you some tea," she said. "Are you hungry, would you like some breakfast? She looked at her guest, "Oh dear Mike, you look terrible."

He felt terrible. "I think I need a shower and a shave first," said Barton, rubbing his hand over his chin; he hadn't shaved since Friday. He caught sight of himself in the hall mirror and looked away. "God I look like a tramp."

"Leave your jacket and trousers outside the bathroom and I'll press them for you," said Irene. "Have you got a clean shirt or do you want to borrow one of Trevor's."

"Sorry to mess up your Sunday, Irene," he said as he sat down at the kitchen table. He didn't really feel very hungry. But it was too late to tell Irene, who was already putting a large plate in front of him: two eggs, bacon, sausage, tomatoes, mushrooms, and hash browns. "You really didn't need to go to all this trouble. A couple of slices of toast would have been fine."

"Speak for yourself Mike," said Trevor Miller. "I'm only allowed the full Monty when we've got visitors, so shut up and tuck in. Sally's on her way over."

Miller had been very firm about it; he'd pick him up at the airport and he was to stay at his house, while they sorted things out. Nobody else apart from Sally was to know that he was back.

"We've got a lot to talk about," said Barton. "I've been talking to my mother about…"

"Wait until Sally's here," said Miller. "This is still about Operation De Niro, so we'll listen to what she has to say first." He gave Barton the best *'I'm in charge'* look that he could and said sternly, "You're still officially off limits, and your personal crusade will have to wait until we square things with Harris."

Barton sighed; there was nothing else to do but wait. He could see that Miller wasn't prepared to rush things. In a way, he was grateful. He knew that he was too involved and right now. Although he resented it, he needed the calming influence of the more experienced man.

Harris could see Barton's frustration, and knew he was going to have a job keeping his protégé in check. "We've got to play this by the book now Mike. I want you to keep a low profile. We're nearly there… let's not blow it now."

Barton nodded, "I know… you're right." Under different circumstances, he could see himself saying the same thing to one of his team.

"If it's any consolation, I spoke to Harris yesterday. He's very interested in your theory about Naismith… he's been talking with the Spanish authorities. They're investigating property development on the Costa del Sol… the whole system… politicians, local councils, banks, developers… it's rotten to the core. It's a money launderer's paradise over there."

When Sally arrived at eleven, the two men were waiting for her in Miller's study. She shook hands with Miller. "Sorry I'm late, sir. I called in to see Jane Barclay on the way." She put her hand on Barton's upper arm and gave it a gentle squeeze. "Hi Mike, are you OK?" She wanted to kiss him, but felt a little uneasy in Miller's presence.

"Much better for seeing you, Sal," he said as he gave her a hug. The thought that Miller was sitting only four feet away didn't enter his mind. "How's Jane?"

As Sally updated them on Jane's condition, Irene Miller brought in a tray of coffee and biscuits. "Thanks for taking her the flowers, Mrs Miller. She really appreciated it."

"Oh! It's the least I could do," said Irene. "I'm just glad that she's getting better." Irene shared the genuine concern that her husband had for the welfare of his officers, and she liked to think that simple gestures like yesterday's visit to the hospital went a little way to easing his burden.

Satisfied that Jane was well on the way to recovery, she left them to get on with business "We'll have a late lunch… about three… is that OK?"

"Sally, I think you'd better start by filling Mike in on what's happened since you last spoke to him," said Miller.

She told them about the developments at the golf club, the leads from Herrera and Debbie King, and Jarvis's arrest. "I was sort of hoping that it was him who whacked Jane," she said, "but he has a cast iron alibi…anyway his prints weren't a match and he's been driving a Range Rover."

"So who else would it be?" asked Miller. "I thought that Jarvis was the last one."

"We're still working on that, sir," replied Sally. "It's got to be someone close to King's organisation though. Everyone who had access to the locker room has been accounted for, except one, and that's a corporate member on King's account. We're still trying to trace the car, there are four possibilities but the leasing records show them all as unallocated. That means, they're probably part of King's pool and we're checking against the surveillance logs to see who's been using them, but it's taking ages. That brings me to the next problem... manpower."

"Look I know what you're going to say, Sally," said Miller, "but I'm still not sure."

"But, sir, we know where the leak came from and we've got everyone banged up...surely we can tell Paul what's going on now. It would really help... my team is knackered. None of them will admit to it, but they're about done. If I could just get a few more bodies to spread the load..."

"I agree with Sally," interjected Barton. "I know there's a bit of a risk with someone still on the loose, but I think if we don't pool what we all know, then the risk of us missing something is greater. I'd rather take the chance and get this thing sewn up."

"Let me think about it," said Miller, "Let's go over everything else. Then I'll decide."

By the time that Irene called them to lunch, they'd covered everything they could think of and worked out a plan of campaign; Trevor Miller was now sure that Barton and Sally couldn't do it without more help, and agreed to talk to Timms the next morning. "But leave it to me. I need to talk to Harris first," he said. "He's still under a lot of pressure to close this by the month end. And you're not in the clear yet, Mike. Getting you back on the case isn't going to be that straightforward... he's got to go all the way to the top."

Before they went through to the dining room, Miller told them not to talk shop over lunch. "It's the one meal of the week that I've always kept for Irene, and I don't want you two spoiling it... agreed?" So they talked about the weather, how nice the garden was looking, and how Barton and Grace were adjusting to their future role as parents. And although, the hour passed by pleasantly, Barton and Sally were both glad when it was over.

After lunch, they resumed their huddle in the study. This time it was Barton's turn to lead. The conversations with Fisher and his mother, what Sally had told him about her conversation with Mary Naismith, his own feelings after meeting the man; everything pointed to a man who wouldn't think twice about murdering an innocent man if it suited his purpose. He repeated what he'd learned about his father and Naismith.

Naismith had been very cold towards James Barton when he first met him and had questioned his suitability to be in charge of police security measures for his election campaign. Although he'd never actually said anything to him directly; he'd made no attempt to hide his racism, and a number of remarks made in James Barton's hearing were particularly offensive. As the campaign had progressed, James started to feel a bit more comfortable. Naismith seemed more at ease around him, even friendly at times. But James was always careful to keep a distance and guard his words; until one day about a week before he died.

"Mum said that Dad came home in a terrible state one night. After an election meeting, Naismith was at the Conservative club with some of his election staff, and couple of friends up from London. They were all very relaxed… having a good time… drinking and joking. Naismith asked Dad to join them. It was late and Dad didn't see the harm in just one drink. Naismith and his friends were talking about the old days… anecdotes about how hard life had been… moaning about how young people today didn't appreciate anything… that sort of stuff. The two men from London kept referring to Naismith as Lenny… Dad didn't think anything of it… he thought it was just a nickname… he'd heard one of the young helpers call him Uncle Lenny a couple of days before. Dad wasn't saying anything… keeping his distance… but at some point Naismith asked him what he thought about something. When he replied, Naismith told him he could drop the 'sir' as he was off duty. By this time, Dad admitted that the one drink had become quite a few… and the next time Naismith spoke to him… when Dad replied he called him Lenny… like the others were doing. Well, that was it. According to Mum, Naismith went mad. She said that the filth that came from his mouth was so bad that even when Dad toned it down, she had trouble believing it. Dad was really shaken up, but next day Naismith behaved as if it hadn't happened and never mentioned it again. Dad put it down to the drink. A week later he was dead."

Barton stopped speaking while he remembered another event; something much more recent; it meant more to him now than it had then. "You know I told you about my first meeting with Naismith? I called him Lenny… Remember Bobby King, telling me to talk to Lenny? Well I got the same reaction… and that's when my troubles started."

Barton was shaking, partly because of his anger at Naismith, partly out of anger with himself: *If I was Trevor, I'd think twice about putting me back on the case. Damn!* His boss was right it was a personal crusade. "I'm sorry Trevor, but I can't let this go… he killed my dad… I'm sure of it."

"Calm down, Mike. Go for a walk, get some air, and clear your head," said Miller. "I need some time to think, and so do you. Stop thinking of yourself and think about what it really means to go on with this." Whatever they had agreed before lunch, Miller wasn't going to let him be part of it; not unless he came to his senses.

"I'll come with you, Mike," said Sally.

They walked down the lane and climbed over the stile to the footpath across the fields. At first, neither one of them said anything; they'd walked about half a mile before Sally took the plunge. "If you prove it, what then?" she asked.

"I don't know. I haven't thought about that."

"Well, it's about time that you did. And while you're at it you should think about who you're doing this for."

"I'm doing it for Dad. I'm doing it for Mum, she deserves to know."

"Your dad's been dead for twenty years Mike, you can't bring him back," said Sally, squeezing his hand tightly. "And your mum, what does she deserve? Will she really want to know the truth? That the man she thinks died a hero was murdered in cold blood, for no reason. Does she want to have to relive it all over again? Does she deserve all that pain? Do you think she wants to wake up in the morning and find her house surrounded by reporters?"

"I hadn't thought about it like that," said Barton.

"No you wouldn't! That's because all you've been thinking about is yourself. You want to hunt down the man who killed you father... see that justice is done... whatever that means... and then ride off into the sunset like in the movies. But this isn't the movies Mike, it's real life... your life and with any luck, the final credits won't be rolling down for another forty years. Have you thought about what you do between now and then... how you'll cope with the guilt, if you break your mother's heart?" she challenged him angrily. "Of course not! Because you're a bloody man and you don't bloody think."

But Barton was thinking now, and by the time they got back, he knew what he had to do. He also knew what he was going tell Miller, which wasn't quite the same thing. He wasn't going to lie to his boss; he just wasn't going to tell him everything.

"So are you OK now?" asked Sally as they walked back along the lane. "That's what you're going to do."

"What am I going to do, Mike?" Miller asked. "Am I going put you back on this? Or do I drive you back to Heathrow and put you on the next plane to the Caribbean? The choice is yours."

"Not much of a choice," said Barton, "but I'll tell you what I want to do and you can tell me if you can go along with it. If you can't, then I'll give you my resignation in the morning."

Miller was taken by surprise. "Don't do this to me, Mike, don't..."

"No... hear me out Trevor. You know that's the last thing I want, but we both know that I'll be a liability if I've got this... OK let's call it an obsession... gnawing away at me." Barton turned and smiled at Sally. "A man's gotta do what a man's gotta do. Huh!"

Sally laughed; Miller looked bemused. "I don't see anything to laugh at," he said. "For God's sake, Mike!"

"Sorry Trevor, private joke. Look, I have to know the truth about my dad; I'm going to find out somehow. If you put me back on the case, I reckon I'll know by the end of the week... I might not have enough evidence to prove a case in court... but I'll know. When I do... when I know for sure... then that's it. I don't want the case reopened, I don't want him charged... I don't want the world to know. I thought I did... but not now. I'll walk away from it. If we can make everything else stick... and we will... he's going to spend the rest of his life in jail anyway." Barton sighed, "And I'll be able to get on with mine."

Miller sat and thought for a moment. This wasn't quite what he'd expected, but Barton seemed to have thought it out. "What makes you so sure that you'll know by the end of the week?" he asked.

"Because of these." replied Barton. He took the packet tied in black ribbon from his jacket pocket. While Miller looked at the cards, Barton took an envelope from his pocket. He opened it carefully and took out a single sheet of notepaper and a small card. His mother had given it to him before he left for the airport. He handed the card to Miller, "I have to go to a funeral sometime this week," he said.

Miller looked at the card and passed it to Sally. Julia's hand wasn't as delicate as Nina Campbell's, but the script showed the same degree of care; she'd written three cards before she'd been satisfied.

Patrick Campbell born 19~02~1963 died 14~05~2003
Beloved husband of my sister Nina
I pray that our Lord will forgive you
Julia Barton

Then Barton unfolded the letter and showed it to them.

Soufriere
St. Lucia
17th May 2003

My dear Nina

I pray that the Lord will give you strength and comfort you in your suffering.

I'm sorry that, all those years ago, I never gave you a chance to explain. I have often prayed for you to forgive me for the way that I treated you that day. But now in your time of grief, I hope that you can understand.

If I hadn't sent you away, I might have been able to understand what you said to me. The man who will give you this letter is my son, Michael. He is a good man with a kind heart. Like your own child, he has lived without his father these twenty years. Tell him all you can, all that you wanted to tell me. Please help him to understand, so that he may find it in his heart to forgive.

And I pray that the Lord will give me the strength to forgive at last.

Your loving sister
Julia Barton

"She's the only lead that I've got left," said Barton, folding the letter and carefully putting it back into the envelope. "You were right Sally… Mum doesn't need to know why Dad was killed. She just wants to close the book."

"And are you sure that's all you want, Mike?" asked Miller. "Look at me, look me in the eye and say it."

"Yes, Trevor, that's all. There's one big difference between me and Naismith," said Barton putting his hand over his heart. "This… he doesn't have one… he doesn't have any feelings. So the only way to hurt him is to take away his money, without it he's got no power. And without power, he's no more than a pathetic, lonely, twisted old man. And every night when the cell door closes, he'll know that I put him there. That's going to be my revenge."

Chapter 30

Monday 19th May

North Middlesex Hospital – 09:00 BST

Barton had spent the night on Sally's sofa, and he borrowed her car after dropping her at the office. Miller had told him not to come into the office until he was called. Things had to be sorted out with Harris first. He also wanted to talk to Timms personally and tell him that Barton was back leading the case. Barton decided to take the opportunity to visit Jane.

As he walked to the main entrance, he passed a man in uniform, putting a ticket on the windscreen of a black Mercedes that was parked in the ambulance parking area. "See that? Some people think they can park anywhere," said the man loudly, addressing his remarks to anyone who might have been in earshot. "Can't you people read the signs?"

"It might help if they could see it," said Barton, pointing to the large skip in the next bay, carefully positioned by the builders to hide the no-parking sign.

He stopped at the florist's kiosk and bought the biggest bouquet he could see. "You men are in generous mood this morning," said the girl as she took his money. "That's the second one like that I've sold this morning and I've only been open ten minutes."

Barton made his way up to the ward and went to the nurses' station. "Can you tell me where I can find Jane Barclay?" he asked, putting the flowers on the desk, "and could you put these in a vase please?"

"She's down on the left in room two, you can't miss it there's a policewoman outside the door," said the nurse. "She's a popular girl today... someone else just brought her some of these."

"Oh! Has she got another visitor? I was hoping to see her on her own."

"That's all right, sir. The gentleman didn't stay... just asked how she was and left the flowers.

Barton was glad to see that Jane was sitting up in bed. She smiled when she saw him and, apart from the large head bandage, she didn't look too bad, "Hello Jane, how are you?"

"Cor! This is a nice surprise. I didn't expect to see you, sir. I thought you were away,"

"Thought I'd better come back… I mean look at you, I can't turn my back for five minutes."

"They say I can go home tomorrow, sir," she said. "It's so boring in here. I can't wait to get back. I know they said I had to rest for at least a week, but I feel fine. If I could come back to the office, I'm sure that…"

"OK, I'll talk to DI Parkinson, but only for a few hours at a time, and we'll chain you to the desk. Look what happens when we let you out."

As Barton left, a thought struck him, and he went back to the nurses' station. "Is that thing on?" he said pointing to a CCTV camera."

"It should be," she replied, "and I hope it is. It's supposed to be there for our safety. You wouldn't believe the abuse we get from some people."

When he got outside Barton went looking for the parking attendant. "Have you got the number of that Merc that was parked over there?" he asked.

"Who are you? I can't just tell anyone, you know."

Barton put his hand in his pocket, but remembered that he didn't have his warrant card. He took out his wallet instead and the man seemed quite happy to settle for a ten-pound note in return for a slip of paper on which he wrote a registration number. Barton looked at the number and called Sally.

"Hi Mike, you can't come in yet. The Chief Super's got Harris in his office now."

"That's all right Sal, I'll stay here a while. I think the man who attacked Jane might have been here. Black S class, index, Alpha – Echo – Five – Two – Romeo – Tango – Golf… is that a match?" He lit a cigarette while he waited for her reply; his first for days, he'd found half a pack in her car. "Right, get the local station to send a car over. I can't look at the CCTV tapes without my warrant card."

National Crime Squad, HQ – 11:00 BST

Barton went straight to his office, where he found Trevor Miller and ACC Harris waiting for him. Sally and Timms were also there, sitting at the table.

"Got him," said Barton triumphantly, putting the two tapes on the table.

"What are these for?" asked Harris.

"DC Barclay's assailant, sir," replied Barton. "I'm pretty sure he was at the hospital this morning." He pointed to the tapes "He's on this one… near the ward, and again on this one getting into his car. I didn't recognise him though."

"I'll get someone to take a look at these, straight away," said Timms. Then he turned to Harris, "If that's OK, with you, sir?"

Harris nodded and Timms picked up the tapes and left the room. He returned a few minutes later and sat at the table with the others.

"The reason that we're all here is to agree how the final stage of this investigation is going to proceed," said Harris. "But first I'd like to welcome DCI Barton back to the fold. Backed up by information from the Spanish police, I'm satisfied with your explanation of the events that led to your suspension and I'm pleased to say that there is no case for you to answer."

Barton grimaced: *Pompous arse, get on with it.*

Harris took a small wallet from his pocket; the wallet that Barton had given to Miller the previous evening: *'You'd better give me your warrant card. Harris thinks I took it off you last week.* Harris pushed the wallet across the table to Barton. "I believe that this is yours Mike. Just be more careful in future... and that goes for you all. The sorts of people that we're up against think they can buy almost anyone these days, so be on your guard, and think before you act." He leaned back in his chair and folded his arms. "Right, lecture over. Now tell me how you're going to finish this thing off."

Barton had been thinking about what he'd discussed with Miller and Sally the day before, and had come up with a few changes to the plan. He was back on the case now, so he decided to take charge. "I'd like to keep more or less the same split as we had before," he said authoritatively. Sally will carry on following the leads that we've had from Herrera and Debbie King... except Paul will know what's going on now. Paul, I'd like you to carry on with Underwood and Nichols and agree the charges with CPS. We'll ramp up the work on all the financial and company stuff and pool all the stuff that Sally's team got from Fisher with everything that Paul has. We'll give Preston and his boys to Thames Valley... they can sort out the murder charges... fight over them with Edinburgh if they want to. They can have Jarvis as well, after Paul's leant on him a bit more."

Everybody nodded in agreement. "Which just leaves Naismith... and I want him for myself." He could see this last remark hadn't gone down well with Miller who frowned and looked at Harris. "Sorry, sir, I'll rephrase that... I would like to take personal charge of the investigation relating to Naismith's involvement. I'd like to talk to you both about how I want to proceed."

Sally and Timms left the office leaving Barton alone with the two senior officers.

"He's sticking his neck out," said Timms.

"It's his neck," replied Sally, "and he knows what he's doing." Barton had gone over it with her the previous evening. Sitting on the floor in her flat as they drank red wine and ate a Chinese take away, she'd realised that she had through to him. What he was now explaining to Harris and Miller was well thought out and made absolute sense. At least that's what she thought, but he might still have a job convincing them. She crossed her fingers and glanced back towards the office: *Good luck, Mike.*

"Well you know him better than me, I hope you're right. Now let's see if they've got anything from those tapes."

"Michael Stevens," said Matt Brady, "who'd have thought it? Look." He ran the tape back for a few seconds and then played it back.

"Are you sure?" asked Sally as he looked at the monitor. "The picture's not that clear. Mind you I don't think I've ever seen him."

"You haven't, but we have," said Timms excitedly, "every other day for the last week. That's him alright."

"Well we'd better get someone to go and pick him up," said Sally.

"No need," said Timms, "I'll be seeing him in court later. What time is Underwood's bail hearing, Matt?"

"With respect, sir, I know that," argued Barton. "I know that I've got a personal interest. But that doesn't alter the fact that I know more about Naismith than anyone else does. I think I understand what make him tick... and what his weaknesses are. I think I can prove his personal involvement in all of this. I don't just mean the business connections... but that he has personally controlled the whole thing and pulls all their strings. I even think that I can get him to admit it."

"You seem to be pretty sure of yourself, Mike, but you still haven't convinced me that you can separate your personal feelings from the job in hand," said Harris.

"But that's the whole point, neither does he. It's just a game to him... fucking with other people's lives... he enjoys it. It's all a bloody game... and I know the rules now. This job shouldn't just be about keeping the politicians happy... locking people up... to make the public feel safe or making a big show of seizing their big houses and their expensive cars to give people a sense of justice being done. They can't even begin to imagine how much money is involved or understand that even if someone like Naismith is put away it could take years going though the courts to track down all his money. This is a war... and we're losing... we're losing because we don't understand that for people like Naismith, it's not really about money, not when you've got more than you can ever spend. This is about power, control... being on top. They use people, manipulate them, corrupt them, destroy them... because they can, because they get their kicks that way... and because they believe they're untouchable. We'll only start winning the war when the people who let them get away with it... the people who cover it up... are prepared to stand up and say no!"

Barton sat down and looked at their faces. He'd blown it; why couldn't he just say what they wanted to hear. "I'm sorry, sir... I..."

"No, that's all right," said Harris. "I could have done without the sermon, but you've got a point. I just wish it were that black and white to our political masters. But someone has to give them what they want, and I don't think that you'd ever want my job... And I certainly wouldn't want yours, but I know that we'd be a lot worse off if you weren't doing it. So go and get on with it."

"Thanks, sir," said Barton with a sigh of relief.

"Just promise me one thing, though."

"What's that, sir?"

"If you are going to make any waves, let me know me know first."

City of London – 14:00 BST

The offices of Blanchard's Bank were situated in Austin Friars, a quiet side street a few minutes' walk from the Bank of England. It wasn't that easy to find, which suited Blanchard's desire for anonymity. Only a simple brass plaque, fixed to the wall beside the doorway announced their presence – *Blanchard & Company, Private Bankers, Established 1788* – There were dozens of small private banks like this in the City, trading on reputations built up over a couple of centuries. Discreetly managing the financial affairs of wealthy clients, who valued their privacy above all else, and who were prepared to pay inflated fees to ensure it. Dave Connor knew that places like this existed, but he'd never had reason to cross the threshold, until now.

The impressive main doors were open and he stepped into a small lobby, where a uniformed commissionaire barred his further progress. In Connor's experience nobody ever looked at a warrant card; sometimes people slammed the door in his face before he'd taken it out of his pocket; most gave it no more than a cursory glance. Not this man; he reached out his hand, took the card, inspected it carefully, held it up and compared the photo to the man standing in front of him. Eventually, when he was completely satisfied, he nodded his head, handed back the wallet, stood to one side, and opened the glass door. "OK you can go in," he said in the voice that he reserved for tradesmen. "The girl at the desk might be able to help you."

Connor had only ever been inside banks with glass screens, high counters, and walls covered in posters advertising loans and savings. The large reception hall that he now entered had none of these. Some twenty feet above his head, a massive crystal chandelier hung from the centre of ceiling. Directly underneath, a young woman was sitting behind a large antique desk, talking on the phone. She raised her head slightly as Connor walked towards her; across the tiled floor.

"Good morning, Sergeant Connor," she said, looking at him over the top of her glasses. "I believe you want to see Mr Edwards. Could I see your identification please?"

Connor handed her his warrant card, and to his annoyance, she went through the same process as the commissionaire.

"I'm afraid he's engaged at the moment. Would you like me to make you an appointment?" she said, in a way that made Connor think he must have brought in something very unpleasant on the sole of his shoe. She turned over the pages of her desk diary, "Next Thursday?"

"I don't need an appointment, miss," Connor said brusquely, wishing that he had brought some dog shit in with him. "Just tell him I'm here, please."

"I'm sorry, Sergeant, but he's very busy you must make an appointment," she said firmly.

Connor started to walk round the desk. "That's OK, I'll find him myself. Where's his office?"

The woman pressed a button on the desk and rose to her feet to stop him. "I'm sorry, but you can't do that... Mr Davis, will you show this gentleman the way out please."

Connor turned around to see the commissionaire approaching. "Now see here miss, I need to speak to Mr Edwards and I'm not leaving until I do. If you prefer I can call for help... I'm sure that you'd rather not have the place full of uniforms, but..."

"Better do as he says Celia," said the commissionaire, before Connor could finish, "...we don't want any fuss."

"Oh! I don't know. Maybe Celia would like a bit of excitement," Connor said sarcastically. "She doesn't look as though she gets very much." He winked at Celia, who tried to hide her embarrassment. "Thank you Mr Davis. I'll wait over there... I'm not in a hurry... shall we say ten minutes, Celia... before I call my colleagues?"

Connor walked towards a large leather Chesterfield, bending to pick up a copy of the Times from a low table. He sat down and watched Celia as she picked up the phone. She spoke for a moment, before getting up and walking towards the staircase. Connor called after her, "Celia."

She stopped and turned, "What!" she snapped.

"I like my coffee black and sweet," Connor winked at her again and deliberately accentuated his soft Irish brogue, "...just like you, my little darling."

Six and a half minutes later, a secretary discreetly entered Jonathan Edwards' office and gave him a note. He apologised profusely to his client and made his way to meet Connor.

"This had better be important, sergeant," said Edwards impatiently. "I'm in the middle of a meeting with a client."

Connor took an instant dislike to the man. Standing there in his hand tailored suit, with a sneer on his face, Edwards looked exactly as Connor had expected and his voice had that air of superiority that he hated. "Is there somewhere private that we can talk, sir?" he asked politely. "Your office perhaps?"

"I told you I'm in the middle of a meeting," snapped Edwards.

"Well I think that it might be a good idea if you told your client to come back another day," said Connor. "This could take some time, I'm afraid."

"Now come on, you can't seriously expect me to drop everything." Edwards protested. "What's this about? I'm busy."

"It's about that white powder that you like snorting up your nose," said Connor, deliberately raising his voice. Celia sat bolt upright as he looked towards the desk and winked at her again. She glared back.

Edwards immediately changed both his expression and his tone. "Do you think we could do this somewhere else?" he asked. "There's a wine bar around the corner." He turned and spoke to Celia. "Ask my secretary to give my apologies to Mr al -Jafra, and cancel my three o'clock, please."

Horseferry Road Magistrates' Court, London – 14:15 BST

Timms knew that there was no way that Underwood would get bail. He sat silently in the court as they went through the motions; Stevens pleaded Underwood's case, the CPS solicitor opposed the request and the magistrates briefly talked amongst themselves before sending Underwood back to Brixton prison. The whole thing took less than ten minutes, and Timms didn't take his eye off Stevens for a second. As the court rose, Timms gestured to one of the court officers, who immediately left the courtroom. Timms spoke briefly with the CPS solicitor, before leaving to join the court officer who was waiting outside with Stevens.

"What's going on?" protested Stevens. "I have to go down to the cells to talk with my client. You're deliberately obstructing me. I could make a complaint…"

"Shut up, you little bastard," snarled Timms. "I'm not stopping you, I'm coming with you. I want to see his face when you tell him he's got to find a new brief."

"What are you playing at?"

"Oh! I'm not playing... Michael Peter Stevens. I'm arresting you on suspicion of assaulting a police officer..."

"Don't think you can get away with this..." Stevens's face turned scarlet, cheeks puffed out about to burst, as he protested. "You can't. I thought we going to do a deal."

"You don't have to say anything, but..." Timms continued with the caution, ignoring Stevens's protests.

"Too late for deal, Stevens," he said. "I've got all the evidence I need." Then, accompanied by a rather bemused court officer, and a very red-faced solicitor, Timms went to tell Underwood the news.

City of London – 14:30 BST

Edwards stopped outside the wine bar. "It's just here," he said.

Connor took one look at the place and carried on walking. "Too busy, we'll go somewhere a bit quieter," he said: *And a bit rougher, you flash bastard.*

The City still had some rough pubs if you knew where to look, and the City Tavern fitted the bill. Situated just off Cheapside, a dingy pub in the centre of an equally dingy square, surrounded by drab, seventies office blocks. But despite its convenience, the office workers obviously chose to go elsewhere for their refreshment, and most of the clientele seemed to be workers from nearby building sites. And, it was definitely not the sort of place that Edwards, was accustomed to. "This'll do," said Connor, as they walked in. He pointed to a table. "Sit there," he ordered. "I'll get us a drink... beer or wine?"

Edwards cast an eye towards the bar and looked at the meagre selection of cheap wines. "Vodka and tonic," he said.

"Pint of Guinness, please pal, and a single V-A-T," Connor said to the barman. "That cheap stuff will do, don't bother with the ice and lemon... and tonic off the shelf, not the fridge."

Edwards poured the lukewarm tonic water into his glass and watched Connor as he licked a thick line of creamy foam from his top lip. "I suppose you're drug squad," he said nervously. "OK, so I do a few lines now and then. But there's no need for all this. What's the big deal? Come on... everyone does it."

"Bit more serious than that," said Connor. "I'm from the National Crime Squad. And I don't care what goes up your fucking nose. But you've been playing with the big boys."

"What do you mean?"

"Who do you get your stuff from?"

"Oh! Come on, man, be reasonable. I occasionally buy a few grammes from the friend of a friend, you can't expect me remember his name."

"Well, I'd remember... if I was giving someone a hundred grand every month. Now, that's a lot of money... even to someone like you," said Connor. "And that's an awful lot of coke for personal use."

"I think you've made some sort of mistake. I told you I just do the occasional line."

"When did you last see Enrique Herrera?"

"Who...? Look, I'm sorry but I don't know anyone by that name. As I've just said, you're making a mistake," said Edwards as he started to stand up. "Now if that's all, I'll..."

"Sit down!" barked Connor. "You know damned well it's not all. Right now, my colleagues are searching your flat in Chelsea Harbour. Now what are they going find? Half a kilo... a kilo... more maybe... let's see Possession of a class A drug with intent to supply... you'll get five years. Maybe more... maybe less... it depends on you."

Edwards knew there was no way that he could bluff his way out of this. He dropped his bravado and shrugged his shoulders. "OK, so what now?"

"I'm going to ask some questions, and you're going to tell me the answers. Give me the right ones and it'll be taken into consideration by the court. Give me the wrong ones and maybe we can find a few more charges to add. Am I making myself clear, sir?"

"OK, just get on with it."

"Herrera? You know him, right?

"I wouldn't really say that. I know of him..."

Connor leaned across the table. "Wrong answer, let's try again. Do you know Enrique Herrera? Let me help you. He sells cocaine."

"OK. I know him."

"You know him rather well, don't you... what, one, two kilos a month?

"Yes."

"How do you pay him?"

"Transfer to an offshore account."

"Just one account?"

"No, several, it changes every couple of months."

"Have you ever transferred any other sums in these accounts for him?"

"Sometimes," said Edwards.

"Robert King? David Nichols? Do you know them?"

"No... but I've heard of them."

"How have you heard of them?"

"I used to know King's daughter. But I've never met him."

"Is King a client? And what about Nichols? Are either of them clients of the bank?"

"I don't know... maybe, all the partners have their own private clients. I might be able to find out. "

"That's better. Now what about Sir Anthony Naismith, is he a client?"

"No... well not personally."

"But he's a client of Blanchard's?"

"Yes. One of our biggest."

"And who manages his account?"

"My boss, Phillip Johnston, he's one of the senior partners."

"Thank you," said Connor. "That wasn't so bad was it? That's all I need to know, for now. I think it's time that we were going back."

"I could do with another drink first," said Edwards, taking his wallet from his pocket. "And not that cheap stuff please,"

"Tell you what, we'll stop off at that poncey wine bar on the way back," said Connor. "You can say goodbye to your pals while we wait." He took out his mobile and called Barton. "We're on Mike. He's confirmed Naismith... not sure about the others... OK, give me a call when you're ready."

"Ready for what?" asked Edwards.

"You'll see," said Connor, smiling. "You'll see."

So would a lot of other people in the vicinity of the Austin Friars that afternoon; the regulars at the Phoenix in Throgmorton Street hadn't had anything so exiting to talk about since the IRA bombed the Stock Exchange.

.

Cheshunt, Hertfordshire – 15:45 BST

Timms switched on the tape. "Interview with Michael Stevens, 19th of May 2003, the time is 3:45 p.m., officers present Detective Inspectors Paul Timms and David Lennox. Mr Stevens has waived his right to have a solicitor present."

"Look, I was coming to see you... you know what you said the other day. I'd thought about it..." Stevens spluttered.

"Was that before of after you knew that we'd got Jarvis?" asked Timms.

"Where were you on Friday, between ten-thirty and ten past twelve?" asked Lennox.

"I can't remember."

"Let me remind you," said Timms. "When the custody sergeant at Tottenham called your office at ten-thirty they said that you were playing golf with a client. So where were you?"

"I don't remember. He rang me and cancelled."

"For the benefit of the tape DI Lennox is showing the suspect a bunch of keys." Lennox put a plastic property bag on the table. "Are these yours?" he asked, "…for the benefit of the tape Mr Stevens has just nodded his head."

"What's this?" asked Lennox pointing to the black plastic key fob.

"My golf club tag."

"For the benefit of the tape Mr Stevens has just identified Cheshunt Golf Club key fob number 97."

"So what?" said Stevens.

"So, the golf club security system records showed that this tag was used on Friday 16th of May," said Lennox. "So where were you, Mr Stevens?"

"OK, I went to the golf club, and then my client cancelled while I was waiting on the practice green. So I changed and left at about eleven-thirty. At about one I got a message from the office asking me to go to Tottenham police station."

"You left at eleven-thirty."

"Yes I'm sure. Maybe a few minutes later, why?"

"Because at about eleven-forty-five, a policewoman was attacked in the men's locker room… but of course you know that… don't you?"

"I just said I left at eleven-thirty," Stevens snapped. "So why would I know anything about that?"

"Do you know anything about access control systems?" Lennox asked. Stevens shook his head.

"I thought not," said Lennox. "So you wouldn't know that they can be programmed to record every time a door is opened. According to the golf club security records, this tag was used to enter the men's locker room from the course at eleven-thirty-six. So when we send your golf clubs and the clothes that you were wearing on Friday to the lab, do you suppose we'll find traces of blood?"

"Look I didn't know she was a policewoman… I didn't mean to hurt her… I just…" babbled Stevens.

"You just what?" said Timms. "You just like hitting women."

"No, it was just a coincidence. Like I said, my client cancelled. I came back into the locker room and I was changing my shoes, when I saw someone opening Mr King's locker. Well I went over to see…"

"With a golf club in your hand?"

"Look, I didn't get a good look at her, she was bending down… she was wearing trousers. I thought she was man."

"And then what happened?"

"I saw what was in the locker. Look I didn't mean to hit her… it just… I don't know… next thing she was laying on the floor. Then I got out fast, I gave Joe Turner two hundred quid to wind back the video tapes and left."

"What was in the locker?" asked Timms. "Whatever else you are Stevens, you're not a fool. So what was so important that it was worth the risk?"

"I was going to tell you… after what you said the other day. I thought we could do a deal. But I had to wait until Warren Jarvis was out of the way…then I was going to tell you."

"So, the anonymous phone call, that was you," said Timms. "I must really have put the wind up you the other day."

"We can still do a deal, like you said?"

"I don't know what you're talking about. Now what was in that locker, or do I have to get a warrant and tear apart everything that this bunch of keys opens."

"Go ahead," spat Stevens. "I want to make my phone call now."

"For the benefit of the tape DI Timms is leaving the room," said Timms as he picked up the keys. "He's all yours Lennox… for the time being."

City of London – 16:00 BST

"Hello again, Mr Davis," said Connor as the old soldier barred his way again. "It's alright I know the way… you stay here I've got some friends arriving in a minute." He gestured to the phone, "Phil wait with Mr Davis and don't let him use that."

Connor held the door open for Barton and Edwards and followed them into the reception hall. "Stay where you are, Celia, and leave that phone," he ordered, as they were halfway across the floor.

"I want to see Phillip Johnston," said Barton.

"You can't…"

"Celia, leave it," said Edwards.

"Thank you, Mr Edwards, when I need you help, I'll ask for it," snapped Barton.

"Now, miss, I'm Detective Chief Inspector Barton… I think you've already met my colleague, Detective Sergeant Connor… and I'm not going to ask you again…"

Barton was rudely interrupted by the wailing of several sirens, followed moments later by the sound of a dozen pairs of boots trampling over the tiled floor. "Ah! My friends have arrived," he said. "Now where was I?"

Barton handed her a search warrant, "This says that I can search these premises and remove… well, pretty much anything I want. Now where is Phillip Johnston?"

"I'll take you," said Edwards eagerly. He didn't sound much like a man facing a five stretch; he seemed to be enjoying himself. "This is just like on one of those TV shows," he said, barely containing his excitement as he led the way up the stairs.

"Well, that was good morning's work, a very satisfactory outcome," said Philip Johnston, as he raised his glass. He was in the boardroom with two of the other senior partners; they'd just shaken hands on a lucrative deal and were celebrating with a very fine Armagnac; unaware that, outside in the ante-room, two very confused looking Saudi gentlemen were being bustled out of the way by a couple of very insistent men in uniform.

"Not now," said Johnston, as the door opened. "I said that we weren't to be disturbed... Jonathan! What's going on?"

"Sorry, we didn't get the message," said Barton as he walked towards the mahogany table. "Which of you gentlemen is Phillip Johnston?"

"I am. Now do you mind telling me who the hell you are?" shouted Johnston angrily.

"I'm your worst nightmare," said Barton. Johnston's partners were speechless as Barton looked at them across the table. "OK, you two can go. My officers will escort you out of the building." Barton picked up the Armagnac bottle and looked at the label. "Why don't you sit down and finish your drink Mr Johnston? I wouldn't want to see a twenty-five year old brandy go to waste." He handed the bottle to Connor. "This might be evidence, Dave... look after it."

Barton led Johnston and Edwards out of the building. "This ought to make the six o'clock news, sir," said Phil Fellows, with a grin, as they passed on the stairs. Barton stood on the steps and smiled contentedly as he watched the two men being bundled into a waiting van. Then he read his prepared statement to the waiting ladies and gentlemen of the press.

As Barton answered questions, Dave Connor took the cap off the black marker pen, he'd picked up in the boardroom. Nobody noticed at the time: but later that evening, anyone looking closely enough at the BBC news would have seen a man in the background, writing something on the brass wall plaque.

Blanchard & Company
Private Bankers
Established 1788
BUSTED 2003

Chapter 31

Tuesday 20th May

Marbella, Costa del Sol – 07:30 CET

Jean Browning sat up in bed and called to her husband. "Peter, come and look at this." She turned up the TV volume and stared at the screen. "Oh God! No! Peter come and look at this!"

"In a minute," Peter Browning called from the bathroom, "can't a man shave in peace."

"It's Blanchard's," she shouted, "Phillip's bank, hurry up Peter you'll miss it… the police have just closed them down."

Browning ran out of the bathroom and froze as he saw scenes, which had been recorded outside the bank the previous afternoon.

"Look Peter, that's Phillip and isn't that the policeman who was here…'

"Oh! Shut up woman, I've got eyes," snarled Browning, filling up with rage. "Shut up and let me listen."

When the phone rang, he turned down the TV volume and picked up the receiver. "Yes, Tony, I've just seen it… OK, I'll see you at the office in an hour."

National Crime Squad, Hertfordshire Branch – 08:00 BST

Barton was already in his office with Timms when Sally arrived. She'd offered him the sofa bed again, but after learning of her run in with Grace, he'd declined. There wasn't much point in going back to an empty house so he'd booked into a cheap hotel near the office for a few nights.

What do you want us to do about the guys we've got locked up?" asked Timms.

"We need to get them talking, Paul. We're getting close, but we're running out of time. Follow the money. You take Johnston," said Barton. "And take the gloves off, Paul. I want him scared. And get someone over to see Nichols. He'll know by now that we've closed his bank. Let's hope that's put the wind up him. He likes the ladies, doesn't he? Why not Send Lorna, she'll soon sort him out.

"Are you ready?" asked Sally. "We don't want to be late."

"Sit down and give me a couple of minutes. We've nearly finished."

"We're going to start on Stevens's office and house this morning," said Timms. "It would help if we knew what we were looking for."

"Jane said she was going to come in for a few hours today. She might be able to remember something," said Sally.

"Good, anything else, Paul."

"Lennox gave me this yesterday. The SOCO found it in the pocket of King's golf jacket." Timms held up a plastic bag with a mobile phone inside. "Surprised you missed it Sally," he said, with a smile. "The phone company are sending over a copy of the call records."

"How did it go yesterday?" asked Sally. "I saw you on the news."

"Like clockwork, Dave did a good job. He's back there this morning. He's taking Edwards with him. He's being very helpful. Didn't have a lot of choice, they found three kilos of coke in his flat," said Barton. "He's going to show them how to get into the computer records."

"It won't be long before Naismith starts trying to move his money. Have you got the financial crime guys lined up, Sally?"

"Yes, there's a whole bunch of them going over to the bank this morning and more waiting to follow up on anything we get from Johnston and Nichols."

"Great... well if we've got all the bases covered, we'd better get going."

Oxford – 11:00 BST

"I don't like funerals," said Sally, as she drove through the gates of the cemetery. "They always make me feel a bit strange... you know... like you know that one day; it'll be you in the box. It's like when you read a book, every time you finish a chapter, you know you're a bit closer to the last page."

"Not my idea of fun either, you can wait in the car if you want," said Barton uneasily. He looked at her, hoping that she wouldn't take up the offer. Earlier, sitting outside the church, he'd been so glad that she'd agreed to come with him. He hadn't given it any thought beforehand; hadn't realised how difficult it would be. He'd tried to get out of the car, but his legs wouldn't move, so they had sat in silence and waited until it was time for Sally to join the tail end of the pathetic little convoy for the short journey to Headington.

Now, as Barton watched the tall young man helping the widow from the undertaker's car, memories came flooding back. Memories, of another cemetery, twenty years before, on another grey day in May; another day like this, when that young man had been him: *Why does it always seem to rain at funerals?*

On that day, there had been hundreds of mourners; today he counted only two. He attached Julia's card to the small wreath of lilies and summoning up his courage, he got out of the car and walked towards the graveside. He'd come here for Julia, but his heart felt for the widow and her son, as he watched them each throw a handful of dirt into the grave. Without a word, he placed the wreath on the ground, and stepped back. He returned to where Sally was standing, and they walked slowly back to the car. Looking over his shoulder, he saw the young man pick up the wreath and show it to his mother.

The minutes that followed seemed like an eternity. As they waited by the car, Barton was shaking like a leaf. "It's OK Mike, you're doing well. I'm really proud of you," said Sally encouragingly, putting her hand on his arm.

Barton wasn't sure what he was feeling, but it certainly wasn't pride. For twenty years, he'd been waiting for this day and now it had come. He'd been waiting all this time to put his ghost to rest; but now, he'd come to the end of what should have been the final chapter, and the book was still open: *Damn you Naismith.*

The young man approached them, "Do I know you?" he said menacingly. "What was that card all about?"

"Your mother knows," said Barton, she'll explain later. He took out Julia's letter. "Would you give her this, please... I'll wait in the car."

A few minutes later, the young man returned. "Mum wants you to come back to our house. Is that alright?"

Barton nodded. He trembled at the thought of it; but it had to be done.

Marbella, Costa del Sol – 11:30 CET

The three men had spent the morning making phone calls that nobody answered, and leaving messages that were not returned; every call traced, every word recorded. Naismith was struggling to hold it together; ignoring the other two men he paced up and down the floor of his office, talking to himself. Every so often, he spat a question at them. Neither Peter Browning nor Colin Marshall had any answers.

"Get on the next bloody plane Peter, you're no fucking use here... get the hell over there and find out what's happening," Naismith shouted in desperation, "...and get those diaries. Find that little arse-licker Stevens, and bring the bastard back here. I'll fucking kill him myself if he's told anyone." He started pacing again. "Well, fucking go then!" he barked. "What are you waiting for?"

Peter Browning didn't need telling again. He got up and hurried towards the door, shaking his head, wondering what good it would do. By the time he got to his car, he'd already made up his mind. He phoned his wife and told her to pack; they weren't coming back.

When Browning had gone, Naismith turned his attention to Marshall. "For Christ's sake Colin, there must be someone you can talk to. What the hell has that boy of yours been doing? He should have told us about this... have you reached him yet?"

"I'll keep trying... but don't blame him..." said Marshall; trying to keep calm. "This must have gone down before he knew anything about it. He'll come through... he always has," he said confidently, unaware that, at that moment, his son was sitting in an interview room being grilled by two officers from the Professional Standards Unit.

Oxford – 11:45 BST

The Campbells lived in a small terraced house in the middle of Oxford's sprawling Blackbird Leys housing estate. Started in the 1950s as a model for social housing, the estate had grown over a thirty-year period and was now home to over thirteen thousand. Like many similar estates in other cities around the country, it had declined rapidly during the 1980s and the familiar signs of decay and neglect were all around. Sally felt decidedly uneasy about leaving her new car at the side of the road and her fears were heightened when a gang of youths appeared from behind a row of lock up garages.

"They're trouble," said Lewis Campbell as the boys approached the car. "They'll have this away in a minute if you park it here." He got out of the car and called to one of the boys. He came over and Lewis said something to him, then he went back to the others and they all walked away down the street.

"I don't trust them. They'll be back," said Lewis. "Better give me the keys. Don't worry, miss, I'll park it in one of the garages."

*Is this where **he** lived?* Barton felt very uncomfortable as he entered the house. It didn't seem right, but he'd come this far and there was no going back.

Nina Campbell, who so far hadn't said a word, offered to make tea and went into the kitchen. Her son returned and invited them to sit down, and then pulled a chair away from the dining table and sat with his legs straddling the seat and his elbows resting on the chair back. He stared at Barton, but couldn't think of anything to say.

Barton and Sally sat, rather awkwardly, at opposite ends of the sofa. Barton had introduced Sally at the cemetery: *'and this is my friend, Sally Parkinson'*, but he hadn't spoken since.

There was long uneasy silence, until Nina returned carrying four mugs on a tray. "I'm sorry," she said, "I haven't got any cups and saucers."

Nothing more was said and silence fell over the room again. Lewis Campbell didn't have a clue who these people were, but his mother had told him that they had something important to talk about, and he was happy to go along with her. He hadn't asked her what or why. He knew that she needed him today and that was reason enough. But, he didn't like the way that the man was looking at him.

Barton was watching the young man; he didn't mean to stare, but it was difficult not to; Lewis looked so like the man who had just been buried.

For Sally, wondering why she had agreed to this, the silence was becoming oppressive. She could see the tension in Barton's face, and knew that he wanted to speak. The emptiness behind his eyes, told her that he couldn't find any words.

Sensing their discomfort and setting her own aside, Nina Campbell began to speak. "Thank you for coming, Mr Barton. This must be very hard for you."

Barton couldn't fail to be impressed this woman dressed in black. She carried herself with dignity. Whatever emotions she was feeling were well hidden. He suddenly felt ashamed at the anger that he had felt towards these two innocent people.

"It was very kind of your mother to send you... you must thank her for me, and tell her she did nothing that needs to be forgiven. It was thoughtless of me to intrude on her like that..: at that terrible time."

Barton bowed his head: *Like I'm doing now.* "I'm sorry," he said "I shouldn't have come... not today... I'm sorry. I should have just sent the flowers. I'll come back some other time."

"It's alright, I don't mind. I'm glad you're here. Don't go. I've got to tell you..." She was pleading with him. Then she looked at her son in the way that only a mother can. "And you too Lewis. It's time you knew. This won't take long, because I don't know much. But I'll tell you everything... I won't leave anything out. When I'm done, you decide Mr Barton. You decide if I can ask your mother... one more time... if she can forgive Patrick."

This was the first time that his name had been mentioned and Barton felt something cold and sharp cutting a nerve. He didn't reply, but he nodded to show that he understood.

"The first thing that you have to know Lewis... is about your dad, my Patrick. The man he killed was Mr Barton's father. That's why he's here."

Slowly and painfully, Nina Campbell began to tell her story. She'd not told anyone before, but she'd lived it every day for twenty years, and remembered as if it was yesterday.

She told them about the night that three men came to the house and took away her husband. Patrick had seemed to know one of the men and he'd let them in. They'd sent her and the baby upstairs. She'd heard them arguing, and a while later Patrick called her to come back downstairs. He told her not be frightened, and that he had to go with the men. One of the men had told Patrick that they wouldn't hurt me or Lewis, as long as he did as he was told. Tears welled in Nina's eyes and she turned her head, away from Barton, away from her son; not wanting either man to see her shame, "But, he lied... he stayed behind... and he hurt me... for three days and nights... he hurt me real bad."

She didn't know what her husband had done until the police came to her house. By that time, the man had gone; he'd thrown some money on the table and told her that if she ever said anything he'd come back and kill her.

"Patrick wasn't a bad man, Mr Barton. I know he had some trouble with the police before I met him. But that was just some trouble over ganja and he paid for that. He was always kind to me and a good father to Lewis. He would never have hurt anyone. He couldn't do that..."

"You said that he knew one of the men. Did he tell you who he was?" asked Barton.

"No, he never did. He just said that he'd met him in prison, when he was a boy, before he met me. He never told me their names, he was scared they'd come back and get me... And, I never told him what that man did to me. He said he didn't want to kill anyone, but they made him do it. They told me that they would kill me and Lewis. He knew he was going to get caught and go to prison... but he was protecting me. That's why he killed your father... to protect me and Lewis.

"I was at his trial," said Barton. "I saw you there. Your husband admitted to being a member of an extreme political group, *WAR... Warriors Against Racism*. He said that the shooting was political... all racists deserved to die." Barton remembered Campbell, standing in the dock; a cold-blooded killer, motivated by hate, who had shown no remorse. "So were these men that you say forced him... were they black activists from the same group."

"No, that was all a lie. Patrick was never interested in politics; he was Rastafari. He just said what they told him. And they weren't black... they were white men. They told him exactly what to do. He had to fire two shots, one was supposed to just miss, but Patrick's hand was shaking and he shot him in the arm. But, they said the second shot was to kill the policeman... your father... that's all I know... I don't know why. Then his lawyer, he told him exactly what to say to the police and in the court." Nina looked at Barton, her eyes begging him to believe her. "I swear it's all true, Mr Barton. He's gone now, why would I lie."

As Barton looked at Nina, his stomach knotted up and bile burned his throat. But, he didn't doubt that what she had told him was true. He'd hated her husband for twenty years; but he couldn't hate a man who'd chosen to take a stranger's life to save his family. But he was burning up with hatred for the man who had forced the choice on him.

"And now they've killed him too," said Nina, her face now betraying her emotions "They said he got in a fight. They said he started it. But I know that's not true... Patrick was never in any trouble the whole time he was in prison." Despair, anger, and confusion coloured her words. "They killed him and I don't know why."

Lewis, who had been sitting silently at the table, got up and sat next to his mother. He put his arms round her to comfort her. Sally looked at Barton and signalled that it was time to leave, but Barton just sat and watched as the young man's tears mingled with those of his mother. He'd been there and he understood how much it hurt. He stood up and gestured towards the kitchen. Sally quietly followed him.

"Give them a moment Sal. I can't leave her like this," his voice trembled and he gripped Sally's hand. She nodded and kissed his cheek. She could never understand how it felt, but she was glad to be there for him.

As they were leaving, Nina asked him again to thank his mother, and Barton promised to tell his mother what she'd told him. He asked her one more question, more out of concern than as a policeman. "Did they ever come back again... did they ever hurt you again?"

"No, they never did, but I still don't sleep some nights. I saw one of them once in London, but I ran before he saw me. He was the one who hurt me. It was about ten years ago, he looked older but I'll never forget his face." She thought hard for a moment, "And I remember his name now. I remember they called him Baz. Does that mean anything to you?"

"Maybe," said Barton. "If I can, I'll find him."

National Crime Squad, Hertfordshire Branch – 17:30 BST

Sally found it hard to concentrate during the de-briefing. They hadn't said much to each other on the journey back from Oxford. She thought that he had seemed remarkably calm and relaxed, and that had worried her, because she knew, it was his way of hiding things. She didn't think that he could go on for much longer; it had to end soon. This was a roller coaster ride like she'd never known before. The previous day he'd been on a high; sharp and alert. The business at the bank seemed to have put him back on top for a while. She'd watched the news, full of admiration for him as he addressed the reporters; the professional policeman, doing what he did best. But today he'd plunged back into the depths. She'd seen the look on his face as Nina Campbell had read him another chapter of the book, and she was worried that he wasn't going to be able to keep his promise. She was really scared that he wouldn't be able to stop himself.

It had been a busy and productive day and, apart from the mountain of paperwork that was needed by the CPS, everyone could see that Operation De Niro was, at last coming to a conclusion. Johnston hadn't even tried to lie; he was a banker not a professional criminal and, after his lawyer had advised him to cooperate, he'd spent all day talking. And they'd been right to concentrate on Nicholls, who was proving to be the weakest link in King's organisation.

Throughout the day they had exchanged and confirmed information with the NCIS. And, as Naismith had frantically tried to contact his associates and move his money, the Spanish police had monitored calls, intercepted faxes and emails, and relayed the information to London. The team at the bank had been checking account and transaction details; following trails that started in London, criss-crossed between the financial centres of Europe, America, and the Far East, and ended in a dozen unregulated financial havens around the world.

The records for the pay-as-you-go SIM card in the mobile phone found in King's locker had been checked. All the calls were to other unregistered mobile numbers, most of them to a number on the Spanish Movistar network.

The searches still hadn't turned up whatever it was that Stevens had taken from the golf club, although Jane had remembered that there'd been a large box in the locker.

There was also a message from Chris Fisher and after the de-brief Barton returned the call. When he'd finished, he took the bottle of Armagnac that he'd liberated from the bank, out of his desk drawer and poured a large measure. He picked up the phone and dialled his mother's number, leaning back in his chair as listened to the ringing tone.

Barton was satisfied, with their day's work. Slowly but surely, the tables were turning. The Puppet Master was losing control. And it was safe for Grace to come home.

Chapter 32

Wednesday 21st May

St Lucia – 02:25 Eastern Standard Time

Grace and Lizzie said their farewells to Julia and Lou, and made their way to the departure lounge. Lizzie was flying back to Boston via Atlanta and Grace had managed to get a ticket on the same flight; she'd planned to stay a couple of days with Lizzie, before flying back to London at the weekend. The two women had much in common and, although they saw very little of each other, had become close friends over the years. Lizzie was looking forward to a girls' night out on the town. "You'll like Boston," she had said excitedly as they had made their plans. "It's got a similar feel to Cambridge."

But now Grace was wondering how to tell Lizzie that she had changed her mind. She'd lain in bed the previous night going over everything that she now knew about this man Naismith; the man that her husband had become so obsessed with. She'd read and re-read the transcripts of the tapes that Mike had made in Spain and the tape that Sally had sent her at the weekend. She'd read Naismith's own words in the manuscript that his mother had given to Sally, noting with great interest Mary Naismith's comments in the margins. And, as she'd told Mike during their long phone conversation, it had all started to add up. "It's no wonder that that little speech he made to you sounded so well rehearsed, it's almost word for word from the manuscript. There's a lot more of course, but I'd say that he'd memorised whole sections of it."

And then she'd thought some more about writing a book. She'd had a few articles published in professional journals, but this was different. A whole book would need a lot more material and that meant more research. She'd looked at a map, Atlanta was in Georgia, and didn't look too far from Mississippi.

National Crime Squad, Hertfordshire Branch – 08:45 BST

Jane breezed into the office looking very pleased with herself, "Lorna I've got it. It was staring me in the face all day. I just couldn't see it. It was like those." She pointed to the pile of boxes that contained Fisher's files. "That's what the other key was for."

"Do you know how many of these there are at Stevens's office," groaned Lorna. "Keep your coat on. All we have to do now is find the one that the key fits. Are you feeling OK? This could be a long day."

Jane nodded; she wasn't going to miss this. She wanted to know what it was all about.

They'd only travelled about a mile when Lorna stopped the car and turned back. "Call DI Timms, ask him who's got Stevens's keys."

Clerkenwell, London – 09:00 BST

Fisher had left a message for them at reception and they were shown into one of the studios; he waiting for them in the control room.

"The tape's still in pretty good nick, considering it's twenty years old," he said "have a look. Not as sharp as digital, but this old broadcast quality video is still better than the stuff you use at home. We've cued it up to start a couple of minutes before the shooting and we can play it as fast or as slow as you like."

Barton looked at the monitors. One of the counters at the top of the screen had been re-set to zero, the other showed a date and time: *14:05:2003 20:11:17*. The frozen image was almost as clear as a photograph. After years of looking at poor quality CCTV pictures, he'd not been expecting anything as clear as this. "Looks good to me, what do you think, Sally?"

"It's a lot better than my video at home," she said, as they sat down.

They watched in horror as the tall figure of Patrick Campbell pushed two people aside and raised his arm. He fired a shot and Naismith staggered backwards. Then, as the mood of the crowd changed and the cheering stopped, Campbell fired again and James Barton fell to the floor of the stage.

Sally watched as panic broke out in the hall. First, the screams, as people started to realise what they had witnessed, then the crowd reacted; shouting, running, pushing and shoving. A tall man stood in front of the podium, holding a microphone, appealing for calm. They ignored him as they clamber over each other in the scrums forming around the exits. Over three-hundred people acting as one; as each thought only for themselves.

Barton saw none of this; his eyes were focussed on only one part of the scene, as he watched two policemen kneeling over the man on the floor; one shouting for help as the other cradled the dying man's head.

Barton raised his head slightly, and for a few moments, his eyes wandered around the screen; briefly focussing on the faces of Naismith and the cluster of men in suits that surrounded him. Then his eyes returned to the horrific tableau at the centre of the stage. He stared through his tears and watched the pool of blood spreading across the floor; watched his father's life drain away.

Finally, as the paramedics lifted the stretcher, he turned his head and looked away. It was all over. He looked at the counter. *00:23:53*

"Could you rewind the tape please," said Barton, "slow motion." He looked at the screen, as the scenes that had unfolded during the last twenty-four minutes, were undone. He looked at the faces at either side of the stage and at the faces in the crowd; hoping to see another face that he would recognise. He stared, as if in a trance, at the surreal images of figures running backwards to take up their original positions; their panic becoming euphoria as they clapped and cheered their candidate. He watched the dying man rise to his feet, and his heart stopped. It was like one of the images from his dream. His saw his father falling upwards, and then jerking backwards across the stage; his movements ungainly, unnatural, as if he were being jiggled like marionette; powerless to resist as the Puppet Master tugged at the strings.

Barton got up and fled from the room, running down the corridor with his hand covering his mouth. At the end of the corridor he flung open a door and ran to the nearest cubicle; he sank to his knees and retched, the bile burning at his throat. He remained there, on his knees, quivering and unable to move, until Fisher helped him to his feet.

"Thanks," said Barton, grasping the edge of a washbasin and steadying himself. "Go back to Sally... I'll be OK... give me a couple of minutes... got to watch it again."

Barton turned on the tap, leaned over the basin, and cupped his hands under the running water. He splashed the cold water over his face, soaking his shirt: washing away the nightmare. As he stood in front of the mirror, taking deep breaths, he saw the look of anguish gradually disappear; to be replaced by one of calm, cold, determination.

"Drink?" Fisher offered him a large tumbler of Scotch.

He brushed it aside, and picked up a glass of water. "No thanks, this is all I need." He drained the glass and then filled it again from the jug on the table. "Sorry about that... couldn't help myself... I'm OK now." His voice trembled only slightly as he spoke.

Sally didn't think he was OK; he didn't look it, nor did he sound it. "We should go, Mike. Don't you think you've had enough?" she said with concern.

"No. I'm OK," he replied, his voice steadying. "I want to have another look… it's alright… it won't be as bad this time."

"What are we looking for?" asked Sally.

"I'm not sure," he replied. "There may be nothing. I thought for a moment that I saw… I thought… I'm not sure."

He turned to Fisher, "Can you wind it back, a bit before the start, and then play it again, please?"

The technician rewound the tape. Barton watched the counter and raised his hand. The tape stopped: *00:05:01*

This time Barton wasn't looking at the main characters. His attention was on a small group of people, standing in the shadows at the back of the stage. "Stop it there," he said, raising his hand. The scene was frozen: *00:01:18*

"Can you go back to zero and replay that part again… as slow as possible?" He moved closer to the monitor. "There stop, stop there," he said excitedly, pointing at a face. "Can you zoom in on that man there?"

The man was standing at the side of the stage, his arms folded across his chest, his right hand resting in the crook of his left elbow. He watched in anticipation as the man gradually filled the screen, becoming more blurred as the image was magnified.

"Can you make it any clearer?" asked Sally.

The technician fiddled with the dials and enhanced the image. Staring from the screen was a face that they both knew; twenty years younger, but unmistakeable: Terry King.

Barton stood up, "OK. Now zoom out again and play it on, slowly." He traced a line on the screen with his finger. Patrick Campbell was looking directly at Terry King. Then King raised his thumb, keeping it pressed against his sleeve, stroking his arm. The movement was so slight that nobody noticed; nobody except Campbell, who began to push his way to the front of the crowd.

Barton clenched his fist; as if he was making victory salute. "See that? We've got him. We've got the bastard."

Sally looked at him; she saw the look of satisfaction on his face and half wished that they hadn't.

Cheshunt, Hertfordshire – 10:30 BST

Miles Kingston met Lorna and Jane at the reception desk. "Terrible business," he said, after the two police officers had introduced themselves.

379

He began to apologise profusely. "I'm so sorry I do hope that are you alright now. You know nothing like this has ever happened here before. Of course, all of our members are all of very good standing. I vet every application myself... so I was sure that it couldn't be a member. But, I understand that you've now caught the man... and he's one of our corporate members, so that's a relief."

Apologies started to turn into excuses, as Kingston explained that he had no means of controlling who the corporate members allocated keys to; an oversight that the committee had pointed out to him the previous evening, when they voted to scrap the corporate membership scheme. The emergency meeting had been called by the chairman of the committee, who was a magistrate. He'd had quite a shock, when Stevens had appeared in the dock: *'You really cannot imagine how embarrassing it was... He was in my court only a few days ago asking me to set bail for one of his clients... I've played golf with the man... this affair could really damage the reputation of the club... you really should have thought of this Miles..."*

The committee had censured Kingston and he hoped that this visit by the police would be the last for a very long time. Lennox had told him of their suspicions about Joe Turner and he hoped that it wouldn't come out. Otherwise, he feared that he'd be up in front of committee again, trying to explain why he hadn't checked his Head of Security's false references.

"You were right," said Jane as she opened Stevens' locker. It was obvious when they'd thought about it. Surely, someone would have noticed if Stevens had walked through reception carrying a large metal box. Lorna had guessed, correctly, that it was still at the golf club, and now Jane was looking at the box again, just as she had a few days before; only this time the person standing behind her wasn't about whack her over the head.

Royal Berkshire Hospital, Reading – 12:45 BST

Sally would soon be receiving several speeding tickets in the post. Barton had driven as fast as the traffic had allowed, ignoring the limits and the cameras. He raced through the gates of the hospital and screeched to a halt outside the main doors. "Find somewhere to park," he shouted as he ran from the car.

Upstairs in the intensive care unit Terry King was drifting in and out of consciousness, as he had been for over a week. He was still on the critical list and the doctors were still not allowing him to be questioned. Barton knew that, but he didn't care, all he cared about was that the man had played a part in his father's death; and now he wanted to know why. He walked slowly from the lift, not wanting to draw attention as he passed the nurses station. PC Nick Kirwan was sitting outside the side ward reading a newspaper. He looked up as Barton approached.

"Good morning, sir, Nick Kirwan, remember me?"

"Get lost, Kirwan," said Barton, as he grabbed the door handle.

"But, sir, I'm not supposed to…"

"Go for a walk," snapped Barton. "Mr King and I need to have a few words."

The young PC didn't need telling twice: *Sod it! I'm not arguing with a DCI.* He disappeared down the corridor, leaving Barton standing alone outside the room.

Barton flung open the door and ran into the room. Terry King's eyes flickered as he realised that this wasn't one of the nurses or doctors, and he tried to make out the face of the large figure standing over him.

"You bastard, you fucking bastard," Barton shouted angrily. "Do you know who I am?"

Although he couldn't see clearly, King could hear, and even his drug-fuddled mind was alert enough to know that this man was trouble. He tried to say something but his mouth was dry and his words made no sound. He fumbled at the call button in his hand, but Barton snatched it from him.

"We don't need any company." Barton said dryly. "I'm Mike Barton. Don't suppose that means anything to you. Think back twenty years," His voice was trembling with rage, but he tried to speak slowly and clearly, "…remember… another man called Barton… a policeman… you killed him. And I want to know why." King's eyes were closed and Barton couldn't tell if he was awake. "Can you hear me?"

King could hear, but he couldn't understand. The cocktail of drugs, pumped into a vein in his left arm at regular intervals, had kicked in again. As he began to lose consciousness, his head slumped forward slightly. Barton took this to be a nod and carried on, unaware that he was talking to himself. "I know you were there… there's a video and I saw you… I saw you signalling to Campbell… And I watched him die… James Barton, Inspector James Barton, my dad…" The words tumbled out of Barton's mouth; accusing, threatening. "I'll make you pay, I'll make him pay, all of you… and Jarvis for what he did to Nina Campbell… and Marshall, I know about him too, the cover up… you'll pay, you bastard…" But King couldn't hear, and even if he had, he wouldn't have remembered; he couldn't remember anything; he couldn't even remember who he was.

Barton stood by the cot, shaking; shouting, repeating himself, again and again; his words becoming more and more incoherent, until he realised that they were being wasted. He looked at King; and then at the machines and the tubes and the wires. "You bastard... you're going to pay, now," he cried out and reached towards one of the tubes.

He felt a hand on his arm. "Mike, don't! He's not worth it." Barton turned his head and saw Sally standing next to him. "Leave it, Mike," she pleaded.

"How long have you been there?" Barton demanded. "I told you to wait?"

"Long enough," she said, tugging at his arm. "Now let's go."

Barton shook free from her grip, and moved towards the cot again. "No Sal... I can't, I..."

This time he felt another hand on his arm; the stronger grip of a man's hand. Then two hands, one on either arm, holding him back. "I think you'd better do what the lady says, sir," said Kirwan. "I think that would be for the best."

Barton stood back and turned towards them, his anger abated. "I wouldn't have done it," he said quietly. "That would make me no better than them. But for a moment... I wanted to."

"It's alright, sir," said Kirwan. "You were never here. I've been sitting outside the door all the time." The young PC showed them to the door. He watched as they walked to the lift, then sat down and picked up his paper.

None of them could have known that the blood clot, formed earlier that day, had nearly reached Terry King's brain. Later, the doctor was to say that it could have happened at any time, and the post mortem would show that Terry King had died from a massive stroke.

When Kirwan filled out his report, that evening, he didn't see any the need to mention King's last visitors.

National Crime Squad, Hertfordshire Branch – 14:30 BST

The office had been a hive of activity since Jane and Lorna had returned from the golf club. Everyone was reading the notebooks; entering dates, times, names, places into the database, and cross checking everything against case notes and old files. This was the proof that Barton had needed; there was no doubt in anyone's mind. King's notes were meticulous and it was becoming clear that, in various ways, Naismith had controlled almost every one of his brother's activities. Lorna was reading one of the more recent entries when Barton and Sally returned. She put the notebook on the desk when she saw them and called them over. "It's all here," she said. "King's diaries... no wonder they were so keen to get them. Look this is the last page – *'4th May 2003. Lenny called – Herrera's on the take - police are on to him – Lenny wants him fixed. I'm giving it the personal touch - tonight – Don't know what to tell Debbie'.*

She gave the notebook to Barton. He studied it for a moment and nodded his head. He flicked through the pages and read a couple more notes at random.

'17th Jan 2002 – 100 kilos C, 50 kilos H – 15 girls - ex Frankfurt – arrived Southampton 5 pm. – Herrera and Milosevic offloaded at Dagenham – confirmed to Lenny.'

'11th March 2002 –confirmation from Lenny – cargo from Bilbao arriving Portsmouth – 8pm – Milosevic to handle 16F + 14M – for Leeds/Manchester.'

"There's a load more," said Lorna. "As far as we can make out he's written down everything he's ever done. If you look in the back of the book, there's like an account of some sort. "

Barton turned to the back pages. They were neatly divided into four columns: *'Date – Amount – Account – Total'*

The last entries read:

'1/5/03 – £2m – 2230561874 GIB- £56m'

'1/5/03 – £1m – 785460001 HK- £32m'

'1/5/03 – £2m – 001357840 GEN – £89m'

'1/5/03 – £1m – 019789023 SH – £73m'

"How far do they go back?" asked Barton.

"Since he was just a kid, the first one's 1944, so he'd have been about six years old. There's a whole pile still in the box, we're only looking at the ones for the last few years."

Barton took what looked like a child's school exercise book from the box, and looked at the front cover: *– Robert James King – Diary 1948 – Private –* he opened the book and leafed through, stopping to read a couple of the entries:

'August 26th 1948 – Lenny came to see me today. Gran let me wait on the corner for him. Lenny told me what he did in America with Henry. They was some bad things but he said it was good fun so it must be ok he said they do things like that all the time in America. He said the niggers are no good and Henry had to punish them. Lenny had some sweets from America. He said I could have some if I didn't tell anyone what he told me. We played football with Georgie and Warren and the others. Lenny got cross when I scored a goal past him and pushed me over. I hurt my knees but I didn't tell Gran. Lenny tore his new coat on the fence and he made me say that I did it and Aunty Mary was cross with me. Lenny says if I want to be friends I have to do as he says. But that's ok because I love him. I didn't want Lenny to go home but Gran said we can go and see him soon.'

'November 5th 1948 – Me and Gran went to see Lenny there was lots of fireworks and a big bonfire with a guy on top. I told Lenny a secret about when I

nicked some money from a shop it was clever Warren and Georgie got the man to chase them and I got the money from the box behind the counter £4. We did splits and I got £2 because it was my idea and its my gang Lenny had a better secret and I gave him five-bob to tell. He said niggers are bad because they have black blood and he made some boys at school push a nigger through a window to see the blood. Then he told me it was a joke because its red like us – don't know how? Then he pushed me over on the ground near the fire where it was hot and I was scared. He had a knife and he said he'd cut me if I told. But I wouldn't ever tell on Lenny he's my brother.'

Barton put the diary back into the box: *Truth and lies.* The truth lay somewhere between a small boy's jottings and an old man's reminiscences. He turned over several more books, until he found the one that he was looking for. He opened the diary and turned the pages:

'12th May 1983 – Lenny wants something big for the news. Wants somebody to take a shot at him – got to look real. Terry knows someone he can set up.

'19th May 2003 – Lenny wants Barton done. Teach them all a lesson. The boys are arranging it.

'24th May – Agreed with Lenny we're doing it at the big meeting tomorrow night. Terry has got Campbell ready - he won't talk to Old Bill – Baz has got his missus and kid locked up – gun can't be traced.'

'26th May 1983 - told Lenny I was sorry he shouldn't have got hurt, but he said it was OK. Terry and Baz in the clear – Marshall fixed things for £10k."

That was all. A man's death arranged and accounted for like a business transaction.

For the next hour, as everybody else busied themselves with the accounts of King's recent past, Barton read though the earlier diaries. Starting with the school exercise books he began to build a picture of the relationship between the two brothers; a relationship very different from the story that Naismith had related to him. The diaries told a story of two brothers who met often during their years living apart; of the younger brother who hero worshipped his sibling and looked forward to their every meeting. Bobby King accepted his elder brother's bullying, took the blame for him, and carried out petty crimes at his behest. As a teenager, the crimes had become more serious and the accounts more detailed; King and his friends had sometimes travelled by train to High Wycombe, where they burgled houses that had been selected by Naismith, who would take half the proceeds. Other crimes were more sinister. Barton read an account of a Jewish shopkeeper in the East End, beaten half to death by the gang as Naismith emptied the till, and another telling of how Naismith had watched as they beat up a black sailor and threw him in the dock to drown, and how good Bobby had felt later when his brother praised them for doing a good job. Dozens of other accounts told similar stories of beatings, rape, and murder; all instigated by Naismith, always the spectator never a participant. Attacks on men and women, young and old, all with one thing in common; they weren't English.

King had kept a record of every meeting, letter, and phone conversation, and, the diaries documented a regular contact between the two brothers until King's wedding in 1963. There was an account of a fight between the two brothers; the fight that Naismith had told him about. But this account told of King finding his new wife in a back room, her clothes dishevelled, fighting off his brother; and how his brother had taunted him with his boasts that he'd already had her, months before and that he could have anything that he wanted. It was the first time that Bobby King had fought back; and the last. The next reference to his brother was a week or so later; King had phoned to apologise.

Barton flipped through more diaries; over the next five years, there were many references to Naismith; but these were mainly notes referring to things that King had read in the papers about his brother's business successes, but other than occasional references to letters that Bobby had written there appeared to have been no contact between the two.

Barton sat and stared at the pile on his desk; an odd assortment of school exercise books, scruffy notebooks and hard cover desk diaries, that represented the early life of Robert James King. The story of a boy, orphaned at the age of nine; bullied, manipulated, twisted and controlled by the older brother whom he adored; growing up to become one of London's most vicious gangsters.

He was lost in his thoughts and didn't hear Sally as she came in. She picked up one of the diaries. "Any good?" she asked.

"Depends what you mean by good," replied Barton. "Nothing to help the case... but they explain a lot. What about the others?"

"October 1970, that's the first reference we've found to Naismith, since their big bust-up in '63. King wrote something about doing a job for Lenny... waste disposal he called it. An American called Ashley Tate... to show them that Lenny meant business. We're checking it out. After that there's a lot more. The bloke he went down for... that one was for Naismith. And then there's your dad... I'm sorry Mike."

"Don't be... we already knew didn't we?"

"There's a lot about business deals involving Naismith," said Sally. "Backs up the stuff Fisher gave us... you know it looks like they were laundering money through Naismith for years. And there's big gap when King was inside... didn't write a lot about business when he was in prison. But it's pretty clear… Naismith has been behind most of what King has had a hand in… for over thirty years."

"OK," said Barton. "Let's see if we can wrap it up tonight. I'll see the Chief Super in the morning and we can work out what else is needed."

Sally couldn't help noticing that Barton seemed very relaxed again. This was the second time in as many days, and it worried her. She couldn't forget the state he'd been in as she'd driven back from Reading. She'd really thought he was over the edge. He'd changed as soon as he'd started looking at the diaries, but she wondered for how long.

"You would have done it… wouldn't you… If we hadn't been there?"

"I don't know… neither do you. I didn't and that's all that counts," Barton replied coldly. "So let's not dwell on it. Shut the door on your way out, I've got some calls to make."

Barton was still in his office when the news about Terry King came through. For a moment he rejoiced, and tasted revenge. Then suddenly the guilt swept over him, stealing all the light from the room, smothering him as though a thick black hood had been placed over his head: *What have I done? This makes me no better than them.* He poured a drink and stared out of the window. As the waves of guilt and shame swept over him, he protested his innocence: *No I didn't touch him… I only talked to him… I didn't touch him.*

As he sat thinking about Terry King, another thought came into his mind: *What if…? No, he couldn't be…? Could he?* Barton rummaged through the pile of diaries, looking for 1962 and 1963. He leafed through the pages until he found the dates he was looking for: *Yes, maybe.*

Barton found Timms and showed him a diary entry. "Has anyone else mentioned this, Jarvis or Underwood maybe?"

"I don't remember anything, but I can check the interview records… see if Matt can remember. Why do you want to know… is it important?"

"Could be Paul," replied Barton. "And while you're at it could you get someone to fish out the transcript of my tapes from Spain, and Sally's meeting with Mary Naismith. Bring it all to my office."

Barton went outside to his car and found the carrier bag behind the passenger seat. When he got back to his office, the transcripts that he had asked for were on his desk. Brady had underlined something on one of the pages. He looked through the other pages, and found what he was looking for. Barton put the four accounts side by side on his desk; reading them again to make sure. It added up; it wasn't conclusive, but he'd charged people on less evidence. He picked up the carrier bag and took it into the squad room.

Jane Barclay was still at her desk. He put the bag down in front of her. "What's that, sir?" she asked.

"A jacket, can you get it over to the lab, straight away? It's got a bloodstain on the back, and…"

Jane listened carefully and wrote everything down. When Barton had finished giving his instructions, she read them back to him just to make sure, "…is that everything, sir?

"Yes. Just tell them it's urgent."

Jane nodded, picked up the bag, and walked towards the door: *When isn't it?*

Memphis, Tennessee – 20:00 Central Standard Time

Grace sat at a window table, listening to the drone of the endless stream of traffic on the interstate. As she waited for her order, she sipped her coffee and looked at the map that she had bought at the airport. She'd circled a small town about fifty miles southeast of the city. She'd arrived in Atlanta that morning with no idea how she was going to find the man; Mississippi was a big place. But she'd called Charlie Henderson and he'd come up trumps. He'd told her where the man lived, or at least where he had lived fifteen years ago. Charlie also said that he'd been born in Marshall County, so there was a good chance that he was still there. A few more calls gave her what she needed; he was a prominent citizen and many people knew him. The final call to the local sheriff's office gave her an address; Henry Patterson, Grand Wizard of the White Knights of the Cross, was living out his final years in a retirement home in Holly Springs.

The deputy had been very helpful and offered to give her directions if she came by sheriff's office, when she arrived in the small town. She'd also learned from him that the nearest airport was Memphis, and she'd managed to get a seat the next flight.

Grace looked at the route that she would take in the morning. It looked an easy run down Highway 78 and she could ask directions when she got there. She reckoned if she left early she could be there by ten; a couple of hours, no more, talking to him; she could be back at the airport by mid-afternoon and have dinner with Lizzie in the evening. It hadn't even occurred to her that he might not want to see her and she was starting to feel excited.

For a while, she had also felt a little scared – she already learned enough to know that Henry Patterson was not a particularly pleasant character – but as she ate her meal and started to run through all the questions, she wanted ask him that feeling passed. After all he was just a frail old man; over ninety years old: *How scary can that be?'*

387

Grace finished her meal and went back to her hotel room. The air conditioner was broken and she opened the window to let in some air. She was too excited to sleep and sat up in bed watching TV, not really knowing, or caring what the programme was, just needing something to distract her mind, to help her sleep. She always found that watching old movies in bed, in a darkened room, had soporific effect and after half an hour she started to feel very drowsy, and switched off the TV set. Away from the main highway, there was little traffic noise and she lay in bed listening to the sounds of the tug boats as they plied their way up and down the great river, until she drifted into a deep sleep; unaware of the messages that were waiting for her on the answering machine in Lizzie's Boston apartment.

Chapter 33

Thursday 22nd May

Chalfont St. Giles, Buckinghamshire – 08:15 BST

Peter Browning read the papers while his wife was making the coffee and toast. On Tuesday, Blanchard's had been on the front pages of every paper; yesterday the business pages were full of comment and analysis; but today it was already old news; and apart from the Times which carried a short piece speculating about the repercussions on City confidence, only the FT seemed interested. He muttered something under his breath and dropped the pink pages onto the heap on newsprint that littered the floor.

His wife put the coffee on the table. "What was that? Is there something else about Blanchard's in the papers?" she asked. Jean Browning just wanted to know what was going on. She didn't pretend to know anything about her husband's business affairs, particularly where her brother-in-law was concerned. All she knew was that her brother was in trouble and it obviously had something to do with Tony: *Why else would he have sent Peter scurrying back to England?*

"Nothing," snapped Browning. "Why can't you just shut up... and you'd better pray that your brother keeps his mouth shut too." He got up and stormed out of the room.

"Where are you going? What about your coffee?"

"Fuck the coffee. I've got things to do."

Jean put her head in her hands and cried as she listened to the front door slam shut. Then the car door slammed, the big V8 growled and she heard a shower of gravel peppering the windows, flung up by the back wheels as the Range Rover lurched forwards, and sped towards the road, leaving clouds of dust in its wake. Her world was falling apart and she didn't know why. Her brother was locked up in police cell somewhere, like a common criminal, and her husband hadn't spoken to her without swearing since they'd left Spain. She'd been to the cash machine yesterday and couldn't get any money from her account, or their joint account. She'd been to the bank to complain and they'd told her the accounts were suspended and taken her cards from her. And to cap it all, when she'd tried pay for the groceries at Waitrose, her credit cards had been refused. Just as she was thinking that it couldn't get any worse, she heard the cars on the drive.

She opened the front door without waiting for the bell to ring, and found herself facing a young woman, flanked by two uniformed policemen.

"Mrs Browning... Mrs Jean Browning."

"Yes, what do you want?"

"I'm Detective Sergeant McLean and this is my colleague Detective Inspector Timms," said Lorna glancing towards Timms who was standing a few feet away. "Is your husband at home?"

"No, you've just missed him. He left a few minutes ago. Why?" Jean said anxiously.

"Blue Range Rover?"

"Yes. But what do want with him?"

"My colleagues will discuss that with him, when they catch up with him," said Timms officiously. "Now in the meantime, we have a warrant to search these premises, and we'd also like to ask you some questions. Shall we go inside?"

Chalfont St. Peter, Buckinghamshire – 08:45 BST

"That's it... up there on the left." Connor said as he pointed ahead to a large sign – *Chalfont Classics – Fine Cars for the Connoisseur*

Barton turned into the forecourt and parked behind the Range Rover. The two men got out of the car and walked towards the showroom. "Nice cars," he said. "I bet that one's worth a few quid." Barton pointed towards a black Ferrari F40 in the window.

"Hundred and ninety-five grand... I'll have two," said Connor, looking at the price on the windscreen.

The showroom doors were locked, and Barton rang the bell. There was no answer so he tried again, and then rattled the door handles. He was about to tell Connor to try round the back, when a battered Toyota pick up pulled up.

A man in overalls got out and walked towards them. "We're closed mate," he said.

"Where's your boss?" demanded Barton.

"Not my boss anymore'" said the mechanic. "I mean we're closed for good. All that lot in there are sold. There's a couple of transporters coming to pick them up later, then I'm out of a job."

"But that's your boss's car. So he's here."

"I wouldn't know about that. If he's here, and not answering then he's busy. I'll tell him you called. But like I said... they're all sold."

Barton took out his warrant card. "I don't want to buy a car. I want to talk to your boss," he said angrily. "So stop pissing about and let us in."

The man shoved Barton in the chest and ran towards his truck. "Nothing to do with me, mate," he shouted. "There's a door round the side, it'll be easier to kick in than the big glass ones."

Connor started to run after the man, but Barton called him back. "Leave it Dave... let the uniforms pick him up."

As the pickup disappeared into the distance, two police cars arrived, and Connor ran up to the first one as it stopped on the forecourt, "Red Toyota Hilux... went that way," he said pointing down the road. The driver turned on the blue lights and the siren and the car sped off towards Denham. A minute later the two occupants of the second car had kicked open the door at the side of the showroom. Suddenly, Browning rushed down the stairs and pushed past them, but he got no further than the doorway. Barton's right foot connected with his shin, sending him sprawling headlong across the tarmac.

"Remember me?" asked Barton, looking down at Browning as he crawled onto his knees.

"Bastard!" snarled Browning, as he staggered onto his feet. "I might have guessed it would be you."

Barton cautioned him, then the two constables took over, and with his hands cuffed behind his back, Browning was bundled roughly into the back of the police car. Barton smiled; and satisfied for the time being, he got into the front passenger seat, leaving Connor to organise the search.

Westminster, London – 10:00 BST

"If you wait here gentlemen, I'll go and find his Lordship," said the usher. He disappeared through a door, leaving the two men sitting in the Central Lobby, the magnificent octagonal hall, at the heart of the great Victorian building that was seat of British government.

"How well do you know him?" Harris asked.

"I knew him fairly well when he was a minister. He was our local MP, but I've only met him a few times since he got his peerage," replied Miller.

"What are we doing here? Do you really think he's got anything to do with this?"

"Until last week, I'd have said no. But Barton's been right about everything else. And he is the chairman of Blanchard's."

"He's also a senior member of the House of Lords and a former Foreign Secretary. God help us if we've got this wrong," said Harris. He was a worried man and he was beginning to have his doubts. He'd spent most of the previous day briefing his boss and the suits from the Home Office. He had operational control and the decision was his; but it had been made abundantly clear to him that, if it went wrong, it was his neck on the block. Barton had kept his promise about making waves; he'd agreed to let Harris and Miller handle this one. He'd told them that he didn't want retribution, the public disgrace would be enough: '...*I want to know that anyone in a position of power, who has helped cover this up, can never do it again. Let them go quietly if that's what the politicians want... but see that they lose whatever power and privilege they have. Let's send out a message.*'

Gerald Browning, Lord Browning of Chiltern had already got the message. He'd had a very uncomfortable meeting with the leader of the party and had already been removed from his position of spokesman for foreign affairs in the Lords; and it would only be a matter of days before the party whip was removed. He was a career politician and this place, and what went on here, had been his life for over fifty years. And now, he was about to become a political outcast. Others had been sent into that wilderness, and had managed to come back – usually with obsequious displays of humility and declarations of remorse; pre-conditions for the prodigal's return, scripted by the party machine – but, he was an old man and he wouldn't have that opportunity.

His involvement with Blanchard's had been well publicised over the last few days, and although he was the non-executive chairman, with no day-to-day involvement in the affairs of the bank, there had been plenty of speculation about his role. The mud would stick. His reputation was in tatters, and as a major shareholder, he was facing huge financial losses. Now the police had come for him, and he wondered what else would come out. If they looked in the right places and asked the right questions, then he could go to prison and at eighty-one, that meant his life was over; nevertheless, he tried to put on a brave face, as he approached the two waiting policemen.

"Trevor, it's good to see you. I nearly didn't recognise you without your uniform," said Browning, trying to make light of the situation. "I appreciate this, you know... friendly face and all that. I've been dreading the thought of men in uniforms. You know... all rather embarrassing."

"Good morning, Lord Browning, let me introduce you to Assistant Chief Constable Harris. We'd like to ask you some questions," said Miller very formally, ignoring the peer's remark. The lack of uniforms was in deference to the place they were in; not to spare Browning from embarrassment. Although, even in plain clothes, it was fairly obvious who they were, and the trio were already attracting disapproving glances from the MPs, peers, and officials passing through the Central Lobby.

"I assume that you'd rather we went somewhere else, sir," said Harris. He didn't wait for a reply. "If you come this way, we've got a car waiting outside."

Browning bowed his head slightly as he followed them from the Lobby, through St Stephen's Hall and the public entrance, and outside into the Old Palace Yard. He looked across the yard, in the direction of the peers' entrance and wondered if he would ever cross that threshold again. He said nothing as he got into the back of the black Jaguar. What he didn't know yet was that the CPS had already decided, under pressure from above, that his prosecution over the Blanchard's affair wouldn't be in the public interest. Harris and Miller were only interested in confirming their suspicions and getting the names of others; there wouldn't be any charges, but he was going to sweat for while before he found out.

Amersham, Buckinghamshire – 10:30 BST

Peter Browning stirred the coffee again, watching the vortex swirl inside plastic cup. He'd been sitting in the room for over an hour staring at the walls and the ceiling, and the coffee was cold ages. The policeman hadn't spoken a word, and Browning found his presence disturbing. The man was standing by the door, but any minute he would walk across the room again and Browning would lose a little bit more of his nerve. "What's going on?" he demanded. "You can't keep me here like this. I want to call my solicitor."

PC Dean Johnson, leaned forward, clasped his fingers together, and pushed his arms out straight; the loud crack from his knuckles was his only reply to Browning's protests. He leaned back against the wall and he folded his arms again, but still he said nothing.

"Where's Barton? How long do I have to sit here? Why don't you say something?" Browning swore under his breath, "Fucking moron," and started to get up, sweeping the plastic cup across the table as he did so, sending the dark brown liquid cascading over the wall.

Johnson leaned forward and walked towards the table, "Sit down, sir," he said firmly; he now had his back to the window and his huge frame cast a shadow over half the room. "Let's not have any trouble now."

Barton had asked the desk sergeant for their biggest man and he'd smiled with approval when saw Johnson, the Thames Valley Police rugby team's star player. Now the big lock forward – six-foot seven, eighteen and a half stones and all muscle – towered above the short, chubby man in the crumpled suit.

Browning didn't need telling twice and returned to his chair, as Johnson leaned nonchalantly against the wall again, and stared at him unblinking. He started to whistle, following the orders that Barton had whispered before he left them alone: '*Don't take your eyes off him, don't say anything, just look menacing and wind him up a bit'.*

Browning might have been even more wound up, if he had known that his father was sitting in the back of a police car, travelling at speed in the fast lane of the M25, only a few miles away.

Harris was sitting in the front with the driver. Lord Browning sat in the back, sandwiched in between Miller and Sally Parkinson. None of them had spoken since they had left Westminster. As they turned off onto the slip road, Sally took out her mobile and called Barton. "We'll be there in about fifteen minutes, Mike... OK. I'll call again when we get there."

Barton entered the interview room with Dave Connor. The two men sat down at the table, facing Browning, and Connor set up the tape. "Interview with Peter Browning, at Amersham police station, the time is 11:27 a.m..."

"About bloody time," snapped Browning. "Now can I call my solicitor?"

"I'm afraid not... not for the moment. Now let's talk about Blanchard's," said Barton casually.

"Go to hell. I'm not saying anything till I've got my solicitor here."

"Fair enough, write down his number and I'll get the constable to call him," Barton passed a sheet of paper across the table. Browning scribbled down a name and number and pushed the sheet back across the table. Barton looked at the paper and handed it to the giant. "OK, so what shall we talk about while we wait?"

"How about cars?" Connor said, with a malevolent smile.

Barton leaned forward, "Yes that'll do. How's the classic car business these days Mr Browning? Must be doing very well, your man said that all the cars in the showroom were sold. Or are you closing down because business isn't that good... liquidating your assets, cutting your losses?"

"You tell me," said Browning. "You seem to know."

"No matter... What I'd really like to know is how much cash you can hide in a car. You know... the ones that you export. " Barton looked at Browning who glared back, but didn't reply.

"What do you think Sergeant?"

"I don't know, sir," replied Connor. "We haven't had time to take them apart yet."

Barton still had his eyes fixed on Browning, who was beginning to look very uncomfortable and grunted at Connor's last remark. "In case you're wondering. Your wife has been very helpful," said Barton. "She gave us the spare set of keys for the warehouse in High Wycombe. Now tell Mr Browning what you found there Sergeant?"

"Thirty-three cars so far… Ferraris, Aston Martins, Rollers, Bentleys and lots more… some of them were in containers ready for shipping. There were eighteen for Moscow… five for a dealer in Spain… Andalus Exoticar, according to the paperwork, and a dozen imports from Spain… same firm."

"Andalus Exoticar… I've heard of them," mused Barton. "That's your friend Brian Jackson's firm, isn't it?"

"So what? We're in the same business. All the paperwork's in order, it's perfectly legitimate."

"Oh! I'm sure it is Mr Browning. I'm sure it is… but then again…" Barton was interrupted as PC Johnson came back into the room.

"His solicitor's on the way, sir," he said. "And there's a phone call for you. DI Parkinson?"

"Thanks, I'll take it at the desk," Barton stood up and turned towards the door. "Sorry Peter, it looks like our little chat will have to wait," he said. "Sergeant, can you finish off and then get this officer to take Mr Browning to a cell."

"For the benefit of the tape, DCI Barton is leaving the room," said Connor. "Interview suspended at 11:43 a.m."

Barton met them at the front desk. "How's it going?" asked Miller.

"Slowly, very slowly, just like we planned… he's getting very rattled," replied Barton. He looked at Sally and smiled. "I can't wait to see his face in a minute. Come on, this way."

Barton led the way to the interview room, and his timing was perfect; when they were halfway down the corridor the interview room door opened and Johnson stepped out, followed by Browning and Connor. Suddenly father and son found themselves face to face. There followed, what Sally Parkinson would later describe as: *'An exquisite moment',* as the two men looked at each other; first in astonishment and then in disbelief.

The old man was the first to speak, "Peter, what on earth are you doing here?" he spluttered. His son had nothing to do with Blanchard's, and his initial surprise had changed to a deep sense of foreboding: *What else is this about?*

"Don't say anything, Dad. Michael's on his way over," said Peter Browning as he the giant led the way back to the cells.

Barton was pleased with himself; very pleased. The encounter had been planned and timed to perfection. Peter Browning would spend the next few hours stewing in the cells, waiting for his solicitor. Of course Barton knew that Michael Stevens wasn't going to show, but they'd let Browning in on that later. Meanwhile they were going to have words with his father, who was looking a very worried man.

"The Superintendent's letting us use his office," said Barton. "I'm sure Lord Browning will find it more comfortable than an interview room."

Barton led the small party upstairs, and after the formal introductions were over, they settled down around a small conference table. Harris sat in the leather swivel chair behind the desk. He was to take no part in the proceedings; his presence was merely to ensure that Barton didn't overstep the mark.

Barton knew where the mark was and, with the latitude he'd been given by Harris, there was little risk of going over it: 'Any questions you like, but no outright accusations, unless I give you the nod'. Barton smiled, it was time to play poker, and the deck was stacked in his favour.

"Thank you for coming to see us, sir. I'm sure that this isn't something that you are used to," Barton said politely, leading in gently. "We won't keep you any longer than necessary, but there are a few questions that I need to ask you."

"That's perfectly alright Chief Inspector," Lord Browning replied, looking more than a little relieved. "It's a most unfortunate business and you've got a job to do. I think you'll find that I've been negligent rather than culpable. Nevertheless as chairman of the bank, I have to accept some of the blame," he said; his faux deference the product of years at the Foreign Office.

"Thank you sir," said Barton: *He really doesn't have a clue. I wonder how long he's been kept out of the loop. Oh well! ...let's find out.* Barton leaned forward slightly, not so close as to be intimidating, but close enough to show he meant business. He looked Lord Browning in the eye, and dealt from the bottom of the pack. "Now I'd like you to tell me everything you know... about your son-in-law... Sir Anthony Naismith, and everything about your relationship with him."

"What the bloody hell are you playing at Harris!" Lord Browning shouted as he looked across the room, glaring at Harris. "You told me this was about Blanchard's." He looked plaintively at Miller, "Trevor..."

"I'm sorry, sir. But we didn't say anything of the sort," said Miller dismissively. "Of course... we need to talk about that as well. But if you'd answer Chief Inspector Barton's questions first, please."

Lord Browning fumed; he was feeling confused and angry now, wondering why nobody had warned him. More to the point, he was a very worried man; he could feel the beads of sweat running down his cheeks: *What do they know?*

"Why don't we start at the beginning," Barton continued, still looking directly at Lord Browning, observing every gesture, every change in expression. "I know it's a long time ago, but could you tell me how and when you first met Naismith."

The peer took a deep breath, and started to draw on the huge reserves of self-confidence, built up over a lifetime in politics. "And why is that relevant?" Lord Browning asked indignantly.

"Fair question," Barton replied, admiring the speed at which the old man had recovered his nerve, but not allowing it to divert him. "OK. We are investigating a number of serious offences... including fraud and money laundering, that involve Naismith, and we are questioning everyone who has had any business dealings with him. That includes both yourself and your son. Now I'll be obliged if you'll answer the question please, sir."

Lord Browning shrugged and bowed his head slightly to avoid Barton's eyes, as he gathered his thoughts and considered his response. It was a long time ago; maybe he could skate over it: *They wouldn't have been able to dig up anything that far back...would they?* He was a politician, a master of the craft, with years of practice at being economical with the truth. He didn't need to lie; just leave a few gaps. He raised his head and looked Barton in the eye. "Alright... but I'm not sure of all the details... it was nearly forty years ago."

"I appreciate that, sir, but if we could get on."

"In 1963, '64 maybe... I was guest of honour at a Chamber of Commerce dinner. I presented some awards... Tony got one for Young Businessman of the Year, or something like that. He wasn't even thirty and he'd already made his first million. We got talking and I told him that we needed people like him to join the party. To be perfectly honest, I didn't really like him that much. He was very arrogant, and there was something very cold, almost sinister about him... but I was fishing for a donation. Yes, it must have been sixty-four, there was an election coming up and we were behind in the polls. I think I got a couple of thousand out of him... a lot of money in those days."

"And he joined the party?" Barton knew the answer, but asked the question anyway, to keep the ball rolling.

"Yes. But, not straight away, he took a bit of persuading... he wasn't that interested in politics... much too busy making money. He joined mainly for the business contacts, rather than any political conviction. But I suppose if I'm honest, that's why a lot of people join." Lord Browning smiled; this wasn't as difficult as he'd expected.

"Business contacts... what sort of contacts?"

"Business contacts... you know... you scratch my back and all that. Bit like the Masons," Lord Browning shot a glance at Harris, "without the fancy dress. And he was a property developer, so it gave him an opportunity to meet a lot of local councillors."

"And he got favours like planning permissions, for his developments?"

"I didn't say that. It just helps to know people."

"And you? Did he scratch your back?"

"Oh! Come on Inspector, you're not that naïve... Yes, he used me, he'd have been a fool not to. I made introductions for him, helped him get his foot in the door. And, before you ask, I got something out of it... the odd board membership, non-executive of course, but some handsome retainers. That's how it works... businessmen need politicians and we need them. Everyone does it... look at Blair and his bloody lot. All that stuff about putting an end to sleaze, and look at them now. It's always the same game... the only things that ever change are the players."

"Is that how you became chairman of Blanchard's?" Barton asked. He looked towards Harris, who now raised an eyebrow.

"Not exactly, I worked for Blanchard's before I entered Parliament. They retained me as a consultant afterwards and I introduced a few clients to them. Of course I had to sever all financial ties when I was a minister... they offered me the chairmanship after I went to the Lords."

"And, did you introduce Naismith to Blanchard's?" Barton looked towards Harris again, this time the ACC shook his head and silently mouthed: *'Not yet'*.

"No, as a matter of fact... well at least not formally. He met Philip Johnston at Peter's wedding." Browning smiled, his answer was economical, borderline, but within the bounds of truth, as he defined them. It was going well, none of Barton's questions had needed an out-and-out lie: *So far so good.*

"On the subject of weddings, how did you feel about him marrying your daughter?"

"I don't really see what that's got to do with you. They got married, she was happy," again, there was indignation in the peer's voice, but some of the words left his lips, coated in doubt. He quickly recovered, hoping that none of them had noticed, "...so I was happy."

Barton had noticed, and sensed that his question had touched a nerve. Now he began to turn the screw. "But she was young... very young, sixteen years younger than him. You've already said that you didn't really like him, and you must have been aware by then that some of his business dealings were... shall we say... not entirely above board. He was already getting a bit of a reputation for walking a fine line with the authorities. And you... you were moving up in politics, needed to be careful about your friends. Business is one thing, but you can't have been comfortable about having him in the family."

"When you put it like that... then I suppose not. But what could I do? Helen wanted to marry him. And, as you say, she was very young, and she was blind to his faults... all she could see was a charming, successful man who gave her anything she asked for." Lord Browning's voice trembled slightly and he looked away towards Harris.

Barton also looked at Harris, and got the sign to carry on. "But, she was only eighteen, still a minor back then. You could have made things difficult. Why did you give your consent?"

"You don't know what he was like. He could manipulate her... he'd have turned her against us. And there would have been a scandal..."

"Scandal?"

Lord Browning shook his head, and his voice trembled. "I had my career to think of... Helen was pregnant, and he used it, taunted me with it: *'Do you want a bastard for a grandchild?'* that's what he said." Any thoughts that he may have had about bluffing his way through were gone from his head, and he wept as he remembered things long forgotten. "And he threatened to spread rumours... that she was promiscuous... that she didn't know the father. I couldn't let him do that."

Barton was stunned, he'd not been expecting this, and he looked towards Harris and shook his head.

"I think we should take a break now," said Harris, taking Barton's cue and rising from his chair. "There should be some lunch, outside. Sally could you get someone to bring it in. And see if you can rustle up some decent coffee." He walked over to the Superintendent's drinks cabinet. "Or perhaps you'd prefer something stronger, sir."

"Just one more question, sir... You said Helen was pregnant, but they don't have any children," Barton hesitated and looked straight at Lord Browning; he needed eye contact; the answer to his question would be in the old man's eyes. He spoke softly, measuring his words, "...what happened to her baby?"

Lord Browning stared back at Barton for a moment, then looked up and gazed at the ceiling. "She fell down some steps and miscarried about a month after the wedding," he gave a deep sigh. "She couldn't have children after that."

"I'm sorry, sir, I didn't mean to upset you," said Barton, genuinely concerned by what he had seen in the old man's eyes.

Lord Browning reached across the table and put his hand on Sally's, grasping it, seeking comfort. "It wasn't an accident... He pushed her," he said in a whisper.

Barton met Timms in the front office, and they found a quiet corner to talk. "Have you finished at the house?" asked Barton.

"About half an hour ago, we've just got back," said Timms. "We didn't find a lot, but there are some interesting family photos... Bobby and Terry King are in quite a few of them. And the IT guys have got his laptop and the computers from the showrooms. They're going through the hard drives."

"What about Mrs. Browning?"

"She's been quite helpful, but I really don't think she knows anything about her husbands business. Or, she's a very good actress. But I don't think so. She's in the interview room now with Lorna."

"OK, Paul, tell Lorna to start asking some more personal stuff. Like how well she gets on with Naismith... And how good... or rather how bad the Naismith's marriage is. Tell Lorna to take it easy... coax her along, but no pressure... Any news from the warehouse, yet?"

"Brady's over there with a crew from Customs. They're going to move the cars to the Customs warehouse and strip them down. It's a bit difficult to check the ones in the containers without taking them out, but the first two they looked at were on the stolen list. Some of the cars in the warehouse are imports, according to the paperwork. Customs did a quick check on the fuel tanks. They were all dry but none of them would take more than twenty litres. We've got that guy you met at the showroom here as well, Dave's interviewing him now."

"Right, I've got to get back to the old man. Give Browning another hour to kick his heels then have another go at him. He's asked for his brief. It's Stevens, so put him straight about that and then start piling on the pressure. In the meantime see what you can get out of that mechanic."

Barton returned to the Superintendent's office, questions turning over in his mind. He hadn't expected to score a direct hit so quickly. Now he needed to be careful; he wasn't sure how far Harris would allow him to push the old man. The remnants of lunch had been cleared from the table. Harris was still sitting behind the desk and Trevor Miller was sitting next to Lord Browning; Sally was missing, but he thought nothing of it; he assumed she'd gone to the ladies. Lord Browning poured himself a large brandy and they started again.

"I've been thinking Barton," Lord Browning said, looking and sounding quite relaxed. "And talking to Mr Harris, I don't think there'll be any charges. So I could walk out of here now."

Barton looked at Harris. What had he said? He couldn't believe that they were going to let it finish here, not when he was so close. But before he got a chance to say anything Lord Browning carried on speaking.

"But, what's the point. My career's over anyway... my connection with Blanchard's has seen to that. And you've made me remember thing's I'd chosen to forget. I don't have much left, but maybe I can keep some self-respect... so if you want to ask more questions go ahead. Ask me anything you like, I'll be honest with you. But I won't talk about my son or my daughter. And whatever I tell you, it stays within these walls... agreed?"

Barton thought for a moment. He already knew that nothing said today was going any further, and now he realised why Sally wasn't in the room. Once again, he looked at Harris, who nodded his head. Suddenly Barton was uncertain of how he should proceed. He wanted to get straight to the point, but he held back. He couldn't come straight out with that question… the reason they were here; not yet. "Tell me sir, what made Naismith go into politics? Did you encourage him?"

"No, definitely not," the old man replied very firmly. "In fact… if I could have, I'd have stopped him."

"Why was that?"

"Because I didn't trust him, I'd realised what kind of man he was. I could see his reasons were purely selfish and we didn't need people like that. Besides he didn't need my help, not at first."

"What do you mean?"

"He'd managed to establish himself in quite a strong position in his local constituency party. He traded on his connection with me, but he bided his time. He didn't show any interest in being nominated for anything. He'd say that his business interests kept him too busy. In the end, he gave in and agreed to stand for the local council. Of course, that's what he'd wanted all along, but he let them think he was doing them a favour. It was only later that he used me to advance himself."

"If you'll forgive me sir, you don't strike me as someone who would let himself be used," said Barton. "From what I've read about your career, I'd have thought that you've used a fair number of people in your time."

Lord Browning sighed. "I can't argue with that Barton, that's the nature of politics I'm afraid. It can be a dirty game… but there are limits… not for him though. I mean you don't use your own family in that way."

"In what way?" Barton asked; probing; sensing that he was getting nearer to the truth.

"He sucks you in, so skilfully that you don't realise until too late. And, then you can't get out. He took my son into business as a director of some of his companies. I was already involved with a couple of them, but I didn't know what was going on. Then he gradually lets you know how some of the deals are done, at first it seemed fairly minor things. Things that you could turn a blind eye to… favours called in… the odd bribe to oil the wheels… nobody's whiter than white. And I had my daughter to think of. But then… then you realise that all the little things suddenly add up to an awful lot… enough to wreck your reputation and then it gets worse. You begin find out that people have been hurt."

Lord Browning paused, picked up the brandy glass and drained it. "Anthony had some rather unsavoury friends… who helped him persuade people… if you get my drift."

"I'm sorry sir, but I need you to be a bit more…"

"Explicit!" cried Lord Browning. "OK if that's what you want. I don't suppose it makes any difference now. People who got in his way had accidents... I swear I don't know any details... he just hinted at it... just enough for me to know he wasn't playing games. But the more I knew... the longer it went on... the more I had to lose. I knew the people that he needed to get what he wanted... to get into the top echelons of the party. He wanted to be Prime Minister... can you imagine that? Trouble was he was a bloody good politician, and they liked him. Then he started on others, and it reaches a point where you're not turning a blind eye any more... you're part of it... they're part of it. He got himself into a position where he was a great asset to the party and at the same time a major liability. Too many people had too much to lose."

"But he resigned in the end. He told me it was to save the party from embarrassment."

"That was the only mistake he ever made. He wanted to be PM, he had it all mapped out... and he thought he was well on his way. He thought he was untouchable, he really believed that Margaret would make him Home Secretary. But she loathed him... his racist views were too extreme for her. The trial gave us the way out, and after we'd tipped of that journalist, we let the paper run the story... but only far enough to provide a reason for the resignation. It was a risk. If they'd dug further there'd have been too much fallout, although nobody knew how much. He let you know there were others in his pocket, but you never really knew who... I had a good idea, but it's not the sort of thing you compare notes about.

But there were plenty of other who weren't, and in the end, they're the ones who stopped him. Right up to the last minute he really believed he could pull it off... the arrogance of the man... he really thought of it as no more than a minor set back. They had to tell him there was no way he could survive and, when he wouldn't listen, Margaret called him to her office and gave him an ultimatum. She was fireproof, we were heading for another big majority, and she wasn't afraid of losing a few votes. Either he went quietly or she'd let things run their course. He'd never be in her government again, so resign, or take the consequences. She told him straight that she could afford to lose people and it didn't matter who else he took to prison with him."

"You mean she'd have been happy to see him prosecuted."

"Well I wouldn't put it quite like that, not exactly happy, but she made it clear to him that she was quite prepared to let the police have full access to the Whip's office. As I told you before politics is a dirty game and the Whips play dirtier than anyone."

"Names... who were these others?" Barton asked the question; although he already knew the answer.

"I'm sorry… that's not part of the deal. Nothing goes beyond the four of us, so there's no point. Isn't that right Mr Harris?"

"That's right, sir," said Harris. "As you say, politics is a dirty game, and we have to pay regard to the public interest." Then looked at Barton, and mouthed: '*Go on.*'

"You already knew that Naismith's brother was Bobby King… before the story came out… didn't you?"

"Of course… although I can assure you that he never told me. But the Whips knew and I dare say Special Branch and MI5 too. Margaret knew and that's another reason he was never going to be Home Secretary… if she'd known earlier he'd never have been a minister. Are we finished now?"

Barton looked at Harris again. The ACC nodded, and then he smiled. Barton was going for gold. "Not quite, sir, there's just one more thing I want to know. Let me take you back to 1983. The general election, the landslide… that was when they first tried to get rid of him wasn't it? Putting him up in one of your most difficult constituencies… bit of risk though… you all expected him to lose, but if he won he'd be the darling of the party."

"You're very perceptive Barton… ever thought of going into politics? It was worth a try… and he was arrogant enough to think he would win."

"But he was losing… nine points behind in the polls… took something pretty special not just to win… but win with a big majority… wouldn't you say? Like riding in on a wave of public sympathy… the voters don't like it when someone actually takes a pot shot at a politician… much as they say they'd like to have a go themselves… he played on that, milked it for all it was worth."

"I told you that's the sort of man he was… the way he behaved was typical… But what has this got to do with me?"

"Oh! I think you know," said Barton calmly. He couldn't believe that he was pulling this off. Inside he was a bag of nerves; his heart was thumping; his blood boiling. Under the table, he was clenching his fist so tightly that his fingernails had drawn blood. "Didn't you ever wonder why?"

"What?"

"Why? If he was losing… why did that anti racist group want to kill him? Wouldn't their purpose have been better served by his humiliating defeat?"

"These people don't think like that… that's a rational point of view. People like that don't think that way… they want to make a grand gesture… they want to shock people… they're terrorists… and they think the normal rules don't apply to them. We have to fight against people like that all the time… it's a constant battle for democracy."

"Bullshit!" barked Barton. "Listen to yourself. You need people like that. If it wasn't for them you bloody politicians would have to face up to real issues. The IRA, the miners, Greenham Common... they gave you an excuse... an excuse for not doing anything about two million unemployed, poverty, street crime, drug addiction, the homeless... things that need real solutions." His fist was still clenched beneath the table; he brought it up and hit the table, leaving a smear of blood on the polished surface. Barton couldn't keep it in any longer. "Now tell me. When did you know!" he exploded. "When did you find out? Or were you part of it? James Barton... the policeman who was killed as part of Naismith's fucking game... he was my father! So, when did you know!" He slumped back in his chair, exhausted, waiting for a reply.

There was total silence and Lord Browning just sat there trembling. He'd been prepared for anything, but not this. Everything else he could live with; all part of the dirty game he'd played his whole life. For nearly twenty years, it had haunted him; the secret that Naismith had shared with him, and then used against him every time he'd wavered. He hung his head, too ashamed to look up. Finally, after what seemed like an age he muttered. "Yes, I knew."

As Barton sat and watched, he regained control. His eyes stared at the man on the opposite side of the table and spoke quite calmly. "I'm sorry, sir. I didn't hear that... could you speak up please."

Slowly, Browning raised his head and his voice, "Yes, I knew... but you must believe me, I swear on my daughter's life that I didn't know until later, after the election. When he told me, I couldn't believe that even he would go that far... and I knew that I couldn't do a thing. He knew that by telling me he had trapped me absolutely and irrevocably. If I said anything, my career would be over by association... and if I said nothing he could make me do anything he wanted."

"Who else knows?"

"I don't know... I didn't tell anyone else and I don't think he did. He didn't need to with the Foreign Secretary in his pocket."

"Yes, I can see that," said Barton. He stood up as if to leave, then he stopped and looked at Lord Browning again. The old man started to get to his feet. He was a broken man but at least he could walk out of the room and go home now. Or at least that was what he was expecting, before Barton spoke to him for the last time. "Gerald Browning, I am arresting you as an accessory after the fact to the murder of James Barton and for conspiring to pervert the course of justice. You do not have to say anything, but..."

"But, you agreed. You can't do this!" Lord Browning protested, looking in vain at Harris and Miller for support.

Barton ignored the man's protests and continued with the caution, "but it may harm you defence if you fail to mention when questioned something, which you later rely on in court. Anything you do say may be used in evidence. Now if you will accompany these officers to the interview room they have some further questions to ask."

Barton walked to the door and opened it. "Details of every dirty business deal. Names of everyone who has ever covered for him... it ends here... understand?" He waited until Lord Browning nodded his head and then closed the door behind him and went to look for Sally.

Holly Springs, Mississippi – 13:00 Central Standard Time

Grace was still trembling as she drove the rental Chevrolet towards the state highway: *He was a frail old man, over ninety years old. How scary could that be?'* Now she knew; Henry Patterson was probably the scariest man she had ever met, and she'd met her fair share of scary people in her job. – Psychopaths, murderers, rapists, sadists, everything in the book – but nothing could have prepared her for a meeting with pure evil. She didn't believe in God; but now she believed in the devil. She'd just spent two hours talking to him.

He'd looked exactly as she had imagined; white hair, a neat white goatee beard, wire-rimmed glasses, crumpled linen suit and a silver topped cane. Just like the old southern gentlemen she'd seen so often on the screen. She'd told him that she was writing a book about Naismith, which was true. He was wary of her, so she told him that she had heard that he had been a great influence on the politician, which was true. When she lied and told him how much she had always admired Naismith's views, he'd smiled at her and told her to pull up a chair.

Henry Patterson was a frail old man in a wheelchair, who barely had the strength to lift his water glass to his lips. But what had come from those shrivelled lips was filth and abuse; the hate with which he spoke was all-consuming. With every word, he had seemed to get stronger, and Grace had felt a little piece of her soul die away.

She pressed the accelerator to the floor: fifty, sixty, seventy miles an hour; breaking the limit, but she didn't care. With every mile she travelled, away from that place, away from him, the air seemed to be cleaner and easier to breathe. She turned on the radio, and listened to the music. It was a country station but it didn't matter. She didn't know the words but she sang along anyway. She just needed to get him out of her head.

Now she understood.

Chapter 34

Friday 23rd May

Amersham, Buckinghamshire – 08:00 BST

It had been a long day and Barton had spent the night at Miller's house again. It had been a restless night. He'd been thinking about Grace and a man he'd never meet. She'd phoned from Boston at about two and they'd spent over an hour talking. He couldn't believe what she'd done and at first he got angry. But then he'd realised what she was saying and all he wanted to do was reach out and hold her: *'I'm going to write that book, Mike. People have got to know. I've started already. I'll send you something with an email'.*

What she told him turned his stomach and he remembered Mary Naismith's words on Sally's tape: *'...that vile American poisoned his mind'.*

All Grace wanted to do was get home as fast as she could; she was catching the first British Airways flight out and he'd arranged to meet her at Heathrow in the evening. He'd told her that they wouldn't have much time; he was flying to Spain on Saturday: *'It'll all be over soon. I promise'.*

National Crime Squad, Hertfordshire Branch – 09:45 BST

Barton had stopped at a sandwich trailer on the way to the office and they were all in the briefing room when he arrived. Everyone stopped talking and began to clap as he walked through the door. He looked around the room. They were all there apart from Brenda. She was still babysitting Debbie King. He looked at their faces and felt proud. What a team. They'd done the job and done it well. It hadn't been easy for some of them, but they'd all seen it through. He looked at the walls and the display boards; charts, photos, maps, the notes written in multi-coloured marker pens, the memos and print outs pinned everywhere. The largest whiteboard was blank, waiting to be filled. They had all the pieces and today they just had to fit it all together. They didn't need to really, not today anyway. But they all deserved to see the big picture and that was what the big board was for. He felt a bit like a general rallying his troops before the final battle, and he knew that for him it would be the final battle, the last time that he'd lead them.

He put the carrier bags on the table. "I got some bacon rolls… hope there's enough to round. Dig in," he said. "Then we'll get started. Who's going first?"

As the day progressed, the board gradually filled, as they each added to the picture. The mood was relaxed and lighthearted. There was laughter and even though the subject was deadly serious they were having fun. There were cheers as every arrest was ticked off, boos when Timms became too pompous, and a few tears when Sally told them about Mary Naismith. Some of them were shocked at what they learned; some of them started to feel sympathy for Debbie King; even for Bobby King when Barton read out extracts from his diaries. The more they heard the more they understood, although it was difficult for some of them to grasp the sheer scale of it all. Barton didn't tell them about Henry Patterson; he didn't want anyone to have any reason to sympathise with Naismith. But when at the end of the day, he told them of the reason for his erratic behaviour and his personal interest there wasn't a person in the room who didn't feel for him. And when he asked for volunteers to help make the last arrests every hand in the room shot up.

At four o'clock the team that was going to Spain was asked to meet on Saturday afternoon; everyone else was told to go home and not come back until Monday… or Tuesday if they felt like it.

Barton sat alone in the room, looking at the big whiteboard. There weren't any gaps left. A few weeks ago he said that he was going to *'Follow the money'* but he hadn't. But they'd followed a man instead, and in a turn of events that none could have expected King had led them to Naismith and the money. When it came down to it the Puppet Master had been beaten by his own ego; his complete disregard for anyone but himself; his contempt for anyone he saw as an inferior and his arrogant belief that he was beyond reach. In the end he was fallible, like all men and in his attempt to cover his tracks, he'd given them leads that would have taken them months to find; if ever.

Would Bobby King or any of the others have given him up? Barton didn't think so. But Naismith had panicked over Milosevic and that had set off a chain of events that even he couldn't control. Warren Jarvis had been ordered to take him out; and later Herrera. Although Naismith hadn't been able to give the orders without the agreement of a Columbian drug baron and the Russian Mafia; contacts he'd made through Gerald Browning, the former Foreign Secretary.

Browning had met Diego Marquez in the eighties, when he'd visited Colombia with a trade delegation. Like most of the Colombian drug cartel, Marquez also had many legitimate business interests and his first contact with Naismith had been as an investor in a property deal. The link with Sergei

Goranovic went back even further. He'd been a KGB general and Browning had first met him when he was a foreign office minister in Edward Heath's government at the height of the cold war. It wasn't unusual for politicians and civil servants at that time to be on friendly terms with their counterparts on the other side; as Lord Browning had told Harris and Miller the previous evening: *'Sometimes when you sup with Devil you need to take a long spoon...but when needs must, you have to share the same cup'*. Thirty years on Browning and Goranovic were still good friends, although Browning had seemed genuinely shocked to learn of the former KGB man's mafia connections.

Had Herrera really been skimming off the top? Or did Naismith merely use that as a way to get to his brother? Had he lied to Marquez to get the killing sanctioned? It didn't matter now; the result was the same. He'd been there when Debbie King had been told about Naismith; how he'd been behind Bobby's death, and Herrera's close shave. He wondered how Juanita would react when she learned that her brother's murder had been agreed to by her husband's father; her uncle. And she would find out; he'd make sure of that.

Had Naismith killed his brother because he'd let him down or did he fear that his brother would give him away? Could he have possibly imagined what it would lead to? King had pointed Barton in Naismith's direction and reawakened the ghosts of the past. And Barton would never let go. But even if Barton hadn't been involved they'd have found King's diaries; eventually. Jarvis would have given them up to save his own skin. He hadn't known that the plan to kill Herrera was a cover for the murder of his best friend. King had arranged the car switch himself, and only Naismith had known the whole plan.

Herrera had led them to the bank and the money. And he still had more to tell them. Once he knew that his sister was safe, he'd give them Marquez's European network.

The Russians and the Colombians might have salvaged something, if Naismith hadn't sent Browning back. The cars belonged to them. In some they'd found cash hidden in the false petrol tanks, in the tyres, and behind the interior trim; twelve million wasn't a lot to them, but it would still hurt; particularly now that they couldn't get at their share of at least twenty times that amount, now locked up in frozen bank accounts around the world. Other cars had the same compartments filled with cocaine and heroin; over three hundred kilos in total. Browning's records showed regular two-way traffic of up to a dozen cars a month in each direction. The quantity was staggering, and news travels fast; prices on the street were already rising fast.

Barton looked at the timeline that they'd drawn along the bottom of the board. Johnston the banker had told them everything; Naismith and King had been laundering money through Blanchard's for over thirty years. The Financial

Crime team had their work cut out. Naismith and King weren't the bank's only dubious clients; several more, suspicious accounts had already been uncovered, and it would take months to investigate all the accounts and identify all of the dirty money that had passed through the bank over the years. Several other NCS investigations had been stepped up a gear on the evidence in the bank's computers, and information was being passed on a daily basis to half a dozen police departments across Europe and the FBI. People who'd never heard of Naismith were going to curse his name.

Barton's thoughts turned towards the innocent people caught up in Naismith's web; mostly women, but wasn't that always the case.

Jean Browning had told Lorna about the Naismith's sham of a marriage. He'd never loved Helen, and whatever she felt for him had quickly turned to fear and loathing after her 'accident'. There was no point speculating as to why she hadn't left him. Grace would probably find a hundred reasons, but they'd all come down to the same thing; Naismith was not a man to who you could say no to; not without paying the price. And so she just closed her eyes and she didn't ask where the money came from. She'd just spent it, lots of it; in compensation for a ruined life. Jean Browning was still so in love with her husband that she refused to believe that he could possibly be involved. Although she too, hadn't asked were all the money came from: *Would things have been different if they had asked?* Barton guessed that it wouldn't have achieved anything, other than to cause them both a lot of pain, and they'd have plenty of that to go though now.

His mother Julia and Nina Campbell, who from a shared tragedy, would now find a common bond of sisterhood.

And Mary Naismith, she had carried that terrible secret for so many years, sharing it only with her son. The son, who on learning her darkest secret, had deserted her and vented his anger by raping his brother's girlfriend; something hinted at in King's diary and confirmed by Underwood: *'He never went against him...he even forgave him after he found out that he raped Carol'.* The son, who had cursed his father, but put the lessons learned from him into practice, as he abused and terrorised his own wife, taking away her unborn grandchild. The son, who had abused her trust with his lies and deceit and in return for her unconditional love, had broken her heart.

She was as much a victim as those who suffered to line Naismith's pockets. The girls, taken from their homes and families, promised a better life only to be forced to satisfy the men who visited the cheap houses and squalid flats, where they lived in fear for themselves and their families. The slave workers, labouring for fifteen hours a day to send a few pounds home to feed their families and living in fear of the gang masters, who sold them to anyone who needed cheap labour and didn't ask questions. The thousands of addicts, whose descent into self abuse was encouraged by ruthless criminals who went unpunished, while the full force of the law hounded them and locked them away for the petty offences they committed to feed their habits.

He felt sorry for, and could possibly forgive, Debbie King. Although she knew little about her father's business, she was guilty by association and had been happy to take his money. But, the arrogant, foul-mouthed gangster's daughter he'd first encountered at the hospital had gone and Barton believed that she was genuinely sorry. He was surprised at how he felt a real affection for her, and he knew that she'd had the same effect on Sally and Brenda. She really cared for Herrera, although he suspected that Herrera was more interested in saving his own skin, and would let her go sooner or later. The two of them had taken a big risk. They'd go free, but they'd spend the rest of their lives hiding. They couldn't be protected forever and they knew it. One day there'd be a knock on the door, or a car accident and they'd disappear. So would Juanita. None of them had a lot to look forward to.

Then there were the others, men who he held them in contempt and would never forget.

How does a man get over betrayal by his best friend? Andy Marshall would leave a wound that would never heal. It would be difficult to trust anyone that way again.

But his sins were insignificant compared to those of his father. Ex-Commander Colin Marshall had also been a friend. He'd also been a friend and colleague of the other man he'd betrayed – DI Colin Marshall had *'lost'* a dozen witness statements, and signed the bogus receipt for the video tape. – And he'd sold out to Naismith long before they asked him to cover up the conspiracy

Gerald Browning, and the other names on his list; how could there ever be a proper rule of law while the lawmakers played their dirty game? How could Barton and thousands of other honest coppers ever be really trusted by the public, when there were men like the Marshall in their ranks and politicians like Browning making the rules?

And as for Naismith. Contempt, hatred, loathing, all came to mind, but no words could sufficiently describe what Barton felt.

He unfolded some sheets of paper; the email Grace had sent from Boston; he'd printed it out during a break earlier in the day. She'd written the first pages of her book and had attached it for him to read.

The Puppet Master
A study of power and control

Dr. Grace Barton BSc, MSc, PhD, AFBPsS
Consultant Forensic Psychologist
Addenbrooke's Hospital Cambridge

Introduction

I don't believe in God, but I have met the Devil. He inhabits the body of an old man who lives in a small town in Mississippi.

I knew he was Devil, because when he spoke the sounds that came from his lips were pure evil. When he looked into my eyes, it felt as if he was sucking out my soul. And when I looked back into his eyes, I saw nothing but a dark black empty void.

I can think of no other explanation; no human being I have ever met has terrified me in the way that this man did. It wasn't just his words, there was nothing that I'd not heard or read before; it was the way that he spoke. It seemed as though every syllable had been coated in vitriol before it left his tongue. Every sound he uttered chilled my blood and I truly felt in fear of my life. And as he spoke; with every word, he seemed to grow stronger; as hatred surged through the arteries and veins of his decaying body, rejuvenating his thin, twisted limbs and nourishing his perverted mind.

He spoke of things that are unspeakable, with pride and excitement. He revelled in his tales of pain and suffering, and showed no hint of remorse, or regret for the abominations he had perpetrated. And he lauded his fellow conspirators as heroes of his evil cause.

He spat expletives, as a snake spits venom – nigger, kyke, wop, queer, cat-licker – although he didn't use these words as insults, for he truly believed that it was not possible to insult those to whom the labels might be attached. He used the words like weapons, cutting deep and wounding as painfully as the sharpest blade. Weapons, crafted and honed to cut into the heart and tear out the soul. Weapons, aimed not only at the wretched victims of his hatred, but at anyone with the slightest essence of humanity. Weapons, used to poison innocent minds, and incite the evil in men.

His creed was simple; anyone not like him could be abused for his pleasure. And for those of a different colour he reserved the worst of his excesses, which he justified as: *'teaching them their place' – The black bitch*, taken into his bed to keep out the chill of the cold night; beaten to death as a lesson to others when she failed to satisfy his lust. *The nigger runt*, pulled from his mother's breast; thrown to his dogs, because he had dared to cry and disturbed the monster's drunken sleep – I could go on, as he did, but the point has been made.

And yet, it wasn't his description of these acts that convinced me. It was that he believed it his sacred duty to educate his own kind. His pupils learned from a syllabus of evil and hatred from the day that they were old enough to listen. And as they grew older they were allowed to watch, and were later initiated into the craft; and to him it was a craft, to be learned, remembered and practised; with relish and without mercy.

I had gone there to talk to him about another man; but I learned about a boy. A young English boy; already damaged by the war and an abusive father; a boy who became his pupil. It took him only a short time, to tell me of the boy's lessons, but the images he left me with may haunt me forever.

– a boy of fourteen, feeding pigs with the genitals of a man who was still writhing in agony a few feet away; while his teacher stood and watched with the bloody knife still in his hand

– the same boy, a year later, watching a man dig his own grave with his bare hands, crawling on his knees; knees shattered by bullets from the gun that the boy held in his hand

– the boy, becoming a man; his 'rite of passage' on his sixteenth birthday, *'a little nigger bitch'* his to rape and abuse, while the men looked on and cheered.

– A year later, he *'graduated'*. He helped as they chained a man to a tree, clamping the manacles around his wrists – the unfortunate man was from another, more liberal state; he was just passing through; his crime, to have taken a white woman for his wife – and he joined in as they raped *'the nigger loving whore'*, taking his turn to hold up the man's head, forcing him to watch. And, when they were done, the teacher placed something in each of the young man's hands and told him to release the man from his chains. The young man hacked off the man's hands with the axe. It was his choice not to use the key.

The man in whose body the Devil lives is ninety-one years old; his memories are rooted in a time of turmoil, over half a century ago; a time that many would rather forget and speak of with shame. But he spoke as if it were yesterday; savouring every graphic detail.

This man calls himself a God fearing man, but he worships no God that I could honour. He calls himself a good Christian, yet he has murdered fellow Christians at worship; burned their churches and set up blazing crosses in the ashes. On the lapel of his crumpled linen jacket he wears with pride a small enamel pin, bearing the emblem of the Ku-Klux Klan. He was Grand Wizard of the White Knights of the Cross; and is still revered and respected by many in his community.

Yes, I have met the Devil. His name is Henry Patterson; he lives in Holly Springs, Marshall County, Mississippi, USA.

Barton folded away the paper and wiped his eyes. A violent coward of a father had deserted him as a child, and a sadistic racist had taken him under his wing, but whatever the influence in Naismith's past, it couldn't excuse what he'd done; the man had made his own choices. Barton got up and walked over to the board. He picked up a black marker pen and with a few very slow, deliberate stokes obliterated Naismith's photograph.

He looked back as he got to the door. "You're nothing any more. You're a dead man," he said as he closed the door and went to meet his wife.

Chapter 35

Saturday 24th May

Duxford, Cambridgeshire – 08:30 BST

Barton woke in his own bed for the first time in over a week. Or at least he was on the bed, fully clothed. Grace was asleep beside him; she still had her shoes on.

It had been nearly midnight when they got home, and Grace was exhausted. She'd not slept properly for two nights. She had tried to sleep on the plane, but kept waking. Every time she closed her eyes, she saw the Devil and the ghosts. Ghosts of men, women, and children; abused, beaten, raped, and murdered because of their colour. She had hardly spoken in the car and the little that she had said made no sense.

Barton remembered lying next to her as she repeated: *'I feel safe now…I feel safe now',* before drifting off to sleep. Throughout the night she'd tossed and turned in her sleep; crying out as the Devil and the ghosts returned. He looked at her now and she seemed peaceful. He knelt beside the bed and undid her shoes. Then he gently took off her jeans and folded them over the back of a chair. She half woke as he pulled the duvet over her and kissed her forehead.

There was so much that they needed to talk about; but it had to wait. Barton needed to be somewhere else and he knew she'd understand.

He packed a bag, then went downstairs to the kitchen and made coffee. He looked for a cigarette, but couldn't find any. He couldn't remember when he'd last had one. He must have given up, but he couldn't remember. He called Grace's parents and asked them to come over. He couldn't just leave her. Not after what she'd told him.

He made another coffee and put some bread in the toaster. He was just finishing the second slice when the bell rang. "Kate! That was quick," he said as he opened the door.

"What do you mean Michael, it's nearly an hour since you called," said Kate Faulkner as they walked into the kitchen. Barton looked at his watch and picked up the cold coffee; he couldn't remember where the time had gone.

He quickly explained the situation to Kate and then ran upstairs to see Grace. She stirred and opened her eyes as he opened the door. "Is that you Mike? What time is it?" she said sleepily.

"About ten. Look, I know it's not good, but I've got to go. Remember I told you on the phone. I have to go back to Spain."

"But I need to talk to you," she said plaintively. "It's important."

"I'll be back tomorrow night. Then it will be over. I'm going to take some time off... then we can talk," he said. "I'm sorry, but I have to go." He looked at her and almost changed his mind; she looked so vulnerable and he knew that he never wanted to leave her again. The moment passed and he grabbed his bag and passport. He bent down and kissed her and she hugged him; like a frightened child.

"Don't go," she pleaded.

"I have to," he said and he kissed the teardrop on her cheek. "It'll be OK. Go back to sleep. Your Mum's downstairs, she's going to stay till I get back."

National Crime Squad,
Eastern OCU – Hertfordshire Branch – 11:00 BST

The team were assembled; bags packed and ready to go. Barton looked around the room and wondered if it was fair on them, not to tell them now, but the he'd made the decision and he wasn't going to take the risk of being talked out of it. They'd know soon enough.

"All the usual suspects then," he said with a smile. "Hi, Brenda, sorry you missed the briefing yesterday, but I'm sure someone will fill you in on the plane." "Right, let's make this quick. We can go over it again tonight."

Sally confirmed that the liaison officers, sent out the week before, would meet them at the hotel. "The local police are watching all four men. They're under virtual house arrest," she said. "They must know that we're coming for them. They just don't know when."

"Well they'll find out soon enough," said Connor. "Who have I got?"

"It's not as simple as that, Dave," replied Barton. "We haven't got them, yet. And we won't... not unless they agree to come back."

"I'm sorry, sir I don't quite follow," said Matt Brady. "I thought we were going to bring them back."

"We don't have any jurisdiction over there... remember that... we have to let the local police take the lead. You work through our liaison team... they know the ropes, you don't. If they don't agree to come with us, some of you could be there for a few of days while the Spanish authorities deal with the extradition requests. If they do come back it's to help with our enquiries, so they are free to change their minds at any time until the plane takes off and you can't arrest them until we're back on the ground at Stansted. This has to be by the book, I don't want any sharp lawyers, getting anyone off on a technicality."

"Got all that, so who's going after who?" asked Connor impatiently.

"That's not been decided yet," replied Barton. "I still need to agree some details with the Chief Super... Oh! And Dave, he's coming with us... so I think you ought to change that shirt, before he sees it."

"What's wrong with it?" asked Connor, looking down at his Day-Glo pink, flowery beach shirt.

"It's bloody awful... you could scare kids wearing that. Or blind them." said Brady, putting on his sunglasses to emphasise the point.

Barton let the laughter subside. "Right, follow me," he said and picked up his bag and led the way to the waiting mini-bus.

"It's just like a school trip," giggled Jane as they boarded the bus.

Connor joined in, "Please, miss, can I sit next to the driver?" he joked in a boyish voice. He was looking at Sally, who was trying to keep a straight face.

"Button it, Dave," said Barton gruffly, not in the mood for joking.

Sally pulled his sleeve, "Lighten up, Mike," she said. "Give them a break. They deserve it."

So did Barton, but he couldn't relax; not yet. He sat alone, at the back of the bus, in a double seat; next to the window. He put his hand over the second seat and shook his head when Sally tried to sit beside him. She took the aisle seat opposite him and watched him for the whole forty-five minutes of the journey. She could see that something was troubling him and wondered what was going on in his head. At the airport, she waited until he'd checked in and then asked the girl at the desk for the adjacent seat. She wasn't going to let him brush her off that easily. But he managed; it was a budget airline without seat allocations.

Barton and Connor killed time by browsing the shelves in the bookshop. Barton stood in front of the best-sellers' display, picking up paperbacks at random, looking at the back covers – he wasn't really interested in buying anything, most seemed to be crime fiction and he'd had enough of the real thing – and then putting them back on the wrong piles, upside down; just for the hell of it.

He joined Connor, who was at the till paying for a magazine.

"Fancy a quick pint, Dave?"

"You buying?"

Barton looked at his glass, it was half-full, but he'd had enough. Connor could manage two pints of Guinness before flying, but it was too much for him. Their flight had already been called and he still hadn't got round to asking his question.

"You not finishing that, Mike?" asked Connor, who was also looking at Barton's glass.

Barton nodded and Connor poured the contents into his own glass. "Crime to waste it..." He drained the glass and set it down, as the last call for the flight was announced over the loudspeakers. "Come on, Mike, we'd better make a move." He started to stand, but Barton's hand was on his arm, holding him back.

"One minute, Dave. There's something I want to ask you."

"OK, but we haven't got long."

"Your dad... and my dad... you know..."

"Sure. They're both dead... and you're going to say that we're doing this because..."

"No! I don't mean... I mean... if you could get your hands on him... get the man who did it. What would you do?"

Connor shrugged his shoulders. "It's history, Mike. Let it go."

"No! Tell me."

It was a question that Connor had asked himself a long time ago, but now it didn't seem important. "Nothing! It's too late. It was different then, there was a war on... people might have called it 'the Troubles', but from where I was, I could see the army on the streets, and people on both sides getting killed... I'd call that a war, and people die in wars. But it's over now. Nobody won and everybody won. Times have changed, Mike. Now it's down to the politicians."

And that was the difference between them; Barton's war wasn't over. "But... when you were there... while it was going on... If you'd caught up with him then, while you were in the RUC?"

"Oh! That's different question, Mike. It's still too late to worry over it. But, then... then, if I'd had the chance, I'd have shot the bastard."

Marbella, Costa del Sol – 19:30 pm CET

They had been had booked into the Don Carlos hotel, about ten kilometres to the east of Marbella. The hotel courtesy coach was waiting for them at the airport, and using the almost deserted toll road it covered the fifty kilometres to the hotel in less than forty-five minutes. Two of the liaison officers were waiting for them at the door; one stepped forward, as the coach stopped, and approached Barton as he got off.

"Evening, sir, I'm John Dixon, liaison team leader... we spoke on the phone yesterday, everything's ready."

Helped by the liaison officers and Connor's fluent Spanish, the whole team was checked in within ten minutes. The liaison team had reserved one of the hotel's private dining rooms and they arranged to meet at reception at nine-fifteen for the final briefing and dinner.

Connor and Lorna laughed when they discovered that they had separate rooms, five floors apart. Sally overheard them talking.

"Your place or mine?" asked Connor.

"Whatever's nearest," replied Lorna, as they walked arm in arm towards the lift.

Sally looked longingly at Barton: *Why can't you ask me that?* She wanted him now, more than she'd ever wanted anyone Then she felt a tingle all over as he put his hand on her arm and spoke to her.

"I'm going up Sal," said Barton "You'd better come too…we've got to be back in half an hour."

Her heart stopped for a moment, before it started to race. But by the time, she opened her mouth to respond, he was gone; already walking across the lobby. She was doing it again. She knew the futility of her situation, but she always let it happen. And she always felt the same – guilty for wanting him, angry because she couldn't have him, hurt because he didn't want her and alone because as long as he was around she couldn't be happy with anyone else. – And she knew it was hopeless. So why, when she expected nothing…? Why, did she always hope for everything?

"Fuck it! Fuck you!" She couldn't take any more emotional overload and as she watched him get into the lift, she made her decision.

The Don Carlos Hotel was between the main coast road and the beach. From the window of his room on the twelfth floor, Barton had spectacular views along the coast to Marbella and of the mountains to the north. He looked towards the mountains rising up beyond the area of Elviria. He quickly located the development high on top of the hills, and traced the line of the road down towards Naismith's villa. He couldn't see the house, but he knew that his adversary was just a few kilometres away; only five minutes' drive from the hotel. He gazed out of the window and thought about his plans for the morning. He knew he'd only have one chance.

After dinner Dixon and the other liaison officers updated the team with the current situation concerning each of the men, answered questions and explained the relationship with the Spanish Police, reiterating what Barton had told the team earlier in the day.

Naismith and Marshall were being watched, and there was an unmarked police car outside each of their villas. Although, there were no formal charges against the men, these were being drawn up by the authorities, mainly in connection with the ongoing investigations into corruption in the Marbella council.

The men were free to come and go as they pleased, but were always followed. The surveillance was quite open and the men obviously knew they were being watched. Marshall was being the most difficult; he'd given his watchers the slip a couple of times, but Marbella was a small place and there was nowhere for him to go. Whatever was going on inside his head, Naismith was no longer showing any signs of panic. He played golf every morning and had visited his office a couple of times, even giving a friendly wave to the policemen who were parked at the side of the road just beyond his gates.

Davenport had a small villa along the coast at La Cala and spent most his time there, or at the local bars. Jackson spent most of his time at the car showrooms in the town, and apart from a trip to Malaga earlier in the week; he hadn't left Marbella. He didn't know that Spanish Customs officers had impounded the three containers that he had delivered to Malaga docks, or that his shipping agent had given all his records to the police.

Barton stood up to address the team. It was time for each of them to find out where they were going in the morning. "OK, let's go over what happens in the morning. They must know that we're coming, but they don't know when. So everybody has to be in place at the same time, and ready to go on my order. Now I'll tell you where you're going and then you can go though the details with the liaison officers. They'll tell you exactly what you have to do." He paused for a moment as Dixon took a pile of envelopes out of his case and put them on the table.

"Naismith," said Dixon, looking around the table as he waited for Barton to tell him who to give the envelopes to.

"That's Dave Connor and me," said Barton. Connor put up his hand and Dixon passed him two envelopes. Connor opened one and put the other on the table in front of Barton.

"Marshall?"

"He's mine," said Miller.

Dixon handed him an envelope. "Who else?" He asked, holding out the second envelope.

"Just me," said Miller. "I want that bastard for myself."

"Davenport?"

"Lorna and Phil," said Barton. "Go easy on him Lorna… he probably hasn't got a clue what's going on. That just leaves Jackson… Paul and Matt, you can have him. He's a right little shit, Paul, so don't be too nice to him."

"What about us?" Jane asked. She sounded disappointed, as she looked across the table towards Sally and Brenda. "What are we supposed to do?

"I was coming to that... I want you and Sally to look after Helen Naismith. I've got a feeling that she'll want to come back with us... even if her husband plays hard-to-get."

"You mean I've given up my weekend for babysitting?" said Jane, sounding even more disappointed.

"It's important, Jane. Mike told me about this yesterday," said Sally. "She's going to need all the help we can give her."

"Sally's right," said Barton. "I want the two of you take care of her. She's going to get a lot of bad news tomorrow."

"What about me then?" Brenda asked.

"I've got a very special job for you, Brenda. I'll tell you about it when we've finished up here," replied Barton.

Brenda nodded in acceptance and spent the next few minutes trying to work out what the special job would be. She was thinking that maybe he wanted her to stay at the hotel as back up. She smiled at the thought of a day by the pool, waiting for the phone to ring.

Barton wound up the meeting. "Each of the envelopes has a list with the names of the liaison team and the Spanish officers who will accompany you in the morning. There's also a booking reference for the nine-fifty flight from Malaga to Stansted tomorrow evening, and, assuming that you get them home, a sheet with the details of the charges that you'll arrest them on when you get back. You'll also find some other useful background stuff. Any questions?"

"Yes, when do we go?" Connor looked at his watch and winked at Lorna. "Not too early I hope. I need my sleep."

"Relax, Dave. This is Spain. They don't like getting up early on a Sunday," replied Barton. "I want everybody in position outside the villas at ten. Your liaison officers will tell you what time you need to leave here. Now if that's all I suggest that you retire to the bar and go through the stuff in those envelopes. You can put the drinks on the rooms."

Barton had spoken on the phone to the Dixon before they'd flown out a week ago, and asked a favour. Before dinner, the two men had talked quietly for a few minutes. They hadn't come for Marquez, but Barton had an interest in his whereabouts. The police were watching the apartment in Puerto Banus and Juanita was there alone. Marquez had taken his boat from the marina and was now in Marseilles, where the French police were watching him.

"Have you ever been to Puerto Banus?" said Barton.

"No, sir," replied Brenda. She looked at her watch. It was nearly midnight and she'd been hoping for an early night. Something told her that the special job didn't involve sitting by the pool.

"Come on Brenda, we're going for a drive," said Barton, "I'll explain on the way."

Barton had arranged the hire car before he left England and signed the paperwork when he'd checked in to the hotel; they only had to wait a couple of minutes for the car to be brought to the front of the hotel. As they drove towards Puerto Banus, he explained about Juanita.

"She'll be in a lot of danger when they find out we've got her brother, and he won't tell us any more about Marquez until he knows that she's safe."

"How do you know she'll come?"

"That's where you come in. You've spent more time than anyone with Herrera and Debbie King, and I'm hoping that you can convince her. You've done a great job with Debbie King, Brenda. I know you can do this."

Barton parked the car at the end of the street. "Stay here, Brenda," he said. "When I'm inside, follow me and I'll meet you in the lobby." Barton got out and walked towards the apartment building. He saw a car with two men sitting in it, parked at the kerb about fifty metres beyond the building. Barton tapped on the window of the car, spoke briefly with the occupants, and returned to apartment building. He looked for the name on the wall panel and pressed a button.

After about a minute, he heard Juanita's voice. *"Ola, quién es?"*

"Juanita, is that you? It's Mike Barton. Do you remember me? Can I come in?" Barton's said quickly.

"No estoy segura… Sorry, English… I'm not sure."

"It's very important. Let me in."

"OK, OK." The electronic door lock buzzed and Barton nervously pushed the door open. He remembered the last time he'd been there, and it felt strange coming back. He went inside and waited for Brenda.

As Barton stepped out of the lift, he could see that the door to the apartment was ajar. "Wait here a minute," he said. Brenda watched as Barton pushed the door open and he went inside.

Juanita was standing in the hallway wearing a thin robe. She let it slip from one shoulder when she saw him. "Hello Mike, you came back," she said seductively. "I hoped you would… I was going to bed…" She stopped when she saw Brenda walk in and stand behind Barton.

"Quién es ella?" she rushed at Barton and slapped his face "Who is she? Is this a trick?" She pushed him back towards the door. "Get out!"

Barton grabbed her by the wrists. "Shut the door Brenda," he said.

Brenda did as she was told: *You obviously didn't tell me everything. This is going to be interesting.*

"That's not why I'm here," said Barton as he tightened his grip on Juanita's wrists. "Now are you going to calm down… or do I have to hurt you."

She nodded her head. "OK," she said. "Let me go, please." She looked up at Barton and her eyes told him that she was frightened; that was what he wanted.

He loosened his grip and led her into the lounge. "Sit down," he said, quietly, but in a tone that let her know it was an order. He let go of her wrist and she obeyed, lowering herself onto one of the sofas. She perched on the edge of the cushion, and as Brenda sat down beside her, Juanita instinctively grasped her by the hand.

"What do you want?" asked Juanita. "It has something to do with those men who watch my house, yes?"

"Yes it does. But don't worry nobody is going to hurt you. They are policemen and they are watching because you are in danger. This lady is a police officer as well, she works for me." Barton moved towards the bar. "Would you like a drink?"

Barton gave the brief details and then Brenda filled the gaps. At first Juanita refused to listen to what they said, but she hadn't heard from her brother for weeks and knew something was wrong. As Brenda told her things that only her brother would have know about, she started to believe them.

She told them what she knew. She admitted that Naismith had set her up with Barton. "It was just a joke, Mike. That's what he told me. I didn't know." She didn't know where her husband was; he'd gone somewhere in the boat and had only called once. He'd told her that her brother had gone back to Colombia.

"What will happen to me?" she asked, despairingly.

Barton didn't pull his punches. "If you stay here, they'll kill you. I don't know what will happen to you if you go home, but your brother cheated them, and you know the sort of people they are."

"Can I come with you?" she said tearfully. "Can I see Enrique?"

"What about your husband?" Brenda asked.

"I hope you catch him. I hope he dies in prison." She got up and took a photograph from the wall. "*Cabron!*" she screamed, as she flung the picture across the room, "*Cabron!*"

"Will you come with us now?" asked Barton.

"Yes, let me pack some things. I don't need much," said Juanita. "It will only take a minute. I'll get my passport." She walked across to another picture and took it off the wall to reveal a small combination safe. She opened the door and put her hand inside.

Barton got up and stood behind her, looking over her shoulder. "What's that?"

She turned round and held up a two bundles of bank notes. "So I can go shopping in England," she said, with little smile.

"We'll look after that," he said, holding out his hand. She handed him the money and her passport, and reached back into the safe. Barton pulled her away when he saw the packet of white powder, and the automatic pistol. "You can leave those here," he said.

Juanita went to pack, leaving Barton alone with Brenda. He took an envelope from his pocket and gave it to her. "The police outside will take you back to the hotel. I've booked her a room. I'll send one of them up to help with her luggage."

"But she said she wouldn't have much."

"Believe me, that lady likes clothes... and shoes. I'll bet she has at least two cases. Now, there are two Iberia tickets to Barcelona in here and five thousand euros. They're open tickets, so you can get any flight, but leave as early as you can. When you get to Barcelona, find a hotel in the city, and check her in for a few days. Go up to the room and stay there for a few hours. She won't need to unpack, because you won't be staying... and make sure that you don't leave by the main entrance. Then take her back to the airport and get a flight to Italy... Milan, Rome... you decide. Stay there for a couple of days, then fly to Brussels or Paris, and get the Eurostar back to London. Have you got that?"

"Do you really think she's in danger?" asked Brenda.

"I don't know, but she has to think so. Now go and tell her to put everything she needs in her hand luggage. She'll have to leave the rest in Barcelona. I'll see you in a few days."

It was two-thirty, when Barton got back to the Hotel; too late to call Grace. He sat in the dark, drinking a bottle of San Miguel from the mini-bar, looking out of the window towards the mountains, focusing on a cluster of bright lights on the hillside; the ring of security lights that surrounded Naismith's villa. He was sure that the hillside had been in darkness, when he'd first sat at the window; it was almost time, and he wondered if he was expected.

He decided to call Grace anyway, but there was no answer and after a minute, the answering machine cut in; he left a message. He guessed she was at her parents' house, but he wanted to be sure and called her mobile. This time she picked up. She looked at the caller display; answered with two words, and hung up. Well at least he knew she was still alive.

He tried to sleep, but every time he closed his eyes, the dream returned, and each time, although the grotesque puppet show was the same, he sensed that something changed. But he couldn't work out what, so he kept closing his eyes, and wandered aimlessly through the dark swirling mists; to look again. Then, just before he woke for the last time, he looked at his hand and saw the knife; reached up and cut his strings.

He looked at his watch; he still had a couple of hours. He shaved and showered; dressed while the kettle boiled and then made coffee. He found some bottles of orange juice and mineral water, from the mini bar, and placed them on the table. Then he sat by the window and looked out towards the mountains again. He drank the coffee and then mixed the orange juice with some water in a tall glass. All the time he kept his eyes fixed on the lights on the hillside, as he went over the plan in his head, working out every twist and turn he could think of; over and over again, until it was right. He knew he'd only have one chance.

The alarm sounded; it was time; he was ready to play the game again. He picked it up the envelope that Dixon had given him and looked at it for a moment. He started to run his thumbnail under the flap, and then he stopped and threw it, unopened, onto the bed. He didn't need it; there was no point in remembering the charges on the list, it didn't matter any more. His jacket was draped over the back of the chair; he picked it up and put it on, he felt inside one of the pockets; it was still there. That was all he needed; Naismith wouldn't be going home... ever.

Chapter 36

Marbella – 07:30 CET

Barton had phoned Sally before he left the hotel. She hadn't been too pleased to be woken up, and she'd felt put out that he hadn't told her about Juanita. She'd probably kill him when she found out that he'd lied to her. He felt bad about it, but it was necessary. "Don't worry. I just want to make sure they get there alright. It won't take me long to get back from the airport. Naismith's place is only five minutes from the hotel, so we'll have plenty of time. But if I get held up, you go ahead as planned. I'll meet you there." He hadn't given her chance to argue, and he ignored his mobile when she rang back.

The dawn was breaking as he drove up the winding road towards the villa. He'd forgotten his sunglasses and he screwed up his eyes as the bright sunlight streamed through the windscreen; he didn't see the taxi following him.

The gates were open, just as Dixon had said; Naismith hadn't bothered to close them for several days: *Is he waiting for me?* A police car was parked on a piece of open ground just beyond the bend and the occupants appeared to be sleeping. Barton drove on; a few hundred metres further up the road he turned round and drove back slowly; holding a map over the steering wheel. If the policemen saw him, he would stop and ask directions; but there was no sign that either man was awake. He slowly rounded the bend and turned through the gates and – had he looked in his mirrors, he might have seen a white taxi driving past – parked the car in the driveway and walked the remaining hundred metres to the house.

Naismith watched the CCTV monitor as Barton approached the house. He pressed a button, swung round in his chair, got up and walked into the kitchen where Maria was making coffee. "Bring my guest down to the basement, when he arrives," he said. "We'll have our coffee in the cinema." It was very early and he didn't want any noise to wake his wife.

The front door was open and Barton stepped warily into the hall: *He is waiting. I'm walking into a trap.* Before he had time for any second thoughts, Maria came out of the kitchen carrying a tray. "*Buenos días, señor.* Come this way, please, *Señor* Naismith is expecting you," she said, and, without waiting for a reply, started to walk towards the stairs. Barton looked at the open front door;

something inside told him he should get out now and come back with the others. Something even stronger was telling him it was too late to turn back; he had to do this alone.

Naismith was lounging in one of the large cinema chairs. "Come in Barton, take a seat," he said nonchalantly. "Forgive me if I don't get up and shake hands... but under the circumstances..."

"Cut the crap Naismith, how did you know I was coming?" Barton said angrily. He bit his lip: *Shit, I'm going to lose it.*

"Come on we can at least be polite. This is what you've been waiting for ... isn't it?" Naismith said, fuming inside at the man's impertinence, but outwardly remaining calm; playing to his advantage. "Thank you Maria, leave the coffee on the side table please." Maria did as she was instructed and left; quietly closing the door behind her.

Naismith continued, "To answer your question... as you know I have my sources. And when I knew you were here, I sent one of the boys down to hotel to keep an eye on you. I had a feeling you'd come alone, and I wanted to be ready."

"It's all still a bloody game to you, isn't it!" shouted Barton.

Naismith raised his hand and Barton found himself looking down the barrel of a 9mm Glock semi-automatic pistol. "Yes, and thanks to you it's proving to be a bloody expensive one. Now sit down," he said coldly, emphasising the word *'sit'*, as though he was addressing a disobedient dog.

Barton sat and looked at Naismith. "Let's get to the point. We both know what you are... what you've done. We both know that this is a charade. I've come to take you back... but we both know that's not going to happen. So I'm not really interested in what you've done. I just want to know why."

"Why?" cried Naismith. He jumped to his feet, and started to pace the floor. "Why? Does there need to be a reason? You see that's the difference... between you and me. You need reasons... you have to be able to explain everything. You look for motives where there aren't any."

He waved his arm, pointing the gun around the room, "That's why I've got all this and you'll never be any more than a boring little policeman... doing as you're told... fighting battles that you can never win... biding your time until you can collect your pathetic little pension. People like you... you'll never understand real power. And all those pathetic do-gooders... like your pretty little wife... looking for reasons... blame the parents... blame the environment... blame the system... blame the Tories for not caring... blame Labour for being too soft. Bullshit! And all those stupid, greedy little people... they'll never know. They jump through the hoops... do as they're told and they never ask why. As long as they get a reward... sometimes money... sometimes, they just want to stay alive.

It doesn't matter... just give them what they want and keep them wanting more. It's all a game... and it's the best game in the world. It gives you a high... better than any of that crap that people shove up the noses or shoot up their veins. You want to know why. Well let me ask you... Why not?"

Barton stood up and turned his back on Naismith. "You're right. I don't understand," he said as he started to walk away.

"Where do you think you're going?"

"It's all over Naismith," Barton said deliberately, as he carried on walking, towards the door. "You can't do it any more. It's finished... You're finished." He stopped and turned back, Naismith looked about to explode and raised the gun, his arm shaking, as Barton continued to mock him.

"Come on, what are you going to do? There's nobody left to do your dirty work... and no money left to pay them off with."

"Shut up and sit down!" snarled Naismith. "You don't think I'm just going to let you walk away... not after what you've done to me." He clasped his left hand around his wrist to steady his arm, and turned the safety catch. "Now sit down or..."

"Or what?" Barton challenged, "What... you'll shoot me? You're on your own now, no one to do it for you. They say it's harder than you might think... to kill a man, in cold blood. Have you got the guts to pull the trigger?"

Naismith walked behind Barton and stood very close, so that Barton could feel the breath that carried his words, "If necessary," he hissed, "...and it's easy to kill vermin. But, I'm not ready for that yet... I don't think it would be very fair on Maria... do you?"

Barton sat down; it was a game and this was the last hand. "Why would that be?" he asked. "I wouldn't have thought that you'd be particularly bothered about the sensitivities of a mere servant."

Naismith looked at Barton, his eyes displaying no hint of emotion. Barton blinked; he could feel Naismith's stare, like cold grey steel piercing into his brain. He thought of what Grace had said on the phone: '...when he stared at me it felt like the Devil was trying to steal my soul. There was nothing behind his eyes... just black and empty'. Barton blinked again, he returned Naismith's stare and saw – Nothing.

Slowly, Naismith started to turn the screw. "You're right," he said. "But I wouldn't even ask a whore to mop up your dirty nigger blood."

Barton recoiled; there was something very sinister in the way that Naismith said that word. This was something beyond the racist insults of the yobs on the streets; Naismith used the word like a weapon; as a sadist might wield a blade to exact pain. He remembered what Grace had written: *Weapons; crafted and honed to cut into the heart and tear out the soul.*

He regained his composure and challenged Naismith again. "So what are you going to do? Take me into the woods and shoot me. Perhaps you'll make me dig my own grave, with my bare hands."

"Now come on Barton, don't be so melodramatic. We're both civilised, educated men," said Naismith. "I'm sure that sort of thing only happens in the movies. I'm not a complete bastard," he waved the gun at Barton and laughed, "…I'd give you a spade. Oh! That's a good one… a spade for a spade. "

Barton didn't to rise to the bait. His plan had been to niggle away at him, to encourage his taunts and his bragging. He was intending to play the game until Naismith had only one thing left to hurt him with. Until he heard the truth from Naismith own lips, he couldn't close the book.

"Maybe you'll kneecap me first and make me crawl into the hole," he said. "Isn't that how Henry Patterson taught you how to do it? I hear you were a quick learner."

Naismith sat back in his chair, and sucked in the air. "So you've been talking to Henry… you have been busy. I won't ask how you found him… or why. Yes, I learned a lot from my stepfather. Would you like to know what else he taught me?"

"Nothing of any value, I'm sure. But go on. I've got all day and you've got the gun."

"So I have," said Naismith as he lunged forward and pressed the barrel of the Glock against Barton's throat. "How does it feel?" he asked, as he slowly moved the barrel upwards and pressed it under Barton's chin. "I just have to pull the trigger and your brains are all over the ceiling. Bye, bye nigger. How does it feel to know that I have the power of life and death? Henry taught me… how to use that power. Shall I tell you how they kept their niggers in their place? Keep them fed, give them a place to sleep, work them hard, and never let them forget you're the boss. It's like training dogs… most learn quickly… come when you call them and sit when they're told. But once in a while there'll be a runt in the litter and it has to be put down. Does that shock you?"

Barton wasn't about to be shocked at anything Naismith said; hurt perhaps but he'd come to expect anything from this man. He was burning with rage but he didn't let it show. "No, I bet you really loved all the stories Patterson told you… Did you get a shock when you found out the truth… that your blood isn't special…? And how about the Jews and the Poles and the Arabs… did you see the colour of their blood… when your brother and his mates beat the shit out of them?"

Naismith's arm lashed out and Barton winced in pain as the barrel of the Glock tore his cheek. Barton took out a handkerchief and dabbed the cut. "That was careless… you nearly got my dirty nigger blood on the carpet."

"So you found my brother's diary... that was very clever of you."

"Not me," said Barton. "Just a boring little policewoman... doing as she was told. Except nobody had to tell her... she worked it out all by herself.... More than Nichols and Stevens could do. Just goes to show... you can train a dog to fetch...but you can't give it the brains to know what it's looking for."

"Very droll, Barton, I hope the young lady concerned has been suitably rewarded," said Naismith. "I take it you've read my brother's diaries. Were they as interesting as I've been led to believe... or did make them go to all that trouble over nothing?"

"Oh! No, they were worth it," Barton replied with a smile that made his cheek ache. "Very comprehensive... your brother had a way with words, clever man... pity you had to kill him."

The game continued; Naismith finding nerves and twisting the knife; Barton defending, content to score the odd point, knowing that Naismith could end it any time. He needed to keep it going; he hadn't got what he'd come for yet and he wondered how long Naismith would make him wait.

"I've had enough of this," Naismith said at last. "It's getting very boring. You seem to know everything... this game isn't worth playing any more." He got up and walked to the table. "But, I've got something to show you... before we take our walk in the woods. And you won't need a spade... there are plenty of holes up there already. Oh! The coffee's gone cold. I'll get Maria to make some more."

While they were waiting, Naismith took a DVD from a drawer and put it into the player. "I'm not sure that you'll like this," he sneered. "But, I find it very entertaining."

Maria bought in the coffee and put it on the table. Naismith asked her to move the table closer, and she put it in front of the two men and poured their coffee. Naismith picked up a cup and took a sip. "Don't let it go cold Barton, it's very good."

Barton picked up the other cup and took a large gulp. The hot, bitter tasting liquid scalded his mouth and throat, temporarily taking his mind off his aching cheek.

Naismith put his cup on the table and took a remote control from a pocket at the side of his chair. "This used to be on tape, but I had it copied. Wonderful things these DVDs, so convenient... and much better than the old tapes, I like the way that get such a clear picture when you can play things in slow motion. Now I got this from an old friend of yours... Colin Marshall. It's very good... but of course I would say that wouldn't I. I'm in it."

Naismith pressed a button on the remote and two panels on the wall slid apart, revealing a large screen. At the press of the next button, the lights dimmed; the third started the DVD player. Barton watched as the film started and played at quadruple speed until Naismith froze the picture. "Now this is the bit that I like," said Naismith. "Watch closely, you don't want to miss it."

Barton got to his feet, knocking over the table. "Is this the best that you can do... I've already seen it. I've got the original. I can tell you the ending."

Naismith pointed the gun at him. "I'm impressed. My people have been trying to find the tape for years. Perhaps you can tell me how you came to find it when we take our walk. Now I don't care if you have seen it. You can watch it again... this time with the benefit of the director's commentary. I think we'll play it in slow motion, and put that handkerchief away... I want to see your face."

Barton lost it and tears rolled down his face as he watched his father die again; and again, and again as Naismith, gloating and boasting, played the scene a dozen times. But this was what Barton had come for; to hear the man's confession. He hadn't expected there to be any remorse; and Naismith's taunting was remorseless, as he enjoyed Barton's humiliation.

When it was over, when Naismith had satisfied his desire for revenge, he turned off the machine and switched on the lights. He looked at the mixture of tears and blood that stained Barton's shirt and jacket, and sneered. The game was over; all that remained was for the victor to take his prize. "Get up. It's time to go," he whispered, prodding the gun into Barton's ribs.

Barton stood up and waited. So this was it; he'd played the game and in a way, he'd won; he'd got what he came for, but it was a pyrrhic victory. If only he'd thought it through. But, he'd been naïve, he never thought that Naismith would go this far; not when he knew it was all over. What would be the point in killing him now?

But, of course, Naismith was right. Barton needed reasons, explanations, and motives; and he'd made the mistake of not thinking like his adversary: *'Why not?'* for Naismith, being able to do it was reason enough.

Barton turned to face his enemy. "OK, you win. Now let's get it over."

Naismith held the gun in the small of Barton's back and they walked out of the room. "We'll use the back stairs," he said. "You can drive... we'll take the Land Rover, there are some pretty rough tracks up there."

They walked through the gym and past the pool. As they reached the bottom of the stairs, Naismith stopped and looked around. "I'm going to miss all this. I have to hand it to you Barton; I've enjoyed our games. I never thought you'd get this far."

"If you hadn't killed your brother, the game might never have started," said Barton with a shrug.

"Yes, in hindsight, that was a mistake. But we all make mistakes and at least I'll live to make a few more."

"It's not the only mistake you made," said Barton. "If you hadn't killed my father, I'd probably have let it drop. My bosses wanted the case closed. We'd have wound things down and they'd have been satisfied with what they had. Like you said... I need a reason for what I do and you gave me one."

"He didn't need to die... the plan didn't call for that. A near miss would have been enough to get the voters behind me. But he couldn't remember his place. He should never have called me by that name. That was unforgivable, and I had to teach him a lesson, make an example of him. So I thought, why not?"

Why not? Barton recoiled, as the two words, said without any feeling, just a throwaway line, exploded like a grenade, and the shrapnel tore through his flesh and shredded his nerves. *Why not?*

Naismith smiled; he could see from Barton's reaction that he'd scored another direct hit. "In a way it was unfortunate... and if that gives you any consolation I actually thought he was a good policeman," he said, looking at Barton and seeing that it was no consolation at all.

"In different circumstances, I might have bought him. But it had to be, and I don't regret it... even if it is the reason that you came after me." He laughed as he twisted the knife again, dismissing Barton's ghost as little more than an inconvenience. "Why worry about it.? Forget it and move on. Like, I've forgotten my brother and all the others... there are plenty more out there, waiting to be bought. You know the only thing that I regret is this," Naismith rubbed his shoulder and laughed. "That bloody man wasn't meant to shoot me, they told him to miss... it nearly ruined my golf swing."

Barton wasn't really listening; he was watching the man on the stairs. He didn't make a sound as he descended the steps, but Barton's eyes must have must have given something away.

Naismith spun round. Too late. Lewis Campbell swung the golf club with all the strength he could muster. Naismith instinctively raised his arm in defence, and then cried out in pain as force of the blow smashed the bones in his wrist, sending the Glock spinning out of his hand. Before Barton could move, Campbell had shoved Naismith out of the way and dived across the floor; grabbing the gun as it bounced towards the pool. He got to his feet and pointed the gun at Naismith.

"Who the fuck are you?" Naismith shouted, as he crouched on the floor holding his shattered and bloody wrist.

Barton looked at Campbell. "Give me the gun, Lewis, don't do anything stupid," he said quietly. "Put the gun down."

"Is this him? Is this the man you told me about?" snapped Campbell, waving the gun towards Naismith. "Get up!"

Barton looked at Campbell and saw a picture of himself as a young man; angry and confused. But now, twenty years on this young man knew the truth and had a gun in his hand. Barton was still angry, and part of him wished that Campbell would pull the trigger. But he knew that this wasn't the way. "Give me the gun, please Lewis. This won't bring your father back."

"He's got to pay, Mr Barton." Campbell was shaking, waving the gun about wildly. "He's got to pay for what he did... they've all got to pay."

Barton had never been so scared in his life. The gun was pointing at him now, and he knew that the safety catch was off; the way that Campbell was waving it about it could go off at any second. The next few moments seemed frozen in time, as Barton remembered everything he had ever learned, the sum of all of his training and experience. Then focussed it all into a five-yard stare; locked onto the young man like a tractor beam. "Don't move Lewis... don't do anything, just stay where you are."

The invisible line between the two of them became a tightrope as Barton put out his hand and gingerly edged forwards; his eyes remaining fixed on the young man; who was staring back at him, twitching but unable to move, like a rabbit trapped in a car's headlights. "This isn't the way Lewis. Think about your mother... they'll send you to prison... could she bear to go through that again?" He reached out and put his hand on the gun barrel. "Give me the gun, Lewis. He'll pay... I promise."

Campbell let go of the gun and Barton breathed a sigh of relief. He slipped the safety catch on, and put the gun into his pocket.

"That's better. Now see if you can find a first aid kit or something. He's bleeding all over the floor."

Barton bandaged Naismith's wrist, taking great delight in causing as much pain as possible, then helped him to his feet. "There, that'll do," he said as he strapped the arm up in a sling. "What was that you were saying about your golf swing? Nearly ruined... I'd say it was totally fucked now."

He turned to Campbell, who was trying to stifle a laugh. "It's OK, Lewis, let it out. Come on, follow me... I've got something to show you, and bring him too."

"Let me introduce you," said Barton, as he shoved Naismith into a chair. "This is Lewis Campbell... we've just been watching his father on screen."

As they sat down on either side of the old man, Barton spoke to Campbell. "How did you get here, Lewis? How did you know where to come?"

"I've been following you. You said he was in Spain so I followed you here. I saw you coming here and followed in taxi. I followed you down here... but when I saw he had a gun I didn't know what to do, so I hid in the garage."

"How long have you been following me?"

"Since just after you came to our house. I got the lady's address off some papers in her car. I went to where she lives and followed her to work. Then I started following you. I'm sorry. Will I get into trouble?"

"No it's alright, Lewis," Barton said kindly. "I think you've already had more trouble than someone your age deserves." He smiled at the young man; he was getting to like him. "Now I want you to look at this." Barton switched on the DVD player. He searched for the scene and pressed the pause button. He got up and moved towards the screen. "Come here Lewis," he said.

Campbell got up and stood at Barton's side. Barton pointed to a face on the screen. "That's him Lewis... the man who came to your house and took your dad away."

"Who is he?"

"His name was Terry King, and he's dead now. This man killed him." Barton looked at Naismith. He sat with a sullen look on his face, nursing his broken wrist, and said nothing. The bravado had gone, but he wasn't broken yet. "Didn't you!" Barton barked.

Naismith nodded and muttered something. Barton took the gun from his pocket and held it to Naismith's head. "I didn't hear you, say it again."

"Yes, I killed him."

Barton put his hand on Campbell's shoulder. "Barry Jarvis, Baz... the man who hurt you mother, and the other man... we've got them locked up and they'll be going to prison. The man who killed your father is already in prison... he'll stand trial for murder and I'll do whatever I can to make sure this one joins him." Barton pressed the eject button on the remote control and took out the disc. "Twenty years Naismith. Twenty years that Lewis and me have lived without our fathers. It was twenty years ago today!" He snapped the disc in two and threw the pieces into Naismith's face.

"Now, get up, we're going for a walk," Barton snapped, jabbing the gun in Naismith's chest. "Come on, Lewis, it's over now."

The three men walked up the stairs into the hall. Barton pressed the gun into Naismith's ribs, "Do you keep any money in the house?" he asked.

Naismith groaned "In the study, over there."

"Lead the way," said Barton, and pushed him towards the door.

Naismith opened the wall safe and stood back. Barton rifled through the contents and took out five bundles of banknotes. He flicked through each bundle and gave them to Campbell. "There's about twenty-five thousand pounds there… not much for a man's life but it might help." He put his hand into the safe again and took out two bundles of euros. "You might as well take these as well… just to help you get home."

Campbell stuffed the cash into his pockets. What do you want me to do now?" he asked.

"Go home, Lewis. Tell your mother she doesn't have to be afraid any more. Take her on holiday… St. Lucia maybe… she's got a sister there. Don't worry about him. I'll deal with him. I promise."

"Thanks, Mr Barton. I'm sorry for the trouble."

"What trouble? You saved my life," Barton held out his hand. "You'd make a bloody good detective… if you ever think of joining the police, come, and see me."

Campbell shook Barton's hand and laughed. "What? Me and Babylon… man that sounds wicked." He let go of Barton's hand and turned towards the door. "I'll be going then," he said. Thanks Mr Barton, maybe I'll see you again.

"Wait," said Barton. He waved the gun menacingly in Naismith's face. "Car keys!"

"What?"

"Your car keys… where do you keep the car keys?"

"In the metal case by the garage door," replied Naismith.

"You heard the man Lewis. You know where the garage is… just take your pick."

As they walked into the garden Barton heard the roar of the big V12, as the Aston powered out of the drive: *Good choice Lewis, that's the one I'd have gone for.*

They sat beside the pool and Barton looked at his watch.

"Expecting company?" asked Naismith.

"Not yet. We've got plenty of time."

"For what?"

"The game isn't over yet Naismith," said Barton, as he put the gun between them, on the table. "Go on, if you think you're fast enough… I thought not. So what does it feel like?"

"What does what feel like?"

"Nothing, nada, zilch, zero… fuck all, because that's what you are and that's all you've got left." It was Barton's turn to gloat, and he was starting to enjoy himself. "Now it's my rules… ready to play old man?"

"Do I have a choice?"

"No… but you don't have to say anything if you don't want to. Just listen… I'm going to twist the knife and watch you bleed."

"You think so." Naismith said defiantly. "I've been playing this game since before you were born. I've broken better men than you, so get on with it. Who cares?"

"Let's start with a few mistakes… maybe some regrets. I know you don't to like to think about your mistakes… but I'm sure that your friends in Colombia and Russia are keeping score. Milosevic… now that was careless… sloppy… not at all like you… it must have been quite an awkward conversation with his bosses. And then there was Herrera, or was he just a way to get to your brother?"

"Where is this leading? Do you really think I give a damn about them?"

"Probably not, and to tell you the truth, I don't either. But Bobby… now that was bloody stupid. And what for…? Why? Oh! I forgot… you don't need reasons. Did you really think he would have betrayed you? He loved you… but I don't suppose that means anything to you. All those years doing your dirty work and he never said a word. Not even when he went to jail for you. So why didn't you trust him? Why did have to kill him?"

"You were on to him… they told me he had those diaries…the bloody fool. I couldn't take the risk."

"They told you… not him then? Who, Jarvis and Underwood? With friends like that, he didn't need enemies. Shall I tell you what I think? Your brother kept a record of everything because he was proud of what he did for you… it made him feel good that he could please you. I can see him now… sitting by the fire in his old age, reading them and reliving the past. Looking back fondly on a relationship that never was… at least not as far as you're concerned. He was never going to tell anybody, least of all me. He was more of man than you'll ever be. I've been thinking about what he said to me, it didn't make much sense at the time, but it does now."

"What are you talking about?"

"Have you forgotten already? That doesn't surprise me… turn the page and write it off… unless of course you can use it to hurt somebody… I'm sorry, talk to Lenny…"

Naismith winced as Barton stressed *'Lenny'*. "Talk to Lenny," Barton emphasised the word again. "I didn't mean to… I let him down…tell him, I love him. Probably not word perfect but close enough."

Naismith grunted. "Load of rubbish… it doesn't mean anything."

"Well there's another difference between us. As far as I'm concerned your brother, sorry half-brother…"

Naismith sat upright, a look of astonishment on his face. "What did you say?"

"That got your attention," laughed Barton. "We'll come back to that. Now where was I? Your brother... we'll call him that... half-brother sounds so awkward... a bit like half-baked... is that what you thought of him? Sorry I'll get back to the point. He was just a gangster, a murderer, and as far as I'm concerned, he was a piece of shit. He probably thought the same about me. But dying men don't need to lie. He was sorry... he thought he'd let you down. I watched him die and he wasn't thinking of himself. He could only think of the people he'd hurt... you... his daughter... and me."

"You!" Naismith sat up in surprise, and then fired back. "What do mean... You? Whatever makes you think that my brother would be concerned about the likes of you?

"There was something else he said, just before he died. I didn't play it to you before, because it wasn't part of his message to you. But you can listen now." Barton reached into his pocket and took out his tape recorder: '*Barton, I'm sorry... I did it for him... Barton... I'm sorry... I didn't want to... I'm sorry, Barton... I had to do it'*.

"You see, I think, he was telling me he was sorry... about my father. He didn't mean to, but he gave you up. If we'd arrested him, he'd have gone down fighting and we'd never have known. But you killed him... and he gave you up without knowing. Or maybe he did? Maybe he decided to fight back, after all those years. Now there's a thought. Whatever, it was a big mistake. Maybe you regret it now... just a bit maybe?"

Barton looked for some reaction, but Naismith's face displayed no emotion. "What are you looking for?" he snorted "An apology?"

Barton knew that he was going to have to dig deeper "Too late for that," he said. "But, never mind. What else have you got wrong? How about loyalty and trust? Do you know what I'm talking about? Maybe I should go and find a dictionary for you. No, let me enlighten you. Loyalty... that's something you can't buy. It has to be earned... or in the case of your brother it's in the blood. Trust... now that's another difficult concept for you. You don't trust anyone... How can you ever be sure you've paid them enough? So let's consider how stupid you've been. Yes, really stupid. Tell me when did your brain stop working?"

Naismith stood up, protesting, "I don't have to listen to this. Who do you think you are?"

"The man with the gun," Barton drawled, reaching out and putting his hand on the grip. "Sit down please. I'll decide what you have to listen to."

"You wouldn't use that. You're bluffing."

"You'll never know until it's too late," Barton said casually "Do you want to take the risk?"

Barton put the gun back on the table, but kept his hand on it. "So you kill the only person whose loyalty is beyond doubt… a man you can trust implicitly… and you're left with incompetent fools, who are only looking out for themselves. Do you know what they were going to do with the diaries? Underwood and Jarvis… Oh! And Stevens… yes we've got him too. They were going to use them… give them to us in the hope of making a deal. Or make you pay a lot of money to keep them buried. Still got no regrets about your brother?"

"Fuck you!"

"Oh! Yes, I was going to tell you… about your brother. Half-brother… now how did I know that? Well, you see there's this nice old lady in Bournemouth…"

"You bastard! Leave her out of this."

"Oh! That got to you… there's someone you care about, then. She told us a lot. I wonder what made her do that."

"Bastard, she's an old lady. How dare you harass her?"

"Oh! But I've never even met her. But you see… your niece has been very helpful to us. And your mother thinks the world of Debbie… she's the only member of your fucking family that she's seen for years. See what I mean about loyalty and trust? And why do you think Debbie has been so helpful?"

"I wouldn't know and I don't really care. For all I know this is just invention.

"She's in love. Love… another word that's not in your vocabulary. She's in love with a greasy little dago drug dealer. I bet that makes you feel good… one of your own sleeping with the enemy. So you can imagine how she reacted when she found out that you'd tried to kill him." Barton emphasised 'tried', and waited for a reaction. Naismith said nothing, his face contorted, and his eyes bulged, his lips quivered, but no words came out.

"That's right… I said tried. He's still alive and he's been singing like a bird. He gave us Blanchard's." Barton laughed, as he watched Naismith's jaw drop. "He gave us your money. And as soon as he knows that his sister is safe he'll give us Marquez and his whole network, and I'll leave you to worry about what that means. Still no regrets?"

"All right, enough. You've made your point. Game over," Naismith blathered. He looked at the gun. "You win, now get it over with."

"Oh! I'm disappointed… I didn't think you were the sort to give up. You didn't really think I'd shoot you. No, I think we'll just sit here and wait for my friends. We can talk a bit more if you like… they won't be here for a while."

Barton looked at his watch; nine-thirty. "They'll be ready about now… they're going to pick up your pals. Marshall's going back to England. You know we really don't like it when one of our own goes bad. Still, you've got to feel a bit sorry for the old boy... he's looking at ten... fifteen years in an isolation wing. Either that or he'll be dead within a month. Not much of a choice is it. I'm not bothered about Jackson. If it was down to me I'd let the Spanish have him. Their jails aren't as comfortable as ours. Still we'll give him a choice. Wherever he feels safer, because I don't think your Russian friends are going to be too pleased when their cars don't show up. As for Davenport... we weren't even interested in him. But then I found out. And perverting the course of justice... well... I wouldn't be too bothered if it was just about buying off witnesses... but coaching Campbell with all that Warriors Against Racism crap... well that made it personal."

"What about me? What choices do I get?"

"Not sure. It's up to you and I want to know a bit more first. About, you and Helen... poor Helen. Oh! I forgot to tell you, we've got her brother and father too. And, no children... she's not got have much left. Anyway, we were talking about regrets. Not having children... does that get to you sometimes? I mean you spend your life building something... you've got it all, except the one thing you can't buy. No kids... you know I could feel a bit sorry for you... except it was your fault. Jean told us about her... accident. I don't think I could live that... knowing I'd killed my child."

The knife had gone to the bone. Barton could barely contain his delight as his opponent threw in his hand. Before his eyes, the man, who not so long ago had held all the cards, became little more than a crumpled shell. Naismith was beaten, crushed, utterly defeated; he had nothing left. And as Naismith wept; real tears, for the first time in over forty years, Barton started to have second thoughts. Maybe this was enough.

"It wasn't my fault, I didn't mean to. We had a row and I pushed her. I didn't mean to but she tripped and fell down the stairs. She just... It wasn't my fault though. Do you know how it feels... to know that you'll never have a son to look up to you... no one to carry on after you... remind people of who you were. People have short memories... if you can't leave something behind... something to remind them... What's the point? You want to know if I have regrets... of course I do... any man would regret that. When I'm gone, it's over... nothing left, no one to remember me, no one to tell their children about me. Of course, I regret not having a son. But you learn to live with it, get on. I couldn't do any thing about, it wasn't my fault."

'It wasn't my fault'. Barton looked at Naismith and then towards the house; Helen Naismith was in there; maybe still sleeping; maybe awake and wondering where her husband was; about to have her life changed; for the better, he hoped. Helen had been grieving for her unborn child for over thirty years, but even now,

Naismith was thinking only of himself, how he felt; there was not a word of consideration for her. *Leave something behind'*, to Naismith having a child had nothing to do with concepts of love and family; a son was a monument to the father: *'It wasn't my fault'*. Naismith had dealt the last hand and was holding Aces and Eights.

"How long have I got?"

"What for?"

"To get ready. You've got what you wanted. When are we leaving?"

"That's not what I want. I'm not taking you back. Why should I make it easy for you? Why waste the taxpayers' money? I don't know who'll get to you first... the Colombians or the Russians... or maybe someone else, who you've shat on and forgotten. I don't really care. I just want you looking over your shoulder for the rest of your life. And every day, when you've got nowhere to go, nowhere to hide, nothing left... and the ghosts come back to haunt you... you'll remember me."

Barton got to his feet and looked at the Puppet Master for the last time; he'd cut all the strings. "But, maybe, if you're lucky my friends will take a different view. They'll be here in a few minutes. But whatever happens, think on this. One of these days you're going to die, and when you go to hell and meet Henry Patterson again... how are you going to explain that you let a nigger put you in your place?"

Barton reached into his jacket pocket and took out an envelope. "I nearly forgot; I brought this for you." He put the envelope on the table next to the gun and walked away. "Game over."

Barton got into the car and turned it around. He drove through the gates and parked by the kerb, just in time to see the cars coming up the hill. Barton got out of the car and leaned on the roof, looking towards the sea. It was a beautiful day and he felt like going for a swim.

The cars pulled up outside the gate. Sally leapt out and ran across the road. "Where the hell have you been? And don't give me that crap about Brenda... I saw her at the hotel." She looked at his face and his bloodstained clothes. "Oh! No! You fool. What have you done?"

Barton tried to smile at her, but his face hurt. "It's alright Sal, we've just been talking. I had a little accident that's all. He's in the garden by the pool. But we may as well go back. He's not coming." He gave her a hug and whispered, "I'm sorry... I wanted to tell you, but I knew you'd try and stop me."

As Barton opened the car door a shot rang out. "I think you'd better get up to the house, Sal," he said. "I think Mrs Naismith would appreciate it. It's all over now."

Barton had given Naismith the one thing that he'd wanted most and taken it away again. Or rather, Naismith had already thrown it away, without ever knowing what he had. Part of him would have liked to have made a big dramatic gesture of handing over the envelope; would have enjoyed seeing his face, as the knife was twisted one last time. The envelope contained the results of the DNA tests which confirmed that Naismith was Terry King's father.

He gave Sally another hug and got into the car. He felt his cheek; it hurt like hell, but he didn't care; the taste in his mouth was so sweet.

Epilogue

Trevor Miller was sitting at his desk; the papers Barton had given him earlier were in front of him. "Sit down, Mike. We need to talk about this."

"I'd rather stand, sir. This shouldn't take long."

"What's this all about?" asked Miller, waving Barton's transfer request in the air. "You can't just walk away. What are you going to do?"

"I'm not sure… back to Cambridge maybe… or the Met? I've written down the options."

"Why? What's all this change in domestic circumstances rubbish?"

"It's not rubbish. I'm going to be a father and I want to be able to spend more time with my family. Besides, I've had enough. This Naismith thing. It's done me."

"Then take some leave. Jesus Christ! You can't throw it all away. You know I'll back you up over Naismith. There's not a man in the service wouldn't want to shake your hand. If it was down to me I'd give you a bloody medal. That's what we do. Keep people safe from scum like him. You're on leave as of now. Bugger off and think about it. Come back when you're ready."

Barton stood his ground; he'd made the decision and he wasn't going to change his mind. Not if they begged him. He took an envelope from his pocket.

"No sir. I can't. And if you won't sign the transfer, you can have this."

"What's that?"

"My letter of resignation… I mean it, Trevor."

"That's blackmail, Mike. Why are you doing this?"

"It's in the letter, you can decide. I'll be waiting outside."

Miller opened the envelope, "Sit down, Mike. You're not going anywhere, till we get this sorted out.

From: Detective Chief Inspector Michael Barton
To: Chief Superintendent Trevor Miller
28th May 2003

Dear Trevor,

It is with great regret that I have to inform you of my decision to resign from my duties as a police officer. It has been my great pleasure and privilege to serve under your command; and an honour to have been entrusted with the command of some of the finest officers I have ever met.

However, recent events have convinced me that I am no longer fit to perform my duties, as I believe the laws that we are duty bound to uphold are fundamentally flawed.

I believe that we are fighting a war that can't be won. I am sure that Operation De Niro will be lauded, by the men in Whitehall, as a great success, but the organisations behind the global traffic in drugs and human beings are too powerful; more powerful than many governments. As long as there is a market and money to be made, there will be other greedy men like Naismith and King who are only too willing to put their snouts in the trough. But they are small players, and they are dispensable. The men who control this evil are untouchable. They will see Operation De Niro as nothing more than a minor setback, until they can resume normal operations. And for all we know, they already have.

I believe that the policies of our government and other democratic states are populist, soft options. And as long as people like us are seen to be doing something they will get their votes. But whilst there are such huge profits to be made, our efforts are insignificant.

What is needed is a courageous and radical reform of the laws.
- *Legalisation of the possession and use of all drugs, with legal supply through properly regulated outlets. If there is no market, there is no profit for criminals.*
- *Reform of immigration laws to allow unrestricted entry to anyone who wishes to live and work here. Allow law abiding, hard working people be here legally, without fear of deportation or reprisals. And put an end to the misery of young men and women sold into slavery and give some hope to the thousands of invisibles living in fear of the people who have smuggled them in.*

I appreciate that many of my superiors will consider these views naïve and simplistic. And I doubt that any of our politicians, whatever their persuasion, have the courage to take such steps, or to even engage in the debate; as this would require them to admit that the problems are largely of their own making.

But until they do, we will simply be swimming against an unending tide of evil; and our efforts to stem the tide will be no more effective than firing peashooters at an elephant.

And, I just can't do it any more.

Yours sincerely
Mike Barton

Miller folded the letter and put it back into the envelope. "Trouble is Mike... you believe all that don't you. But why do you think you're so bloody special? Christ! If every copper, who thought the politicians have got it wrong, was to jack it in... There'd be none of us left. But we get on with the job... we've got enough to do without telling them how to their job."

"But..."

"Let me finish, Mike. You need to back pedal sometimes. It isn't all black and white, and you don't always have to be right. You're a good copper, one of the best. But this bloody obsession of yours to prove you can do it on your own is going to destroy you. You've got nothing to prove... so stop trying so bloody hard all the time. You'll make too many enemies."

"We've had this conversation before, Trevor. It doesn't make any difference."

"I know, but you can't have it all ways, Mike. All this stuff you've written here, you may be right, but the only way that you'll get the politicians to listen to you is to get to the top. And you won't do that without help and you won't do it without learning how to play politics yourself. It doesn't mean that you have to be like Harris and the others, but you have to learn how to deal with them without pissing them off. But maybe it's a bit late for that. Maybe you do need to move on."

"So, that's a decision then, Trevor?"

"Subject to conditions."

"Which are?"

"You take two weeks' leave, as of now. And then you come back and see all the loose ends are tied up. Meantime, I'll ask around, and see what DCI jobs are coming up. Deal?"

"Deal."

Miller put the letter back into the envelope and handed it to Barton. Then he sighed and signed Barton's transfer request. "Good luck, Mike. I just hope that you can find what you're looking for."

As Barton closed the door, Miller opened a drawer and took out another almost identical set of forms. The signature was Sally's; the preferred location was *anywhere* and the reasons *personal*, but he knew why; and he knew she'd change her mind. Her problem had just solved itself.